THIS MAN
MUST DIE

THIS MAN MUST DIE

A BUCK TRAMMEL WESTERN

WILLIAM W. JOHNSTONE

AND J.A. JOHNSTONE

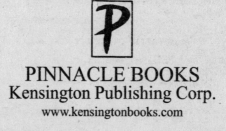

PINNACLE BOOKS
Kensington Publishing Corp.
www.kensingtonbooks.com

PINNACLE BOOKS are published by

Kensington Publishing Corp.
119 West 40th Street
New York, NY 10018

PUBLISHER'S NOTE: Following the death of William W. Johnstone, the Johnstone family is working with a carefully selected writer to organize and complete Mr. Johnstone's outlines and many unfinished manuscripts to create additional novels in all of his series like The Last Gunfighter, Mountain Man, and Eagles, among others. This novel was inspired by Mr. Johnstone's superb storytelling.

All Kensington titles, imprints, and distributed lines are available at special quantity discounts for bulk purchases for sales promotion, premiums, fund-raising, and educational or institutional use.

Special book excerpts or customized printings can also be created to fit specific needs. For details, write or phone the office of the Kensington Sales Manager: Kensington Publishing Corp., 119 West 40th Street, New York, NY 10018. Attn. Sales Department. Phone: 1-800-221-2647.

PINNACLE BOOKS, the Pinnacle logo, and the WWJ steer head logo Reg. U.S. Pat. & TM Off.

First Printing: June 2023
ISBN-13: 978-0-7860-4971-4
ISBN-13: 978-0-7860-4975-2 (eBook)

10 9 8 7 6 5 4 3 2 1

Printed in the United States of America

CHAPTER 1

Buck Trammel ducked his head back just as Verne Ayres cracked off another shot from his pistol. The bullet bit into the doorway less than an inch from where Trammel was standing.

"I already warned you once to stay out of here, Sheriff!" The wild-haired, old prospector punctuated his warning with another shot that split the batwing doors of the Tinder Box Saloon, forcing them open. "I told you I ain't comin' out of here 'til I'm good and ready. And I ain't nowhere near ready yet. This here party's just getting started."

Sherwood Blake, Trammel's chief deputy, tried to pull his boss back from harm's way. "You don't need to be here, boss. Your place is out there, keeping the people back. Let me and the boys handle this."

But the sheriff of Laramie County had no intention of going anywhere. "I was the first one here when it started, and I'll be the last one here when it's over. Where'd you send the others?"

"I have Johnny Welch and Charlie Root headed around to the back door," Blake told him. "The rest of our boys are tending to the crowd out front. Figured you wouldn't want anyone else to wander in here and get hurt."

"You figured right." Trammel lowered his Peacemaker

as he stole a quick glance inside the Tinder Box Saloon. The place was being kept open while it was being redone by the new owner. Ladders and paint cans were set up throughout the interior.

He caught Ayres in the middle of reloading his pistol. The wild hair poking out from beneath the prospector's worn slouch hat was long and gray, matching his overgrown beard.

Trammel's curiosity was rewarded with a rushed shot from Ayres. "I see what you're doing out there. Can't say I ever put much stock in all the big talk I've heard about you these past few years. About how tough you are. How you always get your man. Like I always said, 'The bigger they are, the harder they fall.'"

Trammel had known of Verne Ayres, too, if only by his reputation as a talker and a drunk on the rare occasions he came down from the hills around Laramie. He had always been relatively harmless until that day. "This old fool has almost killed me twice. Where'd he learn to shoot like that?"

"No way of telling with Verne," Blake said. "He never tells the same story about himself twice."

"I can hear you boys plotting out there," Ayres hollered. "It's no use. I've got you right where I want you. Just let me have my celebration in peace and I'll be on my way."

The man could not only shoot but had excellent hearing. Trammel asked Blake, "Any idea what set him off like this?"

The deputy kept his head low but his Winchester ready as he whispered, "Heard from one of the fellas who ran out of there that Ayres was in the mood to celebrate a big strike. Said he'd finally hit the mother lode and was about to buy drinks for everyone in the place. But the bartender said something that turned his mood dark."

That was more than Trammel had known. He was on his

way back to his office in City Hall when he saw customers running out of the Tinder Box like the place was on fire. Given that Adam Hagen was in the middle of changing the place from a brothel into a respectable hotel, Trammel had figured one of the workers might have accidentally started a blaze.

It was not until he heard the shots that he knew it was not as simple as that.

"Send someone to find the bartender and talk to him. I want to know why Ayres is so worked up. He might be able to tell us something that could calm him down."

"I'd be glad to, but we can't do that," Blake told him. "The bartender is lying behind the bar, right next to Verne. He was the first man Verne shot to start this whole mess rolling. The only one who got shot, too, near as I can tell."

Trammel figured bartending was getting to be as dangerous as enforcing the law in Laramie these days. The town was bursting at the seams now that Lucien Clay was in jail and Adam Hagen was buying up every property in sight. The town was filled with people looking for a new start and new ways to earn a living off the boom. "Verne must've found something big to justify this."

"He said he found gold," Blake reported. "Old Verne's been looking for a strike like this all his life, and now he's finally found it. Shame he won't be free long enough to enjoy it."

Both men ducked when another shot rang out from inside the saloon, punching open the batwing doors beside them once again.

"I can still hear you two schemin' out there plain as day. Do yourselves a favor and put the thought right out of your mind. There's no reason for anyone else to get hurt, including either of you. Just let me finish my drinkin' so I can get on back to my claim."

Trammel thought he might have a way to getting Ayres to lower his gun. "Is that what this is, Verne? A celebration?"

"It certainly is," Ayres shouted back. "And I don't appreciate it being ruined. Not by you and not by this sassy bartender, either."

"Help me, Sheriff!" a man cried out from behind the bar. "I'm hurt really bad."

He yelped when Trammel heard Ayres kick him. "And if you don't want to get hurt worse, you'll quit your belly-achin' and let me enjoy this here drink in peace."

Trammel was glad the bartender was still alive. He had to keep Ayres talking. "I thought this was a fight that got out of hand, not a party, Verne. That changes things."

"It does?" Ayres called back. "How do you figure it?"

"The bartender's still alive, so Blake and I don't have any reason to barge in there and take you in. It's just a misunderstanding between a bartender and a customer. Happens all the time."

"Then you boys have no reason to stay out there. Just go about your business and let me leave town on my own steam."

Trammel could not allow that to happen. "It's not much of a celebration with you sitting in there all by yourself drinking alone, now is it? If you promise not to shoot, the two of us would like to come in there and join you for a drink. It's been a while since we've had much cause for celebration around here, and we could use the excuse. Who knows? Your good fortune might rub off on us."

"Sure. And maybe you boys'll buy me a steak dinner with all the trimmings." The sheriff's hopes sank when Ayres laughed. "I didn't get this old by being that stupid, Trammel. You two are just fine right where you are. And

THIS MAN MUST DIE 5

the same goes for whoever you've got sneaking around
behind this place, too. Prospecting's a lonely, thirsty business. I found this claim alone and I'll celebrate it alone. And
I don't aim to allow you or anyone else to swindle me out
of it, you hear?"

Trammel was about to ask him what he meant by
swindling when he heard another voice come from inside
the saloon. "You can hardly call it swindling if it's legal,
Verne."

Trammel could not believe his rotten luck. It was the
man who was renovating the Tinder Box into a respectable
hotel.

Adam Hagen, his part-time friend and a full-time nui-
sance in Laramie. The last man in town who could end this
peacefully.

"Speak of the devil and he shall appear," Verne seethed.
"How'd you get in here, you snake? Slithered under the
door, I imagine."

Trammel took a risk that Verne was distracted and peered
inside. He found Hagen leaning against the doorway next
to the bar. The doorway led out to the front lobby and the
stairs up to the rooms.

As usual, he was wearing a red brocade vest and a
gleaming Colt pistol on his right hip.

"I was upstairs reviewing plans for the place when I
heard the shot," Hagen said. "How're you feeling down
there, Tom?"

"My head is mighty sore, Mr. Hagen," the bartender
replied.

"See what you went and did, Verne?" Hagen said to the
prospector. "You let that nasty temper of yours get the better
of you again. We talked about that the last time, or don't
you remember?"

"I remember everything about you, you scoundrel. Every word you say is poison in my ears. And since this is my party, I say we talk about something different for a change."

Trammel saw Verne gesture toward Hagen with his pistol. "How about we talk about how you tricked me into signing over—"

Hagen drew his Colt and fired twice into Verne's chest.

Trammel had seen Hagen shoot enough times to know he could have cut him down from much farther away. Being as close as he was, there was no question Ayres was dead before he tumbled backward and stumbled over the fallen bartender.

Trammel quickly rounded into the saloon, followed by Blake.

On the other side of the hotel, Deputies Johnny Welch and Charlie Root burst through the front door. Their rifles were at their shoulders and aimed at Hagen.

Hagen switched his aim to Trammel's chest. The smoking pistol hung there for a moment too long for the lawman's comfort. Given that Trammel was over six and a half feet tall, he was difficult to miss and impossible to mistake for anyone else in Laramie. Hagen had clearly seen Trammel and recognized him, too. But the thought of shooting him had entered his mind, if only for a moment.

Hagen slowly lowered his pistol and smiled at the sight of his old friend. "You ought to know better than to barge in on me while I'm working, Buck. I might've shot you in the heat of the moment."

Beside him, Deputy Blake thumbed back the hammer on his rifle. "All the more reason why you ought to tuck that iron away, Hagen."

The gambler's smile held. "What's the matter, Blake? Don't think I could get those two behind me before I took you, too?"

Blake did not budge. "You'll be dead before you try."

"Highly unlikely." Hagen holstered the weapon and held up his hands as he slowly stepped away from the bar. "Never let it be said that Adam Hagen is one to interfere with the law." He glanced behind the bar. "You can come out now, Tom. The bad man can't hurt you anymore."

Trammel motioned for Welch and Root to lower their Winchesters as a bald man popped up from behind the bar and pulled himself over it. He had expected to see a bullet wound but was surprised that all he had was a nasty gash on his gleaming head.

"I thought you were shot," Trammel said as the bartender moved to Hagen's side.

"He would've shot me if he had the chance." Tom pulled off his apron and held it against his bleeding wound. "Verne's pistol went off when he slammed me in the head with that old Navy Colt of his. He didn't shoot anyone."

"Thank heavens for that," Hagen said as he moved the bartender's apron and examined the gash for himself. "I imagined the worst when I heard the shot. Stands to reason why I was in such fear for my life."

Trammel knew that was a lie. He doubted Adam Hagen had ever been afraid of anything in his life. Not when he had a gun on his hip or a rifle in his hands.

Hagen sucked his teeth as he dabbed the apron at Tom's wound. "Verne got what he deserved for treating you this way. I'd be inclined to swear out a complaint against him if he was still alive, but I suppose he's beyond all that now."

"Yeah," Trammel said. "He's beyond a lot of things."

Hagen feigned insult. "That sounds like sarcasm, Buck."

The sheriff ignored him as he walked over to the bar and peered over the side. He saw Verne Ayres crumpled on the floor. Two neat holes still smoldering over his heart.

His dead eyes fixed on the bare ceiling of the saloon. His newfound luck had clearly run out.

"Blake, you'd best get Tom over to a doctor to get that wound cleaned up. Doc Morrison's place is closest. Stay with him until he's been tended to, then get a statement from him for the record."

To his deputies still in the hotel lobby, he said, "Johnny and Charlie, I want you and the others to get statements from anyone else who was in here when it happened. I know the county attorney will want to have all the facts he can muster for his file. Tell everyone to stay outside until I tell them they can come in."

The deputies went off to carry out their respective assignments, paying Hagen particular attention as they passed him. Trammel knew his men did not trust the gambler, and they were right to be cautious.

He waited until Blake had helped the bartender leave before telling Hagen, "You and me are going to have a talk."

Hagen looked down at Trammel's pistol, which was still at his side. "I put mine away, Buck. It's only proper for you to do the same."

Trammel tucked the Peacemaker into the holster under his arm.

"That's better. There are so many guns around town these days. It's getting so a man needs to shoot his way across the street."

Trammel ignored the exaggeration. "The town would be a whole lot quieter if you weren't armed."

Hagen gestured to the side of Trammel's nose. "That scar of yours seems to fade more with each passing week. You wear it well. Makes you look even meaner than you already did, not that anyone could ever accuse you of having a peaceful disposition."

Trammel fought the urge to touch the long scar that ran down his face along the side of his nose. He had received it when Major John Stanton had tried to get away from him a few months back. The assassin had fallen from a roof for his trouble and later died in prison of his injuries.

The scar served as a daily reminder to Trammel of how close he had come to losing his life.

"And that shoulder holster you still insist on wearing," Hagen remarked as he moved behind the bar and grabbed a bottle of whiskey. "When are you going to break down and wear your gun on your hip like a true Westerner? You've been out here long enough. Time to adapt a little to our ways."

"Like shooting harmless old prospectors in a saloon?"

"Calling Verne harmless is awfully generous of you, especially after how he brained poor Tom with that Colt of his." Hagen placed two glasses on the bar and picked up a bottle of whiskey. "I can't have my people treated so poorly. I wouldn't get anyone of quality to work for me if word spread that I let my employees get slapped around by some drunk."

"That isn't why you shot him, and you know it."

Hagen sighed. "But I suppose violence has a tendency to follow us around wherever we go, doesn't it? Wichita. Blackstone, and now here in Laramie. The names of the towns might change, but the circumstances remain the same. You still have a position of authority and I'm still forced to dispatch undesirables."

Trammel watched him place two glasses on the bar as if he was about to perform a magic trick. There was always an elegant air about anything he did, but Trammel had known him too long to believe the façade. His fair hair had already begun to turn white in places, though he was just north of thirty. He kept his beard trimmed and close to his pale skin. He was a shade over six feet tall and managed to remain lean despite a strong appetite for hard drinking and late nights. His light eyes were set deeper than they had been when they first met back in Kansas. Harder, too.

Trammel thought the years had been kind to Adam Hagen in their own way, but not as kind as they might have been, and far kinder than he deserved.

"You didn't have to kill Verne, Adam."

"Of course I did." Hagen poured them a good amount of cheap whiskey. "I was in mortal fear of my life. He pointed his gun at me. I saw you watching the whole thing from the doorway. You saw it with your own two eyes. It's a miracle I wasn't killed."

Trammel did not look down at the glass Hagen slid toward him. "You could've just as easily backhanded him as shoot him."

"And risk poor Tom's life while a drunken lunatic was raving and pointing his gun all over the place? You think too much of my bravery, old friend."

Hagen set the bottle on the bar and reached for his glass, but Trammel grabbed his wrist before he could take hold of it. "You shot him for a reason."

The gambler's eyes narrowed with just a hint of spite. "I didn't claim to shoot him by accident, Steve. And we both know I don't like being handled, not even by my friends."

Trammel released him with a shove. "I heard what he said to you right before you shot him. Something about being swindled."

Hagen shrugged as he took his glass in hand. "The ravings of an old drunk blind with rage and riding high on glory. When Ayers wasn't up in the hills scraping at dirt, he was claiming someone swindled him. Before me, he accused

Lucien Clay of robbing him blind, as if the old sot ever had anything worth stealing. You've been out here long enough to know how those old prospectors are. Always afraid that someone's trying to jump their claim on the off chance they manage to pull something of quality out of the ground. You've seen dozens of men like Ayres come and go. I'm from these parts, so I've seen hundreds. They're as common as horseflies in a stable."

He looked down at the body behind the bar and raised a toast. "To your memory, you old rat. I hope your find was as prosperous as you claim."

Hagen took a healthy swallow of whiskey but was careful not to drain the glass. Trammel knew Hagen was always measured in everything he did. How he drank. How he gambled. How he spent his money and how he made it.

And how he killed. Trammel had never known him to do anything without a reason. He never surrendered reason to emotion, not even when he watched Hagen wage a pitched battle with his family for control of their fortune.

But when Hagen found himself on the losing end, his family ran him out of Blackstone for his trouble. With his brother Caleb and Lucien Clay now in prison for murder, Laramie was left wide open for a man of Adam Hagen's cunning and resources. He was already well underway to building a new empire of whiskey and blood. A piece of a gold claim would only help him reach his aims that much quicker.

Trammel stood upright so his size advantage over Hagen was even more pronounced. "You're not leaving here until you tell me why Ayres thought you were swindling him. And if you lie, I'm going to lose patience."

"Look at you, rearing up on your hind legs like an old grizzly." Hagen set his glass on the bar and tried to rub some circulation back into his wrist. "City living hasn't softened you up as much as I'd hoped. How do you manage to stay so strong?"

"I was born in Manhattan, remember? Laramie barely ranks as a neighborhood where I'm from. Quit stalling and answer my question."

Hagen ran his tongue along the inside of his mouth as he thought it over. "Are you asking me as a friend or as the sheriff of Laramie?"

Trammel knew better than to corner Hagen. If he tried to make this official, he would spend the rest of the afternoon dancing around the question in a blur of words. Any one of the lawyers who had recently moved into town would trip over themselves to defend him in court. Trammel was more interested in the truth than a fight. "I just want to know the truth. Let's leave titles out of it for now."

Hagen considered it before saying, "Fair enough. In that case, I'll tell you. About a month ago, the newly departed Mr. Ayres down there found himself having a particularly bad run of luck at my blackjack table over at the Emerald Isle. You remember the dump. It used to be Lucien Clay's place before I took it over."

Trammel did not need to be reminded of it, nor of Hagen's rapid assumption of Clay's role as the biggest criminal of Laramie now that Clay was in jail for murder. Hagen might have changed the name and fixed up the place, but it was still a den of iniquity as far as he was concerned. "Go on."

"Ayres was convinced his luck was due to turn around. He practically begged me for a some credit, but that was impossible since he was already into me for a considerable sum. Call me a softhearted fool if you wish, but there was something about his desperation that touched me." He tapped the center of his vest. "Right here."

"If you're pointing to your wallet, I'll believe it." Trammel could guess the rest and decided to save them both a lot of time by getting to the point. "You made him sign over his claim to you in exchange for a new line of credit, didn't you?"

Hagen held up a finger. "I only took half. I'm not entirely without scruples. And, as fortune would have it, Ayres wound up going on something of a winning streak. Not enough to entirely erase his debt to me, of course, but more than I had anticipated."

Hagen let out a dramatic sigh as he picked up his glass again. "But I still hold the note, and now that Ayres has departed this mortal coil, I suppose I'm the sole owner of his claim. Alas, the burdens of being the executor of his estate."

"A claim that sounds like it just paid off," Trammel said.

"I wouldn't count on it," Hagen said. "Verne Ayres was a better gambler than a prospector. He wouldn't know the difference between fool's gold and the genuine article if it leaped out of the ground and into his pocket." He offered another toast down to the corpse. "Sorry, old man, but I guess this is one claim that didn't pan out in your favor."

Trammel fought the urge to slap the drink out of Hagen's hand, pull him across the bar, and throw him in jail. He had murdered Verne Ayres just as sure as if he had followed him into a dark alley one night and knifed him to death.

But it was not Hagen's swindling that irked Trammel. Ayres knew the risk of going into debt with a man like Hagen. No one had forced him to walk into his gambling den that night. No one had forced him to sign over his claim to pay for one more turn of the cards. Trammel knew that was where Adam Hagen's true evil lay. He always found a way to use a man's weaknesses against him for his own benefit.

And it was all legal, even if it was not right. "All the money you've got, and you still feel the need to rip off an old grubber like Ayres."

Hagen's eyes slid over to Trammel before the glass touched his lips. "Careful, Buck. I don't respond well to criticism of my character."

But Trammel was not in a careful mood. He had just watched a man get gunned down over a claim that probably amounted to spare change in Hagen's deep pockets. "When is enough going to be enough for you, Adam? You ruined your father and burned his house to the ground. Your brother Caleb is over in City Hall, rotting in the next cell over from Lucien Clay. You're already well on your way to running most of Laramie. You'll be bigger than Clay ever was before long, if you're not already. What more do you want?"

Hagen appeared to think it over as he finally took his drink. He seemed to have made up his mind when he set the glass back on the bar. "More. I want more."

"More of what?"

"I don't honestly know," Hagen said. "I don't know what it is, or if there'll ever be enough, but whatever it is, I want more of it. Land. Gold. Property. Businesses. Women. Today it's this place. Tomorrow it might be something else. Works of art, perhaps. A bigger house or another empire to bring to its knees. All I know is that if it's worth having, I want it. As much of it as I can get. And I'm all too willing to do anything to get it."

Hagen seemed to remember himself and cast off the heavy words with another elegant shrug as he poured himself another drink. "Maybe one day I'll be satisfied, but today, old friend, is not that day."

No, Trammel imagined it was not. But he also knew the day would come sooner rather than later when Adam Hagen came up against something or someone he could not have. A man he could not beat. Something he could not buy at any price. And when he found it, he would pursue it until it finally destroyed him and cost him everything he had.

And once he was ruined, he would gladly start over, for Trammel knew that, for men like Hagen, having something was never quite as sweet as chasing it.

And when that day finally came, Buck Trammel would be there to stop him, or make him pay for all the harm he had done in his life.

He watched Hagen swirl the whiskey in his glass. "I trust none of these details about my Ayers claim will be mentioned in whatever report you give to Judge Spicer?"

"The judge is a plain man," Trammel said. "He's only interested in having me testify to what I see, not what I think, or even what I know. Ayers was armed. He had assaulted the bartender and he *did* point his pistol in your general direction when you shot him. It was legal, but that doesn't mean it was right."

Hagen rested his hand against his chest. "That's a relief. I've had enough dealings with Lady Justice these past few months to last me a lifetime." He gestured toward the glass in front of Trammel. "You haven't touched your whiskey. I know it's not as good as the stuff I usually serve, but it's good enough, given the circumstances. I can even promise you won't go blind."

Trammel pushed himself away from the bar. "No, thanks. Unlike you, I've still got a job to do."

Hagen called after him as he left the saloon. "Don't forget to send the undertaker around when you get the chance. I'd like to reopen as soon as possible, and I can hardly do that with poor old Ayres here, stinking up the place. Though I suppose I could charge admission for people to look at him. Maybe he'll turn out to be worth something after all?"

Trammel decided it was best to ignore the comment. There was never much to be gained by sparring with Adam Hagen, either with words or with pistols. And it was tough to beat a man whose idea of victory changed each day.

CHAPTER 2

The long shadows of his cell's bars were cast along Lucien Clay as he lay on his bunk, lost in thought. It was never truly dark down there in the bowels of Laramie Prison. No matter the time of day or night, there always seemed to be lamplight somewhere, as if the dancing flame mocked his confinement. And without windows to the outside world, it was nearly impossible to measure time, except for the strict schedule the guards enforced each day.

The guards said the constant light in the dingy prison was for the inmates' safety as much as it was for their own. Clay imagined they also liked the idea that it prevented the prisoners from getting much rest. A weakened prisoner is an easier prisoner to handle.

Clay closed his eyes as he thought of the guards. They had been his tormentors all these months. His jailers. But soon, one of them would help him enjoy freedom once more. All he had to do was remain patient.

It was never truly quiet in prison, either. With so many men living in squalor beneath City Hall, there was always someone sniffling or snoring or sobbing or shuffling. His cell was so narrow that he could easily sit against the bars on one side of his cell and touch the other side with his feet. The cell was just long enough to fit his cot and nothing else.

His world had been reduced to a cramped iron cell in the bowels of City Hall.

Clay had been locked up many times in many towns and cities for a variety of offenses. Being a vice peddler had its perils. But none of those places had been as wretched as Laramie Prison. He had not been allowed a visitor in more than a month, not that people were lined up around the block to see him. He had pled guilty to conspiracy to murder Rob Moran, a popular lawman in town. His plea had guaranteed he would not swing for the crime if he agreed to testify against Caleb Hagen, Adam's brother.

Sheriff Buck Trammel had also seen to it that Caleb Hagen was put in the next cell to Clay's, which only added to his torment.

Clay had decided against wasting money on attorneys and appeals and put whatever remained of his considerable fortune to better use. He had planted seeds that had already flowered and appeared ready for harvesting. He reminded himself to remain calm and soon all would be well.

But remaining calm was easier said than done, for in the next cell over, Caleb Hagen's feet continued to scrape against the floor as he constantly paced in his tiny cell. Clay was grateful he was not crying. He usually only did that when it was time to sleep.

"Curses on you for putting me in this mess, Lucien," Hagen said. "Curses on you for telling those infernal lies about me."

Clay had no pity for the man. This time the previous year, Caleb had been the leader of his late father's empire and had looked the part. He may have been raised at the family ranch in Blackstone, but he'd once had the soft look of a New York banker. His face had some of his dead father's sharp features, but any resemblance stopped there.

Too many steak dinners and black cigars had made him thick around the middle and soft in the head.

Months in a cell had transformed Hagen from a captain of industry to a shell of who he once had been. His filthy prison garb hung loosely around his frame and his bearded cheeks had grown fallow from the slop the jailers passed off as food.

"Curse yourself instead," Clay told him for the countless time. "You and your brother-in-law wanted Moran dead as part of your petty family squabble. If you hadn't sent that boy to hire me to have Moran killed, neither of us would be stuck in here now."

"But we can still get out of this." Hagen grabbed hold of the bars, almost pleading. "All you have to do is recant your testimony against me. Tell them it was all a lie. Testify that I had nothing to do with planning Moran's death. Pin it all on my dead brother-in-law instead. He's the one who hired you, not me. And he's dead. No harm can come to him now."

"I'm sure the judge will ignore how convenient that is." Clay stretched on his bunk and clasped his hands behind his head. He could have set his pocket watch by Hagen's daily routines if he had been allowed to keep one. After breakfast and yard time, the pleas inevitably began, followed by whatever scheme he had spent the previous evening cooking up. When Clay remained unmoved by his desperation, Hagen would sputter in angry frustration for the rest of the day until it was time for Deputy Hal Haid to deliver their supper.

Clay had seen the delivery of the food not as an opportunity for nourishment but the chance to set his own plans for freedom in motion. It was the only bright spot in his day, which was quickly ruined by Hagen's whimpering once the guards ordered all candles extinguished for the night.

Clay reminded him, "Testifying against you is the only

reason I haven't been hanged yet. Life sentence was the deal I made, and that's the deal I'm sticking with."

He smiled in the shadows. *At least for now.*

Hagen continued to pace in his cell, like a penned-in bull ready to charge. "Why won't you listen to reason? If you withdraw your testimony, they'll have no choice but to let me go while I'm working with my lawyers on my case. I might even be able to secure bail for you. Tell them Trammel forced you to confess just to frame me. You've got friends in town who can make sure the judge believes that. Everyone knows Trammel's a bully anyway."

Clay had already thought of that. "They'll never believe it. Not now."

But Hagen did not let facts get in the way of his dream. "I'll make them believe it. I'll buy off whoever I must. And once I'm free and clear of all charges, I'll hire the best lawyers money can buy to fight for you in court. Why, I'll have my own lawyer represent you. Free of charge, of course. I'm not talking about some backwoods hick lawyer like they have in these parts. I'm talking about the best legal minds in the country. From Chicago or Philadelphia or New York."

Lucien Clay did not have many joys left to him in life, so his only entertainment was listening to Caleb Hagen constantly claw at the prison walls, looking for a way out. This was at least the tenth time that week that he had made the same offer.

"Do you mean it, Caleb? Honestly and truly? Do you swear you'll get me out?"

Hagen tried to shake the bars in frustration. "I'll have my lawyer draw up papers to that effect if it'll make you feel any better. It'll be an iron-clad agreement."

"Papers he's sure to tear up as soon as I recant my story,"

Clay sneered. "You two would forget all about me before you made it to the station for the next train back to Chicago, or wherever it is you live. No thanks, Caleb. I've got plans of my own."

"Plans?" Hagen's mood brightened. "What plans?"

Clay shut his eyes and cursed himself for saying so much. Any glimmer of hope was bound to lift Hagen's sails. His big mouth would prove risky to his plans. He decided it was time to cut his losses and get some rest. He was expecting a visitor soon and he wanted to be at his best to receive his guest.

"Don't worry about me. Just worry about how your fancy attorney is going to get you out of here. Now, do us both a favor and worry in silence. I'd like to get some sleep before my meeting."

Hagen stifled a yell as he pulled away from the bars and left Lucien Clay alone.

Clay put the temporary quiet to good use and allowed sleep to take him.

When Barney, the elderly prison guard, brought him up to the receiving room later that day, Lucien Clay hated how his visitor looked at him. Pity, with a mix of disappointment. He had never been one to accept pity.

Like Caleb Hagen, prison had done Clay few favors in terms of his appearance. Buck Trammel had shattered his jaw with a single punch the previous year. He had been in ceaseless pain and had headaches and slurred speech for months. He had grown dependent on laudanum to dull his suffering. His mind, once sharp, had soon become lost in a blur of opiates and lost days. He could not help but wonder if he might have refused to play a role in Marshal Rob Moran's murder had he been thinking clearer.

He decided laudanum had not played a part in his decision. Killing the lawman was worth the risk and the great reward promised him.

But Doc Carson had not allowed Clay to have any laudanum during his imprisonment. After passing several bad weeks due to the ill effects of staying off the stuff, he had regained full control of his senses. His jaw was still crooked, which slurred his speech. But he had put his ongoing suffering to good use. It served to push him forward, even when all had seemed lost.

That same determination was the reason this stranger had come to see him today.

Barney looked at the prisoner and the guest with tired eyes as the large visitor stood to greet Clay.

"I'm Frank Bessler, your new attorney." His Texas accent was heavy but cultured. "Pleased to make your acquaintance, Mr. Clay."

Clay shook the big hand the Texan offered. He was a large man, almost the same size as Buck Trammel, though not quite. "Thank you for making the trip all the way from Texas, Mr. Bessler. I appreciate the effort."

Bessler had a healthy, dark beard that made his smile even brighter. His brown suit was clean and devoid of any wrinkles or hints of trail dust. A gold watch chain spanned his broad chest from one vest pocket to the other. Clay caught the faint whiff of shaving cream and hair tonic, which told him Bessler had just come from the barber. A good sign that Bessler might live up to his reputation.

As prisoner and attorney sat, Clay looked back at the prison guard. "Might as well leave us, Barney. My lawyer and I have things to discuss that aren't meant for your tender ears."

The toothless guard gummed his response. "You've got an hour, convict. Not a moment longer."

Clay waited until Barney shuffled into the hall and pulled the door shut behind him, leaving them alone in the cramped room across a crooked wooden table.

Bessler looked amused as he watched the old guard leave. "He looks like he's got one foot in the grave. No wonder you think busting out of this place will be easy."

Clay motioned for him to keep his voice down. "He's old, not deaf. Mind what you say in here. Words tend to carry in prison."

Bessler's look darkened. "And a man in your position ought to mind his tone when he speaks to me. I'm not one of your hired hands, Lucien. Not yet. And you're not the first client I've visited behind bars."

Clay had always bristled at familiarity from the men who worked for him, especially when they happened to be right. Clay was in no position to be haughty, and Bessler knew it.

"Just keep your voice down. I think they already expect I'm up to something."

Bessler's dark eyes narrowed. "What do you mean by that?"

"Meaning I usually don't have visitors these days," Clay explained. "Barney's bound to tell Trammel about it, and he'll get curious."

"Let him get curious. There's nothing wrong with a man in prison meeting with a lawyer. It happens every day."

Clay knew he did not have time to waste on arguing his point. Barney would be looking to take him back to his cell within the hour and they had much to discuss. "According to the notes Mayor Holm got to me, I hear you're good at what you do."

"I am, but we'll get to that." Bessler's smile flashed again. "But first, there's one thing about this whole setup that bothers me. I don't understand how you could've gotten yourself locked up, considering you've got the mayor in your pocket."

Clay felt his anger rise at the thought of it. Old shames rushed to the fore. "Because Buck Trammel isn't in my pocket and he's the one who put me here. Happy?"

"Not yet," Bessler said. "How did you get word to him from your cell? Walt Holm isn't the type who spends much time among prisoners."

Clay saw no reason to keep it from him. "The deputy who brings our dinner each night is a fella named Hal Haid. He used to be one of my best customers before I got locked up. He owed me quite a sum. I promised to forget about his debt if he agreed to take notes between me and Mayor Holm. It was a harmless enough way for him to work off what he owes me. It certainly beats his wife finding out he wasn't always working late."

"You think this Haid character might've read your notes?"

"We always sealed them with wax. Don't worry. If he'd read them, I'd have known."

That seemed good enough to satisfy Bessler. "I'm surprised Walt played along," he said. "He's always been an old church mouse when it came to risking his neck, even back when we rode together."

Clay had always known Walter Holm was a corruptible man. It was why Clay had worked to install him as mayor of Laramie in the first place. He was as greedy as he was capable, which was why Clay had given Holm control of his fortune while he was in jail. Another man might have taken the money and run. But Holm had not wanted to risk Clay testifying in court about how they had worked to the detriment of Laramie for years. A bad reputation was hard for a man to outrun.

"I take it Holm has already given you your fee," Clay said.

"Half, which was more than fair. He said you already had a plan to get out of here without too much bloodshed. He didn't give me any details."

Clay was glad he knew that much. "That's because I didn't tell him everything. He's a politician, and that type isn't always known for their discretion."

"A wise choice," Bessler remarked. "Holm always had a habit of talking too much under the influence of good drink and female companionship. But there's no point in being as guarded with me. In fact, you'll have to be just the opposite if you want me to get you out of here. And you can rely on me to keep anything we discuss confidential. What Holm doesn't know can't hurt either of us. I'm putting my neck on the chopping block right next to yours."

Clay already liked the way Bessler thought. "Did Holm send you the details about my case?"

"He did, and I agree there's absolutely no way I can get you out of here legally. Your sentencing agreement all but makes that impossible. I'm sure you could agree to testify against Holm and all the others you've corrupted here in town, but I doubt it would make any difference to the judge. The best you could hope for is some extra yard time and marginally better food when the mood struck the guards."

Bessler sat forward and folded his large hands on the table. "We both know you didn't pay for me to come all the way here just for my reading of the law. Holm said you had a plan to break out of here. I'd like to hear it."

But Clay needed to know a few things before he could trust him. Even the slightest detail could be the difference between success and failure. "When did you arrive in Laramie?"

"Two days ago," Bessler told him. "I've put the time to good use by giving this town and this prison a good looking-over."

"And?"

"Laramie's not as backward as I'd heard," Bessler admitted. "I saw an old prospector shoot up a place called the Tinder Box just this morning. If a saloon was ever properly named, it's that dump. Doesn't seem to take much for a spark to turn into a blaze in these parts."

Clay frowned at the news. "That's because I'm not around to keep it under control. Adam Hagen took my place, and he isn't nearly as smart as he thinks he is. The Tinder Box always turned a tidy profit when I ran the place. He's going broke turning every saloon into a palace. Thinks he can turn Laramie into another Denver or Chicago."

"I hear Adam Hagen's quite a character. He's Caleb Hagen's brother, isn't he?"

Clay did not want to waste time explaining the complicated lineage of the Hagen family. "Tell me what you make of Trammel and his deputies."

Bessler drummed his thick fingers on the table. "They're good, and Trammel's got no shortage of deputies on his payroll. None of them look like they're easy targets, least of all Trammel."

Clay sneered. "You're not scared of him, are you?"

"Right down to my boots, mister," Bessler admitted. "I've heard talk of plenty of hard cases in my time, so I know the difference between bluster and the real thing. I hear Trammel's not much of a talker, so I'd wager he's the genuine article. Getting you out of here will be one thing. Keeping you out is something else entirely."

Clay could not blame him for being cautious. "What do you make of his deputies?"

"I've watched them work. They're smart. They know how to keep a lid on things without being bullies. They know just how far to push a man to keep him in line without causing a fight. And there's always one of them watching the street, even at night."

Clay did not like the sound of that. "They watch you?"

"I've received my fair share of attention these past few days. A man of my size doesn't exactly blend in, even in a bustling town like Laramie."

The more Bessler talked, the worse Clay felt about his prospects. "Do you think any of them recognized you?"

Bessler waved it off. "Not a chance. This is my first time in Wyoming and none of them looked familiar. The clerk over at the Continental Hotel told me one of the deputies stopped by to look at the guest register. The fool thought the notion of vigilant deputies would put my mind at ease, but I haven't received any unnecessary attention. And before you insult me by asking, they didn't notice me as I looked over the prison. I was very discreet."

"Your idea of discretion could be obvious as far as Trammel is concerned. How discreet were you?"

"I asked for a room at the back of the hotel," Bessler explained. "I told him I wanted something quiet to calm my nerves. The real reason was because the back of the hotel offers a perfect view of this prison. I did most of my work from up there."

Discretion was one of the reasons Mayor Holm had suggested he hire Bessler in the first place. He did not need another gunman like Major John Stanton. The assassin had lived up to his billing when he successfully killed Marshal Rob Moran.

But despite his skill with a gun, Stanton had not been good enough to go up against Buck Trammel in a straight-up fight. Few men were.

No, Clay needed a thinking man to get him out of this dungeon they called a prison.

"What do you think my chances are of breaking out of here?"

"It's possible." His thick Texas accent added a certain level of assurance to his words. "That's not to say it'll be easy. Or cheap."

Clay was not concerned about the price. "Holm will see to it you get your money after I'm free. He's prepared to wire it to any bank you say as soon as I give him the word. Today is Tuesday, and Mayor Holm works out of his law office on Tuesdays. Drop by his office when you leave here, and he'll be happy to give you your money. Tell him this phrase, 'The days are growing shorter.' That'll confirm that I've given him my permission to wire the balance of my remaining funds to the bank in Denver."

Clay thought it prudent to add, "And we'll have no trouble withdrawing it, as long as I'm there with you. In person."

Bessler smiled. "No one's looking to steal your money, Lucien. I've never stolen from a client yet and I don't plan on starting now. Just make sure you're ready to move every night after lights out. I'll be getting you out of here in a day or so at most."

Clay did not like the sound of that. "Don't you want to hear my plan?"

Bessler's chair creaked as he sat back in it. "No, and I never tell a client how I plan to spring them. Like you said, sound has a habit of traveling in jails, and I don't want you getting anxious and trying to help. Holm tells me you're one cold man, but if you start acting squirrely, it might tip off one of the guards. What you don't know can't hurt either of us."

Clay tried to read Bessler's expression, but the lawyer's face was granite. He could remember playing in high stakes poker games that were not as challenging. "Don't make me insist."

Bessler drummed his thick fingers on the table as he thought it over. "I'd tell you, but it's going to cost you extra. Above and beyond what we've already agreed to."

Clay could hardly resent a man for having a mercenary nature. Bessler had not come all the way from Texas out of the goodness of his heart or because he believed in Clay's innocence.

Clay asked him the amount and Bessler told him. Clay agreed to it without hesitation.

And Bessler did not look happy about the easy victory. "That's it? No haggling?"

"My freedom's too valuable to haggle over," Clay said. "I've got the money, so I look at it as an investment. So quit stalling and talk. Barney isn't too good with telling time, so he's bound to be back here any moment."

Bessler seemed just as eager to get down to business and leaned closer to him across the table. "Going out the way I came in here is out. There's a great, big iron door between here and upstairs that's always guarded. If we tried to get out that way, it would mean shooting the guard. Even if I got down here and pulled you out of your cell, getting out would be impossible because everyone would hear the shot. That stairway would turn into a turkey shoot, with us as the turkeys. I don't think either of us want that."

Clay already knew what he was thinking. "That leaves the side door to the courtyard and stalls."

"Agreed, but we'll need to get the timing just right. I saw they have an old Negro man who works as a stable hand in the stalls back there. At first, I thought I might be able to use him as leverage to get inside, but I've been watching him closely. He never comes inside the prison and I don't think he has a key."

"That would be Old Bob," Clay remembered. "He's been working here since before I came to Laramie. They only pay him to stay with the horses. Even fixed up an old shack for himself to sleep in by the horses. I think he likes it. And you're right. He doesn't have a key to get inside. He's got one for those big iron doors that lead out to the street, though."

But Bessler was already past that. "I noticed an old man who goes through that way each night around midnight. Carries a black bag with him that makes me think he's a doctor. I've noticed that he likes to sit out in the courtyard by himself several times a day. Even wheels a chair out with him while he puffs away on his pipe for an hour or so at a time. I don't know why he doesn't just go out front and do it. It would certainly smell better than being next to the horses, but who am I to judge?"

Clay was glad it sounded like Bessler had been telling the truth about watching the place. "That would be Doc Carson. He's always been a solitary cuss. Spends so much time in here that he might as well have a cell of his own. He does most of his smoking and drinking in his office when he's not tending to prisoners. He has bad knees and hates taking stairs when he can avoid it. Says coming in the side entrance is better for his joints. Trammel even comes down to his office to make it easier on him."

"All the better for us. In fact, his predictability is essential to my plan. He always comes back here just before midnight. And each time, he wrestles something awful with those big iron doors into the courtyard."

"He likes to check in on us while we're sleeping." Clay's hopes in Bessler's plan began to dim. "I hope you don't think you can grab him on the street and use him to get in here. He'd sooner let you kill him than allow himself to be taken hostage. He'll cut loose with a holler and draw every gun on the street before you got five paces."

Bessler broke into another wide grin that unsettled Clay. "I know we just met each other, Lucien, but you ought to give me credit for a bit more creativity than that. I've already told you how I plan to do it. You just weren't listening." He pulled his watch from his vest pocket and checked the time. "We've still got a few minutes before the guard comes back. So, you'd best pay attention while I tell you exactly how I'm going to get you out of here. Tonight."

CHAPTER 3

"Steven Trammel, I swear, marriage has made you deaf!"

Dr. Emily Trammel's complaint was enough to finally draw his attention away from his office window. "I'm sorry, honey. Did you say something?"

His wife frowned in that special way that always managed to break his heart. "I've been saying lots of things for the past five minutes, not that you thought they were important enough to listen."

He took another quick look out the window as his ears began to redden with shame. "I didn't mean to ignore you. It's just that something Barney told me is bothering me. That's all."

"You're the sheriff of Laramie," she reminded him. "You've always got something on your mind. If it's not something Barney told you, it's Blake, or something the mayor said that annoys you. I'm talking about something important because it's about you. About your scar."

Trammel ran his finger along the raised pink scar that ran from his forehead down the side of his nose. Adam Hagen had mentioned it back in the saloon, too. The scar had been courtesy of Major John Stanton's bootheel before the assassin had taken his tumble from the roof.

After the pain had subsided, Trammel barely gave it any

thought unless he happened to catch his reflection in the mirror while he shaved each morning.

"What about my scar? It doesn't hurt anymore."

She sighed as she began to repeat herself. "I just got finished telling you that there's a doctor down in Denver who specializes in healing injuries like yours. He's done some impressive work with men who served in the war. I think it would be worth the trip to see him."

"Why?"

"To make that ugly gash on your face less noticeable is why," she said. "Why else would we go see him?"

Trammel knew he must be missing her point but did not know what it was. "Why waste time to go see him at all? I've never exactly been a dandy, Emily. God knows you didn't marry me for my looks."

"Nor for your brains, either, to hear the way you talk sometimes. Don't you want to get it taken care of? Anything he did would be an improvement."

Trammel had never spent much time thinking about his appearance. He had five shirts and two pairs of pants and had been wearing the same boots since Wichita. The scar was not as red as it had been when it first healed. It did not even bother him much unless it was about to snow or rain, and even then, it was little more than a dull ache. "It would take time for us to go all the way to Denver and back. I can't get away right now. There's too much going on here in Laramie."

"There's always too much going on in Laramie." She frowned. "What is it this time?"

He looked out the window again at the bustling Main Street of Laramie. Wagons were making deliveries. Businessmen loped along with laborers and shopkeepers on the boardwalks. The saloons drew steady crowds throughout the day, and it was often difficult to find a free table at any of the new restaurants and cafés that seemed to spring up every day all over town.

He knew Manhattan and Chicago were much bigger and weren't exactly sleepy towns, but more room meant people had more places to go. Laramie seemed to be jumbled together, which only served to pack more people into a much more restricted space.

Laramie was clearly a city on the rise and was beginning to have the same kinds of problems that afflicted larger cities back East.

"Pickpockets and pimps," Trammel said. "Merchants looking to cheat customers. Customers looking to squeeze every dime out of merchants. Drunks, gamblers, drifters. Girls looking to hold up customers."

"So, in other words, it's just another Tuesday in Laramie," Emily concluded.

But it was more than that. "Adam Hagen is going back to his old ways. He gunned down an old prospector in the Tinder Box earlier this morning. Killed him just so he could get control of his gold claim."

"I heard." Emily took her gloves from her husband's desk. "One of my patients was talking about it before I came here to see you. It was Verne Ayres, wasn't it?"

Trammel never ceased to be amazed by the extent of the grapevine of Laramie. "Was he a patient of yours?"

"Don't be silly." She threw one of her gloves at him. "You know I only cater to the women in town."

He laughed as he caught the glove and held it out to her. "Now I remember. You married me for my sense of humor."

She rose from her chair and walked over to her husband to retrieve her glove. "As infrequent as it is." She took the glove from him but did not put it on. She caressed his face with the side of her bare hand instead. "Adam raising trouble is nothing new, Steve. There's something else bothering you. What is it?"

He had never been able to refuse her anything before they were married. Her hold on him had not only deepened after the wedding. She was more striking than beautiful. The strains of early widowhood may have taken their toll on her, but whatever beauty she might have once possessed had been replaced with a strength and determination that Trammel not only admired but needed.

"Barney came up here right before you stopped by. It looks like Lucien Clay's got himself a new lawyer."

"What's so troubling about that? He's entitled to one, isn't he? It's not as though he can do more for him than the old one could. Judge Spicer has already made his ruling, hasn't he?"

"That's what's bothering me," Trammel admitted. "Clay doesn't need to hire a new lawyer. He can't appeal his sentence. And now that Stanton's dead, Stanton's confession is as good as a dying declaration. Clay's already given written testimony against Caleb Hagen, so even if he tries to withdraw his statement now, the judge won't let him. Judge Spicer is just as likely to withdraw Clay's plea deal and see to it that he swings for Moran's murder."

Trammel looked back out the window in time to see the same man Barney had described as he left City Hall. A large man—not quite as large as Trammel, but close. He wore a new brown suit and a matching bowler. He sported a gun on his right hip and a shine on his boots. Frank Bessler obviously took great pride in his appearance.

Emily joined him in looking out the window. "Is that him? He's almost as big as you."

Trammel nodded. "Kind of walks like me, too, and I'm not exactly a lawyer."

"He doesn't seem to have any papers with him," Emily

noticed. "I've never met a lawyer who wasn't carrying a satchel of some kind."

Trammel quietly chastised himself for not noticing that before she pointed it out. "Mrs. Trammel, I think this law business is starting to have an ill effect on you."

"Guilty as charged." She rose on her tiptoes and gave him a peck on the cheek. "Come walk me out. I've got a waiting room full of women who are just dying to tell me about Adam Hagen's latest outrage. Can I expect you home at your usual time?"

Trammel was not so sure, and he hated to break a promise to her. "Probably. But first, I've got to see a lawyer about his client."

Trammel walked Emily down to the boardwalk and noticed Clay's new attorney was taking his time as he walked along Main Street. He had stopped to look in the window of a new clothing store that had just opened in the past week. Bessler was an easy man to spot, even in a crowd.

"That's the fella I was telling you about, Sheriff," Barney said as he came up beside him. "Clay's new lawyer."

Trammel watched the lawyer admire his reflection in the front window of the clothing store. "Frank Bessler, isn't it?"

"An attorney out of Texas," Barney told him. "He's staying over at that new place that opened last month. The Continental."

Trammel had been to the new hotel a couple of times since it opened. It was one of the few places in Laramie that Adam Hagen did not either own or control. It did not have a gambling hall and was looking to be known more for its fancy rooms and good food dining than a saloon, so naturally, Adam was not interested in it.

"Bessler," Trammel repeated. "That name sounds familiar. I think Blake told me about him a couple of days ago, when he checked the hotel registers."

"I saw him write it down in my visitor's notebook downstairs," Barney said. "Can't say I like the feel of him, Sheriff. He's not like any lawyer I've ever laid eyes on, and I've seen all kinds come through my jail. There's something different about him that I can't seem to put my finger on."

Trammel knew Barney had been a guard at the jail for so long, he had taken ownership of the place and its prisoners. Despite his years, he was spry, and his mind was sharp. He kept a close eye on the prisoners and had a keen eye for spotting contraband. Between him and Doc Carson, they helped the deputies run an efficient ship that kept the county's criminal element alive.

"I figure it's a good time to introduce myself to Mr. Bessler, don't you?"

"Not my place to say, Sheriff." Barney was known for preferring to keep his opinions to himself on matters that did not pertain to the prison. "Want me to fetch Blake or one of the other boys to go with you?"

"Not this time. But let them know where I'm going, and to keep an ear out for trouble. You never know what might happen with strangers."

Trammel stepped off the boardwalk and took his time following Bessler, who had since lost interest in the clothing shop and begun to make his way in the general direction of the Continental.

The sheriff easily watched him over the heads of the citizens who were going about their business. Bessler certainly did not carry himself like a lawyer. He moved like a man who knew how to handle himself. Like a man who had plenty of experience in using the pistol on his hip. He wore the gun comfortably and in the perfect position to draw it with ease. He did not pay attention to it as he walked but clearly knew it was there.

Since becoming sheriff, Trammel had constantly reminded himself that Laramie was different from Chicago or New York. Lawyers back East were usually career men who had learned their trade at schools. Except for those who rose through the political ranks, they usually did their fighting in court or with the stroke of a pen instead of a pistol.

Frontier towns like Denver and Laramie tended to draw a rougher crowd of professionals with a more varied background. Many of the men in this part of the country had been in the war and, despite all the years that had passed since, still bore the weight of that experience.

It was clear to Trammel that Bessler had not been a military man or, if he had, was a different sort than Major John Stanton was.

But he was a killer. That much was certain.

And as the crowd around them began to thin out, Trammel decided to see for himself what kind of man this stranger really was.

"Frank Bessler!" Trammel called out at the top of his lungs.

The attorney drew his pistol as he turned in a crouch. Instinct had caused his reaction.

Experience had led him to raise his pistol when he saw Trammel standing alone in the thoroughfare as pedestrians darted away from the scene.

Bessler was fast, Trammel noted. Not as fast as Adam Hagen, but still, plenty fast enough. He was certainly faster than Trammel in the draw.

Bessler stood upright and holstered his firearm with as much ease as he had used in drawing it. "You must be Sheriff Trammel, I presume."

Trammel had not reached for the Peacemaker holstered beneath his left arm. "That's right. I'm Trammel."

Bessler offered an easy smile as he stepped down from the boardwalk to greet him. "You have a unique way of introducing yourself, sir."

"I called out to you a couple of times, but you didn't seem to hear me," Trammel lied. "I was just trying to get your attention over the noise of the street. Guess it came out louder than I'd intended."

"You sought my attention and now you have it." The lawyer held out his hand to Trammel, who shook it. The grip was strong enough to make a point without turning into a contest of strength. "I've heard quite a bit about you since coming to Laramie."

"I get that a lot," Trammel said. "I wish I could say the same for you."

"No reason in the world why you should know about me, Sheriff," Bessler demurred. "I haven't broken the law since I've been here. I'm just a quiet country lawyer visiting a client."

Trammel doubted that. "Given the way you handled that iron, I'd say you're more than just a country lawyer."

"I'm from Texas, sir," Bessler said. "A man can ill afford to be only one thing in Texas. A certain dexterity of the mind and body is called for if one is to live in such places."

Trammel was not exactly sure what dexterity meant, but he made a mental note to find out later. "Mind telling me what a Texas lawyer is doing all the way up here in Wyoming?"

"I already told you. I'm seeing a client."

"Don't have any clients in Texas?"

"This one happens to be a very well-paying client," Bessler added with a smile. "But why do I think you already know who my client is?"

"Lucien Clay," Trammel said. "Interesting choice for a client."

"The ones who pay the best usually are." Bessler slid his hands into his pockets. "I just hope you're not going to ask me to tell you what Mr. Clay and I spoke about just now because we both know I can't do that."

Trammel decided to play a hunch by remaining vague. "I've already got a pretty good idea of what you talked about. There are few secrets in a prison. The truth usually comes out sooner or later."

Bessler did not betray much, but there was just enough of a hint of hesitation for Trammel to know he had come close to the truth.

"I guess it's only fair to warn you that it's a waste of time," Trammel added. "Clay's case, I mean. It's all been settled. I can't think of a reason why Judge Spicer would reopen it. But if Clay wants to waste his money, I'm the last one to try to stop him."

Bessler tried charm. "That makes two of us. I'd hate to be robbed of a handsome reward for my efforts." He leaned closer to Trammel, as if taking him into his confidence. "But I wouldn't trouble myself too much over Mr. Clay's affairs if I were you, Sheriff. My client is all too aware that his legal appeals have been exhausted."

Trammel decided to prod a bit further. "I've always been more concerned about his illegal appeals. Hope you're not troubling yourself over those, either."

"Of course not," Bessler assured him. "I walk the straight and narrow path of the law, Sheriff. And I always advise my clients to do the same, though it hardly benefits me when they do. And speaking of clients, I'm on my way to visit another one right now. Thought I should make the most of my time while I'm here in your fair town."

Trammel figured he had given Bessler a hard enough

THIS MAN MUST DIE   41

time for one day. Anything else he wanted to learn about the stranger could not be discovered through conversation. "How long were you planning on being here in Laramie?"

"Just long enough to make the journey back home to Texas worth the effort, though I'm thoroughly enjoying my stay at the Continental. A lovely place. Quite cozy."

Trammel knew that was all the information he would be able to get from the attorney. "Well, if you find yourself needing anything, you already know where to find me. Stop by my office the next time you visit Clay. I'll give you a tour of the place."

"I'll keep that in mind." Bessler touched the brim of his hat as he began to back away. "I'm honored to have finally had the opportunity to meet you. It's not every day a man like me gets to meet a legend. And with such a charming wife, too."

Trammel took one step forward. "What was that?"

"That woman you bid goodbye to on the street just now in front of City Hall," Bessler said. "I could not help but see your reflection in the window of the clothing store back there. I take it she's your wife." He placed his hand against his chest. "Forgive me if I presumed too much."

Trammel doubted Bessler ever presumed anything. "She's my wife."

"And a doctor, from what I hear. Quite an accomplishment. Don't see too many lady doctors these days. You must be proud."

Trammel knew he was testing him, just as Trammel had tested him by calling out his name on the street just then. "Proud and protective."

"For good reason." Bessler smiled. "A handsome woman. You make a beautiful couple. Too bad she hasn't been able to do something about that unfortunate scar of yours. I heard how you received it. Looks awfully painful."

"Only sometimes."

"That's good to hear," Bessler said as he began to back away, "though I'd hate to meet the man who gave it to you."

"You surely would." Trammel smiled. "He's dead."

"I wouldn't expect him to be running around free as a bird." Bessler touched the brim of his bowler and bid him a good day before continuing his stroll back toward his hotel.

Trammel stepped back onto the boardwalk and watched him blend into the crowd. He knew the Continental Hotel was down that street, but so was Mayor Walter Holm's law office. There was no secret that Holm and Clay were close. He watched Bessler slow in front of Holm's building before continuing toward his hotel.

Trammel thought about having one of his deputies keep an eye on Bessler but decided it would be a waste of time. Bessler was likely smart enough to spot someone watching him. Besides, sometimes the best way to spot a fire was to let it breathe a little.

To let it burn a bit before stomping it out.

CHAPTER 4

"Don't you dare tell me to calm down in my own office," Mayor Walt Holm bellowed. "I'm telling you, Trammel knows we're up to something."

Bessler ran his hand over the bag of gold coins Holm had placed on the table. His gold. His price for freeing Lucien Clay.

"Don't be so dramatic," Bessler told him. "You political types are always so dramatic at the first sign of trouble. Trammel is far too impressed with himself to know anything of the sort. He might suspect something, but that's his nature. I'm not taking him lightly, but I'm not running out of town, either."

"Don't let his size fool you." Holm continued to pace on the carpet of his law office. "He might look like a lumbering fool, but he's far from it. I saw that run-in between the two of you down on the street just now. I might not have been able to hear what you said, but I saw the way you were fencing with each other."

Bessler was glad his performance had been appreciated. What was the use in taking risks if no one saw him do it? "So? What of it? I had a little fun at his expense. Mentioned his charming wife, too. Gave him something to think about."

Holm rubbed his hands in frustration. "You couldn't let it go, could you? You just had to show him how smart you were. Had to show him you were strong enough to take the bait and wriggle yourself off the hook. Still the same showboating dandy you were in the Badlands. You never change."

Bessler always found Holm's discomfort entertaining. He was always so easy to rile. "Surely we haven't sunk low enough for fishing analogies, Walt. You used to be far cleverer than that."

But Holm was not done with his rant. "No one ever got very far by taunting the likes of Buck Trammel. He's much smarter than you'd expect him to be."

"No," Bessler corrected him. "He's just smarter than *you* expected him to be. I'm not in the habit of underestimating my opponents. Not in a courtroom and never in a gunfight. I expect every man I face to be fully capable of stopping me, which is why I always make it my business to have a plan before the deadly dance starts."

"You and your confounded plans." Holm groaned in disapproval. "Clay and Stanton thought they had a plan for Trammel, too. So have about a dozen men who've ridden into this territory to finish him off since he came here with Hagen. Do you know where all their preparation got them? Six feet under the cold earth is where. Why, not even Lucien could outlast Trammel, and Clay is probably the most cunning man I've ever known."

"If he was so cunning, you wouldn't need me to break him out of prison."

"Lucien's in prison because he got overconfident," Holm told him. "His brain was addled by too much laudanum and not enough common sense. He learned the same thing as all the others. Just when you think you've got Trammel cornered, he busts through a wall. What he lacks in finesse, he more than makes up for with brute force. And wherever he is, that scoundrel Adam Hagen is sure to follow."

All this unnecessary worry was beginning to annoy Bessler. "I've already counted on Adam Hagen's interference at some point. I haven't met him yet, but I plan on rectifying that before I set my plan in motion."

Holm stopped pacing. "You're to give that man a wide berth, Frank. That's an order. He's liable to put a bullet in you just for looking at him crooked. That is one bear I forbid you to poke."

Bessler laughed. "You're not in any position to order me around or forbid me from doing anything. You forget I'm not exactly some piker myself. I've done this kind of thing many times before. That's why you sent for me in the first place. I might not have Clay's fame or Stanton's renown, but I'm not one of those Pinkerton thugs that Trammel and Hagen dispatched up in Blackstone, either."

Bessler enjoyed the look of surprise on Holm's face. "Yes, I heard all about those incidents. I had plenty of time to read up on Trammel and Hagen's antics on the long train ride up here, and I've already taken their abilities into account."

It was clear his words were not having the calming effect he had hoped, so Bessler tried a different tactic. An attack of nerves on Holm's part now would only complicate his plans. "You can rest assured I'm not taking either man lightly. I've spent a considerable amount of time studying them and have learned that everyone who has gone up against them have had a single common failing. Just one."

Holm placed his hands on his hips. "Which is?"

"They were foolish enough to face Trammel head-on. Lucien Clay is rotting in a cell right now because he got outmaneuvered by that big ape until it was just the two of them. So did all the men he killed. I won't be making the same mistake." Bessler poked his chest with his thumb. "I won't be staying around long enough to let him corner me. I'll strike early and fast. Lucien and I will be far out of town before the dust settles."

Holm threw up his hands. "Don't tell me the details. People are liable to think I had something to do with this after it happens, so the less I know, the better. I just hope you realize that whatever you're planning won't be as simple as you hope."

But Holm did not need to fear because Bessler had no intention of telling him anything about his plan. Holm's skill had always been in devising a scheme but he could never be counted on to hold his water when things got thick. Bessler doubted years of easy city living in Laramie had done much to steel his resolve.

But as Bessler was relying on him to send Clay's money to Denver once he freed Clay, it might be worth the effort to put his mind at ease. "Lucien wanted me to relay a message to you. 'The days are growing shorter.' I believe that's supposed to be a code for you to release the money with his blessing."

Holm went back to his desk and pulled out an envelope. He removed a piece of paper and began to write.

Until Bessler stopped him. "What are you doing?"

"Writing out an order for John Banner to wire the money to the Bank of Denver, as Lucien and I agreed. It's all been arranged."

"No." Bessler put the first phase of his plan in motion. "There's been a change in that regard. Lucien wants the money shipped overland."

Holm set his pen down. "Overland? You mean by coach?"

Bessler nodded. "His very words. He told me he wants to use the Frontier Overland Company to handle the transaction. I understand they're the best in the territory."

"They are, but that's not what we agreed to in our notes," Holm said. "Wiring the money is fairly commonplace these days, not to mention much more secure."

But Bessler already had an answer ready. "A wire is easier for the authorities to trace. They could put a stop on the withdrawal. Physical gold is easier to divide between us when the time comes for us to go our separate ways. It's just better that way."

Holm looked concerned. "I can't understand why. There's always a risk in taking anything by coach. A wire is much more secure."

Bessler kept the edge out of his voice when he said, "Coach is my client's preferred method, Walt. We should do what he says."

"But that will take some arranging," Holm explained. "We'd have to contact Frontier Overland to have them send a wagon to pick up the money. Then . . ."

"The company is already scheduled to make a stop at the bank tomorrow," Bessler said. "Lucien's money can be added to their shipment. Trust me, it's much better this way. The less time we wait for our money the better. Simply have the bank hold Lucien's gold separate from their other holdings. Like I said, the less time we're stuck in a bank, the better for all concerned. We're picking up a parcel they've been holding for us. Nothing more."

Holm's pen hovered over the paper before he set it aside. "I really should check with Lucien about this."

"By all means," Bessler bluffed. "Provided you can find out before nightfall and provided Deputy Haid can get a message to and from Clay without raising any eyebrows." He pointed to the ornate clock in the corner of the room. "I don't think you'll be able to do that in the half an hour before the bank closes. Lucien will be mighty cross with you if that money's not already waiting for him when we get to Denver. But if you want to risk his wrath, that's perfectly fine with me."

Holm looked at the clock and frowned. Time was against him.

Just as Bessler had planned.

"I'll do it," Holm said as he began to write out the order. "But it's highly irregular and reckless."

He finished writing out the order and called out for a messenger. A young man of about sixteen rushed into the office.

"Yes, Mr. Holm?"

The mayor held out the envelope to him. "I want you to deliver this to Mr. John Banner over at the Bank of Laramie immediately. Not to his clerk, not to an assistant. You are to hand deliver this to Mr. Banner himself. It is of the utmost urgency. Then wait for his reply to my orders."

The boy took the envelope and ran from the office like a dog with a stick in its mouth.

Holm frowned at the open door and got up to close it. "I still don't know why he insists on having me send the entire amount by coach. It's far easier for me to transfer the funds via telegram these days. Faster, too."

Bessler was more than happy to keep Holm in the dark. Using the coach to carry the money was the only reason he had agreed to come this far north in the first place. "I don't know our Mr. Clay well, but he strikes me as a most complicated man of fickle interests."

Holm stopped before reaching his desk. "How did you know the stagecoach was making a stop at the bank?"

Bessler had an excuse ready. "I stopped by the bank before I came over here. Told a clerk I might have a deposit for the stage, and he told me when the next one was going out."

Holm rubbed his chin in thought. "Yes. And it sounds

like the timing works out perfectly with your plan. Almost too perfectly to suit me."

Bessler pocketed his gold as he got to his feet. Holm had just served his purpose. There was no point in wasting any more time with him. After all, he had a man to break out of prison, and not a moment to lose in doing it.

"Lucien Clay and I are beyond your care, Walt. Don't give us another thought."

The mayor winced when Bessler clapped a heavy hand on his shoulder. "I don't have to remind you that you'll need to be careful after all of this. Things are liable to get awfully heated around here once I carry out my plan. I'll have plenty to worry about keeping Clay free. I don't want to have to worry about you losing heart." He squeezed Holm's skinny shoulder hard enough to make him cringe but would not allow him to pull away. "And I won't have to worry, will I, Walt?"

"I've already got my chunk of the money Lucien promised me," Holm said through gritted teeth. "I've got more to lose than you do. You don't have to worry about me."

Bessler released his shoulder and gave him a light pat on the jaw. "Good boy."

Upon returning to his hotel room, Frank Besser began to get ready. He would have preferred to have an entire week to study the prison and town more thoroughly, but the events of the day had made that impossible. Trammel had seen him and grown curious. The longer Bessler waited to make his move, the more likely something could go wrong. Haid could get an attack of conscience. Clay might grow anxious and tip his hand. Mayor Walt Holm's nerves might get the better of him, and even a side glance from Trammel at the wrong time could cause him to spill his guts. Bessler would not give him the opportunity.

He was going to break Clay out of prison that same night.

But as he began to get ready, there was one loose end that dangled just out of his vision like a troublesome eyelash. Adam Hagen. Holm might have been unreliable, but he was not a fool. Both Holm and Clay had made it a point to mention Hagen as a point of concern. From what he knew about the man, their concerns were justified. The saloon owner would undoubtedly play a hand in the aftermath of the events to come that evening, but how capable was he? Hagen was the only outlier. The only man he had not met yet. He was an unknown, and unknowns always troubled Frank Bessler.

The attorney had built his reputation on knowing the answers to the unknowable. He had come to Laramie because he was being paid to do what he did best. To free guilty men from the iron grip of the law. When his skills in the courtroom proved inefficient to the task, his skills with a gun or a stick of dynamite usually got the job done.

Whether it was filing a motion in court or blowing open the iron door of a jail, planning had been the cornerstone of Bessler's success. Surprise was key. Doing the unexpected had proven to be a constant and reliable tactic.

He tended to his weapons. He had long resisted his natural inclination to hire a gunsmith to craft a special gun for him. His flair for the dramatic would have enjoyed having a special gun created just for him. But special firearms often required special ammunition to be effective, and special ammunition was hard to come by for men on the run. And because an empty gun was of little use to anyone, he opted for a standard selection.

He sat at the table beside the balcony and took the

Winchester '73 in hand. He unloaded it, used his gun kit to strip and clean it thoroughly before reassembling it, reloading all fifteen rounds. The rifle was much too large and cumbersome to take into the jail, but it would be essential once they reached open ground in the second phase of the escape.

In fact, he already had an idea of when and where he would use it.

He set the rifle aside and picked up his .41 Long Colt revolver, commonly known as the Thunderer. The pistol had served him well over the years and was the ideal handgun for him to use in such conditions. It was well-balanced and as easy to draw as it was to reload. He hoped he would not be forced to shoot his way out of the jail, but it paid to be prepared for any situation.

After taking the pistol apart and cleaning it properly, he reassembled and reloaded it. He smiled at the sound the bullets made as he slid them back into the cylinder. He held up the loaded gun and examined it. The cold steel looked particularly sinister despite the weak lamplight of his room.

He slid the pistol back into its holster on the gun belt on the table and fed new bullets into the vacant loops on his belt. Then he grabbed his coach gun. The stubby, double-barreled shotgun would be his primary weapon of choice inside the prison. It was small enough to easily conceal under his coat when he was on the street and easy to draw at the appropriate time.

It only carried two cartridges, but the mere sight of it was usually enough to strike fear into whoever it was aimed at. He had seen men Trammel's size frozen in place by the mere sight of it, for a man did not need to be a marksman for it to be effective. And when held against a man's back, even one barrel was guaranteed to be lethal.

He slid both cartridges in place and flicked the weapon shut with a satisfying click.

His modest array of weapons now cleaned and sorted, he moved to the ammunition phase of his planning. He took a box of bullets for the Colt from his saddlebag and dumped them into the right pocket of his coat. He took another box of shotgun shells and dumped them in his left coat pocket. He had seen many men killed as they fumbled for a bullet in the middle of a gunfight. Frank Bessler did not plan on dying in Laramie due to a lack of firing back.

He tossed his loaded coat on the unmade bed and walked out onto the balcony. This would be his last night in Laramie, and he wanted to take one last look at the town before he put his plan in motion. It was already well past sunset, and the town was draped in darkness. No one would see him out there now. He had already made more of an impression than he had planned. Just one last look for good luck.

Bessler enjoyed watching the oil lamps flicker along the wide streets of the frontier town. He could hear the familiar sound of tinny pianos and bawdy singing from the saloons near the hotel. It almost felt like home.

Laramie was a far cry from the general lawlessness of Fort Worth, but there was that familiar element of danger in the air. A feeling that anything could happen at any given moment. That feeling was strong enough to give him pause as he looked out at City Hall and the prison courtyard beside it. His next destination. His destiny.

Yes, timing was essential to his plan. Would he be able to muzzle Doc Carson before the old sawbones could alert one of the guards? Would one of the good citizens of Laramie spot him lingering near the prison and run to tell a deputy? His entire plan to free Clay would be lost if he was discovered before he forced his way into the jail. He would have to make a run for it, knowing he had lost his only chance to earn the rest of his money. Trammel would see to it no one ever got close to Clay again. Such a failure would cost him more than his fee. It would damage a reputation that was already teetering on the edge of respectability.

Bessler did not admire Lucien Clay or think he deserved to be free. The man had been foolish enough, and greedy enough, to involve himself in the Hagen family quarrel. He had arranged for a federal marshal to be gunned down on a city street in broad daylight and had not taken the time to properly hide his hand in the proceedings. Clay deserved to be in prison if for no other reason than his sloppiness.

No, Frank Bessler was not going to break Lucien Clay out of prison because he thought Clay was innocent. He was going to break him out of prison because he needed the money. He needed Clay's freedom more than Clay needed it himself.

His fortunes had turned sour in Texas. A string of defeats in court and an angry judge had derailed his law career. Prison breaks gone wrong in Pecos and Gonzales had cost him money and his standing as a man who always delivered whatever he had promised his clients.

It would have been easy to blame his recent failures on nothing more than a run of bad luck, but Bessler knew it was far more complicated than that. Gamblers could afford to believe in fantasies like luck, but not attorneys. He knew the common factor in all his recent disappointments was Bessler himself.

Perhaps he had grown too confident in his own abilities? He had enjoyed such a long string of success in court and outside of it that he may have become complacent. He doubted he had been in Laramie long enough to truly understand all the shortcomings of his plan, but he no longer had the luxury of time.

Bessler looked over the prison courtyard one last time

and saw the now familiar old railroad lamp hanging outside a shack at the back of the stalls where the deputies' horses were kept. He might not have been able to see much of the courtyard now, but he had already committed every inch of the place to memory. He played out his plan in his mind for the hundredth time and looked for a weakness.

There's no weakness. Stop overthinking it. It's a good plan. I'm good enough to pull it off. By this time tomorrow, Laramie will be a distant memory long behind me and Lucien Clay will be free. We'll hit the stage before it reaches Denver and I'll have more money than I planned. Enough to start a new life anywhere I choose.

Bessler imagined that he and Clay would go their separate ways after they robbed the stagecoach. He would not care what happened to him after that, though he imagined he would probably be caught within a year. Men like Clay never learned to appreciate good fortune. They always returned to the same conduct that had gotten them in trouble in the first place because lawlessness was all they knew.

Just like men such as Trammel only knew the law.

Bessler drew in a deep lungful of air. Ah, the great Buck Trammel. He would never allow Bessler and Clay to simply escape, which was why Bessler had already taken Trammel's pursuit into account. And now that he had finally met Trammel, he had been able to take the measure of the man personally. He would not come after them just because it was his job to do so. He would come after them as a point of pride. It was his duty. It was up to Bessler to use that pride as a weapon against him. His dedication would ultimately be his own undoing.

For Buck Trammel was a city man. A town man. He had been a policeman in Manhattan and had later served as a Pinkerton out of Chicago. His reputation had been built within the confines of civilization. Out in the wild, on horseback, the battle would take place on Bessler's terms and on ground of his choosing. The farther they got from Laramie, the more Trammel would play into Bessler's hands.

But he doubted Trammel would come alone. He was popular in town and would have no problem gathering a posse to run them down. Trammel would insist on leading it, of course, for he would never allow another man to do his duty for him.

Bessler smiled at the thought. He would spring his trap on the big man at precisely the right time. He even had the ideal spot for the occasion picked out in his mind.

And once Trammel was dead, the men who had ridden with him would crumple like old paper. A posse, even one comprised of his talented deputies, would not easily recover from the loss of a great leader like Trammel. He was larger than life, and not simply because of his size. He was a legend in the making. His death would either stop them cold or delay them enough to allow Bessler and Clay plenty of time to hit the bank stagecoach, grab the money, and disappear into anonymity in the large city.

Bessler knew that not even Trammel's death would be enough to stop the chase. If anything, it would make him and Clay wanted men, with appropriately high bounties on their heads. The survivors of the posse would undoubtedly seek to either bring them to justice or avenge their fallen sheriff.

Frank Bessler and Lucien Clay would become two of the most wanted men in the country. Bessler hoped to use his newfound infamy to his benefit. Any man of means who found himself behind bars would undoubtedly want to hire "the Man Who Killed Buck Trammel." He would be able to charge double his current fee for his services. Perhaps even triple.

Bessler leaned against the balcony railing as he dwelled

on the one weakness of his plan. Mayor Walt Holm may likely find himself in a position where he would have no choice but to admit his involvement in Clay's escape plan. If Holm did not talk, his messenger—Deputy Hal Haid— probably would.

But Bessler had already accounted for that eventuality. He would already have a new life in place before either man unburdened their conscience. Bessler already had a new life waiting for him in the safety of Oklahoma City. There was enough chaos in the territory for a man of Bessler's skill to begin a new life. And he would have more than enough money at his disposal to ensure no one got too curious about his past.

Yes, being prepared was its own virtue. And the man calling himself Frank Bessler would never be caught unprepared again.

But he remembered an unsettling part of his discussions that day. The part about Trammel and Hagen being two sides of the same coin. Where one went, the other was certain to follow. He had met Trammel but not Adam Hagen.

He craned his neck to look through the narrow alleyway at the Bank of Laramie clock tower. It was just after nine thirty in the evening. Plenty of time for him to get a closer look at the other side of the coin.

CHAPTER 5

Adam Hagen sipped brandy while standing at the end of the bar of the Emerald Isle. He liked what he saw. To say the newly renovated saloon—formerly known as the Rose of Tralee—was doing great business would have been an understatement. The bar was packed with men standing two deep, and none of them appeared to be in a hurry to leave. Each of his gaming tables had crowds at least three deep as they waited to wager on the spin of a wheel, a roll of the dice, or the turn of a card. Every chair at his poker tables was full and there was no shortage of gamblers anxious to pounce on the first available seat.

Laramie was turning out to be a better investment for Adam than Blackstone. And while he had hoped to be in control of his family's empire by now, a firm hold on Laramie's major vice dens was more than ample compensation. He had come to accept that finishing second place was better than not finishing at all.

Hagen checked his pocket watch and saw it was nearly half past ten. This was normally the time when Verne Ayres would have blustered into the saloon drunk and ready to dance with Lady Luck.

The rugged old dust rat had never fitted in with the high-class clientele Hagen had sought to attract when he refurbished the Emerald Isle. The shabby furnishings and crude paintings were long gone, quickly replaced by elegant drapes and padded seats for the gamblers' comfort. Hagen rolled the barrels of rotgut whiskey down the street to other saloons he owned. This one only served fine liquor and beer that was easier to swallow and offered a more forgiving hangover the next morning.

Even the women Hagen hired to work the floor were of a better disposition than the tired old warhorses Lucien Clay had employed to keep his customers distracted from how much money they were losing.

Adam Hagen knew he may never gain control of his family's empire, but he was building an empire of his own. And Verne Ayres's claim might just prove to be its cornerstone. Hagen would hire one of the men from the claims office to ride out to the Ayres site the next day to judge the value of what he had found there.

Hagen set his snifter on the bar when he saw a large, well-dressed man push through the doors of his saloon. At first glance, he thought it was Buck Trammel wearing his Sunday best but quickly realized this man was just a bit smaller than the sheriff. His black beard was thick but well-groomed. His dark brown suit was of good quality. Good enough for Hagen to hope he might be willing to lose a significant amount of money at one of his many games of chance.

The pistol on his hip looked as if it was kept in good condition, so it was clear to Hagen there was more to this stranger than just money.

Hagen watched him thread his way through the crowded saloon and decided to introduce himself. "Welcome to the Emerald Isle, sir. I'm Adam Hagen. Owner and proprietor of this establishment."

The two men shook hands. "Frank Bessler out of Texas," the bigger man said before adding, "Esquire."

"A man of the law," Hagen remarked. "We always have a warm welcome for attorneys in here. So many of my customers find themselves requiring the services of one at some time or another."

"Services I believe you've required recently," Bessler said, "if what I've heard about you is accurate."

"Anything you hear about me is probably accurate," Hagen said. "The good as well as the bad." He patted a free space on the bar. "What'll you drink, Mr. Bessler? The first one's on me."

"Since you're buying, I'll let you decide."

Hagen flagged down the bartender and told him to pour two brandies. "I hope you don't mind brandy."

"I believe a free drink is the best drink," Bessler said. "I also happen to be partial to brandy and a good cigar."

Hagen was beginning to like the stranger. "Then you've come to the right place. You should join me in the back, where we can enjoy a slightly more refined atmosphere."

Bessler thanked the bartender when he placed two snifters of brandy on the bar. "A refined atmosphere often means more refined tables with equally refined stakes."

Hagen clinked glasses with him. "I am but a pane of glass to your discerning eye, Mr. Bessler. My motives are as transparent and predictable as they are pure."

"Can't say how pure they are, but they're certainly plain enough." The two men drank. "Clarity is often its own reward."

Now that he had hooked him with a free drink, Hagen wanted to haul him into the boat to see how big a fish he was. "What brings you to our fair frontier town of Laramie?"

"Business," Bessler told him. "A client, to be precise. In fact, I believe he once owned this place."

Hagen swallowed his brandy. The stranger had not come to the Emerald Isle by accident or to gamble. He came to play a game of a different sort. "Lucien Clay. I know him well. I heard he had a new visitor at the prison this morning. I didn't know it was you."

"Word certainly travels fast around here, doesn't it? I only met him for the first time today. I'd corresponded with him before coming to Laramie, of course, but meeting a man in person is much better than reading his letters."

Hagen found that curious. "How did he find you? Wyoming and Texas don't exactly share a border."

"I was recommended to him by a former client. I'd never been to Wyoming, though I've heard of its beauty, so I decided to make the trip via train. The beauty of this place has exceeded my expectations."

"I hope you don't have expectations of victory," Hagen warned him. "You won't win any victories by representing Lucien in a court of law. The man's fate has already been sealed as far as the courts are concerned."

"Nothing is ever sealed in the eyes of the law," Bessler said. "Take your brother's case, for instance. I believe he's still awaiting trial after all these months."

Hagen frowned. "Caleb's case is just as hopeless. My brother will never breathe free air again. Something tells me you didn't just happen to wander in here tonight, did you? You came for a reason."

Bessler shrugged easily. "I asked the man at the front desk of my hotel to recommend a place where I could try my hand at cards, and he told me I should come here. He recommended it quite highly."

Hagen made sure the men at every hotel desk in town were well paid to recommend the Emerald Isle to anyone who might have more than a couple of coins in their pockets.

But this was about more than a recommendation. "You came here to play a game of a different sort. And I'm getting mighty curious about what that game might be."

"Poker, faro, roulette," Bessler listed. "I'm also pretty fair at billiards, if you have a table."

"There are plenty of other saloons in town that offer those games and more."

"But none of those places have Adam Hagen." Bessler set his snifter of brandy on the bar next to Hagen's. "There's no reason to make this sound sinister. I'm just trying to get a feel for the town. Of Laramie. Since I'm representing Mr. Clay, it's only prudent that I should get to know something about the place he ran for so long and his former partners."

Hagen could tell Bessler was the type who never left much to chance. The attorney had probably already formed an opinion about him before he walked through the door. It was time to throw him off a bit. "How is old Lucien doing these days? Still having trouble speaking, I trust."

"His jaw has healed quite a bit," Bessler told him, "and he's in surprisingly good spirits despite his current situation. He's hopeful for the future."

Hagen laughed. "I can't imagine why. He's got a life of hard labor and cold gruel to look forward to. At least Major Stanton had the good sense to succumb to his injuries and avoid a life of hardship and toil. I suggest you tell your client to consider a similar approach. I doubt the deputies or guards would rush to save him should they find he hanged himself in his cell one night. I'll even supply the rope."

"I'm sure you would," Bessler said, "but like my mother used to say, 'Where there's life, there's hope.' And I assure you that there's still plenty of life left in Lucien Clay."

Hagen scooped up his snifter. "More's the pity." He

began to do some goading of his own. "What do you think of Clay, Mr. Bessler? Not as his lawyer, but as one man talking to another in a saloon."

"I just met him this morning, so I don't really have an opinion about him one way or the other. I know I like his money, though. Sometimes that can be enough."

"Finally, we're in agreement about something." Hagen let out an exaggerated sigh as he swirled his brandy in its snifter. "Sorry for getting testy earlier. When I learned you were representing Lucien, my blood went up. Given my history with the man, I hope you'll forgive me."

"I don't see why you should resent him," Bessler said. "After all, you're out here free as a bird and he's stuck behind bars when it could easily be the other way around. In fact, I've spoken to a few people who believe you should be in the next cell to your brother."

Hagen placed his brandy on the bar with his right hand while he lifted the lawyer's pistol from the holster on his hip with his left. Bessler had tried to grab it but was too late.

The men around them at the bar grew quiet when they saw Hagen holding the gun.

"What a nice bit of hardware you've brought with you," Hagen said as he let the light play on the gunmetal. "An excellent choice. A Colt Thunderer. I carry one of these myself. An unfortunate name, really. 'Thunderer.' Hard to say when you've had a few too many. The fumbling kind of takes the sting out of it."

Bessler pushed himself away from the bar and grew very still. "You've got fast hands, Mr. Hagen."

Hagen grinned. "And that was with my left hand, sir. Let's hope you never see me pull that trick with my right." He went back to examining the pistol. "It pays to have fast hands in this line of work." He lowered the Colt. "Quite a fancy gun for a lawyer to tote around, even one from Texas. Are you expecting trouble of some kind?"

"I don't think I have to explain to you about the importance of being vigilant. A man never knows where trouble might pop up."

"Or from whom." Hagen looked at the lawyer. "Am I going to have trouble from you, Mr. Bessler?"

The bigger man balled his fists at his side. "Not if you hand over that pistol. Right now."

Now Hagen saw the true man beneath the fine clothes and trim beard. He recognized the glint in his dark eyes. This man was a fighter. He had come to Laramie for more than just a client.

Hagen slipped his finger behind the trigger and allowed the pistol to turn until the handle faced the lawyer. "You keep it in admirable condition. Freshly cleaned, too, if my nose is any judge. You must be expecting trouble this evening."

Bessler took the gun and slowly slid it back into his holster. "A clean gun makes for a clean heart."

Hagen had not heard that one before. "Did your mama say that, too?"

"No." Bessler began to back out of the bar. "I learned that one on my own. Thank you for an enlightening evening, Mr. Hagen." He touched the brim of his bowler. "Until next time."

"I'll be looking forward to it." Hagen allowed his hand to fall to his side near his holster as he watched the lawyer back out of the saloon.

The customers breathed a sigh of relief when Bessler stepped out onto the boardwalk and disappeared from view.

Hagen knew he would probably be seeing Frank Bessler much sooner than he would have preferred.

CHAPTER 6

Bessler walked back to the Continental with purpose but was careful not to run. People, even those coming out of bars at this late hour, tended to remember a man running through the streets. He knew word of his run-in with Hagen would spread throughout Laramie by the following morning. Some might say he had backed down from the gambler.

But after the events that would follow later that night, the people of Laramie would remember Frank Bessler for an entirely different reason. Now that he knew the measure of both Trammel and Hagen, it was finally time to set his plan in motion.

Bessler passed the front desk of his hotel and saw the night clerk was already beginning to nod off. The clock in the lobby told him it was a quarter past eleven. He did not have a moment to lose.

Bessler took the carpeted stairs two at a time up to his room. He changed out of his suit and left it on the bed, opting for the more rugged clothes he had worn on the train. Faded pants and an old brown shirt. He would be traveling light and decided to leave the fancy garb behind. Once he got his hands on the stagecoach's money, he could buy a wardrobe full of suits if he chose to do so.

He uncoiled his rope and tied it around his saddlebags

and rifle. He carried the bundle over to the balcony and began to lower it over the railing to the narrow alley below. The space between the buildings was not wide enough for anyone to take that route from one part of town to the other. He knew his parcels should remain undisturbed until he went down to collect them.

Once they reached the ground, Bessler tossed the other end of the rope over the side and went back into the room. He pulled on his coat and slid the coach gun into the large holster he had sewn inside it. He left enough money on the dresser to pay for the room. Never let it be said that Frank Bessler skipped out on a debt. He imagined the gesture would only add to his legend in the days to come.

He did not bother to lock the door when he left and descended the stairs quietly. He glanced at the clerk at the desk as he reached the bottom and was glad to see he had nodded off completely. In the morning, the clerk would be all too willing to lie about what he had seen that historic evening to anyone who would listen. Bessler doubted he would admit that he had slept through the beginning of it.

Bessler walked out the back door of the hotel past the kitchen and headed for the livery stables. When he had checked in two days before, the manager had assured him the animals were guarded night and day by a dedicated stable boy. But as he studied the prison courtyard from his balcony, he had also kept a close watch on the hotel livery. No one tended the horses after dark. Because he already knew this oversight would eventually suit his purposes, he had decided not to complain.

Bessler took a quick look around the stalls. No sign of an attendant. He walked over to the alley and collected his saddlebags, rope, and rifle. He carried them over to the stalls where both horses he had brought to town were kept. He was glad to see the animals had been fed and cared for over the past few days. They would need their strength for the long journey ahead.

He had little trouble finding his saddles and bridles and began to get the animals ready to ride. He slid his saddle-bags over his horse, a roan, and placed his Winchester in the saddle scabbard.

He led his horse and his spare, a sturdy bay, out of their stalls and into the wider alley that fed out onto Main Street. He climbed into the saddle, took hold of the spare's rope, and rode into the thoroughfare. There was little foot or wagon traffic at that time of night. No one saw him take a sharp left.

Most of the windows of the buildings he passed were dark, save for the odd oil lamp that burned somewhere deep within. He rode along the same route he had worked out from his balcony over the preceding two days. He had also walked it both in daylight and after dark. He knew where he was going.

He continued to ride north for three blocks before taking a right. He continued in that direction for an additional three blocks before another right took him directly to his destination.

The rear wall of the prison courtyard loomed high at the end of the street. It was not as tall as the wall of the main yard, where the prisoners were allowed to exercise for roughly an hour each day. These stables were used to keep the horses of Laramie's deputies. Prisoners were not allowed in that part of the facility.

He imagined whoever had built the wall had not envisioned the need to waste bricks on an area that only served the stables. Why would anyone try to sneak into a jail?

Why, indeed.

Bessler rode close to the wall, then climbed down from the saddle and ground hobbled both horses. He needed them to remain in place while he went about setting Lucien Clay free.

He untied the rope from the packhorse and tied a sturdy knot around the saddle horn of his own. Bessler gingerly climbed onto the saddle and used the wall to steady himself as he got his balance. His significant height allowed him to easily see over the top of the wall. The courtyard leading to the side door of the prison was still deserted. The horses in the stalls were bedded down for the night.

He strained to listen for any hint that the stable hand who minded the place might still be awake. The faint sound of snoring carried on the wind told him the man was fast asleep.

Time to move.

He slowly lowered the rope over the other side of the wall. Simply tossing it over might stir the horses, and he knew his presence in the courtyard would spook them soon enough. He did not want to risk waking the stable hand until the last possible moment.

Bessler easily lifted himself over the top of the wall, grabbed hold of the rope, and lowered himself down to the ground without a sound. He had made it.

He paused again at the base of the wall to listen for any sign that he had been detected. Aside from the gentle fussing of the horses at his scent, all remained quiet.

Bessler took his coach gun from the holster inside his coat. He began to move through the darkness in the path he had laid out in his mind days before from the balcony of his hotel. The layout of the stables was easy enough to remember without the benefit of a lamp.

He paused when he reached the small shack where he had watched the stable hand sleep for the previous two nights. His gentle snoring continued as Bessler moved inside. He brought the butt of the gun down solidly on the sleeping man's temple. The snoring stopped. He used two fingers to check for a pulse at his victim's neck and felt he was still alive. Good. Horses were sensitive animals and tended to become skittish around death. It was also bad luck to kill an innocent. Bad for his reputation, too. A reputation that he hoped would be enhanced by what he did in the next few moments.

He stepped out of the shack and moved among the aisle of stalls. The animals had grown a bit more restless since Bessler had stepped into the courtyard, but not enough to arouse attention.

He pulled his pocket watch from his vest and strained to see the time in the weak starlight. It was almost midnight. His timing had been perfect. Not too early and not too late. Only a few short minutes until he met his destiny.

Bessler crouched in the shadow of the stalls. All he had to do was wait and be ready to strike when the moment came.

Dr. William Carson's knees popped as he stood to pull his braces over his shoulders. His hands ached from the effort of tucking his shirt into his pants. His legs hurt when he walked and hurt when he remained still, so he decided it was best to keep moving whenever possible.

He did not need to be a doctor to know that a man of his advancing years should have the good sense to be in bed at that time of night, but he had never been much of a sleeper. He had always preferred to keep odd hours. It kept his mind sharp despite his daily routine remaining unchanged.

Doc Carson did not see the value of following convention for convention's sake. Why remain in bed when there was plenty of work to be done? Why waste time staring up at the ceiling when he could be tending to his patients at the prison? He preferred to check in at night, while the men slept, so he could gauge their condition without their opinions.

He could tell a great deal about their health by listening to the way they snored, how they breathed, and taking note of who was having trouble sleeping.

His time in the army during the War Between the States had taught him that men confined in close quarters were easy prey for diseases like consumption and other afflictions that targeted the lungs. A sickness could sweep through a camp within a matter of hours, and the dank conditions of the prison made such outbreaks likely. Just because these men had been convicted of a crime did not mean they ought to be condemned to a slow, suffocating death. Not if Doc Carson had anything to say about it. And he had plenty to say on the health of those in his care.

His days were spent tending to whatever ailed them, real or imagined. He never ceased to be amazed by the lies they concocted to get out of work duty or to obtain a spoonful of laudanum. Anything to make the slow time of their incarceration pass quicker.

Doc Carson stifled a cough as he pulled on his heavy coat before leaving his room at the boardinghouse. He had been living there long enough to know how to avoid every creaky board in the hallway. There was no point in disturbing the other tenants from their slumber just because he decided to go back to work.

Once outside, he pulled up his coat collar against the brisk night wind blowing along Main Street. His aching bones confirmed that autumn was fast approaching, which made his nightly vigils at the prison even more important. The poor souls sweltered during the summer, but the cold brought other dangers such as influenza and pneumonia. It was best to keep ahead of such things whenever possible. All it cost him was time, and he had plenty of that to spare. Too much time, in fact. Without a wife or family of his own, he was a forgotten man who had dedicated his life to serving other similarly forgotten men.

He listened to the muted sounds from the many saloons that were still doing a brisk business despite it being just before midnight. Laramie had been a much smaller town when he first arrived there almost ten years before. Quieter, too.

But unlike many of Laramie's other longtime residents, Carson did not resent progress. Change was an inevitable part of life and, in his opinion, necessary. Change was as unavoidable as the snows that would soon begin to blanket the town.

Carson clutched the top of his coat shut from the cold while he dug his key to the courtyard gates with his right hand. The double doors to the courtyard and stables were large iron affairs that met in the middle. He remembered back to when the courtyard wall and doors had been constructed, about eight years previously. The walls had been built quickly and poorly. The mortar between the bricks was beginning to crumble in several places. The iron doors and their hinges were rusty from years of exposure to the elements and prone to sticking. They also shrieked like a banshee each time they were opened or closed.

He slid his key into the lock and began his twice daily battle to wrench the right door open. He could have entered the jail easily enough through the front of City Hall, but the stairs down to the prison caused his knees to ache. He struggled to pry the door outward just enough to allow him to slip through before using all his weight to pull it shut and locked again. He would try to remember to ask one of the guards if they could apply some oil or grease to the hinges when they came on duty the following morning.

Carson glanced over at the stalls to see if Old Bob might be awake, but he only saw shadows. The stable hand was hard to rouse once asleep, and the doctor envied him for it.

The horses seemed a bit more anxious than normal, but he imagined they had caught the scent of something on the wind. Perhaps a coyote or a wolf on the outskirts of town.

The great bell in the Bank of Laramie clock tower began to peal twelve times to mark midnight as Carson reached the side door that led into the prison. The iron door was installed before the courtyard wall had been built and was of much better construction. He undid the lock, and the door swung inward easily and without sound.

The clock tower bell was still ringing when a sharp blow to the back sent Doc Carson tumbling forward into the prison. He landed flat on his face and, for a moment, wondered if one of the horses had broken loose from one of the stalls and kicked him.

He realized his mistake as soon as he felt cold gunmetal pressed against the back of his neck.

A man spoke as the echo of the last gong from the clock tower faded. "Don't make a sound, old-timer. Just do what I say and no one gets hurt."

Carson's mouth went dry as fear crept into his bones. He could not have made a sound had he wanted to.

He heard the side door close behind him before a rough hand grabbed hold of his collar. His attacker pulled him to his feet as easily as if he was a rag doll, then pressed the gun into the small of his back.

"Take me to Clay's cell," the man whispered. "Do it quietly. If you let out a cry for the guards or make a sound, I'll pull both triggers and cut you in half. Nod if you understand me."

Carson quickly nodded and began to lead his attacker down the aisle that led to Lucien Clay's cell. He may have spent his life in a prison surrounded by convicted criminals, but he had rarely known fear like this since the war. His entire body had gone numb. He thought he would have fallen over if the man had not been holding him upright.

Most of the prisoners were sleeping, but even in the dim light, Doc Carson saw Lucien Clay was on his feet, ready to go. His long, stringy gray hair hung over eyes that were alive with excitement.

Doc Carson remained quiet when the gunman pulled him to a halt and pushed him flat against the bars next to Clay's cell. "Hand over the key to his cell. If you drop it, I'll hurt you."

Carson did not realize until that moment that he had managed to keep the key in his hand when he was knocked over. He held it up for the man to take, which he promptly did. The man switched his gun to his left hand as he unlocked Clay's cell door.

Carson shut his eyes. The sound of the opening door sounded like defeat. He did not want to see the man who had attacked him. He did not want to see Lucien Clay free. His panicked brain made him hope they might forget Carson was there if he just remained still long enough. Quiet. The doctor had never been a religious man, but he found himself praying that he would survive whatever came next.

Carson shut his eyes even tighter when he heard Clay's cold voice in his ear. "You know what I've always liked about you, Doctor? You're punctual. A man could set his watch by the schedule you keep."

Carson held his breath as Lucien pushed his face harder against the bars. "I just hope you're smart enough to keep doing as you're told. Are you going to keep doing what you're told, Doc?"

Carson nodded as best he could with his face pressed so hard against the bars.

"Good boy," Clay whispered. "I want you to keep quiet

and lead us out the same door you just came through. Move nice and slow. If you make a sound or let out a cry for the guards, you're a dead man. Do what you're told and you'll probably live. Understand?"

Carson nodded again before Lucien took a firm hold on his collar and yanked him off the bars. The doctor thought his heart stopped beating when he heard one of the prisoners begin to stir from his sleep.

"Lucien?" a prisoner called out. "Is that you? What's happening?"

Carson had not realized his attacker had pushed him against Caleb Hagen's cell door. And now the convict was awake.

Clay kept the doctor moving. "Hurry up," he whispered. "Get going. Don't stop until I tell you."

Carson shuffled toward the door as quickly as his wobbly legs would allow.

"Lucien?" Hagen said, louder now as he slowly stirred from sleep. "Is this it? The jailbreak? Take me with you, Lucien. I have money. I have power. I can help you!"

Lucien Clay was practically pulling the doctor to move faster as Carson heard the hushed voice of his attacker tell Hagen, "Just sit there and keep your mouth shut if you know what's good for you."

Carson reached the end of the aisle and led them toward the side door to the courtyard as Caleb Hagen began to bellow.

"Lucien!" Hagen's desperate wail seemed to fill the prison. "Take me with you! You can't just leave me here like this! Lucien!"

Clay threw Doc Carson against the courtyard door as the rest of the prisoners began to wake due to Hagen's shouting. He knew at least one of the guards must have heard it by now.

"Open it!" Lucien shouted. "Open it now!"

Carson's hands shook as he fumbled with the bolt but managed to get the door open.

Clay pushed him into the courtyard and grabbed hold of his collar before he fell. "Stay with me, Doctor. We're not done with you yet."

Carson heard the gunman behind them say, "Climb the rope over the back wall. I've got horses waiting on the other side. I'll be along in a minute."

The doctor somehow managed to keep to his feet as Lucien Clay dragged him toward the wall.

Carson finally found his voice. "Please, Lucien. Don't make me climb that rope. My legs . . ."

"I know all about your knees, Doc," Clay said. "You're doing fine. Just a little while longer. I'll be sure to tell Trammel how cooperative you've been."

Carson felt a surge of pride he did not know he had. "He'll never let you get away with this. That man will hunt you to the ends of the earth."

"Good." Clay laughed. "I'm counting on it."

When they reached the back wall of the courtyard, Clay shoved Doc Carson, causing him to fall to the courtyard.

"Take care of yourself, Doc," Clay said as he began to climb the rope. "Wish I could say it's been fun getting to know you better."

Doc Carson gasped as he tried to get air back into his lungs. He had just managed to get on all fours when he heard heavy boots running toward him from the prison. He thought it might be a guard coming to rescue him until a sudden heavy weight on his back forced him flat on his stomach.

Carson thought he might have been kicked but quickly

realized he had been used as a stool for the escaping gunman to scale the wall.

The doctor managed to glance up at the man as he disappeared over the top of the wall. He was big. Almost as big as Buck Trammel, but not quite.

Carson cursed himself for lying on the ground like a newborn foal. He should run back inside to tell the guards and the deputies what had happened. That Lucien Clay had escaped. But he was too winded and too frightened to move. Too tired. Too sore. Too old.

The best he could manage was to roll over on his side as a great roar rose from within the prison. The guards must be restoring order by now. They would see Lucien Clay's cell was open and run out to the courtyard to find him. They would see Carson slumped beside the wall and bring him inside.

His nightmare was about to end. His prayers had been answered. He had survived.

But Carson's stomach sank when the side door of the prison flew open, and three convicts spilled out into the courtyard. He remembered his assailant had remained behind while Clay forced him to open the door.

The gunman must have used his key to unlock the cells and allow the prisoners to escape to keep the deputies busy while he and Clay made their escape.

The first three convicts in the courtyard were quickly followed by three more, then ten. It did not take long for most of them to run toward the rusted courtyard doors leading out to the street. At first, they tried to pull it before pushing against it, though something kept them from getting it open.

Doc Carson knew they had not seen him yet. He began crawling toward the safety of the horse stalls when he heard one of the prisoners cry out, "Look! The doc's on the ground over there. Let's grab him!"

Carson shut his eyes and covered his head as the group of convicts closed in on him. Dirt was kicked up into his face as rough hands grabbed at his clothes and pushed him against the same wall over which Lucien Clay had just escaped.

His prayers had not been answered after all. His waking nightmare was far from over. It was only just beginning.

CHAPTER 7

Buck Trammel swung his legs out of bed and pulled on his pants as soon as he heard shouts out on the street. He had just managed to slide his feet into his boots when he heard someone pounding at the door downstairs.

"Steve?" Emily asked, still in the grip of sleep. "What's going on?"

"I don't know." Trammel pulled a shirt over his head. "But I'm going to find out."

He took his shoulder rig from the dresser and put it on. He took his Peacemaker and slid it into the holster under his arm as he rumbled down the stairs. He took his hat from the peg by the door and found a winded Deputy Sherwood Blake waiting for him out on the boardwalk in front of the house, rifle in hand.

"We've got a breakout," Blake reported. "Looks like a bad one."

Trammel pulled the door behind him and broke into a run for the prison. The street was quickly filling up with citizens heading in the same direction. There was nothing like a bit of chaos in the middle of the night to rouse people from their beds.

"How many got out?" Trammel asked Blake as the deputy ran beside him.

"Looks like all of them, from what I saw before I came to get you. The doors between the prison and City Hall are holding, but prisoners have flooded the courtyard by the stalls. Hal Haid and some other men were keeping the doors shut when I came to fetch you."

Trammel cursed as he had slowed down to dodge people in his way. None of them seemed to understand their lives might be in danger.

He was able to look above the crowd and see Deputy Hal Haid and three civilians had their backs against the iron doors leading to the stables. Even from more than a street away, Trammel heard fists pounding on the iron and saw his deputy and the others straining to keep the doors from opening.

Trammel knew he did not have a moment to lose. He broke into a dead run and knocked anyone aside who was in his way. He managed to get a fair amount of momentum before launching his large frame against the center of the doors. The sudden impact was enough to knock the prisoners backward and flatten the doors shut.

But the doors quickly began to rattle once more as the prisoners resumed their pounding.

"You got here just in time, boss," Haid told him over the noise. "They were about to break through just now. They're not giving up."

Trammel flipped himself so his back was flush with the doors. "Neither am I."

Another pounding shook him and the three others, but they remained in place. When Blake caught up to him, Trammel said, "Did you send anyone around to the back to grab them if they climb over the wall?"

"Johnny Welch and Charlie Root are back there minding things," Blake said, "but I know some of them already got away. Brillheart and Bush are minding the door downstairs, but the men haven't tried to come that way yet."

Trammel's mind flooded with questions about how this could have happened when another surge from the prisoners rocked him forward. There would be plenty of time for answers as soon as he restored order.

"Leave Bush to mind the doors and bring Brillheart with you up to the offices," Trammel told Blake. "Get ready to fire down into the courtyard when I give the signal. Hurry!"

Blake ran off to carry out his orders as another blow almost bounced Trammel, Haid, and the two civilians with them off the door. The impact was much heavier. It felt like they had found something to use as a ram.

"They must've gotten hold of one of the horses," Trammel concluded. "Probably got it to start bucking and kick the door down."

A crowd of men had formed in a semicircle on the street in front of the courtyard entrance. Two burly teamsters stood out from the other onlookers.

"Need a hand, Sheriff?" one of the men asked. "You boys are looking mighty tired."

Another horse kick rattled the doors, and the teamsters took that as their cue to lend their size to the effort.

Trammel looked up when a thin stream of dirt rained down on the brim of his hat. "Are they dumping something out on us?"

"That's the mortar between the bricks," Haid said after another impact. "These doors might hold, but the wall around us is crumbling. A couple of hits like that and this whole mess will fall right on our heads."

Trammel heard fear in his deputy's voice and saw it on the faces of the four men now helping them keep the convicts at bay.

"Let 'em come, Sheriff," a man yelled from the gathering crowd. "We'll beat 'em back."

The people cheered as Trammel shouted, "Just stay where you are!"

Another impact rocked the doors before several bricks tumbled from the top of the walls. Hal Haid was right. One or two more like that and the whole thing was bound to crumble.

"Clear the way!" a familiar voice shouted as Trammel saw Adam Hagen force his way through the spectators. He was carrying a Winchester and had his pistol on his hip.

"Never thought I'd be glad to see you," Trammel said as another blow rattled his teeth. He thought he could feel the doors begin to pitch forward a little.

"Save the compliments for later," Hagen said. "What do you want me to do?"

There was only one way he thought they might be able to put a stop to this. "After the next hit, I'll pull the door open. You stick your rifle in the opening and start firing inside."

Hagen brought the rifle to his shoulder and moved into the middle of the four men struggling to keep the door closed. He aimed where the space would appear. "Open when ready."

After another blow toppled more bricks from the wall, the two teamsters helped Trammel pull open the door just far enough for Hagen to slip his rifle through. The gambler cut loose with several shots that sent up a cry from the mob in the courtyard.

Trammel pulled the door open wider, and Hagen quickly slid into the courtyard. Trammel pulled his Peacemaker and followed right behind him. After Deputy Haid joined them, the teamsters pushed the door closed.

Trammel stepped over the bodies of three fallen prisoners,

on the ground near the courtyard gate. Like the civilians on
the street, the convicts had formed something of an arc
around the gates. It appeared that most of the prisoners
were crammed into the courtyard. Those who were not
crouching before him were trying to scale the back wall by
the horse stalls.

He glanced up at the windows of City Hall and saw
Blake and Brillheart aiming rifles down into the yard.

Trammel leveled his heavy Peacemaker at the center of
the mass of prisoners. He searched for Lucien Clay but did
not see him.

"It's over," Trammel shouted at them. "Get back to your
cells right now and I promise no one else will get hurt."

The mob parted as a man atop a horse burst through the
crowd and charged at Trammel, Hagen, and Deputy Haid.

All three men fired at the same time. All three shots hit
the rider in the chest, causing the animal to rear up as its
rider fell. The horse managed to keep its balance and trotted
through the prisoners back toward the familiar safety of the
stalls in the courtyard.

The convicts quickly filled in the space where the rider
had fallen. Trammel noted that each of them had the vacant
look of tired and desperate men. Men who had lived without hope for so long that they had forgotten its meaning.

But now that they had enjoyed a brief taste of freedom,
they would not be content to go back to prison life.

Trammel knew then that they would never return to their
cells willingly. But he could not back away from them now.
He pointed up at his deputies in the windows above. "Those
boys will open fire on the next man who takes another step
toward these gates. Call this off now and you have my word
there won't be any reprisals from me or my men."

"Your word?" A coarse, mocking laugh rose from the

middle of the courtyard. "We have something much better than your word, Trammel. We have a guarantee."

The mob parted as one of the prisoners jostled his way to the front. Trammel winced when he saw Caleb Hagen had a thick arm around Doc Carson's neck. The doctor's face was covered in blood and filth.

Adam's aim faltered at the sorry specimen that was his brother. "Caleb? Is that you?"

"The very same," Caleb sneered. "Good of you to stop by to visit me like this. Guess it took a prison break to bring you around."

Since becoming sheriff of Laramie County, Trammel had made a point of walking the prison at least once a day to keep an eye on things, but he had never noticed the stark change in Caleb Hagen's appearance before. His reddish hair, which had once been tamed by hair tonic and careful combing, had grown wild. His beard was an unruly, weedy mass. His stocky frame had withered on his bones and his eyes had a wild, desperate look.

Those sunken eyes settled on Trammel. "We've all heard your demands, Sheriff, but now it's time for you to listen to ours. We're not going back to our cells tonight or any night. We'd rather die than let you and those henchmen you call deputies let us rot in that dungeon you call a prison again."

The prisoners let loose with a cheer of support.

Trammel eyed them closely. Caleb Hagen was uniting them.

"We've had enough of your slop and poor treatment to last us a lifetime," Caleb yelled over the crowd, "so we have our own kind of deal for you. The three of you down here with us and the two deputies up in the windows drop your guns, turn around, and go tell the good citizens of Laramie we're getting out of here. You're going to tell them to stay back and let us leave. If you do that, you have my word that no harm will come to the good doctor here. I'll be sure to cut him loose as soon as I'm out of town."

Trammel aimed his Peacemaker at Caleb's head. It would be a difficult shot from this distance with Doc Carson in the way, but not impossible.

"And if I refuse?" the sheriff asked.

"Then a great many of us will die, starting with the good doctor here." He proved his point by tightening his grip on Doc Carson's throat, making him cry out. "Then it'll be you, Trammel. Followed by my dear brother next to you."

Trammel took careful aim. The desperate look on Doc Carson's face almost willed him to do it.

The prisoners around Caleb crouched like animals about to spring, and Trammel knew they had made up their minds to run at him. The weight of the situation had pitched too far to one side. Momentum was against him. There was no way to avoid blood now.

"Well?" Caleb asked. "What do you say?"

Trammel allowed his pistol to answer for him and fired at Caleb.

Adam began shooting from his right. Deputy Haid from Trammel's left. Blake and Brillheart did the same from above.

The courtyard descended into madness as the prisoners charged forward with a roar, knocking aside their fallen comrades.

Madness descended on the courtyard as all Hell broke loose.

Trammel quickly emptied his pistol into the mass of prisoners as he fought to keep his footing against the rushing mob. Unable to take time to reload, Trammel used his big pistol as a club to beat a path toward the fallen Doc Carson.

Adam and Deputy Haid had also stopped shooting and

resorted to using their weapons and fists to fight against being overwhelmed by the prisoners making a mad dash for freedom.

From their spots up at the windows, Blake and Brillheart had been forced to stop firing when the convicts got too close to their comrades.

Trammel rushed into a clear space in the chaos to find Doc Carson on the ground. He was careful to step over him to prevent him from being trampled by the herd of humanity. Trammel flattened a charging prisoner with a backhand.

The sheriff turned when he heard a terrible crack and saw the embattled wall collapse in a cloud of dust outward into the street. The gates he had fought to keep closed slammed down into the thoroughfare with a loud clang as prisoners climbed over one another and the rubble in a mad dash for freedom. True to their boasts, the civilians had not only held their ground but waded into the tide of escaping convicts.

Trammel hoped the volunteers who had helped him keep the gates closed had gotten clear before the entire mess toppled on them. He looked around for Deputy Haid as prisoners cleared out of the courtyard but saw no sign of him.

Adam Hagen tended to Doc Carson. "Can you stand, Doc?"

Carson grabbed Trammel's leg and tried to pull himself up but fell back to the ground.

"Cover me." Trammel ordered Hagen as Trammel tucked his Peacemaker back in its holster and lifted Carson off the ground. Adam and his Winchester led the way as Trammel carried the doctor to the side door of the prison.

Three prisoners were on their way out when Hagen leveled his empty Winchester at them. "Get back inside or die right here."

The three men turned around and ran back inside.

Hagen held the door open as Trammel carried Carson to the doctor's office and laid him down on the examining table. Hagen stood watch over the hallway beside the half-closed door.

"You boys don't have time to worry about me," Carson told Trammel. "You've got prisoners to round up. Those people out there will kill them if you don't."

But although Trammel was not a doctor, he saw that Carson was in a bad way and continued a quick examination. "Are you shot? Does anything feel broken?"

Carson yelped when Trammel touched his ribs, but a quick check of the rest of his body showed no other wounds except a nasty gash on his head.

Trammel grabbed the nearest bandage he saw and held it against the wound. "Keep pressure on it to stop the bleeding."

Carson pushed his hand away with surprising strength. "I know that. I'm the doctor here, remember?"

Hagen said from the doorway, "Sounds like he's just fine, Buck."

Doc Carson grabbed Trammel's arm with his free hand. "You've got to get after Clay. He's the one who started all this. Had help, too."

Trammel had figured Lucien Clay was at the center of this mess. "How did he manage it?"

Carson winced as he held the bandage to his scalp. "He had a man waiting to jump me out in the courtyard when I came back to make my nightly checks. I didn't get a good look at him, only a glance as he was going over the top of the back wall. He was big, Buck. Almost as big as you."

From his spot at the door, Hagen asked, "Did he sound like he was from Texas?"

Carson did not have to think about it. "I suppose he did, come to think of it."

Hagen reloaded his rifle as he kept an eye on the hallway outside the office. "That sounds like Frank Bessler. I knew I should've shot him when I had the chance."

Trammel was not aware Hagen knew him. "You met him, too?"

"He stopped by to see me over at the Isle about an hour ago. Seemed awful willing to pick a fight with me, but I wouldn't oblige. I thought it was strange at the time, but now it makes sense. He was either getting up enough courage to pull this stunt or he wanted a good look at me before he did it."

Trammel knew he should mount up and ride out after Bessler and Clay right then, before they got too far, but the crisis in town made that impossible. He had to restore order to both the town and the prison before he could even begin to think about running down Bessler and Clay.

And judging by the sounds carrying into the prison from the street, Laramie had already begun to tear itself apart.

Carson made a feeble attempt to push Trammel away. "Go on, Buck. Get out there. Bring this town to heel like you should be doing. I'll be fine."

Trammel knew the doctor was right. "Stay right where you are, Doc. I'll send someone to keep an eye on you as soon as I can manage it."

Hagen left the office before Trammel. Together, they raced off into the heart of the chaos.

CHAPTER 8

As soon as he stepped over the rubble of the ruined courtyard wall, Trammel saw a group of people clustered in the middle of the thoroughfare. The sheriff and Adam pushed their way through the crowd and saw the two teamsters from the door and some other men had ten prisoners lined up against the wall of a warehouse across the street. The prisoners had been badly beaten and were sitting with their heads buried in their hands.

"We've already got a bunch of them rounded up for you, Sheriff," one of the men called over to him. "We're awfully sorry about what happened to your man over there, but we didn't notice him until after everything quieted down. A real shame. He was a brave boy."

Trammel followed the direction in which the man was pointing and saw three civilians gathered around a body lying atop the rubble.

It was difficult to identify him through the blood and dirt at first, but as Trammel stepped closer, he saw the tarnished star pinned to his vest. It was the mangled body of Deputy Hal Haid.

And his gun and gun belt were nowhere in sight.

Adam Hagen looked away from the carnage. "That poor kid."

One of the elderly men was all too eager to repeat what he had seen. "I saw the whole thing, Sheriff. I watched them carry him out here kicking and screaming before one of them picked up a brick and pummeled him to death. Savages. Heartless, soulless savages, every single one of them."

Trammel forced the loss of a good man from his mind as he listened for any sounds that might tell him where he should head next. "You see which way they were headed?"

"They scattered in all directions, like dust in the wind," the elderly man told him. "And there was no shortage of good Laramie men and women hot on their heels." He pointed behind himself. "We heard some shots coming from that direction just before you showed up just now."

Trammel knew he would find plenty of trouble in any direction he chose, so the sound of gunfire was probably the best indication. He took off running in the direction the old-timer had told him. Adam Hagen followed close behind.

When he reached the corner, Trammel saw Deputies Johnny Welch and Charlie Root had taken cover behind the porch of a house located in the middle of a street. Trammel and Hagen ran toward them, only to be forced to dive when someone began shooting at them from inside.

Both men crawled toward the deputies on their elbows until they reached Welch and Root.

Trammel said to Root, "I thought Blake sent you two to grab up prisoners as they jumped the wall."

"And we were in the middle of doing just that when someone started shooting at us from here," Deputy Root said. "I think some of the prisoners got hold of a gun."

Deputy Welch added, "Some civilians are keeping an eye on the prisoners we grabbed. Got about ten of them, near as we could count before the shooting started."

Trammel did the math as he began to reload his pistol. Twenty of the fifty prisoners had been accounted for. That meant more than half of the convicts were still on the loose. He had no intention of being pinned down here while prisoners openly ran through the streets.

Once he finished reloading his pistol, Trammel told them, "Follow me."

Trammel got to his feet and hit the closed front door with his shoulder. The door burst open, causing a woman inside to scream.

He looked down the hall and saw the back door in the kitchen was open.

"They went out that way, Sheriff. Three of them. And one of them has a pistol!"

Trammel rushed by her and ran out the door. He saw three convicts running away from the house as fast as their legs could take them. One of them turned and fired a quick shot at Trammel that missed wide. Trammel knew he would never hit him in the dark and gave chase. He heard Hagen and the two deputies running right behind him.

Trammel called back to his men as he ran. "Welch, you're faster. Grab the one with the pistol."

The deputy darted past him and knocked two of the prisoners to the ground before tackling the third.

Trammel quickly reached the first two men Welch had knocked down and saw one of them trying to bring up a pistol.

Hal Haid's pistol.

The convict screamed when Trammel pinned his hand to the dirt beneath a heavy boot. "You the one who did that to Hal?"

The prisoner struggled to pull his hand free, which only caused Trammel to put more weight on it. He heard the bones begin to give way, and the prisoner cried out in pain.

Trammel aimed the Peacemaker down at his temple.

"You beat one of my men to death, didn't you? You miserable son of a—"

"Buck!" Hagen called out as he tried to get Trammel's attention. "Don't do it. Not here. There are too many people watching."

Trammel did not care who saw him. He had the man who had caved in Hal Haid's skull dead to rights.

He thumbed back the hammer of his pistol. "Let them watch. Let them see what happens to anyone who kills one of my men."

"Don't do it, boss," Deputy Root said as he picked up the second prisoner who Welch had knocked down. "Hal wouldn't have wanted it that way. And neither will you when you calm down."

Trammel felt the big pistol begin to tremble in his hands as he fought against his instincts. "Then somebody better hurry up and pry that iron out of his hands before I change my mind."

Hagen plucked the pistol from the prisoner's grip and tucked it into his pants before grabbing him by the neck. "He's not going anywhere, Buck. You can get off him now."

Trammel reluctantly took his boot from the convict's hand and allowed Hagen to pull him to his feet, handing him over to Root. "You and Welch should run these three back to their cells, then fetch the men you caught coming over the wall. A couple of teamsters grabbed about ten more out front, across from where the wall fell. Buck and I will spread out and bring back whoever else we find."

Trammel battled his rage to keep his hand from shaking. "Stay in the prison after you get all men secure. Tell Blake and Brillheart to come out and help us hunt down the rest. We've got a long night ahead of us."

The four men ducked as more shots echoed somewhere in the near distance. Trammel knew he had nothing short of a complete disaster on his hands. He had lost at least one deputy, possibly more. He had seen at least three prisoners dead. Even with help from the citizens, he would count himself lucky if he found half the prisoners who had managed to escape. And it would be a miracle if they did not hurt or kill anyone.

And none of this would have happened without Frank Bessler and Lucien Clay. The two were already long gone from Laramie, undoubtedly riding hard toward the timber where the two men would lose themselves while plotting to make their next move.

Trammel would not rest until both escapee and accomplice swung for what they had done that night. He did not know if they would swing from Judge Spicer's gallows or the nearest tree, but he would see to it they paid. For what they had done to his prison. For what they had done to Laramie. And for what they had done to poor Hal Haid.

CHAPTER 9

Frank Bessler pulled up on the reins as he and Clay reached the timberlands outside Laramie. They had ridden at a brisk pace for more than an hour and it was time to give the animals a rest now that they had reached cover. If anyone was chasing them, they would be hard-pressed to find them in the dark.

Clay pulled his horse to a quick stop as he sped past Bessler. "What's wrong with you? We've got to keep going."

"We'll get moving again in an hour or so, after these horses rest for a spell." Bessler climbed down from the saddle. "They need a good drink of water, too. No one's following us and they won't come looking for us until morning. That gives us plenty of time."

Clay looked back toward Laramie. "We're still too close to town. Trammel's probably leading a posse to come after us right now. He won't let the dark stop him."

"I don't imagine it would," Bessler admitted. "But those prisoners I freed from their cells will stop him long enough for our purposes. We'll rest now. Dead or tired mounts won't do us any good out here."

He led his horse over to a stream and it began to drink.

Clay reluctantly climbed down and joined him. "You don't have any idea what we should do next, do you?"

Bessler had not expected Clay to be easy, but they were off to a contentious start. "We're wanted men now, Lucien. We've got to think everyone we meet will be out to hang us or shoot us for whatever reward they put on our heads. That's why we can't risk taking the train to Denver to get your money, so we'll need to keep these animals in fine shape if we hope to make it. We won't be passing through any towns either, for bullets or provisions. Can't risk it."

"What'll we live on?" Clay asked. "Are we going to have to shoot our dinner?"

"Jerky and hardtack's all I brought with me," Bessler said. "We'll be riding along water, so we won't go thirsty. It's not much, but it'll be enough to keep us lean."

He had already buried supplies on the trail up ahead, but Clay did not need to know that. He could not afford to trust him until after they had split the money. "We'll travel light and travel fast, just like you wanted."

Clay looked as if he did not understand what Bessler was telling him. "But Trammel . . ."

"The sheriff is going to be kept plenty busy rounding up all those convicts I let loose back there. It'll probably take him the rest of the night and a good part of the morning before he can even begin to think about coming after us. We've got your neighbor to thank for that. If he hadn't woken up and started wailing, I would've just brained the doctor and headed for the hills. That fool made my plan better. Walt Holm will be smart enough to delay Trammel even longer, which will only give us a better head start."

Bessler could tell that Clay had not considered that and did not care for the idea now that he had. "I never liked relying on other people for my own luck. I think we could get a little more out of these mounts if we push them a little harder for a while longer."

"You can do what you want with your own animals

when you have them, Clay. But the horse you're riding is mine. And since you don't have any money to buy him from me at present, he's not going anywhere except over to this stream to drink. You and he's not going anywhere until I say."

Clay led the animal to the edge of a stream, where it eagerly began to drink.

Bessler laughed. "You really don't like taking orders from anyone, do you, Lucien?"

"No. I've been giving them for so long, I've gotten out of the habit of obeying."

"It's only temporary. As soon as we get your money, you'll be your own man again. Just remember, you didn't only pay me to free you, but to help you stay that way."

Clay had not warmed to the idea and seemed eager to change the subject. "How many men do you think you freed back there?"

"Just the four at the end of your row," Bessler admitted. "I handed the key to them and told them to free the rest. I'll bet that's what they did. How many men in that prison anyway?"

"About fifty, near as I can figure. It was only built to hold twenty, until they built a bigger territorial prison. Guess they never got around to it. They were fixing to build it up in Blackstone, but King Charles killed that idea before it got started. Said he didn't want his town spoiled by a bunch of criminals."

Bessler might never have been to Wyoming, but he had heard plenty about King Charles Hagen. "Funny that his boy wound up in the prison he fought to build. I wonder if any of those boys back there freed old Caleb or just let him whimper in his cell out of spite. I hope they let him go. He might prove to be a useful distraction to Trammel."

The chaos he had undoubtedly left in his wake had

been a welcome surprise to Bessler. The situation had deteriorated so quickly when Caleb started yelling that Bessler released the prisoners on a whim. Fifty escapees would be enough not only to plunge the entire prison into chaos but all of Laramie with it. There was no way so many prisoners would sheepishly return to their bunks just because Trammel told them to. That would mean bloodshed. The more blood and confusion, the more obstacles Trammel and his men would have to clear before setting their sights on chasing him and Clay.

Bessler clapped his gloved hands as his heart filled with delight at the thought of the mess Trammel would have to clean up. Holm had been worried that Trammel would discover the extent of the relationship between Holm and Clay. But with Laramie falling apart all around them, the details would become blurred in the fog of accusations that would descend over the town. He only hoped Mayor Holm saw the gift they had just placed in his lap. Holm might've been weak, but he was a smart-enough politician to use the situation to his advantage.

"Stop gloating," Clay said as he sat on a large rock beside the stream. "There's nothing to smile about until we reach Denver."

"Don't be so glum," Bessler chastised. "We got away clean, didn't we?"

"We got away," Clay clarified. "We're not free yet. You only kicked over a viper's nest back in Laramie. We'll have plenty to worry about once Trammel picks up our trail. He'll probably be waiting for us in Denver."

"That's what I'm counting on." It was time to let him in on the grander plan. "Because we're not going to Denver. Your money will never make it that far."

Even in the darkness of the wood, Bessler could feel

Clay's hard eyes bore a hole through him. "What did you just say?"

"Your money will never make it to Denver," Bessler repeated. "We're going to get it long before then."

Clay slowly got to his feet. "You mean Holm didn't send the wire like he promised?"

"He sent it overland by armed coach. Just like I told him to."

Bessler moved his hand to the gun on his hip when he heard Clay shift his weight in the dirt. "Don't go doing anything stupid, Lucien. It's all part of my plan."

"Whatever scheme you're hatching better be smarter than lousing up my plans to get my money."

Bessler was disappointed in Clay. For a man who was known for his cunning, he was shortsighted. "We'd never have been able to touch that money if I'd done it your way. They've got telegraph wires strung up all over the territory now. The same wire that would've carried your money would've carried information for our wanted posters. If Trammel hasn't already sent our names and descriptions to Denver, they will by this time tomorrow. They'll probably put a nice reward on our heads, too. Every man with a badge on his chest or a gun on his hip will be out to find us in the hopes of a payday. Every bank clerk, too. They'd have a guard cover us until the law got there, even if I shaved my beard and changed my appearance."

Bessler sensed some of the fight go out of Clay as he continued to explain himself. "I had them send your money by coach because they won't just be hauling your money, but other valuables for the Bank of Laramie. I happen to know the route the coach will take and where we're going to hit it."

"How could you possibly know that?"

Bessler decided to keep that information to himself.

"You'll get every penny you've got coming to you and so will I. We'll split whatever else we take off the coach between us. You'll walk out of this a richer man than you intended, Lucien, as will I."

Bessler had not known his client long, but he knew the type. They never remained quiet for long, and when they did, they were either plotting a scheme or were suitably impressed by a scheme they had just heard. He took Clay's silence as a compliment.

"How were you fixing to split the money?" Clay asked. "Aside from mine, of course."

Bessler smiled in the darkness. It always came down to the split with men like Lucien Clay. "Sixty-forty in my favor seems fair."

"Considering it's my money we're risking, I'd say fifty-fifty is closer to the mark."

"I'm sure you would." Bessler had no intention of splitting his haul down the middle. Clay would be lucky if Bessler didn't cut his throat and take the whole bundle with him. Clay might have been a dangerous man back in Laramie, but he had spent the last several months in a prison cell. Every free breath he drew now was borrowed time.

But they still had to ride together for a while, so there was no reason to spoil it now. They still had to contend with Trammel and whatever posse he cobbled together to pursue them.

"You'll have plenty of time to make your case for a larger share, Lucien. For now, let's just enjoy the quiet."

Bessler knew Clay was incapable of enjoying the quiet. A new goal had presented itself. A problem to ponder.

His next statement was almost predictable. "I'll be needing a gun."

Bessler ignored the question. "Holm managed to get one

of your girls to pack some of your old clothes for you. You'll find them in your saddlebags."

Clay remained where he was. "And the gun."

"We'll see. For now, get changed out of those prison rags. I can turn my back if you're modest."

Clay cursed him in the darkness as he began to get dressed.

CHAPTER 10

It was well past noon when Dr. Morrison finally convinced Trammel to sit for an examination. Despite all the people in Laramie who needed medical attention, Emily had brought her colleague to City Hall to personally tend to her husband.

Dr. Thomas Morrison was a youngish man in his thirties, with curly, dark brown hair and wire-rimmed spectacles. His natural serious expression only grew more so as he took a closer look at the sheriff's condition.

Trammel yelped and pulled back when Morrison touched the left side of his swollen jaw. The sheriff used his tongue to force two loose teeth from his gums and spat them into the wastebasket by his desk.

"That ought to help with the pain in your jaw," Morrison said as he looked at Trammel's hands. "Your knuckles are swollen, and you've taken several hard blows to the head. Your eyes aren't as responsive as I would like, and they seem to have trouble focusing. I think you might be concussed. The scar along your face is healing. You're lucky it didn't reopen during the fight."

"It wasn't a fight," Trammel corrected him. "It was a prison break. There's a difference."

"Not according to your body. Ligaments sprain and break no matter what caused them."

Trammel rolled his neck, causing the bones to pop, and he suddenly felt like he had slept for hours. "Nothing I haven't lived through before."

Morrison and Trammel had never met before, but the doctor seemed to understand he could not force the issue. "If you were a normal patient, I'd order you to have bed rest, but since Emily already warned that you won't listen to me, I won't waste my time."

He reached into his medical bag and produced a dark bottle of pills. "This is a bottle of salicin. They prescribe this for pain in France and it seems to have some benefits. It might agitate your insides, so I suggest you take it with food. And if you really are concussed, you can't allow yourself to fall asleep. If you do, you might never wake up."

"No need to worry about that." Trammel took the bottle of pills. "I won't be sleeping any time soon, Doc."

Morrison shut the medical bag and threw his coat over his arm as he spoke to Emily. "I hope you'll have better luck than I did in talking some sense into him. He'll listen to you before he listens to me."

"Don't count on it," Emily said.

But Trammel was not ready to let the doctor go just yet. "I know you were tending to Doc Carson before you came up here. How's he doing?"

"He's about the only man in Laramie who's in worse condition than you," Morrison said. "Several of his ribs are broken. His skull is cracked and he's having great difficulty breathing. I imagine one of his lungs is punctured and in danger of collapse. He'll require constant care for the foreseeable future. He'll have to remain immobile in his office for a few days until he's well enough for me to bring to my office. I've already taken the liberty of talking to some of the other doctors in town, and we've agreed to take up some of the good doctor's duties here in the prison while he recuperates."

Trammel knew Doc Carson was in a bad way. "How's his spirit?"

Morrison's eyebrows rose at the question. "Distant. Perhaps even troubled, which is to be expected. He's survived quite an ordeal, as have you. Be sure to take time to be good to yourself, Sheriff. You're a big man, but no one's big enough to ignore their body for long. Graveyards are full of men who tried."

The doctor bid Emily a good day as he left Trammel's office.

Emily went to her husband and gently placed a hand on his arm. "I hope you'll listen to him, Steve. You need to take care of yourself."

Trammel knew she was right, but this was no time for him to think of himself. "I've got to meet with Mayor Holm in a few minutes, then do another tour of the town. Right before you grabbed me, we just got word of a group of convicts who tried to grab a wagon to make a break for it. A bunch of civilians almost beat them to death."

She stroked his face with the side of her hand. "I think you might have a fever. That means infection."

He gently lowered her hand from his forehead. She was the first glimmer of peace he'd enjoyed since the uprising started.

He looked up when he heard a knock at his door. "Come in."

Deputy Sherwood Blake said, "Sorry to interrupt like this, boss, but the mayor's asking for you."

Trammel's shoulders sagged. As always, Holm's timing was impeccable. "Tell him I'll be along in a minute."

He took his wife's hand and kissed it. "You'd better go

help Morrison and the other doctors with the wounded around town. Don't worry about me. I'll be fine."

He pushed himself off the desk and felt his wife's hand on his arm. "Worrying about you comes with the ring you gave me, Steve. Promise me you won't let Holm push you too far. I don't want you losing your temper. You've been through quite an ordeal, too."

Trammel would try but knew better than to make a promise to her he did not know he could keep.

Hagen smirked while Holm raged at him. He always took great pleasure in annoying people, and the mayor was proving more entertaining than he had hoped.

"I told you to get out of my office, Adam. Whatever I have to say to Trammel, I'll say alone."

But Hagen refused to allow his friend to face the wrath of a desperate politician. "I heard you the first three times you said it, Walt. And I've ignored you each time for a reason. There's not a man in this building who can make me leave, least of all you. I have every right to be here as a concerned citizen of Laramie. I helped Buck and his deputies round up a lot of escapees. I feel my actions last night will add some clarity to your inquiry."

Holm scowled at him. "This is not a query, sir. It's a reckoning."

"Whatever it might be, I'm here for the duration. Besides, you and I have some matters to discuss."

"Matters?" Holm recoiled. "What matters?"

"They can wait," Hagen said. "At least until after Buck Trammel has had his say."

They grew quiet when Trammel entered the office. He had to duck his head as he stepped through the door.

"Shut it behind you, Trammel," Holm ordered. "You're not going to want anyone else to hear what I have to say."

The sheriff did as he was told and took his seat next to Hagen. "What are you doing here?"

"Lending moral support and giving evidence on your behalf."

Holm laughed. "Of course. Trammel and Hagen. Hagen and Trammel. Where one goes, the other is sure to follow. Like pestilence and death."

"Or like politics and greed," Hagen added.

"There's no reason to be so dramatic, Walt," Trammel said. "We've almost got the town back under control."

"After it suffered because of your incompetence," Holm said. "How many men were we holding in the prison downstairs as of last night when the trouble began?"

"Fifty," Trammel reported.

"And how many have we returned to their cells?"

"Forty-three. Six were killed trying to escape. Only one got away clean."

"The worst one," Holm observed. "Lucien Clay."

Hagen saw Trammel wince as though he had been slapped. "The prisoners I've spoken to told me it started with Clay. It looks like he had help from his lawyer, Frank Bessler. Near as we can figure, Bessler climbed over the courtyard wall, busted Old Bob in the head while he slept in the stables, then jumped Doc Carson when he came back to make his rounds at midnight. Bob's alive, but he might lose an eye. He's our stable hand, not that you'd know him."

Holm's eyes narrowed. "I'm the one who hired him ten years ago during my first turn as mayor, so don't you dare try to portray me as an elitist, Trammel. It won't hide your culpability in all this."

"What culpability?" Hagen shot back. "Lucien Clay and

Frank Bessler are to blame for this, not Buck. No one has ever broken out of that prison. No one has even tried. Not successfully anyway."

"Until last night, when Lucien Clay broke the mold." Holm sounded almost happy to say it. "Have you had the chance to take a good look around town this morning, Sheriff?"

Trammel had been on the street for nine straight hours without a break by that point. "I have."

"It looks like a battlefield out there," Holm went on. "Three civilians died when that wall toppled over. We lost six more good people to desperate convicts who were allowed to run wild through the streets while you stood by and watched it happen. The fact that you managed to capture any of them at all is nothing short of a miracle."

Hagen sat forward in his seat. "Buck wasn't standing by. He was keeping the courtyard gates closed while—"

Trammel cut him off. "My deputies worked themselves to the bone to bring back every single one of those prisoners alive. And any convict who took a life will be tried for it."

Holm went on. "I haven't even begun to contemplate the tragic loss of Deputy Hal Haid. Another victim of your incompetence."

Hagen felt the rage that coursed through Trammel's body. "Hal died doing his sworn duty. And the man who killed him will swing for it. So will Lucien Clay, Frank Bessler, and anyone else who helped them pull this off."

"Helped them?" Holm sat back in his seat as if he had been pushed. "What makes you think they had help?"

Hagen heard a change in the mayor's tone. Something was odd about it. "What an interesting idea, Buck. I think you should continue with that thought."

Holm turned on him. "No one cares what you think,

THIS MAN MUST DIE   105

Hagen. If Clay had any help, it probably came from your lousy brother. He was one of the ringleaders who grabbed Doc Carson, wasn't he?"

The mayor pointed a thin finger across his desk at Trammel. "Don't you dare try to turn this into a conspiracy. There's no one else to blame for what happened here. Those men broke out of your prison. Clay never would've made it out alive if you had been doing your job. He's a known, convicted criminal with allies throughout the territory. Did you expect him to simply accept his fate? Men like Clay don't have any respect for the rule of law any more than your friend here does. Of course he tried to escape. It's his nature. Just like it's supposed to be your job to stop him. You've got as much blood on your hands as either Clay or this Bessler, assuming he's even involved."

"He's involved." Hagen spoke through gritted teeth. "You can bet your life on it."

The mayor was undeterred. "I *did* bet my life on it, Adam. I bet my life and the life of every other citizen of Laramie that the great Buck Trammel was up to the challenge of keeping us safe. I should've known he wasn't up to the job. That's a mistake I intend on correcting right now."

He looked directly at the sheriff. "You're fired, Trammel. As of this instant. Leave your star on my desk and get out of my office immediately. You're through in Laramie."

If Adam Hagen had forgotten how quick his large friend could move, he was reminded of it when Trammel reached across the desk, snatched Holm by the chin, and ripped him from the chair in one fluid motion. The mayor's feet barely touched the ground as Trammel slammed him against the wall behind his desk.

"If anyone's got something to answer for today, it's you, Holm. You were in on this, weren't you?"

"Let go of me," Holm demanded as he struggled to get away.

But Trammel kept him pinned against the wall. "Everyone knows you've been in Clay's pocket for years. No one wanted to do anything about it. Maybe it's time someone did. Maybe that someone is me."

"You're through in Laramie," Holm croaked as best he could with his jaw in Trammel's grip. "You're fired!"

Trammel gripped the mayor's jaw tighter. "You're not the only one who's been doing some thinking. I saw Bessler on the street yesterday. He was heading toward the Continental, but he didn't go straight there, did he? Your law office is on that street, isn't it?"

Hagen decided to take a risk and advance Trammel's argument with a lie. "There's no point in denying it, Walt. I can produce several witnesses who saw him go into your building."

"Lies!" Holm rasped. "Blatant lies! You two are just covering up for each other."

"Facts," Trammel said. "I've been wondering how Clay could've managed to send for Bessler. I read every letter that leaves the prison before they get sent out. It wasn't his lawyer, because he fired him months ago, and it doesn't take months to get here, not even from Texas."

"Unless he walked," Hagen offered. "And we know Bessler didn't walk. I checked with the railroad. He took the train, along with two horses. He used one of those horses to help Lucien ride away last night. He planned this and you helped him."

Trammel took Holm from the wall just long enough to adjust his grip to his collar before slamming him back against it. "It was you, wasn't it? Clay told you to send for Bessler, didn't he? Tell me how."

Holm struggled to say, "You can't prove that. You can't prove any of that."

Trammel tightened his grip. "We'll see about that. I'm going over to the bank to have a talk with the bank president. I'm going to ask him who's in charge of Clay's accounts, and I'll bet he's going to show me a piece of paper that has your name on it."

"You can't do that!" Holm tried in vain to break Trammel's grip. "Those records are confidential. You'll need a judge to . . ."

Trammel pushed him harder against the wall. "I can be pretty convincing when I want to be."

Hagen could see Holm was starting to break and decided it was time to move things along. He stood up and made his way over to the mayor's bookshelf. "Have you ever heard the old saying about the truth setting one free, Walt? It's one of my favorite verses of the Bible. I've always had a great love of reading, even as a boy."

He tapped one of the books on Holm's shelf. "I can see you do, too. Then again, I'd imagine that comes with your profession, what with you being a lawyer and all. Wonderful thing, a book. A good book anyway. I love to lose myself in a good story. One can learn so much from reading, particularly when the writer knows a subject well. When I first returned to the territory, I acquired quite an interesting book from the late Madam Peachtree. You remember her, don't you, Walter? Used to work with Lucien Clay?"

Hagen enjoyed the look of fright on Holm's face as he began to move toward him. "It was her masterpiece. Her magnum opus, if you will. It told a grand, soaring tale as old as time itself. A wonderfully annotated story of greed and corruption set right here in our frontier Eden."

As Trammel kept the mayor pinned against the wall, Hagen flicked Holm's nose. "Your name is in it."

"More lies." Holm strained. "If you had anything like that, you would've used it by now."

Hagen leaned on the wall next to him and folded his arms. "I never needed to use it until now, but alas, you've given me no choice. The late madam had your name in her book of corrupt politicians. Coded, of course, but it's a code I easily deciphered. And I'll have no trouble proving my case once my persuasive friend here gets the bank to allow me to look at their records. Clay always liked to brag that he had you in his pocket back when we first formed our partnership after Madam Peachtree's demise. I'll be more than happy to take the trouble to verify it if you continue to be difficult."

Trammel let up just enough pressure on Holm's throat to allow him to speak. "What assurances do I have that you won't do that anyway?"

"None in the world except my word as a gentleman," Hagen said. "But as I'm not much of a gentleman, let's leave it at this. If you don't come clean, Trammel will throw you out the window. We'll tell everyone it was due to your grief over what happened last evening. No one will question it as no one particularly likes you."

The mayor flinched when Trammel went to grab him again. "Fine! Clay told me to send for Bessler."

"How?" Trammel growled. "You've never even been down to the prison."

"It was Deputy Haid. He passed notes between me and Clay. That's how we communicated in secret."

Trammel punched the wall less than an inch from Holm's head. "You coward. Trying to pin this on a dead man."

"It's true!" Holm yelped. "He gave the prisoners their dinner. Clay would pass a note to him and Haid would deliver my response. He owed Clay a lot of money. He did it to work off his debt. He didn't know what Clay was planning to do. That was between Bessler and Clay."

Trammel released Holm and staggered away as if he had been struck. But the truth had landed harder than any punch. "Haid did that? Why didn't he tell me?"

"It was harmless," Holm told him. "Clay would have ruined him if he'd breathed a word to anyone. He never talked to Haid about helping him break out because he knew he'd never go for it. I didn't even know the particulars. They must've made the decision when they met yesterday."

With Trammel distracted by the news, Adam saw Holm was beginning to gain the upper hand, so he quickly stepped in to stop it. "But you knew Bessler was going to break Clay out of jail, didn't you?"

"That's why I sent for him when Clay asked for my help. That's what Bessler does. When he can't get a man out of prison legally, he finds a way to break him out. I didn't know the specific details and I didn't know when. Bessler's always been able to get a man out without hurting anyone, so something must've gone wrong."

Adam knew what had gone wrong. "My brother panicked when he realized what was happening and started begging them to take him with them."

Holm's lower lip began to quiver. "No one was supposed to get hurt. Bessler was always careful. That's why I thought he was the best man for something like this."

But Adam Hagen knew that was only part of the story. "You know where they're going, don't you?"

Holm shook his head, but Adam closed in on him. "Clay's too careful to make a break just for freedom's sake. He'll never go back to jail again, and staying free takes money. He was sitting on a nice pile when he went to prison and you're the one who's been watching it for him, haven't you?" The more Adam spoke, the more it made sense. "Where did you wire the money, Walt?"

"I didn't wire any money," Holm said.

Trammel grabbed his lapels and pulled him toward the window. "I've had enough of your lies."

Holm could not speak fast enough. "I wanted to wire it, but Bessler told me Clay didn't want that. He told me to send it overland instead."

Hagen gestured for Trammel to stop. "That makes sense. We'd be able to trace a wire. We could have the bank put a hold on it if we found out where it was." Yes, that sounded something like Clay would do. He would be too smart for that. "Where did you have the money sent? And don't tell me you don't know because we won't believe you."

"It was sent by an armed coach this morning," Holm said quickly. "From the Bank of Laramie to the Bank of Denver. It's just a sealed pouch that's to be held in the vault until it's picked up. That's where they're going, but I don't know how. You must believe me!"

"After you take out your cut, of course," Hagen said. "How much?"

The mayor swallowed hard. "I keep twenty percent for my trouble. The rest went directly to Clay."

Hagen cut loose with a piercing whistle that made Holm grab his left ear. "Twenty percent. My, you have been busy, haven't you, Walter?"

Trammel had overcome the initial shock of his late deputy's betrayal. "Bessler's going to hit that stage, isn't he?"

Adam could see that Holm had not considered it. "I don't know. He didn't tell me that much, but now I suppose . . ."

Trammel released him with a shove. "I'm heading over to the bank to find out how that money's getting to Denver. If we find where the money's headed, we find Bessler and Clay."

The sheriff did not bother to close the door behind him.

The mayor sagged against the wall as he began to try to rub feeling back into his neck and face. "I hope you don't expect me to thank you for getting that animal to let me go."

Adam was all too happy to disappoint him. "Oh, you're not free, Walt. Not by a long shot. You've still got me to contend with, and you and I must come to an understanding."

Holm blinked. "What sort of understanding?"

"An understanding that involves silence. Yours as well as mine. I'll even throw the sheriff's cooperation into the bargain. But it won't be cheap."

"Cheap?" Holm repeated. "What in the devil are you talking about?"

"It's not complicated." Adam eased him back against the wall. "It's not even illegal. You're going to give me sixty percent of whatever you took from Clay as part of your fee. In exchange, I'll agree to keep quiet about your hand in last night's unpleasantness. And don't try to shortchange me, because you know I'll check. If you lie, I'll be most unhappy."

Holm began to sputter a protest, but Adam quietly drew his pistol and held the barrel against his lips. "No talking, Walt. Not yet. In exchange for my generosity in allowing you to live and keep your reputation, you'll promise to keep our plans to yourself. You won't try to warn Bessler or Clay. In fact, if you go anywhere near a telegraph office, I'll have you killed. You and whatever unfortunate poor soul you send on your behalf. I'll have my people watching you closely until my return. Nod if you understand."

Holm nodded quickly.

Adam withdrew the pistol and slid it back into his holster. "Good boy. Continue to play your part in this tragedy and I promise all will be well."

Hagen began to step away but stopped as another

thought came to him. "And if it's all the same to you, we'll forget that business about you firing Buck. We're all under a considerable strain right now, so we'll mark it up to excitement. Don't you agree?" Hagen smiled. "This is the part where you agree, Walt."

"Yes, of course," Holm said. "It was just nerves."

"Good boy. And don't forget that you're not a brave man, Walt. Cunning, perhaps, but not brave. Remember that when your pride begins barking at you once we leave."

Hagen thought he heard the mayor begin to weep as he left him alone in his office with only his guilt to comfort him.

CHAPTER 11

Trammel watched John Banner turn pale after he told him about Clay's money.

"Good heavens," Banner said from behind his desk. "I wish you had come to me earlier, Sheriff Trammel. I might have been able to stop the coach before it left this morning."

Trammel could not do anything about that. "How long since the coach left town?"

Banner pulled out his pocket watch and confirmed the time. "It left four hours ago at first light. It always leaves early on Wednesdays. The driver likes to make good time on his first day."

At least he knew what he was up against. "Is he going straight to Denver or is he making other stops?"

"I don't know." The bank president came around from behind his desk and went to a framed map of the Wyoming Territory on the wall. "I've been using the Frontier Overland Company for years and Tucker never tells me the route he plans to take. That would be Tucker Cobb, the owner of the company. He's got a partner, too. Butch Keeling rides shotgun with him. Also a partner."

Trammel did not care about the stagecoach company, only what it was carrying. "Where do you think he's most likely to stop next?"

Banner pointed up at the map. "There are at least six banks that I know of between here and Denver. Cobb could decide to stop at any of them or at none of them. There are also several mining towns and ranches between here and Denver where he might make a payroll delivery or pick up a deposit. Frontier Overland has many customers in this area, though we've gotten out of the practice of sending large sums by coach these days. It's easier to wire money to a bank now that we have the telegraph. Quicker and safer, too."

Trammel would have cursed his luck if he thought it would have done any good. "And you didn't think something might be wrong when Holm told you to move all of Clay's money by coach?"

"No, because it wasn't Mr. Clay's money," Banner told him. "It was in one of the many accounts Mr. Holm has with us. He often handles large sums of money for his clients. I would have needed to look at the account history to see if it had once been Mr. Clay's money. I had no reason to do that. I would have alerted you had I suspected anything, Sheriff."

Trammel did not know Banner well, but he had a reputation as an honest man. That was rare for a banker. He had no reason to think he was lying.

He pointed up at the map. "Let's say Cobb and Keeling don't stop the stage between here and Denver. What route would they take?"

Banner looked at the map. "Your guess is as good as mine. Tucker Cobb is the best coachman in the territory. He's known for being careful and diligent. He's never lost a shipment to bandits in the ten years he's been in operation. The trails between here and Denver are littered with the bodies of men who were foolish enough to try to rob him. Butch Keeling, his partner, is a dead shot. Not too many bandits get close to the coach when he's riding shotgun."

Trammel had heard of Cobb and Keeling but had never met them. "They'll both have to be good if Clay and Bessler are going after them."

"Bessler?" the bank president repeated. "The lawyer who came to take up Mr. Clay's case? I knew someone helped Clay escape, of course, but I didn't think Bessler had anything to do with it."

"Well, he did," Trammel said, "and he's the biggest question in all this. We can look on a map and guess where they might go next, but since I don't know the man, I can't be sure."

Mr. Banner went back to his desk and took a piece of paper. He studied the map closely as he took pen in hand and began to draw a rough outline of the map on the wall. "I don't know what route Tucker Cobb will decide to take, but I've ridden with him several times on the way to Denver. The stage company keeps a couple of stations along the route so they can switch out horses during a hard ride. They pay a station manager to keep horses available for the line to use on a more infrequent basis. I'll place a dot on this map for each station I know about between here and Denver. Maybe it'll help you narrow down where Cobb might be headed."

Trammell doubted the map would help but thanked him for the effort. The stagecoach already had a head start of several hours. He had no idea where Bessler and Clay would strike. There was an awful lot of ground to cover between Laramie and Denver, and he doubted he would find them before they struck. Trammel knew he would need to hire a good tracker if he had any hope of bringing them in.

Bessler would probably head for Texas, which did not tell him much. Texas was a large state, and a man with money could easily disappear there. Texas was also well out of his jurisdiction—as was Denver, for that matter, though the law in an adjoining state would likely be more under-standing. Texas was practically a country of its own.

Clay did not have any roots and could plant himself any-where. If he made it to California, he could disappear for-ever.

Trammel would have a devil of a time finding them if they stuck together. It would be much harder if they split up.

Trammel took Banner's hand-drawn map and thanked him for his efforts before leaving the bank.

He was not surprised to see Adam Hagen waiting for him outside.

"What did Banner tell you?" Hagen asked as he walked with Trammel.

"He sent Clay's money on to Denver four hours ago. If I don't hit the road now, I'll never catch them."

"We'll be ready to ride in an hour," Hagen said. "I've already got some of my men packing provisions for us."

Trammel knew Hagen had not been waiting for him out-side the bank just to enjoy the morning air. "You're not going anywhere. I'll ride out with Blake and Welch. I need you here to keep an eye on things."

"They'll be needed here because I'm going with you," Hagen countered. "I've seen you out on the trail, remem-ber? I saw how you handled yourself on the way to Black-stone from Wichita, remember? You needed me back then every bit as much as you need me now."

Trammel had been frustrated at every turn since the moment his boots hit the floor around midnight. Hagen was not making it any easier. "I'll be fine. Blake's hunted down plenty of men before."

"But not with you," Hagen reminded him. "You'll need every deputy you've got to stay here and keep the town in line. A lot of men will be looking to test the boundaries after what happened last night. And since I can't talk you out of going after Clay, I'll have to go with you."

"Catching fugitives is my job, not yours," Trammel reminded him. "You can help by keeping the criminal element in town from killing each other until I get back."

"Blake's a good man, but he's not me," Hagen persisted. "You've seen what I can do out in the open, and no one knows the ground between here and Denver better than I do, not even Blake. I'm also the only one who can get you to listen to reason out there. You're a tough man, Buck, but you're still a tenderfoot out on the trail. You'll need me with you when you come up against Bessler and Clay. You know I'm right."

Trammel did not like the feeling of control slipping away from him so quickly. He did not like admitting Hagen was right. He remembered their ride from Kansas to Blackstone and all the obstacles they had overcome together. Despite their differences in the years since, he and Hagen had always made a formidable team.

That did not mean he thought it was a good idea. "How would it look if I let you ride out with me after you killed Verne Ayres? Everyone knows your history with Clay. They'd think I was letting you come along to settle a score. Maybe even cover some of your crimes by killing him."

"I've never made a secret of who or what I am," Hagen reminded him. "In Blackstone or here in Laramie. I don't care what people think and neither do you. I only care about doing whatever needs to be done. We both know you've got a better chance of catching Lucien and Frank if I ride out with you. I'd hate to see you killed on account of something as fickle as public opinion."

But Trammel had no choice but to care. He was no longer the lone lawman of Blackstone. He was a sheriff responsible for the largest county in the territory. The people's opinion about his judgment mattered. Just because Mayor Holm was corrupt did not give Trammel license to do whatever he wanted.

But he was risking more than his life by going after Bessler and Clay. Whatever reputation he had would suffer if he was unable to capture them. People would doubt if he was up to the job. And, for all his faults, Trammel could not think of a more capable man than Adam Hagen to help him find them.

"They've already got almost a day's head start on us," Trammel reminded him. "You said you'll be ready to ride out within the hour?"

"I am." Hagen grinned. "And I've already got some good horses picked out from the stable. I might even manage to throw in a surprise or two along the way."

Adam broke off to tend to his business, and Trammel shouted after him, "No surprises, Adam."

"Just one," Hagen said over his shoulder. "You've got to allow me a little fun. Trust me, you'll like it."

Trammel decided there was no point in arguing. Bringing Bessler and Clay to justice was more important.

Trammel carried his rifle and a box of bullets with him as he went down into the prison to check on Doc Carson. He found Sherwood Blake standing guard in the hallway outside the doctor's office.

"How's he doing?" Trammel asked his deputy.

"Shaken," Blake told him. "Not his usual self, which is to be expected. We're all a bit off after last night. Losing Hal was a heavy blow."

Trammel knew a lot of things about Deputy Hal Haid would hurt if they ever came to light. But whatever he had done, it should not have cost him his life. "I know. I can't believe he's gone, either."

"And I still don't know how Clay could've gotten word to that lawyer," Blake went on. "I've been turning it over again and again in my mind. We read every letter Clay ever wrote before we sent it. We never would've let a letter get past us."

Trammel saw no reason to burden him with Hal Haid's role in delivering messages between Clay and the mayor. "I hear you're handling the funeral."

"After his wife left him, Hal didn't have any family besides us. We got the preacher to read over him before the burial tomorrow morning." He glanced at the rifle the sheriff was toting. "Looks like you'll be missing the service. I hear you and Hagen will be riding out after Bessler and Clay this morning."

Trammel was about to ask him how he had heard but remembered word traveled fast in prison. He could not expect his deputies to be immune. "That's what I came down here to tell you."

"Do you think taking Adam Hagen with you is wise?"

"No," Trammel admitted, "but I need you here in town to run things while I'm gone. I'd prefer to have you with me out there, but your place is in Laramie. The people respect you, and they'll listen to what you tell them to do."

Blake checked the hallway for anyone who might be listening before saying, "Hagen's a stone-cold killer, Buck. You saw him gun down Verne over his claim yesterday. If he kills Clay, it'll look like you two were getting revenge. It'll be much cleaner if you and I go."

"He knows Clay and how he thinks," Trammel said. "I'll need that knowledge if I have any hope of catching up to him. Just like I need you to stay here. You're the law in Laramie until I get back. I'll worry less knowing the town is in good hands and I can't think of any man who could do the job better than you."

Trammel knew how much Blake had resented him several months before, when Trammel first became sheriff. Blake had worked for the position for years under the late Rob Moran. It could have been argued that he should've been sheriff instead of Trammel.

But the two men had earned each other's respect in the months since. Trammel could not think of a higher compliment than to give Blake control of the town in his absence.

He was glad Blake saw it that way. "I won't let you down, boss."

"I know you won't. And I hate to miss Hal's funeral, but I'll pay my respects to him when I get back." He handed his deputy his rifle before stepping inside Carson's office. "Keep an eye on that for me while I look in on Doc."

Trammel barely recognized Doc Carson, propped up on pillows in the bed he kept in his office. His head and arms were heavily bandaged. His breathing beneath the sheet that covered him was shallow. He had never noticed how slight the doctor was before now. He always seemed so sturdy when tending to the prisoners. He had a quality of permanence about him.

But now, as he was laid out beneath blankets, Trammel decided the doctor looked closer to death.

Carson opened his eyes and looked over at Trammel. "Well? Are you going to just gape at me or are you going to come in here?"

Trammel pulled over a chair and sat beside his bed. "I've seen you look better, Doc."

"Don't let appearances fool you," Carson said. "I feel much worse than I look."

Trammel imagined he did. "I told you that you were in a

bad way when I carried you in here earlier. Sorry to see I was right."

"Not as sorry as I am." Carson closed his eyes briefly and grunted from pain. "I heard you got most of the men back in their cells. Excellent work, though I doubt Holm appreciates it."

"Blake and the boys deserve all the thanks. I just wanted to stop by before I took off after Clay."

"I knew it was only a matter of time before you did. I'm surprised you've remained in town this long. Where do you think he is?"

"Somewhere between here and Denver." Trammel did not have the time to explain all the details and did not think Carson wanted to hear them. "I'm bringing Hagen with me to help pick up his trail."

When Carson frowned, Trammel thought he might give him a lecture about Hagen, but he did not. "I've had plenty of time to think about the break and I'm sorry for having caused all this trouble." The doctor turned to face the wall. "If I'd been paying more attention when I came back for my rounds, I would've seen that big fella waiting in the shadows to jump me. I might've been able to give out a shout to let the guards know what was happening. But it all happened so fast that I never had the chance. And when it happened, I couldn't make a sound."

Trammel could feel regret coming from the older man like a fever. "I don't want to hear that kind of talk. You didn't do anything wrong and none of this was your fault. If you'd left your keys in a cell or forgot to close one of the doors, you might deserve some blame. But you've gone that way hundreds of times. You had no reason to expect to get jumped like that. Bessler does this kind of thing for a living. You never stood a chance."

"It only takes one mistake," Carson whispered almost to

himself. "When the prisoners grabbed me out there in the courtyard, it was like they didn't even know it was me. After all the time I'd spent caring for them, all the good I did for them, it was as though it didn't even matter. *I* didn't matter. I was just a thing to them. I never expected them to turn on me like that. To hurt me. Caleb, maybe, but not the others."

Trammel had seen what regret could do to a man. How it could eat away at his soul until there was hardly anything left. How it destroyed everything in its path, so all a man could remember was the darkness it left behind.

Trammel had battled more than his fair share of such poison and had paid the price. He did not want to see this good man succumb to the same fate.

"We work around some pretty bad men, Doc. They aren't all good and they aren't all bad. They're not devils and they're not angels, either. Life just kind of shaped them that way, just like it shaped you and me into who we are. Locking a man up isn't the best way to make him pay for his mistakes, but until someone comes up with a better one, we're going to keep on doing it. That's why you're going to keep giving them the best life they can expect while they're here. Maybe even a better one than they deserve. Not because of who they are, but because of who you are."

He rested his hand on the doctor's shoulder. "There's no shortage of blame to go around for what happened last night, but you don't deserve any of it. No one thinks you did anything wrong. Not me, and you shouldn't either."

Trammel was not sure Carson had heard everything he just told him. "Caleb Hagen. He was always so meek. Weak, even. But out there, he was the worst one. The look in his eyes. He was like a man possessed of some evil. Tell me he didn't get out."

Trammel had seen the same look in Caleb's eyes when

he grabbed hold of Carson right before the great rush happened. There had been a dark fire in his eyes as he threatened Carson's life. A fire Trammel had sought to extinguish with a single bullet but had missed.

"Caleb's back in his cell, and he won't be grabbing you or anyone else anymore. But you don't have to worry about that now. Concentrate on doing what the other doctors tell you to do. They're lined up to take care of you. I'll ask Emily to look in on you from time to time. You know she's always been fond of your old stories."

Trammel's stomach turned when he saw a single tear escape Carson's eye. "I'll have plenty of new stories to tell her about last night. Not all of them pleasant or entertaining."

"And she'll be happy to hear them." He took the man's hand and gave it a confident shake. "I'm going to kill Clay for what he did to you, Doc. I swear it."

Carson kept looking at the wall. "I know you will. I only wish it helped me feel better. I don't think anything will ever make me feel good again. Not the way it used to. Not after all this."

Trammel let go of his hand. He hated seeing such a good man torture himself so. "I can't promise you it will. All I can promise you is that justice will be done."

As he lay in his bunk in his cell, Caleb Hagen had never known such pain was possible. Everything hurt. His head throbbed from the throttling it had received when the men trampled him. His left shoulder felt as if it had come out of its socket and had not been put back in place properly. His right arm felt broken. Pain stabbed him in the chest whenever he gathered enough strength to breathe. And when breath came, it felt like he was inhaling through a wet blanket.

Only his legs felt reasonably normal, though both ankles were swollen. He feared they might be sprained.

He had gone hoarse from calling out for help hours ago. Or had it only been minutes? Time had ceased to have any meaning for him since the deputies found him out in the courtyard and dumped him back on the cot in his cell. He had to keep his eyes shut tightly out of fear he might see his cell spin again and make him sick to his stomach. No one had been by to clean the mess he had already made, and he doubted caring for him was high on their list of priorities. Not after what he had done to Doc Carson.

He was not sure if he was awake or asleep when he heard someone calling his name. Was it Lucien? Had he returned to rescue him after all?

"Poor Caleb," the voice mocked him. "Poor, forsaken Caleb."

He recognized the voice from the countless nightmares that had dominated his sleep since those first days of his incarceration. *Adam?*

"Poor, crushed Caleb," Adam continued. "Trampled underfoot like the miserable insect you've always been. Even as a boy, Father saw the weakness in you. Do you remember? The disapproving look whenever he watched you ride. The disgust at how awkward you were when it was time to gather the herd. How he mocked your stammer when you read your lessons and how slow you were at math. No matter how hard you tried, you could never quite measure up to his exacting standards, so you made your own. None of it was ever good enough for him. You were never more than a tool to him, no more or less than the sharp edge he used to scrape the mud from his boots."

Caleb knew this had to be real. No nightmare could be so cruel. Adam was here outside his cell. Why was God tormenting him so? Hadn't he suffered enough?

Adam kept talking. "And now look at you. As powerless and small as ever. Fate has cut you right down to size as fate is known to do. The whole world can finally see you're nothing more than the crushed, flattened thing you've always been. If I had a better opinion of you, I might be tempted to bribe one of the guards to let me put you out of your misery. After you grabbed poor old Doc Carson like you did, they might even allow me to do it for free. But I'm not going to do that, Caleb. I'm not going to be that merciful, and neither are they. No one will come to tend to your wounds. No one will repair your broken bones or salve your cuts and scrapes. They're going to forget about you, Caleb, just like the rest of the world has already forgotten about you. Your wife. You're going to spend however long you have in this world right where you are until your injuries finally claim your life. And they will claim you, Caleb, for no one or nothing else will."

Caleb willed his eyes to remain closed. *Make it stop. Make it stop!*

"I doubt you'll still be alive when I get back to town, so this will have to serve as our farewell, though it's hardly a fond one. I only hope you'll remember, for however long you have left, that I was the only one who always saw you for what you truly were. And now the world sees it, too."

Caleb kept his eyes shut as he listened to his brother's footsteps as he walked away. Each step felt like another nail being driven into the lid of his coffin.

And despite the great pain it caused him to do so, Caleb Hagen screamed into the darkness for all he was worth.

CHAPTER 12

Trammel stepped out the side door of the prison into the courtyard. The blood of the fallen and the maimed still stained the ground, though the remains of the dead had been removed. The horse stalls and stables were still standing, and the animals seemed to be calm.

The collapsed wall was an ugly gash in the view leading out to the street. Much of the brickwork had been cleared and piled in the far corner of the courtyard. The large metal doors he had fought to keep closed earlier that morning had been placed against the building like a child's forgotten toy. Now, in the clear light of day, he saw how dented and warped both doors had become. He was surprised they had withstood as much punishment for as long as they had.

It was not until he focused beyond the broken brickwork that he saw a familiar man sitting atop a gray horse in the thoroughfare. Another horse laden with the burden of provisions stood behind him.

John "Hawkeye" Hauk touched the brim of his hat. "Nice to see you again, boss. Mr. Hagen sent me a wire letting me know you were heading out after Bessler and Clay. He figured I might want to tag along. He was right."

Trammel smiled for the first time since he could remember.

His former deputy from Blackstone was always a welcome sight. "For once, Adam figured correctly."

"I told you it would be a good surprise," Adam Hagen said as he led two gray horses out from the stalls. They were already saddled and ready to be ridden. "Our young companion there has our packhorse and we're ready to leave on your order."

Hagen handed Trammel the reins of the second horse, and the sheriff climbed into the saddle.

Hagen said, "I assure you the pale horses I've procured are merely a coincidence and are not a biblical reference. They're simply the best mounts I could find in the stables, though I think they'll fill the bill nicely."

Trammel noticed the horse Hagen had given him was the larger of the two, undoubtedly chosen to bear his considerable bulk. He gestured over to the packhorse Hawkeye was tending. "Looks like you got plenty of supplies."

"Enough to get us all the way to Denver without stopping if it comes to that," Hagen said as he got into the saddle. "More than I suspect we'll need, but at least we won't have to worry about running low on anything. Got plenty of bullets, too, though I'm sure you already brought plenty."

Trammel had, though he did not think it was possible to have too much ammunition when going up against the likes of Frank Bessler and Lucien Clay.

"How do you expect to pick up their trail?" he asked Hagen.

"I've already tracked them from behind the wall back there to the edge of town," Hagen said. "I'll read the ground as best I can from there. I expect they rode slower in the night right after the escape, so we'll catch up to them sooner than you might think."

Trammel remembered the map Banner had drawn, dug it out of his shirt pocket, and handed it to Hagen. "This is where a few of the stagecoach stations are located between here and Denver. It might help you make the right decisions. Keep it with you and let's get moving. I'd like to make up some ground before nightfall."

Without another word, Hagen rode his horse through the gap in the ruined wall and took the lead.

Trammel followed and, upon reaching Hawkeye, shook hands with his deputy before following Hagen. "Who's minding things up in Blackstone while you're out here with us?"

Hawkeye brought his mounts next to Trammel. He pulled the packhorse behind him on a lead rope. "There's not much to tend to in Blackstone these days. With Mr. Hagen down here in Laramie, Blackstone's become a mighty quiet town. There are still some of the Hagen family's constables around to keep an eye on the place. I expect they'll be able to live without me for a week or so. And if not, I'll set things right when I get back."

Trammel was glad to hear it. Hawkeye had changed quite a bit from the awkward young man he met on his first day in Blackstone. He had grown into his responsibilities as a deputy and proven his mettle several times when situations got thick. Trammel knew a man of Blake's experience would have been a better choice to go up against the likes of Bessler and Clay. But he could not think of a better man to trust with his life than John Hauk.

"Let's just hope you're not gone for too long. With Adam sniffing them out, I'm hoping we can run down Bessler and Clay well before they reach Denver."

"With Mr. Hagen scouting for us, we're bound to find them," Hawkeye said. "And they'll be mighty sorry when we do."

Yes, Trammel certainly liked the man Hawkeye had become.

They rode in silence along Main Street and passed the building where Emily kept her office. The boardwalk was as crowded as every other doctor's office he had seen in town since sunrise. People suffering from ailments, real and imagined, looking to be tended to and share stories about the part they had played in the great prison break.

He chanced a look at the line of patients waiting outside Emily's office in the hope he might catch one last glimpse of her before he left town.

He knew making a special effort to say goodbye would be difficult for them both. He did not want to risk her talking him out of it. He knew she would tell him to send one of his many deputies to run down Bessler and Clay. That his place was here in Laramie, not out on the trail hunting fugitives anymore. He feared she would remind him of what he had promised her when he became sheriff of Laramie. That he would finally leave the more dangerous work to others and enjoy life for a change. Life with her.

But Lucien Clay was a problem Trammel had allowed to fester for far too long. Now it was up to him to make it right. Blake and any of the other deputies were certainly better suited for the assignment. He would have wagered they could ride and track better than he ever would.

But Walter Holm had been right when he said that protecting Laramie was his job, and he could not trust it to anyone else. Bessler and Clay had to answer for what they had done. For the lives that had been lost and the havoc they had wrought. And it was up to Buck Trammel to see to it that his debt was paid in full.

His breath caught when Emily stepped out onto the boardwalk as he and Hawkeye rode by. She returned the young man's enthusiastic wave, then saw her husband riding beside him. And the packhorse loaded down with supplies for the trail.

His heart sank when he saw her expression change as she realized where he was going. He expected her to run toward him in a last attempt to keep him from going.

Instead, she brought her hand to her lips and kissed it before holding it aloft in the hopes that the kiss would find him.

He touched the brim of his hat and continued to follow Adam Hagen as he led them out of town. He did not look back. He did not dare.

CHAPTER 13

Lucien Clay and Frank Bessler crested a ridge that offered a view of the valley below. There was still a fair amount of daylight left, and while they had put a good bit of distance between them and Laramie, Clay knew they could cover a fair amount of ground before it grew too dark to travel. Trammel was likely after them by now, and Clay wanted to continue to press whatever advantage they still had.

But Frank Bessler was in no such hurry. He closed his eyes as he drew in a lungful of mountain air. "Drink it in, Lucien. Isn't it wonderful? Free mountain air. There's nothing quite like it."

After more than a day of riding, Clay was beginning to think his rescuer was a bit touched in the head. "The air's the same back in Laramie."

"No, it's much different here." Bessler closed his eyes and lifted his face toward the warmth of the sun. "Can't you sense it? The excitement? The chase is on. Trammel has left Laramie to hunt us down."

Clay looked behind them. Fortunately, all he saw were the same rolling hills over which they had just ridden. Ground that was far too open for his tastes.

"I don't see anyone coming."

"Not yet, but he's back there. And unless I miss my guess, Adam Hagen will be with him, too. He won't allow his dear friend to ride into the wilderness without him. I'm looking forward to meeting him again. We have a score to settle, he and I."

Clay did not care about settling scores, just about staying free and getting his money. "This doesn't look like the kind of route the stagecoach will take."

Bessler opened his eyes as if he had just been disturbed from a dream. "I know where we'll find the stagecoach, Lucien. Don't worry about that. It's already been arranged. We have plenty of time."

Clay's rescuer's demeanor was beginning to grate on him. "If that's true, I say we ought to keep on riding while we still can. I'd rather be there early than late. And if Trammel's already after us, I don't like being out in the open like this."

"But we *are* early. Not for the stage, but for a much more pressing appointment." He lowered his face and looked at Clay for the first time in miles. "Trust me. I haven't lost all my senses. I've taken us over open ground for good reason. It makes us easier to track."

Clay was beginning to grow more than just concerned. "I'm no plainsman, but even I know we've left a trail a blind man could follow."

"That was by design," Bessler told him. "I want them to find us."

"What?" Clay remembered Bessler had refused to give him a gun when he asked for one. Now he knew why and wished he had insisted. "Quit talking in circles and tell me what you're up to."

"Must I explain everything to you?" Bessler sighed heavily. "Fine. I'm going to hang back here for a bit while you ride on. I'm going to buy us some time with Trammel.

And this is the perfect spot for it. The same one I told you I had picked out back when I visited you in the prison."

Clay might not have a gun, but he had always been more than fair with his fists. He was certain he could drop the bigger man with one well-placed punch if he had to. And he was beginning to think he might have to. "How do you figure?"

Bessler spread out his hands across the vista as if he was granting it to Clay. "Allow me to present Ennisville."

Clay looked over the rocky hillside and had to squint hard to see a tiny settlement in the valley below. He had to squint because there was not much to see. He could barely make out a crooked old building and what appeared to be some canvas tents scattered near it.

Clay was not impressed. "Looks like the backside of nowhere to me."

"Prison has not dulled your vision, Lucien. There's not much to the place, I'll give you that. It's little more than a ghost town, used by fur traders and Indians mostly, but it serves our purpose nicely. We're not going anywhere near the town, but Trammel and Hagen won't know that. They'll pause here long enough to see the town and wonder if we've gone down there."

Despite the cool air, Clay felt a bead of sweat break out along his brow. It still did not sound like much of a plan. "And it won't take them long to figure out we're not there, before they pick up our trail again."

"That won't happen because they'll already be dead." He pointed down toward rocks jutting out of the ground just below them. "These will provide nice cover for me when I ambush them. They won't see me before I take my first shot. Or my second. And the lack of cover will give me ample opportunity to finish off whoever's riding with him."

Clay looked around. "This doesn't look like an easy place to ride out of in a hurry."

"There's a narrow path that runs among these rocks. I'll have my horse down there waiting for me. When the deed is done, I'll climb down and ride out to meet you at camp."

Now Clay was sure Bessler had lost his mind. "You mean we're going to split up? I'm not one for outdoor living, Bessler."

"Just follow my directions and you'll be fine," Bessler assured him. "You're going to take the supplies and ride down this incline. Stick as close to the ridgeline for as long as you can and keep on going with the sun on your right. Stop in the woods after dusk and make camp near the town, but make sure you keep a low fire. I've put some matches in your saddlebags. I don't think anyone will stumble upon you, but it pays to be careful. If I'm not back by morning, break camp and keep heading in the same direction. I'll have no trouble following you and I'll be along as soon as I can."

"And what happens if you don't show up?"

"Then you'll just have to make your own arrangements," Bessler told him. "I'd wait a few months before you try to get your money from the bank in Denver, and hope the clerk isn't paying attention. But I don't have to tell you how to handle such things. You've always been enterprising. Don't worry. It won't come to that. Nothing's going to happen to me. I'll meet you on the trail as soon as I deal with Trammel and then we'll see about getting our money."

Clay still did not like the idea of parting. "We're already way ahead, Bessler. Don't get cute. I say we keep pushing on and put more space between us and Trammel. I haven't seen anyone get over on him yet by trying to be fancy, myself included."

But Bessler's mind was set. "We'll be much safer if our

pursuers are busy tending to their wounded or if they're dead. I don't want to have to worry about them catching us while we're taking that stage. And even on the off chance that I miss them here, they'll have no choice but to ride with much more caution. They'll be expecting an ambush awaiting them behind every rock they see and every wood they ride through. Their caution will only slow them down. A few moments time now will pay a handsome dividend for us later. After we hit the coach and get our money, we'll go our separate ways. Any survivors will have to decide which of us to track, but by the time they make up their mind, we'll be long gone."

Clay may not have agreed with it, but it was clear that Bessler's decision was final.

"Everything will work out fine, Lucien. We have the elements of time and surprise on our side. We've laid a trap for them and they're going to ride right into it. You've benefitted from my schemes so far. Trust me a little longer and you'll see that all will be well."

Clay had no choice but to follow the big Texan's lead. For the moment. "If things happen like you say, it just might work."

"Of course it will work. I thought of it, didn't I? Time's wasting. Keep heading south and I'll find you as soon as the deed is done. Just be ready to move fast come first light. We won't have a moment to lose once I get there."

Clay continued along the ridge, just as Bessler had told him. He did not have anything to lose except his life. And that was not worth much these days.

Adam Hagen had some trouble picking up Bessler's and Clay's trail in the muddled tracks outside of town, but they proved easier to follow the farther they rode away from

Laramie. The two fugitives had taken a southernly route and moved practically in a straight line since.

Perhaps too straight for Hagen's preference. He did not trust what he was seeing. He knew the tracks were true. Not even a man of Lucien Clay's cunning could fake such a thing.

No, Hagen did not trust the trail because it had been too easy to follow. The men had chosen to ride through open land when there were plenty of trees that would have offered better cover. They had avoided streambeds in favor of open ground, which only made them easier to track.

It was as if Bessler was leading them precisely where he wanted them to go. He was lulling them into a false sense of comfort so Trammel and his men would lower their guard somewhere along the many miles between Laramie and Denver. It felt like a trap.

Smart, Hagen said to himself as he read the ground. *But I'm smarter.*

He pulled his Winchester from its scabbard and brought his horse into a trot when he spotted the remnants of a campsite among a stand of trees ahead. The area was clearly deserted, so he did not signal for Trammel or Hawkeye to join him. They would catch up to him at their own pace.

Hagen climbed down from the saddle and walked around the site before crouching to take a closer look at the remnants. He picked up a half-burned prison uniform from the ashes and knew it had belonged to Clay. No attempt had been made to hide the garment. A wise man would have buried it, along with any evidence of the fire.

Neither Bessler nor Clay had bothered to do either. Clay was a city man, so he might be forgiven for the oversight, but Bessler was too careful to have made such a mistake. He had wanted the clothes to be found.

Hagen stood when Trammel and Hawkeye rode toward him.

The young deputy was encouraged by the rags Hagen was holding. "Looks like we're right on their trail to me."

Hagen allowed it to drop into the ashes. "I already knew that before I found this."

Trammel said, "Seems awful careless to leave it out in the open like that."

"That's because it is." He had already learned as much as he could from the site, so Hagen climbed back atop his horse. "I'll continue to ride ahead, but all of us need to keep an eye on our surroundings. I think Bessler and Clay are lulling us into a trap they could spring on us at any moment. It's never a good sign when the trail of desperate men is this easy to follow."

Trammel began to reach for his Winchester, and Hawkeye joined him. Hagen told them to stop. "There's no reason for that now. Just pay attention to our surroundings. Call out if it's too quiet or too noisy or just doesn't feel right. Bessler's proving to be much craftier than I already thought he was."

Because there was no reason to remain there, Hagen got back on his horse and continued to ride. Trammel and Hawkeye followed close behind.

Trammel said, "You told me you had a chance to kill Bessler back in Laramie. When did you meet him?"

"Minutes before he broke Clay out," Hagen said. "It was as though he was trying to feel me out to see what kind of man I was. It didn't make much sense to me at the time, but it does now. I surprised him by taking his gun from him, too. I was a fool to give it back to him. I won't make that mistake again."

Young Hawkeye seemed encouraged to hear that. "You'll do worse to him next time, Mr. Hagen."

Hagen kept his eyes moving along the horizon. Bessler and Clay were out there somewhere waiting for them.

"Don't get too cocky, Hawkeye. Arrogance has killed more men than bullets. Remember that."

He dug his heels into the flanks of his horse and pulled away before Hawkeye tried to encourage him further.

CHAPTER 14

After only his second night outdoors, Lucien Clay was already tired of the wilderness. He was huddled over a small fire, hoping it was not high enough to draw attention.

He had never been one for sleeping outside, not even before he came to Laramie. He had first come to the territory as a wrangler for a group of Jayhawkers out of Kansas. He had not known much about herding livestock when he signed on to the wagon train, but the wagon master had been in desperate need of men. Having his own horse and saddle and being able to ride was enough to get him the job.

He had spent many nights under the stars when time allowed, but he had never grown fond of it. The trappings of civilization, even a mining camp in the hills, were more suited to his tastes. He hated the cries of coyote or the wolves baying at the moon. They only grew quiet after a kill, and Clay always feared that one night it might be him who caused their silence. Their howling hunger did little to sooth the nerves of the cattle and the fear of stampede always hung in the air.

Every river they crossed tried to drown him or sweep away the livestock. Every rain froze him to his core, even on a warm night. The memory of constant hunger and filth had never left him.

But although the experience was in his distant past, it had prepared him to accept his life in prison. To take each day as it came and to accept that there was nothing he could do about his condition until the right moment came. He never doubted that he would be free one day and refused to allow discouragement to nest in his stomach.

He had put his time in Laramie Prison to good use. He spent hours watching Doc Carson treat the prisoners. He paid close attention to how he minded his keys, half-expecting the aging doctor to leave them somewhere he could easily lift them and make his escape. But Carson was never quite as forgetful as Clay wished him to be. He always returned his key immediately to his pocket after each use.

The deputies who tended to the prisoners always showed distain for their charges. Deputy Sherwood Blake was the worst. Although he never dealt with the convicts directly unless there was a problem, fear of his wrath was enough to keep them in line. Even the slightest infraction might be enough to cause a man to be locked out in the yard for an entire day. Such punishment was rarely meted out during nice weather and was usually reserved for the coldest nights or insufferable summer days.

It was not until Hal Haid rotated onto the dinner shift that Clay finally saw a possible way out of his predicament. At first, he wondered why the deputy tended to shy away from him. He never missed an opportunity to allow one of the other deputies to deliver his dinner. It had taken Clay a few sleepless nights spent in thought to remember why. And when he finally remembered, it was as if the sky had opened and manna descended from heaven.

Hal Haid once was one of his customers. He never was much of a drinker by Clay's recollection but had never shied away from trying his luck at his gambling tables or with one of the sporting ladies in Clay's employ. He'd had a full beard then. He was stockier, too, which made it more difficult for Clay to recognize him.

He remembered Haid's luck ran short at the tables and, like most gamblers, he begged for a line of credit. Clay usually frowned on the practice—collecting on a debt was always messy—but when he learned he was a deputy, Clay allowed him to gamble to his heart's content. It was always good to have a lawman in his debt. Rob Moran always was above such corruption, but even pillars of the community were only as good as the ground on which they stood. And in a town like Laramie, the sheriff had to stand on the shoulders of his deputies.

Once Clay recognized Haid, he reminded him of his debt and pressed him into service as a courier between himself and Mayor Holm. Those hastily written notes were the reason he was breathing free air that evening.

He closed his eyes when the night wind shifted, carrying with it the sounds and smells from the nearby town. Ennisville, Bessler had called it. Agony would have been a more accurate name, for it reminded him of all he had lost during his time in prison.

He had not seen a woman in six months, nor touched a drop of whiskey. Doc Carson had refused to even give him medicine when his throat became inflamed, citing orders from Sheriff Trammel himself.

Now he found himself within shouting distance of civilization, and although it was not much of a town, it was better than nothing. He did not have a penny on him and Bessler was wise enough not to leave him any money, but such were practical concerns. The sudden hunger for company and liquor overwhelmed him, as though he were one of those baying hounds that haunted his dreams from his time as a trail hand with the Jayhawkers.

He remembered Bessler's warning about staying in camp and waiting for his return, but a man could not live on advice alone.

There was a town nearby. People. Food and drink. Bessler might be right about there not being much to Ennisville, but to Lucien Clay, it was Paris. He had been denied anything good for far too long. That night, he would slate his thirst. Caution be damned.

Clay got to his feet and patted the dirt and dust from his clothes. He saddled his horse in the dark and rode in the direction of Ennisville. He knew it would be difficult to find his camp again in the darkened woods, but he used the weak glow of the Ennisville lights to guide him in a relatively straight line to town.

When he broke into a clearing, a cloud rolled past the moon, allowing him to see a large rock beside a tree. He looked around the area and saw no other landmark like it. He looked backward between the trees and saw a flicker of flame from his humble campfire. He fixed the image in his mind and hoped it would be enough for him to find his way back later.

Clay rode closer to town and paused in the shadows to take a closer look at the settlement. Bessler was not exaggerating when he said it was little more than a mining camp. Most of the place was comprised of canvas tents on either side of a muddy spit of land that served as a street. Someone had attempted to lay planks to allow easier conveyance from one side of the street to another, but the mud had swallowed them whole.

One tent bore a sign that said it was the Ennisville General Store. Barrels and crates undoubtedly filled with supplies were piled beside it. The proprietor was undoubtedly somewhere close by, keeping an uneasy watch on his goods. Clay would be sure to stay far away from the place.

Clay imagined the other, smaller tents pitched nearby served as shelter for the few unfortunates who called this place home. He did not know what one might do for work here and he did not care. He had concerns of his own.

A ramshackle building on the right side of the street was obviously a saloon. An old freight wagon sat rotting in the mud beside it. The place seemed to have been cobbled together by whatever planks the builders had been able to find. But welcoming lights burned brightly behind its crooked windows, and the stench of stale beer thrilled his senses.

He had seen enough to imagine it was safe and rode his horse over to the front of the saloon. The remnants of a hitching rail sagged in the cloying mud, but Clay tethered his animal to it anyway. Depending on how receptive the locals were to him, he might not be there long.

He pushed open the lopsided doors and saw the place lived down to his expectations. The bar was a sparse affair, nothing more than a plank nailed atop a couple of beams of wood.

The only men he could see were gathered around one of the three round tables in the place.

An old man who looked like he might be a Cheyenne sat alone at a small table in the far corner of the saloon, nursing a glass of whiskey. He was the only one who looked up when Clay walked in, and his eyes hung on him like death.

A bald man with a thick red beard and an equally impressive belly sat in the middle of the circle dealing cards to five men who watched his nimble hands go to work.

"Evening, stranger," the dealer said. "If beer is your poison and cards are your game, you've come to the right place. If you don't care for either, best take your business elsewhere because that's all we've got in store."

None of the men bothered to look at Clay, though one of

them said, "As long as you're not too picky, because the beer tastes like skunkweed and the dealer's lousy."

The dealer continued to shuffle cards, unfazed by the criticism. "You can take up your complaints with Queen Victoria if she ever waddles though my front door, Hoppy. No one's got a gun to your head. You can head back to your claim and complain to your wife if you don't like the way I run this place."

"As if she'd have him," one of the other gamblers said.

"Besides, you're better-looking than she is," said another, to the laughter of the others.

The dealer raised his bushy eyebrows and looked at Clay as he shuffled the cards. "You gonna say something, friend, or did you just come in for the scenery? Don't have much of that around here, I'm afraid. Come to think of it, we don't have much of anything here in Ennisville, but you're welcome to whatever we have, provided you can pay."

The first man said, "Old Red here will even let you take him for a twirl around the floor if you've got a penny in your pocket."

Red slapped his hand on the table. "The price is ten cents, you mangy old drover. I had to raise my price. Times are tough in these parts."

The men laughed easily at the bad joke, but Clay remained standing alone like a child looking at a jar full of hard candy back in Laramie.

Red set the cards aside and sat back in his chair. It was only when his impressive girth shifted that Clay saw a pistol stuck in the side of his pants.

"Not much of a talker, are you, friend?" He thumbed back toward the Cheyenne sitting alone in the corner. "I've already got one customer who doesn't say much. Chief might as well be made of wood for all the words he says.

We can't have two quiet men in here. Bad for the ambience, you might say."

A new thought seemed to come to Red. "Are you one of them mime fellas? I saw one of those boys when I was last in New Orleans near five years ago. Just stood up on stage doing all sorts of odd motions with his hands. One of the most unsettling things I ever saw. Kept expecting him to sing or dance or tell a story or two. But nope, he just made a fool of himself. Had to keep my partner from shooting him out of spite." He slapped the arm of the man next to him. "That was Steve. Remember him? Lanky fella with the lazy eye. He would've put on a better show than that quiet fool."

"I remember," confirmed the man next to him. "Died two years ago with the fever."

Red waved off the unpleasant memory and turned his attention back to Clay. "If you're a mime, you can keep on traveling, because we've got no use for your kind here. Could use a piano player, though, if we had a piano. The last player we had in here took it with him when he lit out for California last spring. Never thought he was serious about leaving until he showed up with a wagon one day and hauled it away. I was so shocked, you could've knocked me cold with a feather."

"I don't play the piano," Clay said. "Cards have always been more my game."

Red opened his hands in mock amazement. "He speaks after all. It's a miracle, boys. I told you Ennisville was sacred ground, but none of you heathens ever paid me any mind."

One of the gamblers was growing restless. "Just shut your mouth and deal the cards."

Red shook his head in disappointment. "Now, is that any way to treat our guest? He's come all the way here from . . . Where'd you say you're from again?"

"I didn't say. I'm from nowhere, I guess."

"Even better," Red decided. "He's come all the way from Nowhere, and here you are being rude. I don't know why you're in such an all-fire hurry for me to deal anyway. You always lose."

Red raised his chin in Clay's direction. "What can I get for you, mister? Dealing with these boys has given me an unnatural thirst."

"Beer sounds good." Clay could not remember a time when it sounded better than it did now. "And I'd like to try my hand at whatever you're playing, except I don't have any money."

The five men around the table joined Red in taking a closer look at the stranger. Clay imagined he did not look like much to them. Not much of a threat. Not much of a gambler. Just a man who walked into a saloon in the middle of nowhere in the dead of night without a penny to his name or a gun on his hip.

"No money, you say." Red chewed it over. "Got anything to trade?"

"No."

Red looked past him outside. "That your horse tethered in front of my place? You could use that as collateral. My eyes ain't what they used to be, but it ought to be worth a glass of beer or two at least."

Clay noticed the Cheyenne in the corner was still looking at him. It made him feel as though the old Indian could see through him. He did not like that feeling.

"Can't expect me to get around without a horse," Clay said. "How about we play for something more interesting?"

"Sounds promising," Red allowed. "Like what, for instance?"

"My life."

The five men slowly backed away from the table. Clay saw that none of them were armed, but they were nervous that he might be packing. He held his hands away from his sides.

"I'm not carrying a gun or a knife." He slowly turned so the men could get a good look at him. "I don't expect any charity and I'm not asking for any. I've just been in a bad place for a long time. Too long, to tell the truth."

Red ran his hand over his beard as the men stood on either side of him. They looked like they did not know what to do. Clay was just glad they had not thrown him out yet.

"I'll give you the beer if it means that much to you," Red said.

But Clay shook his head. "I just told you, I don't want charity. I want my chance at a turn of the cards. If I win, I get my beer. If I don't?" He nodded at the pistol tucked in Red's pants. "I'll deserve a bullet. What I'm wearing and my horse ought to be enough to cover the cost. I'm willing to risk it. What about you?"

Clay enjoyed the confusion that washed over Red and his customers. They were catching the sickness he had brought in here with him. The thrill of risking everything for seemingly nothing. That feeling where the unthinkable not only became tangible, but something close to fun. Where the threat of death made life worth living.

He imagined they had probably ambled into the saloon for another forgettable night of meaningless chatter and bad beer. Clay had given them more than they had bargained for just by walking into the place.

Red looked at his customers. "What do you say, boys? Think it's a worthwhile wager? A man's life over the turn of a card?"

"Nothing's cheap," one of the men observed. "If he wants to put it on the table, I say let him."

Another man said, "Not like we've had much in the way of entertainment around here in quite a while."

Red's mind was made up, and he gestured toward a chair one of the men just vacated. "You might as well make yourself comfortable, mister. It looks like we have ourselves a game."

Clay moved to the chair like a thirsty man dove at a running stream. He had not realized the strength of his own hunger until that moment. He did not care if he won or lost, only that something was at stake. Everything was.

He looked past the men at the Cheyenne in the corner. He was still looking at Clay, but not as if he was interested in whatever game the white men were playing. It was as though he was simply biding his time while he waited for something else to happen. Something more.

Clay shook it off and hoped the Indian did not get his wish.

"The name of the game is vignt-et-un," Red told him as he resumed shuffling the cards. "Brought it back with me from that trip to New Orleans I told you about earlier. I hear they play it in France. It means—"

"Twenty-One." Clay was dizzy. He could practically smell the ink on the cards. It had been so long. "We call it black-jack where I'm from."

"From a little place called Nowhere." Red grinned as he shuffled the cards. "See? I was listening." Red placed the deck on the table. "Cut."

Clay kept his hands from shaking as he took the deck, cut them, then shuffled them with a practiced speed that made the men gasp. He finished his impressive display and placed the neat deck in front of Red. "Now deal."

"I see this ain't the first time you've played cards." Red cracked his knuckles as the men moved in closer. "Mighty fancy. Let's see if luck fancies you enough to let you win a hand."

After Red finished dealing the cards, Clay had two kings. Red had a two of clubs.

The men cheered.

"Good start, mister," one of them said. "Luck is sitting on your shoulder."

"Split it."

Red's grin disappeared. "You're sitting on twenty right there. You're more than halfway to winning."

Clay felt his blood rushing through his veins. "You deaf or just stupid? I'm not interested in being halfway to anything. I told you to split it."

Red split the two face cards and dealt two more, slapping each one in front of him.

Clay stretched out his hand and turned over one of the cards. It was an ace. Twenty-one.

The other was the nine of spades. Nineteen.

"He won!" the men shouted in unison.

Red turned over his cards. With the two card he had showing, the next was a four of diamonds. At six total, his next card was a jack of clubs. Sixteen. He dealt another card. A jack of hearts. He'd lost.

Clay had won.

Red sagged in his seat and let out a breath he had not realized he was holding. The others gathered around Clay, eager to slap his back and shake his hand, hoping some of his luck might rub off on them.

Clay looked over and saw the Cheyenne was still looking at him. His blank expression had not changed.

The praise from the strangers meant nothing to him. All he wanted was another hand. Another chance to risk it all. To feel like he used to feel back when he was someone.

Red clapped his hands like a fat kid with a new toy. Clay had never seen a dealer so happy to lose. "Mister, I almost shot you when you split those two face cards."

Clay had never placed much stock in "almost." "I'd like that beer now, if my credit's still good."

Red threw his head back and laughed. The others were all too eager to join in. "I'd say you're entitled to more than that. Two beers coming right up."

The men followed Clay to the plank bar, eager to tell each other about what they had just witnessed even though all of them had seen it for themselves. Clay imagined they would be talking about that night for the rest of their lives.

Red filled up each man's mug from the barrel behind the bar, but beckoned Clay to follow him to another table away from the others. "Let's you and me have a talk over here in private."

Clay looked longingly at the four mugs of beer Red carried with him. They passed by the old Cheyenne, who had taken a sip from his glass while Clay was not looking. His presence was more unsettling now, especially after he had risked his life.

"Does he just sit there like that all night?"

The saloonkeeper laughed. "Don't mind Chief. He's just an old trapper who used to cook here when we had a going trade. He's kind of like our good luck charm. If someone gets sick, he's mighty handy with the herbs and such. He doesn't bother anyone, and he always pays, unlike some of my other customers."

Red had barely placed the mugs on the table before Clay took one and drank from it deeply.

He could not disguise the sigh that escaped him after the first swallow. He could not remember having tasted anything so good. It quenched a thirst deep in his soul.

Red watched him from across the table. "How long did you spend inside?"

Clay licked the beer from his lips, not wanting to miss a single drop. "Is it that obvious?"

"Obvious enough to a man who knows what to look for," Red said. "I've spent my fair share of time behind the iron. How long were you in for?"

Clay sagged as the beer hit home. He was not drunk but relieved. "Does it matter?"

"Not particularly," Red said. "And notice I didn't ask what you were in for."

Clay had noticed. He just did not care. "Guess that part doesn't matter, either."

"As long as you had a good reason for it, and men like us usually have a good reason for the things we do, even if it happens to be against the law."

Clay might have laughed had he not been busy draining his glass. Red owned a broken old saloon barely worthy of the name. Lucien Clay had once owned the finest gambling dens and restaurants in the territory. He'd had his opium brought by Chinese directly from the docks in San Francisco. He had made more money in a week than a man like Red could have dreamed about had he been given five lifetimes.

Yet despite the different roads they may have taken, life had led them both here. In Red's saloon, drinking bad beer after a hand of blackjack. Perhaps water seeks its own level after all.

Clay would not laugh at Red. If he managed to survive the next few weeks, it might be him on the other side of a table, talking to a stranger without anything to lose.

"It's nice to meet someone who understands how rotten life can be."

Red pointed in the direction of the men at the bar. "Each of those boys over there are good men in their own way. One of them is a trapper. The rest work in the mines scattered about these parts. They work hard and try to do the best they can, but they don't know what it means to live. And

I mean really live. Not just earn enough to get your next meal or see you through to the next winter. I mean stake a claim and do anything you have to do to defend it. I think you know what I'm talking about."

Perhaps it was the effect of the beer or the excitement, but Clay did not have the slightest idea what Red was talking about. He did not care about anything except the second beer Red had placed on the table. Clay grabbed it and began to drink from it.

Red took Clay's avoidance as an encouraging sign. "I don't think you just happened in here this evening by accident. I think you came in here for a reason."

Clay agreed with him there. Beer and gambling. He wiped his mouth with the back of his sleeve. "I told you why I was here when I first came in."

"I'm talking about more than that." Red's eyes gleamed with promise. "I'm talking about a bigger reason. People don't just accidentally find themselves in Ennisville. They're always either on their way to something or running from something. And I think you've got something in store. Something big. And even though you might not know it yet, you'll be needing a partner. If that's the case, I'm your man."

Clay pitied Red. The bartender had clearly been stranded out here in the backwoods of the territory for so long that he had lost touch with reality. Clay had Frank Bessler as a partner, which he counted as one partner too many.

But Clay knew he would need all the friends he could get if Bessler did not kill Buck Trammel. He decided to play along with Red's delusions. He looked back to confirm the men at the bar could not hear them before asking, "What kind of work are you up for?"

"Name it and I've done it," Red told him. "Banditry, gun work, and almost anything else you can think of. Got chased up here from New Orleans a while back, but I always like to keep my knife sharp."

Clay knew the territory was filled with men like Red. Men who believed they were capable and dangerous, willing to risk their lives for the sake of a payday. But just because Red was not unique did not mean he could not be useful.

"You get many travelers through here? Men on their way to Denver?"

Red stroked his beard as he thought it over. "We're not exactly a stop for the stagecoach and we've got no railroad near here, but we do a fair trade with men going to and from Denver. Particularly the kind of man who's anxious to keep out of sight for one reason or another."

Clay had already had his fill of beer, so he decided to cash in whatever goodwill he still had with Red on another gamble. "There might be men coming this way. Men who are looking for me."

Red licked his lips. "Want me to get rid of them for you?"

As if you could, Clay thought. "Not in the way you're thinking, though I'd appreciate it if you told them I was heading east. Tell them you saw it was me and two men riding with me." The more Clay thought about it, the more he liked the idea. Three was a nice number to throw them off.

"But you're not heading east, are you?" Red said it as more of a fact than a question.

"I am," Clay lied. "I'm not looking to outrun these men. I'm looking to draw them in so I can surprise them and finish them off before they catch up to me."

"You can count on me, friend." Red laughed and clapped his hands again. He was delighted to be included in Clay's scheme. "What'll they call you when they get here? Who should I be looking out for? What do they look like?"

Clay did not want to risk describing Trammel. Even if Ennisville saw half the visitors Red had boasted about, word about Trammel would have certainly reached him. Red had agreed to help confuse unknown strangers but might think twice if he knew one of them would be Buck Trammel.

"I don't know who they'll be or how many there'll be," Clay admitted, "and I hope I never do. I've managed to keep ahead of them so far. But you'll know them when they get here. I'm not even asking you to lie. Just to aim them where I need them to go."

Red offered a curt nod. "Consider it done. Just do us both a favor and don't say a word of this to the boys up at the bar. They're not the most dependable types for something like this."

Clay smiled. But Red was more than dependable. The most gullible always were. "I'll keep that in mind."

He finished his beer and was ready to leave when Red pushed one of the two remaining beers on the table toward him. "So, how do I find you afterward?"

It was not even a real plan, but Clay already had an answer for that question, though he had to be careful. To sell it as genuine, he could not be too obvious or Red might grow suspicious. "Are you sure you're ready to leave all this behind? You've got a nice corner of the world carved out for yourself here."

"Nothing I'm not willing to leave behind in the same amount of time it takes me to throw my stuff on the back of a horse. Just tell me when."

"I don't know the answer to that," Clay admitted. "And I won't know until they get here. Could be tomorrow. Could be a couple of days from now, if they come at all. Just make sure you point them east and, if you're still willing, trail after them, but be ready to move fast. We'll catch them in between us and finish them off. But I'll be firing blind, so you'll need to be careful."

"Don't worry about me. I've done this kind of thing before plenty of times." He extended his hand across the table. "What's your name, mister?"

Clay had been lying to him all this time and saw no reason why he should tell him the truth now. "Frank Bessler. But let's keep that between us."

After the two men shook on it, Clay grabbed the mug of beer and drank from it until it was dry. He savored every swallow. He imagined it would have to last him quite a while after the real Bessler took his shot at Trammel. If Bessler returned, they would have to hit the stagecoach with his money and lay low for a while. If Bessler did not come back, Clay would have to stay clear of civilization for a while, until it was safe to try to get his money from that bank in Denver.

Clay set his mug on the table and shook hands with Red again. He kept his voice low as he said farewell. "Thanks for the beer. See you along the trail, partner."

"Thank you, Fred. You can count on me."

Clay rose and noticed the old Cheyenne was still watching him. It was impossible for him to see what he thought. He was neither interested nor disinterested, but he did not look away, either.

Clay shook off the chill that ran down his spine and bid the men at the bar a good evening as he went outside without stopping to shake their hands. They seemed disappointed, but they had served their purpose. They were witnesses.

He untied his horse from the sunken rail, climbed into the saddle, and rode east, just as he had told Red he would.

About a quarter mile out of town, he turned back and rode behind the tents and saloon to avoid being seen.

He could hear the men inside laughing as they told one another about all the stranger had just done. They had no choice but to repeat it to themselves; there was no one else to listen.

Clay felt a warmth inside his chest he had not known since he had been locked away in prison. It was not from the beer he had consumed, or even from the hands of black-jack he had won.

Lucien Clay had corrupted another soul, this one named Red. It was so easy, he could not claim it as much of an accomplishment, but at least his trip into town had not been entirely in vain.

He found the rock in front of the tree he had used as his landmark and made it back to his humble camp without in-cident. After securing his horse and removing the saddle, he pulled a blanket over himself and fell off to sleep with only the crickets and the stars to keep him company.

CHAPTER 15

Frank Bessler sat between two rocks as he took in the glorious scenery that surrounded him that morning.

He regretted that he had waited so long to come to Wyoming. He had heard about its majestic beauty for years from cowpunchers who returned with grand stories of drives they had led through the territory. The untamed lands and the barely tamed towns. The women were friendly, and the whiskey overflowed. The place seemed to stamp the souls of even the hardest men he had represented who'd traveled there and back.

Bessler had always envisioned Texas as the place where he would spend the rest of his life. The flat lands. The broiling summers. The hive of activity that was Fort Worth and the rough charm of San Antonio. The same old clients getting into the same old trouble year after year. He knew the judges he could buy and those he could not. His life had settled into a predictable rhythm in such an untamed land.

He had come to think of Texas as an in-between kind of place. Not quite civilized and not quite savage. Not quite American, but not entirely Mexican, either. It was the land where one country blended into another. He found that aspect comforting. He had always known there was more to the world than Texas, of course, but Texas had always been big enough to be his world. He had come to believe the land was as essential to his being as breathing.

But from where he sat now, along a rocky ridgeline from where he waited to murder a man, the wonder of Wyoming's beauty captured his soul. He found himself mourning the death of something that had never lived until that moment. A dream of calling such a place home.

Now that he had seen Wyoming with his own eyes, he knew he would have settled here years before had he allowed himself to explore beyond the boundaries of his beloved Texas. But his decision to aid Clay in his escape had made any move to Wyoming impossible now. He was already a marked man after engineering the prison break and killing Trammel would only increase the price on his head. He would never be able to return to his old life and remaining here would be nothing short of suicide.

The night and sunrise he had spent on the ridgeline caused him to decide he was done with Texas for good. Perhaps he had already known that when he agreed to help Clay escape. There was no reward for a man to spend his entire life in one place. No one gave you parole for time served in a town. Life's rewards came from serving a purpose. A cause.

There was nothing left for him in Texas anymore. He knew his future would be out here among the endless mountains and glorious sunsets. He would see what he could make of himself in such a place. Montana or Oregon. And once Trammel was dead and the stagecoach robbed, he would have enough time and money to make his new dreams come true.

He had spent the cold night nestled among the rocky outcroppings, gnawing on the beef jerky he had stashed in his saddlebags and drinking the water from his canteen.

It was hardly a feast, but he was not seeking comfort. He was there for a reason, and it was better to remain focused on the task at hand. He had slept lightly and remained mostly awake and aware of his surroundings.

He did not take it for granted that Trammel and whoever might be riding with him had camped for the night. He could not afford to bank on their complacency, especially if Adam Hagen was with him. He may have only spoken with Hagen for a few moments back at the saloon, but it was evident the man was as crafty as he was capable.

Hagen was not like Clay, whose dangerous demeanor weakened the farther he got from civilization. In Laramie, Lucien Clay was a man to be reckoned with. He could corrupt the order of a town to his advantage. Out here in the wild, he was just a scrawny man ill-suited for the chaos of nature. Trammel might fare a bit better out here, but only due to his size and his grit.

To borrow a gambling term, Hagen was the true wild card in his plan. Visiting him on the night of the prison break had been a risky but rewarding endeavor. At least he had a sense of the kind of man he was up against and had adapted his plan accordingly. Only time would prove if he was correct.

Bessler tensed when he heard the unmistakable sound of an approaching horse. He grabbed his Winchester and slowly stood just high enough to see beyond the rocks that granted him ample cover.

He saw Adam Hagen riding toward him along the tall grass that he and Clay had covered the previous day. The dandy sat tall in the saddle. His brocade vest looked even gaudier in the morning light. His flat-brimmed hat was angled downward as he studied the tracks and droppings their horses had left, leading him toward the ridge.

Bessler raised his rifle to his shoulder. *That's it, Hagen. Just keep coming. There's nothing to concern you here.*

His pulse quickened when he saw only two riders following at a distance. One of them was much larger than the other and, although he could only make out their silhouettes from so far away, he knew one of them had to be Trammel.

The third member of the party did not look familiar to him. Given his much smaller size and the fact that he was trailing a packhorse, Bessler knew he was of no consequence to his plan.

He watched Hagen pay particular attention to the tracks Lucien had left when he had headed south to make camp. The saloon owner was already well within range of his Winchester, though Trammel had just entered the limits of his marksmanship. Bessler refused to rush the shot. He took careful aim as the sheriff rode closer into his trap.

Bessler remained still as he watched Hagen stand up in his stirrups and look over the ridge to the valley below. The morning light was still weak enough to conceal him among the rocks, but it was strong enough to reveal the tiny town of Ennisville below. The town would be the most logical place to hunt for Bessler and Clay.

Hagen brought his horse around and beckoned his companions to join him.

Bessler tensed as he watched the two riders break into a trot. Trammel was finally in range.

He took careful aim at the big man, who only grew into a larger target as he rode closer. Just before he passed under his gunsight, Bessler squeezed the trigger.

The rifle recoiled as he watched the impact of the bullet jerk Trammel back in the saddle. Bessler levered in a fresh round as, from the corner of his eye, he saw Hagen pull his rifle from the scabbard beneath his left leg.

Bessler fixed his aim on Trammel once more. He was

sagging forward in the saddle as the third rider came to his side. He had been hit and his horse had slowed.

Bessler fired again, and this time, his bullet knocked Trammel backward from his horse. The third rider dropped to the ground to tend to his wounded companion.

Bessler flinched as a bullet ricocheted off a rock a foot away from his head. He had been so taken by his success that he had almost forgotten about Hagen.

Bessler shifted his aim in time to see Hagen riding back to Trammel, twisting in the saddle as he cracked off another shot at the ridgeline. He fired blind and the shot sailed harmlessly overhead and into the valley below.

Bessler drew careful aim on Hagen as he levered in another round and fired. The gambler cried out and spilled from the saddle.

Bessler, unsure if he had hit Hagen, worked the lever again and peered out into the tall grass for the spot where he had seen the gambler fall. It was difficult to spot him, but he saw a flash of movement—a hand?—and squeezed the trigger once more.

Another yelp from Hagen told Bessler he had hit his mark.

Trammel and Hagen were down, if not dead.

Bessler looked up when he heard a guttural cry rise from the grass and saw the third rider had regained his horse and begun to charge toward him. He had his pistol in his hand and aimed in Bessler's general direction.

The lawyer smiled at the sight. *How noble. How brave.*

The young rider had selected the wrong weapon. Bessler knew he was still well out of range for the pistol to be of any use as Bessler took his time to prepare his next and final shot.

He ejected the spent round, took aim, and allowed the screaming rider to speed closer. He judged the man to be scarcely older than a boy. But if he was old enough to ride with the likes of Trammel and Hagen, he was old enough to accept his fate.

He centered his sights on the center of the boy's chest and squeezed the trigger.

The horse reared up, causing its rider to fall off its back before it, too, fell among the tall grass. The packhorse he had been leading remained far behind.

Bessler finally lowered his Winchester and allowed himself time to admire his work. Three men had ridden after him. All three had fallen under his gun. And one of them was the great Buck Trammel.

His work was done.

He knew prudence dictated that he should go out to make sure each of the men were dead, but something held him in place. *Everyone who thought they had Buck Trammel beaten found out too late that they didn't.*

Bessler knew he had put two bullets into Trammel. He was down, but the big man undoubtedly still had some fight left in him.

Fate had smiled upon him that day. There was little to be gained by risking more than he already had.

As Bessler turned to make his way down the rocks to his waiting horse below, the ground beneath his boots gave way. He managed to hold on to his rifle as he found himself sliding down the rocky slope until he crashed on the ground beside his horse.

His back ached from the rocks that had raked his back during his fall, but he was alive. He was already sore when he tucked his Winchester back into the scabbard on his saddle and he rode away along the narrow path as quickly as he dared.

He grinned through his pain as he finally reached level ground and heeled his horse's flanks to go faster.

His plan had worked perfectly. He had won.

Buck Trammel was finally dead.

CHAPTER 16

Hawkeye was not sure if he was alive or dead when he came to and heard a voice calling his name. He remembered someone had shot at them. He remembered seeing the sheriff get hit and Mr. Hagen, too.

He had the warm, metallic taste of blood in his mouth and began to fear he was dying. He thought he could still hear the echo of that last shot above him.

Hawkeye ran his hands over his chest and face and cried out when he lifted his hands to see them covered in blood. But he did not feel any pain. Was this what it felt like to be dying?

"Hawkeye!" The voice was much louder now, and he recognized it as Mr. Hagen. "Are you hit?"

"I think so." He frantically moved his hands along his body, but nothing hurt. But where had all the blood come from?

He lifted his head and braced himself for the agony that was sure to follow. But there was no pain, just a dull throbbing across his back from when he had hit the ground.

"Keep your head down!" Mr. Hagen shouted. "He might still be out there. Don't move. I'm headed your way."

But Hawkeye was too worried about his condition to heed the advice. He looked over his body and failed to see a wound. He rolled over on his side and was sure he had not been hit.

It was not until he saw the remains of his horse's head that he realized the blood was not his, but the animal's.

Mr. Hagen parted the tall grass as he crawled over to him. "You're not hit. The blood's from your horse."

"Did he get you?" Hawkeye asked.

"No, but he came close. That spill I took was just play-acting."

Whatever relief Hawkeye might have felt was quickly pushed aside by his concern for the sheriff. "The boss got hit. Twice. I'd better go see how bad."

Hagen reached out and pulled the boy back to the ground. "Stay low and stay here until I call for you. That lowlife might still be waiting out there."

Before Hawkeye could protest, Hagen was already on his feet moving at a crouch. He saw the two remaining horses and the packhorse had gathered near a group of trees, nosing the grass around their hooves as if nothing had just happened. Maybe things were not as bad as he feared.

But that notion died the moment he heard Mr. Hagen call for him. "Buck's been hit. Get over here now!"

Hawkeye forgot all about the gunman who might be waiting to finish them off as he sprang to his feet and ran back to where he saw Mr. Hagen crouched over the sheriff. He tore off the left sleeve of his fancy shirt and pressed it against a bleeding hole in Trammel's chest.

Hawkeye froze where he stood. The sheriff had been shot. He had never seen him look so flat and helpless before, and the sight made no sense to him. He had to still be dreaming. This could not be happening.

He heard himself ask, "Is he dead?"

"He will be if you don't get over here and keep pressure on this wound."

Hawkeye crouched beside Trammel, who tried to lift his head as he asked, "What happened?"

Mr. Hagen grabbed Hawkeye's hand and pressed it hard against the balled-up sleeve covering the holes on the right side of his chest. "I'm not going to lie to you, Buck. You've been shot twice."

Trammel allowed his head to drop back to the ground. "Is it bad?"

"It's not good." Hagen tore his other sleeve and made another ball with it before holding it against the second hole just below the first. This time, Hawkeye did not need to be told what to do and he pushed down on it. His hands were quickly growing red from the blood seeping through the fabric.

Hagen said, "I need to feel behind you to see if the bullets are still in there. This is going to hurt, so yell as loud as you need to."

Hawkeye shut his eyes as he put all his weight on the wounds. He had never seen so much blood before, not even in all the scrapes he and the sheriff had survived back in Blackstone. The stench of it might have turned his stomach if he'd had anything in it. They had only stopped for a few hours the previous night and had not taken the time to eat anything.

Trammel cut loose with a yell Hawkeye did not think was possible as Mr. Hagen dug his left hand beneath the sheriff's right shoulder. When he pulled out his hand, it was slick with blood.

Hawkeye turned his head and gagged.

Mr. Hagen worked fast. "I think the bullets passed right through you, but I can't be sure until I turn you over." He reared back on his haunches and undid his belt. He pulled it free from the loops and doubled it over before putting it in Trammel's mouth. "Bite down on this as hard as you want. It'll help some with the pain."

Hawkeye felt his hands begin to shake as Mr. Hagen told him, "I'm going to need you to help me roll him over on his belly. He's going to scream something awful, but it's for his own good."

Before Hawkeye could agree, Hagen began to pull Trammel toward him. The deputy had never appreciated how heavy the big man might be and it took all his strength to help flop him over.

The sheriff spat out the belt and his screams filled the air around them before he fell silent.

Hawkeye recoiled. "Good Lord, we killed him."

"He just passed out," Mr. Hagen said as he examined the wet holes on the back of Trammel's vest. "Looks like the bullets passed right through him. That's good in the long term, but he'll bleed to death if we don't find a way to stop it."

He ripped open his fancy vest and pulled his shirt over his head. "I'll do what I can to try to stop it, but he'll die for certain if we don't get him help fast. I need you to get on one of those horses and ride down to that town down in the valley. Leave the packhorse. It'll only slow you down. Get someone to help and get a wagon, too, if they've got one. We'll need it to move him."

Hawkeye was still too taken by the sight of so much blood when Mr. Hagen shoved him hard. "Ride, boy! Ride like the wind and get back here as fast as you can. Go now!"

Hawkeye was on his feet without realizing it and running faster than he thought he was capable. He practically leaped onto the horse's back—he was not sure who it belonged to—and dug his heels hard into its flanks.

He might not have been as good with a gun as the sheriff

or Mr. Hagen, but he knew he could ride plenty fast. He used the reins to slap the horse's neck to get it to run quicker. But no matter how hard he hit the animal, it could not run fast enough to suit him.

He forgot about whoever had shot at them and if he might be waiting to finish them off. Nothing else mattered except getting to town and finding the sheriff some help.

Rider and horse raced down the ridgeline and rounded into town. People had already come out from the canvas tents on either side of a muddy span as an old Indian man approached him with his arms outstretched.

"Whoa, boy, whoa," the stranger said as Hawkeye brought the horse to a stop just before the man took hold of the bridle. "We heard all the shots ring out down from the ridgeline. What happened?"

Hawkeye knew his words were coming out in a jumbled rush. "Somebody ambushed us from up in the rocks. One of my friends is hurt. Sheriff Trammel. Someone's got to come quick or he'll die."

The old man took a firm grip on the horse. "Climb down and come with me. I've got a couple of mine already hitched to my wagon. Get on and we'll go fetch your friend."

Hawkeye got off the horse and ran over to an ancient buckboard that looked like it might break apart if he touched it.

The Indian ran past him and climbed into the seat. "Better climb aboard if you're coming with me."

The deputy had barely sat down before the man snapped the reins, sending the horses into a trot. The wagon creaked and groaned as the animals ran up the incline, pulling man and wagon behind them.

Hawkeye watched the lines that crisscrossed the older

man's face grow deeper as he asked, "Did you see the man who shot your friends? What did he look like?"

"Never saw him, the coward," Hawkeye spat, "but he sure got a mighty good look at us. Shot Sheriff Trammel twice in the chest and killed my own horse, too."

"Guess that explains all the blood on your face."

The team crested the hill, and the Indian cracked the reins again. He did not know how the Indian was able to get so much out of the horses as his own had been winded by the time he covered less than half the distance and none of the weight.

The team sped up when it reached the flatlands and Hawkeye pointed in the direction of where Mr. Hagen was tending to the sheriff. The Indian brought the team to a quick halt when he pulled up alongside them before jumping down from the wagon. He reached in and pulled out a leather satchel as he joined Mr. Hagen beside the fallen sheriff.

Hawkeye never felt so useless as he simply stood there and watched the men try to save Trammel's life.

"You a doctor?" Mr. Hagen asked the stranger.

"Reckon I'm the closest thing to one you can expect to find in these parts." The Indian removed the shirt Hagen had been pressing against the wounds and examined the holes on Trammel's back. "Bullets went straight through from the front?"

"They did and they're bleeding bad," Mr. Hagen confirmed.

The stranger opened his satchel and dug out two lumps of dirt wrapped in cloth. "We'll have to plug these wounds first before we load him into my wagon. He'll bleed to death before we get him back to town if we don't."

Hawkeye was disappointed to see the Indian had two lumps of green dirt about the size of a fist.

"That's all you're gonna do?" The young deputy could hardly believe what he was seeing. "We could've done that already if all you were going to do was pack dirt in him."

Hagen glared up at him. "Shut your mouth, boy. You don't know what you're talking about. Let the man work."

"It's not just dirt." The old Indian gestured for Mr. Hagen to help him struggle to pull off the sheriff's vest before he tore his shirt up the back. He broke the clumps apart and applied them to the wounds. "This is special dirt. It's got medicine to it."

After tending to the back wounds, the Indian gestured for Mr. Hagen to help him roll Trammel onto his back, where he used his hands to paste more dirt to the wounds in his chest.

"Was he like this when he fell or did he pass out?" the stranger asked Mr. Hagen.

"He passed out when I rolled him onto his belly."

"Good. He'll need the rest because this is going to hurt." The Indian looked back at Hawkeye and said, "Help us lift him and get him into my wagon. I won't be able to do anything else for him out here."

Hawkeye helped the stranger lift Trammel from the left while Mr. Hagen strained to lift him from the right. If the sheriff had seemed heavy when he had helped to roll him over before, he was completely deadweight now.

The three of them grunted from the effort it took to lug Trammel the short distance to the back of the wagon. After they succeeded in rolling him inside, the stranger hopped into the flatbed with the sheriff and said to Hawkeye, "I hope you can drive a wagon, boy, because I need to tend to these wounds some more."

"I'll do it," Hagen began to climb up into the wagon, but

the old Indian pushed him back. "Go get both your horses and bring them back into town. You might be needing those supplies before long."

Hagen cursed as he ran off to retrieve his animals while Hawkeye took up the reins. He snapped them hard across their rumps, and both horses set off at a good run. They took the incline a little too fast to suit him, but the old rattling wagon remained on the narrow path. They took the turn into town easily, and Hawkeye pulled them to a stop in front of the same building where the wagon had been before.

Mr. Hagen was right on their heels with the packhorse and was already helping the stranger to pull the sheriff from the back by the time Hawkeye made his way around to help them.

Together, the three of them struggled to bring Trammel inside the building, which Hawkeye quickly realized was a saloon.

"Set him down here," the stranger told them as soon as they were inside the door. "I'll get something from my room to help him. Stay with him, boy. Keep talking to him. Let him know you're there."

Hawkeye knelt on the floor beside Trammel, unsure of what to do. He took hold of his hand and began saying anything that came to mind. "You've got nothing to worry about, boss. These good folks are going to fix you up as good as new before you know it. You'll be back after Clay in no time."

Mr. Hagen touched the dirt on top of the wounds and examined his fingers. "Moss. That's good. That's very good."

Hawkeye was about to ask him what was so good about it when a bald, fat man with a long red beard walked out from the back of the saloon. "What in tarnation is going on out here?" He pointed down at the sheriff. "You can't bring him in here. Roll him back outside. This is a saloon, not a hospital."

Mr. Hagen stood up and had his gun in the fat man's face before Hawkeye had seen him draw it. "Unless you want it to become a morgue, you'll shut your mouth and get back to wherever you came from."

The Indian came out from the back carrying another bag and knelt beside the sheriff. "I'd do what he says if I were you, Red. These boys have had a trying time of it, and I don't recommend you testing their patience."

Hawkeye watched the fat man hold up his hands as he slowly backed away from Mr. Hagen's gun. "Sorry, fellas. Didn't mean any harm. We just don't see many men who've been shot is all."

Mr. Hagen did not lower his pistol. "Whiskey. Full bottle. Now."

Red ran behind the bar, grabbed the first bottle he saw, and brought it back to Hagen, who placed it on the floor beside the Indian without taking his gun off the bartender.

"Figured you could use that to clean your tools."

"My tools are always clean," the Indian said as he peeled away some of the moss and placed it next to the wound. "But I appreciate the gesture." Without looking up from Trammel, the Indian spoke to Hawkeye. "Boy, you and your friend ought to step outside and get some air. There's nothing more you can do in here for now. I'll come get you when I'm done."

Hawkeye gently lowered Trammel's hand to the floor and got to his feet. The man called Red had already backed up behind the bar and Mr. Hagen holstered his gun.

Mr. Hagen kept looking at Red as he asked the Indian, "He going to live?"

The man reached into his bag and patted the open

wounds with a dry cloth. "Won't know for a while yet. Only time will tell, but I'm doing everything I can. I just hope it's enough."

Hawkeye had never seen Mr. Hagen look so grim, not even after he had gotten himself shot up back in Blackstone. "If he dies, you die."

If the Indian took offense, he hid it well as he kept examining the wound. "I already figured as much. Now go on. I'll be out to see you in a while. You can threaten me some more then."

Hawkeye urged Mr. Hagen to leave with him as they stepped outside. He was surprised to see that everyone had gone back into their tents or wherever they lived. If this were Laramie or even Blackstone, the street would have been full of curious folks anxious to find out what had happened. Who had been shot and who had done the shooting. But he imagined this place, whatever it was called, didn't have the same kind of permanence to it that those larger towns had. People could afford to be curious with four walls around them and a roof over their head. Minding one's own business was better in a place as fragile as this appeared to be.

Hawkeye's mouth suddenly felt dry as the excitement began to leave him. "Mr. Hagen, I've never seen the sheriff look so bad."

Mr. Hagen was looking over the street as though he was getting a feel for their new surroundings. He did not look himself as he stood in his undershirt, streaked with dirt and blood and sweat. He did not look as calm and capable as he always did in town, with his fancy vests and clean clothes. He looked leaner. Meaner, even.

"Neither have I, Hawkeye. Neither have I."

The words had not been meant to provide any comfort

and they didn't. "But he'll pull through, won't he? He's strong. The strongest man I've ever seen."

"No one's strong with a hole in him, much less two. All we can do is hope that old heathen in there knows what he's doing." He rubbed his fingers together in thought. "He put moss on the wounds. Helps cut down on infection and stops the bleeding. Saw needles and thread in his bag, too. That's good. Better than burning it closed. Maybe he's not a butcher after all."

Hawkeye lowered himself against the wall of the saloon until he sat on the ground. He had not had time to grasp everything that had just happened to them until that moment. About seeing the sheriff get shot. About charging at the shooter like he had. It had just seemed like the right thing to do at the time. He had not even thought about getting shot.

"Is it always like that?" Hawkeye asked Mr. Hagen.

Hagen had been thinking about something else. "Is what always like what?"

"Like that, back there. Is it always that fast? That bloody?"

"You've been in a fair number of scrapes," Mr. Hagen reminded him. "You know each time is a bit different."

Hawkeye supposed he was right, but there was something different about this time. "Everything always just kind of happened before. I could tell something was going to happen long before it did. But this just came out of nowhere."

Mr. Hagen scowled. "It didn't come out of nowhere. A man was waiting in the rocks to gun us down. And he almost succeeded. Still might, depending on how Buck pulls through."

Hawkeye drove his elbow into the wall in frustration. He hated being so young. He hated not being able to do the things the sheriff and Mr. Hagen could do.

"We've got to stop them." Hawkeye fought back the

tears that choked him. "We have to stop Bessler and Clay before they do this to someone else."

"I know," Mr. Hagen said. "And I aim to do that just as soon as I can."

CHAPTER 17

Bessler was surprised it had taken him so long to catch up to Clay on the trail. He found the spot where he camped the night before easily enough, despite the fugitive's admirable efforts to bury it. It was not good enough to completely hide it, not from his discerning eye. Not from Hagen's either, though he happily reminded himself that neither Hagen nor Trammel would be troubling them from now on.

He found Lucien Clay ambling alone in a generally southern direction when he called out to his partner in evil deeds.

"Look at you. Riding through the wilderness all by yourself. Keep this up and we just might make a plainsman of you yet."

Clay did not stop his pace as he continued riding. "You sound awfully cheerful for a man who spent the night sleeping on a bunch of rocks. Find anything for your trouble?"

"Three plump partridges who never knew what hit them." Bessler beamed. "Riding along through the meadow like they didn't have a care in the world. I happily put them out of our misery."

Clay stopped riding. "You mean it? Trammel?"

"Hit him twice by my reckoning." Being able to say it out loud made his victory taste twice as sweet. "Watched him drop from the saddle like a bale of hay. Hagen, too. Each man caught two bullets apiece, but it was ammunition well spent."

Clay looked like a man who had just been shaken out of a dream. Bessler found it almost comical.

"And the third man?" Clay asked. "You said there was a third."

"A boy, really, but he's dead, too. I only count him as a half, considering he was so young."

Clay urged his horse to get moving again and fell in beside Bessler. "Buck Trammel and Adam Hagen. Both dead. I can hardly believe it."

"You can believe it as surely as you can believe anything in this old world."

"You're sure?" Clay pushed. "I mean, you checked afterward just to be certain?"

Bessler was almost insulted. "I've shot many men before, Lucien. I know when I've put a man down."

"Putting him down is one thing. Making sure he stays down is something else entirely, especially when those men are Trammel and Hagen."

"I hit them, and they fell," Bessler assured him. "Even if I only wounded them, we'll have our money and be on our way long before they can catch up with us. But don't trouble yourself, Lucien. Their ghosts disturbing our sleep is our only concern."

Clay had clearly heard him, but the words had not done much to convince him. Bessler wrote it off to shock from the good news. The two men had been a thorn in Clay's side for so long, he could not quite grasp that he was finally done with them.

Bessler knew trouble was funny that way. First, a man fought against it, but as time passed, he gradually came to depend on it, as if it had become as much a part of him as a hand or a foot.

"Cheer up, Lucien. Today is a happy day, for now we can turn our gaze to far more lucrative matters. We're finally going to get our hands on all that money we've promised each other."

Bessler thought the prospect of money would snap him out of it and he was glad to have been proven right when Clay asked, "You mean we're going to hit the stage? Did you find out where it is back in Ennisville?"

"I already knew where it was going to be long before Ennisville." In fact, Bessler had made arrangements with the Frontier Overland Company via telegraph when the train from Texas made a stop before reaching Laramie. "And if you promise to quit worrying, I'll be more than happy to tell you all about it. But there'll be time for that. For now, just enjoy our ride through creation and rejoice in the knowledge that all our troubles are behind us. And the partnership of Bessler and Clay is nearly at its end."

"The partnership of Clay and Bessler sounds much better."

Bessler allowed him to have it his way. For now.

Hagen watched the man called Red push away the bowl Chief had placed in front of him.

"I don't need food. What I need is customers, and I can't hardly expect anyone to come in here now that I've got a dying man on the floor. People come in here to get away from real life, not to live it."

"People don't come in here at all anymore," Chief said as he returned from the kitchen and placed a bowl in front of Hawkeye, then Hagen. "And the few who do come in aren't looking to escape anything except their wives and boredom. That man on the floor isn't hurting your business any. When the thirst gets too bad for them, they'll be back. Those wretches would drink over a pile of dead skunks."

Hagen was about to ask the old Indian about Trammel's condition again, but he ambled back into the kitchen before he could do so. The Cheyenne had refused to answer his questions after tending to the sheriff, but Hagen would make it a point to press him for an answer when he returned.

"There's a time for answers and there's a time for eating," was all the Chief had said when he finally stood up from tending to Trammel. "If I'm hungry, I know you are, too. News is better received on a full stomach."

Hagen had been frustrated by the lack of response, but there was not much he could do to force the man to tell him. Besides, he was right. He and Hawkeye were hungry.

Hagen might not have been a doctor, but it was clear that Trammel was still breathing and had grown much calmer since they had brought him into the saloon. His wounds had stopped bleeding and he was resting as peacefully as he could expect given he was on a saloon floor.

Hawkeye dug into the contents of the bowl with a fork and barely took time to chew. "You ought to have some, Mr. Hagen. It's delicious."

Hagen was ravenous. They had not taken the time to eat dinner the previous night and had not eaten that morning when they had broken camp and resumed the hunt for Bessler and Clay. No one had expressed having much of an appetite. Hagen had not realized how hungry he was until that moment. But he needed more nourishment than food could provide. He needed answers.

When Chief returned from the kitchen carrying a bowl for himself, he sat at the same table with Hawkeye and Hagen. He paid them little mind as he began to eat the food he had prepared.

Hagen decided to prod him a little. "Is this some Cheyenne delicacy you've prepared for us?"

Chief grunted as he began to eat. "An ancient feast passed down to me from my elders through the generations. Venison stew."

"Tastes like deer meat to me," Hawkeye said.

Adam Hagen smiled for the first time all day. The boy's innocence could be comforting at times.

Hagen could tell Chief would not allow himself to be riled, so he began to eat. Hawkeye was wrong in his description. It was not just good. It was delicious.

"This is quite good," Hagen said. "I'd say you're a man who knows your way around a kitchen."

The Cheyenne neither stopped eating nor looked up from his bowl. "I should. I used to be the cook here, back when we had customers who were interested in doing more than drinking their meals. I like to keep my skills sharp or else they'll go to waste. Waste is a sin."

"Sin?" Hagen remarked. "I didn't think Indians believed in the notion of sin."

"They don't, but I do. I was raised in a missionary school back East. Taught me how to read and write and about the Bible."

Hagen looked at his long, silver braids and his rough, deerskin clothes. His turquoise necklace had a tooth and a rough-hewn crucifix dangling from it. "You don't dress like a Christian man."

Chief kept eating. "The missionaries taught me many things, but I never forgot who my people are. Not much cause for fine clothes out here. You found that out for yourself earlier today when your friend got hurt."

"About that," Hagen said. "Why won't you tell me how he's doing?"

"I didn't say I wouldn't tell you. I said I was hungry. Trying to save a man's life is hard work. An empty stomach makes a man careless."

Red pounded his table, making his bowl jump. "I ain't running a hospital around here." He pushed himself away from the table and stormed outside.

"An empty stomach also makes a man irritable." Chief continued to eat his stew. "I've tended to your friend and stopped his bleeding. I sewed up the places where he was bleeding inside the best I could and closed him up again with thread. I've dressed his wounds with moss and clean bandages. That's all I can do. All anyone can do. Now we'll watch him for signs of fever sickness."

Hawkeye lost interest in his meal and set his fork aside. "Do you think he'll catch a fever, Chief?"

The Cheyenne thought it over as he chewed his deer meat. "A barroom floor's not the best place to treat an open wound, but I did my best. All we can do now is watch and wait. If you're a godly man, praying might not hurt."

Hagen was not in a prayerful mood as he continued to eat the stew. "I noticed you haven't asked us why we're here."

"I was too busy trying to save the sheriff's life to have polite conversation. I also don't ask questions when I already know the answer."

Hagen found that curious. "And what answers do you think you have?"

"You're hunting two men. One shot at you. The other is a tall, thin man with long, gray hair. A man with dull black eyes who carries death around his shoulders."

Hagen pushed his bowl away from him, his appetite suddenly gone. "You've met Lucien Clay."

"You mean he was here?" Hawkeye slowly took the fork from his mouth. "He must still be close."

"He told Red his name was Frank Bessler, but I imagine that's a lie." Chief picked up his bowl and drank the gravy from it. "He put on quite a show in here last night. He gambled his life for a hand of cards and a beer."

Hagen was not surprised. "That sounds like Clay."

"It wasn't much of a bet," Chief admitted. "The men were playing blackjack and Red wouldn't have killed him even if he lost. Red's a killer, but he's usually more of a sport about it, especially when he thinks a man could do him a good turn."

Hagen drummed his fingers on the table. Lucien certainly had a knack for making allies wherever he went. "And I'd wager Red and Clay had quite a conversation after the floor show."

Chief said, "They sat right at this very table and had themselves quite a talk. I couldn't hear what they were saying, but I can read lips well enough. Clay told him he'd be riding east. I think he told Red to follow him, but I can't be sure. He saw me looking at him and turned his head away from me when he spoke."

Hagen knew there was more the old Cheyenne was not telling him. "What makes you say that?"

Chief folded his arms across his chest. "Red's usually an even-tempered man. He doesn't change much from one day to the next. But ever since that stranger left, Red's been restless. Anxious, like a strong horse straining against a rope. That's why I think Clay offered to let him go with him. He planted an idea in his brain that's beginning to flower."

Hawkeye looked confused. "Think it's got something to do with us, Mr. Hagen?"

Hagen practically knew it. "Only one way to find out. And only one way to make sure he doesn't cause any trouble while we're here."

Hawkeye and Adam jumped when Chief produced a

large knife from beneath his buckskin shirt and buried the blade in the top of the table.

"Can't let you do that, mister."

Hagen enjoyed a display of bravado as much as the next man, but not when their lives might be at stake. "That's an impressive knife. You forget I have a pistol."

"And I'll bury that knife in your chest if you pull it or take one step toward Red," Chief answered. "He might not be much of a man, but he's been good to me over the years. Didn't run me off when people quit coming here. Always gave me a place to stay and a roof over my head. I expect I've been good to him, too, hunting for him and feeding him like I do. I guess I don't owe him much, come to think of it, but I won't have you killing him over something he might do. He's been in this godforsaken town for as long as he has for a reason. This place is as much a part of him as it's part of me. He could've left years ago but never has. I can't say why. He's had more than his share of offers to go elsewhere."

"Touching," Hagen said, "but I'm more concerned about him harming my large friend on the floor over there."

"As you should be," Chief allowed, "but I can't let you take his life on account of something that might or might not happen. You and Trammel and the boy are under my protection for as long as you're here. So is Red. He is for now, anyways, until he does something to change that."

Hagen thought he could draw the pistol on his hip before Chief could get hold of the knife, but he was not certain. "And if he does something to change that?"

"I'll handle it. You've got my word on that. Just like you have my word that if you touch that pistol, you'll be dead before it clears leather."

Hagen laid his hands flat on the table. The old man's expression had not changed since the first moment he had seen him. Not from the effort of placing Trammel in the wagon. Not while he watched him tend to Buck's wounds. And not now, while he had just threatened his life.

His look may not have changed, but there was a steel in his manner he could see. It had always been there but came to the fore now that he needed to use it.

"Maybe I'll have the same luck as Clay?" Hagen wondered aloud.

Chief slowly shook his head. "He was playing against Red. You're playing against me. There's a difference."

Hagen doubted he could have beaten him to the knife. Now he was almost sure Chief would kill him. "I give you my word I won't strike first."

"If it comes to that, you won't have to strike at all." Chief nodded toward the door. "Clay rode east when he left here last night, but something tells me that was more for Red's benefit than the truth. I spotted some fresh tracks my horses didn't make out back. If you're looking to find out where Clay's going, I'd start there. Might want to put on something before you go. It'll get awfully cold at night now that the leaves are changing."

Hagen had not said anything about riding out after Clay, but he had not had to. Chief obviously knew the kind of man he was and what he had to do. It made him feel better about leaving Trammel and Hawkeye in his care.

"Don't worry about me," Hagen said. "I always pack with any circumstances in mind."

"I imagined you would. How are you fixed for food?"

"I have enough."

Hawkeye caught up to the conversation. "You mean you're leaving before the sheriff is fit to travel?"

Chief answered for him. "He has to go, boy. Clay and Bessler are miles away by now. He didn't ride all this way just to follow them. He aims to capture them, and he can't do that by sitting around here watching Trammel. Your friend won't be in any shape to sit up, much less ride a horse for days, assuming he lives. It'll be at least a week before he can even think about getting in a saddle again. Not if he has any hope of those holes in him mending properly."

Hagen felt a pang of pity for Hawkeye as he was torn over what he should do. Should he stay to help protect Trammel while he recovered or live up to his duty as a lawman? He made it easy for him.

"You can't come with me, Hawkeye. Chief here is right. I'll have to ride hard and fast if I hope to catch up to Bessler and Clay. I can't do that if I'm worried about you when things get rough. I'd feel a lot better if I knew you were here keeping an eye on Buck for me. Buck would appreciate it, too."

It was clear the boy agreed, though pride prevented him from admitting it. "It might be the right thing to do, but it ain't right."

"Right doesn't play into it. If it did, we'd still be back home, and Clay would still be rotting in prison. We didn't call the tune. We just have to dance to it."

Hagen did not want to encourage the youth to argue any further, so he stood up. His decision was final. To Chief, he asked, "I owe you anything for tending to the sheriff?"

Chief watched him stand. "Leave your supplies here. You'll be able to travel lighter that way. You can pay me whatever you think is fair when you get back. But make sure you come back. I don't want to be stuck looking after this kid for the rest of my life. I'd like to enjoy some peace in my old age."

Hagen might have laughed if the circumstances had been different. "I'll take that as your way of wishing me luck. Don't worry about me. I know how to take care of myself."

He rested a firm hand on Hawkeye's shoulder. "Keep an

eye on this old heathen for me. Make sure he doesn't take to hopping around sprinkling dust all over the place. Buck needs his rest."

Hagen left the table before Hawkeye could argue. Hawkeye was glad when Chief put him to work. "You'd best clean up these tables, boy. Help pay for your room and board until Hagen comes back to fetch you. We're not running a hotel around here. Not anymore."

Hagen reached the front door of the saloon and paused to take a final look at Trammel. He was pale, but his breathing was steady. He had been through quite an ordeal. Two bullets to the chest would have been enough to kill most men.

But as the sheriff had proven to him time and time again, Buck Trammel was not most men.

He had no idea if Trammel could hear him when he said, "Live, my friend. I'll get Bessler and Clay one way or the other."

As he stepped outside and dug out a new shirt from his saddlebags, he wondered if he had said the words for Trammel's benefit or his own.

Chapter 18

Lucien Clay had begun to think Frank Bessler did not have the slightest idea where they were heading. They had been meandering through woods and clearings for hours while his rescuer insisted on whistling a song without a tune.

Bessler stopped suddenly in a clearing and held up a hand, signaling for Clay to stop.

"There she is, Lucien. Our ticket to gold and riches lies straight ahead."

Clay nudged his horse beside Bessler and looked in the same direction. Just as he had back on the ridgeline, he was forced to squint to see what Bessler was looking at.

A line of wooden fences contained a small herd of grazing cattle. Beyond it sat a sprawling ranch house made of logs. The place had clearly been added on to over the years, but the original part of the home was still evident. The logs that made up its construction were lighter and more weathered than the rest of the place.

"Looks like a house to me," Clay observed.

"Right you are," Bessler said. "And it also happens to be the place where we will find our money."

Clay glanced at Bessler. Had he not been watching him

for the past several hours, he might have thought he was drunk. "My money's on a coach, not under the floorboards of some old house."

Bessler smiled. "Right again, Lucien, but in this instance, the money will be coming to us. I arranged it so. I scheduled the coach to make a special stop right here later today." He pulled out his pocket watch and checked the time. "Within two hours, as a matter of fact. We're not as early as I would have liked, but early enough for our purposes. Come follow me. I'll introduce you to my friend."

Before Clay could ask more questions, Bessler took off toward the log home.

When Clay caught up with him, he said, "I didn't think the stage made special stops."

"The larger stage companies don't make a practice of it," Bessler told him, "but the Frontier Overland Company does. That's the company the Bank of Laramie uses."

Several drivers for the stagecoach line had stopped in his saloons over the years. He knew the company's owner, Tucker Cobb. He knew the man who rode with him, Butch Keeling. And they did, indeed, make special stops for ranchers and mining companies. For a handsome fee, of course.

"How'd you know about them?"

"I got that idiot Holm to tell me all about them when he wrote me about you," Bessler explained. "Tucker Cobb prides himself on being able to deliver funds securely any-time and anywhere. Now you know why I insisted on the money being brought to Denver overland instead of by wire. Cobb thinks he's going to be picking up a deposit from a rancher too fearful to bring his money to Denver unguarded. He isn't counting on our plans of making a sudden and complete withdrawal."

Clay did not like it. It sounded too easy, and stealing money was never easy, especially from the likes of Cobb. "Tucker's a mighty crafty character. What makes you think he'll fall for it?"

"Because they've already been to this ranch many times," Bessler assured him. "Ben Fletcher owns this spread, and he just happens to be an old acquaintance of mine who owes me a favor or two. He used to ride with me. With Walt Holm, too, before he found politics. I got Fletcher out of a few tight spots in our day. You could say I'm the reason he has all this. If it hadn't been for me, he'd still be breaking rocks in a prison yard in Texas. Helping us get your money is his way of returning the favor. For a small percentage of our take, of course."

Clay certainly did not like the sound of that. "A cut from your end of the take, not mine."

"Of course," Bessler said. "It didn't take much to convince him to help us. Fletcher thought about ripping off the stage himself many times but decided against it. Robbing bank wagons doesn't exactly fit in with his new life as a respectable, honest rancher. His loss will prove to be our gain."

Clay could not deny it was a neat plan. Perhaps a bit too neat for his liking. "Seems awfully convenient that all this has fallen so neatly into place all of a sudden."

Bessler pulled back on the reins, bringing his horse to an abrupt stop. Once again, Clay had to compensate, and it took him a bit of effort to keep his horse under control.

Clay did not like the way the lawyer was glaring at him. "What's gotten into you?"

"I don't like being interrogated, Lucien."

"It's my money we're talking about. My hide, too. I've got a right to some answers, especially when you're the only one around here who seems to know the questions before I get around to asking them."

Bessler let out a heavy breath. "Do you know how many men Walt Holm contacted to get you out of prison?"

"No."

"Five that I know of," Bessler told him. "Every one of them turned him down flat because they knew it would mean going up against Buck Trammel. I was the only one who agreed to take it on because I already knew how I'd do it. If I didn't already know Ben Fletcher, I never would have taken the job because I wouldn't be sure how I would get your money, much less live long enough to spend it. I didn't come up with this plan because of you, Lucien. I rescued you because I already had a plan in place."

Clay held up his hands in surrender. He had never thought Bessler freed him out of a sense of justice, but it helped to finally know the reason he had agreed to help him at all.

"That's the first straight answer you've given me since I met you."

"Let's just hope it's the last one. I find the truth can be awfully tiring, don't you?"

Bessler got his horse moving again and Clay once again fell in behind him. For once, they had agreed on something.

They rode around the fence line and headed straight for the house. Clay noticed that, despite it being a cold day, there was no sign of smoke from the chimney.

"Looks like your friend's not at home."

"He and his men are tending to his cattle in another field on his property," Bessler explained. "I told him I didn't want them anywhere near here when we did the deed, and

Fletcher was more than happy to agree. He doesn't care what we do as long as it doesn't lead back to him. We'll have to clean up our mess before we leave, which isn't too much to ask, all things considered."

Clay had expected Bessler to ride around to the front of the house but was surprised when he climbed down at what appeared to be the back door. The two men tied the horses to a hitching rail when Bessler said, "Check in the barn to see if Fletcher left any horses behind. We could do with some fresh mounts. I'll go inside and get a fire started. No reason we can't be comfortable while we wait."

Even after all the months he had spent in prison, Clay still resented being told what to do. He hated being told when to sleep and when to wake. When to go outside and when to submit to an examination by Doc Carson. Bessler's fancy airs did little to make it easier to take, but he had no choice but to obey until he had his money. After that, Clay would decide if he would make the attorney pay for his familiar tone.

He walked over to the barn and struggled to pull the sliding door open. He had not been used to manual labor even before prison, so it took him greater effort than usual.

After finding the barn empty, he looked around the gentle rises and rolling hills of the Fletcher spread. Birds chirped somewhere in the distance, while a few head of cattle grazed in the pasture near the barn. There was a simple beauty here he imagined appealed to some people.

Clay stifled a yawn. He would rather be dead than be forced to endure so much endless quiet.

He trudged through the mud toward the back door of the house. He paused beside Bessler's horse and checked the saddle. He had hoped the lawyer might have forgotten to take his rifle inside with him and saw that he hadn't. Pity.

One squeeze of the trigger and he would have increased his portion of the take from the coach to 100 percent. But Bessler was not that careless. As his attorney had reminded him many times since the jail, he had a plan.

But so did Lucien Clay. And it did not involve riding away from the Fletcher place with only that which Frank Bessler decided to give him.

CHAPTER 19

From the perch of his stagecoach, Tucker Cobb slowly lowered his binoculars. He did not like what he saw. He did not like it one bit.

Butch Keeling looked over at his partner. "What's got your dander up?"

Cobb did not like to be pulled from his thoughts, especially when those thoughts had not yet completely formed in his mind. "What makes you think my dander's up?"

"The way you set your jaw on end," Keeling told him. He was from Arkansas and, like most people from that part of the country, was given to speaking his mind. "You always do that when you see something you don't like. Kind of like the way you grind your teeth when you sleep. Means something's chewing at you. Can't tell you how many nights I've lost sleep on the trail on account of all that grinding. At least it helps keep me awake when it's my turn to stand watch."

"You're not paid to sleep anyway," Cobb chastised his old friend. "You're paid to be watching the road for bandits."

"Hard to do that without a good night's sleep," Keeling said. "Even harder when you won't give up that fancy spyglass of yours."

Cobb handed the binoculars to his partner so he could see for himself. "What do you make of it?"

Keeling worked the knob as he brought the image into focus. "Not much to make anything of it one way or the other. A scrawny fella with long, gray hair is walking out of the barn and into the Fletcher house. Kind of looks like Lucien Clay, but seeing as how Clay's in prison, that's not likely."

Cobb had seen that, too, and reached the same conclusion. "The question is why."

Keeling continued to look through the binoculars. "Why what?"

Cobb was beginning to wonder if the man had been paying attention to anything he had said for the past few minutes. "Why is that man going inside that house?"

"It's cold out," Keeler reasoned. "Maybe he wants to get something to eat or sit by the fire some. Truth be told, a pot of coffee would really hit the spot right now, it being as cold out here as it is."

Cobb took the binoculars away from him. Such a valuable pair of looking glasses was too important to leave in Keeling's hands. "That's not what I'm talking about. How many times have we stopped here at the Fletcher spread over the years?"

"Four or five times," Keeling said without giving it much thought. Cobb had always been impressed by how he could remember such details, but often forgot what day it was. "Each time went off without a hitch. They even offered us coffee, which I'd gladly accept right now."

"Fletcher offered it to us," Cobb reminded him. "Does that scrawny fella you just saw look like Ben Fletcher to you?"

Keeling ran a rough hand over his bony face. "Can't say as he does. I remember Mr. Fletcher being a might bigger than him." He held out his hands away from his stomach and made an oval motion. "Bigger in the belly, I mean."

Cobb pointed down the hillside toward the log house.

"That man we just saw looks like he hasn't had a good meal in months. And in all those times we've been here, when have you seen a ranch hand walk into that house? Fletcher never let his men so much as stand on the porch, much less walk inside like they had the run of the place. Made us drink our coffee up here, remember?"

"He certainly did," Keeling said. "Saw plenty of his men back in that pasture we passed on the way here, though. One of them might have been Fletcher, come to think of it."

Cobb did not have to think of it. He knew that man was not Ben Fletcher. He knew of the trouble they had seen back in Laramie, though the bank president was too eager to get them on their way to share any details.

"Fletcher's not in that house," Cobb concluded. "And I've got a feeling that skinny fella down there really is Lucien Clay."

Butch Keeling continued to rub his chin as he thought about it. "Maybe Mr. Fletcher's sick. Could be that fella is tending to him while he's getting better. Could be that Mr. Fletcher's getting on in years and has decided to treat the men who work so hard for him in a better way." He rubbed his hands on his arms against the cold. "Not everyone treats their people like mules like you do, Tucker."

Cobb scowled at him. Keeling always chose the worst time to be difficult. Cobb handed him the binoculars again. "Take another look. And this time tell me what you don't see. I'll give you a hint. Look at the top of the house."

Keeling began to look through the field glasses once more. "No birds. Maybe he went and got himself a cat."

Cobb tried to grab the glasses back from him, but Keeling pulled away. "I see what you're getting at now. No smoke from the chimney."

The wagon driver sometimes thought Keeling tried his patience on purpose. "That's what worries me most. Not only is Ben Fletcher not given to showing his men kindness, but what man in his right mind sits in a house in this weather without a fire to keep him warm? If he was in there and sick as you say, he'd be sitting right beside a roaring fire. I know I would."

Keeling handed the glasses back to his partner. "Not much gets past you, Tucker. Guess that's why we've managed to stay alive for as long as we have."

Cobb opened the lid of the wagon box on which they sat while driving the team and placed the glasses back in their pouch. "If you had to live by your wits, you'd starve."

"Then I guess it's lucky for me I can shoot better than you," Keeling observed.

There was no arguing with him on that score. Because despite all the many ways he enjoyed teasing Butch Keeling, he had never met a man who could match him in a fight. Be it pistols or rifles or knives or fists, his partner rivaled only himself in ferocity and effectiveness. Tucker Cobb may have been the brains and brawn of the Frontier Overland Company, but Keeling provided the rest of the aspects that made theirs a successful concern.

Tucker Cobb had spent the last ten years building a reputation for being able to transfer large sums of money from one part of the territory to the other. He always managed to do it safely and had never lost a penny to bandits or misfortune. That was not to say that every assignment had been easy or had gone without incident, but in his business, if the ledger was balanced to the penny at the end of a run, he had done his job well.

His chosen profession had taught him much in the past decade. One of the lessons Cobb learned was to listen to his instincts. And he had ignored them since they had left Laramie.

Tucker sat on the wagon box. "I never should've taken this run, Butch. Something's been off about it since the start."

Keeling remained standing, preferring to watch the approach and the road behind them. "Hauling large amounts of money ain't exactly safe work, Tucker. If we wanted safety, we should've been lawyers or such."

The dangerous aspects of their profession had never bothered Cobb before and they did not bother him now. "I didn't say I was afraid. I said there's something wrong with this entire setup. Not many people send such large sums overland these days. They wire the money."

"A practice that promises to run us out of business before too long."

But Cobb had more immediate concerns. "First, we get that strange telegram from Ben Fletcher telling us to pick up a deposit. Then, a couple of days later, Mr. Banner at the Bank of Laramie said his client insisted on moving all this money by coach. Doesn't that seem like a coincidence to you? Sounds awfully convenient to me."

"You've always handled the business end of the operation," Keeling reminded him. "I just go where you bring the horses and shoot anyone who tries to get in our way. I leave the thinking and the decisions to you."

Tucker continued to puzzle over the coincidence in his mind. He'd had large shipments before. But the timing of this had bothered him since the beginning and had gnawed at him every day since. He had ignored his instincts for the worst reason of all. He and Butch needed the money.

Seeing the ratty-looking stranger entering the Fletcher home had done little to ease his concerns. Tucker Cobb had never lost a shipment before and he was not about to start now.

His mind was made up. "We're not going."

Butch grew still. "You sure about that, Tucker? It'll cost us money and we're in dire need of funds right about now."

Tucker did not need Keeling to remind him of their rotten financial situation, but all the money in the world did not do a dead man any good. "It feels wrong. It feels like we're riding into something. You feel it, too, don't you?"

"Can't say I disagree with you, if that's what you're asking," Butch admitted. "But I'd best remind you that we've got four awfully tired horses here. We were counting on changing them out for fresh ones at the Fletcher spread."

That was another part of what he had seen that bothered him. "You see any horses waiting for us down there?"

"No," Keeling admitted, "and that's mighty troubling. I'm not saying we should ride into anything. I'm saying we should think about what it'll cost us, and I don't mean the money. It's been hard traveling between Laramie and here, and these animals are about done in. I'd say we might be able to get twenty more miles out of them, maybe less if we set them to running. This road we're on only leads in one direction: right past the Fletcher house. If that mangy fella is Lucien Clay and he's waiting to jump us like you think, it'll mean we'll have to move past them at a hard run. They're liable to come after us. If there's only one or two of them, I can probably handle them. But if it's more than that, we could get stuck in the flatlands with no cover and no prospect of securing fresh mounts."

Tucker Cobb knew every trail of the Wyoming Territory like the back of his hand. He knew every way station and cow path wide enough to fit his stagecoach, and some that were not.

"We could make Claro Station before nightfall if we're careful. We can get a new team there and continue to Denver."

Butch said, "We can double back if you want. Switch out the horses at Emperor's Pass."

Tucker knew that was not an option. The man who ran that station loved to gossip. Once word spread that the Frontier Overland Company had been forced to double back, their already suffering business would become the laughingstock of the territory. Cobb's stock-in-trade was his reputation. They could no sooner turn back than he could make his horses take wing and fly to Denver.

"We'll press on," Cobb decided. "The sun will be setting in a bit. If they come after us and we can manage to stay ahead of them long enough, we just might be able to lose them in the darkness."

"It's risky," Keeling said, "but I'm with you if that's what you decide to do."

It was. Cobb gathered up the reins as Butch took his seat beside him. "You want me up here with you or down in the coach?"

"Up here is best. You can flop over on the roof if you need to get them off our tail."

Keeling set the shotgun beside him and took his Winchester rifle in hand. "I'm right here, boss. Same as always."

Cobb released the hand brake and snapped the reins. There was no sense in putting off the inevitable any longer than they already had.

CHAPTER 20

Adam Hagen had plenty to think about as he tracked the fugitives through the wood. The path the two men had taken was interesting. The old Cheyenne medicine man had been telling the truth. Clay had, indeed, ridden out of the saloon to the east only to make a wide circle behind the town and head west. Hagen rode past the remnants of a campsite without bothering to stop. He doubted he could learn anything from whatever the fugitives might have left behind and did not want to waste time.

He and his packhorse had ridden at a good clip since leaving Ennisville and he knew he must be closing the lead Bessler and Clay had on him. Bessler probably figured he had left his pursuers for dead after his ambush outside of town. He would be riding easier now as he and Clay plotted where they would hit the gold-laden stage.

Hagen found the route they had chosen was curious because there were better places on the way to Denver where they could attack the coach. He did not need to look at Mr. Banner's hand-drawn map to think of half a dozen stations where the Frontier Overland Company was likely to stop to switch out tired horses. All of them were directly south of where the tracks led.

Instead, Bessler and Clay continued to ride due west.

The woods were too thick for them to have spotted the coach as it passed, and they had not chosen the path at random. They had ridden with purpose and at a slower pace.

Bessler was taking them somewhere intentionally, which meant he had probably already laid a trap for the Frontier Overland Company men. The question was where, and Hagen knew the answer must lie somewhere ahead.

As he continued to ride in that direction for the rest of the day, he thought long and hard about where Bessler might spring his trap. There were no shortages of ridges and rocky outcroppings from which he could ambush the stage, but the companies were not foolish. They tended to avoid such places, preferring to stay in open ground whenever possible. They usually stayed away from heavily wooded areas and steep inclines that would only slow their pace and tire their horses.

Claro Station was to the south of this general direction, and stages were known to stop there on long journeys. Perhaps that was where Bessler and Clay were headed. Attacking them at a station might prove to be a challenge for two men, especially if there was more than one stage stopped there. But Bessler had managed to break Clay out of prison. Perhaps he thought a way station would be much easier?

Hagen kept the idea of Claro Station in the back of his mind while his eyes remained on the trail. He would only find the men if he followed where they had gone, not where he thought they might be or where he hoped they would go.

Instinct caused him to stop as soon as he reached a clearing. The memory of Bessler's ambush was still fresh in his mind. Even the most peaceful scenes and most unlikely ground could prove dangerous.

He paused and sat still while he listened to what the land could tell him. He heard birdsong in all directions. The wind blew his way, and he caught the scent of cattle in the air.

A farm or a ranch was close. A relatively new ranch, for he had not known of one in this part of the territory. Much had changed since he left Wyoming for West Point all those years ago.

He pulled his Winchester from beneath his leg and slowly rode out of the clearing. He squinted into the distance and saw a log ranch house with a fenced-in pasture to the side of it where cows grazed beneath a darkening sky. A thin stream of gray smoke rose lazily from the chimney. Someone was home.

Bessler's and Clay's tracks led right to the place. He doubted they would have been able to ride past it without at least looking it over. Clay had been unable to resist the temptation of civilization back in Ennisville. Perhaps he and Bessler were inside, holding the rancher and his family hostage right now? Hagen gripped his rifle tightly. The family might be in trouble, but their misfortune could prove to be Hagen's gain. Men in a house were easier to kill than in open land.

He was looking over the ground, deciding on the best way to ride up to it without being noticed when another thought came to him. Perhaps this was part of Bessler's trap for the stage? He had not just happened on this ranch. He and Clay had ridden straight for it. Perhaps he had arranged for the Frontier Overland stage to make a special stop here under the premise that a deposit would be made. Tucker Cobb was known to make special stops at ranches and mining camps for a fee.

Yes, Hagen thought, that was something a man like Frank Bessler would come up with. That meant the rancher and his men would be in on Bessler's scheme. And it *would* be Bessler's idea. Hagen knew Clay's influence extended between towns and cities, not ranches.

Hagen would remain close by until after dark, when he could more easily—and safely—take a closer look at whoever might be inside that log house.

He was about to dismount and find a vantage point from which he could watch the house when a great cry echoed in the valley below. He moved his horses closer to the edge of the hill and saw a stagecoach with a four-horse team sprinting down a slight incline along a hill beside the house. He was too far away to tell for certain, but he knew it must be the Frontier Overland stage. Clay's money would ride right past the house, and it did not look like it was going to stop.

He heard the echo of the coachman cry out as he cracked the reins to urge the animals to run faster. As the coach darted past the house, rifle shots rang out from the front of the place. Hagen was still too far away to know for certain, but it sounded like only one gun was being fired.

Hagen smiled from the hillside as he watched Bessler's careful plan fall apart before his eyes.

Hagen saw the shotgun rider leap onto the top of the coach and lie flat on the roof as he returned fire. He snapped off a quick volley of shots at an impressive rate and wisely stopped shooting when the coach sped out of range.

Hagen squinted as he saw a large man run out into the front yard and shoot in vain at the fleeing coach. It was undoubtedly Bessler. And his money was getting away.

He disappeared back into the house just as Hagen watched the back door open and saw a man dart outside. He ran to the two horses hitched to a rail behind the house and climbed into the saddle.

That had to be Clay. He had not seen the man in almost half a year, but even at this distance, it was evident how much prison had taken out of him.

Hagen watched as Bessler joined him out back and

practically leaped into the saddle before the two of them sped off in pursuit of the fleeing coach.

Hagen patted his horse's neck. "Hope you're ready for some fun, boy, because things are about to get interesting."

He dug his heels into the horse's flanks and raced down the hill to join the battle.

Bessler had almost rejoiced when he looked out the window and saw the stagecoach coming down the hillside toward the cabin.

But his stomach dropped when he realized it was moving too fast to stop. The driver had somehow sensed a trap and was about to speed away.

"What's going on?" Clay shouted as Bessler took his rifle and ran to the front door.

Bessler had no time for questions and even less for answers. He threw open the front door of the house and brought his Winchester to his shoulder. He took aim at the coach as it quickly drew near.

He knew trying to hit the driver or the shotgun rider was pointless, so he aimed at the easiest targets. The horses.

Bessler rushed his first two shots and was carefully taking aim for his third when a bullet buried itself in the wooden doorframe next to his head. He dove to the porch floor when another quickly followed it.

The coach driver cut loose with a throaty roar as he drove the team onward. Bessler brought up his rifle and fired from the prone position up at the wagon box. His bullet bit into the wood of the coach, just below the Frontier Overland Company sign painted above the doorframe.

He levered in another round and aimed at the shot-gunner, but the man had already scrambled onto the top of the coach and cut loose with a series of shots that peppered the ground and floor around him.

Bessler's last shot was blind and may have nicked the rear wagon wheel as the coach raced by. He could hardly remember seeing a man work a rifle so fast.

Bessler knew his chances of a payday were dying with each passing second, so when the shooting stopped, rage led him to scramble to his feet and fire in vain at the fleeing coach. Each of his bullets fell well short of their intended target, and he yelled after it from a part of his being he did not know existed.

"Did you hit them?" Clay asked from the cover of the doorway.

"Get back to the horses," Bessler ordered. "We're going after them!"

Clay ran back through the house as Bessler followed, feeding more rounds into his rifle from the store he still had in his coat pocket. A sharp sting rose from the back of his head and along his back, forcing him to stop reloading to check what had happened. His hand came away from the back of his neck bloodied.

He removed his hat and saw a hole had passed through the rear top of it and through the brim. That rifleman had come within a hair's width of shooting him in the head. If he'd had the time, he might have counted himself lucky. But there was no time for such consideration, and he ran through to the back of the house to join Clay outside.

He jumped into the saddle and brought his horse around as he began to give chase. He thought he caught some movement down the hillside out of the corner of his eye but discounted it. There was nothing he could do about it anyway. He had a fortune to catch.

Bessler was careful not to allow his horse to run all out

as the coach raced ahead. He looked back at Clay, who was whipping his horse's neck with the reins to little effect.

"Easy, Lucien, easy."

"Easy?" Clay sneered, frustrated with the lack of response from his mount and the sight of his fortune escaping. "That's my money up ahead!"

"And we're not letting it out of our sight," Bessler assured him. "That team has been running flat out for almost a mile now. They're close to being played out, so they're bound to slow down soon. If we keep our pace steady, we'll catch up to them well before it gets dark."

Clay cursed the unresponsive animal, but Bessler was glad he had stopped whipping it. He might need the escapee before this was over, especially the way the shotgunner seemed to be able to fire Clay might prove valuable if for no other reason than to stop a bullet meant for him.

Bessler slowed his horse to a trot and Clay's horse followed suit. The coach was a good half mile ahead of them by his reckoning and had been forced to slow down due to a bend in the road.

"Now's the time to close in on them," Clay said. "They'll reach that woodland ahead if we don't take them now."

Bessler was beginning to grow annoyed by Clay's constant complaining. "Let them reach it. Those trees will afford us as much cover as it does them. It's too dense in there for them to stray off the road much, if at all, and the branches are too low for them to move at speed. They'll be stuck in there with tired horses and a heavy wagon. Be patient, Lucien. Let's see what they do. Their next move will tell the tale."

Bessler slowed his horse as he saw the coach do the same. The road the team had taken from Laramie had been an arduous one. If the past was any predictor, he imagined the coachman had planned to switch out his team at the Fletcher spread. Bessler had made that impossible.

The wind shifted, and he caught the scent of ponderosa pine and horse sweat from the trail up ahead. The coach had slowed down to a crawl. They would be lucky if they made it as far as the pine trees, but they would not be going much farther. Not before dark, at least.

"Keep going, weary travelers," Bessler said. "Keep going. We'll catch you soon enough."

Clay's horse fought as its rider struggled to maintain control. "My money's getting away and here you are, wasting time by quoting poetry."

Bessler reached down and grabbed the bridle of Clay's horse. "This is still my show, Lucien, and you'll do as I say, or by God, I'll—"

A bullet struck the ground in front of his horse's hooves, kicking up dirt and sending the animals scampering away in opposite directions. Bessler rode in a wide circle, while it was all Clay could do to remain in the saddle.

"Get back!" Bessler ordered him. "We're too close to them."

Another shot landed just a bit farther than the first, and Clay had the good sense to join him several yards away.

"That's got to be Butch Keeling," Clay said. "I knew he could shoot, but how can he hit us from that far away? Even I know we're not too close."

But Bessler knew. "The wind's in his favor. And we're up against a man who's obviously skilled with a rifle."

After riding backward several more yards, Bessler climbed down from his horse. "The wind has died down. We'd better stay here for a while. Once it gets dark, we'll walk our horses into the woods and circle around them. They'll have the coach as cover, but we'll have a lot more ground to work with. Should prove interesting."

Clay jumped down from the saddle and spat on the ground. "I'm for it as long as I get my money."

"Did you hit them?" Tucker Cobb asked his partner.

Butch Keeling frowned from the roof of the coach as he lowered his rifle. "Can't stay as I did. The wind helped some, but they were a might out of range. Put some fear into them, though. Scattered them, too. They'll stay back there for the time being."

Cobb looked up at the sky. "Won't be long before dark now. It'll get even darker sooner when we reach those pines."

But Keeling had begun to factor that into his thinking as soon as Tucker decided to run past the ranch house. "Might as well let the horses move into the trees at their own pace. We'll feed them while it's still light out. We ain't going anywhere, and those fellas out there know it. The big one is smart."

"Wish I'd been smart enough to see it before we got there," Cobb said. "Would've saved us a lot of bother."

Keeling had ridden with Cobb for almost a decade and had been his business partner for nearly as long. He imagined he had come to know the man better than he knew himself. He never did something without a good reason, and he had agreed to make a special stop at the Fletcher ranch for a good reason. Banks using the telegraph to move money between them had taken a sizable chunk out of their business. They could always go back to taking passengers, but money was easier to move than people. Travelers needed more comfort and preferred a place to stay each night. In some ways, they needed more care and tending than the horses that pulled the coach. Money did not care about comfort, and neither did Cobb and Keeling.

He knew they were in a fix, but their situation would not improve if his partner was too hard on himself. "That big fella would've killed us if it hadn't been for that big nose of yours being able so sniff out trouble. We're alive because of you and we're going to stay that way if I have anything to say about it." He patted his rifle as he climbed down to kneel beside Tucker in the wagon box. He wanted to keep a close eye on the men they had left behind them. "And it just so happens that me and Winnie here have plenty to say on the subject."

Cobb allowed the team to move forward at its own pace as they ambled into the pines. The branches weaved a tight knit over the road, and it was almost as dark as night. "At least it was only the two of them. I'm glad Fletcher's bunch stayed out of it."

Keeling found the fact cold comfort. "He was in on it, though. We'll be paying him a visit on our swing back through Laramie. I intend on having a long, unpleasant talk with that man. I don't care how many of his boys are with him, neither."

"You and me both."

Keeling saw something in the distance behind them and nudged his partner to stop. "Hold them up for a minute, Tucker. I see something coming."

Cobb sagged in his seat. "Guess I was hasty in thinking Fletcher's bunch would stay out of this."

Keeling waited until he was sure of what he was looking at. "It's only one man. I can't tell if he's seen them yet, but they look like they've seen him."

Tucker flicked the reins instead of snapping them, putting a bit more speed into the tired horses. "He has his troubles and we have ours. Might as well get deeper into these trees and get ready for them when they come."

Keeling did not know the stranger riding up on the others, but he wished him luck. He was going to need it.

CHAPTER 21

Adam Hagen stopped behind a rise when he saw Bessler and Clay scatter. The echoes of rifle shots from the coach had begun to die away, and he took great enjoyment in watching the two criminals scramble like a couple of scared cats.

You're up against it now, Hagen said to himself. *Got yourselves caught between two hard cases.*

He could hardly believe his luck as he saw the two riders climb down from their horses. They thought they were well out of range now that the coach had proceeded to head straight into the pines. Bessler had undoubtedly decided it was time to rest their horses as night drew nearer.

Hagen had been careful to keep his animal fresh. The fugitives were now on foot with tired mounts.

This was the good fortune he had been seeking since Laramie. If his time in the cavalry had taught him anything, it was how to press an advantage.

Now was the time.

He heeled his horse into a full gallop. The animal responded with everything it had, seemingly eager to break the slow pace they had kept up throughout the day.

He pulled his Winchester free as he watched Bessler and Clay finally catch sight of him when he was about five hundred yards out.

Clay remained frozen where he stood, holding on to his horse's reins like a stunned stable boy. Hagen had suspected Bessler had not been foolish enough to give him a weapon, and he had been right. Clay would have started shooting if he had been armed. It was in his nature.

Just as he knew it was Bessler's nature not to panic. He watched him pull his rifle free and begin to take aim at the charging Hagen.

Three hundred yards.

Adam brought his rifle to his shoulder and snapped off a quick shot. It was difficult to hit anything from atop a horse on a dead run, but his bullet struck the ground just to Bessler's left as the man took a knee. Close enough to cause his horse to bolt.

Bessler was calm. Too calm.

Hagen veered his horse to the left, realizing too late that Bessler had him dead to rights.

Bessler's shot missed, but the gunfire and Hagen's sudden change of course caused the animal to rear up. The ground gave way beneath its rear hooves, sending animal and rider slamming down into the grass.

Hagen heard the sound before he felt the pain and knew his left leg was broken.

He had managed to hold on to his Winchester through the fall and kept it as pain lanced through his body. The horse almost throttled him as it fought to get back up. His horse had barely made it ten feet before a second shot from Bessler sent it crashing down for a final time.

Hagen's eyes filled with tears from the pain spiking through his leg. He planted his face close to the ground and screamed his agony into the dirt. He only hoped the soil had been enough to mask his injury to the men he had been chasing.

"Well, well, well," Bessler mocked him from afar. "Seems

like you're a mighty difficult man to kill, Hagen. Sorry about the horse. I was aiming for you."

Hagen forced himself to swallow his agony as he strained to look in the direction of Bessler's voice. He had fallen on good ground. It was a slight rise to the left of the fugitives. He could see the top of Bessler's head and judged he was about maybe ten feet above them. He might have been able to make a stand there had he not been pinned like one of the many butterflies his sister once had in her collection.

Bessler continued his torment. "Guess I should've had the good sense to finish you off back at the ridgeline. But if there's one thing about Frank Bessler you'll soon find out, it's that I rarely make the same mistake twice."

It took all of Hagen's will to slide his elbows beneath him and bring the Winchester to his shoulder. The world swam before him as he used every ounce of will he had to block out the pain and take careful aim at Bessler. He was standing now and coming toward him, grinning.

"Careful, Frank," Clay called to him. "He's not dead yet."

"A situation I aim to rectify right now."

Bessler's grin faded as he racked the dead round from his rifle.

Hagen levered in a fresh round and, in his delirium, saw Bessler split in two. He aimed at the center of the mirage and fired.

Bessler cried out as he was jolted to the right side and fell from view.

Hagen might have taunted him, but the pain spiked through to his head and began to throb. He barely managed to eject the spent round in case Clay decided to finish the job.

Hagen blinked his eyes clear and watched as Clay struggled to get the bigger man to his feet. He held the rifle by the barrel in his left hand while he did his best to keep Bessler propped up with his right. The horses had backed away from them during the shooting, and they were forced to lumber toward them.

It might have been comical if Hagen had been in a better state to enjoy it.

He was panting heavily now as he tried to focus. His hands began to shake as he aimed the rifle between the two men. He did not care which one he hit. He just had to get off another shot before he passed out.

The butt of the Winchester slammed into his shoulder when he squeezed the trigger, but he heard Clay yelp and knew he had hit one of them. Hagen strained to keep his head up long enough to see Clay limping as he helped Bessler climb atop his horse.

The former saloon owner was forced to use the rifle as a walking stick as he hobbled over to his horse, pulled himself into the saddle, and managed to disappear into the trees. Hagen did not know what propelled Bessler, but whatever it was, it gave him the presence of mind to follow Clay into the pines.

Hagen allowed his head to drop to the grass and he lost his grip on his rifle as he lost his grip on consciousness. The black that consumed him was welcome.

CHAPTER 22

Red was beginning to think Chief and that Hawkeye brat would never leave the saloon, but they finally had.

The time was perfect. It was growing dark outside. He had not lit the lamps, so no one could see inside the saloon. His few regular customers were either still working or just about to have their supper. No one should be coming in for quite some time. By then the deed would be done.

He had made himself scarce after losing his temper earlier. He knew he had run afoul of Hagen by talking the way he had about Trammel. He had never met the man before but knew him by reputation. If even a quarter of what he had heard about the sheriff was true, he doubted he could beat him in a fair fight. But there was nothing fair about life in the Wyoming Territory. Out here, the strong survived by preying on the weak.

And Buck Trammel was not only weak, he was also standing in the way of his chance at a new life. The stranger who had turned his place on its head the previous night had a dark light about him. A light that drew Red like a moth to a flame.

He knew he had remained in Ennisville for far too long and it was time to move on. He had convinced himself that he was content to spend the remainder of his days entertaining trappers and drinking his fill. It was one of the few benefits of owning a saloon in the middle of nowhere.

But he had not touched a drop so far that day because he finally had something better to do. Last night, that stranger had come in from the dark and left more than a couple of empty mugs and a good story behind him. There was something about him that had given Red hope. He had a goal. The promise of a new life somewhere far away from here. To be part of a gang again. To be feared. All he had to do to get it was help the stranger a little.

He had failed his test against Hagen earlier, but Trammel was a different story. He had barely moved since Chief and the others brought him into the saloon. The blanket over him rose and fell weakly. Red had seen men with less serious wounds die. He doubted Trammel would last the night in his condition.

But Red always had been an impatient man who preferred a sure thing. Trammel was standing between himself and his future, but not for long. He would deal with the whelp after he finished off Trammel. He hoped Chief had the good sense to stay out of it but would deal with that if he had to. One problem at a time.

He went behind the bar and grabbed an old towel to help him dispatch Trammel. A few seconds of struggle and no one would know what had happened. Chief would figure he simply died in his sleep.

Red balled up the towel as he approached Trammel. The sheriff still looked intimidating even though he was unconscious. His lantern jaw was as crooked as his nose and his large hands were flat on the blanket across his chest. Red would not even have thought about crossing him had he been on his feet.

The floorboards creaked as he dropped to a knee beside him and used the bar towel to wipe away the sweat that now dappled his brow. He had begun to place the sopping towel over Trammel's mouth and nose when the sheriff's left hand shot up and snatched him by the throat.

Red gagged and dropped the towel as he clutched at the hand that was choking him. He had been in brawls before when men had tried to strangle him to death, but he had never felt anything like this. The grip only grew tighter as his eyes bulged from the effort of trying to breathe.

Trammel opened his eyes and glared up at him.

"You ought to be quieter if you're gonna try to kill a man in his sleep."

Red gurgled as he struggled in vain to break the wounded sheriff's iron grip. He pounded the arm at the elbow, but it would not bend. He tried to pry the fingers from his throat, but they were like a steel band around his neck. He tried to pull away, tried to fall back, anything to get free. But the arm would not move. It would not allow him to move, either. Trammel had locked him in place while he killed him.

Red could feel his life begin to slip away and, with it, his will to keep fighting. His lungs burned and his throat ached, and Trammel's grip grew still tighter until Red heard something pop deep in his throat. His head sagged and his life ebbed away.

Red's last thought was that he was dying in his own saloon, propped up like a scarecrow in a forgotten field.

When Trammel was sure the man was dead, he pushed his lifeless body away from him. He pawed the wet towel off his chest and threw it on top of his would-be assassin. He forced himself to sit up with great effort as he heard someone enter from the back of the saloon.

He heard the old man who had been tending to him say,

"You start cleaning those chickens, boy. I'll go check on your friend."

Trammel looked up at him when he appeared in the doorway. Despite the darkness of the saloon, he recognized the man. The deep lines of his tanned face had become familiar to him in his few moments of awareness. He had spoken to him in a low and steady voice while he treated his wounds, though Trammel had no memory of what he said. He only knew it had been enough to keep him anchored while pain and sleep took him.

Trammel noted the man's face remained impassive as he looked down at him and the dead man on the floor beside him.

"What happened?"

"He did something stupid." Trammel bit off the pain that webbed through his chest as he struggled to sit up. "It cost him his life."

The old man nodded. "I can see that."

"Sheriff?" Hawkeye called out before pushing past the old Indian. "You're awake!"

"Looks that way." Trammel held up a hand to stop the boy before he fell on him. He was still groggy and needed some time before he was ready for Hawkeye's enthusiasm. "That fella over there tried to change that."

Hawkeye stopped when he noticed the body on the floor. "Red? What happened to him?"

"He tried to kill me." Trammel began to examine the stitched wounds on his chest. "I stopped him before he did. Who is he anyway?"

"He owns this place," the old man told him. "Or at least he did while he was alive."

Hawkeye knelt beside the body and checked for a pulse. "His neck is crooked."

"I broke it." Trammel flexed his sore left hand. "Guess I

got carried away. Should've just knocked him out so I could question him later." Now that he had a chance to take a closer look at him, he knew he had never seen him before. "Why'd he want to kill me?"

The old man came to him and eased Trammel back to the floor. "A man was in here last night. A gray-haired man with dead eyes who poured poison in his ear. Poison about you, I think, and the promise of a better future if he killed you and your friends."

Trammel winced as the old man examined his own handiwork. Gray hair. Dead eyes. "Sounds like Lucien Clay to me."

Hawkeye said, "That's what Mr. Hagen thought right before he rode out after him and Bessler. We think Bessler was the one who shot at us up on the ridge. Why, if it wasn't for Chief here, you might not have made it."

Trammel watched the man checking the stitchwork on his chest. "That what they call you? Chief?"

"Among other things." His examination was done. "I know you'll be wanting to sit up, maybe get on your feet. Don't do it. You've got two big holes through the middle of you, mister. The damage is more on the inside than the outside. The only way to heal that is through rest and time."

"Too bad I don't have either." Without help, he rolled over and pulled himself to his knees before standing. He used the wall to keep his balance as Hawkeye came to his side to help steady him.

"Chief is right, boss. You need to rest. We can get you something more comfortable than the floor if you want."

But Trammel would hear none of it. "How long since Hagen left?"

"About six hours ago." Chief folded the blanket he had used to cover Trammel. "Soon after he helped bring you here. He was anxious to get back on the trail of the men you were following."

The old man picked up the sack of grain that had served as Trammel's pillow and carried it into the back room of the saloon.

"Has it really only been a few hours?" Trammel fought not to wince as pain shot through his chest. "I feel like I've been asleep for a week."

"You got shot just after dawn," Hawkeye told him. "Mr. Hagen went after Bessler and Clay when Chief told him he'd done all he could for you. I know what you're thinking, boss, and I'm begging you not to go. You're in no fit state to walk, much less ride a horse. Give it a few days. Until tomorrow morning at least. Mr. Hagen can handle himself until then and you sure could use the rest."

Trammel shook off a wave of weariness that washed over him. He had been hurt and shot many times in his life, but he had never felt like this. "Bringing in Bessler and Clay's not Hagen's job. It's mine. They already had a big head start on us this morning. Now, they're probably a day ahead. If they haven't hit that stage yet, they soon will, and once they do, they'll split up and it'll be twice as hard to catch them." He had to lean on a chair to keep from falling over. He had never felt so weak, but he could not give into it. "It might already be too late as it is. You'd best get the horses ready. We'll be riding out after him right now. There's still plenty of light left for us to make up some ground."

Trammel struggled to lift his head when he heard a group of men talking out on the street.

One of them called into the saloon. "Look at how dark it is in there, boys. Guess old Red's gotten too cheap to buy lamp oil."

"Or matches," said another. "He'll probably start charging us for spitting on the floor next."

Trammel forced himself to stand upright. He did not know these men or their intentions. He had no reason to fear them but had no reason not to, either. They sounded like they were friends of the man he had just killed, and once they saw what he had done to Red, he doubted they would ignore it.

One of the men pushed open the door and stepped inside. "Where are you, you old bottom dealer?"

Four men piled up in the doorway behind him when they saw Red's body on the floor. His vacant eyes were staring up at the ceiling. His neck at an unnatural angle. Too severe for there to be any hope he was still alive.

Their gaze and surprise slowly moved beyond their dead friend on the floor and ran all the way until they were looking up at Trammel. He imagined he looked like quite a sight just then. The long scar across his face and the two stitched holes in his chest did not exactly make him look welcoming.

"What happened to Red?" one of them asked.

The sight of the five men bunched together blurred before him, but he willed himself steady. "He's dead."

A man in the center of the group mouthed his words before he managed to give voice to them. "How?"

"He tried to kill me," Trammel told them. "I couldn't have that. And unless one of you boys are anxious to join him, you'll help pick him up and carry him out of here. And you'll do it right now."

"And just who are you?" a third man asked, then pointed at Hawkeye. "And who's that boy with you?"

Bile rose in Trammel's throat, but he swallowed it down. "That boy is Deputy Hauk out of Blackstone. And I'm Buck Trammel."

He could tell by their reaction that the name meant something to them. He was glad, because he did not think he had the strength to explain it to them.

The first man who had spoken said, "Mister, I don't care

if you're Wyatt Earp himself. You had no cause to go killing old Red."

"He had plenty of cause," Chief said from the end of the bar. "Red tried to kill him, and the sheriff here had every right to kill him first. That stranger you all were so fond of last night put thoughts in Red's head and he was just dumb enough to believe him. Now do what the man told you. Carry Red across the street, out behind the general store. I'll be over there in a while to see that he's tended to properly."

The men did not seem any more eager to obey Chief's instruction than they had Trammel's. But they reluctantly crowded around Red's corpse and managed to lift him. With great effort and groaning, they carried him outside.

Trammel wiped sweat from his brow before propping himself up once more with the help of the chair. "I'm grateful, Chief, but we'll be getting on our way. I guess my shirt is gone, and since I didn't have time to pack another, I'd be grateful if you'd lend me one of yours."

"You might want to be heading out of here, mister. You might even have to, for all I know, but your body has other plans. You're drenched in sweat and you can hardly stand on your own two feet. You won't get fifty yards before you take another spill out of the saddle. Best come back here and sleep in Red's bed. I don't think he'll be having much use for it now."

Trammel gripped the chair tightly. "I said I'm going and that's final."

"Tomorrow," Chief said. "I'm not arguing with you. I'm just telling you what I see. You're a big, strong man, but no one's strong enough to stand two holes in them like you've got. You can either get back here and go to bed or me and the boy will have to drag you back here after you pass out. I've lugged around your heavy carcass enough for one day. You ain't exactly a sparrow feather."

"And you're no chief."

"Never said I was. That's just the name Red put on me." He beckoned Trammel to come to him. "Quit being stubborn. We both know you're not going anywhere."

Trammel hated admitting defeat. Not in Manhattan, or when he was a Pinkerton. Not when he was in Blackstone and not since he came to Laramie.

But despite the will that had carried him through every trial he faced, he knew he could not fight his own body.

Hawkeye looked relieved when Trammel said, "I want you to wake me up at first light, you hear me? I don't care how deep I'm sleeping. Understand?"

"I understand, boss." Hawkeye took his arm and helped ease him off the chair. "Let's get you comfortable before you fall down."

Trammel was glad for the help and used the bar to balance himself as he walked toward Chief.

"What's your name anyway?" the sheriff asked him as he passed.

"Doesn't matter." He took Trammel's other arm and led him into the back room. "Maybe I'll tell you tomorrow, if you're still alive."

Trammel settled for that. It gave him something to look forward to.

CHAPTER 23

Tucker Cobb had chosen to take first watch. Keeling was a light sleeper anyway, and Cobb doubted he could have slept if he tried.

The night was unexpectedly warm after such a cold day, and they had not needed to build a fire. He resisted his dire urge for coffee—his nightly ritual—and took a pull from his canteen instead. He never allowed whiskey on a business run like this. They only drank beer at the stations when there was nothing else available. He preferred to keep his wits about him when guarding a large shipment. He preferred to act as though an attack was always just about to occur. That night, he just happened to be right.

Cobb remained on his feet and stood against the coach. He kept the team hitched up but stopped them in a spot where there was grass for them to chew on. Keeling kept watch while he watered them from his hat from a barrel strapped to the back of the wagon.

He knew the darkness of the pines could play tricks on a man's eyes, as well as his mind. The sky high above the trees was gray and cloudy, blotting out the moon. He did not react to snapping branches or rustling coming deep from somewhere within the wood. Many creatures called the forest home, and he and his coach were just guests passing through.

It was not the sound that troubled him but the lack of it. Animals grew quiet when they sensed a change in their world, which was why Cobb found the rhythm of the wood comforting.

The two men who had tried to ambush his coach were out there somewhere in the darkness. He and Keeling had seen what happened to them following their run-in with the lone rider who had surprised them. He knew both bandits had been shot but doubted they were dead.

Cobb knew the man who shot them was wounded, too. Keeling had seen him take a nasty spill from his horse. He was probably out there right now, crippled and alone, if he was still alive. That part of the territory was dangerous enough for a man on his own, much less if he was injured. His natural inclination was to ride out and help him, but Cobb was in no position to be charitable. He was not on his own and he had not been riding through the countryside for pleasure.

He had been paid to bring the bank's money from one dot on the map to another. He had been paid to ensure it arrived at its destination safely, which was exactly what he intended to do. Besides, he needed his tired team ready to ride at a moment's notice if the bandits tried to do something. Riding off alone to check on the fallen stranger would practically invite them to attack. Both he and Keeling were more than handy with a gun, but going up against two men alone was dangerous business.

He offered up a prayer for the man's well-being and stood his post. The bandits were out there somewhere in the darkness looking at him right now. He could practically feel their glare. They were shot up and wounded, but a desperate man was the most dangerous there was.

If they were foolish enough to move against him and his charge, Tucker Cobb would be ready to give them more than they bargained for.

From behind the cover of a fallen tree, Lucien Clay bit off a scream as he tied the tourniquet tighter around his calf. Hagen's bullet was still deep inside the muscle, and Clay knew it was only a matter of time before it became infected.

Which was an even better justification for why they should hurry.

Clay would worry about the bullet later. For now, he was more concerned about getting his money.

Clay kept his voice to a whisper as he once again tried to convince Bessler to act. "One of them is bound to be asleep by now, Frank. I say we hit them and hit them hard."

"And I said not yet," Bessler said through gritted teeth. "Just give it a bit more time."

Clay did not know what Bessler was waiting for. He was not the one who still had a bullet in him. Earlier, Hagen's shot had ricocheted off the barrel of Bessler's rifle before scraping the left side of his cheek. He had a deep, nasty gash just below his eye. Aside from suffering from dizziness and shock immediately after it happened, Clay knew there was nothing wrong with him.

"You take the rifle," Clay said, "I'll take the coach gun. Between the two of us, we'll blast that stage to pieces, along with anyone in it. We'll take all the money and head out. Why wait?"

"You're getting as bad as that whimpering fool I found in the cell next to you back in Laramie," Bessler said. "I didn't say we're *not* going. I just want a better look at where they are. It's tough to tell with the shadows. I think one of them is still in the coach. The other's probably outside, but

I can't tell which side of the coach he's on. We ought to know that before we pop up from behind this log and start firing. We'll only get one good chance at this."

But Clay could hear a subtle change in Bessler's voice that made him think there was much more to it than that.

He quickly realized this was the first time since the jailbreak that Bessler was not in control of a situation. He was the one who grabbed Doc Carson and used him to get into the jail. He had also laid in wait to ambush Trammel and the others at the ridgeline.

Clay had only seen Bessler attack, but on that day, he had been forced to defend himself. His trap for the coachmen at the Fletcher spread had failed. Hagen had surprised them by catching up to them, and they had barely escaped with their lives.

Clay knew Bessler was not waiting for anything. He was just scared.

Lucien Clay was not about to remain hiding, waiting for Bessler to find his nerve. His money was out there on that coach, and he was going to take it with or without him.

He grabbed Bessler's rifle and slid over the top of the log. His calf was on fire, but he ignored Bessler's whispered pleas for him to come back. He hobbled uneasily through the dried leaves and twigs that littered the forest floor. If anything, his wound made his steps more deliberate and quieter.

He limped slowly toward the vague outline of the coach. He could hear and smell the team of horses still hitched to it. The driver could send them running again at a moment's notice, which was all the better reason for him to strike now.

He crept toward the back end of the coach, hoping to catch the outline of whoever was standing guard. If Clay was in this man's position, he would have stood against the coach to blend in with it.

His eyes had long since adjusted to the darkness, and he thought he could make out the shape of a man by the rear wheel. He was not certain, but it was close enough for him to take the shot.

Clay raised the rifle and aimed into the darkness. But his calf felt as though it was on fire, and he was forced to move to a nearby tree for support. He had to make his first shot count.

Now that he was steady, he once again raised the rifle and was glad to see the shadow had not changed. The man was still standing there. He could practically see him.

Clay's fortune was at hand.

He squeezed the trigger.

A loud click. Nothing happened. He had forgotten to lever in a fresh round.

He felt an impact knock him to the ground as a rifle blast lit up the night. Bullets peppered the tree he had been leaning against and filled the air above his head.

Bessler yelled into his ear. "I told you to stay down."

Bessler took the rifle from him and quickly returned fire.

From his spot on the ground, Clay heard a loud creak that sounded like a door open, followed by a series of flashes that could only be rifle blasts.

Bessler dove flat on the ground and crawled away as Clay heard the hand brake thrown and the snap of the reins. The coachman was moving out!

More bullets hit the trees and ground around where Bessler had landed as the coach lurched forward. Clay saw a barrel strapped to a small platform at the back of the coach and knew that was his way on. If he could just reach it, he could climb onboard, crawl over the top, and knock the driver from his perch.

He scrambled to his feet and began to chase it. He had forgotten about his wounded calf until the pain stabbed through his leg and caused him to collapse. He landed face-first in the dirt but looked up in time to see a man crawl out of the coach and climb up into the wagon box.

His money was gone. He had lost his chance.

He looked up when Bessler burst from the darkness on horseback. The animal kicked dirt on him as it hit the path and galloped after the fleeing coach. If that coward was not giving up, Lucien Clay certainly would not.

He bit off the pain as he got to his feet and hobbled back to where they had stashed their horses. The coach driver had not unhitched his horses, so Bessler and Clay had decided to leave the saddles on their mounts. He gripped the saddle horn and cried out in pain as he pulled himself up into the saddle.

He kept his wounded leg out of the stirrup and joined the chase to steal back his money.

CHAPTER 24

Tucker Cobb had to lean forward to avoid being whipped by pine branches as they sped through the dark forest.

"You hit?" Keeling asked him.

"No, but I think the water barrel was. The coach took a beating. What about you?"

"Nary a scratch. Too bad the same can be said for those fellas back there. They're on our tail right now."

Cobb had been waiting for something to happen, and when he heard the metallic click, he reacted. Whatever plan the bandits had been waiting to spring on them had fallen apart and they had been lucky to escape unharmed.

"How many of them are there? I only saw one."

"So did I," Butch said. "The big fella. I saw the other one got hit in the leg when that stranger happened on them, but I doubt he's dead."

Tucker did not know, either, and it was not worth thinking about. "Leave them be for now," Tucker told his partner. "These branches are too low for you to climb up on the coach, and the trees are too close to the road for them to get around us. If one of them climbs on the back, you know what to do."

Butch Keeling kept his rifle ready as the branches scraped

them. He had to hold on to his hat to avoid it being swept away. "How deep into the forest do you think we are?"

"I stopped us just about in the middle," Tucker said as he kept his eyes on the road. He was driving blind, but these horses had traveled this route before. He was counting on them being able to see well enough to avoid running into the trees. The branches above them had begun to thin out, and some of the gray light from the sky allowed him to see a bit better. "I'll have them run flat out once we get into open ground. Be ready for them to make a move then, probably to our left and away from your gun."

"Just keep her steady, old-timer. I know what I'm doing."

They were the same age, so Tucker did not take it as an insult.

He turned his face as sagging branches raked him when they cleared the forest, and the gray-lit nightscape came into view. Cobb knew the ground between here and Claro Station was relatively flat. He would have welcomed it normally for the sake of his horses, but with bandits on their heels, it was a problem.

He cracked the reins and set the team running at a full gallop as Keeling moved up to the roof of the coach.

Cobb was about to ask Keeling if he had spotted anyone, but his question was answered when he heard his rifle begin to fire. He was shooting to the left, just as Tucker had thought.

He was surprised when his partner stopped shooting as quickly as he had started. He might have thought he had been bounced clear off the coach if his boots weren't still over his right shoulder.

"What's wrong?" Cobb called out to him.

"Got nothing to shoot at," Butch said as he slid back down beside him. "He just stopped chasing us."

That did not sound right. "Maybe you hit him."

"I don't think so." Keeling began to feed more bullets into his rifle. "I got close but didn't see him drop. And his horse didn't throw him, either. He just decided to pull up, but he's still back there."

Cobb had been running the team hard for close to a mile and slowly eased up on the reins. They had to keep moving, but he did not want to risk having one of them falter and wreck the coach. One misstep on the dark road would be disaster, and he had already pushed them harder than he wanted.

"Keep an eye out for them, but I think that'll be the last we see of them before we reach Claro Station."

Keeling finished loading his last round into the Winchester. "How long you figure before we get there?"

"At this pace?" Cobb did a rough calculation in his head. "About two hours, maybe less. Well before sunup. We'll change out the team and make the last push on to Denver. See if we can't hire on some men to ride with us while we're there."

"I don't think we will, but you've always been a more hopeful man than me."

Cobb just hoped the team lasted that long.

Frank Bessler had decided to stick to the road as he allowed his horse to move at a slower pace.

He would have throttled Clay had he been there. The fool had been too anxious and too greedy to listen to reason back in the woods. If he had just waited a bit longer, Bessler could have avoided this. He had been planning to shoot at least one of the horses to keep the coach from running off like it had. He would have worked his way around to the other side and hit the coachmen from the left and the right.

But the impact from Hagen's bullet had scrambled his

brains, and he had a tough time putting his thoughts into words. The plan was there, but the words had refused to come. Clay had taken it as indecision and took matters into his own hands. He had not even thought to make sure the rifle was ready to fire before he acted.

He did not bother to look behind him when he heard another horse approaching. He knew it must be Clay. Even if Hagen had recovered, he did not have a horse. And even if he had stolen Clay's, Bessler knew he would have started shooting already. Clay might have done the same if Bessler had been foolish enough to allow him to have a gun.

Clay slowed his horse roughly as he joined Bessler on the road.

"You keep treating that gelding so roughly," Bessler said, "he's liable to throw you. You'll have a busted neck to go along with your bum leg."

"You were chasing them!" Clay shouted in the darkness. "Why'd you stop?"

"Because I'd chased them as far as I could," Bessler told him. "That shotgunner is quite a shot. I didn't want to risk getting hit because it isn't necessary."

Clay pounded his leg in frustration and immediately regretted it. "But if you'd caught them, we could've been splitting the money by now."

Bessler threw back his head and laughed. "Good old Lucien Clay. Still thinking like a tinhorn saloon rat. The money's just there waiting for us to take it. All we have to do is kill them and it's ours. Why didn't I think of that?"

"You weren't doing much thinking back there in the woods. Quaking in your boots is more like it."

Bessler drew the coach gun from his coat and held it an inch from Clay's face. He had not thumbed back the hammers.

"The next time you speak to me that way, I'll kill you. I

don't care what it does to my reputation. I don't care if Holm doesn't give me the rest of my money. I'll leave you where you fall and take all the money for myself. Is that clear?"

Clay had not pulled away from the shotgun. He kept looking forward as he rode beside Bessler. "You think you're the first man who's ever pulled a gun on me?"

"No, but I'll be the last unless you learn some respect. Now answer my question."

"You've made your point, so get that gun out of my face."

His point made, Bessler tucked the gun back inside his coat. "I wasn't planning on chasing them out of the forest, but it just so happens that it works to our advantage. Those horses are plenty tired now, and they'll have no choice but to switch them out soon. The only place they can do that given the direction they're headed is Claro Station."

"Which is exactly where we didn't want them to go." Clay had managed to keep the venom out of his voice when he said it. "There'll be men there. And fresh horses."

"A man," Bessler allowed. "The man who tends the place. Maybe a couple of helpers. He may have horses, he might not. The coach trade in this part of the territory isn't what it used to be since they put the railroad in. There's a good chance they'll have to wait for new horses to come in."

"That's a mighty big 'if,' Frank. The way our luck is running tonight, I wouldn't count on it."

But Bessler had not finished his thought. "Let's say the station agent has a fresh team just waiting for them. It'll still take some time for them to hitch them up and get them ready. The two men with the coach will be as hungry as we are by now and are bound to stop long enough to get something to eat. Maybe get some sleep. If they do, we'll be ready for them when they leave, and this time we do it my way. We shoot the horses first, take the money, and move on."

Bessler expected Clay to begin picking apart his plan but was glad when he continued to ride on in silence.

"It'll be going on sunrise by then," Clay said. "Any customers in the station are liable to be sleeping. Could make it easy for us to take them before they know what's hit them. We might come out of this richer than we planned."

Bessler smiled. Clay was always scheming. Enough was never enough for the likes of him. "Sounds like something to look forward to, doesn't it?"

CHAPTER 25

Trammel had to keep his legs wide in the stirrups to maintain his balance atop the former packhorse. The Peacemaker holstered under his left arm felt heavier than normal, but at least it was on the opposite side of his wounds. His head throbbed, though not as much as it had during the night. He still had waves of blurry vision, but he managed to blink his eyes clear.

He knew he was in no condition to ride, much less ride after two desperate men like Bessler and Clay, but he did not have a choice. He had already lost too much time in this pursuit, and he did not dare trust their capture to Adam Hagen.

It was not that he did not think Hagen could kill both men. He was almost certain he could if it came down to it. Trammel was afraid of what he might do afterward.

It was that concern that had prevented Trammel from falling asleep despite his wounds. He had spent most of the previous evening staring up at a crooked ceiling from a dead man's bed. A bed that had belonged to the man he had strangled to death earlier that evening.

He may have been shot, but he refused to be a patient. He might have needed rest, but he did not have the time. Lucien Clay was out there somewhere free while Trammel lounged in bed. The man who had shot him was free, too, and that burned in Trammel's belly hotter than the two holes in his chest.

He could not let that stand, not even if it meant his life. He could not live with himself if they killed someone else just because he had not been able to do his sworn duty.

Which was why he had rousted Hawkeye out of bed well before dawn and told him to get ready. Chief had already been awake, perhaps in anticipation of the sheriff wanting to leave. He gave him a buckskin shirt that was a bit too tight but fit him surprisingly well.

Chief had helped Hawkeye prepare their two remaining horses for the journey, along with a small bag of bandages and a poultice for his wounds. They had been forced to leave behind most of the supplies they had brought with them, taking only what they could fit into their saddlebags. He might not have been much of a tracker, but even Trammel knew they would have to travel as light as possible.

"Be sure to change your bandages twice a day," the old Cheyenne told him. "And keep this moss on your wounds. Hagen followed the others on a path that leads to the west. You should stay on it until it gets brighter, then see if you can pick up his trail from there. You won't have to stop to eat or sleep, so you'll probably catch up to him in a day or so if you're lucky."

Trammel had expected Chief to try to stop him from leaving, but he had not. He simply gave Hawkeye the medicine and went back into the solitude of the saloon without another word.

Hawkeye had been silent since they had left Ennisville, a condition Trammel knew better than to write off as weariness.

"I guess you're angry with me," Trammel said as the sky slowly began to brighten with the coming day.

"More disappointed than anything, I guess. You should've let Chief tend to you for a while longer. Mr. Hagen can handle himself just fine."

"Mr. Hagen's liable to handle himself too well," Trammel said. "And help himself to that money if he gets his hands on it."

"He wouldn't do that. He knows you wouldn't want him to."

Trammel knew the young deputy looked up to him and Adam alike, though for different reasons. He admired Trammel for having faith in him and teaching him how to fight. He admired Hagen's flashy style, quick wit, and even quicker gun. But he did not know Adam beyond the image he showed the world. It was time for the boy to grow up a bit.

"Guess you didn't have the chance to hear about what he did in Laramie the day before he sent for you."

"I guess not, seeing as how I was in Blackstone at the time."

Sass, Trammel thought. The boy was developing some backbone. "I watched him kill a prospector named Ayres in a saloon. The old boy was looking for a fight. Some might say he had it coming, and maybe he did, but that's not why Adam shot him. He shot him because he wanted his claim. A claim that looked like it was about to pay off."

Hawkeye grew flustered. "Mr. Hagen wouldn't do that. He wouldn't kill a man unless he had a good reason."

"He had a good reason," Trammel said. "The oldest reason there is. Greed."

Hawkeye looked away as they continued to ride. "You're just like everyone else. The folks in Blackstone. The people in Laramie. His own family. I thought you were different. You're supposed to be his friend."

"I'm as much a friend to him as anyone can be," Trammel

said. "I'm not trying to turn you against him, Hawkeye. I'm just trying to tell you why I'm doing this. Adam's a more complicated man than you give him credit for. Nothing's ever a straight line with him. There's always another angle to consider, no matter what he does. You saw that for yourself when we worked in Blackstone together."

"He's always been kind to me," Hawkeye said. "Never saw him kill a man who didn't have it coming, and it sounds like that Ayres fella was practically asking to get shot."

"Maybe he was," Trammel allowed, "but that doesn't mean greed couldn't have played a part in it, too. I don't care if Bessler and Clay live or spend the rest of their lives in jail. But I do care what happens when men like Adam can get rich by also doing some good."

"Did you ever think he might be going after them for what they did to you back at the ridge?"

"I'm sure that's part of his reason. Maybe even a bigger part than I'm giving him credit for. But it's not necessarily the whole reason, and you need to keep that in mind."

The sky began to brighten quicker now. Ribbons of deep purples and bright pinks filled the horizon. It was shaping up to be a pretty morning, too pretty for him to waste arguing with Hawkeye.

"Anyways, I was just trying to explain why I wanted to hit the trail as early as I did."

"You didn't have to bother," Hawkeye said. "I might be young, but I ain't a kid anymore, boss. I've been through plenty since you hired me on, and I can make up my own mind. And I already knew why you were out here before you said it. You're here because it's the only way you know how to live. You can't change your nature any easier than those buzzards circling over there can become ducks."

Trammel peered past the boy and saw a group of buzzards soaring high over a flat bit of land. They had their wings stretched out as they coasted on the air in a lazy circle. He knew that could only mean one thing. Someone—or something—was dead.

"What direction do you take that for from here?"

Hawkeye snapped out of his indignation and took a closer look. "Judging by the sun, that would be south. Why?"

He did not have to consult the map Mr. Banner, the bank president, had drawn for him back in his office. "That's the direction the bank stagecoach was set to head."

Hawkeye pointed to the hoof prints and horse droppings they passed. "But Mr. Hagen clearly rode this way. Straight on toward those hills up ahead."

Trammel knew Hawkeye was already a better tracker than he could ever hope to be, but the sight of the buzzards circling to the south stuck out in his mind.

And as he peered into the distance, he thought he saw why.

"That look like a trail to you?" he asked his deputy. "See how it snakes around and shoots out toward those trees in the distance?"

Hawkeye shielded his eyes and looked in the direction Trammel was pointing. "Seems to be, now that you pointed it out, but I can't see what those birds are circling over."

"Something dead," Trammel said. "Or someone. Let's ride over and find out."

Before Hawkeye could protest, Trammel steered his horse off the trail and rode down the hill to the spot the buzzards had chosen. He thought he might pass out when he reached for his Peacemaker and pulled it free from its holster. The pain was almost enough to make him drop it.

But it only served to make him grip it tighter and heel his horse into riding faster. Hawkeye followed close behind.

As he closed in on the spot, Trammel could see a large lump atop a slight hill that was clearly a horse on its side. And as he grew closer still, he saw a man facedown on the ground a few yards away from it. He recognized who it was immediately.

"Adam!" Trammel called out as he reined in the horse and jumped down from the saddle.

Hagen struggled to look behind him as he grabbed his rifle but cried out from the effort and dropped the Winchester.

"You shot?"

Hagen squinted at him through the pain. "What are you doing here? You're supposed to be in bed."

Trammel was checking him over as Hawkeye joined him. "Mr. Hagen! What happened?"

"It was Bessler," Hagen told them. "My horse rolled on me when he shot at me. I think I hit him. Clay, too, but I don't think I killed them. They're not still there, are they?"

Trammel looked around but did not see any sight of them. "Looks like they're gone. Which leg is it?"

"My left," Hagen said. "I think it's broken."

Trammel ignored the pain coursing through his chest and told Hawkeye, "Ride into those pines and bring back the thickest branches you can find. We need to set his leg."

The young deputy began to go for his horse until Trammel grabbed his arm. "Keep your rifle handy. Bessler and Clay might be in there and wounded, so be careful."

Hawkeye told him he would before he got in the saddle and rode toward the pines.

"That poor boy," Hagen said. "All he's done this whole time is tend to us like an orderly." He allowed his head to sag. "I tried rolling over on my back, but it hurts whenever I do. I've been just lying here like a dead fish since it happened."

Trammel checked Hagen's left leg. The part between his hip and knee seemed fine, but the leg was crooked below the knee. He touched it lightly, but Hagen still jumped.

"Doesn't look like the bone is sticking out," Trammel

told him. "You might've just busted your knee, but I won't know for certain until I roll you over."

"Two holes in your chest and now you're a doctor?"

At least Adam was in good spirits. "I might not be much of a plainsman, but I've seen plenty of broken arms and legs. I know what to do."

"Too bad you don't take your own advice. You should be in bed right now instead of riding all over creation. I've seen how you track a man. You just as easily could've ridden past me as found me."

"Lucky for you I'm stubborn." Trammel thumbed up at the sky. "We saw the buzzards circling up there. Only would've been a matter of time before they got bored with your horse and tried to take a piece out of you."

"I heard them." Hagen patted his rifle. "I was planning on serving them a lead appetizer when you showed up. Leave it to you to spoil my fun. Your timing was always lousy." He rested his head in the grass. "Why didn't you stay back in Ennisville, Buck? You'll die bouncing around out here and Bessler and Clay will get the credit."

"Not likely." He kept an eye on the distant pines, anxious for Hawkeye's return. "How'd you get close enough to shoot at them?"

"They were chasing a stage from a ranch house back there. Looks like we were right about them planning to rob the stage, but the driver must've caught on. They chased the stage into those pines over there, then stopped. That's when I came along and took a shot at them. I think I shot Bessler in the shoulder, and Clay's got a bullet in his leg. I passed out before I could see for sure. They were gone by the time I woke up. I heard a lot of shooting in there during the night, but I don't know how it turned out."

Trammel listened for any sound that showed his deputy might have stumbled across them, but he did not hear any gunfire. "We'll see what Hawkeye saw when he comes back. At the very least, you slowed them down a bit. At the most, one of them might be bleeding out somewhere in those trees right now."

Hagen asked, "Got any idea what the date is?"

"Can't say as I do," Trammel said. "Why?"

"Because I'm going to mark it on a calendar, for this is the day Buck Trammel became a philosopher."

Trammel did not have to do much thinking or philosophizing to be glad to see Hawkeye ride out of the woods back toward them. He had a cluster of thick branches tied to his saddle. "That boy listens."

"Listens better than you," Hagen said. "Has more sense, too."

Trammel walked out to greet his deputy and began to look over the branches he had gathered. "Good job, Hawkeye. You got more than we need, but they won't go to waste. We can use the rest to make a fire later."

Hawkeye climbed down from his horse. "I got the thickest I could find on the forest floor. We can cut some more down, but it'll take time."

"These should do nicely. Come over here and help me keep Adam still while I set his leg. He's going to be in an awful lot of pain, so put all your weight into it."

Trammel and his deputy crouched on either side of Hagen. Buck took one of the thinner branches and had his friend bite down on it. "I'll be needing my belt to hold your leg in place, so I'm afraid this stick will have to do you. I can try to knock you out, but my right arm's still not right. Might only break something on the first punch."

Hagen took the wood but did not bite on it. "Just do whatever you've got to do and get it over—"

He cried out when Trammel grabbed hold of his leg and twisted it back in place before he was ready. The sound of sinew and bone moving was almost worse than the sudden pain.

The sheriff directed Hawkeye to place two large branches on either side of Hagen's leg while he pulled his belt tight around them. Trammel slid another branch over the front of his knee and at the back before tightening it enough to make him scream again.

He told Hawkeye, "Hold his leg and keep it from flopping while I turn him over on his back toward you."

Trammel took Hagen by the left shoulder and hip and easily flipped him over onto his back while Hawkeye kept the left leg straight as he eased it down. Both were waiting for Hagen to wail again in agony, but he had not made a sound.

Hagen seemed just as surprised as his handlers. "That doesn't hurt nearly as much as I expected it would."

"That's because I don't think your leg's broken," Trammel told him. "I think your knee was just knocked out of its socket. It'll still hurt, but if we keep it bound up like we have it now, it should hold until we have Chief look at it."

Hagen seemed to forget about his injury quickly. "Chief? That would imply I'm going back to Ennisville."

"Didn't mean to imply it," Trammel said. "It's an order. Hawkeye here'll take you back while I keep on after Bessler and Clay."

"That's not going to happen," Hagen said. "You've fixed it so my leg can't move. There's nothing that old heathen can do for me that you haven't done already. We're going on after them together."

"Now look who's being stubborn." Trammel had been afraid he might say that. "A one-legged gambler and a one-armed sheriff will be a sorry sight. I made it this far and I can make it a lot farther if I'm not worrying about you."

Hagen stretched to his right and picked up his rifle.

"None of us will be going anywhere until we handle that bunch I see riding toward us right now."

Trammel and Hawkeye looked behind them and saw a line of riders approaching across the flatland.

"Now who are those boys?"

Hagen began feeding fresh rounds into his Winchester from slots on his gun belt. "We'll be finding out soon enough. Just make sure you give me a clear shot at them. Hawkeye, you break off to the left with your rifle. Buck, you stay on your left. They're riding in a line, so . . ."

"The leader's probably in the center." Trammel stood up and pulled his Peacemaker from the holster under his left arm. The movement did not hurt as much as it had earlier, but it still hurt plenty.

He counted five men on either side of the center rider. Eleven in total. Normally, it would be acceptable odds, but neither Hagen nor Trammel was in good condition. Hawkeye might have to make up the difference if things went wrong. Trammel could not allow it to come to that.

He kept his pistol at his side as he walked away from the others to greet the riders.

The leader of the line of riders stopped about twenty yards away from Trammel, and his men did the same.

The man Trammel took as the boss of the outfit was older and much heavier than those who rode with him. His dark beard was streaked with gray and white. His skin had the tanned, cracked look that befitted a man who had spent most of his life in the saddle. The men with him looked to be Mexican, and Trammel thought they might be vaqueros.

The leader of the group was the only one who spoke. "What are you boys doing on my property?"

"Didn't know we were on anyone's land," Trammel said. "Didn't see anything posted on the road. Who are you?"

"I don't see as how that has anything to do with my question, mister."

Trammel tapped the star on his borrowed buckskin shirt. "Most people answer when a lawman asks them a question. I'm not inclined to repeat myself."

"The name's Ben Fletcher and my land goes for about a day's ride behind me and ends right in front of those pines over yonder." Fletcher leaned forward and crossed his hands atop the saddle horn. "I answered your question, now you answer mine."

"My friend's horse threw him yesterday," Trammel told him. "Tore up his leg some. We were just helping to fix it before we can get him back to a doctor."

"This whole wide prairie and he just happens to get himself crippled here on my land."

"I'm hardly a cripple." From his spot on the ground, Hagen worked the lever of his Winchester. "I was thinking the same thing about that coach that almost got robbed on your place. All this land where two fellas could've hit it and they picked your spread. Mighty convenient."

When Fletcher reached for the pistol on his hip, his men joined him.

Trammel raised his Peacemaker and aimed it at Fletcher. "They pull, you die."

The rancher gripped his pistol but did not pull it. "You shoot me, these boys will cut you down."

"We'll see about that. You won't be in any position to care if they do."

Fletcher remained still. "You pointed to that star on your chest but never told me your name."

"Buck Trammel," he told him. "Out of Laramie."

The rancher's eyes narrowed. "Out of Blackstone, too, as I recall."

"You recall correct. Now get your hand off that pistol

and tell your men to do the same. No one needs to die here today."

Fletcher let go of his pistol and slowly brought his right hand up for his vaqueros to see. "You heard the sheriff, boys. Leave your irons where they are. We don't want any trouble with the law. Which is why I don't know about anyone trying to rob any coach. I was with my boys tending to the herd in one of my fields until just now. We came riding over when we saw you trespassing." He held up his hands. "I know that's not the case now. I was talking about before."

Trammel lowered his Peacemaker but kept it at his side. "How did you come to know Bessler and Clay?"

A flash of recognition before a poor attempt to cover it. "Can't say I know anyone named Bessler, but Clay's from Laramie, same as you. Owns a couple of saloons, I think."

"He did," Hagen said from behind his Winchester. He had not lowered his rifle and neither had Hawkeye. "I own them now."

Fletcher regarded the man with the wooden branches wrapped around his left leg. "Guess that would make you Adam Hagen, then."

"You guess right. So, let's try guessing at something important, like the truth. Why were you helping Bessler and Clay rob that stage?"

The man next to Fletcher spoke up. "Mr. Fletcher here already told you he didn't have anything to do with any robbery or any stage. We've been tending cattle and horses in a pasture on the far side of his property. If we'd decided to rob anyone, they wouldn't have gotten away."

"Sounds convenient," Hagen said.

"The truth often is." Fletcher gestured toward the dead horse nearby. "I take it that was your animal?"

"Shot dead by your friend Bessler."

Fletcher grinned and looked away. "Seeing as how I've always been on the side of law and order, what do you say I give you one of mine? Help get you to someone who can look over that leg for you properly." He spoke to his men. "How about you boys head back and pick out a good, steady animal for Mr. Hagen to ride. I'll stay here until you get back. But hurry. We've got plenty of chores to do and the day's only getting started."

The men turned and rode back the way they had come without so much as a sideways glance at Trammel or Hagen or Hawkeye. Fletcher had given them an order and they were following it.

Trammel could not help but notice it. "You've got those boys well trained." He kept his pistol flat against his leg.

"If you'd been any other men, they wouldn't have left my side so easily. But seeing as how you're Trammel and Hagen, they let it be." He looked over at the young deputy. "Who are you?"

"Name's Hawkeye," the young deputy said.

The name seemed to mean something to the rancher. "I have heard of you."

Trammel was more interested in correcting another mistake Fletcher had made. "Why'd you lie to us about knowing Bessler? And don't bother denying it. I could tell you recognized the name."

Fletcher looked around to make sure his men were out of earshot. When he confirmed they were, he said, "Let's say me or one of my men happened to know Frank Bessler." He held out his hands, as if to encompass his land. "From a long time ago, before all this."

"Sounds like a story," Hagen said. "We're more interested in facts."

Trammel motioned for Hagen to be quiet. "Go on."

"Say this fella got a letter from Bessler, saying he wanted his help in setting up a score on a stage on a certain day."

Trammel understood what he was trying to tell them. "I'd say the fella was a fool for not telling the law about it."

"But say this fella stood to earn quite a bit of money just by letting him use his house while he was far away. He didn't have a hand in it, but he didn't stop it, either, because he wanted nothing to do with Bessler. He's a man full of trouble and death follows him wherever he goes. If he refused him, he might go ahead and do it anyway. Might run off some of his livestock and burn down his house out of spite."

Trammel was content to play Fletcher's game for the moment. "I'd say, if this fella was a rancher, he'd have ten men or more to keep that from happening."

"It would seem that way," Fletcher allowed, "but this fella knows Bessler pretty well. He knows thirty men wouldn't be enough to stop him once he decided a man is an enemy. He knows how to repay a kindness as much as he knows how to avenge a slight. Let's say this fella thinks Bessler is part of his past and it's best to keep him there."

Trammel motioned for Hawkeye and Hagen to lower their rifles as he gingerly tucked his Peacemaker back under his left arm. "I wish I could talk to this fella and ask him if he knew where Bessler and Clay might be."

Fletcher nodded toward the pine trees behind them. "I doubt he would know for certain, but the coach has stopped here many times in the past. And if it's old Tucker Cobb driving this run, he'll be headed straight for Claro Station, a few miles in that direction. He'll be looking to change out teams and get something to eat. There's not much to the place, but you can bet he's there before he presses on to Denver."

Trammel saw a rider approaching them from the ranch house while trailing a bay on a lead line. It looked like Hagen would be getting to ride after all.

"You ought to tell this friend you've been talking about that, if his story checks out, he probably won't have anything to fear from me. But if I find out he had a hand in any of this, I'll be back. And he won't be happy to see me."

"If I see him, I'll be sure to tell him."

The rider from the ranch handed the reins of the spare horse to Trammel. "Feel free to return him whenever you're done. He's a good animal. Good luck to all of you."

Trammel assured him they would, and he watched Fletcher and his man ride away.

Hawkeye took the animal from Trammel. "Even I could tell that man was lying."

"I've always said you were perceptive beyond your years," Hagen said as he laid his rifle on the ground. "I never trust a man who talks around things instead of coming right out and says them."

"He got us a horse for you," Trammel said. "That'll have to be enough for now." He held out a hand down to Hagen. "You want to try getting up on your own or do I have to carry you?"

Hagen hesitated as he tried to stand. "This is going to hurt, isn't it?"

"You lose your nerve when you fell off that horse? I never took you as a man who shies away from a little discomfort."

Hagen took firm grip of Trammel's left hand, and both men grunted from the effort of pulling him upright. Trammel's right side burned and Hagen hopped on his right leg while his left remained immobile.

Hawkeye surprised them by laughing. "Guess neither

of you will be winning any dance contests anytime soon, but at least you're alive."

Hagen swept his hat from his head and hit the young deputy with it. "No one likes sarcasm, kid. Now, get my tack off that horse and put it on this one. We've got men to catch."

CHAPTER 26

Cobb watched Guillermo "Charlie" Ramirez rub the sleep from his eyes as he opened the wooden gates to Claro Station. The horses were exhausted by the time they pulled the coach inside the thick adobe walls that surrounded the main building and corrals.

The Mexican did not bother to close the gate behind him as he trudged over to greet Cobb and Keeling.

"Morning, Tucker. Wasn't expecting to see you again so soon." He walked past the coach and began looking over the horses. "Never saw a team of yours in such sorry condition, either. They look just about done in. Guess you boys ran into some trouble on the way here."

"You could say that," Cobb said as he stood on solid ground while Butch jogged to the gates to close them. "I'm afraid we might have brought some with us, too."

"Seems like it." Ramirez watched Butch quickly close the wooden doors and throw the wooden bar across them. "How many this time?"

"Two of them, but don't let that fool you. Those boys are plenty of trouble."

Ramirez whistled as he circled the stage, pausing by the bullet holes that pockmarked the back of the coach. "Looks like your water barrel took the worst of it. That rear right wheel, too."

Cobb normally made it a point to know the condition of his horses and his wagon, but events back in the pine forest had prevented him from doing so before then. Three of the spokes had been hit by the rifle and were chipped. The wood beneath the rim was cracked, but the metal around it was holding.

"Think it'll last us until we make it to Denver? We're in a bit of a hurry."

Ramirez ran his hands over the spokes and the wheel itself as he made his judgment. "It might, but I can have one of my boys give you a new one. Outfit you with a new barrel, too."

Cobb was pleased to hear it. "How are you fixed for horses?"

Ramirez clapped the dirt from his hands. "I've got a few, but only two are in good condition. Had a stage roll through here yesterday on its way to Denver, and they cleaned me out. The ones I have are a day or so away from being fit for travel."

Cobb's stomach sank at the news. "Only two?"

"Afraid so," the station agent said. "Every stagecoach outfit in the territory has been struggling since they put in the railroad. I don't have the livestock I used to have. You're more than welcome to go over to the corral and look them over for yourself. You might be able to find a couple who could get to Denver if you wait until tonight, but with men on your trail, I wouldn't suggest it."

Cobb thought it over. "You said you had two good horses?"

"A freighter traded them out a week ago," Ramirez explained. "You might be able to make the trip on two horses, but lugging a coach this size, it'll take you longer. And if you had to make a run for it . . ."

Cobb had heard enough. "I know. It's risky." Ramirez knew horses better than he did. If he said they could not make the trip, it was true.

Cobb hit the side of the coach out of frustration. "Of all the lousy luck."

"Calm down," Butch chastised him as he joined them beside the coach. "We're in better shape now than we were this time yesterday. We've got high walls and a safe place to hole up." He clapped a hand on Charlie's shoulder. "Not to mention this man's fine Mexican cooking to line our bellies. No, sir, not a bad condition indeed."

Ramirez called over two of his station hands and gave them orders in Spanish. They promptly began to unhitch the team and lead the weary horses into the barn, where they would be tended to, wiped down, and fed.

Their condition wounded Cobb deeply. He hated to push good horses to the limit, but events on the road had given him little choice. He hated being stuck at the station even more.

"I don't like this, Butch. I don't like it a single bit. We've got a schedule to keep."

"We wouldn't be doing anything except feeding worms right now if it wasn't for you," Butch reminded him. "Be glad we've got anything to keep at all."

Cobb took no comfort in his words. "I don't like being stuck here like this. And I don't like giving the two who've been dogging us a chance to catch up. I imagine we'll be safe enough while we're in here, but we'll have to move on eventually."

Butch did not seem worried. "We handled them easily enough so far. They threw their best at us, and it still wasn't enough. We know the land between here and Denver better than they probably do. Until then, we rest, eat, and push on."

Cobb usually relied on Butch's optimism to keep his spirits up. They had survived dozens of scrapes against greater odds before and had always managed to make it to where they were going. But he could feel there was something different about this time. "I don't like allowing them to catch their breath like this. It might be only two of them out there, but anything could happen while we're in here."

"Charlie said he's got two ready to ride," Butch said. "We could borrow some saddles from him, split the gold between us, and set off for Denver on horseback. We could make it in a day and we'd travel a lot faster without that big old coach slowing us down."

Cobb had already thought of that. "The load's too big for horseback even if we break it up. It'd be too bulky, especially if we had to run for it. Besides, I like having the coach as cover in case we need it."

"They don't have food," Butch pointed out. "They don't have bullets and they don't have shelter. We get good horses we can push on to Denver in a day. We'll have Charlie tell his men to mind the ground around the station. They'll give a holler if they see anything. We can take the fight to them if we have to. End this now instead of running away from them like we have."

Had they been rolling empty, Cobb might have considered it. But they had been entrusted with the bank's money, and it would take both of them to get it to Denver safely. He would not risk their lives unless he had to. It was not about striking first. It was about not striking at all.

"We're not going anywhere for a while," Cobb decided, "and we both think better on a full stomach. Let's head inside and see what Charlie's serving. We'll talk about this later."

"I think that's the first good idea you've had all day." Butch pushed past him. For a thin man, he had a fearsome appetite.

Cobb took a final look around the compound. The walls were thick and stood higher than a man. Even the big man who was pursuing them would have a difficult time climbing it without being seen. And even if he made it over the top, he would have quite a fight on his hands with nowhere to go.

They and the valuables they were hauling were as safe as they were liable to be. At least, for now.

He went into the station building before Butch ate everything in sight.

"Well, we're too late," Clay spat as he watched the wood gate to the station close. "We should've hit them again before they got in there, but you wouldn't have it. That rangy fella's in there right now with the coach driver and my money."

"Our money," Bessler reminded him. "And the situation isn't as hopeless as you make it out to be."

Sometimes Clay wondered if he and Bessler were watching the same events unfold. "They're behind high walls, getting fresh horses and filling their bellies. We're stuck out here, low on ammunition and without so much as a crust of bread between us." He grabbed his leg as his calf ached something awful. "And in case you've forgotten, I've got a bullet in me."

But Bessler did not seem to be bothered by his partner's discomfort. "Where you see problems, I only see possibility. In fact, I only see assurances for the first time since we left Laramie."

Clay had finally had enough of his double talk. "I swear,

if you don't speak plainly, I'm liable to knock you right off that horse."

"Follow me." Bessler brought his horse off the road and began to ride toward the station. "Don't be afraid. No one's watching."

Clay could not believe the lawyer was brazen enough to approach the high walls of the station. But he was right. No one appeared to be looking over the top.

Bessler did not bother looking back at him as he explained. "Walls can provide protection, but they also keep a man from seeing what's beyond them. Look at us. If we had a stick of dynamite, we could light it and toss it over the side."

"But you didn't think to bring any dynamite."

Bessler ignored the comment. "We have something else going for us: the element of surprise. They're in there now, eating and resting. Perhaps they're getting a team of fresh horses ready to ride. Perhaps the station has none to give them. But we know exactly where they are and they can't exactly sneak out of here without us seeing them, now can they?"

Clay had not thought of that. "No, I guess they can't."

"There's only one way in and one way out," Bessler went on as they rounded the first corner of the wall. "They'll be vulnerable as soon as they leave, and that's when we'll hit them. Back in the forest, you moved before I could shoot the horses, but we won't make the same mistake this time. We'll cut them down, strand them, and finish them off. We've still got more than enough bullets left to do the job. Don't worry about that. As for food, there's game around here. We'll hunt for what we need. We don't have to worry about being quiet because they already know we're out here waiting for them."

He looked back at Clay and smiled. "We have time on

our side, Lucien. Time can play some awfully nasty tricks on a man, even dangerous men like those two coachmen."

They rounded the back wall of the station, and Clay was glad there wasn't a gate there. Maybe Bessler knew what he was talking about after all. One way in. One way out. It just might work.

"I'll see what I can do about killing a deer or a rabbit for our breakfast," Bessler said. "I still have some jerky left to hold us over. If we fail, perhaps our friends will bring something with them."

There he went, talking foolish again. "Friends? What friends? We don't have any friends here."

"Not yet," Bessler said, "but I have a feeling that will change soon. Ben Fletcher is bound to get back to his ranch this morning, and when he sees that I haven't left any money for him, he'll be angry. He's not the type who likes being slighted, so he's bound to come looking for answers. And when he does, it won't just be us out here but Fletcher and whoever he decides to bring with him."

Just when he began believing Bessler had a plan, he said something crazy like that. "You're sure fond of pinning your hopes on chance. What if he doesn't come back until tomorrow? What if he doesn't care enough about the money to come looking for us?"

"Ben Fletcher only cares about money," Bessler told him. "Always has and always will. His time out here might've changed him a little, but no one changes that much. Don't worry. He'll be here. I know the man. And when he does, those high walls will begin to feel like a prison to anyone unfortunate enough to still be inside them."

They rounded the back wall and began riding back toward the front. "It'll be like shooting fish in a barrel." Bessler patted the wall as he rode by it. "A nice, adobe barrel."

Clay heard horses approaching the station at the same

time Bessler did. "Riders. Quick, get off the horses and walk them over to the brush over there. I want to see who it is."

Bessler scrambled out of the saddle and led his horse into the thick overgrowth that surrounded the station. Clay rode his horse into it and had to use a tree to help himself climb down.

His calf felt like it was on fire as he hobbled over to join Bessler at the tree he was crouched beside.

He watched three men approach the station on horse-back. One of them was riding with his left leg jutting away from the horse. The rider in the lead was a youngster who seemed to ride easier than his two companions.

But Clay did not need to be able to make out the face of the third man to know who it was. A large man who held the reins with his left hand while his right arm hung loosely at his side.

"Buck Trammel," he seethed. "He's still alive!"

"Shut up," Bessler told him. "They're close enough to hear us."

They were, indeed, closer, and Clay recognized the rider with the outstretched leg as Adam Hagen. He figured the boy must be Hawkeye, Trammel's deputy from Blackstone.

Clay could scarcely believe what he was seeing and pushed Bessler in frustration. "I thought you said you killed them. They look dead to you?"

"They don't look prosperous," Bessler observed as he watched them ride closer. "Trammel looks like he's about ready to pass out and Hagen's got a broken leg." He surprised Clay by laughing. "They might as well be dead for all the good they'll do those coachmen."

Clay grew quiet when he heard Trammel call out, "Hello in the station. This is Sheriff Buck Trammel. Let us in. We have business here."

Clay watched for a few anxious moments as the wooden doors were pushed open and the three men rode inside. Bessler had been right. Trammel was pale and his face was slick with sweat. He looked like he might drop at any moment.

For the first time since he had left his cell, he felt he might just find a way to get his money and rid himself of Trammel once and for all. "I hope you're right about Fletcher. We could use his help."

"He'll be here." Bessler stood up. "If not for us, then for himself."

CHAPTER 27

Trammel recognized the broad man with the bushy gray mustache standing in the station building. He was glaring at him as Trammel handed the reins of his horse to one of the station agents. A dinner napkin was still tucked in the collar of his shirt, and he had not bothered to wipe the remnants of his meal from his chin.

"You're Tucker Cobb, aren't you?" Trammel asked him. "I'm Buck Trammel."

"I know who you are, Sheriff." Cobb scowled at Hagen, who Charlie and Hawkeye were helping down from his horse. "Can't say I approve of your companion, though."

"And a blessed morning to you, too, Tucker," Hagen said once he reached solid ground. "Still as elegant as ever. Judging by that mess on your chin, I take it you're enjoying the chili."

"And judging by what you did to Ayres, I'd say you're nothing but a low-down killer."

Trammel saw a tall, rangy man with a week's worth of stubble walk out into the doorway beside him. "I'd mind my words if I were you, Hagen. You ain't talking to a half-drunk prospector right now."

"Butch Keeling, as I live and breathe," Hagen gushed as he struggled to maintain his balance on one good leg. "I should've known you'd be here. Where one goes, the other follows. Like passed wind and the stench of cut cheese."

Keeling stepped past Cobb and out onto the porch. "I see that busted leg hasn't softened your mouth any."

"Nothing wrong with my gun hand," Hagen said. "If you want to do something about my mouth, now's your chance. Given my infirmity, you might even manage to clear leather before I kill you."

Trammel had heard enough and stepped in between the coachmen and the gambler. "We've got plenty of trouble waiting for us outside. We don't need any of it in here."

Butch pointed past the sheriff toward Hagen. "If he doesn't start any trouble, there won't be any."

"There won't be any trouble," Trammel told him, "because I won't allow it."

Tucker Cobb plucked his napkin from his collar and began to wipe the food from his face. "You boys look like you've already had more than your fair share. I've never seen a man look so pale and still be walking around. Which one of them got you? That big feller or the skinny one with the long, gray hair?"

"The big one." Trammel had gotten so accustomed to the dull ache from his gunshot wounds, he had forgotten they were there. "His name is Frank Bessler from Fort Worth, Texas."

The name clearly meant nothing to him or his partner. "What about the lanky fella with the gray hair?"

"Lucien Clay."

The coachmen traded looks before Cobb said, "That fella who broke out of prison back in Laramie?"

Hagen laughed. "Just how many Lucien Clays do you know, Tucker?"

Cobb ignored him. "We knew something was wrong

when we pulled into Laramie that morning, but Mr. Banner was eager to send us on our way."

"Even if he had told us it was Lucien Clay, why would he hang around these parts after he was free?" Keeling said. "If it were me, I would've hotfooted it out of the territory instead of holding up stagecoaches."

"He can't go anywhere," Trammel explained, "because you've got all his money. That's part of the load you're bringing to the Bank of Denver."

Cobb stopped wiping his chin while Butch sagged against the doorway. Trammel knew they had not known that part. Now that they did, everything made much more sense.

"Too bad Mr. Banner didn't think to tell me that," Cobb said. "I might've hired on more men to ride with us had I known."

"Hire them with what?" Butch asked. "We're nearly broke, and no one worth anything would've ridden with us unless they got half up front."

"Still could've been done. I have friends in Laramie who would've trusted us." He looked over Trammel and Hagen. "You boys look like you've had quite a time of it. Guess you've got Clay and this Bessler fella to thank for that."

Trammel was glad to see some of the tension fall away from the situation. "I got shot twice in the chest by Bessler and Hagen busted his leg trying to catch them after they chased you into the pines back there."

Cobb's eyes narrowed as he looked at Hagen. "That was you who charged them?"

"Seemed the right thing to do at the time," Hagen said. "I suppose I got caught up in the moment and got careless." He patted the branches strapped around his leg. "I paid for it."

"That big fella can shoot," Butch said. "Not as good as me, mind you, but you're lucky he didn't kill you."

"Yes, what a blessing." Hagen hobbled toward the door and Hawkeye helped him. "Now, if you two have left anything for us, I'm going to get something to eat. I'm starving."

Butch got him up to the boardwalk and helped Hawkeye bring him inside, leaving Cobb and Trammel alone.

Cobb gestured up to the brightening sky. "Looks like it's shaping up to be a beautiful day."

Trammel looked around. It was the first time he had been to Claro Station. The adobe walls around the grounds were high, but he wondered if they were high enough to keep Bessler on the other side. And even if they were, they still had a serious problem.

"Only one way in here and one way out," Trammel observed. "We're boxed in here while we've got two men waiting to shoot us as soon as we leave."

"Agreed. Though Butch said it looks like Hagen put a bullet in Clay's leg, which might slow him up some."

Trammel was not hopeful. "If Clay's breathing, he's dangerous. Bessler, too. We'll be riding into a cloud of lead as soon as we open those gates. There's only two of them, but they'll be enough, especially as banged up as we are." Another troubling thought came to him. "Don't know why they didn't shoot at us when we came in just now."

Cobb looked encouraged. "Maybe they left."

"More likely we surprised them," Trammel said. "They want that money you're hauling and they won't stop until they get it."

"I was afraid you might say something like that," Cobb admitted. "The station agent only has two horses ready to ride, and that wagon requires at least four good horses. Maybe we could hitch up two of the ones you rode in here? Use the third horse as an outrider."

Trammel did not think much of the idea. "The outrider would be the first to get shot. We could all pile into the wagon and shoot back from there."

"That wagon is already loaded down with gold for the bank," Cobb told him. "If we put men back there, we'll need a six-horse team, and we don't have that."

Trammel had been afraid he might say something like that. But then he thought he might be approaching this from the wrong direction. He was thinking about what they did not have instead of what they had in their favor. "Our three mounts are in good shape. Combine that with the two horses you say the station has, that means one horse per man. I say we split the money between the five of us and dart off in different directions. Bessler and Clay wouldn't be expecting that, and they couldn't chase all of us at once. Some of us are bound to get away."

But the coachman was already shaking his head as Trammel laid out his plan. "Butch and I already thought about that. Even if we split the haul five ways, the gold's heavy enough to weigh down the horses. Whoever Bessler and Clay chose to run down wouldn't stand a chance. The rest might be able to make it, but you'll be sentencing one of us to a death. I don't know about you, Sheriff, but that's a price too high to pay."

Trammel cursed and walked away from him. He was not so much angry with Cobb as he was frustrated by the situation. "Did the station agent tell you when they're getting fresh horses?"

"Charlie doesn't know," Cobb said. "Could be today. Could be a week from now. We might be able to leave tomorrow with four of them, but it'll be a big risk. I've seen the horses with my own two eyes. Whoever had them before pushed them to the bitter end. They'd die before we got halfway to Denver, if they lasted that long, and my coach is too heavy for only two horses to pull."

Trammel looked at the walls, then looked at the heavy wooden doors. If they'd had such doors back at the prison, he doubted things would have gotten out of hand.

He had to find a way out of here. Even if Charlie had provisions for a week, they would still have to leave eventually. He doubted Bessler and Clay could survive in the open for that long, but they likely knew it, too. And the longer he waited, the closer they would come to desperation. Bessler had already proven how dangerous he could be when he had time to plan.

"There's only one way to handle this and it won't be easy. How many men does Charlie have working for him here?"

"Two old Mexicans who tend to the horses," Cobb said. "I wouldn't count on them for much in a fight."

"I don't need their guns," Trammel told him. "I need their eyes. I want one man on each of these side walls, looking for any sign of Bessler and Clay. Sound, smoke, fire, anything. Have them come get us if they see anything. If they do, we'll head outside and finish them off once and for all. Hit them before they have the chance to hit us."

Cobb's perpetual frown deepened. "Doesn't sound like much of a plan. You're shot up, Hagen's got a busted leg, and that boy you brought in here is mighty green. That'll leave most of the heavy work for me and Butch to pick up. I'll go with you, but I'll have to put the question to Butch. We're equal partners in this business and I don't speak for him."

But after seeing how he squared up to Hagen, Trammel knew Butch Keeling was spoiling for a fight. And if his reputation was to be believed, he would be a welcome addition. "Don't worry about details. Just get Charlie to post his men on those walls like I told you. And hope they give us something to shoot at."

After dropping the deer, Bessler was glad Clay had not made a fuss about building two fires in two different places.

He dug out a hole and placed rocks around the first one. A large rock above it helped disburse some of the smoke. It was large enough to cook the deer meat, but not enough to alert the station to their exact location.

After they had eaten their full, Bessler led their horses to a second spot closer to the station walls, where he proceeded to build a much larger fire in a clearing. He placed their saddles around it to make it look more like they had decided to bed down there.

But this fire was not for cooking meat. It was meant to bring prey to them.

From behind a nearby log, Bessler kept his voice low as he explained his plan to Clay. "Our bellies are full and, by now, so are there's. They know we've got them trapped in there, and it's only a matter of time before they try to do something about it. They'll be looking for us, and this fire is close enough to the wall for the smoke to show them where we are. Or at least where we want them to think we are."

Clay did not appear to be convinced. "You fooled them once back at the ridgeline, Frank. Trammel's a crafty one. He won't fall for the same thing twice."

"I don't need him to, but one of those coachmen might. Maybe they'll send out the station agent to look it over. Whoever they send will be walking right into our trap."

"And if they don't send anyone at all?"

Bessler had already thought that part out ahead. "Then we'll use it as a distraction while we work our way around to the gates. They'll try to sneak out, maybe even tonight, and head around the other side toward Denver. They'll think we're right here. They won't expect us to be waiting for them."

Clay looked as if he had plenty to say on the subject, but their conversation back on the road had caused him to hold his tongue. Looking down the twin barrels of a shotgun tended to make a man more cautious with his words. "We've got nothing else to do but wait, so it's as good a plan as any."

Bessler reached inside his coat and handed the coach gun to him. "Don't fire until I tell you to."

Clay took the gun, cracked it open, and checked the cartridges inside. "It's loaded. I guess you've decided to trust me."

Not on your life, Bessler thought. "Just follow my lead and try not so shoot me by accident."

Clay snapped the shotgun shut. "I wouldn't dream of it."

Bessler motioned for him to be quiet when he heard the unmistakable sound of a branch cracking nearby. It could have been an animal or one of the men from the station. Only time would tell which.

Bessler took hold of his rifle and closed his eyes as he listened to what the overgrowth might tell him about who was out there. Another snap, only this one was much closer.

He opened his eyes and saw Clay had remained motionless beside him.

A rustle of leaves told him it was probably just an animal.

But the sound of a rock striking a tree told him it was human.

Bessler placed a hand on Clay's shoulder, willing him to remain calm.

More sounds of rustling grew louder. The rock had been

a test to see if they might panic and shoot. Whoever it was had decided to investigate the campsite. Bessler would make sure their curiosity would cost them dearly.

Clay pointed to a spot in the brush that shook. Bessler peered at the spot and saw a dark mass within the leaves. He held up a finger to signal Clay to wait. He could easily hit the figure from this distance but first wanted to be certain he was alone.

He took a quick look around to see if anyone else was in the overgrowth with them. He could not see anyone, but that did not mean they were not there.

Bessler brought his rifle to his shoulder and aimed at the dark mass in the bushes. If it moved again, he would shoot.

The shadow shifted to the left.

Bessler fired.

The shadow dropped as the area around them erupted with the sound of squawking birds taking flight at the sound of gunfire. Bessler kept his aim steady as several shots rang out from their right.

Clay ducked behind the log but remained ready to shoot as a bullet struck a tree next to them, sending splinters of bark and wood on top of them.

The shooter made no secret of his movements now as Bessler heard a great thrashing through the overgrowth. Whoever it was had begun to move away from them and back toward the station.

Bessler looked for something to shoot at, but no target presented itself. The lawyer did not want to fire a second time out of fear he would mark their location. When he heard boots running along the compact dirt by the walls, he knew the man had escaped.

And although there still might be another man hiding nearby, Bessler's instincts told him it was all clear.

He was about to investigate what he had shot at when

Clay surprised him by saying, "I'll go. You're a better shot than me. Cover me."

Bessler remembered he still had a bullet in his calf, but it did not prevent Lucien Clay from climbing over the log and slowly hobbling over toward where the dark mass had been. He moved at a crouch as he limped to the spot. Bessler kept his ears sharp and his rifle ready to fire at the slightest sound. He would not put it past Trammel to have a second man waiting to ambush them.

He watched Clay bend with great difficulty before he limped back into the clearing. He was carrying a horse blanket.

Bessler stood as his partner allowed the blanket to drop open. "Good shot, Frank. Too bad it wasn't one of them."

Bessler walked over and took the heavy blanket from him. "Smart, Trammel. Real smart. We'll just have to be smarter. And next time, we will be."

CHAPTER 28

Trammel was holding the horse in place when Buck Keeling climbed back over the wall.

"Charlie's Mexicans were right about where the fire was," Keeling said when he reached the ground. "It was too good to be true, but I'm glad we checked it out. He was lying out there waiting for us, just like you said he'd be."

Trammel could not take all the credit. "That blanket was a nice touch, Tucker. Gave them something to shoot at besides old Butch here."

"I've pulled that old trick before," Cobb said. "I'd rather lose a blanket than a man. At least we know they're still out there waiting for us."

But Trammel already knew that. "Did you see where they were hiding?"

"They only shot once," Butch said as he patted the dust from his knees, "so I couldn't tell for certain. They're getting smarter and more careful."

Trammel put together what he had learned about Bessler and Clay since leaving Laramie. "That shot sounded like it came from a rifle. Back at the jail, Doc Carson said Bessler kept a coach gun trained on him the whole time. I've seen him carry a pistol. That means they have at least three guns between them. He only wasted one shot on our ruse,

THIS MAN MUST DIE 271

so we've got to believe they've still got plenty of rounds left. The three of us plus Hawkeye can walk around well enough, but Hagen's out. We'll have to find another use for him. I sure wish he was able to move around better. The odds would be in our favor if he was."

"Too bad we can't hurt them with words," Keeling observed. "That boy has the sharpest mouth I've ever seen."

Trammel thought he might be onto something. "Maybe he can. Come on, let's see how he's doing."

The three of them walked back into the main building. This station was like several other station buildings Trammel had seen before. The main dining room was to the left, where a large iron stove stood in the corner. It provided warmth in the colder months and a place where Charlie prepared meals for customers.

To the right was a room with ten beds where travelers could sleep. It was a far cry from the luxury Adam Hagen sought to offer his guests in Laramie but served its purpose.

Trammel entered the dining room where Charlie had untied the branches Trammel and Hawkeye had bound around his knee. Hagen gripped the armrests of his chair tightly as Charlie gingerly worked the leg.

Cobb helped himself to a mug of coffee on the dining table. "What's the verdict, Charlie?"

"I know horses better than humans," Charlie said as he slowly raised Hagen's leg until it was straight, "but a knee's not much different from a fetlock. It doesn't feel broken, though the muscle around it is swollen."

Hagen tensed as he gripped the armrests even tighter. "It sure hurts like it's broken. Just don't take me out back and shoot me."

"I don't think we could spare the bullet," Charlie said. "No cause to, either. I'd say you should stay on it as much as you can. Keep bending it so it doesn't lock up on you. It should get better in a couple of days."

Charlie got up. "At least that's what I'd do if you were one of my horses."

"How encouraging." Hagen rolled down his pants leg and slowly began to flex his knee. "Though I have to say it feels better now that it's not bound up. But enough about me. How'd your hunting go, Butch?"

"Got shot at, but they missed me," Keeling said as he helped himself to some coffee. "They're still out there, though."

"I could've told you that before you left. Clay won't budge until he gets his money. He'd rather die than lose it."

Cobb said, "Then he's in for quite a disappointment, because he's not getting it. That money's bound for Denver and I'm getting paid to see that it gets there. If he wants it after that, he can take it up with the bank."

Trammel knew this was not getting them anywhere. "I was thinking you might be able to help us out, Adam."

"How?" Hagen asked. "By toddling out there and letting them shoot at me? I doubt they'll be kind enough to step out and give me a crack at them."

"By doing what you do best," Trammel said. "By setting that mouth of yours loose on them. If you can manage it, I'd like to get you over to that gate so you can talk at them some. Get under their skin. Tucker, Butch, Hawkeye, and me will be on the wall, waiting to shoot anything that moves. They've been careful up until now, but if anyone can make them lose their temper and make a mistake, it's you."

"Cute, but it won't work." Hagen pushed himself out of the chair and put some weight on his left leg. He refused any help as he took a tentative step. "I never thought I'd say this, but I can sympathize with Lucien right about now. My leg's plenty sore, but at least I don't have a bullet in it. He does, which will mean he can't get around much better than I can. If the bullet's still in his leg, he'll start getting a fever soon, if he doesn't have one already. The longer this goes on, the more this becomes a one-man act. That's not good news. Unfortunately, Bessler has already proven just how dangerous he can be on his own."

Cobb was about to argue, but Trammel held up a hand to silence him. He knew it often took Hagen a while to work around to his point. "What do you think we should do?"

"I heard you and Tucker talking before outside about splitting the load and riding off in different directions. I know Tucker said that's not possible, but there's no reason why two or three of us can't make a break for it. Trammel and I will stay here with the money while Cobb, Keeling, and Hawkeye ride back to Laramie, get Blake and some of the deputies, and bring them back here. Bessler and Clay took a winding route to get here. If you were to ride straight back to Laramie, you could make it before dark and bring them back here before breakfast."

Trammel did not like the idea of sending anyone out into waiting guns, especially given how gifted Bessler had proven himself with a rifle.

But short of any other options, it sounded like it just might work.

"I'll go," Hawkeye said. "Even if Mr. Cobb and Mr. Keeling won't, I'll do it."

Keeling said, "Tucker's always done the thinking for our outfit. I'll do whatever he says, but it should do the job."

Trammel saw all eyes in the dining room had settled on Cobb. "What do you think of it, Tucker?"

"I don't think much of it at all, but without fresh horses to break out toward Denver, it's the only chance we've got. But we'll have to leave right now if we're going to leave at all."

He spoke to Charlie. "Have your men get three of the best horses you have saddled and ready to ride. Do it fast. Our lives depend on it."

The station master ran outside and began to give orders in Spanish to the two men on top of the walls.

Trammel was beginning to think this might be a good idea after all. "Hawkeye, I want a count of every bullet we've got. Take only what you need. We might have to use the rest of it to defend this place. Bessler and Clay will know something's wrong when you tear out of here."

Hawkeye was about to go to the barn to get their saddle-bags when Charlie blocked his way. "It doesn't look like anyone's going anywhere, Sheriff. We have company. Come look. Quick!"

Charlie did not need to tell Trammel to hurry. He ignored the growing ache of his right side as he followed the station master to the adobe stairs that led up to the narrow ledge along the top of the wall.

When he got there, one of the Mexican stable hands was pointing beyond to the road that led to the station.

Trammel gripped the top of the wall when he saw no fewer than ten riders coming their way. And although they were still too far to see their faces clearly, Trammel recognized the stout lead rider with the dark beard flecked with silver and gray.

Cobb and Keeling joined him on the narrow ledge.

"No," Cobb said as the riders came into view. "It can't be."

But Trammel knew it was true. "Ben Fletcher and his men. Looks like they've come to get their money after all."

Fletcher brought his horse to a stop in the middle of the road as his men broke into two lines on either side of him. They rode past him as they enveloped the walls of the station.

"Looks like we're surrounded," Trammel said.

"I make ten of them," Cobb said. "With Bessler and Clay, that's an even dozen."

Keeling had brought his rifle with him and began to aim it down at Fletcher. "Let's cut the odds in our favor."

Trammel grabbed the barrel to keep him from raising it. "Not yet. It might come to that, but let's see what they do first."

Fletcher looked up and tipped his hat to Trammel before riding into the overgrowth.

Butch Keeling pulled his rifle free from Trammel's grip. "You're going to regret not letting me kill that man."

But Trammel already had regrets. "I should've done it myself when I had the chance. You'd best get down there with Hawkeye and divvy up those bullets. They'll be making their first run at us come nightfall and we'll need to be ready."

Trammel was left alone at the top of the wall, suddenly feeling like the last man on earth.

CHAPTER 29

Ben Fletcher enjoyed the look on Frank Bessler's face when he rode his horse through the overgrowth. It was a curious mixture of surprise and anger. He counted himself lucky. Not many men had lived after seeing that expression on Bessler.

The rancher climbed down from the saddle and extended a beefy hand to the lawyer. "Good to see you again, Frank, though you don't look happy to see me."

Bessler looked at the hand but did not take it. He kept his flat against the holster on his hip. "What are you doing here, Ben?"

"Why, I just came to get all that money you promised me in your letter," Fletcher said. "You remember? The part where you promised me twenty-five percent of whatever you took off that stage?"

"And I was intending on getting it to you," Bessler said. "But things didn't go as I planned."

"I saw that," Fletcher said. "When I got back to my place this morning, I didn't see any money, but I found Trammel and Hagen on my spread. The years have not been kind, Frank. I can remember a time when you could've taken a stage all by yourself and did on more than one occasion."

Bessler's eyes narrowed. "The stage driver got spooked

and rode past the house. We chased them, but they got away. It's been known to happen."

Ben Fletcher liked seeing Bessler embarrassed. The lawyer had gotten him out of plenty of trouble back when they rode together in Texas and Indian Territory. He had gotten Fletcher into plenty of trouble, too, but Fletcher had forgotten all that once Bessler sprang him from prison.

Fletcher kept teasing him. "But you've always been such a careful boy, Frank. And I was counting on that money. I only let you use my place for the ambush because you were so sure you could take that stage easy enough. Now, I'm not only out of money I was counting on having, but my name is at stake. What do you think will happen to me if that sheriff and that stage ever reach civilization? Cobb knows me, Frank. Trammel and Hagen, too. They'd have a warrant sworn out for my arrest before they had the saddles off their horses."

Bessler's jaw tightened. "I told you I'd get you your money."

"Haven't got it yet." He made a show of looking Bessler over. "All I see is you and a skinny saloonkeeper who looks about done in." Fletcher laughed as he finally cast his eyes on Lucien Clay. "How are you doing, Lucien? You don't look so good. Still carrying Hagen's bullet in your leg?"

Clay leaned against a tree. His forehead was covered in sweat. He held a coach gun at his side as though it was an afterthought. "I remember you. You hurt one of my girls at the Rose of Tralee."

"And your bouncer made me pay handsomely for the privilege," Fletcher said. "I should've gone back and had my boys burn that place to the ground. I guess living out here for so long has softened me up as much as it has old Frank here."

Bessler pounded his holster in frustration. "I had a plan,

Ben. There's only one way they can get that coach out of the station, and we were going to ambush them as soon as they made a break for it."

Fletcher had figured as much when he saw the wooden station doors shut on the ride there. "Sounds like a good plan. Getting in there would be tough for only one man. Old Charlie Ramirez knew what he was doing when he built that place. Ever been inside?"

"Can't say as I've had the pleasure."

Fletcher knelt, picked up a stick, and began to trace a box in the dirt. "This is the wall. Made of adobe, and thick enough to stop anything you can throw at it short of a cannon ball, and we don't have any cannons. Can't burn it, either. A couple of boys tried that a few years ago and it didn't do a thing."

He drew smaller squares in the middle of the box. "The station building is here, and the stables are over here. None of them are against the wall, and there's nothing between the walls and the buildings except wide-open ground. Even if you managed to climb over it, you'd land without cover." He drew a large "X" through the box. "Like I said, Charlie knew what he was doing when he built the place. But we've got one thing in our favor beside numbers. The ledge that runs along the top is very narrow. Too narrow for them to put too many men up there at once and not enough space for them to fire from if they do."

But Bessler had not been following his drawing. "That's why we were going to hit them as soon as they made a run for it."

"You mentioned that." Fletcher tossed the stick aside as he stood up. "That could take days. Longer than you'll want to wait, and longer than that pimp you brought with you has. He'll be dead by this time tomorrow morning unless one of my boys pulls that bullet out of him."

Clay mumbled something before his body sagged and he collapsed to the ground.

Fletcher laughed. "I'll be more than happy to shoot him if you want. Or cut his throat, if you want to save the bullet. Free of charge, for old time's sake."

Bessler knelt beside Clay and placed the back of his hand against the fallen man's forehead. "He's burning up. He was fine a minute ago."

"That's the lead in him. Let him die. We don't need him anymore. One man won't make a difference for what we need to do."

"I need him alive," Bessler said as he turned Clay over onto his stomach. "It won't do me any good if he's dead."

Fletcher laughed again. "Frank Bessler and his blessed reputation. Still worrying about what people think of you. If that stage in there is half as rich as you claimed in your letter, you'll have enough money to buy whatever kind of reputation you want."

Bessler balled his hand into a fist and pounded the dirt. "A reputation is all a man has in this world. Help him, Ben. Or get me some whiskey to clean my knife and I'll do it. You owe me that much."

"After you put me in this position, I don't owe you any-thing." But Fletcher knew he might need a man of Bessler's skills to get his money, so he relented. "Ramon! Get over here. I need you to dig a bullet out of a man's leg."

One of Fletcher's vaqueros stepped through the over-growth and picked up Clay as easily as if he were a rag doll. In Spanish, he said, "Someone's already got a fire started over there. I'll work on him, but I can't promise he'll live."

Fletcher did not expect him to. "Just get the bullet out

and burn the wound closed. It doesn't matter to me if he lives or dies."

Bessler stood up to follow the man to the fire, but Fletcher stopped him by grabbing his arm. "Let the man work, Frank. He's done this before."

Bessler looked at the hand on his arm. "You know I don't like people handling me, Ben."

The rancher let him go. He was a much bigger man, capable of killing him with one punch if he pushed him too far too fast. "And I don't like having to ride out here looking for the money you owe me. That means we're going to have to come to some arrangement."

"We've already got an arrangement. Twenty-five percent of what we take off the wagon. Aside from Clay's money, of course."

"That was for the use of my ranch," Fletcher told him. "Now that I've had to work harder for it, it's only fair that my share is larger. We split the whole thing right down the middle. Fifty-fifty."

Bessler did not even consider it. "No chance. Clay will never stand for it."

"He's in no condition to stand for anything right now," Fletcher reminded him. "He might not even last until night, and he won't if I tell my boys to finish him off." He took a step closer to Bessler. "I didn't just bring all these boys to get that money, Frank. I brought them to keep you from driving a hard bargain. If you let your temper get the better of you, I promise you'll get a hundred percent of nothing but dead. Fifty-fifty is fair." He held out his hand to him once more. "And this time, I'll be insulted if you don't take it."

Bessler scowled at the hand and at the man who was offering it.

He shook his hand. "You have yourself a deal."

"A wise decision, Frank. You always were the smartest one in the gang. Even smarter than Walt Holm."

Bessler pushed his hand away. "Now it's your turn to be clever. How do you plan on getting that money? We've lost the element of surprise."

"By the oldest way there is," Fletcher told him. "Fear."

CHAPTER 30

Trammel was still standing atop the wall, trying to get a sense of where the newcomers were located, when he watched Fletcher ride back into the middle of the road. He was alone, but Trammel knew there could be as many as ten rifles on him right now.

He eased his Peacemaker from the holster under his left shoulder and held the pistol just below the top of the wall.

"Nice morning, ain't it, Buck?" Fletcher called up to him. His voice was loud but calm.

"That's Sheriff Trammel to you, Fletcher."

"Have it your way," the rancher said. "I didn't come here to argue. I came to make a deal with you. A fair one at that."

Trammel leaned against the wall. "Let me guess. We agree to hand over the money to you and you'll let us live."

"I see you've played this game before," Fletcher answered. "And yes, that's about the long and short of what I'm proposing. You give us the money and you get to live. We don't want to kill you and we don't want you shooting any of us. I know your reputation and I've heard what you can do. I don't want blood. I just want the money. I'll even sweeten the pot for you."

Trammel thought it was almost comical. "You'll split some of it with us for our cooperation."

Fletcher grinned as he shook his head. "I'm not that generous, Sheriff, but I'll give you something just as good. I'll give you Lucien Clay."

Trammel gripped the top of the wall. He had not been expecting that.

"He means nothing to me," the rancher went on. "Less than nothing. He's in a bad way from that bullet in his leg, but I've got one of my boys tending to him now. He's already got the fever and he might not live much longer, but once my man patches him up, I'll be happy to hand him over to you. I'll even kill him if you want. My way of being neighborly and all."

Trammel realized it was a good offer. He had not come this far to protect the stagecoach. He had ridden in pursuit of Bessler and Clay. Even if he brought Clay's corpse back to town over a horse, the territory would know that Laramie was a town of law and order. The money was Cobb and Keeling's concern, not his.

He decided to test Fletcher's generosity. "What about Bessler? He's the one who sprang Clay from prison. He's a wanted man, too."

Fletcher rubbed his beard, as if he was giving it some thought. "How about this? If you agree to hand over the money right now, I'll give you Bessler as part of the bargain. That way, I won't have to split anything with him." He held up a finger. "But you'll have to give me your word on it right this instant or there's no deal."

Trammel was impressed with Fletcher. The man had a knack for getting straight to the heart of the matter. "We give you boys the gold and you and your men hand over Bessler and Clay. You ride off and go back to your ranch like nothing happened."

Fletcher offered a wide, generous smile. "I did it once and I'll do it again. What's your answer? We have a deal?"

From behind the wall, Trammel thumbed back the hammer of his pistol. "Even with everything we know about your hand in all this. You'll just let us go?"

Fletcher's broad grin faded, and Trammel had his answer.

"No deal." He raised his Peacemaker and fired twice down at the rancher. Both shots hit him in the chest, causing him to buck in the saddle before dropping to the ground.

Trammel ducked as bullets began to pelt the top of the wall as Fletcher's men called to one another to get their boss.

The sheriff knew the walls were too thick for the bullets to penetrate and slowly began to walk down the stairs to join the others.

He stopped when he saw Cobb and Keeling in the courtyard below. They were aiming Winchesters up at him.

"You made a wise decision, Sheriff," Cobb said as he began to lower his Winchester. "We'd have blasted you over the top of that wall if you'd agreed."

"You'd have tried," Hagen said as he and Hawkeye stepped out from the station building doorway. Hagen had his pistol trained on Cobb while Hawkeye had his rifle on Keeling. "But would have paid dearly for it."

Trammel tucked his Peacemaker back in the holster and patted the two men on the shoulders as he walked between them. "Save it for Bessler, boys. You'll have plenty to shoot at come dark."

Frank Bessler tried not to gloat as he stood over Fletcher's corpse as the vaqueros mourned the loss of their leader. He had warned Fletcher to be careful with Trammel. He had ignored his advice and paid the ultimate price.

Fletcher's men were sullen and unemotional as they

looked down at their fallen leader. The man who had been attending to Lucien Clay's wound when Fletcher was shot spoke first.

"What do we do now?" he asked in Spanish. "Do we stay and fight for the gold or go back to the ranch, bring the cattle to market, and go our separate ways?"

"If we take the money," one of the vaqueros said, "we don't have to go back to the ranch. We'd already be rich."

"Richer than you imagined." Bessler surprised them by speaking Spanish. He hardly considered himself a linguist, but he had managed to pick up enough of the language to get by. "I had a deal with Mr. Fletcher. A seventy-thirty split. I offer the same to any man who agrees to help me get that money."

Each of the ten men said they were with Bessler.

The first vaquero who had spoken told the men to get back to their positions around the station. Once they broke away to carry out his order, the man approached Bessler. "My name is Ramon. I run the crew at the Fletcher place."

The two men did not bother shaking hands. "You were the man who treated my friend Lucien. How is he?"

"He is very sick, señor. His leg is on fire."

"They seem like capable men. Are they?"

"For this kind of work? Yes. Many of them have done this kind of thing before. It will not be easy to get the money, but it is not impossible."

Bessler already had an idea about how they could get inside, but he was eager to hear what Ramon thought. "What's your plan?"

"The wooden gate is the only weakness in the station. I say we burn them with some of the lamp oil Mr. Fletcher told us to bring."

"It's not subtle," Bessler said, "but it's the only thing I can think of that might work."

"The doors will burn and send smoke inside the station if the wind blows the right way, but we will not attack the station from the front. As the men try to put out the fire, we can use the smoke as a distraction while we climb over the walls, kill the gringos inside, and take the money."

Bessler thought waiting for them to make a run for it was a better plan, but there was something to be said for a more direct approach. Another coach or set of travelers could be due to come to the station at any moment. And although he was sure the vaqueros could handle anyone who happened by, every encounter posed its own risk. Fletcher had said it was difficult for men in the station to fire down at them from the walls, but Trammel had just proven it was not impossible.

"There are five men in there who can fight," Bessler reminded him, "and that doesn't include whoever's working in there."

"Don't worry about the workers." Ramon grinned. "I know Charlie Ramirez. He will not risk his life or the lives of his cousins. They will live here long after the gringos leave. They will hide in the stables with the horses and only come out when the shooting stops. We have nothing to fear from them."

Bessler liked the vaquero's bravado, but it could prove to be dangerous. "You saw what Trammel can do. He won't make it easy. The men with him are good fighters. They will not just give up the money."

"But they will give it up, señor, and we will be rich. The gringos are fighting to defend something that does not belong to them. My men will fight for the future that money will give them. It is very difficult to kill such a dream."

Bessler still did not think much of Ramon or his men.

But perhaps they could distract Trammel, Hagen, and the others just long enough to give him a chance at grabbing the money. Even if they all died in the attempt, it was a risk Bessler was willing to take because it cost him nothing.

But he thought of a way he might be able to improve his chances a bit. "I've got an idea that might tilt this in our favor."

CHAPTER 31

Trammel joined Hagen and Hawkeye on the porch of the station building. Hawkeye leaned against a porch post as he kept an eye on the doorway while Hagen sat on the edge of the porch while he slowly flexed his sore leg.

Hagen grimaced through the pain. "I thought that station keeper was out of his mind when he told me the leg wasn't broken, but the more I walk around, the more I think he's right. It's starting to feel better already."

"Glad I was wrong." He was happy Hagen was not as hurt as he had first believed, but he had other concerns. "Thanks for your help just now. Things got messy with Cobb and Keeling."

"We weren't going to let them shoot you, boss," Hawkeye said as he watched the station building. "Still won't."

"I can't say I hold it against them," Hagen said. "You're out here to bring in Bessler and Clay. Tucker and Butch are here to protect the money. It's understandable there'd be conflict. The key is to find a way to resolve it."

Trammel had not needed Hagen to tell him that. "I guess this is what you army fellas call a siege. Ever been in one before?"

"A couple," Hagen told him. "Real nasty business. They

can drag on for a while, and things can get mighty ugly when they do. I've always thought the best medicine was to end them before they can get started. You had the same inclination when you let Butch climb over the wall and look around when Charlie's men spotted that smoke. You should keep following that instinct now."

Trammel was not sure what he was getting at. "How?"

Hagen nodded toward the wooden gates. "Our predicament now isn't all that much different from with the prisoners back in Laramie. They made a break for it when they got the chance, and we should do the same now. Bessler's going to try to burn that gate, and when he does, we'll be trapped in here. They're too smart to come in right away unless they climb over the walls while it's burning. But if we move now, before they're set, we might stand a chance of getting away."

Trammel's hopes sagged. He thought Hagen had been spending his time thinking of something different. "Charlie said he's only got two horses fit for pulling the stage and Cobb agrees with him. Our horses aren't draft horses, Adam. They wouldn't get far."

"We don't need them to get far," Hagen said. "Just far enough to give us a fighting chance before this mess turns into a massacre. You've tried to shoot men from horseback. It's not as easy to do as the dime novels back East make it sound. The next station is about twenty miles from here, but the Fletcher spread is less than ten. I'd wager there are plenty of good horses there. And we'd have plenty of room to make a stand. I say it's worth the chance to make a run for it."

Charlie Ramirez came out of the station building and sat down on the porch next to Hagen.

"Eavesdropping is a nasty habit," Hagen told him.

"My station, my rules," the Mexican said. "It just so

happens I was listening to what you said just now, and it makes sense. I don't want my place burned any more than you boys want to get trapped in here. It'll turn into the Alamo, which was a good day for Mexico but a bad day for everyone inside."

Trammel was encouraged. Maybe Hagen's idea was not so bad after all. "You got any horses that could make it that far?"

Charlie scratched his head as he thought about it. "Now that they've had some rest, maybe. I couldn't do it, and neither could either of you, but I've witnessed Tucker Cobb get more out of an animal than any other stage driver I've ever seen. If it can be done, he can do it."

Charlie held up a stubby finger. "You boys might make Fletcher's place, but that'll be as far as they'll take you tonight. I'm not responsible if one or all of them falters, or what happens to you boys once you get there. Hole up and keep your heads down. They won't be able to take you anywhere else for another day at most."

Tucker Cobb and Butch joined them on the porch. "You boys are doing a lot of talking about what I can and can't do. Thought it was time I set you straight. We're not going to the Fletcher spread. The Frontier Overland Company only goes in one direction, and that's straight ahead. We're not going to backtrack to land those boys know better than we do and I'm not getting trapped in a dead man's house. I've got a schedule to keep, and I intend on keeping it. So, we're going to break out of here just like you boys have been saying, but we're going out there, banking left and heading on to English Station to the south. And we're going to do it right now with the horses we've got."

Keeling spoke to Charlie. "Pick out six of the best horses you think can make the trip and have your men hook them up to the stage. We're going to bust out of here as soon as possible and—"

Keeling stopped talking when he heard a man from beyond the walls begin to shout in Spanish. Trammel had never learned the language, but judging by Charlie's expression, whatever the man was saying wasn't good.

"It's Ramon, Fletcher's top hand," Charlie said. "He's not speaking to you, but to me and my cousins. He's saying we don't have to die for you. That if we come out right now, we won't be harmed. They're offering us a hundred dollars after they take the money. They're offering us two hundred dollars if we kill you right now. We can ride back home with them as rich men. It's a generous offer."

Charlie fell silent as he listened to more of Ramon's edict. "Now he's saying that if we don't come out, they'll not only kill us but all our family still in Mexico." Charlie stopped listening. "I don't have to tell you the details. He's describing some very nasty things."

Keeling said, "Best get them busy, Charlie. They're liable to get spooked if you don't."

Charlie got to his feet and beckoned his cousins to him. As Ramon kept making threats, the three men began to lead horses from the corral.

Trammel knew it was almost time to go. "Everyone had better make sure your guns are loaded and you've got plenty of bullets ready for reloading. Don't waste shots when we tear out of here. You won't hit anything anyway. Tucker and Butch will be on the wagon. Hagen, Hawkeye, and I will ride alongside. Keep your head down and your horse moving. Tucker, we'll follow your lead south. Just make sure you take the straightest route between here and English Station."

"I don't need you or any other city boy telling me how

to handle a team," Cobb said. "You boys just do your best to keep up."

He stepped down from the porch and began helping Charlie and his cousins with the horses.

"Don't mind him," Keeling said. "He always gets like this before a dangerous run. If we can make those two turns out of here without getting shot, we might have a chance. Catch them flat-footed and off their horses. I'll do my best to whittle them down some once we start, but I imagine there'll still be plenty of them on us quicker than we'd like. You boys be careful. Hope to see all of you at English Station."

He surprised Trammel by stopping long enough to offer his hand to him. "No hard feelings, Sheriff. About that business just now."

Trammel shook the shotgun rider's hand. "None at all, Butch."

He joined the other men as they began to bring the horses to the stage.

"What a lovely sentiment." Adam smiled. "A bit of brotherly love to take with us on the task ahead."

Trammel shook his head as he went inside to gather his things. Hagen could ruin any occasion. "Hawkeye, help get our horses ready and cinch those saddles tight. We've got some hard riding ahead of us."

But Trammel stopped when he caught the unmistakable odor of burning wood.

Hagen got to his feet as Hawkeye pointed toward whisps of smoke that had begun to seep beneath the wooden gate. "Looks like they've started, Sheriff."

"Guess that means we'd better hurry up. Get those horses ready. Now!"

* * *

Ramon Ochoa did not trust the gringo Bessler. He was a big man with nasty eyes that never settled anywhere for long.

But as he watched the fire take hold on the station doors, he knew the plan would work. If the Mexicans inside had not been frightened before the fire, they certainly would be now. They were peasants, after all, and valued their lives above all. They would not risk death—and their families—for a few gringos who probably did not even know their names.

Ramon got on his horse and began to ride a circuit around the station walls. "We're going over the walls," he told them as he passed. "Get ready to move when I tell you."

He had just managed to complete his circle when he saw Lucien Clay had gotten to his feet and begun to limp through the overgrowth. He had almost forgotten about the gray-haired man with the hole full of poison in his leg. The infection from his wound had already spread through his leg. He would probably be dead before morning, if he lasted that long. Had he been a generous man, Ramon might have killed him, but he needed his bullets for more important targets.

He rode back to the front of the station and saw the smoke beginning to grow thicker as it spilled over the wall. In a few moments, the smoke would be thick enough to blind or choke anyone inside and it would be time for his men to make their move.

Fletcher had been a man willing to take risks. He would have sent all ten of them over the wall, hoping to overwhelm the gringos. Ramon would be much more cautious. He would send only five men over the wall and keep five outside with him to handle anyone who tried to escape. He imagined Bessler would do whatever he wanted. Ramon would be sure to deal with him as soon as the shooting started, or if he ceased to serve a purpose.

Ramon heard shouting from inside the station and knew his plan was beginning to work. The gringos were terrified by the fire and were undoubtedly doing their best to try to put it out. He would have his men move inside soon.

He rounded the corner to the front, but his horse shied away from the heat and the flame just as the burning wooden doors flew open. Several horses spilled out, panicked by the inferno raging behind them. Bessler shouted curses as a six-horse team barreled between the burning doors and quickly rounded the corner to the left.

Ramon had just gotten his mount under control as three riders burst out from the station and followed the coach. He did not bother shooting at them as his horse was bucking too hard from the excitement to get a decent shot.

He raised his voice over the shouts of his men, telling them, "They're getting away! Get on your horses! After them! After the money!"

He did not see any sign of Bessler as he brought his horse around and finally began chasing after the escaping coach.

His vaqueros stopped firing on his orders and ran to their horses as Ramon sped by. The last rider was the large man he had seen Fletcher talking to back at the ranch. The sheriff he had called Trammel. He was riding slower than the others and was a much easier target. He would be the first to fall.

Ramon followed him as he disappeared around the back of the station walls. He brought his horse into a gallop in pursuit of the fleeing men. The coach was moving much faster than he had thought capable, and two riders on either side of it struggled to keep pace. Trammel brought up the rear.

Ramon had always told his vaqueros that trying to shoot

a man from a galloping horse was a waste of a good bullet. But Trammel presented such a large, slow target that he could not resist. He drew his revolver and began to take careful aim at the man in front of him.

Trammel turned in the saddle and leveled his Peace-maker in his direction before firing. Ramon did not have time to react before the lead bullet struck him in the chest. Reflexes made him pull back hard on the reins and sent his horse crashing to the ground amid a cloud of dust and dirt.

Ramon was flat on his back as his men sped past him. He thought one of them was Bessler, but he could not be sure. He watched his own horse get back to its feet and trot away.

He searched for his wound and found a bleeding hole in the center of his chest. He did not feel any pain, but he could not feel his legs, either. His lungs felt heavy, as if they were filling up with liquid. He knew he was dead. As dead as Lucien Clay soon would be.

He heard a horse draw to a stop nearby and hoped one of his men had decided to come back for him. Dying was a nasty business and he did not like the idea of slipping away alone.

He saw the outline of a man against the sun. He had long gray hair, and Ramon wondered if it might be one of the angels his *abuela* had told him about when he was a boy.

But when the man stooped to take his pistol from him, Ramon Ochoa knew this was no angel. It was the man he had just seen wandering through the overgrowth. The dead man Lucien Clay.

Beads of sweat dripped from his brow as he took the gun and hobbled back to his horse. Ramon would have pleaded with him to kill him had he been able to speak, but his lungs were so full. So heavy.

He allowed his head to drop to the dirt as he watched the man ride away and wondered if they might meet again soon.

CHAPTER 32

Trammel kept his head down as he was peppered by chunks of earth as he trailed behind the coach. He steered his horse to the right and kept the animal running.

Hawkeye was moving at a dead gallop in front of him, while Hagen was off to the left. Cobb was up in the wagon box of the coach, snapping the reins as he whipped every ounce of speed out of the six-horse team making a mad dash for English Station. If one of those tired horses took a wrong step, the whole stage would be wrecked.

He saw Butch Keeling climb out onto the top of the coach with his rifle in hand. "Here they come, boys. Hot on our heels!"

Trammel had never been in this situation before and looked toward Hagen to see what he did next.

"Keep going!" the gambler shouted back. "We'll try to slow them up."

Trammel watched Hagen slowly pull on the reins, and Hawkeye followed suit. Trammel sped past him as he tried to gradually slow his horse's momentum. He was far from a capable rider and did not want to risk being thrown.

By the time he managed to bring his horse around, Keeling had begun firing from the coach.

Hagen's horse had stopped. He had pulled his rifle and

was aiming back at the men speeding toward them. Trammel kept his pistol in hand and counted nine of them in pursuit and closing fast.

Hawkeye was riding toward them and held his rifle against his shoulder with one hand. He fired as Hagen did, and two riders on the edges fell from the saddle. Trammel could not allow his deputy to ride alone.

Seven left.

Trammel's horse would not grow still, so he slapped his heels into its sides and got it running again. He ducked as the lead vaquero shot at him, though the bullet sailed past him. Trammel returned fire, but his bullet, too, went wide.

The distance between them closed fast as the bandit shot at him once more. Trammel thought he had his horse's gait timed well enough and placed his next shot more carefully. A red stream passed from the charging rider's back, causing him to drop his rifle and continue riding past him.

Trammel kept his eyes on the riders coming his way as Hawkeye and Adam each cut another man down on their respective sides.

Four left.

Trammel saw Hawkeye drop his shotgun as he reached for his pistol. The sheriff watched his young deputy fumble the grab and drop the pistol. He tried to stop his horse to retrieve it when a rider rammed his horse into Hawkeye's. It was only then that Trammel realized that rider was Frank Bessler.

Bessler's mount was stunned by the impact, and he struggled to maintain his seat in the saddle. Trammel cut loose with a savage yell and began to fire as he sped toward him.

Two of his rounds hit Bessler's horse, causing it to buck and scream. Bessler held on to the reins with both hands as Trammel's gun clicked empty. He swiped at the man as he sped by but missed. By the time he reined in, Trammel saw Bessler climb down just as the horse collapsed beneath him.

Trammel dropped his Peacemaker and grabbed the Winchester tucked beneath his right leg. He saw Hawkeye had just gotten to his feet as Bessler moved toward him.

"Bessler!" Trammel said as he dropped from the saddle and brought his rifle to his shoulder. "Let him go."

Trammel fired as the lawyer balled his fist and delivered a roundhouse right to Hawkeye's jaw.

The boy staggered back a few feet before he fell. Trammel had rushed the shot and missed.

Bessler turned and began running at him.

Another shot from Hagen caused a vaquero to fall from the saddle and land on the ground just in front of Trammel, spoiling his shot.

Bessler barreled into Trammel with enough force to make him drop his rifle as the two of them tumbled to the ground. His chest burned with pain renewed as Bessler rolled away.

"I've had just about as much of you as I can take, Trammel!" Bessler shouted as he kicked at the sheriff's head.

But Trammel managed to roll away and pushed himself to his feet. Bessler tackled him again, though this time did not roll away. He grabbed Trammel's buckskin shirt with his left hand and belted him with a nasty right. Trammel heard his neckbones crack from the impact.

Bessler pulled him up by the shirt again and brought back his right hand to deliver another blow. But Trammel blocked it with his left arm and dug his right thumb into Bessler's eye.

The outlaw lawyer's grip on his shirt slipped as he batted Trammel's hand away. The sheriff grabbed at Bessler's neck with his left, but the big man's neck was too thick for him to get a decent hold.

Trammel summoned all his remaining strength to bring his right knee hard into Bessler's ribs, knocking him off balance as he fell over onto his side. The pain burning in his chest almost caused him to black out, but he knew Bessler would kill him if he did.

Trammel used his elbow to push himself back upright and wrapped his arms around Bessler's throat like a vice. He used the pain thundering through his chest to squeeze his neck that much tighter. The lawyer struck back at him with large heavy hands that struck his temple and almost made him lose consciousness.

But Trammel did not pass out and he did not let go. He held on as he remembered Doc Carson's frightened face. As he remembered Deputy Hal Haid lying dead in the gutter following the prison break Bessler had planned. As he remembered the Ennisville bartender's face as he tried to smother him in his sleep.

He tightened his grip and continued to squeeze harder as if his life depended on it because he knew it did. Bessler's blows grew weaker and slower the longer Trammel held on until his arms went slack.

Trammel looked up when Hagen yelled at him. "Let him go, Buck. He's out cold, if he's not already dead.

Trammel slowly released his lock around Bessler's neck and pushed him away, allowing the unconscious man to flop to the ground. Much to Trammel's disappointment, he appeared to still be breathing.

"I'd better go check on Hawkeye," Hagen said as he began to limp toward the fallen deputy. "Bessler hit him mighty hard."

But Trammel saw a more immediate threat in the form

of another rider approaching them from the direction of the station. "We've got a straggler."

Hagen forgot about Hawkeye and joined him in looking at the last rider coming toward them. A painfully thin, gray-haired man was slumped forward in the saddle. The horse was taking its time loping along, more interested in the grass on the ground than the rider on its back.

"That's Clay," Trammel said as he struggled to get to his feet.

"It surely is." Hagen raised the rifle to his shoulder. "This is almost too easy."

Trammel grabbed the barrel and forced it down. "Don't waste the bullet. He might already be dead."

Hagen tried to pull the rifle free but failed. "And if he's still alive?"

Trammel took the rifle from his friend. "Then he doesn't look like he'll be for long. Go check on Hawkeye. I'll take care of Clay."

Hagen let him have the rifle but limped toward the lumbering horse. Trammel went with him.

They caught up to Clay several yards away. Hagen took hold of the bridle while Trammel pulled Clay down from the saddle. The escaped convict was mumbling to himself, his clothes damp with sweat.

Hagen looked down at the dried blood on Clay's pants leg. "That's just about the best thing I've seen all day."

Trammel placed the back of his hand against Clay's forehead and quickly pulled it away. "He's got a bad fever. That wound's probably infected. We'd better get him back to Charlie's place to get tended to."

"Why?" Hagen asked. "You don't mean to save him, do you? Not after all this. All he's done?"

"I rode out here to give him justice, and that's what I'm going to do by bringing him back to Laramie. I don't care if he lives or dies, but that's what I'm going to do. Bessler, too."

Hagen kept holding on to the horse's bridle as Trammel lifted Clay and dumped him over the saddle. He uncoiled the rope and used it to tie Clay's hands and feet beneath the barrel of the horse. Hagen handed Trammel his knife so he could cut the rope.

Trammel stood up and braced himself against the horse. His chest ached and he felt dizzy. Some blood from his wounds had begun to seep through his buckskin shirt.

Hagen said, "You're in no shape for this, Steve. Just shoot Bessler and leave him here. The judge is only going to hang him anyway."

"That's what judges are for." Trammel shook off his dizziness and took a moment to look around them. The ground was littered with Fletcher's men who had been chasing the wagon. Their horses mingled with Trammel's and Hagen's, unbothered by the carnage around them. Sometimes, Trammel envied animals more than humans.

"Doesn't seem right, does it?" Trammel said aloud. "All this death over a coach full of gold."

"Save the sentiment for church." Hagen gestured at Bessler. "Your sparring partner is waking up. Unless you're anxious for a rematch, I say we grab one of these stray horses and truss him up like you did Clay. He's liable to be a lot less cooperative than Lucien."

Trammel coiled the remaining part of the rope as he headed toward Bessler. "Probably going to need more rope."

Hagen smiled as he hobbled behind Trammel, pulling the horse with him. "A bullet would be easier."

CHAPTER 33

Tucker Cobb decided the events of the day were good enough reason to break a cardinal rule of the Frontier Overland Company. With their coach secure at English Station, the two coachmen rode back to Claro Station to check on Trammel, Hagen, and Hawkeye.

They rode through the patch of ground where the men of Laramie had cut down Fletcher's vaqueros. Bodies littered the ground, stripped of guns, rifles, gun belts, and bullets.

"Looks like Trammel and Hagen made it."

Tucker was not surprised. "Their type always does."

Butch leaned over to look at one of the dead men in the grass. "I'd say Charlie picked them clean. Guess he took the horses back to his station, too."

"They looked like fine animals," Cobb said. "I'm sure they'll fetch a fair price. The guns, too. Can't begrudge a man making a profit, especially after they cost him a pair of good doors."

Butch rode beside his partner in silence. Neither man thought to take off their hat to honor the men who had fallen here. They had killed the four riders Hagen and Trammel missed. They had gathered up their horses, but not their pistols. Tucker would be sure to do that before they rode on to Denver the next morning. The company could use all the money they could get.

"You decide if you're gonna tell the sheriff the bad news we got back at English Station?" Butch asked.

Tucker had been thinking about nothing else until they came upon the field of dead men. It was a difficult thing to tell a man the life he had known was over. Tucker had been forced to start over again several times in his life, but that was the cost of life on the frontier. Freedom in exchange for certainty. He had no regrets.

"He's tough enough to take it," Tucker said. "It's best if he hears it from friends rather than a stranger."

"We ain't exactly his friends," Butch said. "We were fixing to shoot him, if you'll remember."

Tucker remembered. He doubted he would forget anything about that day for as long as he lived.

"Let's pick up the pace. Bad news doesn't wait on any man."

The two rode quicker, and Tucker found the journey much more enjoyable. At least no one was trying to kill them.

When they reached Claro Station, they found the scorched doors open but still standing. Charlie Ramirez and his two cousins were examining the damage.

The station master offered them a warm greeting when they saw him. "Ah, my friends! I thought you had made it."

"We didn't think we'd find you in good spirits," Butch said after they shook hands with Charlie. "Them fancy doors of yours are ruined."

"But still standing." Charlie beamed with pride. "Just like my station."

The man's cheerful disposition was why Cobb had always been fond of him. "Trammel and Hagen inside?"

"With their prisoners tied to my front porch," Charlie

told them. "Their young friend is a bit worse for wear, but he'll be fine. They're in the dining room now, enjoying a well-deserved meal. Go in and pay them your respects. I'm sure they'll be pleased to see you."

Tucker and Butch rode into the courtyard and found Bessler and Clay tied in a sitting position against two sturdy porch posts.

Bessler was tied across the middle, his hands bound behind the post. His legs were straight out in front of him and tied at the ankles. A handkerchief served as a gag to keep him quiet, though his eyes burned with rage.

Clay was tied in a similar fashion, but his chin was against his chest and his shirt looked as though someone had dunked a bucket full of water over him.

Butch was the first one to notice the condition of Clay's right leg. "Looks like his run-in with Hagen cost him a limb."

Tucker looked away when he saw Clay's right pants leg was flat. Amputations always affected him poorly, even when a man deserved it. "I just hope he lives long enough to swing."

They tied their horses to the far porch post. Bessler struggled against the ropes as he turned his head and mouthed muted curses at them as they entered the station building.

They found Trammel and Hagen sitting at the main dining table. Plates of half-empty food and a bottle of whiskey between them.

Hagen patted his mouth with a napkin as he watched the two coachmen approach. "Well, if it isn't our old friends Cobb and Keeling. A close call with death seems to suit them. They look better than when they left."

"It hasn't dulled that fancy mouth of yours any," Butch said. "Still chirping like a robin, ain't you?"

"And why shouldn't I?" Hagen asked. "Our foes are bested. The men who tried to kill us are either dead or imprisoned, and my prospects for the future have never been brighter. When word spreads about what happened here today—and I'll see to it that it does—we'll be famous. People will come from all over to shake hands with the men who survived the Carnage of Claro Station. They'll trip all over themselves waiting to meet Brave Buck Trammel and Heroic Adam Hagen. I might even have a song written in our honor."

Tucker ignored Hagen as he grabbed the bottle of tequila he knew Charlie kept hidden behind the bar for special occasions. He picked up two glasses and brought them over to Trammel's and Hagen's table. "How's your young friend? Charlie tells me he got hurt."

"Bessler hit him pretty hard," Trammel said. "He's inside now, sleeping it off. He'll be fine with some rest. How'd you boys fare with the ones who got past us?"

"We took care of them." Cobb placed the two glasses and the bottle on the table. "Butch got three and I got one who tried to climb on the coach. Say what you will about those boys, they were determined. They were probably quality hands, too. Every one of them."

Hagen finished his whiskey. "The greed for gold has brought many a man to rack and ruin. That would make a fine name for a song, wouldn't it? 'The Greed for Gold.' Somebody get me a paper and pencil. I should write this down. Could have a musical revue on my hands!"

But Tucker could feel Trammel was studying him. And he noticed the sheriff had not touched his whiskey. "Why so glum, Tucker? I didn't expect you to be singing songs like Adam here, but things aren't as bad as all that. You got your coach to English Station, didn't you?"

"Yeah. It's locked up and being guarded as we speak." He took the bottle of tequila and poured two drinks for him and Butch. Hagen shoved his empty glass toward him, and he reluctantly filled it. "You'd best drink that whiskey down, Buck. I'm afraid you're going to need it."

Trammel grew wary. "I prefer to take bad news straight, Tucker. Why don't you tell me what's gnawing at you?"

"Don't say I didn't warn you." Cobb set the bottle on the table and took a telegram from his shirt pocket. "They gave this to me after I secured my coach at English Station. They've just had a telegraph line put in." He handed the yellow paper to the sheriff. "I only wish it delivered better news."

Hagen set his glass aside as he sat up straighter in his chair. "What does it say?"

Tucker did not have the heart to tell him. "It's Trammel's news. It's up to him to share it if he wants."

He watched Trammel's expression closely as the sheriff read the telegram. He looked for a hint of emotion. Sadness. Anger. Relief. Anything that would show some emotion.

But, as he suspected, Trammel read it over a few times before refolding it and handing it back to Cobb. "Much obliged for the information, Tucker. Thanks for telling me."

Hagen looked like he was about to burst. "Well? What is it?"

Butch looked away.

Trammel said, "I got fired. The telegraph was sent to every station and telegraph office in the territory. By order of Mayor Holm and the city elders, I'm no longer sheriff of Laramie and have no official capacity whatsoever. Effective immediately. Sherwood Blake is acting sheriff now."

Hagen pounded the table, causing some of the tequila to slop over the rim of their glasses. Tucker knew that at another time, Hagen would have bemoaned the loss of good liquor. But now was not such a time.

"Holm, that miserable weasel," Hagen seethed. "I'll kill him for this. I'll gutshoot him and leave him where I find him."

"No, you won't," Trammel told him. "They hired me, and they can fire me. This star comes off just as easily as it goes on. I knew that when I took the job. They needed to blame someone for the jailbreak, and that someone is me." He took his glass of whiskey and downed it. "Can't say I hold it against them, seeing as I was the one responsible for the prison. Or at least I was until now."

Tucker saw Hagen was not ready to give up so easily. "But we rounded up all the men who escaped. And you're bringing Bessler and Clay back to face trial. I'm sure Tucker and Butch here will attest to that, won't you, boys? That ought to count for something."

Trammel set his empty glass on the table. "It counts plenty. It counts as far as the people of Laramie say it counts. Justice will be served. It doesn't say anything about serving me."

"That don't make it right," Butch said.

"Justice doesn't have to be right," Trammel answered. "It just has to be carried out. And that's exactly what I'm going to do. Star or no star. As soon as Hawkeye's fit to travel, we're bringing back Bessler and Clay. After that, I'll worry about me."

Tucker had heard of Trammel's bravery and dedication to duty before, but he had never seen it with his own two eyes. He had known many men who had worn a badge and carried a gun, but few seemed to appreciate what it truly meant. Buck Trammel was not such a man.

He held out his hand to the former sheriff and hoped he

would take it. "It's been an honor riding with you, Buck. And it might not count for much, but you have my admiration."

"And our respect," Butch added.

Trammel shook hands with both of them. "That means plenty, boys. And I appreciate it." He looked at the bottle of tequila. "And since I'm not a lawman anymore, how about you pour me some of that cactus juice."

CHAPTER 34

A large crowd gathered on Main Street as word quickly spread around Laramie that Buck Trammel and Adam Hagen had returned with Frank Bessler and Lucien Clay in tow.

Hagen rode out in front, while Hawkeye led Clay, who was barely able to sit upright in the saddle. Trammel led Bessler's horse. The big man's hands had been tied to the saddle horn, and the gag was still in his mouth. He tried to kick at the spectators who hurled curses and rotten fruit at him.

The crowd parted for Hagen and the others as they rode straight to City Hall, where Mayor Walt Holm and Sheriff Sherwood Blake stood to meet them. Blake had a Winchester set on his hip, standing guard next to the mayor.

Deputies Brillheart and Root took the reins of the prisoners and led them into the prison courtyard. Trammel was glad to see the wall was almost half rebuilt.

Hagen rode his horse close to Holm and looked down at the man from the saddle.

Blake stepped in between them. "Don't do anything stupid, Adam."

Hagen ignored him as he glared down at Holt, who would not meet his gaze. "I'm not going to kill you, Walt.

Not today. But I'm going to take everything you love away from you. Your office. Your good name. Your livelihood. I'm going to make you watch as I burn it all in front of you. I'm going to make you watch the wind carry off the ashes. That's a promise."

Hagen brought his horse around and tipped his hat to Buck. "You know where to find me."

The crowd quickly parted as Hagen rode through them.

Trammel and Hawkeye climbed down from their saddles. No one came to tend to their horses, so Hawkeye held the reins of both.

He could feel a tension run through the crowd as they waited to see what would happen next.

Blake swallowed hard as he moved between Holm and Trammel. "Same goes for you, Buck. I didn't want it to happen this way, but I won't let you lay a finger on the man."

Trammel had never doubted he could take Blake in a fight if he had to, but his quarrel was not with the acting sheriff. He spoke loudly for the benefit of the crowd as he said, "I took an oath to bring law and order to Laramie and that's what I've done. Frank Bessler and Lucien Clay have been captured and brought back to stand trial. Mr. Adam Hagen and Deputy John Hauk risked their lives and endured great danger to help me do that. This town owes them a debt."

He unpinned his sheriff's star from his bloodstained buckskin shirt and held it out to Holm. "You wanted this. Here it is."

The crowd began to jeer and curse as Holm turned and began walking up the stairs of City Hall.

Blake reached for it, but Trammel closed his hand. "You wanted it," Trammel yelled to him. "You can at least be man enough to take it from me."

Hawkeye stepped forward and threw his star on the ground. "You can have mine, too, while you're at it."

Holm stopped halfway up the stairs, as if frozen in place. He clearly felt all the eyes of the town on him. After a long moment of indecision, he kept going as curses and catcalls rose from the crowd.

Blake remained in place as Trammel watched Holm disappear inside the hall.

"Guess he doesn't want it after all," he said to Blake. "No offense to you, Sherwood, but I'm only going to give this to him."

Blake scrapped the dirt around Hawkeye's star with his boot. "Guess you haven't heard."

"I heard," Trammel told him. "I got the telegram in Claro Station the day before yesterday. Tucker Cobb was supposed to send you a telegram from English Station that I was coming back with Bessler and Clay. Didn't you get it?"

"Oh, we got it," Blake said. "And the mayor got more trouble than he was bargaining for. Seems you're a lot more popular around here than he thought. When word spread that he'd fired you, me and the boys had quite a time keeping these people out of City Hall and dragging Holm out by the scruff of his neck. He had no choice but to promise them that he'd let you keep your star. He wasn't happy about it, but that's the way it is."

Hawkeye said, "So the boss can keep his job?"

"Sure can." Blake toed the deputy's star toward him. "No reason why you can't keep yours, either. We've got enough trouble around here without having to worry about sending a man up to Blackstone now and then."

Hawkeye quickly scooped up his star and pinned it back on his shirt. "That's good news, ain't it, boss?"

The crowd that had gathered around them began to cheer as Trammel opened his hand and looked down at his star.

He had never thought he would see it again, much less still be sheriff of Laramie.

The cheers gradually unified into a single word. "Trammel. Trammel. Trammel."

Blake stepped aside and broke into a grin. "You'd better put that on, boss, or we're liable to have another riot on our hands."

The cheers rose as Trammel climbed the steps. He had never been one to seek attention or acclaim, but after everything Bessler and Clay had put him through, he had to admit it felt good to be appreciated.

The crowd cheered when he held up the star for all to see. And when he pinned it on his shirt, they threw their hats into the air.

His breath caught when he saw Emily was standing next to Blake and Hawkeye and quickly ran down the stairs to embrace her. None of the pats on the back or praises from the townspeople felt as good as her arms around him.

"Looks like you get to keep your job," Emily said.

He held her as tightly as he dared. "As long as I have you, I have everything."

TURN THE PAGE FOR AN EXCITING PREVIEW!
Smoke Jensen settled in Colorado to build a legacy for
his wife, Sally, and their family. But before the
Sugarloaf Ranch became legendary across the western
frontier, the Jensens had to survive
a Wild West infested with barbaric men who sought
fortune and glory while killing with violent glee.

**JOHNSTONE COUNTRY.
WHERE DYING AIN'T MUCH OF A LIVING.**

Building a ranch takes heart and grit. Smoke and Sally
Jensen are more than capable of meeting the challenges
of shaping the land, raising the livestock, and establishing
their brand. But Smoke wasn't always an entrepreneur.
He's more apt to settle accounts with a fast draw than a
checkbook. And when he learns his old friend Preacher
has been ambushed by outlaws, he wastes no time
saddling up and hitting the vengeance trail with his
fellow mountain men Audie and Nighthawk.

Preacher's attackers have taken over the town of
Desolation Creek, deep in Montana Territory.
Their scurrilous leader, Vernon "Venom" McFadden,
has his men harrassing terrified homesteaders and
townsfolk to get his hands on nearby property that's
rumored to be rich with gold. Smoke and his helpmates
drift into town one by one with a plan
to root out Venom's gang of prairie rats
and put the big blast on each and every one.

**National Best-selling Authors
WILLIAM W. JOHNSTONE
and J.A. Johnstone**

DESOLATION CREEK
**A Smoke Jensen Novel of the West
On sale now, wherever Pinnacle Books are sold.**
Live Free. Read Hard.
www.williamjohnstone.net

Visit us at www.kensingtonbooks.com

CHAPTER 1

When a bullet zipped past Smoke Jensen's ear, leaving a hot, crimson streak in its wake, he had a realization.

Trouble sure had a way of following him.

He hadn't come to Big Rock with anything on his mind other than taking care of his business, maybe saying hello to a few friends, chief among them Sheriff Monte Carson and Louis Longmont, and then getting on back to the Sugarloaf.

Of course, his wife, Sally, had it in mind to do some shopping, but that was harmless enough, except for the damage it did to his pocketbook. So, no reasonable explanation existed as to why he found himself smack-dab in the middle of a shooting scrape.

Or rather, *another* shooting scrape.

The last thing he wanted was trouble. He wasn't the type to just stand idly by when bullets were flying, though. He might catch one of them. Or worse, innocent folks might get shot. So, he drew his Colt with lightning speed and took aim at the man who had just emerged from the general store.

A wisp of powder smoke still curled up from the muzzle of the gun in the man's fist. He had already shifted his focus elsewhere after firing that first round. Evidently, he caught

Smoke's movement in his peripheral vision and turned his attention back in that direction. He leveled his weapon and sneered.

"I wouldn't," Smoke said.

The warning fell on deaf ears and the man's finger twitched, ready to squeeze off another shot. Smoke's keen eyes saw that, and his gun roared first.

The bullet hammered into the fella's chest, sending him backward as his feet flew from beneath him. He landed flat on his back. His fingers went slack and he released the revolver. Smoke ran to the gun and kicked it away. One quick glance told him the gesture hadn't been necessary, although erring on the side of caution was always better.

A scarlet ring was spreading on the man's dirty, tattered shirt. Dull, glassy eyes, with the life fading from them, stared up at Smoke.

"Who in the—" Smoke began, wanting to know who he had just shot, and why.

He didn't have time to finish the question as another shot rang out from inside the general store.

"Sally," he said, working to rein in the worry he felt rising in his chest. He swung his gun up, while quickly stepping away from the dead hombre, who lay sprawled out in the middle of the street. Eager to check on his wife, who'd gone inside the store a few minutes earlier, Smoke was about to close the gap between himself and the structure, when the door flew open again.

Another gunman burst onto the store's porch, spinning wildly as if trying to assess his surroundings, but not moving cautiously enough to gain a true lay of the land. This gave Smoke all the time he needed to dive behind a water trough. He reached the cover just in time as the panic-stricken gunman sent two wild shots into the air. As far as Smoke could tell, no one was hit. Most of the folks who had been on the boardwalks or in the street had scrambled for cover when the shooting started.

Just who was this fella and what was he all fired up about? Maybe, Smoke thought, he could end this without any more bloodshed. He didn't care for the fact that a fresh corpse was only a few feet away. Smoke didn't hesitate to kill when necessary, but he didn't take any pleasure in it. If he had his way, he'd never be mixed up in gunplay again.

Smoke rested his arm on the trough and drew a bead, his hand steady, his aim sure.

"Put that gun down!" he called. "No one else has to get hurt. Or worse."

A few townspeople were hustling around, trying to get out of the line of fire. Two old men who'd been sitting on a bench, enjoying the shade the boardwalk's overhanging roof offered, dove off the side and onto the ground. Smoke had to chuckle, realizing the impact had probably jarred the old-timers. They were in one piece, though, and didn't have any bullets in them as they crawled beneath the porch. Thankfully, it seemed as if everyone was out of harm's way.

Until the little girl dashed past.

Smoke hadn't even noticed her before now. She couldn't be any older than six, but might have been as young as four. She was a little thing, and scared, as she screamed for her ma. She tried to make it off the porch, but the gun-wielding hombre extended his free arm and scooped up the child, jerking her back onto the porch before Smoke could react.

The man held on to the girl tightly, using her as a shield as he swept his gun from side to side. She squirmed and kicked her legs as she continued screaming, but she had no chance of escaping the man's brutal grip.

Smoke regretted not having put a bullet into the wild-eyed varmint as soon as he laid eyes on the man. That would have ended this before he had a chance to grab that poor child.

"I'm gonna get out of here!" he yelled. "You all hear me?"

Smoke caught a glimpse of movement up the street and swiveled his head to see Sheriff Monte Carson hurrying toward the scene, with two deputies following him. Unfortunately, the crazed gunman on the porch noticed them, too, and sent a shot in their direction. Monte and the deputies instinctively split up as the bullet whistled between them. Monte took cover in one of the alcoves along the boardwalk, while the two deputies crouched behind a parked wagon.

The little girl screamed even louder after the shot, but her captor only tightened the arm he had looped around her body under her arms.

"Shut up!" he snarled at the girl. He turned his attention back to the sheriff and yelled, "Stay back! I swear I'll put a bullet in this here child's brain!"

Smoke's blood was boiling. He'd encountered some low-down, prairie scum in his day, but anyone who would hurt a child was the worst of the worst. He had to smile, though, when the girl started writhing even harder beneath the man's arm. She tried throwing her elbows back and even sent a few more kicks toward him, but his strength put an end to the struggle quickly. Still, Smoke admired her fighting spirit. He aimed to tell her as much, too. He'd get a chance, since he would never let that little girl die.

"What is it you want?" Smoke called.

He wasn't the law in Big Rock, but with the sheriff and his deputies pinned down and unable to get closer, he was in the best position to act.

"I want out of here," the gunman said. "I want to make it to my horse down yonder, climb in the saddle, and get out of town without any trouble!"

"Sure, friend," Smoke replied in an affable tone. "Just let the young'un go and you can mosey on out of here. No one will stop you."

The man's lips curled back, revealing jagged yellow teeth. "That ain't how this works. She comes with me. I'll leave her down the trail when I'm free and clear."

Smoke's back stiffened. He couldn't let the hard case ride out of town with that little girl. If she was carried off by him, she was probably as good as dead.

"My daughter!" a loud, terror-stricken voice screamed. "He has my daughter!"

The hard case swung his gun hand around to cover the panicking woman who ran out of the store next door, holding her dress up as she sprinted. Her feet kicked up gravel and dust, but she didn't slow down any, until the man jabbed his gun toward her.

"Don't come any closer! I'll shoot her!" He jammed the hard barrel back against the child's skull, causing her to cry out. She tried reaching for her mother, the gesture causing the woman to cry even louder and stretch her arms out, too, as she skidded to a stop in the road.

Smoke had seen more than enough. He couldn't get a shot off, though. He was good—probably one of the best there was—but even he couldn't guarantee a clean shot under these circumstances. It was just too risky. And he'd be damned if any harm came to a child because of him.

But he couldn't *not act*, either.

The street was eerily silent. Smoke could see the two old-timers crawling quietly beneath the porch, headed toward the gunman, obviously intent on intervening. There was an opening where they could get out, not far behind the man. Smoke hoped it wouldn't spook the varmint, causing him to shoot the child.

Smoke cast his eyes toward the sheriff. Monte Carson

peered around the corner of the alcove where he had taken cover, but he made no move toward the gunman. His deputies stood motionless behind the wagon, following his example.

The tension was thick. Normally, Smoke was as calm as could be in situations like this, but now his heart felt as if it might beat right out of his chest. Perhaps the child's presence did it. Or maybe his not knowing what had happened to Sally. Had that shot he'd heard earlier hit her? Was she okay? Heaven help that crazed outlaw if she wasn't. Whatever the reason, his nerves were a bit more frayed than usual.

He fought hard to control his emotions. He needed to proceed with a clear head. He didn't give a damn about his own life.

Right now, that little girl was all that mattered.

And Sally.

Smoke drew a deep breath, exhaled slowly, and fought down his anger. Now wasn't the time to be blinded by rage. A wry smile tugged at his lips as a plan began to take shape inside his mind. What he needed was a distraction. Maybe those two old-timers would give it to him. They were edging closer, shifting beneath the porch and looking as if they were ready to scramble out and spring up at any moment.

Just like that, though, in the blink of an eye, the old men and Smoke's plan became irrelevant.

The outlaw had taken a few steps back on the porch, toward the store's door. He never bothered to check behind him.

That had been a mistake.

A bottle broke into a dozen pieces as it crashed against his head. One jagged shard tore into his scalp, slicing away the flesh and leaving a hot, wet, bloody streak.

Out of instinct, he dropped the child. She leaped off the

porch as quickly as possible and into her mother's arms. For a moment, Smoke feared the outlaw would trigger his gun, but the man just pawed at his flowing wound. Confusion registered in his eyes as he swayed unsteadily on his feet. His gun slid from his fingers.

"What the—"

He tried spinning around, but didn't have a chance before a second bottle smashed into him, sending him to the ground, out cold.

Smoke was already at the porch now, his gun still drawn, when he realized who had saved the day.

There in the doorway, with the neck of a broken bottle in her hand, stood Sally.

CHAPTER 2

"What on earth is going on here?" Monte Carson asked.

Smoke finished thumbing a fresh cartridge into his walnut-butted Colt and then pouched the iron. "I was wondering that myself." He looked to Sally and arched an eyebrow. "Here I was worried about *you*, and I should have been worried about *him*." He jerked his head toward the unconscious gunman who lay on the porch's puncheon floor.

One of the sheriff's deputies was standing over the downed man, relieving him of his weapons. A small derringer was up his right sleeve, along with a knife in one of his boots. The deputy then rummaged through the man's pockets and pulled out a wad of greenbacks and waved them toward the sheriff.

"Those are mine!" Don Baker said.

He was a large, easygoing man who ran the mercantile, along with help from his clerk, Ike Hairston. Ike was out on the porch now, too, and hurried to the downed brigand. He reared his foot back, but Sheriff Carson stopped him.

"You can't kick him now. He's laid out cold!"

"Well, I oughta," Ike said, and then his voice trailed off into a consortium of jumbled curse words. "They tried to hold up the store."

"They didn't *try*," his boss corrected him. "They did rob us. Would have gotten away with it, too, if it hadn't been for Jensen."

"Which one?" Smoke said with a smile. His eyes darted to Sally, who was now off the porch and checking on the terrified mother and child.

"Thank God she's okay," Sally said, rubbing the girl's back.

The two old-timers had rolled out from under the porch and, after considerable effort, were finally stumbling to their feet.

"Sheriff, I think Walt done broke his backside," one of them said.

The other groaned as he rubbed his rear end. It took considerable effort for Smoke to control his laughter, and one look at Sally told him she was having the same struggle.

Monte seemed somewhat annoyed when he said, "Will someone just tell me exactly what happened?"

"I'll tell you," Ike said, still red-faced with anger. "Those two no-accounts came in the store, acted like they were shopping, but then drew their pistols and demanded the money from the register. They were also trying to take off with a few supplies, jerky and coffee, mostly." He jabbed a bony finger toward the dead man in the street and said, "He got spooked and told his partner they had to get out of there. That's when he came out shooting!"

"That explains your ear," Monte said, looking at Smoke.

Smoke remembered the close call and touched his ear. It stung a little, but the blood had dried now. He'd had a lot worse done to him over the years.

"Guess I was in the wrong place at the wrong time," Smoke said with a chuckle.

"Or the right place," Monte said. "He may have hit someone with those wild shots, had you not taken him down. Reckon the town is obliged to you for that. Once again."

Smoke nodded.

It seemed as if Monte took every opportunity he could to state how much the town of Big Rock owed Smoke. In fact, Smoke was mostly responsible for the settlement's founding, having led an exodus here of folks escaping from the outlaw town of Fontana, several miles away. They had fled to escape the reign of terror carried out by brutal mine owner Tilden Franklin and his hired guns.

Now, a couple of years later, Franklin was dead, and Fontana was an abandoned town, nothing left but moldering ruins, while Big Rock was growing and thriving. Monte Carson wasn't the only one who gave Smoke a lot of the credit for that happening.

Smoke, however, wasn't interested in accolades. He was thankful when the storekeeper started talking again.

"Anyway," Ike Hairston continued, "that spooked his partner inside the store and he started shooting, too."

"Anyone hit?" the sheriff asked.

"No, but he plugged the dang cracker barrel!" Ike said. He looked as if he wanted to kick the man again. His anger subsiding, he shrugged and said, "That's when he came out onto the porch, and, well, you saw the rest."

Sally was at Smoke's side now. They joined Sheriff Carson in examining the two outlaws. Both wore dirty, torn homespun and it seemed as if neither had bathed in a long while.

Smoke thumbed his curled-brim hat back, revealing more of his ash-blond hair, and scratched his forehead. "Looks like these two had fallen on hard times."

"Explains why they were so desperate," Monte said with a frown. "Still doesn't give them call to carry on like this."

"Sure doesn't," Smoke agreed. "Reckon they could have gotten a meal just about anywhere here in town."

Smoke wasn't exaggerating. Big Rock was a friendly community, where folks could find plenty of help if they needed it. Smoke might have even given the two work at the Sugarloaf, had they dropped by. Of course, the fact that one had held a little girl hostage showed he was *not* simply a good man who'd fallen on desperate times, so Smoke doubted if they'd had any intent on working for an honest day's wages.

The one Sally had laid out was now starting to groan as he came to.

"Let's get him on down to the jail," Monte told his deputies. "I'll send for Doc Spaulding to patch him up."

"He needs to take a look at my rear, too!" Walt said, still rubbing his derriere.

"Maybe he can get you one of those sittin' pillows," the other old-timer said. "Feels better than resting your cheeks on a hard chair, that's for sure!"

Monte rolled his eyes and mumbled, "Lord help me." He turned his focus to the corpse, which lay in the street, and winced as he saw that flies had already started to gather. "I'll get the undertaker down here, too. I'll look through the wanted dodgers I have back at the office. Could be that you have some reward money coming, Smoke."

Smoke snorted. "A bounty-hunting Jensen? Now that's a thought."

"Don't you go getting any ideas. We don't need any more trouble," Sally said. "Besides, you're a rancher. Remember?"

Smoke held up his hands in mock surrender. "Believe me, I've had my fill of trouble. I'm not looking for more." His smile disappeared as he turned his gaze toward the sheriff. He scratched his strong, angular chin and asked, "Do I need to stick around and appear before Judge Proctor?"

"Nah," Monte said. "This is pretty cut-and-dried. The way I figure it, you did the town a favor. You too," he said, smiling at Sally. "Smoke, you sure married one with a bit of sass in her."

Smoke laughed, nodding in agreement.

He certainly couldn't argue that point.

The ride back to the Sugarloaf was seven miles and Smoke didn't mind the journey one bit. The country was mighty pretty, and he had an even prettier woman by his side. As he guided his black stallion, Drifter, beside the buckboard Sally drove, he took a moment to soak it all in.

She had an infectious smile, which he never tired of. Her brown hair hung in bouncing curls. With Sally set against the backdrop of the rugged Rocky Mountains, Smoke wondered if he'd indeed been shot back in Big Rock and was now in heaven.

"What are you looking at?" Sally said, though her smile hinted that she already knew the answer.

"The woman of my dreams," he said without hesitation.

She smiled even wider. "And what are you thinking about?"

Smoke laughed. He made a show of looking around and said, "Well, I suppose I could tell you, since there's no one else around."

Now Sally laughed loudly. "Easy. We've got a few miles to go before we're back home."

"Like I said, there's no one else around."

Sally cast him one last devilish grin before turning her attention back to the trail before her. Smoke did the same.

They rode in silence for a few minutes before he said, "That was some stunt you pulled back there, walloping that owlhoot like that. You could've been hurt."

"And that little girl could've been killed."

"True," Smoke admitted. "Reckon I can't be too upset."

"Upset? You knew I was a handful when you put the ring on my finger."

Smoke chuckled. "That I did. And I wouldn't have you any other way. I just want you to be careful, is all. I intend to grow old with you."

"Of course," she said. "I'll be sitting by your side on the porch in our rockers. We can look out over the Sugarloaf. It will be massive by then."

"You have big plans," he said.

"*We* have big plans," she said.

"Yep. And they don't include gunfighting, that's for sure."

She gave him a pointed stare. "It really bothered you, what happened back in town?"

He nodded. Drifter continued to pick his way over the trail, staying beside the buckboard, moving at a measured pace. It seemed as if the horses were just as content to enjoy the pleasant evening as night fell around them as Smoke and Sally were.

The falling sun painted the picturesque landscape in pink and yellow hues. A cloud of gnats hovered just off the road. A few grasshoppers leaped in the brushy grass to Smoke's left. Smoke sucked in a lungful of air and held it a moment, enjoying the smell of the upcoming summer. Something about this time of year called to him. Something peaceful. Thinking about peace, he said, "I just hope this valley is tamed one day, and sooner rather than later. I've had more than enough gunplay to last me a lifetime."

"There will be peace around these parts soon enough," she said. "Men like you and Preacher have worked hard to make this land safe for decent folks. One day, our children will thank you for it."

Smoke smiled once again. He sure liked the sound of that.

Children.

Of course, if they turned out anything like their pa—or ma, for that matter—they'd keep him and Sally on their toes.

They finished their trip in silence, content to simply be in each other's presence. The relaxing ride did wonders in washing away the unpleasantness that had occurred back in town, and by the time they arrived home, it was already nothing but a memory.

That peacefulness didn't last long, though. Upon riding up to the house, Smoke realized they had company. Two saddle mounts he didn't recognize, along with a couple of pack animals, were tied in front of the log ranch house.

Something stirred deep inside his stomach, telling him that all was not well. He remembered that realization he'd had back in town when the shooting had started.

Trouble just had a way of finding him.

**Other sexy, steamy reads from
GENA SHOWALTER
and HQN Books**

GENA SHOWALTER

THE DARKEST SEDUCTION

Lords of the Underworld

HQN™

Recycling programs
for this product may
not exist in your area.

ISBN-13: 978-0-373-77657-3

THE DARKEST SEDUCTION

Copyright © 2012 by Gena Showalter

www.Harlequin.com

Printed in U.S.A.

Dear Reader,

At long last, I'm pleased to bring you the story of Paris, keeper of the demon of Promiscuity. Yes, I finally feel as though I've tortured him enough. After all, since the Lords of the Underworld were first introduced, Paris has

1) Lost the only woman he was able to bed more than once

2) Given up his chance to find her by choosing to save one of his friends instead

3) Formed an addiction to an illicit substance

4) Choked out any light of goodness inside himself

5) Turned into a war/fighting machine

His road to happily ever after has been paved with blood, sweat and tears. Mostly mine. Fine. Mostly his. Whatever. *Semantics.* Anyway, I knew he deserved something, and someone, special. In fact, I had an idea for him and sat down to write it. Four tries later—with three hundred pages in the trash—he showed me exactly what he wanted. Okay, fine (again). I finally gave in and did things his way. And you know what? He got the "special" I wanted for him.

The characters had so much more depth than I expected, and as they interacted the puzzle pieces began to fall into place—I saw why he wanted what he wanted, and for the first time in a very long time I heard Paris laugh. (I heard this in my head, of course, but laughter is laughter.) He'd found his "mine," and she was and is exactly what he's needed all along.

Will I ever stand in my characters' way again? Well, yeah. (Hey, at least I'm honest.) But this one time, giving in proved to be the best thing I could have done.

I hope you are as satisfied with Paris's story as he is.

All my best!

Gena Showalter

THE DARKEST SEDUCTION

Throughout the years I've learned that family matters. I've been blessed with one of the most amazing families EVER. They love me, support me, and they are always there when I need them. The bond you see between the Lords, as well as the bond between the Harpy sisters? That's what I have with my family, and I am beyond grateful. So this one is to my husband and children, my mom and dad, sisters and brothers, in-laws (who are so much more than that), nieces and nephews and crazy aunts and uncles. I love and adore you all!

Acknowledgments

From family to friends, I am blessed. To Jill Monroe, Kresley Cole and P.C. Cast. I love you, ladies!

I speak, and the humans tremble in fear. I speak, and my people rush to obey—and yet still they seek to destroy me. My salvation rides the wings of midnight, and my burden she carries. My rage she unleashes, delivering damnation to all with a single swing of her sword. I speak.
—A passage found in the private journals of Cronus, king of the Titans

Speak all the hell you want. I'm taking what's mine.
—Paris, Lord of the Underworld

PROLOGUE

"HIS RAGE..."

"I know."

High in the heavens, Zacharel watched the world below him. Watched as the once genial Paris murdered yet another of his enemy, the Hunters. How many victims that made in the past hour alone, the angel could not say. He'd long since lost count. And even if he paused to do the tally, the answer would have changed a second later as yet another body fell to the slick, blood-coated blades the warrior wielded.

Of course, the panting, sweat-soaked Paris spun to engage two others, his motions fluid, lethally graceful... as unstoppable as an avalanche. At first, he played. A punch, cracking bone. A kick, smashing lungs. Laughing, spouting the worst of curses. Soon none of that was enough for the demon-possessed soldier, and he danced his blades over the tendons in their ankles, hobbling his prey for easier elimination.

Paris had made himself Bait to purposely draw these Hunters to him. They'd come eagerly, happily, intending to steal the vile demon tethered inside him and finally end him. So Zacharel could not fault the warrior for what he did to defend himself, even as several new bodies joined the already mountainous pile enveloped by a sea of crimson and black. And yet, he could not commend the warrior, either.

These were not mercy slayings or even carried out in the name of a cold and calculated vengeance birthed in the bowels of an equally cold rage. No, these were a spew of fire, hate and desperation hotter than anything hell had ever created.

"He is like a poisoned apple," Zacharel said to the angel beside him. And because Paris was bonded to the demon of Promiscuity, his pruning belonged not to the humans he lived amongst but to the Deity's angels, who policed different realms of evil. "Poison of this nature spreads slowly but corrupts absolutely."

Beads of ice fell around Zacharel, as they always fell around him these days, his breath misting in front of his face. Every crystal was to be a reminder of his own crimes, so recently brought to his attention. But unlike Paris, he did not wear misery like a winter coat, hugging it close to his body, relying on it, feeding it, helping it grow. Zacharel cared for nothing, not anymore.

In his quest to destroy the demons that had ruined his life, he had slain "innocent" humans, and this was to be his punishment—to carry his Deity's displeasure with him always.

"As succulent as others consider this particular apple," Lysander proclaimed, "they will be willing to taste anything he offers."

Zacharel moved his gaze to the man who had taught him how to survive on the battlefield. The elite warrior was a muscled tower of unwavering strength. He wore a long white robe, his majestic wings like rivers of molten gold. Zacharel's ice raged around him, too, though not a single flake dared land on the man. Perhaps, like myriad other creatures, the crystals feared him—and rightly so. In their world, he was judge and jury, his word law.

"Do we remove temptation?" Zacharel asked. For centuries he had acted as Lysander's executioner.

"I will not order his assassination, no," Lysander said, resolute. "At the moment, Paris is redeemable."

Unexpected. Even with the great distance between the heavens and the earth, Zacharel could hear the grunts and groans Paris elicited, the screams of his enemies. The pleas for mercy that would echo into eternity, forever unheeded. And as determined as this Lord of the Underworld was, this was only the beginning.

"What will you have me do, then?"

"Paris searches for his woman, intending to free her from the Titan king's enslavement. You will aid him, protect him and protect the girl. The moment her ties to Cronus are cut, however, you will bring her here, where she will live out the rest of eternity."

Even more unexpected. The command smacked of leniency, something Lysander had shown to only one other demon-possessed immortal in all the millennia of his life: Amun, Paris's friend. And only because Bianka, Lysander's Harpy mate, had asked.

She must have requested this second favor, as well, for it was widely known that Lysander was powerless against her wiles. But even a besotted groom, tasked as he was with governing the heavens, responsible for all that transpired there, should not have asked another angel to do this deed. Aid a demon? Bring another here to live? Horrifying.

Zacharel offered no objection. And despite the fact that he had never experienced desire himself, he would do his best to cure Paris of his so that, when the inevitable break with the female came, the warrior would not return to his rage.

"Paris will protest her loss." After everything the warrior had done to find and save her already, everything he would soon do…oh, yes, he would protest—using those dripping blades to make his case.

"You must convince him that he will be better off without her," Lysander said.

"Will he be?"

"Of course." There was no hesitation in the pronouncement, lending it an edge of fiery truth. An unnecessary edge, for Zacharel knew Lysander would not, could not, lie.

"And if I fail to convince him?" He had to ask, needed the penalty riding heavy on his shoulders, driving him to succeed.

Eyes of pitiless navy frosted over, revealing the iron depths of Lysander's warrior core. "We are lost, for the greatest war the world has ever known now brews. The girl will lead us to our victory—or our enemy to theirs. It's as simple as that."

Very well, then. When the time came, Zacharel would take her. No matter how Paris was affected.

Paris would hate him, and would, perhaps, do more than rage. There was no stopping that, not when so much darkness swirled inside him, a rot in his soul, far worse than any spiritual poison. But that wouldn't stop Zacharel from fulfilling his duty.

Nothing would.

CHAPTER ONE

PARIS TOSSED BACK THREE fingers of Glenlivet and signaled the bartender. He wanted an entire hand and by right or might, he'd have it. Except soon after the single malt was poured, he realized an entire hand wasn't going to cut it, either. Fury and frustration were living entities inside him, frothing and bubbling despite his recent fighting.

"Leave the bottle," he said when the bartender made a move to help someone else. Hell, suddenly Paris doubted every drop of alcohol in a ten-mile radius would do the trick, but hey. Desperate times.

"Sure, sure. Anything you say." Shirtless Boy Wonder released the bottle and beat feet.

What? He looked *that* dangerous? Please. He'd washed off the blood, hadn't he? Wait. *Hadn't he?* He looked down. Shit. He hadn't. Crimson streaked him from head to toe.

Whatever. He wasn't in a human bar, so no "authorities" would have a beef with him. He was in Olympus, though the heavenly kingdom had recently been renamed Titania. Once only gods and goddesses had been allowed here, but when Cronus reclaimed the realm, he'd changed things, allowing vampires, fallen angels and other creatures of the dark to come and play. A nice little screw you to the previous king, Zeus.

Call the bartender back, Promiscuity said. *I want him.*

Promiscuity—the demon trapped inside him, driving him. Irritating him. *Remember when I wanted fidelity? Monogamy?* Paris replied in his mind. *Well, we don't always get what we want, do we?*

A familiar growl sounded in his head.

Whaa, whaa, pout, pout. He downed the second alcoholic offering and quickly chased it with a third. Both scorched so good he enjoyed a fourth. The potent alcohol razed his chest, burned holes in his abdomen, and flooded his veins. Nice.

And yet, his emotions remained as dark as ever, the edges of that bone-deep fury and frustration unsmoothed. His inability to save a not-so-innocent woman he should hate—*did* hate, at least a little—but also hungered for, body and soul, drove him, a constant whip against his flank.

"If I asked you to leave, would you?" a monotone voice said from beside him. A voice accompanied by a blast of arctic air.

He didn't have to look to know that Zacharel, warrior angel extraordinaire and infamous demon-assassin, had just joined him. They'd met not long ago, when the feathered axman had come to Buda to off Paris's friend Amun. Had old Zach actually succeeded, two crystal blades would have been drilling into his spine at that very moment.

I want him, the demon said.

Screw you.

Finally. We're on the same page.

Really hate you right now.

Once upon a time, the demon had spoken to Paris with annoying frequency. Then the stupid sex fiend had stopped, merely urging Paris to bed this person or that person, no matter their gender or Paris's own feelings toward them. Now, the talking had started up again and it was worse than before, because he wanted everyone, *especially* the ones Paris felt no desire for.

"Well?" the angel prompted.

"Leave, when I had to beg Lucien to bring me here and I know he won't be so accommodating next time? No, but I'd damn sure want to know why you gave a crap about my location."

"I do not care about your location."

True story. Zacharel didn't care about anything, a fact you learned real fast in your dealings with him. "That's my point, so get lost."

As Paris nursed a fifth whiskey, he studied the smoke-stained mirror in front of him, covertly panning the area behind him. Bejeweled chandeliers hung from the ceiling. The walls were rose-colored marble, veined with glittering ebony, the floor a sparkling stretch of crushed diamonds.

Throughout the room, men and women talked and laughed. From minor gods and goddesses to fallen angels trying to work their way back into their saintly fold. *Good luck with that in a bar. Morons.* Anyway. There was probably a demon or two sprinkled among the masses, but Paris couldn't tell for sure.

Demons were as sneaky as they were evil. They could skulk around in their own scales, proudly showcasing their horns, claws, wings and tails—and getting decapitated by warrior angels like Zach. Or they could possess someone else's body and skulk around in *their* skin.

Paris had thousands of years of experience with the latter.

"I will leave, as you so succinctly suggested," Zacharel said, "*after* you answer another question for me."

"All right." Something else Paris knew from experience: angels were freakishly stubborn. Better to hear the guy out, otherwise he'd find himself with a new shadow. He turned, facing the dark-haired stunner with eyes the color of jade, and sucked in a breath. Never ceased to amaze him, how magnetic these celestial beings were. No matter their gender—or how mind-numbingly dull their personalities—they drew and held your attention, every damn time. For some reason, Zacharel did so with more intensity than most.

But the magnetism wasn't what caught Paris's attention this time. Majestic wings arced over the angel's broad shoulders, a turbulent fall of winter clouds with streams of gold winding and curling throughout, snowflakes raining from the tips like glitter in a globe.

"You're snowing." *Captain Obvious, that's me.*

"Yes."

"Why?"

"I can answer you, or I can ask my question and leave." Dressed in the long white robe that was customary for his kind, Zacharel should have looked innocent and prissy. Instead, he looked like the Grim Reaper's evil twin: emotionless, as frigid as the snow he shed and ready to kill. "Your choice."

No thought necessary. "Ask."

"Do you wish to die?" Zacharel said it as simply as he'd said everything else, mist crystallizing in front of his mouth, creating a dreamlike haze and reminding Paris of the breath of life. Or death.

Definitely ready to kill, Paris mused. "What do you think?" he asked, because honestly? He didn't know the answer anymore.

For centuries he'd fought to live, but now, now he constantly threw himself into the fire and waited to be burned. *Liked* being burned. What kind of sick prick had he become?

Unflinching, the angel held his gaze. "I think you want one particular woman more than you want anyone—or anything—else. Even death…even life."

Paris pressed his tongue to the roof of his mouth. One woman in particular: the not-so-innocent one.

Her name was Sienna Blackstone. Once a Hunter and always his enemy, for Hunters were an irritating army of humans who hoped to rid the world of Pandora's demons. Then fleetingly, she'd been his lover. Then dead, gone. *Then* she'd been brought back from the grave, her soul merged with the demon of Wrath. Now, she was out there. Somewhere. And she was suffering. Cronus had enslaved her, thinking to use her demon to punish his adversaries, and now that he'd lost control of her, he thought to torture her into submission.

Paris might dislike the things Sienna had done to him, and yeah, as he'd already admitted, part of him might even hate the woman herself, but even she did not deserve the cruel, vicious—eternal—punishment being meted out.

I will find her, and I will *save her.* From Cronus… from himself. Right now, Paris simply couldn't get past the fact that she was suffering. Once that part of the equation was dealt with, he would stop thinking about her. He had to stop thinking about her.

"So I want her," he ended up saying to the angel. Sienna was not up for discussion. "BFD."

"I will pretend I know what that means." Zacharel shook his wings, more of that pure, glistening snow raining down. "As for you, I think that, despite your own desires, your demon wants anything with a pulse."

"Sometimes even a pulse isn't a requirement," he muttered, and damn if that wasn't the truth. Sex, as he'd taken to calling his dark companion, wanted anyone and everyone—but only ever once. With the exception of Sienna, Sex would not allow Paris to harden for the same person twice.

Why could he have Sienna again? No damn clue. "But again, so?"

"I think, even though you crave this particular woman, you slept with your friend Strider's future wife. He is the demon of Defeat, and your actions made his courtship of the Harpy very difficult."

"Hey. You're entering dangerous territory here." Not that Paris had anything to apologize for.

The one-nighter had happened weeks before Strider and Kaia hooked up. Or had even thought about hooking up. Therefore, Paris had done nothing wrong. Technically. And yet, he now knew what Kaia looked like naked, and Strider knew that he knew, and that meant all three of them knew Sex tossed out naked images of the girl every time they were together. A consequence Paris loathed, but couldn't stop.

Zacharel's dark head tilted to the side in a reflective pose, all the more mysterious because of the mist that continued to form with his every exhalation. "I meant only to point out that you have clearly moved on to other conquests and that you are hardly discriminating in your choices, which makes me wonder why you still pursue your Sienna."

Because Sienna had been Paris's one and only shot at monogamy. Because he'd inadvertently brought about her death. Because he'd felt like he lost *everything* when she died.

"You're annoying," he snapped. "And I'm done talking to you."

Still the angel persisted. "I think you feel guilty about every heart you break, every dream of happily-ever-after you crush, and every bit of self-loathing you encourage when your partners realize how effortlessly you overcame their reservations. I also think you are overindulged and pathetic, and that you have no business crying about your problems."

"Hey! I've never cried." Paris slammed his glass on the counter with so much force the bar split down the center and the cup shattered. Blood welled from the slices in his palm, but the sting was minimal. "And you know what? I think you are seconds away from finding pieces of your body scattered in all the corners of this bar."

Then, while he's down, we can have him!

Zip it, Sex.

"Uh, here you go," the bartender said, Johnny-on-the-spot with a clean rag he thrust in Paris's direction. His arm shook. He was still afraid of Paris.

I want—

I said zip it! "Thanks, man." Paris fisted the material, applying pressure to the slivers of torn tissue before anyone could scent him and the oh-so-special pheromones his demon excreted.

One whiff of the intoxicating aroma, and everyone around him would become unforgivably aroused, uncaring about where they were or who they were with. Mostly their hunger would be for *Paris,* and though that would have been an especially craptastic outcome tonight considering he was operating under a time crunch, he would have enjoyed rebuffing the males with his fists.

Except…the pheromones never enveloped him. He frowned. Sex wanted everyone he'd spotted tonight. Why not take advantage of his ability and force the patrons to want him back?

Paris returned his focus to Zacharel, wondering if the angel was somehow responsible.

Those eyes of the rarest jade narrowed to tiny slits. "I think you hope to save your Sienna, and that is a good thing. I think you mean to keep her, and that is not. No matter how intensely you crave her, no matter that she might be your only chance at forever, your demon will eventually ruin her, for humans were never meant to battle demons, and at heart, she is still a human."

"What about her own demon?" he snapped.

"If one is bad, two is surely worse."

"Enough!" If they continued on this path, his fury and frustration would rise up and consume him. He would lose sight of tonight's goal. "I'm not going to keep her." He would. He *so* would if given a chance, and if she would have him, of course, but hell, she wouldn't have him.

"Good. Because this particular woman would not like the man you have become."

Snorting, Paris shoved his free hand through his hair. "She didn't like who I was." And now, after he'd irrevocably stepped over the line between right and wrong? Please.

He'd known his actions were reprehensible, and he'd stepped over anyway. He'd killed, callously. Seduced, methodically. Lied, cheated and betrayed. All of which he would do again and again.

"Yet you still rush to save her," Zacharel said.

Yeah. He was as big a moron as the fallen who frequented this place. Whatever. He *knew.* Didn't care. "Look, I don't answer to you. I don't have to explain myself. And what's with all the questions? You said you only had one more."

"I have asked only the one. The rest have been observations, and I have one more of those to offer." Zacharel leaned into him and whispered, "I think, if you continue on this destructive path, you will lose everything you have come to love."

"Is that a threat?" Paris fisted the collar of the angel's robe. "Go ahead and try something, winger. See what—"

Air. He was fisting and yelling at air.

Little growls sprang from his throat as he lowered his arm to his side. The only reason he knew Zacharel had been here was the temperature of his hands. They were practically frostbitten.

"Uh, who were you talking to?" the bartender asked, faux casual as he cleaned an already clean counter.

If an angel didn't want to be seen, an angel wouldn't be seen. Not even by his brethren, fallen or otherwise. So only Paris had seen Zacharel this go-round. Great. "Myself apparently, and we prefer to chat without an audience."

Was Zacharel still here? Paris wondered. Or had he materialized somewhere else? And what was the purpose of all that talk of Paris needing to stay away from Sienna? The angel shouldn't care.

Paris dropped the rag and turned the rest of the way to face the crowd. Several warriors were scowling in his direction—why?—dangerously close to ruining the room's elegance with the blood they were tempting Paris to spatter. He massaged the back of his neck, forcing thoughts of Zacharel and his threat into hiding. He had bigger and badder to deal with. He was here for Viola, the minor goddess of the Afterlife and keeper of the demon of Narcissism. She should have popped in already.

Maybe she'd heard he was coming and bailed, and if that was the case he couldn't blame her. He and his friends had once stolen and opened Pandora's box, unleashing the evil from inside. As punishment, they were cursed to host the demons they'd released within themselves. Unfortunately, there'd been more demons than naughty boys and girls to contain them, and when the box had disappeared in the chaos, the leftover evil spirits had needed homes. What better recipients for the Greeks to select than the unlucky, unable-to-run inmates of Olympus's—*Titania's*—immortal prison, Tartarus?

So, yeah, Paris was partly responsible for Viola's dark side. She'd been one of those unlucky prisoners. He wasn't entirely responsible, though, considering the girl was a criminal once considered dangerous enough to be forcibly kept away from the very gods and goddesses who were often praised in mythology books for their most vicious deeds.

What crime Viola had committed, he didn't know and didn't care. She could slash him to ribbons, as long as she gave up the information he craved. The final puzzle piece needed to at last save Sienna.

According to the Hunters he'd slain just this morning, Viola came here every Friday night to hustle immortals at pool and rave about her awesomeness over a few beers. Apparently, said Hunters had been watching her, intent on nabbing her and "persuading" her to join their ranks. So, in a way, she kinda owed him.

Where the hell is she? he wondered again, searching for the telltale long blond hair, eyes the color of cinnamon and a killer body that could—

Appear in a puff of white smoke.

There, in front of the bar's only entrance, stood a luscious woman with long blond hair and eyes the color of cinnamon. Paris straightened, his nerve endings zinging with anticipation. Just like that. Prey located. Target acquired.

CHAPTER TWO

I WANT HER, SEX SAID as Paris studied Viola.

Of course you do, he replied dryly.

The tendrils of smoke that had marked Viola's appearance now curled away from her, thinning out to reveal a slinky black dress. The thick straps on her shoulders veed to frame heavy cleavage before dipping past her pierced navel. The micromini skirt stopped just below the hem of her panties.

Was she even wearing panties?

Paris yawned. He'd been with gorgeous women, ugly women, and everything in between. One lesson he'd quickly learned: beauty could hide a beast, and a beast could hide a beauty.

Sienna belonged to the beauty-hiding-a-beast category—at least to him. While he'd been crazed with desire for her, she'd been plotting his downfall. And maybe he was as bad as his demon because part of him found even that side of her sexy. A reed-thin female had bested a battle-hardened warrior, and he thought that was hot as hell.

And okay, yeah, she considered herself plain and maybe once he would have agreed, but from the beginning, there'd been something tantalizing about her. Something that drew him, held him captive. Now, anytime he pictured her, he saw a flawless gem with no equal.

Concentrate. A command from the demon, who still wanted the minor goddess, and a reprimand from himself.

Viola flipped the length of her silky hair over one sun-kissed shoulder and scouted her surroundings. Men openly gaped. Women tried to hide their jealousy with (unconvincing) blank masks. She paused on Paris, looked him up and down, her lids narrowing, and then, shockingly, she dismissed him and continued her visual sweep.

The last time his demon had failed to attract a potential bedmate, he'd met Sienna shortly thereafter. Could that mean...what if... His anticipation intensified until his bones vibrated. He would get his answers—*tonight*—no matter what was required of him.

He closed in on Viola, schooling his features to reveal only admiration as he went over his plan. Charm first, if he could actually remember how to be charming. Force second, and yeah, he definitely remembered how to go that route.

Ignoring his approach, Viola bent down and slid a glittery pink phone from inside her black leather boot. Moans of approval erupted behind her, and men high-fived each other, as if they'd just received a glimpse of heaven. Even immortals could be childish. *Never me.* Unaware or unconcerned, she danced her nimble fingers over the phone's tiny keyboard.

Paris frowned. "What are you doing?"

As an opener, the question totally blew, as did his accusing tone. But if she thought to summon help, someone to fight him, or even a Hunter to kill him, she'd soon find herself his hostage, *as well as* his informant.

"I'm Screeching. That's the immortal version of twittering or tweeting or whatever you lower beings want to call it," she said without glancing up. "I've got over seven bazillion followers."

O-kay. Not what he'd expected. He'd spent a lot of time with humans, and knew they enjoyed sharing their every inane thought with the world. But a Titan who did so—that was new.

"What are you telling them?" Was Cronus among the seven bazillion? Was Galen, the head honcho of the Hunters? And how many was a bazillion?

"I maybe might be kinda sorta telling them all about you." A grin lifted the corners of her plump red lips as she continued type, type, typing. "'Lord of Sex is filthy and looking to score. I'm not interested, but should I help him rack up points with someone else?' Send." She focused those haunting auburn eyes on him. "I'll let you know when the results come in. Until then, is there anything else you want to know about me before I walk away and ignore you?"

Lord of Sex, she'd said. Sooo. She knew who he was, *what* he was, but she wasn't running from him, wasn't tossing insults at him and wasn't screaming for his execution. A great start. "Yes, there is, and it's a private matter very important to me." Subtext: *don't you dare Screech about it!*

"Ohhh. I love private, important matters that I'm not supposed to talk about but do, because I'm such a giver. I'm listening."

Despite her convoluted confession that she meant to tattle, there was no more typing. Good. He proceeded. "I want to see the dead. How do I make that happen?" Sienna was a soul without a body—a soul he couldn't sense in any way. Only those who communed with the dead could see, hear and touch her. But rumor was, Viola knew a trick that rendered the ability unnecessary.

She blinked, and he noticed that her lashes were painted a glittery pink to match her phone. "Let me tell you what I just heard. Talk, talk, talk, *I*. Talk, talk, talk, *I*. Well, what about *me?*"

His jaw clenched. There was being charming, and there was being a sucker. He wasn't a sucker. Well, not all the time. "I'll tell you about you. You can see the dead. Now you're going to teach me how to see them." An order she would do well to heed.

Her nose wrinkled. "Why do you care about seeing souls? If they're still here, they're causing trouble and—oh, oh, wait." Clap, clap, jump, jump, twirl. "I've already figured this little mystery out because I'm highly intelligent. You want to see your slain human lover."

Instantly his fury flashed to the surface, hot enough to blister. He didn't like anyone speaking of Sienna in any fashion. Not Zacharel, and certainly not this strange minor goddess with a penchant for gossiping. Sienna was his to protect, even in that capacity. "I—"

"Tsk, tsk. No need to confirm my genius assumption." Viola patted his cheek, all syrupy sweetness for his mental handicap. "Especially since I can't help you."

She tried to walk away.

He caught her wrist. "Can't or won't?" There was a big difference. The first he could do nothing about. The second he could change, and if she pushed him, she would discover the lengths he was willing to go to, to do just that.

"Won't. See ya." Oblivious to the rage she threatened to unleash, she jerked from his hold and practically skipped to the back of the bar, her perfect ass swaying, the heels of her boots clicking.

Incensed, he followed her, shoving aside anyone who got in his way. Grunts, groans and growls abounded, the predators in the crowd taking exception to his brute-force tactics. No one attempted to stop him, however. They sensed a far greater predator in their midst.

"How do you know who I am?" he demanded the moment he reached Viola. They'd start there and work their way to the mind changing, just in case one was dependent on the other.

She performed another twirl, making a production of it, as if she were a model at the end of a runway. He was a tall man used to towering over women, but Viola was a tiny fluff of five feet nothing and he *dwarfed* her.

Sienna, on the other hand, was just the right height. Standing, or on his knees, or lying down, he'd reach all the best parts of her, no problem.

"I know everything there is to know about the Lords of the Underworld," Viola said. "I made the entire horde of you my business when I escaped Tartarus and learned you were responsible for my condition."

She *did* blame him for the demon she'd been stuck with, then. And she smelled of roses, he realized with a jolt, the gentle scent suddenly clinging to his sinuses, very nearly drowning him in a warm sense of peace.

Lucien, the keeper of the demon of Death, could do the same thing to his enemies, calming them just before he struck a life-ending blow.

Paris's fury and frustration quickly chased that peacefulness away. "Stop that."

"Wow, that's a dark scowl. And not a very good look for you, I must say," she added, then caught a glimpse of her coral-painted fingernails and studied them in the light. "So pretty."

Touch her.

He tuned out his demon and decided he'd give the charm/sucker thing one more shot. Because, honestly?

He had yet to intimidate this female in any way. If this next attempt failed, he would let loose his beast in full force—and he wasn't talking about Sex. There was darkness inside him now, so much darkness, and that darkness would drive him to do what was necessary, no matter how vile.

He had no one but himself to blame, for he'd opened himself up to it. Just a fraction at first, like a crack in a window. But the funny thing was, once you welcomed in a breeze, there was no stopping what came next. A wind, a storm, thunder and lightning, until you could no longer reach the window to close it—and didn't really want to anyway. That's what this new darkness was. Evil in its purest form, an entity very much like Sex, urging him on.

Lie, cheat, betray, Paris thought. Here, now, like all the other times before.

He leaned down, softening his expression, forcing his demon's desires to seep through his pores. Forcing his blood to heat and the musky scent of arousal to drift from him, as sultry as champagne, as heady as chocolate. If Sex wouldn't use those pheromones, Paris would. He hated doing this, because, like everyone else, both he and Sex became mindless, flesh-hungry beings at the first whiff. Worse, the memories of what he forced people to do…to crave…

"Viola, sweetness. Talk to me. Tell me what I wish to know." His tone was a sensual caress, blissful and sure, and yet, even with the pheromones affecting *Paris,* he wanted only one woman and Viola wasn't her.

"I meant to thank you for my demon," she went on, as if he'd never spoken. As if he did not currently smell like pleasure walking. "He's the best! But then halfway to Budapest to track down your fortress, I forgot all about you. I'm sure you understand." She fluffed her hair, looking away from him as she waved to someone at her right. "So, anyway, now that you're here, thanks. Feel free to relay that to the others. Now you'll have to— Argh! Who put a mirror there?" she ended in a screech.

Undiluted rage blazed from her expression for a single heartbeat, followed by rapturous ecstasy as she studied her reflection.

"Look at me." She angled one way, posed, then angled another and posed again. "I'm *gorgeous.*"

"Viola." Seconds passed, but she never stopped admiring herself. She even blew herself a kiss. Fine. They'd do this the other way. "I can make you beg for my touch, Viola. In front of everyone. And believe me, you *will* beg. You will cry, but relief will never be yours. I'll make sure of it. But do you know what else? That's not even the worst of what I'll do to you."

Several seconds ticked by, but she never offered a reply.

Fury...

Frustration...

Darkness...rising... He wanted to strike, to hurt, to kill.

He inhaled, held, held...smelled an infusion of roses... released the breath. Okay. Good. This time he was able to allow both emotion bombs to fizzle before detonation, calming him.

Perhaps Viola couldn't help herself, he realized suddenly. As he knew very well, all of Pandora's demons came with a major flaw. This could be hers. She was Narcissism, after all, a lover of self.

Testing his theory, he stepped in front of her, blocking her view of the mirror. Her entire body stiffened. Her gaze darted left and right, as if searching for interlopers who might have tried to harm her while she'd been incapacitated. No one had approached, and the tension drained from her. She breathed easier.

"I will *gut* the culprit!" she whispered fiercely.

Bingo. Her flaw, and one she clearly reviled.

"Concentrate on me, Viola." He gripped her by the shoulders, squeezing harder than he'd intended and shaking her until those cinnamon eyes rose to meet his. "Tell me what I want to know and you'll walk away from this unscathed."

Still not the least bit intimidated, she shrugged off his hold. "*So* impatient. I should be used to it by now, but alas. Men falling all over me…still a burden."

"Viola!"

"Fine. Let's see what my worshippers have to say sooner rather than later, shall we?" She lifted her phone and read the screen. "Four hundred and eighty-five votes for *Help him by giving him my number.* Two hundred and seven votes for *Are you stupid, climb him like a mountain,* and one hundred and twenty-three votes for *He's mine, bitch, walk away.*" She looked up at him, another smile taking root. "The little people have spoken. Yes, I will tell you about the souls."

Urgency overrode his relief. "Tell me, then. Now."

"Hey, you. Demon scum." The harsh voice rang out from behind him.

Annnd one of the guys Paris had bumped into earlier was finally acting out. Paris ground his molars. His hands returned to the female's shoulders. "Viola. Tell me." She would tell him, and he would leave, finally beginning his search in truth.

"Get your hands off my female!"

Or not. Unleashed aggression dripped from the male's

tone, and the need for violence quickly resurfaced inside Paris.

Restrain yourself, common sense counseled. *Victory is within reach.* "A friend of yours?"

"I have no friends." Graceful fingers reached up and hooked several tendrils of hair behind her ear. "Only admirers."

"I'm talking to you, demon." The male again.

Need rising…higher and higher…a thick black cloud that would not dissipate until blood ran in rivers at his feet. "If you want this admirer to survive, flash us out of here." Popping from one location to another with only a thought always made him sick, but sick was better than distracted.

"I don't," she said. "Want him to survive, that is."

"Are you listening to me, demon?" The tone was harsher, and far more determined. "Move away from her and face me. Or are you a coward?"

The cloud enveloped his mind, a single thought suddenly consuming him. The male was an obstacle in his path, blocking him from Sienna, and obstacles were to be eliminated. Always.

Another small voice of reason whispered through him, a beacon of gold amid an endless stretch of midnight. *Zacharel… Current path… Destruction…*

"Look at yourself in the mirror, goddess," the male commanded. "I don't want you to see what I do to the demon."

Even as a curse tore from her mouth, Viola obeyed, angling around Paris as if she couldn't help herself and hated herself for it. Just like that, she was once again enraptured by her own image, pinkie-waving and blowing kisses.

The golden whisper was destroyed. Death became inevitable. Paris pivoted on his heels to glare at his opponent.

Soon, blood would flow.

CHAPTER THREE

PARIS HAD GOTTEN ONE FACT wrong. He didn't have an opponent. He had opponents. The knowledge caused a heady rush of eagerness to flood him. The day just kept getting better. Earlier he'd slain a handful of Hunters, and this hour's selection—aka dessert—was a trio of fallen angels, each one bigger than the last. They were without shirts—the new fashion?—their scarred backs visible in the mirror at the top of the wall.

The frothing trio formed a solid wall of muscle on the other side of the bar, their arms crossed over their chests, their legs braced apart to evenly distribute their weight. A classic I'm-about-to-hurt-someone stance.

I want them, Sex said, as if that were some big surprise.

"You will not walk away," he warned the men. Lately, he couldn't afford to leave survivors. They had a nasty habit of returning for revenge.

"I've seen you around," the one on the left said. "You smile and women fall at your feet, but I'm gonna change that when I rip your spine out of your mouth. *Then* I'm gonna tell your enemies where you are. Yeah, I know who you are, Lord of Sex. I also know the Hunters want the privilege of killing you."

The one on the right flashed a grin, total I've-lost-my-wings-and-I'm-glad evil. "Yeah. I like that idea. Maybe

I'll sign up with them, just to watch what they do to you when we're finished, you dirty—"

The one in the middle, the biggest one, placed a hand on Rightie's shoulder, silencing him. He had a bright white halo tattooed around his neck. That could mean he was only recently fallen, that he still had ties with the angels or that he liked to reminisce. Whatever. He would experience the same fate as his friends. "Less words, more pain."

"Yes, more pain," Paris agreed. He unsheathed his two favorite daggers, the clear, crystal blades glinting like rainbows in the light.

"Hey, no arsenals allowed inside," the bartender bellowed. "Only fists."

The entire bar stopped and quieted, clearly intent on watching.

"Feel free to try and pry mine from my grip." That would mean more opponents, more bloodshed. More satisfaction.

"Unfair advantage," someone else called.

Exactly. If you weren't cheating, you weren't trying. But, all right. Even lost to the decadent taste of violence as he was, Paris knew how to pretend to play nice. He commanded the blades to vanish from view while still remaining in his hands. Magical as they were, they obeyed.

"I don't care what weapons you use," Halo said.

"You shouldn't have come here." Leftie unfolded his arms. "This is our territory, and we're taking it back."

"Now, we'll make sure you never return." Rightie fisted his hands, cracking his knuckles. "This is gonna be fun."

"Fun. Yes. For me." Paris approached.

The trio approached.

All four met in the middle. The moment Paris was

within reach, he kicked Leftie while punching Rightie. Leftie hunched over, gasping for breath. Rightie died. Paris had punched with his invisible blade, sinking hilt-deep into the bastard's carotid.

One down. Two to go.

Halo swung a meaty fist, but the low, straight line Paris had made with his body caused the former winger to encounter only air, the momentum spinning him around. By the time Paris jerked upright, Leftie had regained his stamina and jumped on him, attempting to rip out his trachea with claws that hadn't been there a moment ago. Through dumb luck or talent, Leftie managed to angle his wrist when he realized Paris was shifting position, hitting the tendon that ran from neck to shoulder instead. There was a brutal rending before Paris shoved him off, the bastard taking hunks of skin and muscle with him.

Paris didn't release him, though. He held on tight, even as Halo got back in the game and hammered at his face. He stabbed Leftie with a quick *jab, jab*. Kidneys first, to shock and disable. Heart second, to kill. Leftie died just like his friend.

Two down. One to go.

Paris released the now-lifeless body, heard the *thump* as it landed. Grinned. All the while, Halo continued to whale on him. Crack, crack. Pain in his eye, pain in his lip. Blood cascaded down his chin, stars winked through his vision, and Sex retreated to a hidden corner in his mind. Each new point of contact threw him backward into tables, knocking down glasses, chairs and people.

Finally he managed to dodge one of those fists. He regained his balance and spun low, intending to slash Halo in the back of the knee and hobble him. But the once heavenly being was used to dirty demon tricks and spun as well, darting out of the way just before contact.

An arm's length away from each other now, they straightened and glared. Paris had yet to land a single blow on the man. He wanted to land a blow. *Would* land a blow. Then, when Halo was immobilized, Paris would slice him from navel to neck.

From the corner of his eye, he caught a flash of alabaster, a ripple of molten gold amid the feathers of an angelic warrior, and the snow that had become Zacharel's closest companion.

The man desires his woman as you desire yours. You would punish him for that?

The words drifted through Paris's mind, rays of light scented with hope. To his shock, the darkness thinned and he thought, *No, I don't want to punish a man for going after the woman he craves. Even if* I'm *the obstacle he faces.*

"I'll probably regret this," Paris said, gripping the invisible blade hilts tighter, just in case, "but I'm willing to let you leave. This is a one-time offer. Leave and live. That's it. No negotiation."

Halo scowled, his chin lifting, dark gaze narrowing. Whatever his name, there was no denying his punk-rocker appeal. His hair had been dyed the same pink as Viola's phone and lashes. Tears of blood were inked at the corners of his eyes. A ring of steel protruded from the center of his lower lip. "I'm not leaving. She's mine, and I will not allow you to have her, to use and discard her when you finish with her."

Everything always came back to that, Paris thought, disgusted with himself and his demon's need for sex. But then, the guy had said the one thing guaranteed to demolish his no-negotiation boast, so they'd try this a different way. "Does Viola want you in return?"

A hiss of fury. "She will."

Same thing Paris had once thought about Sienna. Still did, if he were being honest. He hoped that there was something he could do or say that would change her mind about him and she would come around, want him the way he wanted her.

Did the fallen angel have a chance at success? Did *he*? Females were the most stubborn creatures ever created.

"Just so you know, I don't want Viola." He stepped to the left, again and again until they were circling each other, every second bringing Paris back to the man he used to be: honorable, concerned, valiant. This wouldn't last, he knew, but he ran with it while he could.

"You lie!" Halo's nostrils flared with the force of his inhalation. "I, who never before craved a woman, could not resist her. *Everyone* wants her."

"Again, not me. I'm here for info that will help me save *my* woman. That's it."

A heavy pause as Halo flexed and unflexed his fingers, debating the truth of Paris's claim.

Circle, circle. "Information only," Paris reiterated. "I swear."

"No." He gave an abrupt shake of that pink head, his stubbornness a rival to that of a female. "I do not believe you. You carry the evil nature of a demon. You won't be able to help yourself. You will lust after her, take advantage of her. Bed her."

No, he wouldn't. He was too close to Sienna, and he would wait for her as long as he could and survive. Fine. So maybe the truth was—he might. Survival had caused him to do terrible things. Maybe he should point out that

Viola carried a demon, too. But then, Halo was past the point of thinking logically.

Paris sighed, the darkness rising again. "We finish this, then."

Paris...

"No!" he gritted, blocking Zacharel's voice from his head. "I tried your way. It didn't work."

He and Halo leapt at each other, meeting in the middle. Just as before, those meaty fists hammered at Paris. While the beating felt like stampeding demon hooves on his face, Halo's midsection was left wide-open. But rather than take the kill stabs as Paris had done with the others—some of Zacharel's light must have stuck around after all—he swept his arm low and sliced into Halo's thigh, barely nicking his femoral.

Still the beating continued to rain, the fallen never registering the fact that he was going to bleed out if he didn't leave and stitch himself up. Arms swinging, legs kicking, they fell into a table, toppled to the ground, rolled. Broken glass cut at Paris's arms, his back. He landed several searing blows, accidentally slicing with his blades, until finally he sent Halo stumbling backward, out of range.

Halo stood, gasping for breath as he stepped forward once, twice. Then he stopped and frowned with confusion. At last his knees gave out. He dropped like a stone in the ocean. His once-tanned skin blanched to an unnatural chalk-white, his tattoos dimming. His eyes were suddenly fever-bright.

Fallen angels did not heal like immortals. They healed like humans: slowly. Or not at all.

"You...you..."

"Won." Done, done and done. All three were felled. "Get some help, and you should recover just fine."

"But you…" Incredulity bathed Halo's punk-rocker features. "You won through cheating. That was a blade I felt. Multiple times!"

"Hate to break it to you, big boy, but cheating happens a lot. You might want to try it yourself. Besides, you said you didn't care what weapons I used."

There was muttering behind him.

Paris raised his arms and spun in slow motion. The crowd had yet to disperse, more concerned with collecting bets than escaping notice. "Who's next?" Blood dripped from his still-invisible daggers, pooling on the floor.

Suddenly they all had somewhere else to be. The sea of faces parted, giving him a direct view of Zacharel. The angel had his arms crossed over the wide expanse of his chest. His expression was troubled.

"Still here?" Paris arched a brow in challenge. "You want a piece of me, too?"

Frowning, silent, Zacharel vanished.

Seriously. Why the interest?

Does it matter? Urgency shooting through him, Paris stomped to Viola, who still studied herself in the mirror. He sheathed his weapons and jerked her toward the door. "Come on."

It was definitely time to go. One, he didn't want to risk anyone else deciding to fight him. Two, seeing him talking to her might be more than Halo could handle. And three, she might have changed her mind about telling him what he wanted to know. He'd have to get physical.

Halo watched her with longing in his eyes—and just before the door closed behind Paris, hatred. Yeah. The dude would be back for revenge. *Shoulda killed him.* He still could. But Paris opted not to return to finish the job.

If Zacharel reappeared and kicked up a stink, his game plan would be screwed.

"Hey," Viola said, at last snapping out of her trance. She tugged at his hold. A cool wind blew past them, caressing the silky length of her hair along his arm. "What do you think you're doing?"

I want her, Sex said, peeking from the shadows of his mind.

On a mission here. "I'm getting you to safety," he lied. "You don't want your admirers to swarm you, do you?"

She tugged harder. "Of course I do. Here's a lesson about women. We like to be admired from afar, and then complimented up close."

He seriously did not need lessons. "I meant your admirers weren't paying you the proper homage. They don't deserve your exalted presence."

And wouldn't you know it. Her resistance ended there. "You make an excellent point."

Of course, she'd missed his sarcasm.

He arrived at an abandoned alley and stopped. Perfect. The moon was so close he had only to reach out to trace the soft, orange-yellow edges. Clouds were closer still, enveloping him in a fine, dew-scented mist. Though the area was well-lit, no one passing by would see what transpired within the narrow space.

He rounded on Viola, pressing her against the solid gold bricks of the building, invading her personal space to gain her full attention. Except, her attention had already moved to her phone, her fingers flying over the keyboard.

I want, I want, I want!

I hope you rot and die.

"'Lord of Sex is bloodier than before and...ick... swollen. My eyes are not amused.' Send."

He claimed her phone and, rather than smashing it as instinct demanded, returned it to the inside of her boot. "You can Screech about this later. As for right now, you're going to talk to me. What can I do to see the dead? Remember, your worshippers insisted you tell me."

A pout of those lush lips, but she said, "Burn the body of the soul you wish to see and save the ashes. Speaking of, did I ever tell you about how I once saved the ashes of a—"

On and on she droned about what she'd done, then about herself, her life, and Paris tuned her out, a curtain of hope forming around his mind. He'd already burned Sienna's body and saved the ashes. At the time, he hadn't known why he'd done so; he'd only known he couldn't part with what remained of her. And ever since, he'd secretly carried a small vial of those ashes in his pocket.

Somehow, he must have suspected he would need them.

When Viola at last quieted, he said, "There's more to seeing a soul than saving the ashes." There had to be. A few weeks ago, Sienna had escaped Cronus, had hunted Paris down, yet Paris hadn't seen her.

He never would have known about her arrival if William the Ever Randy, another being who could commune with the dead, had not been with him and casually mentioned the dead girl at his feet. Of course, Cronus had swiftly tracked her down and dragged her back to her prison.

An act the Titan king would pay for.

"Duh, of course there is. Mix the ashes with ambrosia and tattoo the rim of your eyes," Viola said. "You'll see her, I promise. If you want to touch her, tattoo the tips of your fingers. If you want to hear her, tattoo the flesh behind your ears, blah blah blah. I remember a time when I—"

Once again he tuned her out. This he could, *would* do. Tattooing one's self with the ashes of the dead might be disgusting to most people, but Paris would have done a lot worse. "Will I smell her? Taste her?" he asked, interrupting Viola's monologue.

"Only if you tattoo the inside of your nose, lips and top of your tongue. One time, in Tartarus, I—"

"Wait."

Enough! I don't want her, Sex suddenly piped up. *Find someone else.*

Well, well. For once they were in agreement. "Is there anything else I should know? Any consequences I should be aware of—"

"Paris."

The familiar voice came from behind him. Paris whipped around, sickness already churning inside his stomach. Whenever Lucien visited him, bad news was quick on his heels. "What's wrong?"

CHAPTER FOUR

LUCIEN, KEEPER OF DEATH, stood tall and strong, a power-ful presence even through the haze of mist that envel-oped him. Like Viola, the warrior could flash from one location to another with only a thought. His dark hair was a mop of tangles sticking out in spikes. His eyes—one blue, one brown—were bright with concern. Dirt smudged his scarred cheeks, and there were rips in his wrinkled shirt and pants.

"Since I told you not to come back for me until I texted you, I take it that's not why you're here." Out of habit, Paris palmed his blades. "You better start talking."

Lucien's gaze strayed to Viola. "Get rid of her first."

The "her" in question straightened her spine with a jolt. "Oh, no, he didn't. I'm not some pretty a man can just toss aside whenever—oh, hey. You're Anya's man." The indignation left her, and she waved happily. "Hi! I'm Viola. As if you couldn't guess. My reputation for awesomeness precedes me, and I'm sure Anya has men-tioned me countless times."

She knew Anya, the minor goddess of Anarchy? A woman who had more balls than most men—because she'd cut them off the guys stupid enough to get in her way and kept them as souvenirs. Well, of course Viola knew Anya. They might have "minor" in their respec-tive titles, but they were both major pains in the ass.

Lucien's dark brows drew low. "No, she never—"

"Stops talking about you," Paris rushed out, halting his friend before he insulted the egomaniac. He ran his hand along the front of his neck, his fingers taut as a blade, the universal sign for *cut that out or die*.

"Yes," Lucien lied, frowning. "She mentions you all the time."

Viola laughed, a tinkling sound of amusement. "No need to state the obvious, you darling boy. As if I'm not aware of how often I come up in conversation."

"You should probably Screech about seeing Anya's man," Paris said. "Maybe describe him. Post a picture. Whatever."

Expression serious, she said, "Ixnay on the picture. Those are reserved for *my* image, otherwise my fans get twitchy. But the other thing...totally. Description is one of the many areas I shine in, since I shine in everything." She grabbed her phone and typed away. "Hair of indigo and eyes of crystal and chocolate, he stands before me..."

Paris met Lucien's confused stare. "She's the keeper of Narcissism, and she only registers conversations about herself." Clearly. "You can talk freely with me."

Lucien's eyes widened, and he studied Viola anew. "Another keeper? How did you find... Why isn't she...? Never mind. Doesn't matter right now." His focus whipped back to Paris. "I'm here because Kane's missing."

The sickness returned to burn a path up Paris's chest, stopping to play a game of tonsil hockey in his throat. "How long?"

"Just a few days. He and William were together. Someone captured them, took them into hell to execute them. Maybe Hunters, maybe not. Another group attacked the first. William says the cavern they were in collapsed and knocked him out before the men could do anything to him. When he woke up, he was in a motel room in Budapest. Without Kane."

Paris rubbed a hand down his face. "Is Kane still... alive?" He had trouble speaking that last word, much less thinking it. If his friend had been slain while he'd been chasing tail, he would never forgive himself.

"Yeah. He is. He has to be."

Because they couldn't stand the thought of living without him. "You putting together a posse to search for him?"

"That's why I'm here."

"Who do you have so far?"

"Amun, Aeron, Sabin and Gideon."

Nasty fighters, all of them. If Paris were missing, he'd want the same guys looking for him. Seriously, the only team capable of getting better results would be Jason Voorhees, Freddy Krueger, Michael Myers and Hannibal Lecter.

Amun was the keeper of Secrets, and there was no greater warrior to have on your side. The man was like a worm in your brain, able to ferret out in seconds information you'd buried for years. In fact, there was *nothing* anyone could hide from him. So Kane's location? No prob.

Aeron was the former keeper of Wrath. He'd recently been beheaded and given a new body, and that's when his demon had merged with Sienna. But even without his darker half, Aeron liked to make his prey squeal before he moved in for the kill. Anyone who'd hurt Kane would pay. Repeatedly.

Sabin was the keeper of Doubt, a warrior of unparalleled strength and determination, and he had a vicious streak that caused hardened criminals to soil their pants in fear. He got into your head, reminded you of your weaknesses, and basically turned you into a slobbering bag of self-recrimination before he savagely murdered you—with a grin on his face.

And Gideon, well, he was the keeper of Lies. He dyed his hair blue, was tattooed and pierced, and had a warped sense of humor very few others got. His new favorite game involved casting his demon from his body and into his enemy's, then sitting back and watching the human destroy himself as the evil consumed him.

Paris almost felt sorry for whoever had taken Kane. Almost.

"So, you in?" Lucien asked.

"I—" *Hate this.* He wanted to say yes. He did. He loved his friends. More than he loved himself, even more than Viola probably loved *her*self. (Speaking of, the damn woman was still typing, and from her mutterings, she was telling the world how the Lord of Death found her far more attractive than the goddess of Anarchy.) His friends had fought beside him, bled for him and always had his back.

They'd do more than take a bullet for him. They'd take a life—even their own. But... "I can't," he said, whether he'd be able to forgive himself or not. "Not right now. There's something I have to do first." His resolve, that cloud of darkness, still swirled inside him, driving him. He'd come this far; he couldn't back out now.

Lucien nodded without hesitation. "Understood." There was no trying to change Paris's mind, no making him feel guilty, which meant there was no better friend. "You want help with your mission?" he added, and damn if Paris didn't start to feel guilty anyway. "If you're headed into something dangerous, I'm happy to volunteer William."

William, Anya's best friend and someone Lucien

would love to see stabbed in the back. And heart. And groin. Willy wasn't possessed by a demon, but according to gossip he was the devil's blood-brother, as well as related to the Four Horsemen of the Apocalypse.

Gossip was probably right. Nothing scared William. Nothing bothered him. And the cherry on top? If Willy ever opened a closet door and the boogeyman jumped out, it was only the boogeyman who'd be scared.

"Bring him to me," Paris said. "He owes me." William had let Cronus take Sienna without a fight. As far as Paris was concerned, the guy was now his slave for life.

"Done." Lucien's gaze shifted to Viola, who was *still* typing. "What about her? We can't let her run around on her own. Cronus *and* the Hunters would doubtless love to snatch her."

Cronus hated the Hunters, and the Hunters hated Cronus. Both sides were searching for the remaining demon-possessed immortals, each hoping to recruit more than the other, and neither would shy away from using brute force to get what they wanted. Paris enjoyed the idea of screwing both parties over.

"Take her," he said, placing his hand on Viola's shoulder, meaning to shake her and gain her attention.

The action, innocent though it was, startled her, and between one heartbeat and the next, she went from gorgeously angelic to looking like the demon inside her. Two horns extended from her scalp. Red scales replaced her skin, and her eyes glowed like radioactive rubies. Sharp, deadly fangs protruded over her lips. Her nails grew into claws. The scent of sulfur overpowered the scent of roses, a scarlet mist wafting from her, stinging his nostrils, making *his* demon whimper like a newborn baby.

With a roar of white-hot rage, she sank those claws into Paris's wrist and tossed him so hard he smacked into the building next door, its solid gold bricks cracking and plumping filigree into the air.

Oxygen abandoned his lungs. Stars returned to his line of vision. What. The. *Hell?* When he was able to focus clearly, he saw that Viola was Viola again, exquisite, blonde and innocent.

"Oops. My bad." With a tinkling chuckle, she stuffed her phone into her boot. "Touching the merchandise isn't allowed. Ever. Now, did you need something from me?"

Lucien pinched the bridge of his nose. "This is gonna be fun. I can tell."

"Do you mind going with Lucien?" Paris asked her as he lumbered to his feet. Every new breath scraped his lungs against his ribs. Worse, the wound in his neck had opened. With one toss, she'd done far more damage to his body than the three amigos inside the bar had. "He'll take you to Anya and you two girls can, uh, catch up." He'd thought to force her to go. Now? He'd beg if necessary.

"Seriously?" Viola clapped, twirled and threw herself into Lucien's arms. "Yes, yes, a thousand times yes! I'm going with you, but only if you promise to stop and pick up my pet, Princess Fluffikans, on the way. Small word of warning, though. You're about to fall madly, passionately in love with me, and Anya will be utterly heartbroken."

It was far more likely that one of the other—single—warriors would fall madly, passionately in bed with her, but now wasn't the time to point that out.

Lucien fought off her octopus-like arms, scowled at Paris, and vanished with Viola jabbering about her majorly awesome awesomeness. Paris didn't bother staying where he was. Death could follow the spiritual trail he left behind, easy, and meet him somewhere else.

Time to do a little tattooing.

The mortal and immortal worlds were scarily alike. Titania was a thriving metropolis of shopping centers and restaurants, brimming with entertainment of any and every kind. Didn't take Paris long to gather the necessary tattooing equipment and a spare set of clothes, and settle into one of the motels he'd been amused to discover existed here. Apparently even immortals liked to have secret assignations.

As he waited for Lucien, he ate because it was de rigueur. A sandwich, and he had no idea what was strapped between the bread. He got himself off because that was necessary for his demon. He hadn't had sex today, and the orgasm was like an injection of strength. Strength that wouldn't last, not like the adrenaline rush that accompanied intercourse, but whatever. He'd take what he could get.

He showered, cleaned off the blood and the wealth of other things clinging to his skin. A lot of humans had died under his blade today. Hunters, his enemy. Mostly males. More and more, they were recruiting females. Paris wondered what would have happened if he'd met Sienna on the battlefield, or if he'd ever attempted to interrogate her.

If she'd lived long enough, that's what he had planned to do to her. *After* he'd bedded her again. Would he have hurt her? He liked to think no, but…damn. He couldn't be sure. She'd known things she shouldn't. Where he was, why he was there. How to distract him, what to use to drug him, an immortal unaffected by human toxins. Now he knew she'd gotten her info from Rhea, Cronus's wife and the true leader of the Hunters. Not directly, he didn't think, but filtered down through the ranks. But even if he hadn't known, he wouldn't have concerned himself with questioning her this time around. He just wanted her.

Safe, right? You just want her safe? A sneer from Sex.

Whatever. Paris toweled off and looked himself over in the steam-fogged mirror. He'd lost a little weight, had bruises under his eyes, a few scratches on his cheeks and neck. His hair wasn't exactly even. He'd trimmed the strands himself, just kind of chopping anytime a piece fell into his eyes. What would Sienna think of him now? Despite everything, she'd been attracted to him before. Would she still be attracted to him? Right now, he might be a little too feral for *any* woman. Very mountain-man meets post-traumatic stress survivor.

But what if the impossible happened and she did, in fact, want him again? For real, with no hidden agenda. What if she simply craved his body inside of hers? After all, she'd fought her way free of Cronus's prison and come looking for him.

Lowering his guard would be stupid. He couldn't trust her. Not really. He could take her, yeah, that was still on the menu. If he could still get hard for her while he was around her. Only time would tell. And if he could—and he thought he could, considering he was hard merely from thinking about her—maybe he could even stay with her a few days. If so, would his hunger for her finally wane? Or would it continue to intensify? Would he be able to let her go when the time came?

What if she *wanted* to stay with him?

He yearned for that. So damn badly he yearned for that. But like Zacharel had said, Paris would ruin her if he kept her. Not for the reasons the angel had given, but because if he and Sienna were ever separated and he couldn't get to her, he would cheat on her. He would have to. His other choice would be death, and on the scales of life-versus-death, cheating—surviving—won every time.

He knew that firsthand, had once tried to sustain a relationship with a woman. Susan. He'd had her, knew he couldn't have her again, but had craved something more and had pleased her in other ways. He'd genuinely liked her, had enjoyed her company—but had ultimately cheated on her, hurting her worse than anyone else ever had.

And here was another slap of truth: if he cheated on Sienna, he would destroy everything they had managed to build, as well as her heart, her sense of trust and any hint of innocence. He would be worthy of every dark deed she then committed against him—yet still he wanted her.

The situation was *so* messed up.

Scowling, he slammed his fist into the mirror. Jagged pieces of glass fell, shattering further when they hit the floor, surrounding his discarded weapons and glistening like diamonds in a sea of destruction. Blood dripped from his knuckles as he palmed and sheathed the blades at his wrists and ankles and holstered the guns under his arms. At this rate, he'd soon be carving himself up like Reyes, the keeper of Pain. Anything for release, for a moment when he didn't have to wonder or worry about anything but his injuries.

Whatever. He'd gotten used to wondering and worrying. They were his constant companions now, and without them, he'd be utterly alone. Paris dressed in the new clothes he'd bought, a black shirt and black pants. Where he was going, night reigned no matter the time of day. He needed to blend.

Not long ago, he'd snuck into Cronus's secret harem

and seduced one of the concubines, trading sex for information. Paris now knew Sienna was being held in the Realm of Blood and Shadows, part of Titania but…not. The realm was a kingdom within this heavenly kingdom, invisible to most and protected by evil. To enter was to die, blah, blah, blah.

Paris could find the realm on his own, no problem. He'd gotten very good at bribing his way through the heavens, even the hidden areas. Finger-combing his wet hair, he padded to the desk in the living-room-slash-bedroom. He sat down and spread out his new tattoo equipment. Part of him wished he was out there, killing Hunters or already making his way into the Realm of Blood and Shadows. These delays sucked.

To his immense relief, Lucien found him a short while later, appearing in the center of the room. "I felt bad for stiffing you with Willy, so I brought you a prize."

Death shoved the drenched, protesting William in Paris's direction, then motioned to Zacharel, who stood at his other side. The "prize," as though he was something out of a Cracker Jack box.

"Actually," Zacharel said in that cold voice of his. "I brought myself. Lucien was hunting you, and I saved him the time and trouble."

Paris popped his jaw. "Thanks tons," he said to Lucien, ignoring the angel. "Mean that."

William, my sweet William! I want him, Sex said, practically spraying drool through Paris's mind. Sex *always* wanted a piece of the guy. Not that Paris had ever admitted that aloud. Not that he ever would.

"So sad I can't remain," Lucien said with mock pity. "By the way, Viola's pet, Princess Fluffycakes or whatever, is a Tasmanian devil *and* a vampire. You're lucky

I'm leaving without slitting your throat." Once again, the warrior vanished.

As tiny snowflakes swirled around him, Zacharel eyed the room with distaste. "What are you doing here?"

"Seriously man, it's a dump," William added. "When I'm in the heavens, I only ever stay at the West Godlywood. Can we at least request a suite?"

No, they wouldn't be playing either man's version of the Q-and-A game. They would be playing Paris's. "Why is it always snowing around you lately?" he demanded of Zach.

"There is a reason."

So not helpful on any level. "Will you share it?"

"No."

"Are you following me?"

"Yes."

At least he didn't try to deny it. Not that he could have. Angels spoke the truth, and only ever the truth, which made Zacharel's earlier threat to kill him all the more real. "Why?"

"You are not yet ready to hear the answer."

Paris loved that kind of cryptic crap, he really did. "If you're going to stick around, make yourself useful and tattoo the rest of me." For the lines around his eyes, he needed a steady hand. "Then you can help me kick ass and not bother with names."

Zacharel leveled him with a frown as fierce as the flurry of snowflakes storming from the ends of his wings. "I have never tattooed anyone before. I'm likely to mar you."

And yet, he would still do a better job than William, no question. "The worst you can do is poke out my eyes, but that's hardly a concern since they'll grow back. Eventually."

That frown deepened, minutes ticking by. "Very well. I will do this for you."

"Yes, you make yourself useful, angel boy. Meanwhile, I'll be in the bathroom." William's jet-black hair was dripping wet and plastered to his face. There was a fluffy white towel wrapped around his waist, displaying muscles that rivaled Paris's own, and a tattooed treasure map that led to his man junk. Looking at him, you could see the makings of a temper so savage anyone who miraculously survived an encounter with him would end up needing therapy. And diapers. "I've *got* to finish deep conditioning my hair."

Or maybe *not* so savage.

No matter. Paris had never been closer to finding and saving Sienna. With these two warriors at his side, he'd succeed. Guaranteed.

CHAPTER FIVE

SIENNA BLACKSTONE, newly crowned Queen of the Beasts, Princess of Blood and Shadows, and Duchess of Horror, stood with her back pressed into the crumbling stone wall of the castle she unwillingly called home. Her wings were heavy, constantly pulling at recently formed tendons and bones, making her ache, cringe and, humiliatingly enough, sometimes cry.

The wings arched over her shoulders and draped down her sides in a cascade of midnight, their spiky tips now reaching the floor. She remembered seeing these very wings on Aeron, the previous host for the demon of Wrath. On his muscled, grimly tattooed body, they had appeared soft, gossamer, as weightless and beautiful as storm clouds. On her slight frame, they overpowered and overwhelmed and she had trouble finding her balance.

Sadly, that wasn't the worst of her problems. Cronus, god of gods (according to him) and all around asshat (according to her), paced in front of her, ranting and raving. Saying he was "upset" would be the equivalent of saying the Atlantic was a rain puddle.

When she'd first met him, he'd looked like a codger of an old man, complete with gray hair, wrinkled skin and stooped shoulders. Now he was *GQ* flawless and barbarian tough. Dark chestnut hair hung to strong, wide shoulders. Skin of the smoothest texture was tanned to the perfect shade of bronze. He'd also ditched his prissy toga in favor of a black mesh shirt and black leather pants.

The change was gargantuan—and creepy. She wanted to ask why he'd gone this route, then offer to punish his stylist free of charge. Did she dare? Heck, no. The ranting and raving would morph into a straight-up savage beating. At least, that's the impression he gave.

"I saved you," he snapped, death in his timbre as he stomped one foot in front of the other, back and forth, back and forth. "I strengthened you. Gifted you with your demon. And how do you repay me? By constantly refusing to obey me. It's unconscionable!"

Gifted? *Really?* If the new definition of *gifted* was *cursed forever and ever with misery and pain,* then yeah, he had. "I obeyed you," she reminded him. *At first.*

"At first," he said, parroting her thoughts. *His* was an accusation that lashed like the sharpest of whips. "And only because you were compelled. You've since learned to block me."

True. And that she had was a testament to the iron-hard rigidity of her stubborn core. With only a thought, this huffing, puffing being could render unending pain. With a wave of his hand, he could vaporize entire cities. Something she would do well to remember.

Sienna chose her next words carefully. "To be fair, you tricked me." Okay, so maybe she hadn't chosen carefully. At least her tone had been as flat and unaccusatory as possible.

A narrowed flick of his gaze nearly buckled her knees. "How so?"

She pressed more of her weight into the wall. "You promised I would see my younger sister."

You look so pretty, Enna.

Really?

Really. You're the prettiest girl in the whole wide world!

Skye, her only sibling, a little girl she'd adored with her whole heart, had been abducted years ago, never to be seen or heard from again. Sienna missed her terribly, prayed she was healthy, whole and that she hadn't suffered incomparable cruelties.

"Yet you merely teased me with a glimpse of her," she added, rubbing her stomach as she always did when she thought of her sister, reminded of yet *another* girl, someone else she'd loved and lost, the— She cut that thought off before it could form. *I won't break down in front of this creature.*

Cronus ground his molars. "That glimpse… I should have known it would come back to haunt me." He paused, a low growl bubbling from his throat. "I guess I should at last admit the truth, then. I showed you an illusion of your sister, nothing more."

Wait, wait, wait. An *illusion?* Sienna bit her tongue. Why would he… How could he…? No matter the question, the answer was simple. To play her like a piano, as Paris had once said to her *about* her. *Bastard* wasn't a vile enough word for this beast.

Steady, calm. "Is she even alive?" Sienna gritted out.

"Of course."

There was no *of course* with Cronus. He lived by his own set of rules, and he didn't always abide by those.

Every time he appeared before her, her demon showed her the despicable things he'd done throughout his life. The lives he'd taken, striking down not just his enemies, but his own people, humans, *anyone* who dared defy him. And he'd stolen, oh, had he stolen. Ancient artifacts, powers that belonged to others, women. He had no shame. No limits.

"How do I know you're telling the truth now?"

"You won't. Your demon will."

A suspended moment as she searched inside herself. Wrath was calm, not worked into a frenzied need to punish him for lying. That glimpse of Skye had indeed been an illusion, but Cronus did believe she was still alive. Sienna gritted her teeth, saying, "Bring her to me, the *real* Skye, and let me keep her, *then* I'll do anything you ask."

"No."

"Why?" She stamped her foot. It was childish, sure, but she had no other way to express her displeasure with this man. "Do you, a supposedly all-knowing being, not know where she is?"

In a blink, he was a mere whisper away, scowling down at her, his breath fanning over her. "Enough about your sister! Aren't you curious why I gifted you with Wrath? You, a fragile, dearly departed female who had upset one of my strongest warriors? Aren't you curious about my desire for your willing participation in my war?"

Do not suggest the king of the Titans needs a breath mint. She gulped. *And don't you dare think about the warrior you upset. Don't you dare think about Paris.* Oh, no, no, no. "Y-yes." And now she was stuttering? *Grow some lady balls, Blackstone!*

Red flashed in Cronus's eyes. Demon-red. A fiendish crimson that made her think of blood mixed with nuclear toxins. Not only was he the king of the Titans, but he was also possessed by Greed—and right now, his demon was at the wheel, driving his actions, his words. Around her, the castle shook, his anger rattling its very foundation.

"You know the Hunters. You know how they operate. You were once a part of their cause."

"I know." As if she could ever forget or absolve herself. Once she'd even borne the symbol of infinity on her wrist, their mark. A permanent reminder of their "goals." In this spirit form, she had no tattoos but the butterfly around her wings, and for that, she was immensely grateful. "The same is true for thousands of others."

Except those thousands of others actually had no idea they were fools, or that they were expendable, nothing more than puppets on strings. Like she had been—until she'd gotten a bitch slap of truth and clipped those strings with brutal proficiency.

Soon after Wrath's possession of her, Cronus had whisked her to a Hunter compound. Because Cronus could shield himself from prying eyes and humans could not see her, no one had noticed them. Just as she'd seen the king's sins play through her mind, she'd seen the transgressions of the Hunters. Thefts, rapes, murders, all in the name of "good." That she had once been a (supposedly vital) part of their cause, that she had once aided them...

Punish them... Steal, rape, murder...

There he was. Wrath. Her dark companion. Even remembering what he'd seen, and being worlds apart from those responsible, he urged her to seek vengeance against the Hunters. To show no mercy, no forgiveness for even the innocent among them, for all the harm they had caused, to hurt them far worse than they had hurt others.

Punish...

Cringing, she covered her ears with her hands. "Shut up, shut up, shut up," she chanted. Sometimes she could resist him; sometimes she could not. That's when he would overtake her, and her world would go black. For a little while, at least.

Though she was cursed to remain inside this deteriorating monstrosity of a castle, somehow Wrath was not. When he was in control of her mind, they could leave. He would use her body to castigate others however he wished.

Days later, she would wake up with blood on her hands, coating her skin. Of course, memories of what the demon had done would then deluge her. Sadistic, stomach-curdling things. And yet, nothing—*nothing!*—he had forced her to do was more disgusting than what the Hunters were doing to innocent humans.

Humans. How odd her new vernacular was to her. Once *she'd* been a human. Such a foolish human. *How could I ever have thought the goal of the Hunters was the* elimination *of evil?*

Well, okay, that was easy. As a teenager, she'd seen a vile demon in action—or what she'd thought was a demon—and the experience had freaked her out, convinced her that such evil was the reason her sister had been taken. Combine that with the shock of learning that humans were not alone, that there was an entire world of creatures at work around them…

The whole other-world thing had proven to be true, at least. But the rest, the demon she'd seen? While they did in fact exist, she hadn't encountered one that night. Her Hunter boyfriend had drugged her—his preferred method of recruiting—created the perfect atmosphere to elicit fear, and her hallucinating brain had filled in the rest. Afterward, he'd fed her fear with stories of the evil they could fight and the good they could do, saying she might even be able to find and save her sister.

What he'd failed to tell her: humans made their own decisions, influenced by demons or not. They decided to embrace the dark or run into the light.

Not all Hunters cloaked their malevolence with righteous determination; she knew that, she did. Some were genuinely sincere in their desire to rid the world of evil, and wouldn't create their own to do so. But the fact that she had once willingly contributed to such a warped cause, well, she would never get over that fact. Worse, *she* had hurt Paris, a warrior who would give his life to protect the ones he loved.

There was no stopping the next flood of thoughts, each revolving around the man she had once harmed beyond repair. She had struck at Paris when he was at his weakest. Worse, she would have aided in his cold-blooded murder if he hadn't escaped with her.

During that escape, she was shot down and she'd even blamed him for that, thinking he had used her body to shield his own. Oh, how she had despised him. Now, she despised only herself.

No, that wasn't exactly true. She also hated the Hunters and everything they represented.

Cronus wanted her to punish them. Her demon wanted to punish them. *She* wanted to punish them. But Cronus refused to simply unleash her. Instead he demanded she return to their midst and spy on Galen, the leader's right-hand man, as well as the keeper of Hope. Yep, a demon was second-in-command of the demon slayers, and none of them knew it. They thought he was an angel.

"As devoted as you were to the Hunter cause in life, Galen will believe you wish to rejoin him in your death," Cronus said, as though reading her thoughts. Maybe he had. "He will welcome you with open arms."

"He won't be able to see me."

"He will. Leave that to me."

"He won't wonder why I'm demon-possessed? *How* I'm demon-possessed?"

"He knows. My wife, *his* leader, told him. But he is overly confident of his appeal and his strength, and he will think *he* is watching *you*."

"In that case, he'll never tell me anything."

"No, he'll feed you false information, and the truth can be garnered from that."

"What if he asks me to prove my loyalty to him?"

"He will."

And she would be forced to comply to continue her ruse. Would he ask her to hurt the warriors she now wished to aid? To hurt innocent humans? Well, the answer to both was the same. Never!

Look at me. Once a human who didn't know about the supernatural, then a Hunter in the midst of it all, hating the demons I chased, and now I'm one of those demons—and hoping to aid the others. "Sorry, but I'm gonna have to stick with my first answer."

Another flash of red streaked through Cronus's eyes, brighter than before. If she was intelligent, she would view that red as a stoplight for her resistance.

Why start acting like a smartie now? "That's a big-time no, in case you forgot," she said more firmly.

"Your human superior ordered you to sleep with Paris," he growled, "and you did. Do not try and act self-righteous with me."

Yes, but her attraction to Paris had been immediate and overwhelming. She had yearned for him.

Yearned for him, even though she believed his demon was responsible for infidelity, the breakup of marriages, teen pregnancies, rapes and the rampant spread of STDs. Even though Paris had been, and would always be, at the head of a never-ending parade of lovers. A fact driven home by a coworker who had watched him for days, snapping pictures of all the women he bedded, then showing those pictures to Sienna after she'd brought him in. And yet she'd still had to fight a wave of jealousy, an emotion she never should have felt in the line of duty.

Had she mentioned her mental incompetence?

"If he asks you to kill for him, seduce him into bed instead," Cronus said. "That will save you from having to do something unpleasant."

They certainly had different definitions for *unpleasant!* "You'd be better served demanding I bring you Galen's head in a magical box of starlight while riding on the back of a Pegasus through a rainbow, because he won't want me sexually. I've never been the type to attract a man's attention."

She knew what she looked like. Hazel eyes too big for her face—ordinary. Lips also too big for her face—unappealing. Freckled skin—unfashionable. And wavy brown hair that was neither silky-straight nor perkily curly—ordinary, unappealing *and* unfashionable.

Cronus remained undeterred. "You're right. You haven't."

The truth can't hurt you, she told herself—while hurting.

"But then," he went on, "your looks will not matter. Galen will be attracted to your demonic power. He'll want to control you, to feed you all that false information, to use you. Yes, the more I think on this, the more I like it. You will sleep with him."

She ran her tongue over her teeth. "Killing Galen will destroy the heart and soul of the Hunters far more effectively than pleasuring him."

"Yes, but dying is not his fate."

"What's his fate, then? What is it, exactly, you think he can do for you?"

Silence.

Deep breath in…out… "Okay, there are two problems with your plan. Galen's a douche bag, and I suck in bed." Wait. That hadn't come out right. "I mean, even if he only wants me for my demonic power—" just saying the words grated "—or because he thinks he can feed me false info, or control me or whatever other reason you think up, he'll never come back for seconds because we'll both be embarrassed by our performances, and the entire plan will be moot."

The only reason she'd garnered Paris's interest was because he'd been desperate to get laid—by anyone!—in order to survive. "Galen is more likely to laugh at me than tell me his secrets."

Perfectly trimmed brows arched, fixing the king's features in a patronizing expression. "You can be trained."

"So can dogs, but they'll only bite you." She would do far worse.

A beat of silence as he absorbed her taunt. "Woman, you frustrate me! I'm not asking you to willingly submit to torture. I'm merely asking you to allow a man to have you in the name of duty—as you have allowed before."

"That's too big a commitment for me. I kill him, or I do nothing to him."

"Galen is an immortal warrior who has spent thousands of years on a battlefield. How do you propose you kill him, hmm?"

"Just leave that to me," she said, mimicking his earlier words. "And, hey, here's another idea. Why can't *you* kill him? I thought you were all-powerful."

"Enough!" With a scowl as dark as a moonless night, Cronus slammed his fists on either side of her temples, creating holes in the wall and causing bricks to fall and dust to plume in the air.

Rattle…rattle…

Great. The entire castle was shaking again.

"How dare you, a slave, question me? I am your master, your owner. The arbiter of your fate. I answer to no one."

Except to your wife. With the royal sovereigns, hurting one always hurt the other, pain slithering across the bond between them. But Sienna wasn't going to remind him of that little gem. "I don't care who you are. I will not align myself with Galen."

Before she could so much as blink, Cronus fit his hands around her neck and squeezed until she could no longer breathe, until her lungs burned and her throat felt scaled by acid. *Rattle, rattle,* went the walls, as if the entire structure might collapse from within. "I can be the executioner of your soul, and you will cease to exist in every way, or I can be your savior, granting you a measure of peace at long last." Tighter…tighter…then, abruptly, the pressure eased. "Remember that, for you are the one who will decide your ultimate fate."

She barely curbed the urge to feed him both of her knuckles. "Whatever I decide," she snapped, uncaring of the consequences, "you're still an asshole."

Surprising her, he gave a grin full of teeth. "Aren't I, though?"

At one time, Sienna had been mild mannered, afraid of hurting anyone's feelings, desperate to smooth any and all ruffled feathers. Maybe the demon's bad mood had bled into her. Or maybe the waspishness came courtesy of knowing just how worthless her entire life had been. Either way, she had never had more to lose—or cared so little.

"You should have picked someone else to host Wrath. Because…wait for it…*my answer is still no.*"

Rather than adding fuel to the seething cauldron of his

temper, her words seemed to make him back down. His features softened, the murderous rage draining from his gaze, his taut lips sliding back over his teeth. He lowered his arms.

Shocking.

"No," he said, gentle, so gentle now. "There was no better choice than you."

Her heart drummed fitfully in her chest. Though she was dead, her spirit self had developed a heartbeat, a need to breathe, the moment the demon had entered her soul-body. Unfortunately, this meant she could feel pain and if cut she would bleed.

"Why me?" she finally asked. "You have to tell me *something*."

"Do I?" He turned, offering his profile and ignoring her question. "In this realm hidden from the rest of the heavens, where no one will ever find you, I don't *have to* do anything."

A muscle drummed rapidly in his jaw, and before she could reply he added, "Do you enjoy living here, Sienna?"

"No." Not because she was magically compelled to remain inside this castle, but because he'd done what he could to make her time here a misery. Including digging deep inside her mind and yanking out the worst of her memories. Those memories played out like movies in every room, a never-ending stream of persecution, guilt and shame.

Every day she relived Skye's abduction. How she'd failed to save her sister from the man dragging her away. Every day she witnessed the loss of the baby she'd been unable to bring to term, something she *hated* remembering, would never willingly dwell on. Every day she saw her foolish betrayal of the beautiful Paris. How she'd hurt the first man to ever make her crave *more*. How she'd condemned him simply because of his race.

"That's too bad. Because you will remain here until you agree to return to your flock and become my spy."

Back in the air went her nose. "If those are my choices, I'll stay here forever."

Cronus tossed her another grin, a cruel twist of his lips that lacked any hint of amusement. "Is that so? What if I told you that I picked you *because* of your sister?"

"I would demand to know why." Her eyes narrowed to tiny slits, the king of Titans in their crosshairs. He was tricky, without morals and utterly devious. She had to be careful. "I would also point out that you could have played that particular card sooner."

"Not if I feared you would obsess over her and forget my purpose. Now, however, you have left me no choice."

She feigned nonchalance and buffed her nails.

He hissed at her. "What if your precious Skye once lived with Galen? What if she bore him a child?"

Take me swimming, Enna. Please, please, please. I'll never ask for anything ever again.

"I don't believe you." The denial gasped from her, a croak of dismay. *He's lying. He has to be lying.* "Show her to me." She forced herself to add, "Please," though the word was gritted.

He wasn't done. "What if Galen is the only one who knows where they are? What if he tortures them? What if becoming his whore is the only way for you to learn the truth? The only way to save them?"

"I—I—" Had no answer. *He's lying!* The scream of desperation echoed through her mind—her own, not her demon's. She had to stay strong. Had to insist he present at least a modicum of proof before she reacted.

"Think about all I have told you, my darling Sienna. I

will return soon and we will discuss any new duties you might wish to take on." With that, he disappeared, there one moment, gone the next.

Sienna sank to her knees, her strength leaving with the king. Her eyes burned, her chin trembled. Her wings pulled and folded in ways they shouldn't, and a sharp cry escaped her. *Every* damned *day* was a new lesson in horror for her.

Tears trickled down her cheeks, scalding her skin. How much more could she take? How much longer until she broke?

For Skye, she'd do just about anything, and Cronus knew that. Skye was all she had left, having somehow become both sister and daughter in her mind. Made sense, though. She'd only known her sister as a little girl, and the baby she'd lost, a girl as well, had never gotten the chance to grow out of infancy. And the possibility of a niece or nephew? Yeah, she'd do anything.

Cronus knew that. No wonder he'd reined in his temper. He didn't have to hurt her physically to get what he wanted. No wonder he'd chosen Sienna for his games. She was still a puppet, the strings she thought she'd cut anchored to another master's hand.

Worse, there was no way to fight this one.

CHAPTER SIX

PARIS SPRAWLED IN an unfamiliar bed, one hand at his side and gripping a crystal blade, the other draped over his forehead, shielding his eyes. After a few days of traveling, closer than ever to his goal, he was in another motel in Titania, with Zacharel…somewhere, and William snoozing peacefully on the bed beside his.

In quiet moments like this, Paris's mind always hopped the Memory Train, taking him back to when he'd first met Sienna, and tonight was no different. He remembered walking the streets of Rome, in desperate need of a lover, every woman he encountered shooing him away as if he were repugnant. Then someone had rammed into him from behind, and weak as he'd been from the lack of sex, he'd nearly fallen flat on his face before he'd managed to right himself.

"I'm so sorry," he'd heard her say, the sensual rasp of her voice thrilling him on every level.

He turned slowly, afraid that if he moved too quickly he would frighten her and she would run away like the others. Papers were scattered around her feet, and she crouched, trying to gather them. First thing to register was dark hair curtaining a face hidden by shadows.

"That'll teach me to read and walk at the same time," she muttered.

"I'm glad you were reading," he said, bending down

to help her. "I'm glad we ran into each other." More than she would ever know.

Her heavily lashed lids lifted, and her gaze met his. She gasped. He reeled. She was on the plain side, with eyes and lips too big for her face and skin dotted with uncountable freckles, but she possessed a grace and presence so few mortals could ever hope to attain.

"Your name doesn't start with an A, does it?" he asked her, suddenly suspicious of fate and master plans. Maddox had recently become a sap for a woman named Ashlyn. Lucien had abandoned his manhood for Anya. Paris refused to do the same for anyone.

Her brow puckered in confusion, and she shook her head, that fall of dark hair waving around her delicate shoulders. "No. My name is Sienna. Not that you care and not that you really asked. Sorry. I didn't mean to just blurt it out."

"I care," he replied huskily, thinking he would have the best time stripping her. One, her clothes bagged on her, hiding the secrets of her femininity. Two, she was skittish, her babbling charming, and he expected a similar reaction in bed. "You're…American?"

"Yes. Vacationing here to work on my manuscript. Again, not that you asked. I can't place your accent, though."

"Hungarian," he said, giving her the simplest answer. The Lords had been living in Budapest for a while, and there was no way to explain—without sounding crazy—that he spoke languages she'd never even heard of. "So you are a writer?"

"Yes. Well, I hope to be. Wait, that's not right, either. I *am* a writer, but I'm not published yet."

Now, of course, he knew the truth. She wasn't a writer.

The pages of her romance novel had merely served as a launch pad for their sensual conversation, nothing more.

When she'd next asked him to grab a coffee with her, he'd said yes, already throbbing with need for her. They'd talked and laughed the entire time, and he'd enjoyed every moment of it. He'd relaxed with her, something he hadn't been able to do with very many others. But she had a contagious smile, a keen wit, and that grace of motion that matched her demeanor.

Meanwhile, his demon shot out wafts of his pheromones, so there'd been no great difficulty in convincing her to rent a hotel room with him. Or so he'd thought at the time. Along the way, she had pretended to change her mind. Or hell, maybe she *had* changed her mind. Maybe she'd fallen in like with him, too, and had decided not to hand him over to her Hunter brethren. But sex fiend that Paris was, he'd pressed her for more, dragging her into an abandoned alley and kissing the breath out of her.

That's when she drugged him, using a needle hidden in one of her rings. He'd woken up strapped to a gurney, naked and groggy. She had crouched in front of him, and he'd assumed the Hunters had taken her prisoner, too. Until she'd said four little words that changed the nature of their relationship.

"*I* locked you up."

His brilliant reply? "Why would you do something like that?" He still hadn't wanted to believe this woman he so craved had something to do with his current circumstances.

"Can't you guess?" she asked. She angled his head to the side, and, studying his neck, traced a fingertip over a sore spot. Puncture wound, he'd realized, the answer to her question slipping into place, taking root.

"You're my enemy."

"Yes." Then she'd added with a frown, "The wound isn't healing. I didn't mean to jab you with the needle quite so forcefully. For that, I'm sorry."

His eyes narrowed on her, feelings of betrayal and disbelief whisking through him. "You tricked me. Played me like a piano."

Again, "Yes."

"Why? And don't tell me you're Bait. You're not pretty enough." He'd said it to be cruel, but now, remembering, he cringed. No wonder she had later done what she'd done, said what she'd said.

A blush stained her cheeks. "No, I'm not Bait. Or rather, I wouldn't have been to any warrior but you. But then, you don't care who you screw, do you, Promiscuity?" Every word had dripped with disgust, his charming, babbling romance writer long gone. But the grace… oh, that she couldn't banish.

"Obviously not." When her blush deepened, he added silkily, just to taunt her further, "Aren't you afraid I'll hurt you?"

"No. You haven't the strength. I made sure of that."

Her newfound resistance to him, no matter how poorly he acted, irked. Females adored him, always. Well, almost always. "You enjoyed yourself while you were in my arms. Admit it. I know women, and I know passion. You were on fire for me."

"Shut up," she snapped.

Good. He was getting to her. "Want to give me a go before your friends show up?"

After that particular jab, she had stomped away from him, but she hadn't left the room. Remaining a safe distance away, she admitted her status—Hunter—and detailed exactly what her friends planned to do to him.

"We're going to experiment on you. Observe you. Use

you as Bait to capture more demons. And then, when we find Pandora's box, we're going to draw out your demon, killing you and trapping the monster inside."

Warrior that he was, and as many battles as he'd fought, he'd known to show her only indifference. "That it?"

"For now."

"You might as well kill me then, sweetheart. My friends won't surrender themselves to save little old me."

"We'll see about that, won't we?"

When he realized antagonizing her wasn't helping his cause, he switched to seduction, his default setting. He projected sexual images into her head, something he hated to do. *Didn't* do anymore. He couldn't live with himself afterward. And as she had pictured what he wanted her to picture—the two of them together, naked and straining toward climax—her breathing became choppy, her nipples hard underneath her shirt. A white shirt that did nothing to hide the lace of her bra, proving she had a secret sensual side.

He'd almost had her, but in the end, she'd wised up. He'd made the mistake of continuing to call her sweetheart, an endearment he'd used on countless others, and she'd known it. After that, it hadn't taken her long to figure out he used the term because he couldn't remember her name—or anyone else's.

Finally she'd left him for real, only returning a few days later when he was a few breaths away from death. That's when she at last stripped for him, at last pleasured him.

That's when he killed her.

CHAPTER SEVEN

THE NEXT MORNING, Paris stood at the highest edge of a cliff overlooking the Realm of Blood and Shadows, his body poised for war. Finally, he'd found his destination, hidden in a far corner of Titania, its portal invisible to everyone but William. What do you know? The guy had his uses.

Now Paris would find Sienna.

His blood boiled with the fury he'd suppressed for far too long. His muscles burned with startling ferocity, and his bones vibrated with the need to act, to hurt someone. Multiple someones.

Soon.

Sharp gusts of wind blustered, doing nothing to scatter the shroud of thick, black mist surrounding him, seeping inside of him. The scent of aged copper filled the air, leaving a moist film in his nose. Muted shrieks echoed from every direction, so many shrieks of pain. Above, the moon formed a sallow hook, its ends frayed, hemorrhaging into an endless expanse of unforgiving night. Below, an ocean of crimson tears frothed and hissed, creating a second symphony of anguish.

And there, in the center of it all, perched a nightmare of a castle. Dark stone crumbled. Withered ivy with dagger-sharp tips climbed the walls, every leaf reminding him of a spider. The roof knifed into several points, a body staked through the heart and hanging from each, dripping blood onto the glass panes of every window. There were several balconies guarded by multiple gargoyles of every size.

Gargoyles that would, apparently, come to life.

Writhing shadows, slick and oily in appearance, hovered around the entire structure, but they didn't touch a single stone. They maintained a generous distance, as if a rod of iron held them in place. The moment they heard the starting bell, whatever that was, Paris suspected they would burst free and attack whoever happened to be nearby.

"She's inside," he told his companions. "I know it." He wanted to go in, guns blazing. Was desperate to go in, guns blazing and knives slashing, but he couldn't. Not yet, not yet. Information had to come first.

Death was in the details.

"That's great, wonderful, but why am I here again?" William asked, scratching his head. He consumed the space at Paris's left, dressed for the runway rather than the front lines. Silk suit, no weapons. A bottle of conditioner in his pocket. Yeah. Conditioner. Again. For split ends. A little jaunt into hell had "damaged some of the precious strands," so he now carried his "necessary daily treatment" *everywhere*.

Annnd hearing his voice caused Sex to purr like a kitten. It was disgusting.

"I'm still recovering from agonizing physical and mental trauma," William added. The warrior had barely escaped from his encounter in hell, true, but being crushed by boulders and clawed by flesh-hungry fiends was hardly agonizing.

"Just, I don't know, consider this your punishment for abandoning Kane," Paris said. How many gargoyles would he have to battle? He did a quick head count. Fifty-nine from the front. Probably a similar number waited in back. Half of them were as big as dragons, but some were as small as rats.

As William could probably tell him, size didn't always matter. Which of the creatures would cause the most damage?

"I didn't abandon him. Per se." William brushed a piece of lint from his shoulder. "I was pummeled by falling rock and woke up in a motel in Budapest. In my compromised mental state, I thought some demon damsel in heat had taken one look at my amazing body and rescued us, but then Kane thought to remove her from my rugged animal appeal, and so he dragged her out to get coffee, not yet realizing he was simply energizing her for the mattress marathon to come. A marathon with me, in case I wasn't clear on that point."

Paris didn't bother rolling his eyes. Clearly William was Viola's male counterpart. Wasn't that a nice little bouquet of roses?

"Actually, you're here because you owe Paris a favor." Zacharel flanked Paris's other side, the snowstorm now brewing above him. The change had happened the moment he'd stepped into this realm. He still wore his robe, but blades were now strapped all over his muscled body. He was definitely warrior-appropriate. "More than that, you are avoiding your girlfriend."

William gasped with outrage. "First, I don't owe *anyone* a favor. Second, I don't have a girlfriend, you pansy-ass winged piece of shit."

"Don't you?" A blink, all innocence. Zacharel didn't seem to care about the name-calling. "What is young Gilly to you, then?"

Gilly. A human with a crush on William. The warrior claimed they were just friends and nothing more, but if anyone could see secret longing in someone's gaze, it was Paris. And William definitely had a lot of secret longing going on for that girl. Shockingly, though, he hadn't done anything about it. Had only coddled and babied her, which was why Paris hadn't gutted him. Gilly had been through enough in her short life without William turning his lethal charm on her.

Dangerous as a lightning strike, as lethal as a pair of crisscrossing short swords, William whispered, "You're about to find out how your liver tastes, my friend."

"I have tasted it already," Zacharel said, his voice its usual monotone. The snowflakes began to fall in earnest, tiny at first, but growing in diameter. An arctic wind blustered around him. "It was a bit salty."

How the hell was a guy supposed to respond to *that*?

Apparently William didn't know, either, because he gaped at the angel. Then, "Maybe if you added a little pepper?"

O-kay. It was official. William had an answer for everything.

"Enough," Paris said. Just then, he had his inner darkness on a leash. That could change at any moment. This was the closest he'd ever come to saving Sienna. To seeing her again, to touching her, and urgency had him in a vise grip. Which was stupid. He knew it was stupid.

He didn't know her, not really, had only interacted with her those two times, and yet, looking back, he was certain he'd never felt so connected to anyone in his life. He could still remember the delicate rasp of her voice. Soft and lyrical, washing over him, entrancing him. Could still smell her sweet wildflower scent. Could still feel her soft body pressed against his harder one.

Now he wondered if he would even like her on any level but a sexual one. Would he find her annoying? And what about her—would she still view him as evil, even though she herself now carried a demon?

"Let's focus, ladies." *That includes you,* he added for his own benefit. If he could bypass the outside line of the fortress's defense completely, he'd be in perfect condition when he got inside. "Zacharel, you will flash me inside the castle."

"No, I will not."

He scowled but didn't bother asking why. As always, his ears picked up the web of truth woven through the angel's tone. Zacharel couldn't or wouldn't flash him; the reason didn't matter. "William?"

"I've only recently begun to flash myself, and yeah, I'm damn good for a beginner—not that I need to tell you that since anyone with eyes would have noticed— but I'm still honing my amazing skills. There's no way I can cart your carcass anywhere."

Paris stifled a sigh. No flashing with William, either. "Is the water swimmable?"

"Nope. Not only is the water poisonous, but the fiends inside it have a hankering for flesh." William motioned to the dilapidated bridge leading to the front entrance, thick, arched double doors covered in spikes with a clear liquid dripping from their tips. "You have to use the drawbridge, and you have to let the guards carry you. There's no other way."

"I have never battled a gargoyle before." Zacharel shook his head, a dark lock of hair tumbling into one emerald eye. Damp from the melting snow, the hair stuck to his skin. He didn't seem to notice. "But I am certain these will murder Paris before willingly carrying him inside."

As if he were the only intelligent life form left in existence, William splayed his arms. "And the problem with that? He'll still be inside, exactly where he wants to be. And by the way," he added, blinking at Paris with lashes so long they should have belonged to a girl. "Your new permanent eyeliner is very pretty. You'll make a good-looking corpse."

Do not react. He did, and the teasing about his ash/ambrosia tattoos would never end. "Thanks."

"I prefer the lip liner, though. A nice little feminine touch that really makes your eyes pop."

"Again, thanks," he gritted.

He wants us!

Stupid demon.

William grinned. "Maybe we can make out later. I know you want me."

Tell him yes!

Not another word out of you, or—

"Paris? Warrior?" Zacharel said. "Are you listening to me?"

"No."

Zach nodded, apparently not the least offended. "I enjoy your honesty, though I believe you suffer from what the humans call ADD."

"Oh, yeah. I definitely have attention deficient demon."

"Now, changing subjects, since I'm not listening to the angel, either," William said. "Since we're going with my diabolically genius plan, you're gonna have to scale down the cliff and step onto the drawbridge." He tented his hands and drummed his fingers, contemplating the bridge from every angle. "The moment you do, the gargoyles will come to life. They'll attack you. Oh, and the more you fight them, the harder they'll bite and claw you. So, if you remain relaxed, they'll only hurt you a wee bit before they cart you inside to chain to a wall. In theory."

Wonderful. But this was what his woman had to deal with every day. He could do no less. And if the gargoyles had broken her…

Broken… In, out, in, out, he breathed, oxygen scalding his throat, blistering his lungs. He twisted his head left then right to pop the bones in his neck. His fury bubbled to the surface, riding the waves in his veins. He would save Sienna and torch the castle to the ground—along with every living creature inside it.

Zacharel folded his arms over his massive chest, the snow so thick now that none of the flakes had a chance to melt. His hair now boasted strands of glistening white. "How do you know so much about this place and its protectors, William of the Dark?"

William of the Dark? That was new, yet fitting. "Yeah. How do you?" Paris studied the gargoyles in question. They were hideous. The big ones were winged, with ram-like horns, fangs as long as sabers and probably just as sharp, and daggers for nails—on both their hands and their feet. The small ones just looked hungry. Oh, and infected with rabies.

Another piece of invisible lint was brushed from William's shoulder. "Maybe I was once co-ruler of the underworld and sought out all the hideaways of Cronus and his followers, intending to blackmail them, and discovered this little love shack. Or maybe I see the future and knew we'd come here one day. Or maybe the gargoyles once served me, calling me Master Hotness."

Paris read between the lines. "Maybe you once nailed a gargoyle, and she had a big mouth." If there was a bigger he-slut than Paris, it was William.

William gave another shrug. "Or that."

White wings threaded in gold lifted, shook and returned to their place of rest against Zacharel's back. "And what makes you so sure your Sienna is in there, demon?"

Do not react. "I just am." Arca, the goddess he had seduced in Cronus's harem, the one he'd vowed to rescue after ensuring Sienna's safety, had told him there were only two possible locations for her. If Sienna had been taken to the other, her soul would have withered within days. Therefore, she was here. End of story.

"I'll provoke the guards," he said, thinking out loud, "but I won't enrage them. They'll cart me inside, planning to lock me up. I'll free myself before they can, search for Sienna, find her and escape with her. Simple, easy."

Yeah. Right.

"I'll stay here and act as lookout." William nodded, clearly satisfied with the idea. "If you don't return in, say, the amount of time it takes my conditioner to penetrate my scalp, I'll go for help." He snickered. "I said penetrate."

For freakin' real. "Knowing you, you'll forget all about me and head to a salon for a mani-pedi." More than that, Paris wasn't sure Zach would have his back— or stab it. "So, guess what? You're going in with me. Zach will act as lookout."

"Perhaps you've been living in Hungary for so long you've forgotten English and didn't understand what I was saying." First in French, then in Spanish, then in Russian, he said, "I'm staying here, and that's final." William tangled a hand through his indigo mane, frowned when he encountered a snag. Scowling, he whipped out his conditioner, squeezed a few drops onto his fingers and combed the creamy mixture through until he achieved the desired smoothness. "I'm a lover, not a fighter."

"Guaranteed you stabbed your mother seconds after she birthed you. So do me a solid and strap on your big-girl panties because here's the deal. If you walk away now, I will follow you for the rest of your days, seducing every woman you desire away from you."

A heavy pause, rife with fury as cold as the angel's snow. "Fine," William eventually muttered. "I'll go with you, but only because I'm in need of a decent cardio workout."

Good. Paris had meant every word. He hadn't come this far to welcome defeat. He would lie, cheat, destroy, whatever it took. Now, and until Sienna was safe.

He did a quick pat down. All of his blades were in their sheaths. A visual check on his guns ensured the safeties were off.

"Bullets won't kill them, you know," William said. "They'll only cause hissy fits."

"Don't care." Bullets would buy him a few seconds, surely, and sometimes that's all a guy needed to bring home the victory.

William slapped him on the shoulder, sending Sex into rapturous convulsions. "Before we do this, I've got one question for you. And you can't lie. This is too important."

A bit sick to his stomach at what such a debaucher could want to know, Paris cast his attention to the black-haired, blue-eyed he-devil. "Ask."

"Are you going to suggest I kiss you for good luck or strength or whatever it is your sex demon needs?"

That earned the warrior a two-fingered salute.

"So that's a no?" William asked.

Paris worked his jaw. "Here, let me help you off the cliff to the drawbridge." With no more warning, he shoved William over the ledge. He thought he heard a fading, "*So* not cool," from the bastard as he fell…fell…

Splat.

Sex gasped in outrage.

"Not exactly a nice thing to do," Zacharel said, but there was a gleam in his eyes, one Paris had never seen before. Something akin to amusement.

"What's your plan?" Paris asked him.

"Only time will tell."

"You'll wait here, right?"

"Perhaps."

All righty, then. With the angel's cryptic nonanswer ringing in his head, Paris snapped a blade between his teeth and scaled the jagged rocks, down, down, his hands rapidly torn to ribbons. Vines slithered from cracks, stroking over him, attempting to shackle his wrists and ankles. Dangling by one hand, he stopped long enough to slice through the nearest green stalk.

Another soon came at him, and he sliced through it, too. But damn, they were everywhere. One wound around the arm he was using for balance. His heart tripped over itself with dread—and anticipation. He glanced down at the bridge. *No other way.*

Paris carved into the vine holding him, kicked the rocks with his legs and fell. When he hit bottom, he really hit bottom, jarring the air from his lungs.

Suddenly William loomed over him, scowling, snarling and bloody, his suit dirt-stained and ripped. "Do you know. How many strands. Of hair I lost. On my way down?"

Whatever. "Math was never my thing, but I'm gonna say you lost…a lot."

Electric-blues glittered with menace. "You are a cruel,

sadistic bastard. My hair needs TLC and you…you…
Damn you! I've gutted men for less."

"I know. I've watched you." Paris lumbered to his feet
and scanned the rocky bank they stood upon, the crimson ocean lapping and bubbling in every direction. The
drawbridge was only a fifty-yard dash away. "Don't kill
the messenger, but I'm thinking you should change your
dating profile to balding."

Masculine cheeks went scarlet as the big bad warrior
struggled for a comeback.

No more playing. It's D-Day. Soon, I'll rescue Sienna,
Paris thought. Maybe she would stay with him for a few
days. If so, they could make love, over and over again,
and for just a little while, he could pretend they had forever.

Or maybe she would leave him immediately. They
wouldn't make love even once, and he would be forced
to take someone else just as soon as the door shut behind
her.

Who was he kidding? She would definitely leave
him. There were too many obstacles between them. His
demon. Her demon. The fact that he'd slept with her and
then countless others. The fact that he'd inadvertently
used her body as a shield, saving himself. Her former
occupation. The fact that she'd tricked him into lowering his guard so that she could drug him and allow the
Hunters to capture him. The fact that she had watched
as he was tortured. The fact that she hated him.

And maybe, once he'd saved her, he would realize she
was not the one for him. Maybe *he* would be the one to
leave *her.* Maybe he would find that he truly couldn't
sleep with her again. That he'd made a mistake.

Maybe. But he was still doing this.

"One of these days you're going to wake up," William finally said, "and I will have shaved you. Everywhere."

"Won't make a difference. Women will still want me. But you know what else? What I did to you wasn't cruel, Willy." He offered the warrior a white-flag grin. A trick. A lie. "This, however, is."

He grabbed William by the wrist, swung the man around and around before at last releasing him and hurling his body directly onto the bridge. Frayed rope whined, and boards broke beneath his muscled weight.

William lay there, trying to catch his breath and glaring daggers at Paris. On the castle parapets, the gargoyles unleashed a chorus of battle cries.

CHAPTER EIGHT

SHOULD SHE OR SHOULDN'T SHE? Hours had passed since Cronus's ultimatum and departure, but the same question still rolled through Sienna's mind. Should she give herself to Galen, perhaps saving her sister, perhaps succumbing to her captor's deception, or should she continue to resist, possibly causing her sister's continued torture?

Another question, one far more important: If there was a chance she could save Skye, even the most minute chance, shouldn't she take it? She'd vowed to do anything, everything, and Galen fell into the category of anything, didn't he.

Well, hell. There it was, laid bare, with no sugarcoating. The answer was a resounding *yes*. She'd spent her life searching for Skye. If necessary, she would spend her death searching, too. At least now the blinders were off, and she knew the monster she was to seduce.

In bed. With Galen. She tried not to vomit.

She wished she were stronger, more capable, the outcome assured. She wished the battle for Skye could be waged on her terms, without Cronus there to pull her puppet strings.

And maybe…maybe she could arrange that. If she escaped this hellhole before the king's return, she could go to the keeper of Hope, torture him for the information she wanted and then kill him, *without* screwing him.

In theory, that was easy. In reality, it was probably impossible. A bitter laugh—the only kind she had stored inside her lately—escaped, mimicking the sudden chill in the air. She shivered. She'd tried to escape this castle time and time again. While she could open doors and windows that led outside, she couldn't step or crawl beyond them. Her entire body would shake, pain would lance through her, a thousand needles pricking at her, and she would collapse, pass out.

The pain she didn't care about. She could endure. But the passing-out thing? There was no way to combat that.

She was curious to know whether or not someone else could pass through. And the good news was, there were three candidates upstairs who could put that question to the test. All she had to do was free them.

Time to pay them another visit, she thought with a shiver that had nothing to do with the cold. And *what* had caused such a huge drop in the temperature?

Her wings scraped the scarred marble floor as she lumbered down a hall, around a corner and into the wide, spacious ballroom. Her heart sank when the walls fell away and the memories Cronus had plucked from her mind began to play out. At her left, a young Skye began screaming for help. At her right, a horde of Gargl, as she'd heard Cronus call the gargoyles that served as sentries here, dragged a slumped-over but very much awake Paris.

Sienna stopped, a sudden lump growing in her throat. *Paris.* Her body went hot and cold at the same time, goose bumps spreading over her skin, embers igniting in her veins. Cronus certainly knew how to torment her, didn't he? He knew exactly what images would drive her mad.

And this one...whoever created him had outdone himself. How hauntingly lovely Paris was. No mortal could ever hope to compare to him. No other immortal or mythical god could ever measure up. He possessed a face designed for the luxuries of the bedroom as well as the savagery of the battlefield. Eyes of vivid blue seductively lined with kohl she'd never before seen him wear, and hair a concerto of colors. Black, brown, even a few strands of flax. A tall body, muscled in the most delicious way.

He was perfection personified, and he was nothing more than a mirage. Still, she wanted to run to him so badly, to smother him with kisses as she begged for his forgiveness.

Forgiveness she did not deserve.

At least he wasn't injured in this memory. A small comfort, but she had to take them where she could find them.

Another vision unfolded behind Paris, a second horde of Gargl carrying a second dark-haired warrior. This man was just as tall as Paris, just as muscled and, miracle of miracles, almost as lovely, but *he* was definitely injured. Bite marks covered his arms, and horn punctures created a canvas of pain on his chest. Odd. She'd never had a vision of him before. Didn't even recall meeting him.

Her gaze returned to Paris. Two of the Gargl were… humping him? Yes. Their tongues were hanging out, their lower bodies gyrating against him. Why would Cronus show her something like that? To make her jealous? Of the Gargl?

Something was…off about this, she thought.

Before she could puzzle it out, Wrath slammed against her skull, again and again, distracting her. Her temples throbbed in tune with his motions even as the heat cranked up inside her, defeating the cold, leaving her sweating and flushed. Any time a memory of Paris materialized, both the demon and her body reacted this way.

Heaven...hell... Always when they saw flashes of Paris, Wrath uttered those two words. *He can help us.*

"I know he can," she whispered, no longer surprised when she found herself talking to the beast. "And he is certainly our heaven, isn't he?" Her only ray of hope.

Well, well. Look how far she'd come. From hate to... love? Did she love him? Surely not. She hardly knew him. But if he were more than a cruel, heartless trick meant to bring her to heel, she could have learned about him, she thought wistfully.

"Sienna?" Paris's voice, deep, harsh, rasping, uniting them once again.

Another shiver raked her as her gaze locked with his. Her entire body jolted with awareness. *Enough,* she almost shouted. *You've tortured me enough. I concede.*

"Sienna!" It was a hoarse cry layered with desperation and expectation. "Sienna!"

"Enough!" There was no holding the command inside this time. Tears burned her eyes. Her chin trembled, knocking her teeth together. She fisted the edges of her shirt lest she reach out to touch him as the Gargl carried him past her.

In the beginning, she had believed the illusions to be real. She had thrown herself into them, her failure to connect destroying pieces of her—the only pieces she still liked.

Heavenhell. Help. Help!

"Sienna!" Paris fought so fervently against his captors, twisting, turning, kicking, hitting, that one of his shoulders popped from its socket. "I'm here for you. I won't leave without you. Sienna!"

HEAVENHELL. HELP!

She felt as if iron balls churned in her stomach, their swift motions tossing bile up her throat. She released her shirt to dig her nails into her thighs, cutting skin, trying to reach bone. *Steady.* Though she wanted to do something, anything to calm Paris, she knew the more she did, the more he would fight. *This isn't real. He isn't real.*

"Sienna!"

Finally the group disappeared around the corner, and if they had been real, they would have been headed for the dungeon. Paris continued to rage, and she very nearly chased after him, mirage or not.

"I'm sorry," she rasped. "So sorry."

Wrath whimpered.

Though she wanted to collapse, curl into the fetal position and sob, she forced her mind to clear and her feet to move in the opposite direction. Just like that, another memory flickered to life, playing beside her as she walked. Her long-deceased mother sat in the dark, nursing a glass of vodka.

I wish you *had been the one taken!* Great, gut-wrenching sobs. *I'm sorry. I didn't mean that, honey. I'm so sorry.* Slap. *I hate you! Get away from me.* More sobs. *I'm sorry. I shouldn't have hurt you.*

Other families had suffered similar grief, similar fights, and Sienna tried not to let this recollection affect her. And anyway, it was safer than the vision of Paris. Still, she did her best to tune it out and concentrate on her task. Freeing the demon-possessed immortals upstairs, learning from them.

Cronus might have commanded the Lords to find and capture the other hosts of Pandora's evil, but the Titan king had never stopped searching himself. Now, three were chained in the bedrooms above. Obsession, Indifference and Selfishness. And not a one of them knew she was here.

Because she hadn't yet learned to fly and wasn't sure she'd ever develop the strength to do so, Sienna climbed the winding staircase. The tips of her wings caught in the frayed carpet at least a thousand times, razing her already sore muscles. Her thighs burned from the exertion necessary to propel herself upward. Twice she had to pause to hunch over and catch her breath.

When she reached the landing, she squared her shoulders, lifted her chin. The warriors up here sensed weakness of any kind, even if they couldn't see its source. And when they sensed weakness, they beat at the clear, invisible doors that contained them, tossed out the vilest of obscenities and vowed all kinds of retribution, as if she were responsible for their confinement.

Come on, come on, you can do this, you can make it. Look what you've survived already. The pep talk worked. *There you go. Good girl.* The first bedroom she passed was Cameron's. Hadn't taken Sienna long to figure out he was host to Obsession. He was a creature of habit and because it was twilight, he was stretched out on his floor, doing push-ups. Up. Down. Up. Down.

As always, seeing him caused Wrath to erupt in a frenzy of movement. Pain exploded through her head, a precursor to images the demon would next throw into her mind. Violent images from Cameron's past. Bloody battles, a woman in his arms, limp, dead, then one of himself, cursing at the heavens, screaming…screaming… vowing revenge…

Sienna hurried past, but not before the very real image of his bronzed, glistening skin, sweat dripping along the sexy ridges of his muscles, was seared into her brain. His hair was a richer, deeper shade of bronze and plastered to his head. His eyes were downcast, but she knew they were a startling lavender rimmed with silver.

In the room next to his was Púkinn. Indifference. Upon seeing him, Wrath went lethally quiet. A reaction Sienna didn't understand, and the demon wouldn't explain.

Púkinn's Egyptian heritage shone through the sharpness of his bone structure and the sensuality of his dark eyes. His hair was long, black and straight as a pen. The rest of him, however, was more beast than man. Horns stretched from his scalp. His hands were permanently clawed, his legs muscled and furred.

Cameron called him Irish, because, despite his looks and ancestry, his voice dripped with the seductive accent of the isles. Sienna thought of him that way, too.

Finally, she reached Winter's room. Selfishness. Wrath was ambivalent about her, neither tossing out images nor shooting out lances of menace, something else Sienna didn't understand.

Winter had her hip cocked against the jamb and her arms crossed over her middle. Her coral-painted nails drummed a steady song of impatience. She looked so much like Cameron they had to be blood-related. Bronzed skin, bronzed hair and lavender eyes rimmed with silver. Mile-long legs, curves that weren't just dangerous but fatal.

The lushness of her femininity would have been a perfect contrast to Paris's exquisite masculinity.

Sienna tensed, the thought alone causing thrums of jealousy to wrap around her chest and squeeze. *He's mine.*

No, he wasn't, she forced herself to think, and he would never be. She'd tried to reach him, but he'd been unable to see her. And that was probably for the best.

After everything she'd done to him, all the ways she'd hurt him, he would never be able to trust her.

"Who the hell is out there?" Cameron growled. He'd become obsessed—naturally—with ferreting her out. And perhaps she shouldn't have visited so many times, but even before today, she'd planned to free them. Somehow, some way. "I know someone's out there. Reveal yourself. Now."

"We're dealing with one of Cronus's spies, I'm sure," Winter said, her voice as smooth and sultry as a caress. Her gaze almost, but not quite, met Sienna's. "I heard him talking earlier."

"I...will...gut...you," Cameron seethed. He wasn't talking to Winter, but to Sienna. He might grouse at Winter, snap at her and sometimes even scream at her, but he never threatened her. And if anyone could find a way to slay a ghost...thing—or whatever she was— Sienna was willing to bet it was Cameron. Because, and here was a shocker, he wouldn't stop until he had what he wanted.

"Do your tirades never end?" Irish asked, that accent giving her a case of the oh-mys.

"Actually, Irish, you mythological douche," Winter fired back, "they don't, and he's going to tirade all over your ass if you don't shut your mouth."

"Someone should have spanked you a long time ago, little girl." Irish.

"Touch her and you'll soon be eating your own balls. And they'll just be the snack pack. Main course will follow." Cameron.

Sienna didn't mind their bantering. This was mild in comparison to what they'd thrown at her. Besides, they only had each other. And while they loved to snipe and snark at each other, they united the moment Cronus appeared, their mutual hatred bonding them.

She held out her hand, reaching for the clear shield that blocked her from Winter's room. Contact. She sighed when the barrier refused to yield. Yesterday she had palpated the top half, searching for any vulnerable pockets. She'd found none. Today she would tackle the bottom half.

"Sienna!" Paris's voice echoed off the walls. "Sienna! Where the hell did you go?"

Something lurched in her chest, and she was once again fighting tears. *Damn you, Cronus.* Of all his torments, this was the worst. Her hands continued to move along the shield, quaking now.

"Sienna!"

Those scalding tears flooded her eyes and splashed down her cheeks, leaving burning tracks. The memories had never followed her before. When she moved to a new room a new one would appear, one horror exchanged for another. This was the first ever to dog her.

And…she stilled, frowned. This couldn't be a memory, she realized, the answer to her earlier concern finally slipping into place. As far as she knew, Paris had never been to this castle, and she'd never seen the Gargl anywhere else. So, the two had never fought in her presence.

Could he… Was he…

Her heart skipped a beat.

"Sienna!"

Another beat.

"Who *is* that?" Winter demanded.

"Another prisoner?" Cameron.

"And who's this Sienna?" Irish.

They heard Paris's voice. They had never seen or

heard the memories before. This wasn't… This couldn't be… Her heart stopped altogether.

"Sienna! Damn it." *Grunt, bang.* "Get off me, you perverted bag of stone." *Bang.* "Sienna!"

This wasn't a memory, wasn't a vision. This was real and happening right *now.* Paris was here. He'd come for her. Was searching for her, trying to get to her. A second later, her heart kicked back into gear, slamming into a too-fast rhythm, making her pant. The Gargl might have hurt him, might be hurting him even now.

"Paris!" Panicked, she straightened and raced down the hall, down the steps. Just as before, her wings caught on the carpet. Her momentum propelled her forward, onto her face. She cringed, moaned, but two seconds after she landed, she was back on her feet and sprinting. "Paris, I'm here!"

If he continued to fight the Gargl, they would have his organs as snacks. She'd seen it happen too many times to count. And once they tasted a man's insides, nothing and no one could stop the ensuing feast.

She quickened her step and prayed she wasn't too late.

CHAPTER NINE

CRONUS FLASHED TO HIS private bedchamber in his favorite secret palace, gripping a puny, wretched Hunter by the scruff of his neck. The moment the wall murals appeared at his sides, a large bed crafted from the darkest ebony materializing in front of him, he shoved the Hunter to his knees, maintaining that hard grip. A thick crimson carpet kept the action from fracturing the human's kneecaps, the only mercy the man would receive this day.

Atop the bed, chains rattled. The naked female bound to the posts spotted him and struggled to free herself. Of course, she failed. The chains were not just reinforced steel; they were mystically enhanced. And really, she only had herself to blame for her confinement. Cronus never would have captured her if she hadn't come here with the intention of seducing and chaining *him*.

Had he not been in possession of the All-Key, she would have succeeded. Now, nothing could restrain him.

Grinning, he studied her. Dark hair tangled around bruised shoulders, evidence she had struggled long before his arrival. Skin usually the color of flawless cream was now amusingly sallow. When eyes a mix of crystal and crimson flashed absolute hatred at him, his grin widened.

"I will *massacre* you for this," she snarled. Before he had time to respond, she calmed, returned his grin with a wicked, wanton one of her own, and purred, "But only after I play with you a bit."

"Now, now, darling." Cronus *tsk*ed under his tongue. If any female were capable of harming him, it was this one, but he would *never* admit it. "Is that any way to greet your husband of countless centuries?"

Rhea, queen of the Titans, eyed him as if he were an animal—and she wanted to wear his pelt as a victory coat. "A better way to greet you would be with a sword swinging at your neck."

He waved his hand through the air as if he hadn't a care, the action so patronizing it was sure to reignite the fuse of her temper. "Careful, my dearest. You're in danger of protesting too much."

"Argh!" With her demon, Strife, flashing ruby-colored scales and gnarled bone under the surface of her skin, she intensified her struggles. "You will pay for this."

"So you've said innumerable times. Alas." He let out a mocking sigh, barely audible over her raspy panting. "How you humiliate yourself, my heart of hearts, but do go on. My favorite part comes when you realize nothing you do, nothing you say, will aid you, and you sag in defeat."

Despite his taunt, she did indeed continue to fight. And as his own wrists and ankles throbbed in protest, he lost his amusement. He was connected to this horrid creature. Connected in a way he could not escape.

When someone injured her, *he* was injured also. No matter where he was or what he was doing. Likewise, when she experienced pleasure, so did he. Yes, he always knew when she bedded another man. But then, she always knew when he bedded another woman.

Perhaps that was why they despised each other so passionately, and why they had chosen opposite sides of the war that raged between immortals and their human enemy. Cronus had aligned himself with the Lords of the Underworld, and Rhea the Hunters.

"Death is too kind for you!" she spat just before sagging against the mattress as he'd predicted, perspiration dotting every inch of her body and making her glow.

He enjoyed seeing her this way. Helpless, naked and utterly unable to protect or cover herself. She had lush breasts with lovely tawny tips. A soft belly, and even softer thighs. And once upon a time, he truly had loved her. He would have given her anything, would have given *everything,* to make her happy. Actually, he *had* given everything.

Though he'd known better, he had shared his throne with her. Had even shared his godly abilities. He'd hungered for her so absolutely, he hadn't wished to exist if she could not be by his side, ruling with equal power.

As the centuries passed, however, she began to change. From sultry to grasping, from kind to cruel, her thirst for power surpassing his own. Ultimately, she betrayed him in an attempt to usurp him. *She* was the reason he'd been incarcerated inside Tartarus. *She* was the reason the Titans had fallen to the Greeks. At least the ones she'd aided in rising up against him had betrayed her in kind.

Now, nothing would save her from his eternal wrath.

"It's that time again, my pet," he said, all hint of his softer emotions gone.

During one of their many altercations in prison, after he had killed her lover and she had killed his, they had vowed to never again harm those closest to the other, and a vow given was unbreakable. Therefore, Cronus could not touch her precious Galen or any of Galen's top advisers—though Cronus had finally found the bastard's lair, as well as his first in command, the new keeper of Distrust, Fox. In turn, Rhea could not touch any of his Lords.

They could, however, harm the minor foot soldiers. As he would soon prove.

"Your choice, Rhea. I beat you, or I kill one of your Hunters."

The human kneeling at Cronus's side jerked at the threat, mewling sounds seeping from his bloody lips, but he never spoke a word. Just a guess, but that could be because Cronus had already cut out his tongue.

Cronus wanted Rhea to choose her punishment, and he didn't care that he would, essentially, be punishing himself. Causing her to suffer overrode all other concerns. "Which is it to be?" Every day he offered her the same choice, and every day she gave the same answer.

"You think I care about a fragile, useless human?" She lifted her chin, her narrowed gaze remaining on Cronus, completely lacking in fear or mercy. "Kill him."

A whimper escaped the Hunter.

No, her answer had not changed. Cronus could have beaten her anyway, and perhaps one day he would. For the time being, he liked giving her what she asked for. Liked thinking she would be haunted by her selfishness for decades to come.

"Very well." Cronus stretched out his free arm, summoned a sword from nothing but air, and struck. The Hunter's head fell to the floor with a thump. His body quickly followed.

The scent of copper coated the air.

Rhea's thunderous expression remained the same, untouched by remorse. "Do you feel better now, my stallion? Do you feel like a big, strong male?"

Bitch. He would not allow her to gain the upper hand.

"Do you care nothing for your ever-dwindling army? The very men fighting for *your* cause."

One bare shoulder lifted in a casual shrug. "I feel the same for my army as you feel for yours, I'm sure. Nothing."

No, he did not care for his Lords, but he respected their strength and determination. Or rather, he had. Lately the warriors were too busy falling in love, too concerned with their own petty squabbles, and now too busy rescuing Kane, the keeper of Disaster, to heed Cronus's orders. Still, they were a buffer between Cronus and eternal death, so he needed them.

He frowned at the thought of all that had transpired to bring him to this moment. Long ago, the first All-Seeing Eye under his command—a being capable of seeing into heaven, hell, past and future—had prophesied that a man filled with hope would fly to him on wings of white and behead him. At the time, Galen had not yet been created. Therefore, Cronus had assumed an angel assassin would come for him, which was why he'd pitted himself against the Deity's Elite soldiers. War had broken out—among angels and gods, Greeks and Titans—and even those on earth had suffered.

Weakened from the ceaseless fighting, Cronus found himself defeated by Zeus and thrown into Tartarus. Soon afterward Zeus created the Lords, Galen among them, to serve as his personal army, ready to defend him should the Titans rise up from their moldering prison. But in a fit of foolish pique, those same warriors opened Pandora's box, unleashing the demons from within and raining down more havoc on a world still reeling from the heavenly war. When Zeus meted out their punishment, decreeing that each would house a demon inside himself, Galen was paired with the demon of Hope, wings of white sprouting from his back. *Then,* upon Cronus's escape from the immortal prison, the newest All-Seeing Eye had painted the same future that had earlier been foretold, this time *showing* Galen's victory over him.

What the first Eye had told him—and the newest did not yet know—was that there was a way for him to save himself. A woman with wings of midnight, who had lived among his enemy but craved a life with his allies, was to be his salvation.

That woman was Sienna. Everything about her fit the Eye's description, from her appearance to her circumstances.

Therefore, she had to do as the Eye had said she must do. Reign by Galen's side, despite her desire to aid the Lords. Only she could keep Galen's attention, though she didn't yet know how or why and Cronus wouldn't tell her. Only she could hold her own against Rhea, if ever his wife got free. Only she could stop the Lords from attacking Galen, for killing the keeper of Hope would not stop the prophecy from coming to pass. His demon would be given to someone else, and that someone else would then become the white-winged slayer of the Titan king.

"I will escape, you know," Rhea said, and she sounded confident.

Whether that confidence stemmed from her abilities or his capitulation, he wasn't sure. Didn't care. He rubbed a thumb over one brow, another dismissive gesture. "No, I do not know. I've never seen so weak a goddess."

Only he could unlock her chains, and he planned never to do so. Among her most recent crimes, she had convinced her sister to become his mistress and spy on him. Another reason for Cronus's insistence that Sienna do the same to Galen.

"One day..." she gritted out.

He moved to the side of the bed, away from the dead body and closer to his hated wife. "You will ruin me. You will imprison me. You will... What other threats have you issued, hmm?"

"I will peel away your skin, spit on your bones and dance in a pool of your blood."

"Sounds like a truly spectacular evening. Until then, I think I'll have a bit of fun." With a single wave of his hand, he summoned one of the countless females currently residing in his harem. A redhead with deeply tanned skin and roses in her cheeks appeared beside him. Unlike some of the others he owned, she truly enjoyed attending to his needs.

Today she wore a transparent drape of silk and lace, jewels that had once belonged to Rhea and a smile brighter than any sun. Seeing the Titan queen so helpless on the bed, and knowing she herself was a favorite of his, she puffed with pride, flipped her hair over one shoulder, and waved smugly.

Rhea hissed.

And that's why I chose her, he thought with an inward grin.

Recognizing the diamonds curling around the girl's neck, Rhea released a spew of curses.

"Majesty," the girl said with a curtsy, talking over the queen to prove how little she mattered. The fragrance of citrus wafted from her. "What can I do for you?"

"You can show the woman on the bed how much your man pleases you." He waved her in front of him, where he bent her over, her face right in front of Rhea's.

"Does *she* not please *you?*" the girl asked.

The queen gave another hiss and tried to bite her.

"Enough of that." His gaze on his wife, he lowered

the zipper to his leather pants. He despised wearing such constrictive clothing, but Rhea found this type of garment attractive, and his need for vengeance far surpassed any desire for comfort. "You know what you must say to stop this from happening," he told his wife. Rhea must only concede defeat, vowing to forever obey him.

"I'll die first."

"Very well."

He took the servant, and the pleasure was intense—and he would never admit it was so satisfying only because he kept his eyes on his wife. She, however, closed her eyes to *block* his image. No matter. She felt every sensation along with him, and that was enough. For now.

When he finished, he righted his clothing with hands trembling from the force of his release—which was humiliating; a king should recover swiftly—and sent the grinning servant away.

"Bastard," Rhea said on a panting breath. "I hate you. With all of my being, I hate you."

"As I hate you."

A smile of genuine amusement suddenly curled the corners of her mouth. "You know, Cronus, darling. You did not enjoy your whore half as much as I enjoyed mine."

The words were carefully calculated, a stinging blow to his masculine pride. But he was careful to keep his own expression equally amused. "You know, *darling*," he said. "You might have enjoyed your men, but you only ever had them once before I found and killed them. I, on the other hand, am already looking forward to having the redhead again tomorrow."

CHAPTER TEN

FANGS IN HIS ARMS. Claws in his legs. Horns jabbing into his stomach. At least, Paris seriously hoped that it was horns jabbing into his stomach. For a while, some of the gargoyles had ground on him like dogs in heat as their friends attempted to chain him down. *Won't gag.* He would have allowed the restraints—if he hadn't seen Sienna. She was here. Alive. Unfettered.

She'd looked at him, had met his gaze, and sadness had wafted from her. Sadness and regret, and even horror. The horn-rimmed glasses she'd once worn were gone, her eyesight probably perfect in the afterlife, but her features were the same. Big hazel eyes, plump red lips. A flow of mahogany waves, now to her waist.

His woman. His *mine.* One by one his friends had fallen in love, and he'd been so jealous. Now, here was the woman who'd fascinated him as no other. He'd thought, *Must reach her...must wipe away the horror...*

Sex had thought, *Must have her.*

Now his demon retreated into the back of his mind, the coward, as Paris fought his way free of the gargoyles to run after her. In an instant, his captors swarmed him, their fervor intensified. He tossed one, then another, then another still, slamming the rigid stone bodies into walls. They recovered instantly and returned to him. More clawing, more jabbing.

They slowed him, but they didn't stop him. He was

weak and growing weaker, because he hadn't had sex all day. Didn't think he'd had sex yesterday, either. He'd already forgotten. Whatever. Sienna was here, and with one glance, he'd gotten hard for her.

He *could* have her again. No question about that now. He just had to reach her.

As the darkness rose up inside him, clouding his mind with thoughts of destruction and death, he offered no more resistance, allowing it to drive him deeper and deeper into the place where only demolishing the obstacles in his path mattered. These gargoyles wanted to keep him from his woman. They did not deserve to live.

One step, two, three, the things clawing at his thighs, his calves, hanging on to his ankles, he eked his way into the ballroom. All the while he punched at heads, kicked and stabbed at middles. Stone cracked. Pieces scattered on the floor.

"Sienna! Where—"

She flew around the far corner, her dark hair tangled behind her, her hazel eyes wild and bright. In a blink, the world slowed down and he noticed details he'd missed before. Her lips were more swollen than usual, with droplets of blood dried at the corners. A bruise colored her cheek, a blue-black testament of the pain she had been forced to endure. One of her obsidian wings was bent at an odd angle, clearly broken.

She'd been hurt. Someone had hurt her.

Red mixed with the black, both swimming so thickly in his brain they compromised his line of vision. Shimmers of rage sparked a thousand must-kill-must-protect fires, each one warring with the others. In his veins, his blood was molten, turning jerky movements into fluid, lethal arcs.

With a roar, he tossed away two other gargoyles. He

grabbed another by the neck and punched, punched, *punched,* creating a hole in the creature's cheek, the rest of the stone chipping away bit by bit. Still the creature fought Paris's hold, teeth chomping at his fist.

"Let them chain you," Sienna shouted. "Please, just let them chain you."

She wanted him bound? Hated him as much as he'd feared? No matter. Her command and plea were discarded, his determination unwavering. *Must kill...* Punch, punch. *Enemy must die.* Punch, punch, punch. Stab. *Obstacles must be eliminated.* Punch, stab. Debris flew in every direction. The gargoyles forgot about their desire for pleasure, or whatever they'd felt while writhing on him, and went on full attack, no longer going easy on him.

Sienna reached him, smelling of wildflowers and... ambrosia? He inhaled deeply. Oh, yeah. Ambrosia's sweet, sweet perfume permeated his skin, overshadowed everything else, including the need to kill, but oh, he now wanted to imbibe. Had to imbibe. His mouth watered, even as he wondered why she would smell of the immortal drug he had forced himself to stop using not too long ago, when he was hurt during a fight he would have won if he'd been clearheaded. His injuries had almost caused him to miss his appointment with a goddess to purchase his crystal blades, and he'd decided then and there to stop using. Thankfully, he had gone through the worst of the withdrawal already; he couldn't afford to go through it again. He would stop caring about anything but his next fix.

Want her. As close as she now was, Sex perked up, pouring strength straight into Paris's system and changing the direction of his own thoughts. *Must touch her... must have her...*

For once, they were in agreement.

"You have to let them chain you." When she attempted to jerk two of the gargoyles away from him, they turned on her, some biting, some clawing, some head-butting her. Her knees collapsed under their weight.

Another roar ripped from his throat. She had tried to save him? The very idea was foreign to him. Ignoring the beasts still attempting to subdue him, he concentrated on the ones climbing on top of her. He grabbed one and threw. Grabbed another, threw.

"Run!" he commanded her.

The beasts returned to him in a snap. He tried to knock them away, clearing a path for her, but she didn't run. She lay panting, her limbs unmoving, not even trying to shield herself.

Her watery gaze pleaded with him. "Please, Paris. Be still. Don't fight."

Heated breath caught in his throat, and though every instinct he possessed screamed to continue fighting, continue hurting anything and everything in his way, he planted his heels on the floor, sheathed his blades and lowered his arms. She had tried to save him; he would trust her.

He would surrender.

For a moment, the beasts took full advantage, converging on him like flies to honey. *Steady.* Like Sienna, he remained unmoving. Shockingly, the fighting frenzy soon eased. The gargoyles latched on to his arms and once again began dragging him to the prison where they'd already locked William.

Sienna lumbered to her feet and followed, never allowing eye contact to break. A good thing. If she had, he would have erupted all over again. *Can't lose even that much.*

"They'll leave you alone after they chain you." Her voice trembled, pain in the undercurrents. "They simply have to complete their task, and then you'll be free to do whatever you want."

Want her...

Despite his injuries, he hardened a second time, his demon's scent wafting from him, a rich chocolate mingled with the most expensive champagne. If he'd needed more proof that he could have this woman again, here it was. He could have her as many times as he wanted her, however many times she would allow him. He was awed. He was vindicated.

He was undone.

Finally, he was with the woman he craved above all others.

The beasts not holding his limbs leapt back on top of him, grinding, rubbing against him in that disgusting way. Harder this time, and much more determined. Even their need to complete their duty and chain him couldn't override his demon's allure, he supposed. He tuned them out, kept his focus on Sienna.

She was here—he would never tire of the thought—and she was breathtakingly lovely, the essence of all that was feminine. Even dirt-smudged and blood-caked as she was, he'd never seen a more exquisite female. His mind had not built her up during their separation. On the contrary, his mind had not done her justice. Those hazel eyes glittered with swirls of emerald and copper, hints of summer and winter combined, framed by spiky jet lashes. Her lips were bee-stung and utterly wicked. The kind women paid to have and men paid to use.

Her hair wasn't too dark or too light, but the perfect shade of russet streaked with shimmers of the purest gold. The locks were longer than before, with waves as mesmerizing as those in an ocean.

Her freckles had lightened, but they were as decadent as ever, a treasure map for his tongue. The rest of her skin, cream and rose petals, glowed as if she had swallowed the sun. Her body, so slender, so elegant, was as graceful as a ballerina's. Her breasts were small, but they would fit amazingly well in his big hands as he tongued her nipples. Her legs were long and would wrap around his waist, holding him tight.

Mine, he thought. *Mine.*

Take her. Sex had abandoned the *I wants* and *I needs,* and was now all about the commands. As if Paris would argue. One question plagued him, though. Would being with her a second time actually strengthen him?

Around the corner, William waited—and he was grinning, his electric-blues calling Paris all kinds of stupid. He had broken free of his chains, as Paris should have done to avoid the beating, and waved as Paris passed him. The beasts paid him no heed, still clinging to Paris and proving Sienna's claim. He relaxed. So close to holding her, to touching her as he'd dreamed.

Oh, the things he wanted to do to her...

She might push him away; she might not. Either way, at long last he would find out.

CHAPTER ELEVEN

PARIS WATCHED AS WILLIAM flowed into motion beside Sienna. Still she didn't look away from him and he wondered what thoughts she entertained. Was her body reacting to him, as his was reacting to her?

Blood-spattered walls framed her, and Paris cursed. He would have given anything to see her surrounded by silks and velvets. Would make it so, before he let her go. A vow, even as the thought of letting her go made him want to howl.

"Nice to see you again, Sienna," William said, as pleasantly as he was able. The frost in his eyes belied his endearing facade.

Paris tensed. If the warrior hurt her...

"We've met?" she asked.

For a moment, William radiated absolute bafflement. Then his expression cleared, and he offered a sugar-sweet smile. "It distresses me that you don't remember, but I don't mind reminding you. Allow me to paint the scene. We were in Texas, and you were crouched on the concrete like a dog, holding on to Paris like a leech." His cruel, sneering pitch was meant to intimidate her, to put her in her place for everything she'd done to Paris.

"Tone," Paris snapped. She might have done him wrong, but he would not allow her to be disrespected.

Sienna shrugged, apparently unconcerned by what the

warrior had said. "You'll have to forgive me for not notic-ing you back then. Next to him, you're kind of homely."

William choked on his own tongue.

For the first time in forever, Paris grinned with true amusement. The only other time he'd witnessed such spunk from her was when she had drugged him. He hadn't liked it then, but he liked it now, especially since it was directed at someone else.

William caught his breath and added, "Just so you know, I'll kill you if you harm him in any way. And I don't care how much it will upset him." So calmly stated, there was no arguing the warrior's intent. "Paris has proven to be stupid where you're concerned, and that means his friends have to pick up the mental slack."

There went his amusement. An animalistic growl left him, his lips peeling back from his teeth. Darkness rising again…rage returning… Paris struggled to free his arms, intending to wrap his fingers around William's neck and squeeze. No one threatened Sienna. No one. Ever.

You don't really want to injure him. Stop. A plea from deep inside himself, where remnants of the old Paris must still reside. William's loyalty was a nice surprise, and something he appreciated on a visceral level.

Where Sienna was concerned, however, Paris was not exactly rational, and his struggling intensified. *Must defend her…*

The gargoyles stopped dragging him, stopped hump-ing him and returned to fighting him, shoving him to the floor and into a pile of bones. They raked at him with their claws and teeth.

"See?" William splayed his arms, his point proven. "Stupid."

Biting the inside of his cheek, Paris forced himself to chill a second—third?—time. He huffed and he puffed like the big, bad wolf he was, knowing he would be given a chance to make his point about Sienna later, when he could get to his knives. His friends could do and say anything they wanted to him, but not to her.

Once again the creatures lost interest in the battle and resumed the trek to the prison.

Sienna and William continued to follow, and soon Paris's wrists and ankles were shackled to a crumbling stone wall in a four-by-four chamber devoid of any luxuries. Claws scraped the floor as the creatures filed out, each squawking happily about what they clearly considered a job well done.

Sienna severed visual contact and collapsed at his side, her trembling fingers working at one of the metal bands. He could have freed himself. Or hell, William could have freed him, but Paris liked having those soft, elegant hands on him. They were his favorite part of her body, every movement an exotic dance.

On a raspy catch of breath, she said, "They're tasked with chaining anyone who survives the walk from drawbridge to castle, and once that's accomplished, they lose interest. You'll be free to move about the place as much or as little as you want."

He closed his eyes for a moment, letting her voice drift through his mind. Husky, low, a caress he'd missed more than he'd realized. He could listen to her forever.

Did part of him still hate her? Yeah. Definitely. Hated what she'd done to him, hated what he'd done *for* her. Hated how strongly she affected him. And beneath all the hate, he resented that she hadn't seen beyond her *own* hatred to choose him all those months ago, the way he'd chosen her.

He would have taken her home. He would have pampered her. At least, that's what he told himself now. He

wouldn't contemplate what he would have done to her
before the pampering commenced. Wouldn't think about
the interrogation he'd planned or the chains he'd imagined buying for her.

"I'm having trouble… I can't… The fall must have
hurt worse than I realized." Her voice had thinned to a
mere wisp of sound, barely audible. "So…sorry…" Her
hands fell away from him, and she slumped forward, her
slight weight resting on his chest.

"Sienna?" he demanded, but there was no response.
Anyone who could see and touch her could injure her
spirit form; he knew that. And the gargoyles had certainly been able to see and touch her. But without a heartbeat or need to breathe, she should rebound quickly.
Right? Except, the bloodstains around her mouth…*how*
had she bled? he wondered now.

"Must have fainted from the sight of my beauty," William remarked with a sigh. "There goes the tickle fight
I had planned."

Ignoring him, Paris yanked one of his arms, ripping
the chain from the wall. He wrapped that arm around
Sienna's waist, holding her against him, keeping her
steady.

She fit him perfectly.

After he ripped the other arm free, he eased her to her
back and peered down at her, his heart causing a riot of
sensation in his chest.

Her head lolled to the side, and she was pale, paler
than before. Another rip, followed by another, and his
ankles were free. Then he jerked at the cuffs themselves
until they fell away. *Then* he did what he'd wanted to do
since the first moment he'd seen her. He touched her,
smoothing the hair from her brow. Her skin was as soft
as it appeared, and warm, so wonderfully warm. He'd

craved a moment like this so desperately, had dreamed of it over and over again, and had nearly killed himself a hundred times over to have it. To his delight, reality was so much better than the dream. More than feeling her heat, he smelled her scent all around him, enveloping him. The wildflowers, the coconut sweetness of ambrosia, both creating a heady musk of arousal.

Why ambrosia? He couldn't get past that. Was she a user? If so, he'd bet someone, like, say, Cronus, had forced her to become one. She wasn't the type to willingly fall into drugs. From what little he knew about her, she liked order and craved control.

I'll protect her from further abuse, he thought next. She was his. For just a little while, she was his.

Sex jumped up and down. *Take her, take her, take her.*

Instinct demanded he obey. Still he resisted. *Not like this. Not while she's out.*

A sigh of frustration, maybe even a muttered *you're no fun* as Paris looked her over, shielding her from William's gaze as he moved her clothing out of the way to check for injuries. Every newly revealed inch of skin acted as a lick of flame to Sex, causing the demon to hiss and shake. *Or maybe you* are *fun.*

Though Paris admired the body beneath him just as fervently as his dark companion, he hissed and shook for a different reason. Another rise of darkness, another increase of boiling rage. Beneath fading bruises, his woman was as fang-and-claw-mark-ridden as he was, blood oozing from her in tiny rivers of pain.

His next mission crystallized. Finding out how to hurt the gargoyles and then making them pay for every mark.

Really making them pay, he decided when he spied a deep, angry gouge in her side. He sucked in a breath to try and calm himself down, but he inhaled so sharply his lungs felt like mini-vacuums, drawing the air in with commando force. His muscles tensed, his head fogged all over again and his mouth watered. He could actually *taste* the ambrosia in the air. Frowning, he bent down and sniffed along the line of her neck. The closer he was to her, the stronger the scent became.

"Kinky," William said.

"Can you be serious?"

"I *was* being serious. I always figured you for the in and out type. Kinda stealthy, leaving the girl wondering whether you'd even been there or not. But I didn't know you were quite *this* stealthy."

"Nice to know you've considered my sex life," he grumbled.

"Hasn't everyone?"

"Screw you."

"Again, hasn't everyone?"

"This is pointless." Another sniff. The fog thickened, Paris's brain practically swimming through it. Could the fragrance originate in Sienna's blood? Yet another sniff, another infusion of that ever-thickening fog. Yeah, it was definitely in her blood—and a lot of it. More than even an addict could handle. Her scent was as strong as if she were actually growing in an ambrosia field.

Which should be impossible. Right? Ambrosia was harvested in special meadows elsewhere in the heavens, as far from this dark realm as the moon was from the earth. Lavender petals were plucked from the foliage, the clear, intoxicating liquid squeezed out before those petals were dried and turned into powder. No one could handle the liquid, not even immortals, and humans certainly couldn't handle even the powder.

But Sienna wasn't human anymore, was she.

He was ashamed to admit he was tempted to bite her,

to drink her down and savor every drop. He'd walked the path of addiction, sprinted it, really, but he had somehow managed to skirt the edge of need during his journey here, knowing his wits were required to succeed. If only that would lessen the sweet, tantalizing lure of her right now…but no.

"As interesting as this is, and honestly, I don't mean to interrupt your seductive process," William said, airquoting the last two words, "but are you gonna get to the good stuff or what?"

"I thought I told you to shut it."

"No, you told me to screw you, and that was five minutes ago. A lot's changed since then. Like, I'm currently bored."

Biting his tongue until he tasted copper, Paris finished his search for injuries. And shit, there was another shot of desire—his own rather than his demon's. He shouldn't notice those lovely pink nipples, shouldn't notice the soft dip of her belly or the trim length of her legs. Shouldn't be counting her freckles, already planning his tongue's attack. (He would start with the darker ones on her stomach, and work his way to the lighter ones on her thighs.) He was a bastard. He was sick, disgusting. He should be whipped.

When she woke up, she'd take care of that for him, he would bet.

Hate myself. "She's already dead," he gritted out. He noticed her right wrist no longer bore the tattoo of infinity, a symbol the Hunters used. "Why is she bleeding? Shouldn't she heal as quickly as we do?"

"Oh, now you want to talk to me?" the warrior quipped.

"Just answer the question before I cut out your tongue and nail it to the wall."

"You've really lost your sense of humor, you know that? But okay. Fine. I'll play along. She's dead, yes, but she's also possessed by a demon that is very much alive. His heart beats for her. His blood fills her veins. I shouldn't have to explain demon physiology to *you*. And what the hell is that smell? It's mouthwatering. A real party for my—"

"Stop breathing!" Paris didn't want anyone else breathing her in.

"O-kay. Possessive much?"

"Let's get back to the subject that won't get you maimed. She's possessed by a demon, yes, but she's also a dead human spirit. So…"

"So, you're still able to touch her."

To borrow the bastard's phrasing: Obvious much? "What I'm asking is, will she heal?"

"Yeah, because her demon will heal. And here's a little tip for the next person held captive by your stunning conversation. You should have started with that and saved us time and trouble."

Okay. Okay, then. Good. She would heal. Paris scooped her up in his arms—pissed all over again with the gargoyles. What they'd left on him…was now on his woman.

Sex adored the contact and purred his approval.

"I'm taking her upstairs, looking for a bedroom." Paris would clean and bandage her. If she didn't wake up and demand he leave her the hell alone first. "You're not invited."

As much as he wanted her awake, looking at him, talking to him, he hoped she slept through the cleaning. He was desperate to get his hands on her, really on her. Yeah, he was a sick, sick bastard. But that wasn't the main reason, he told himself. He didn't want her to feel any pain while he doctored her.

He studied the chains for a split second, thinking it might be a good idea to tie Sienna to a bed while he had the chance. That way, she couldn't run until after they'd discussed a few things. But he hadn't come all this way, done all those things, only to enslave her himself. His goal was, and had always been, her freedom.

And shit. She might not run from him. Earlier she had ignored him, had watched as he'd passed her, but a few minutes later, she had rushed to his rescue. Whatever the reason for the change, she hadn't sought to get rid of him.

He rubbed his cheek against the top of her head, luxuriating in the feel of her silky hair before carrying her out of the cell. The gargoyles hadn't bothered shutting the iron bars that would have kept him and William inside. At least until they'd picked the lock, that is.

"You're such a wuss," William said, pacing beside him. "I hope you know that."

"Really? I'm not the one carrying conditioner around."

"Maybe that's why your hair has so many split ends."

"Tell me about your hair one more time. You'll wake up bald."

"That's a ridiculous thing to say. We both know I'd have your guts spilled before you ever got the razor near me." William raised his chin. "By the way, only a real man can accept his feminine side."

"I don't know who fed you that line of garbage, but I can promise she's laughing at you right now."

"Surprise! It was your mom—after I boned her."

A mom joke. How original.

The gargoyles were no longer in the ballroom. Paris hadn't noticed the interior before; he'd been a little too busy getting his ass kicked. Now he had a look around. It was dark, crumbling like the rest of the place, with blood dried on the walls and bones tossed about haphazardly.

Up the stairs they climbed, the carpet threadbare in multiple places. On the new rise were statues, a lot of damn statues. Male, female, old, young. Only thing they had in common were their expressions of horror.

"I take it you're gonna be busy for a few hours, since I suspect that's how long she'll be out and you can do your thing." William brushed his fingers over a large pair of alabaster breasts. "I mean, that's the reason I'm not invited to join you, right?"

"You better shut your mouth while you still have a head." Even as irritated as he was with William's suggestion, pulses of desire shot through Paris at the thought of being alone with Sienna and touching her as easily as William had touched the statue—little flames he wasn't sure whether to douse or welcome.

"Shout if you need me. Like, if she's too much for you."

"That day will never come." Paris veered left as the warrior veered right. "By the way, if you knock on my door, you better be dying. 'Cause if you're not, you soon will be." He shouldered his way into the first room he came across. His luck was holding, because it was a furnished bedroom. All he had to do was remove the thick layers of dust and the tarp draping everything.

Or maybe he should leave the tarp. Because when Sienna woke up, this might become a war zone.

CHAPTER TWELVE

KANE, KEEPER OF THE DEMON of Disaster, could not believe his luck. Usually his life took the express train to hell, whether he'd purchased a ticket or not, with rocks falling on his head, lightbulbs shorting out and holes opening up at his feet. Stuff like that could really mess with a guy's mind, so over the years he'd developed a philosophy that had saved his life: bad shit happened, but whatever, he would deal and move on.

Now he was actually *in* hell, but he wasn't being tortured. He wasn't being questioned, and catastrophes weren't occurring. He was being worshipped. By demon minions, sure, but worship was worship, right? Their scaled, clawed hands caressed him, their horned heads rubbed against him gently, and the rest of their bodies... he wouldn't think about.

Mine, Disaster whispered inside his head, pride bubbling to the surface and washing through Kane's entire body.

Yeah, Kane knew these minions belonged solely to Disaster. Long ago, the High Lord had lived in this section of hell, had ruled here, and then had chosen to leave it all behind and escape. And even though thousands of years had passed since that time, the connection hadn't faded. The minions, or lesser demons, had sensed their leader inside of Kane and rescued him from his attackers.

Currently Kane was perched on a throne of the

freshly…excavated bones. Okay, okay. That was a nice way of saying the bones used to belong to the Hunters who'd thought to hurt Kane, and only a few days ago they'd been plucked out. And, when you considered the fact that Kane's shirt and pants were made from the tanned and leathered skins—because of the heat, the process had been swift—well, a chair of femurs? No biggie.

They were gifts, the minions had said. And like he could really say, "Thanks, but I'd rather have a toaster." In return, all they wanted was his sperm.

Yeah. That's right. His baby juice.

Seemed his demon had once possessed a jealous streak and, true to his name, had caused a disaster that wiped his male minions from existence. Only females remained and they were desperate to procreate with their favorite Evil Overlord.

Kane hadn't had sex in centuries; the act was simply too risky for his partners. So yeah, his body was primed and ready. Gnarled the demon hands might be, but they still stroked and gripped just fine. His mind, however, was *so* not on board.

"Back up, ladies," he commanded. He could have been nice about it, sure, but something he'd learned was that demons only responded to strength. Nice wouldn't get him crap.

Still, he expected a fight. Instead, moans of disappointment echoed and contact ceased. They obeyed him, inching backward. But they lingered nearby, prostrate, still reaching for him, clearly hoping he'd change his mind.

Inside his head, Disaster prowled with purpose, unhappy with the distance. The females belonged to him, they were his right, and he wanted to mate with them. *Take,* he said.

No. Kane wasn't the type of guy who could walk away from his kids, even half-demon ones, and that's what he'd have to do in this situation.

Take!

I said no. He'd rather find a way out of here. But every time he stood, and no matter what he said while he was standing, within seconds the females would swarm him, pushing his pants around his ankles. He wasn't sure whether Disaster had trained them to react so swiftly, or if Kane was just special.

Two things he *was* certain about. His friends were worried about him, and they were searching for him. He didn't want them coming down here, risking their lives when his was no longer in danger.

Take one, then. Just one.

Ah, so they were supposed to negotiate now, were they? Well, the answer was still a resounding hell no. But…maybe he could pretend, Kane thought. Maybe if he picked one of the females, got her alone, he'd have a better chance of sneaking out of the cavern.

His gaze skated over the kneeling, writhing bodies. Some had horns protruding from their spines, some had pointed wings. Some had red scales, some had green. Beyond them was the cavern, blood caked on the jagged rocks, fires blazing in every corner, and screams of the damned floating on the hot, sulfur-scented air. When he found a smaller body with no horns *or* wings, her scales on the lighter side of jade, he pointed.

"You." If for once in his eternal life, his good luck held, she would be a weak link.

Gasps of surprise. Hisses of jealousy.

"I want you," he reiterated.

His chosen stood. Her legs were twisted, facing the wrong way. Her feet were hoofed, and when she smiled, he saw a mouthful of bloodstained fangs. Disaster slammed against his skull, *bang, bang,* desperate to leave him, to touch her, to pound inside her.

Mine. She's mine!

And just how would the bastard react when— hypothetically—Kane nailed her? Murder Kane, the same way he'd once murdered his own people? Probably. Because if he managed to end Kane's life, he could remain here, a place he'd once fought to escape but now realized he missed. Sure, if that happened, Disaster would be crazed from the loss of his human host, but the demon would be free to screw whoever he desired, all by himself.

Talk about a messed-up sitch.

Demon Girl limped to the throne, and the wanton gleam in her eyes suggested she intended to climb Kane like a carnival pony the second she reached him, while everyone watched.

Bang, bang. Disaster was on board with that.

Kane shook his head and extended a hand, palm up, to stop her progress. "Nope, sorry. Don't come any closer."

A frown pulled at the corners of her mouth as she obeyed.

"Privacy," he said. *Bang, bang.* Harder, faster. "I want to...take you in a tent." He wasn't sure what verbiage these demons would understand.

"Massster?" Her forked tongue swiped over too-thin lips.

"I will not take you out here." Or anywhere. *Bang, bang.* Damn it. His demon needed to settle the hell down. "So, build me a tent." *Bang.* "All of you." *Bang.* And hell, maybe, with his present run of good luck, he wouldn't have to wait for its completion. Maybe the females would be so distracted during the building of the tent, he could stomp out of the cavern while yelling, whistling, whatever, and they wouldn't notice.

"Tent?" she asked, still so clearly confused.

"Yes. I want one. Build the tent now, and you can have babies later." *With someone else.*

Bang! Bang!

Most of the minions rushed away to gather the necessary supplies, shoving each other out of the way, but a few stragglers remained behind, staring at him. And by *a few,* he meant a little over one hundred. He sighed. So, there'd be no stomping, yelling or whistling his way out.

He wished he were more like Paris. Wished he could plow through them—in bed and out—and be stronger for it while remaining emotionally distanced and unconcerned with the consequences.

Of course, then he'd also be a drug addict obsessed with finding the woman who'd tried to kill him, but at the moment, drugs and obsession seemed like a nice change of pace. And damn. When Kane got home, he was gonna be teased mercilessly about his precious seed, his needy harem girls, and his refusal to fertilize their petunia patches.

Bring it, boys. At least he'd be home.

Home... The word echoed through his mind, a wave of foreboding slamming through him.

Something was about to happen, he realized with a twist of sickness. Something terrible was about to happen. A disaster...a tragedy of the worst sort...inside the fortress in Buda, where all the Lords and their significant others lived. *His* fortress. His demon knew it, sensed it, and in turn, so did Kane.

He was on his feet and running for the exit, not slowing even when multiple females latched on to him and held on for the ride.

CHAPTER THIRTEEN

VIOLA TRAILED AFTER the gorgeous warrior named Maddox as he carried his very pregnant wife, Ashlyn, up the stairs, past naked portraits of his friends holding rainbow-colored ribbons and stuffed teddy bears. This was the fourth time one of the Budapest residents had foisted her off on someone else, and she couldn't understand why no one wanted to spend more time with her.

From Lucien to Anya, whom she'd met in Tartarus centuries ago. They'd been cell-block-B mates. Anya had always been jealous of her, of course. Who hadn't—and wasn't? Earlier today the minor goddess had pretended not to recognize her, but Viola had taken the lie for what it was. A plea to hear all about Viola's magnificent life.

An hour later, Anya had handed her off to Reyes and his Danika. Viola was still puzzling over Anya's parting words to the couple. "Here you go. Take her. And you're welcome. You won't need to stab yourself to please your demon for at least a year, Reyes."

Just how was Viola supposed to have pleased an anguish-happy fiend like Reyes? He was possessed by the demon of Pain, yet she was perfectly...perfect, a joy to look upon and listen to, a veritable fount of shiny, priceless pearls of wisdom, with a keen sense of fashion and a knack for home decorating.

Speaking of those little life skills, she'd already decided to put them to good use. From now on she would be dressing everyone here, as well as redesigning their mansion's interior and exterior. And she wasn't even going to charge them—more than a few hundred thou.

Her eyes filled with tears as her hand fluttered to her heart. She was *such* a giver.

At one time, centuries ago, she'd done something not so giving and sent herself catapulting into a shame spiral, but she couldn't recall what that something was. She never did. Her demon stored negative memories away, hiding them from her. Anything to continue her love affair with herself. As if she would ever end it.

Anyway. An hour into *their* conversation, Reyes had handed her off to Aeron's angel, Olivia. And fifteen minutes after that, Olivia had sweetly suggested that Viola shouldn't deny Maddox the pleasure of her company. Five glorious (for him) minutes later, Maddox had stomped away, muttering something about finding his wife and Viola could join him if she insisted. So, here they were, headed to the couple's bedroom.

"I'm sure I could whip up some kind of mechanical chair that would cart your wife around," Viola told the warrior. He was shirtless, and the crimson butterfly tattoo stretching across his shoulder blades—the mark of his demon—seemed to be scowling at her. "I'm handy with tools, as you probably guessed, and your back is probably strained from her *massive* weight."

Ashlyn smothered a laugh with one hand, but she failed to smother Maddox's snarl with the other.

"She is light as a feather," he snarled. "I enjoy carrying her. I also enjoy having her all to myself."

"Okay, but it's your back's funeral. In a few years, you'll probably need a brace." Oh, yes. His tattoo was indeed scowling at her. A gnarled, skeletal face had formed between the wings, fangs extending from a tiny mouth. The edges of the wings sharpened into dagger-like points, curling toward her.

Cool, but in no way comparable to hers. The front of her butterfly stretched along her chest, stomach and legs. The back of her butterfly stretched along her shoulders, thighs and calves. A total body tat that glimmered with the radiance of crushed pink diamonds.

Ashlyn's honey-colored eyes found her over Maddox's muscled shoulder. "He's not trying to get rid of you—"

"Yes, I am," Maddox said.

"—he's just cranky," the human finished.

Viola's brow wrinkled as she attempted to figure out how the poor, addled pregnant woman could have come up with such a preposterous idea. Get rid of her? Please. Men, women and children, mortals and immortals, fought to keep her by their sides. "Don't worry your pretty little head about me," she said. Wasn't that what humans said to one another to prove they weren't offended by stupid ideas? "I'm sure he's simply overwhelmed by my magnificence."

Maddox was the one to scowl this time, tossing the dark expression at her before stopping in front of a closed door. But then Ashlyn giggled and his gaze shot to her face. His entire body softened, melting like an ice cube in the summer heat.

A pang throbbed in Viola's chest. She thought back, but couldn't remember anyone ever looking at her like that, as if she were the morning sun, the midnight moon, and every star perched in the endless sky. Even though she'd had thousands—no, bazillions!—of admirers.

"Where's your dog?" Ashlyn asked.

"Princess Fluffikans is exploring these new surroundings without any hindrance from mommy."

. "That explains the screaming downstairs," Maddox muttered.

Ashlyn kissed her husband on the lips, then reached out to twist the knob. The door creaked open, and Maddox carried her inside. Fresh, clean air wafted to Viola. Out of habit, she scouted every inch in a single sweep, searching out all the mirrors and reflective surfaces. To the left was a vanity, and she made a mental note to avoid it, even as her demon urged her to close the distance…to take a teeny-tiny peek…just one, just for a second, because she would look so very beautiful….

She gritted her teeth. Dewy flowers spilled from colorful vases balanced on every piece of furniture in the room except the bed. Flowers *had* been woven in the wrought-iron bedposts, though, twining and clinging like ivy.

A portrait hung in the center of the far wall. And sweet heavens. Viola approached the thing slowly. The attention to detail was stunning. She could only take in a little at a time, studying one small section, looking away, then turning back to study another, repeating the process again and again until she'd gone over every inch.

In it, Ashlyn lounged in a lush, jewel-toned garden, flower petals in her hair, draping her body and dripping all around her. But the petals were not actually petals; they were faces. So many faces. The warriors here, their women, faces Viola didn't recognize and others she did—including her own. She quickly looked away from her own image, deciding to ponder its presence at a safer time.

One of Ashlyn's arms was bare, her skin tattooed to her elbow. Flames and snowflakes twisted together, and while the flames should have melted the flakes and the flakes should have doused the flames, the two somehow fed off each other, growing in color and intensity the higher up her arm they moved.

There was a reflective pool in front of her, and Maddox peered at her from its murky depths. Ashlyn reached for him with that tattooed arm, a silver ring winding along her index finger, glowing majestically.

Viola's nerve endings tingled. She'd seen paintings like this one before, but couldn't recall where or when. What she did know: every color, every face, every inch *meant* something. For real. This was symbolism at its finest. Only she didn't know how to decipher it.

"Who painted this?" she asked, her awe unmistakable. She straightened, turned away from the portrait before she lost hours of her life puzzling over the thing. Same as she lost hours every time she caught sight of her own image.

"Danika, Reyes's woman," Maddox muttered.

Danika. Hmm. Now that the painting was behind her, Viola allowed herself to question her inclusion in it. She'd met Danika for the first time this morning. The female appeared human, but after seeing this, she knew there had to be more to her. "It's an exquisite piece."

"Her work always is," Ashlyn said proudly.

"She sees into the future?"

"We will not discuss that," Maddox said.

So yes, she did. "She'll want to paint one of me all by myself, of course. I'll have to check my schedule and make sure I have the time to pose for her." *If not, I'll make time. Must question her. Must learn more about myself.*

Another giggle from Ashlyn. Another scowl from Maddox.

He'd placed his female on the bed and tucked the covers around her. Now he smoothed the hair from her brow, as gently as if he were caring for a fragile infant. "What do you need, sweetheart? Name it, and it's yours."

Dainty fingers rubbed at that swollen belly even as a soft smile played at her plump lips. "I would really, *really* love an orange. Just one this time, though. Last time this particular craving hit, you brought me the entire grove."

"I will bring you the best, most succulent orange you have ever tasted." He caressed her cheek for a moment, as if he couldn't bear to look away from her. Then he forced himself to do so and shot Viola a threatening glare.

"You will guard her with your life. And if you hurt her, even accidentally…" His hands fisted at his sides.

"Can't think of anything vile enough?" Viola thought for a moment. "May I suggest disembowelment? You can hang me from the ceiling with my own intestines. That would be really gruesome."

He gaped at her.

"Word of warning, though. Intestines are pink and pink is my best color. Wait. Who am I kidding? All colors are my best color. So, if you go that route, be ready to fall in love with me all over again."

His mouth snapped shut, a grimace contorting his lips. "That's it. I'm staying. Viola, you go find the orange."

"No way. Unless we go together and you carry me." All that walking had caused her feet to throb.

He looked at the door, then Viola, then the door, then Viola again.

Oh, come on. "Your resident angel already told you that I'm pure of heart, can be trusted, blah, blah, blah." That had surprised Viola, because she wasn't sure she'd ever been pure of heart. The fact that the warriors believed the dark-haired girl without a moment's hesitation had *really* surprised her. Supposedly, they were the most suspicious beings on earth. "Oh, and bring me an orange, too, but put it beside a hamburger and fries. I skipped lunch."

After issuing a few more threats to her life, he finally stalked from the room.

"Overprotective momma grisly," she muttered. "Geez."

"Have you never been in love?" Ashlyn asked.

"Hello. I'm not a fool."

"Is that a yes, then?"

"Um, yeah, that's a no."

A serene smile met her vehemence. "Why so much horror at the prospect?"

The ache in her chest returned. She rubbed and rubbed, nearly peeling off her shirt and the skin underneath, but the damn ache persisted. "I don't know." Time to change the subject. "I'm thinking about planning a singles' night here at my new home—fingers crossed it's forever—and letting the unattached warriors court me." She strolled to the bed and eased onto the edge. "Maybe a speed-dating-type thing, since I usually can't stand a man for more than a few minutes at a time. Afterward, I'll give the ones I like a rose and the others will have to pack their bags and leave the fortress permanently."

"Hmm. Well." Ashlyn tapped a finger against her chin, the corners of her lips twitching as if she were fighting another laugh. "Believe it or not, there are only a few singles left."

"Like who?"

"Well, let's see. There's Torin."

His image rose in Viola's mind. White hair, black brows, brilliant green eyes. Gorgeous face and muscled body. "He'll do. You may continue."

"Well, not that he's not wonderful, but I should warn you there's a potential drawback to dating him. He's the keeper of Disease, and he can't touch another living creature skin-to-skin without causing a plague. You wouldn't get sick from him because you're immortal, but in turn you also wouldn't be able to touch another living creature without passing on the illness. Besides him, that is."

Viola rubbed her tongue against the roof of her mouth. "You're right. I wouldn't get sick if I touched him. I'm sure you noticed how killer my immune system is. But even still, I'm not sure I want someone so flawed worshipping at my temple. Who else is there?"

"There's Kane, but he's..." Sadness dulled Ashlyn's amber eyes. "He doesn't date. Says it's not worth the hardship."

"He'd change his mind for me, of course, but that's not why you're sad, right? I believe I heard something about him being missing."

"Yes."

"Don't worry. As soon as he finds out I'm here, he'll find his way back. Even if he's dead. I don't like to brag, but that's happened a few times before. I'll just shoot out a quick little Screech, and boom. The race to reach me will begin."

Rather than cheer the girl up, her reassurances tossed worry into that storm of sadness. "Uh, you're not supposed to Screech," Ashlyn said. "Remember?"

Viola's shoulders slumped. That's right. Within five minutes of arriving here, Lucien had dragged her to the luscious Torin's bedroom and told the guy to check out her blog and website—evidently he was the resident computer guru. Afterward, both men had issued the same warning. Screech or post anything online about her location or her new BFFs and she would never be allowed back.

"Who else?" she asked.

Ashlyn nibbled on her bottom lip. "There's Cameo, but I'm pretty sure she likes men."

Viola shook her head. "I could change her mind, no problem, but I'm so over that stage of my life. Who else?"

"There's William the Ever Randy. He's not a demon keeper, but he's some kind of immortal."

William the Naughty Boy Toy. Oh, yes, she knew him. Like Anya, Viola had met him in Tartarus. "He's more than immortal, but whatever." He was also arrogant, conceited and highly annoying. "I'll put him in the maybe category."

"More than immortal? What does that mean? He's claimed to be some kind of god a few times, but I always assumed he was bragging, padding the truth. Which is—"

"Enough about him. We're talking about me. Who else can I date?"

Annnd a return of the nibbling. "There's Paris, but he's kind of obsessed with another woman right now."

"The dead one. Yeah. I know. I could still change his mind, but I don't think I want to, because…" There was a reason, wasn't there? As Viola pondered the answer, she clinked her teeth together.

Paris had asked her how to see the dead, and she had told him. Then he'd asked her something else, but Lucien arrived and ended their conversation. What had he asked? She tuned her mind's radio in to their past conversation, and her eyes widened as the answer at last slammed into place.

Consequences. He'd wanted to know if there would be consequences for tattooing himself with Sienna's ashes.

Oops. She'd let him get away without telling him that yes, there would be.

Oh, well. It wasn't her problem. It was his.

CHAPTER FOURTEEN

DAZED, SIENNA WALKED down a long hallway. Just as her past had played along the walls of the castle, Paris's past played *here,* a concerto of colors, faces, voices… limbs. On both sides of her, above and below her, women writhed, so many women. At first, she saw them smiling, heard them laughing, each one eager for what he offered, quickly falling for his charming facade.

Why wouldn't they? Whatever they wanted, he gave them. A touch, a kiss, a lick. A gentle ride. A rough pounding. He made love to all of them, knew exactly where to stroke and taste for maximum pleasure. He knew precisely the right amount of pressure to use as he kneaded their breasts, their thighs. Soft for some, firm for others.

He knew what position to place them in. On their backs, their hands and knees, right side up, upside down. Knew some wanted slow, and some wanted fast. They loved him for it, their pleasure unparalleled.

Then he left them and they cried with gut-wrenching sobs, their bodies heaving, their hearts breaking as the grief overcame them. Interspersed throughout the females were males. Paris had been with men, too, and he'd left them in the same condition as the women. They wanted him, and though they were not his preference, he took them so that he might survive. Afterward, they asked him to stay and he bailed.

One woman, Susan, was a beauty he'd truly cared for. He'd tried to make a relationship with her work, but Paris, being Paris, had hurt her in the worst way, choosing survival, as always, over her heart.

When Sienna caught an image of herself, she stopped, gasped. There, practically overshadowed by the other images, Paris was strapped to her boss's table, naked, the lights dim, and she was on top of him. She didn't need the vision to serve as a reminder. She would never forget.

She had been unable to see him, needing the darkness to relax, and he had alternated between snapping at her, hating her, hating himself, and aiding her, moving his hips to increase her pleasure. Now, however, she saw into his mind. Part of him had hoped to punish her afterward. Part of him—the deepest, most secret part—had wanted to hold on to her and never let go. To him, she had been a balm unlike any other.

Nausea rose, threatening to erupt. He had thought such beautiful things about her, and still she had condemned him.

Wrath slammed into her frontal lobe, urging her forward. To see more, to see all. She stumbled along, her feet as heavy as boulders.

Other scenes bled into the image of her and Paris, and someone must have cranked the volume control because suddenly she heard grunts, groans, moans and screams. Screams of pleasure, of pain and even of fury. Accusations were hurled, followed by pleas.

The pleas were followed by curses.

Sometimes, when Paris could find no one willing to be with him, his strength would wane, his will to live would wither and his demon would pull free of his reins. A dark, rich scent would seep from Paris's pores, intoxicating everyone nearby, luring them closer. These people would flock to him, regardless of their previous reservations about him or their disgust for casual sex. They would take him, or allow him to take them.

When this happened, Paris always battled intense guilt, because he knew the dastardly thing he was doing—but he took whatever was offered anyway.

These bedmates did not cry when he left. They watched him through narrowed eyes, detesting him, shamed by what they'd done with and to him, horrified by what they would soon lose. A loved one's respect.

He *had* broken up marriages, had committed adultery and performed sexual acts that left him cold and shaken. He then allowed those same sexual acts to be performed on him. A self-imposed punishment of sorts, she thought. All of that she could have guessed. But what astonished her? He detested himself far more powerfully than any of the humans ever had or could.

Oh, Paris, she thought. He was heaven and hell, just as Wrath had said, wrapped in the same luscious package.

Sienna wanted to cover her eyes to block the sights. She wanted to scream and scream and scream to block the sounds. *Everyone* in the crowd was crying now. Even Paris. Their tears poured from the ceiling, raining down, battering at her. But her hands remained at her sides and her mouth remained shut, her feet moving automatically. Her body was no longer connected to her brain.

Wrath wanted her to know, and so she would know.

The volume cranked up another notch, a shriek resounding at her left, spine-chilling, nauseating. All of the tears ceased. Another shriek sounded, then battle scene after battle scene came to life. Blood, a canvas of scarlet. Blades glinting with menace. Guns firing one after the other. Bombs exploding. Limbs separating from bodies, guts spilling. Death, so much death. Each delivered by Paris.

Paris, the FedEx deliveryman of Pleasure and Fatality.

There was no guilt here, however. No shame. Only cold, hard logic. Kill or be killed. No room for emotions or regrets. No hope for something better. This was it; this was the card he must constantly play. Fight for what he wanted or curl up and die.

He would not curl up and die.

Even though Sienna's own demon seemed to like Paris on some level, Wrath, being Wrath, still hoped to castigate him for all the wrongs he'd committed. The demon urged her to sleep with Paris and leave him. To break his heart. To make him sob and beg for another chance with her. Then, of course, would come the stabbing, hurting him as he had hurt so many others.

No! No, no, no. She jerked free of whatever leash the demon had used to bind her to his will and flattened her hands against her stomach, as if the puny action could settle the sickness still churning there.

"I will not punish him," she shouted, proud of her strength and conviction. Paris had done all those things, yes. And no, there was no excusing him. Though he'd been influenced by the evil creature inside him, he was responsible for his own decisions. He could have found another way.

But who was she to condemn anyone? Had *she* yet found another way? No.

Wrath offered no argument, and she frowned. That was unlike him. Usually he threw fits until she caved. But then, perhaps Aeron, Wrath's former keeper, had already fought and won this particular crusade. After all, Aeron and Paris had lived together for centuries, plenty of time for the demon to have either gotten a taste of what he desired or to have been berated into submission.

If ever she met Aeron—and if he could actually see her and didn't try to kill her—she would ask. She would do anything to return Wrath to him, too, despite the fact that such an action would kill her.

"Sienna." Warmth drifted over her cheek, sliding along the line of her jaw.

Her nerve endings perked up, firing back to life, making her skin tingle.

"Wake up for me. Come on, that's it, that's the way."

Yes. That voice…sexual and primal, blatant in its masculinity…a summoning finger she must follow. Where the voice originated, pleasure awaited her. So much pleasure.

She blinked open her eyes. Things were hazy at first, but the more she blinked, the better she could see. She was inside one of the second-floor bedrooms of the castle. The air was musty and yet chocolaty and—Paris loomed above her, peering down at her.

Breath snagged in her throat. He was just so beautiful, his face flawlessly chiseled. He could seduce anyone, anywhere. His hair was the richest shade of black, the purest shade of brown, with lighter strands woven throughout like ribbons of gold. His eyes were a wanton crystal, his lashes so thick and black they weighed down his lids, keeping them at half-mast, forever come-to-bed tempting. His lips were lush and red, and perhaps the most decadent part of an already decadent man. His skin was like crushed diamonds mixed with honey and cream. Pale, yet kissed with shimmers of the sun.

He bore a few scratches and had shadows under his eyes, but neither acted as an imperfection. They simply enhanced his appeal, adding depth. Lover, warrior…

protector of those of his choosing. And he was here. With her.

"How are you feeling?" he asked, the words scratchy now, as if there were glass shards stuck in his throat.

Was that a note of concern she detected? If so, this must be a hallucination. Paris wouldn't care for her well-being. Not after everything that had happened between them. With a shaky hand, she reached up and pressed her fingertips into the rose tinting his cheeks. Solid, warm. Real.

She gasped out a startled, "You really are here."

"Yes. I... Yes." His pupils expanded, concealing all the blue with a spiderweb of black, before snapping back into place. "How are you feeling?"

"Fine." There was a slight twinge in her stomach, a definite ache in her wings, but nothing that was un-manageable. A perk of being undead as well as Wrath's host, she supposed. No matter the severity of her inju-ries, death had no hold on her and she healed quickly.

"I cleaned you up, bandaged the worst of your wounds." Guilt layered his tone, a deeper flush bloom-ing across his cheeks. Those pupils expanded again, stay-ing that way—nope, they snapped back.

She'd never seen eyes do that. "Thank you." She moved her hand to her hair, grimaced when she encoun-tered tangles. She must look like total crap. "And you? How are you?" Her question trembled with the same in-tensity as her hand.

"Fine," he parroted, offering no more than she had.

He straightened, increasing the distance between them, though his hip remained pressed against hers. One of his arms slid forward and stopped beside her rib cage, taking the brunt of his weight.

They stayed like that for a long while, silent, looking at each other, then looking away.

This was…awkward. Really, *really* awkward. They hadn't seen each other in so long, and the last time they had, well, things had not ended well. *No one but yourself to blame,* she thought sadly.

"A lot has happened since we were last together," he began, then lapsed into silence as if contemplating all that had occurred.

"Yes," she agreed, though she had spent too much time contemplating it already.

"I know you were given a demon. What I don't know is how you're handling him," he said, staring somewhere far, far beyond her shoulder.

"We have our moments."

"He shows you the sins of others?"

"Yes."

"And forces you to punish the wrongdoers?"

"Yes."

He nodded. "Aeron, the guy who had Wrath before you, used to hate that. He would resist for as long as he could."

"And then Wrath would overtake him," she grumbled.

"Yeah."

"I have the same problem." Usually she saw the images of a person's sins while she was awake, and things would progress from there. She would fight the urges and win, or she would fight the urges and fail. She wasn't sure what to make of the fact that she'd seen Paris's transgressions while she was asleep.

Another bout of uncomfortable silence ensued. There was so much to say, but she didn't know where to begin.

"Paris," she breathed at the same time he sighed and said, "Sienna."

They stared at each other now, searching, unsure. *Annnd* once again silence reigned, so heavy she could feel the weight of it pressing her deeper into the mattress. Her heart careened against her chest in a useless attempt at escape. If the damn thing had been hooked to a battery, she would have pulled the plug. Anything for relief from this suspended, anxious sensation, fear of sending Paris fleeing preventing her from saying all the things she'd imagined saying to him.

"You go first," he said, a muscle ticking in his jaw.

Very well. She could do this. *She could.* "I just wondered how you got here and why you…why you came for me." And he had definitely come for her, and her alone. Why else would he have shouted her name like that? Did he hope to punish her for what she'd once done to him?

His eyes narrowed. "I changed my mind. I'll go first. Tell me why *you* came to *me,* that night in Texas when William saw you at my feet. William being my *homely* friend." Through those slitted lids, she saw that his irises had frosted over, the darkness still evident. His expression became granite-hard, ruthless determination cloaking him.

The man who sat before her now was not the one who'd fought the Gargl to reach her; he was not the one who'd taken such care with her wounds. And he *had* cared for her wounds. She'd been cleaned, bandaged, just as he'd said.

No, the man who sat before her was the one she'd first met in Rome. The one who had kissed her one minute and woken up strapped to a torture table the next. The one who had cursed her with one breath, and praised her with the following.

Whoever he was, she wouldn't lie to him. She would never lie to him again. "I needed help," she admitted, "and Wrath knew where you were, how to reach you. He had taken over, and I came to there at your feet."

"Do you still need help?"

"With Wrath? Yes."

He nodded, losing that knife edge of ruthlessness. "I'm sorry I couldn't see you that night."

"You have nothing to apologize for."

"Anyway," he said after clearing his throat. "I figured you would have trouble adapting, though you're doing far better than I did at this stage, so I asked Aeron if he had any tips for you. He said you'll have an easy time of things if you feed the bastard a little bit every day. Someone lies to you, you lie back. Someone cheats you, you cheat them back. Someone hits you, you hit back."

How willingly he offered the information. He didn't make her beg. Didn't taunt her because he knew and she didn't. And Aeron hadn't withheld the information, when he had to hate her for taking his companion—and they *had* been companions. Wrath had been an extension of him, still missed him to this day. But as grateful as she was for the advice...what a terrible way to live, she thought. "Thank you for that."

"Welcome," he said stiffly. Then, "Do you still think I'm evil and in need of snuffing out?"

"No! You're not evil." That she had ever placed the man in the same category as the demon... She was so very ashamed. How foolish she'd been. How gullible. "I'm sorry that I ever thought you were."

The visual perusal he next gave her peeled away her clothing, leaving her bare, trembling. "And I should believe you?"

He would never trust her, but then, why should he? "Being paired with Wrath, well, my eyes were opened. I saw the truth for the first time. The things I did...the things I'm urged to do…you've been dealing with that for thousands of years, and still you fight. Doubt me all you want, but I vow to you now." To stop herself from reaching out to him, she fisted her hands at her sides. "I will never hurt you again."

In his hooded eyes she saw flecks of anger, a blaze of arousal. Then, nothing.

He looked away from her, gaze landing on the room's only window. There was a crack in the thick, black curtains, a single ray of moonlight slipping inside. Then he offered a shrug of one strong shoulder. "You asked why I came for you."

Disappointment rocked her. A response to her vow would have been nice. But then, she didn't deserve it. "Yes."

"I— Damn it. I couldn't let you suffer."

He couldn't…let her…suffer…oh… Here was a mercy she was no longer capable of offering to others, so she knew how precious it was. Tears sprang to her eyes and tracked down her cheeks, a trickle at first, then a flood. Until her body was heaving with the same force as the women in that dream hallway. Until she couldn't see the bedroom or Paris.

What happened to growing a pair of lady balls? Breaking down now, in front of him, was humiliating, but she couldn't stop.

Her shame exploded, little pieces tossed into every corner of her body, saturating her. All her life, she'd only ever been able to rely on herself. Her mom's alcoholism, which had started right after Skye's abduction, had eaten away at any love the woman had felt for Sienna. Her dad had eventually taken off and started another family, forgetting the little girl he'd left behind.

Then in college, she'd begun dating Hugh. He'd listened to her stories about her past, offered sympathy and aid. He'd told her about himself, and his belief in the supernatural. When she expressed doubt, he promised to show her—and he had. She'd been scared yet thrilled at the same time, because then she'd had someone to blame for every single one of her troubles.

How freeing that had been. How marvelous to realize that her mother wasn't at fault. Her father wasn't at fault. *She* wasn't at fault. How soothing to think her parents would have loved her still if not for the evil the Lords had brought into the world. So, yeah, she'd jumped headfirst into the good-versus-evil game.

And yet, the Hunters had gunned her down to get to Paris.

Paris, who hadn't wanted her to suffer.

Her sobs emerged so powerfully, she was soon hiccupping, eyes and nose running freely, and that sent her embarrassment to a new level. Stalwart arms wrapped around her, careful not to brush against her fragile wings, lifting her, drawing her into a hot, muscled chest. His heartbeat hammered as swiftly as hers.

And wouldn't you know, that made her cry even harder.

"Calm down," he commanded, clearly uncomfortable. And wow. You would think a man who'd been with as many women as Paris had would know how to finesse one who was nearing hysteria, but no. He patted her back a little too roughly, then glared down at her when she failed to obey him.

How could he *not* want her to suffer? How could she ever have judged him so harshly?

"Sienna. Stop this."

"Can't…help…it. Did such…terrible things to…you. And you…you're here. And you're being so *nice*."

A pause, as if he couldn't quite digest her words. Then, very gently, he said, "But I did terrible things to you, too. Didn't I?"

CHAPTER FIFTEEN

SIENNA TOLD HERSELF TO SHUT UP, to lock down tight, but the words poured out of her of their own accord. "You were going to have sex with me and walk away. Not the most chivalrous behavior, but that hardly justifies being drugged, tortured and nearly killed. I tricked you, let them hurt you. And then I raped you. I think I raped you." She choked, but still the words kept coming. "I'm sorry, Paris. I'm so sorry. I know that's not good enough. Nothing I say will ever be good enough, but—"

"Sienna."

"I'm sorry. I am. And afterward, when I was dying, I blamed you, but it wasn't your fault. I told you I hated you, and I'm so very sorry for that, too. You didn't deserve any of it."

Another pause. His hands began to move down her back, caressing now, before sliding back up again, soothing her. "You didn't rape me," he said, and there was a surprising tinge of amusement in his tone. "I wanted you. I wanted you so damn badly, even though I didn't want to want you." Or maybe she'd imagined the amusement. His timbre was now an abrasive rasp.

"I slept with you because I was told to, because I wanted to destroy you," she said.

"I slept with you to strengthen myself."

"But I still wanted you," she added in a soft whisper. His fingertips pressed into the muscles just under the rise of her wings, but the pressure eased all too soon. "And I still wanted you. That's one of the reasons I took you with me when I got free, because I wanted to be with you again."

Another sob left her. "I thought you used me as a shield, and I...I..." Well, crap. The sobs became so great her voice box finally closed up.

He pressed a kiss into her temple. "I didn't use you as a shield. Not intentionally, at least. I'm sorry for how things ended, so very, very sorry. If it helps, I've punished myself a thousand times, will probably punish myself a thousand more. Had I known what would happen, I would have left you there...and come back for you later."

The last was offered hesitantly, as if he feared her reaction to such a truth. "I'm glad."

An eternity passed just like that, the two of them clutching at each other, the silence no longer prickly but calming. And, okay. Maybe she was the only one doing the clutching, but he didn't seem to mind. He continued to caress her.

She hadn't realized how much she'd craved contact with another body until just that moment. That the body belonged to Paris, well, that made it even better. He was so strong, and smelled so sweet, and if she wasn't careful, she would soon be rubbing her cheek against his chest, burying her nose in the hollow of his neck and twining herself around him like a vine.

When at last she quieted, exhaustion set in and she just kind of sagged against him, her head resting on his shoulder. Her eyes were swollen, heavy, her nose stuffed up, and her throat raw from her tears.

"Better?" he asked.

"Yes, thank you. I...I... Paris." Her lips parted, and

she inhaled through her mouth. "Despite everything, you came here to help me. You put yourself in danger."

"Danger is nothing to me." His voice had become gruff, as if he disliked the direction the conversation had gone in.

Danger might be nothing to him, but she'd seen him with his friends. *They* were everything to him, and still he'd left them to save her. A surreal—and even more shaming—realization.

What did his unwillingness to let her suffer mean? Did he, dare she hope, have feelings for her? Crave something *more* with her? Though she wasn't ready to release him, she did just that, pulling back, taking another deep breath and drawing in the dark-chocolate scent of him. If the movement hadn't disrupted the angle of her wings, lancing a sharp pain through her, she would have sat there, savoring him, drowning in a sudden burst of arousal, for hours.

Frowning, Paris maneuvered the gossamer extensions of her wings into a more comfortable position. He was infinitely careful, his every motion checked. When he finished, he eyed her warily. "Better?" he asked again.

He *had* to have feelings for her. Impossible, and yet, possible all the same. "Yes, thank you." She looked down at her hands. They were wringing her shirt, twisting and wrinkling the material, yet she hadn't realized she'd moved them. She should ask him about his feelings. She should—

"Why did you walk away from me when you first saw me?" he asked, his tone curious rather than accusatory. "When the gargoyles had me."

"I thought you were a hallucination. A memory. They're like film reels, playing around me in a never-ending stream."

His frown deepened, pulling those lush lips tight over perfect white teeth. "Even now?"

Her gaze darted around the room, and she could only gape. She saw crumbling stone, portraits draped by sheets, but no memories. "No. It's just you and me." Probably because they couldn't steal her attention away from Paris. "Paris, I want to tell you things. About the Hunters. Things that could help you and your friends. I—"

"No," he said, cutting her off.

"But—"

He gave an abrupt shake of his head. "No," he reiterated.

"I don't understand."

"I don't want you to tell me anything about them."

"But…why?" Even when she had been poised over his helpless body, moving on him, even when he had rightly blamed her for his condition, he had not peered at her with such harsh resolve. Red flickered through his eyes, those shadows once again dancing through his irises.

She didn't have to consider the problem long before the answer slithered into place, a boa ready to suffocate its prey. He thought she would mislead him, send him straight into a trap, and there would be nothing she could say to convince him otherwise. That hurt, but then she deserved that and more.

Not knowing what else to do, she shied away from the topic. "How can you see me, hear me? Touch me? You couldn't before."

The red faded, the shadows stilled. His pupils did that expanding, contracting thing, taut rubber bands ready to snap.

"I learned a few tricks about the dead," he said. "That's all."

And he wouldn't share those tricks or anything else with her; his tone made that clear. An ache ignited in her heart, dropped into her stomach and guillotined every bit of happiness his presence here had wrought.

"Did you also learn how to break a curse and bust someone out of a castle they can't leave?" she asked. Good. Back to business. *Without* another breakdown.

A terrible stillness came over him. "I knew you were trapped here, but I'm still not sure how."

"Do you know where here is?" She could guess, but the answers that came to her made her sick.

"A hidden kingdom in the Titans' section of the heavens."

Her eyes widened. "Heavens? Really? I would have bet somewhere in hell."

"What happens when you try to leave?"

"There's some kind of invisible block. I approach a door or a window and I hurt, and if I remain in front of the portal for too long, I pass out. But sometimes… sometimes Wrath takes over and the blocks fall away. I end up outside the castle's walls, not too far from here, I don't think. And I do things. Terrible things," she whispered. "Then I come back here, I can't stop myself. I step inside and the blocks immediately go back up."

He reached out as if he meant to cup her cheek, to offer comfort. Then he growled, low and guttural, and his arm dropped to his side. That made her want to erupt into a fresh round of sobbing, but she didn't allow herself the luxury. Not even when he jerked to a stand, stalked to the window and tossed the curtains aside, the distance a great chasm between them—symbolic.

Dust wafted around him. A few tugs, and he had the pane lifted. Hot, pungent air drifted inside, stinging her nostrils. He palmed a blade, extended his arm into the darkness—and met no resistance.

Others *could* leave, she realized. Only she was trapped.

He slid the glass into place and spun to face her. He didn't return to her side, but leaned back, propping himself against the wall. The bulge of his muscles stretched the black material of his T-shirt. His pants hugged his thighs—and an impressive erection.

Could he possibly...want her? The way she wanted him?

Who are you trying to fool? He's the Lord of Sex. He probably has that reaction with everyone.

"Can you let Wrath take over your body without taking over your mind?" he asked, a catch in his voice.

She forced herself to meet his eyes as heat flashed in her cheeks. "I, uh... He takes over both, but I've never just let him. I don't always win, but I always fight him."

"Stop fighting him. Let him take over your body, but try to maintain some kind of tether to your mind."

Her mouth fell open, snapped closed. Just like that, he wanted her to allow the being that thrived on punishing *everyone* to consume her, to drive her every action? "You don't understand what would happen if I did that."

He gave a bitter laugh that did nothing to mar his masculine perfection, and everything to enhance it. Maybe because with the unveiling of his bitterness came a need to kiss him better. "Oh, but I do."

Yes, she supposed he must. "Wrath hurts people. *I* hurt people. And what if I hurt *you*?"

Melted steel in his eyes, bubbling from his voice. "I can take care of myself, and I want to get you out of here."

"I want that, too." Just not enough to risk hurting

him. And really, her demon wasn't the only—or even the worst—worry. Her eyes widened. How could she have forgotten, even for a moment? "Cronus," she gasped out. "If you help me, Cronus will come after you. I'm surprised he hasn't already."

"Way I hear it, he's been too busy to concern himself with me." Paris grinned, slow and wicked. Eager. "But he and I are due a reckoning, and we'll soon have it."

Her hand fluttered to her throat. "Not on my account. I don't want you—"

"Do you have any family?" he asked, interrupting her. "Anyone I can take you to once I get you out of the heavens?"

She blinked. He'd saved her, still felt desire for her if his erection was any indication, but he didn't intend to keep her, or even be with her. He wanted to foist her off as quickly as possible. Of course. Stupid, stupid Sienna for ever hoping otherwise.

They couldn't make anything work between them, anyway. She knew more about his demon now and knew Paris couldn't sleep with her again, despite...*that*. Right? He was a one-time only joyride. *Right?*

"Sienna," he snapped. "Eyes on my face. Please."

The heat in her cheeks rose to scalding as she jerked her gaze away from his man business a second time. "I'm sorry. I didn't mean to make you feel like a piece of meat. I was just lost in thought."

"About my di—uh, junk?"

"Well, yes."

His jaw dropped with the force of his astonishment, and she had to wonder why the god of sex would find such a revelation so unbelievable.

Anyway. What had he asked her before? Oh, yeah. Her family. "No. There's no one who could take me in, no one who could even see me." As she spoke, she looked the rest of him over. He was still cut from the Gargl, the wounds now scabbed. He had healed, but only slightly. And his skin had lost a bit of its glittery sheen. Was he weakening from lack of sex? That's what had happened in the Hunters' prison.

"When was the last time you had a woman?" she asked, trying to act nonchalant about a very sore subject between them.

The frost she'd seen earlier fell over his entire body. His eyelids narrowed, the gleam in those ocean-pretty irises flint hard.

"I don't remember," he gritted out.

The confession relieved and thrilled her, she was ashamed to admit. He was clearly hurting. "Well, I'm... uh, I'm, you know...available. For you. If you can, I mean. And if you, you know, want me and can use... that on me." How pathetic she sounded, but she wanted to touch him again, to be with him one last time. Even if she had to reduce the act to a simple clinical procedure. "I owe you." Or a favor between pseudo-friends.

The ice thickened, cracked, thickened again, as if a battle raged inside him. The ice won. "Really? You're *available* to me? You owe me?" He popped his jaw. "Thank you for that *generous* offer. How could a guy like me ever refuse?"

A guy like him? "I didn't mean—"

"Just so you know, I didn't come all this way to enjoy your *availability* or to collect on a debt. So, while I can, in fact, screw you again, I hope you'll understand when I do the unthinkable and pass. But don't worry, I'll still help you. Screwing me isn't a requirement."

She chewed on her bottom lip to stop herself from responding. *Deserved, deserved, deserved,* she told herself again. And maybe his refusal was a good thing. He still resented her. And as he'd already proven, he didn't trust her. Being with him, and watching him walk away afterward, would slice her into pieces so jagged she'd never be able to fit herself back together.

More than that, she had to go after Galen. The thought hit with so much force her entire body shook. She had toyed with the idea, but hadn't decided officially. Now, she saw the truth. She'd told Paris she had no family, but what if she did? And what if only she could save them? If there were the slightest possibility that Galen was torturing her sister and her child, Sienna had to act, which meant she might have to…do things with him. Necessary things. Things she wouldn't be able to bring herself to do if she forged any kind of bond with Paris. A white-hot toxin flooded her veins, stinging.

"You look disgusted and scared," Paris said, his voice as sharp as any dagger. "Why?"

"Neither emotion is for you," she said quietly. Never for him. Not anymore.

A hard knock sounded at the door, followed by the homely guy's rough timbre. "Paris. This isn't exactly life and death, my man, but things are quiet in there so I figure you haven't quite learned how to undo her bra strap. Give it a rest and come out here. You have to see this."

Paris looked like he'd just been granted a reprieve from a firing squad. He straightened. "On my way," he called. He stood there for a moment, grinding his molars, thinking about something unpleasant, judging by the expression on his face. Then he stalked to the bed and held out his hand, helping her lumber to her feet.

His calluses abraded her palm in the most delicious way, and she shivered. "Thank you."

"Whatever." He didn't lead her out, but leveled her with a fierce frown. "Don't try to leave my side. Understand?"

Was he afraid she'd run from him? Afraid she'd tell someone where he was so they could kill him?

Deserved, she reminded herself. What really sucked about the whole situation was that she couldn't ask for a second chance with him, or even an opportunity to redeem herself. As she'd just realized, they were already doomed, her path already decided.

Another realization struck. That same path could give him what he wanted more than anything. Victory against the Hunters. Not that he would ever know the part she'd played. If Cronus had his way, Paris would assume she was Galen's mistress. His sexual toy. And…and she would be, at least until she learned the truth about Skye. Then she would kill him, as *she* wanted, no matter the consequences to herself.

"Sienna," Paris snapped, drawing her back to the present.

She peered up at him. No matter how things shook out, she was going to lose him, and that was a hard fact given that she'd only just found him again. But for today, she was with him. That would have to be enough. "I won't leave your side."

CHAPTER SIXTEEN

GALEN, KEEPER OF HOPE, leader of the Hunters, leisurely explored the rooms inside his enemy's fortress. He'd only recently healed from battle wounds he'd received courtesy of the Lords of the Underworld. Now it was time for payback.

The blade he held was new and had never seen a single moment of action. Today, that would change.

"—shut that damn thing up," Cameo, keeper of Misery, was saying as she snaked around the corner and stomped past him. Draped as he was by the Cloak of Invisibility, she failed to spot him.

He studied her as she passed. In all the centuries since their creation, she hadn't changed. She had long, dark hair made for fisting, and the slim body of a dancer made for screwing. Her eyes were liquid silver—and made for dangling from his necklace. "If you don't, I will stab both of you. And let me tell you, one-point-eight people die every second. I never mind adding to the tally."

Maybe she *had* changed. The low, raspy resonance of her voice carried the heavy burden of a world's worth of sorrows. Enough to spring an ache in his chest, one that promptly seeped outward, invading more and more of him. In the heavens, her voice had brought only pleasure.

Scowling, Galen tucked the length of his wings into his sides and pressed against the wall. The action caused a white feather to loosen and drift to the floor, no longer hidden by the Cloak. He bent to pick it up, stopped.

A short, curvy blonde clutching a black dog...thing darted after Cameo. "All's I'm saying is that with a little makeup you could look like my country cousin rather than my undernourished uncle. Maybe no one's told you this, but bags are meant to be carried in your hands, not under your eyes."

The—mutant dog's?—head twisted, twisted, its beady eyes locked on Galen. A lethal growl rent the air, fangs spearing its lower lip. Evidently the Cloak's magic did not work on all creatures. (What *was* that thing?) He flipped it off, and it yipped.

"Hush, princess. Mama's teaching Beauty 101 to the clueless. Besides, we don't want the silly Lords upset with you again, do we?"

Galen didn't recognize the blonde or her ugly "princess." What he did know? The Lords welcomed only a select few into their exalted midst. That meant she was either a new addition to the Lords' army or a warrior's girlfriend. Pitiful how many of the once-stalwart men had fallen in *lurrÅ¿ve* recently.

Whatever or whoever she was, she would die like the others.

The duo and their not-quite-canine companion stormed into one of the bedrooms. A door slammed. No alarm was sounded.

His scowl melted into a grin. They couldn't see him, but they could have sensed him. That they hadn't meant this would be easier than he'd thought.

Strider, the idiot, had given the Cloak of Invisibility to the Unspoken Ones, beings so vicious, so evil, even Hercules would have trembled in fear at the slightest mention of them. Cronus had enslaved them before his own imprisonment, had once thought to control them. In turn, they wanted him dead. Now they were trapped on their private island in Rome and reduced to bargaining.

A point in Galen's favor. They knew he was destined to remove the Titan king's head, and so when he visited their island, they sought his support. Their first gesture, giving him the Cloak. Their second, teaching him exactly how to use it. He'd assumed it was a shield against prying eyes, but he'd assumed wrong. The Cloak was also a weapon. A very effective one at that.

He needed every advantage he could get, even if that meant aligning himself with the worst creatures ever to roam this earth. His men were disappearing right off the streets, never to be heard from again. His queen had disappeared, as well. He'd had no contact with her for weeks.

She knew him well enough to know he looked out for Number One. He would betray anyone to get what he wanted, and if she'd decided to walk away, to betray him as he'd betrayed so many others, that was her problem. He would go after her the same way he continued to go after her husband. With everything he had.

Galen planned to rule the heavens. *And I'll succeed this time.* He knew it, but then, he always "knew" his plans would work. His demon could convince anyone to do anything—and Galen was included in that number. Hope built up everyone's dreams, then laughed when those dreams came crashing down.

But it wasn't Hope driving him this day. It was Jealousy. His other demon.

Oh, yes. His former friends might not have been bright enough to figure this out yet, but Galen was possessed by *two* of Pandora's demons.

Because he had convinced his fellow warriors to steal

her box, because he'd then betrayed them, thinking to become leader of the Elite Guard himself, taking Lucien's place, he'd committed two crimes. Therefore, he deserved two punishments. Or so Zeus had said when he'd set about pairing each Lord with their demon and restoring order to the heavens.

He *despised* having two demons. Hope built him up only to tear him down, then Jealousy would rile him back up, whispering things like, *That male has a female, yet we are far better. Why don't we take her from him?* Hope would then fill him with an urge to do just that, to take, the need becoming a living thing inside him, every ounce of his being certain he would succeed—but somehow always falling short of victory.

Well, today he would not fail.

Today he landed a stunning blow to his enemy.

He would steal away Legion, the devil-woman they'd once sent to kill him. The she-cat who had seduced him. The innocent virgin who'd been living inside a porn star's skin. She'd screwed him within an inch of his immortal life before biting him with her poisoned fangs. While he had writhed in pain, she had left him to die, only to be carted into hell thanks to a deal with her maker gone bad.

Galen had hunted her, but the Lords had found her first. They'd brought her here, and Galen wanted her back. Wanted to have her again. Wanted to punish her. To kill her and cut the tether she seemed to hold him on.

He was sick of wondering about her, sick of thinking about her.

How many warriors had she given herself to since her return?

Yeah, like that. He was sick of imagining her with

a thousand others, sick of the constant rage of jealousy concerning her.

He would discover the answer, though, and if any of the Lords had enjoyed her luscious body, they would pay a higher toll than their friends. Oh, each and every one of them would die, but some would scream for months before he took their heads.

Except…he searched the fortress from top to bottom, looked in every chamber, accounted for every warrior still in residence—and not even Torin, who monitored the place, noticed him—but there was no sign of the girl.

Very well. He'd go with Plan B. He would take a page from the Unspoken Ones' book and "bargain" before he struck.

Despising the delay, he stalked to Maddox and Ashlyn's bedroom and ghosted through the wood. He wasn't just invisible, he was insubstantial. Maddox, keeper of Violence, was no longer inside. His very pregnant female reclined on their bed, reading a book to her unborn babe. A babe Maddox would be desperate to save.

Ashlyn was a pretty thing, with hair, skin and eyes the color of a honeycomb. Truly, she was as golden as the moon on the brightest of nights, and she was delicate and fragile as only a human could be. Her voice was soft, lilting, and filled with love.

No question, Maddox would move heaven and earth to get her back.

Galen padded to the side of the bed and pushed the Cloak from one shoulder. As he materialized, another grin quirked the corners of his mouth. Ashlyn noticed him and quieted, her entire body jolting with fright.

"Galen," she gasped out.

"Scream for me, little Ashlyn," he said, reaching for her. And she did.

WILLIAM KIND OF EXPECTED to be pulverized the moment Paris emerged from the bedroom. Fists hammering at his face, teeth ripping at his jugular, something menacing like that since he'd dared to interrupt the happy reunion. After all, madness and mayhem were a Paris Lord staple. What William hadn't expected was a half grateful, half thunderous stare, but that's exactly what he got.

"What did you want to show me?" the Lord of Sex snapped.

Paris had moved mountains to get here. Had done things that made a reprobate like William look like a choirboy, all to save the girl he currently had tucked into his side. And that he was holding her hand as if she were a life raft and the flood had come, rather than swinging at the man who had just cock-blocked him…well, that was just weird.

It could mean one of two things. Paris had already had sex with her, so there'd been nothing to block. Yet only an hour had passed since their parting. So *that* would mean Paris was quick on the climax trigger and, as many ladies as he'd nailed, William would bet the guy could go all night and then some.

Option two was slightly more likely, but still improbable. Paris hadn't known what to do with the girl and had wanted to bail.

But why would he want to bail? For that matter, why, with every second that passed, did he appear more pissed than ever? Had Sienna turned him down flat?

Impossible, William thought next. She was clutching Paris's hand as desperately as he clutched hers.

William raked his gaze over her. She was pale, her freckles stark in contrast, and she was a bit shaky on her feet. Hmm. Studying her like this, he wondered what Paris saw in her.

At first glance, and hell, maybe even at second, she appeared plain. He looked deeper, though, and that's when the delicacy of her bone structure became evident. What's more, those hazel eyes were large and unbelievably lovely, the perfect blend of emerald and copper. Her hair was a waterfall of mahogany, cascading around her. And her lips…yeah, he would have committed a few crimes himself to have those fit around his shaft.

She was on the slender side, small-breasted and even underweight, but damn if she didn't call on every protective instinct a man possessed.

"Are you just going to stare at her?" Once again Paris snapped the words. This time, menace poured from him, the threat of attack very real.

Now William doubted his face would be the only thing rearranged. His favorite appendage would be on the receiving end of a nice little slice and dice. *Sooo.* The biggest he-slut ever created was possessive as hell over a woman who'd once wanted to kill him. Talk about comeuppance. But then, wasn't that what Wrath specialized in?

Paris took a step toward him, the menace intensifying. "I asked you a question."

William cut off a grin and held his hands up, palms out, questions rolling through his mind. How much did Paris really want the girl? Did he regret coming here? How much influence could she wield over his emotions? Was the plan still to get in, get out and get rid of her? Only one way to find out.

"Answer me," Paris snapped.

"Nope," William said. "I don't just plan to stare."

A growl erupted from the warrior. They both knew he'd just implied he meant to do more.

Good. Maybe William would survive what came next,

maybe he wouldn't. "I like your shirt," he said, directing
the compliment to Sienna. "I *really* like your pants." She
wore a plain white T-shirt, dirt-smudged and torn, and
baggy cargo pants. Her tennis shoes were missing laces.

"I… Thanks?" Her brows knit with her confusion.

"May I make a wardrobe suggestion, though?"

Another growl sounded from Paris before she could
reply, a hand darting out and wrapping around William's
windpipe. Pinpricks of red glowed inside those ocean-
blues. No, Paris's irises were no longer blue. They were
black, no difference between pupils and the rest. "Are
you now implying her clothes will look better on your
bedroom floor?"

So. Much. Fun. "Who, me?" He couldn't breathe, so
the words squeaked out. No, Paris did not regret coming
here.

"Paris," Sienna said, utterly calm. "I know I have no
right to ask this, but will you please not kill him? I'm not
a fan of the rotting body scent."

Tighter…tighter…then the pressure eased, fell away.
"Show us what you found."

Interesting. She wielded a *lot* of influence. He wondered if Paris realized how much—and exactly what the
warrior thought of the development. But no matter what,
William assumed the plan was still of the get-rid variety. No relationship lasted without trust, and these two
had not a spark of it between them. Even as Paris eyed
William like a slab of beef to carve for dinner, he kept
Sienna in his crosshairs, as if afraid she'd bolt, or even
do a little carving of her own.

"Come on, or you'll be ticked I didn't show you
sooner." William turned on his heel and marched down
the hallway and up another flight of stairs to the third
floor. He didn't have to look back to know the couple

followed him. Paris's booted footfalls reminded him of stampeding buffalo.

He slowed his pace and Paris came up beside him. At some point, the warrior had picked Sienna up. She was cradled in his arms, her wings tucked around her, her head resting in the hollow of his neck. Even more interesting was the fact that she hadn't uttered a complaint.

Her gaze met William's, steady as a rock. She frowned. "Wrath goes silent around you. He doesn't show me any of your perceived sins. Why is that?"

Oh, no. He wasn't veering down that conversation path. Not with a former Hunter and a dead, though brought back to life, newly possessed whatever the hell she was. "You'll have to ask him."

"I did."

He pressed his tongue to the roof of his mouth. "And?"

"And he offered no response, so I decided it's because you have to live with yourself, a punishment worse than anything Wrath could mete out."

Miracle of miracles. The demon wasn't tattling on him. "The answer will just have to remain a mystery, then. Oh, and a word of warning. Smart mouths really crank my chain. Keep talking dirty to me, baby."

She rolled her eyes.

Paris inserted himself into the conversation with a hesitant, "Did he show you mine?" That he didn't threaten William proved the depths of his uncertainty about what Wrath might have broadcast.

William had seen Paris aroused (not on purpose), playful, pissed off, blood-soaked, stubborn, drugged out, relaxed, stressed and everything in between. But he had never seen the warrior frightened. Just then, Paris was frightened, his expression haunted, his muscles knotted over bone.

"Yes," she replied so quietly he had to strain to hear.

A taut beat of silence. "Do you want me to put you down?"

"No!" Color flooded her cheeks when she realized just how loudly she'd shouted the word. "No. I like where I am."

From a mouse to a lioness. Adorable really, and William thought he might make a pass at her when Paris finished with her. Because, even as fierce as Paris was about her, he would let her go. Resolve had bled into the fear. Even though Paris had suspected she would not want to be touched by a man who had done the things he'd done, even though she had proven him wrong and that had to be a relief, he was determined to live without her.

"I just meant that, uh, my back hurts," she added. "I need your support."

"Like a good jockstrap," William said, patting his boy on the shoulder. "But then, that's Paris for you."

Even with Sienna in his arms, Paris managed to give him a two-fingered salute. Mentally, of course, but William saw it all the same.

"I should have asked him to finish you off, rather than to let you go," she muttered. Then, "Are we heading to the fifth floor?"

Ah. So she knew what was up there. "Yes."

"Why?" Paris asked.

"You'll see," William replied.

Sienna opted to ruin the surprise. "Other demon-possessed immortals are up there."

"Other demon..." Paris increased his speed, leaving William eating his dust. "Are they armed?"

"No," she said, "but they're trapped."

"Show me."

"That's what *I* was trying to do," William muttered as

he chased after them. One day it would be nice for someone to place *him* first. Not a lover, though, and not the girl who haunted his dreams. The girl he would protect with his life now and always. She wasn't meant for him.

His one true love would die—or kill him. It had already been foretold, and there was no other option.

CHAPTER SEVENTEEN

CAREFUL TO KEEP HIS MIND on the situation at hand, rather than on his aching, needy body, Paris stopped in the center of the fifth-floor hallway. He was shocked by what he found. Only Sienna's slight weight in his arms, her tropical, feminine scent in his nose, her silky hair brushing against his skin, grounded him.

Funny, that. The magnification of her drugging scent should have sent him flying straight into a round of withdrawal—or chewing at her neck. Instead, the need to protect her, even from himself, beat everything else.

There were three immortals up here, a female and two males. They stood at the back of their rooms, staring at him, making no moves toward him. He'd never met them, which meant he hadn't locked them in Tartarus before his possession. Still, they were glaring at him. Did they know who he was? *What* he was?

I want them, Sex said.

Wow. What a shock.

A whiny *I'm becoming weaker by the minute* followed.

Believe me, I know. How he longed for the days when Sex retreated into the land of silence and led him simply through urges. *Now, do me a solid and stuff it.*

That's what I'm trying to do!

Crude bastard.

Like Paris was really any better. Over the years Paris had slept with thousands of different people for thousands of different reasons, and not all of them had been about passion. He truly needed to take a woman, like, yesterday, and that's one of the reasons he was here, to be with Sienna again. But he hadn't so much as kissed her, even though he was desperate to do so, because he didn't want to be with her for any reason *but* passion.

Mutual desire mattered.

She desired him, yes. At least, he was pretty sure he'd caught the scent of her arousal while she'd offered to "service" him, but he'd treated her shabbily. She'd looked at him with those sad, watery eyes, hopeful for forgiveness, and he'd snapped at her.

Damn it, he didn't want her apology or her gratitude. Didn't want her pity, and certainly didn't want her to want him because of his demon's pheromones. Had he taken her up on her offer, gratitude and pity would have been in that bed with them, as well as anger, distrust and regret. He hadn't done the ménage thing for a long time.

Maybe he should have taken what he could get, though. Waiting was kind of stupid. Case in point—his current weakness. More than that, Sienna might not give him a second chance. She might run, as he'd feared. It was just, she wasn't like any of the other women he'd been with, and he didn't want to treat her as if she were.

What makes her different from the others?

The question sprang from deep within him, throwing him. She was gutsy, but so were others. She was witty, but so were others. She was sometimes sweet and sometimes spicy, but again, so were others.

Mmm, spicy.

Stupid Sex. Anyway. Sienna was also guarded, yet vulnerable. Determined, yet kind. She was willing to go to any lengths to see a mission through to the very end.

Just like him. She had seen visions of his past, yet had thrown no judgment his way.

Once, Paris had asked Aeron exactly what the demon revealed in regards to him. The reply had been brutal: *all the hearts you've broken, all the tears you've caused.* That's what Sienna had seen and forgiven. So, yes, she was different, and he liked those differences.

She stiffened when Paris returned to the first door from the landing. That suggested there'd been conflict between her and the man inside. So, of course, Paris studied the guy intently. He was tall, muscled and glaring more fiercely than the others, as if Paris were already tagged and under a microscope. Handsome, if you were into deeply tanned skin and freaky bicolored eyes. Not that Paris was jealous or anything.

But just how much time had the guy spent with Sienna?

"That's Cameron. He's the keeper of Obsession," she said with a tremble.

A tremble born of fear…or desire? *I won't ask. I won't.* With the way they'd left things in the room, and hell, with the things Paris had done since their first parting, the answer wasn't his business.

"Has he ever touched you?" Damn. He'd asked, and with a whole lot of force.

She looked surprised. "No. The same invisible doors that keep me inside the castle keep them imprisoned in their rooms."

Her voice. Would he ever get enough of it? His ears hummed with sensation every time she spoke. "Did you want him to touch you?" He had to stop this.

"Never!"

A beautiful reprieve. "Then he can live," Paris muttered. He repositioned her in his arms, reached out and, yep, sure enough, there was an invisible block preventing him from entering the room.

"So you're not going to murder him? That's quite generous of you," she said dryly.

Irreverent humor from her, with him, was a shocker every time. In each instance they'd been together—and granted, there weren't many—things had been serious between them, gravely so. He liked that she now felt comfortable enough to tease him.

"I try." He stopped at the second doorway.

"This is Púkinn, aka Irish. He's bonded with Indifference," she informed him.

Indifference was half man, half animal. Horned, clawed and furred. Something out of a nightmare. For real. The man beast just looked Paris up and down and turned away, as if Paris were of no importance.

At the third door, Sienna twirled the ends of her hair around her finger. "Here we have Selfishness," she said with a hint of…anger? Or the same stinging jealousy he (hadn't) felt?

"She's very pretty, isn't she?" Sienna asked.

"Yes." The female had the same bicolored eyes as the first male, the same deeply tanned skin. She was attractive, there was no denying that, but he hungered only for the woman in his arms.

"Her name is Winter."

"That's great. How long have you been here?" Paris asked, looking down at Sienna instead of the immortal. Her lids were downcast, her lashes causing shadows to tumble over her cheeks. "How long have *they* been here?"

"I've lost track." The pink tip of her tongue slid over her mouth, leaving a glistening sheen of moisture. "They were here first, though."

I want to taste her. I will taste her.

His blood heated another degree. *Get in line.*

With all of Paris's experience, he was clueless when it came to this woman. What would soften her toward him totally and completely? Not just light a fire under her sympathies, but truly seduce her? She had changed since they'd last met in Rome, but she was still just as much of a mystery to him.

That she'd cried, that she'd apologized, that she'd sounded sincere, all were far more than he'd ever un-expected from her. Try *hell had just frozen over* shock-ing. But she had, on all three counts, and she'd looked at him like she'd never looked at him before. As if he were a man worthy of affection and attention. As if he weren't some dirty, disgusting thing on the bottom of her shoe. As if *she* wanted to protect *him*.

How the hell was he supposed to deal with that? How was he supposed to react?

Was he a fool for wanting to believe her? Hell, not wanting to, but actually doing so.

Maybe he shouldn't have been so offended by her offer to service him. Maybe he should have just taken her up on it. He'd had her on a bed. He could have stripped her, spread her legs and pounded inside her. Her hands would have been all over him, her passion cries ringing in his ears.

He cut off a bitter laugh. He was all twisted up, con-fused, waffling and contradicting himself. He didn't trust her; he trusted her. He wouldn't touch her without pas-sion; he'd touch her any way he could get her. And shit. Why hadn't she run from him, despite her vow? Or was she too busy regretting her offer to service him to launch into motion?

And really, what did that mean to her? That he could

take her here, now, anytime, or that she would go down on him? *Don't think about that.* He'd just get hard again.

The bitter laugh escaped. Make that, just get harder. His erection had yet to dissipate, acting like a heat-seeking missile as the female immortal strolled to her doorway, her hips swaying in a totally feline way. Didn't matter that Paris wasn't attracted to her. His demon saw, his demon wanted.

Part of him had hoped that being in Sienna's presence would stop this kind of thing from happening. But, no. Even though he could have her again, his demon still sought other women and always would.

I'm such a prize. No wonder she'd once hoped to slay him.

As carefully as he was able, he set Sienna on her feet. When she moved to his side, he dragged her back in front of him, pressing his erection between the curves of her ass. He hissed at the beauty of the pleasure. Pure, undiluted. Yet...

She had stiffened, he realized. At least she didn't jump away, and she didn't chastise him. Eventually, she even softened against him, as if she was exactly where she wanted to be. Well, hell. She must have feared he'd set her away from him, rebuffing her, and that's why she'd gone board-rigid—and why she'd relaxed when he hadn't. Talk about an ego boost. He wanted to beat his chest King Kong–style.

"Tell me what you know about them," he said, barely stopping his hands from flattening on her stomach, burrowing under the waist of her pants and seeking the warm, wet heart of her.

"About who?" the immortal in front of him asked. "And who the hell are you?"

One question answered, at least. They didn't know him, either. "Wasn't talking to you," he said.

The female splayed her arms. "Then who? You're alone."

"Like hell I'm—"

"They can't see me," Sienna interjected. "I've listened to some of their conversations, and that's how I know who and what they are." As she spoke, her stomach growled.

The sound gave him the excuse he needed. He moved his hands to her belly and rubbed. "Hungry?"

"Yes."

Then he would feed her. He would like that, he thought. Would like knowing he was fulfilling at least one of her needs. "What do you eat?" What *could* she eat?

"I don't. And it's only recently, within the last few weeks, that I've developed an appetite." She covered his hands with her own, her skin growing clammy. "Cronus brings me a glass of something sweet once a week. He forgot this time."

A glass of something sweet. Sweet. *Sweet.* The word echoed in his mind, an answer to one of his earlier questions sliding into place. *His* stomach bottomed out as he said, "Is it transparent, with tiny purple beads floating inside?"

"Yes." Her neck craned, allowing her to look up at him, and he watched as her brow wrinkled. "How'd you know?"

That *bastard!* Paris kept the curse inside his head and his expression neutral. "Does it taste like coconut, this liquid?" he asked, ignoring her question.

"Yes. But again, how did you know? Do you know what it is? He's never told me."

Yeah, he knew what it was, and now understood why she smelled as delicious as ambrosia. Cronus had done more than enslave her. He had condemned her. And he would pay. Oh, would he pay.

For better or for worse, though, vengeance would have to wait. Cronus liked to visit Torin, keeper of Disease, and have the computer genius find things for him. Currently he wanted cell locations for the Hunters, and had given orders for the Lords not to attack. Torin was giving him the info, all right, but only a piece at a time, as per Paris's request, keeping the king busy traveling back and forth between the heavens and earth as he stalked his prey and did whatever he did to them. That way, he had little time for Sienna. But "little" had been too much.

I should have gotten here sooner. There was no way to fix the damage that had been done to Sienna. There was no cure for what ailed her. Paris would have to tell her, have to prepare her for what would happen when she was out of here and on her own. Not now, though. She would be upset, and rightly so. More than that, he wanted to first taste her blood to be sure.

"Yo. Dude. Who the hell are you talking to?" the immortal demanded. "Don't make me ask again."

"Or you'll what?" he snapped. "Flip me off? Call me names?"

Winter opened her mouth to respond, and judging by the fire in her eyes, the words would scorch, but then her gaze shifted to Paris's right and her lips pursed in disapproval.

Oh, goodie. William had just decided to throw himself into the convo.

"You again," she said, and she did not sound happy.

"I know," the warrior replied with a heartfelt sigh. "You're so lucky to see me twice in one day. You're honored by my presence, yada, yada, heard it all before. Let's just move on, shall we. I don't handle fawning very well."

She flashed a scowl full of fangs, and Paris did a double take. Fangs? She was a vampire? He knew such creatures existed, knew William liked to bed them, but he'd never met one himself.

"They're not going anywhere, and Sienna's hungry," he said. "Let's find the kitchen. I—"

Suddenly the immortal female stumbled backward, landed on her ass. Her skin leached of color, and as she crawled farther and farther from the doorway, her gaze began moving throughout her chamber. She was babbling about shadows and pain. The same babbles erupted from the other doorways.

Sienna dug her nails into Paris's arm, a great shuddering wave moving through her. "No. No, no, no."

"What?" The panic spread into him. He forced her to turn, to face him. "What's going on?"

"They're coming." Her eyes filled with horror as she peered up at him.

"Who is?"

"The shadows. The pain."

"I don't understand."

"I think I do," William said, all hint of teasing and self-praise gone. "And if I'm right, we're in trouble, Paris." Never had he sounded more solemn. "Hold on to your girl, because I'm not sure how many of us will be walking away from this."

CHAPTER EIGHTEEN

"WHERE'S MY WOMAN! My...woman...need...her..."

Viola watched as the hulking black-haired giant tore down the other half of the entertainment room. The TV, pool table and an odd assortment of other things had been destroyed already. So had everything in the room next door, and the room next to that one. She knew because Maddox had busted down the walls between them, giving her a clear view into the other side of the fortress. Only rubble remained.

The other warriors jumped on the giant, again, knocking and pinning him down. Still he fought, screaming viler curses than she'd ever heard, even from the prisoners locked in Tartarus. Last time, his friends had lost their hold on him. This time, they managed to keep him there. Still, she was kind of scared, a foreign emotion for her.

"Where is she? I have to find her!"

The last word left him, and he just sort of collapsed into the mess, sobbing so hard his ribs had to be cracking. Tears filled her own eyes, but she blinked them back. He wanted his wife back, the loss of her destroying him.

"We'll find her," someone said.

"She and the babies will be unharmed."

"Be at ease, friend."

The warriors spoke calmly, but even she heard the tension and doubt in their voices. Maddox cried harder.

Viola felt like a voyeur. She felt useless. There was too much emotion here, too much loss, and she'd never handled this kind of thing well.

"Stay calm, we all have to stay calm."

"We'll have answers soon, and we can head out."

"Just a few minutes more."

"He has her," Maddox managed to say between shudders. "That bastard has her. I don't know where to look. There's no sign…nothing… Just the feather, just the feather."

One by one the warriors released him, and inched backward. Maddox stayed down by choice, his hand moving over his face to shield his eyes from the too-bright light overhead. How deeply he must love his woman and their unborn babies. Viola had suspected when she'd watched them together earlier, but seeing *this* proved she hadn't realized the limitless depths.

"We'll go hunting," Cameo said, speaking up for the first time since they'd heard Ashlyn scream and Maddox roar.

Viola wished the female warrior hadn't spoken then, either, and had to rub her chest to ward off the ache Cameo's shattering voice always left behind.

"Tonight," the one named Reyes growled. There was a deep gouge in his neck, blood dripping from it. "No later."

"We managed to get hold of Amun, and he's on his way back to Buda." Strider, the fiercest in the room, was actually trembling. His gaze kept returning to his wife, who stood a few feet away with her sister, as if he needed to reassure himself that she was here and well. "He'll learn something. Point us in the right direction."

"And if not him, Lucien will handle this," Anya said,

ever the proud girlfriend. Lucien had taken off to track
Galen's spiritual trail.

"Galen wouldn't dare hurt Ashlyn or the babies."
Haidee, Amun's girlfriend, paced back and forth, back
and forth, too agitated to remain in one place.

"Gideon and Scarlet are coming home with Amun.
Scarlet can tell you if the babies are still…still…" Aeron
scrubbed a hand over his closely shaved scalp. He was
supposed to be with the others, searching for Kane, but
had remained behind for some reason no one would tell
her.

Viola hadn't been here long, but she'd memorized the
warriors' names, faces, demons and abilities. Scarlet was
the keeper of Nightmares and by entering the dream
world, she could search for a specific person's mental
doorway. A closed doorway meant they were asleep. An
open doorway meant they were dreaming. No doorway
at all meant they were dead. But Maddox and Ashlyn
were bonded, one destined to die when the other died,
so no one had to wonder about her. The babies, however… *Don't go there.* Scarlet could also murder people
while they dreamed, killing them in real life. Perhaps
Galen would take his last breath tonight. Then again,
perhaps not. If Scarlet could enter his dreams, she would
have done so already, but Viola guessed that something
blocked her.

I could take him.

Enough of that, she thought with a scowl. Once she
hopped on the train to self-love, there was no turning
back.

She concentrated. The warriors. Yes. They didn't trust
her, and she was a little surprised they hadn't turned
on her, blaming her for this catastrophe. She was the
stranger, after all, and the kidnapping had happened soon

after her arrival. But then Olivia, the angel who'd made them relax about her presence the first time around, had said Viola wasn't responsible in any way, and they'd all believed her without question.

Besides Olivia, Scarlet, Anya, the still-pacing Haidee and Danika, who had her arm around a girl named Gilly, there were two Harpies, half-sisters Gwen and Kaia. Gwen belonged to Sabin, and Kaia to Strider. The pair had their heads together as they whispered. Galen was Gwen's father, and, if Viola's superior hearing was on target—and it always was—Gwen planned to hunt him down herself, crack open his ribs and rip out his black, rotted heart. Just her little way of making up for the lenience she'd once shown him.

"That Torin guy didn't get any recordings of Galen?" Viola asked, recalling his wall of computers and monitors.

No one looked her way or paid her any attention.

Her demon scraped sharp, pointed horns against the inside of her temples, and she bit back a moan. Ignoring her was the fastest way to gain Narci's attention. And when Narci's attention was locked…oh, stars above. Trouble followed. Always. Viola didn't want her other half intruding on this heartbreaking event, determined to make everything about her.

"No, there are no recordings," a soft, gentle voice said from beside her.

With a gasp, she spun. She hadn't heard anyone approach, but now a tall, slender female with long, blond hair was at her side. The girl looked fragile…haunted. Pain consumed those dark eyes. More pain than any one person should ever have to bear. She watched Maddox, a tear streaking down her pale cheek.

Viola thought she'd interacted with everyone in the

house, but this girl was new. She had a blanket draped around her, the material clutched tight to her chest, her knuckles without a shred of color. "Did you talk to him? To Torin?"

The girl's chin was trembling too violently for her to speak; she shook her head.

"Then how do you know about the recordings? Better question—who are you?"

More tears tumbled. They had to burn, because whatever path they traveled, they left red welts behind. "I'm… I'm Legion." Such a soft, soft whisper.

Legion. Ah, yes. Once a demon who had made a deal with the devil. The devil that granted her a human body. A deal she'd lost, forcing her to return to hell, where she was tortured in the vilest of ways, raped, abused, passed around and tortured some more.

Viola looked at the girl. Really looked at her, the way only she could. Past skin, past bone, and into soul. Legion was dying. Actually, some part of her was already dead. Her will to live had been obliterated. She was a brittle leaf hanging on by the thinnest thread, the next cold wind all that was needed to pull her loose and finally send her tumbling away.

By nature of her birth, Viola could be that wind. All she need do was reach out, curl her fingers around Legion's wrist and draw her close. Not usually so simple, and not usually so easy; but then, willingness made all the difference. A deep breath in, and there would be nothing remaining of Legion's soul. She would cease to exist on every level.

Perhaps Viola had stared a bit too long or a bit too intently because Legion began to quake, shifting from one foot to the other, and then, when that wasn't enough, inching away.

"I won't hurt you," Viola said.

Legion stopped as if she'd shouted. Poor, broken girl. A china doll already shattered. She drew the blanket closer, trying to fold herself within and hide.

"Lucien." Anya's relief was palpable, filling the room after the keeper of Death appeared.

Viola turned, watching as the minor goddess threw herself in her man's arms. He hugged her with unyielding strength, their love a tangible thing. Once again Viola's chest ached. She wanted that. Wanted that so badly she would kill to have it. But, of course, she could never have that. She was destined to love herself, and only herself.

Everyone else in the room quieted, waiting to hear what the warrior had to say, so tense their bodies were ready to snap. The scarred warrior looked them over, opened his mouth, closed it.

"Just say it," Maddox commanded. He'd worked his way to his feet, was checking the clip on one of his guns. "Tell me what you learned."

Lips compressed, Lucien gave the room another sweep. This time he stopped on Legion, who had bravely eked her way back to Viola's side. "Legion, sweetheart," he said, his tone so gentle he could have been talking to a child locked in a closet, afraid a monster waited under her bed, "go on up to your room. This isn't for you. All right? Okay?"

After everyone turned to face her, and she had wilted under the attention, she spun and ran away. Several agonizing heartbeats passed before Maddox broke.

"Tell me. Now."

Lucien drew Anya deeper into his body. "Galen didn't try to hide. He knew I would follow his trail, and so he waited for me to catch up. Ashlyn wasn't with him," he added as Maddox opened his mouth to say something.

"He said I would no longer be able to follow him, that I'd found him only because he'd let me get that far. And he was right. Afterward, I tried. I failed. I'm sorry."

"Tell me!" Maddox had stashed his gun and now clutched two blades. One of them he held by its body rather than by its hilt, and his palm had already sliced open. He didn't seem to notice as blood dripped, dripped. "Finish it."

A stiff nod. Lucien looked as if the words were being jerked out of him, and the jerking hurt. "He said she's safe, for now, and that he'll send you a video of her to prove it. He said…he said…if we want her back alive, we'll trade Legion for her."

Viola wasn't sure anyone else heard the gasp and frantic footfalls beyond that shattered wall, but she did. And she knew. Legion hadn't gone up to her room. She'd hung back and listened. Now, though, she was at last running for her chamber, no doubt seeking sanctuary between its walls.

The warriors argued, words shooting between them with rapid-fire precision.

"Where does he want to meet? When?" Maddox.

"Rome. The Temple of the Unspoken Ones. Tomorrow. Midnight." Lucien.

"Take me there. Now." Maddox.

"Be sensible about this." Strider. "Those bastards are hard-core, and if they're on his side—"

"I don't care! Get that through your heads. I don't care about anything but my woman and my children. And you *will* take me there, and I *will* hunt him down, and when I find him I *will* kill him. Do you hear me? Take me to that island. You have five seconds to flash me or I'm catching the red-eye, and there's no one in this world or the other that can help the mortals who get in my way."

Deciding not to wait for Lucien's reply, Viola snuck out of the room. No one noticed, and that once again pricked at Narci.

Be a good girl, she told her other half, *and I'll show you how pretty you are.*

The demon bounced up and down inside her head. *When?*

Soon.

Now. A whine.

Soon.

Now. A demand.

Never.

Soon? Another whine.

Soon. You drive a hard bargain. Viola followed Legion's spiritual trail—Lucien wasn't the only one with such a talent—flashing herself into the bedroom. The girl was pacing, her hair flying wildly behind her. She hadn't abandoned the blanket, but clutched the material ever closer.

"I can't, I can't, I can't. I can't leave. I can't go to him."

"Legion," Viola said gently. Yes, she was uncomfortable with other people's feelings, but she'd peered at this broken doll's soul and wanted to help.

How odd. Once, Viola had fed on souls, on their energy. She had drained them, ended them. One day, though, she'd taken the wrong soul at the wrong time— the only terrible memory she'd managed to retain—and found herself imprisoned in Tartarus. Then, of course, she was paired with Narci and the only soul she'd been able to feed on was her own.

Like an immortal's limb, her soul kept growing back and she kept feeding on it, but it never grew back in its entirety because she never actually stopped eating. For lack of a better word. So, basically, she was half of a person, as well as a spiritual cannibal, and she never ever concerned herself with others.

Why had she come here again? She should leave.

Those dark eyes found her, tears catching in equally dark lashes, and Viola's feet rooted in place. "I can't. I can't do it. *I can't do it.* He'll want to touch me. Hurt me. I…can't."

Legion raced to her bathroom, hunched over the toilet and vomited. Viola's feet tugged free, but still she didn't leave. She walked into the bathroom and held back the girl's hair, only to realize she hadn't actually vomited. She had dry heaved. Poor thing. She probably hadn't eaten a decent meal in weeks.

Hours seemed to tick by in endless misery. Between each of her heaves, the girl sobbed. And when she wasn't sobbing, she was shaking so violently her teeth chattered. No one ever came to the door, and Viola decided the Lords had opted not to trade the girl for Ashlyn's safe return.

Finally, blessedly, Legion's outburst drained her. She slumped over the toilet, her tear ducts tapped out.

Viola stepped away, and those red, swollen eyes followed her.

I really must leave now, she thought. She'd stayed far too long, the sense of unease returning. "I'll tell the warriors you're a no-go, okay?" Maddox might try and slay her for her efforts, but Narci would dig the attention, so whatever.

"I can't go, I can't go," Legion whispered. "He was here, I smelled him, knew he was here, but I couldn't make my voice work, haven't spoken since I got here, couldn't even scream, even though I wanted to scream and scream and scream. I hid under the bed. I should have screamed, I should have screamed."

Her words were heavy on the guilt, an emotion Viola refused to tangle with. "Yeah, so, uh, good luck with that. It was nice meeting you and everything." One step, two, she backed her way out. She didn't do the friendship thing. Ever. With anyone. Especially not broken china dolls that would require way too much time and effort.

Legion's tear ducts clearly hadn't dried, because a new waterfall began. "I can't leave Ashlyn with him, either." She sniffled, gulped. "Ashlyn is so nice, and the babies, she let me feel them kick once. She's due any day. She needs to be home. Maddox needs her to be home. What should I do?"

So badly Viola wanted to reach for her phone, Screech the question and follow the ensuing flood of advice, but much as she yearned to leave this room, she wanted to stay in the fortress.

For all their faults, the Lords hadn't tried to take advantage of her. Hadn't tricked her into looking into a mirror, and they utterly adored her. And okay, maybe that last one wasn't the truth and merely came courtesy of her demon, but nothing was a lie if you believed it. Therefore, the Lords did, in fact, adore her.

"I think you should, uh, follow your heart?" Oh, ick. That sucked. Like, majorly. The girl didn't know what her heart wanted, which was why she was asking for guidance.

"What would you do?" Legion asked.

She could weave a pretty speech about always being willing to help others, Viola supposed. The guys downstairs would probably prefer that. Only problem was, lying to anyone but herself created messes. Viola hated messes.

"I would save myself, no matter the cost to those around me. But then, I've only ever cared about myself, so…" She shrugged. "It's up to you. Who do you love more? Yourself, or the ones who took you in?"

CHAPTER NINETEEN

STRIPPED AND PINNED to a boulder, Kane gritted his teeth at the humiliation. Hadn't taken the minions long to catch him after he'd bolted. His *innocent little* chosen had been the worst of the lot, ripping out his Achilles tendons, hobbling him.

Now everyone in the crowd took turns attempting to steal what he'd refused to give.

He wouldn't give them what they wanted. He wouldn't. But how much longer could he survive the torment? The pressure was building, so intense it was painful.

You've survived this kind of thing before. He could survive this. *Breathe, just breathe.* His lids were squeezed together, his blood molten in his veins. All the while, his demon laughed inside his head. *Laughed.* Enjoying the disaster as it happened.

Maybe surviving wasn't the right path, he thought, the humiliation morphing into rage. Kane had never liked his demon, but now, now he hated the creature with every fiber of his being. He wanted to be free of it, and that meant dying. He wanted to punish Disaster for taking pleasure in his misery, regardless of the fate that would befall him.

And he would. Yeah. He would do some punishing. No matter what he had to do achieve the desired end, he would do.

PARIS CROWDED SIENNA into the wall, leaned down and got in her face. Her breath emerged choppily, her eyes were wild and her pupils dilated with panic. Sex enjoyed the contact, was already begging for more. Paris tuned him out and kept things as nonsexual as possible. Sienna was too upset for more.

"You have to hide," she said, the words emerging brokenly. "I'll try to draw them to me, away from everyone else. Okay? Yes? But you really, *really* have to hide."

He cupped her jaw, forcing her to peer up at him rather than scanning her surroundings for a hiding place. As if he would ever hide from an enemy and leave a female to fight for him. "What's coming? Talk to me, baby." He knew she wasn't too keen on endearments from him—at least, she hadn't been before—but then, he'd never called another woman his baby. Only sweetheart and honey, meaningless words like that, and never with such a note of affection.

Those lush lips parted on a gasp, and she blinked in bafflement. "Baby," she whispered, and he decided she liked it. There'd been a note of reverence in *her* tone. Calm suddenly smoothed out the panic. "The shadows. They dart through the walls, and they feed on us. All of us. Even the gargoyles hide. There are so many of them. They'll cover you, they'll be all you see, all you know, and they'll eat at you."

Corporal shadows with a hunger for flesh. He thought he'd traveled every corner of the heavens, but he'd never heard of such a creature.

William had, though, because he muttered, "Oh, shit on a brick. This is bad. Exactly what I feared."

Paris met his troubled gaze. "What do I need to do?"

"Just stay where you are." The grim-faced warrior reached up and unsheathed a knife from behind his shoulder blades, then sliced his arm open from elbow to palm. Instantly crimson flowed. He closed the distance, bent down to the floor, and smeared a bloody circle around Paris and Sienna. "Don't step out of this, do you hear me? Both of you, *stay there*. Disobey me, and you'll regret it."

He didn't wait for a reply, but sprinted to the entrance of the female immortal's room and dashed his wound across the clear shield separating them. The female was too busy clawing at her walls to notice. Before William reached the second room, his wound closed and he had to make another incision. He painted a line of blood over that shield, as well.

He didn't make it to the third room.

Just as Sienna had predicted, shadows burst through the walls. In a snap, it was lights-out, the black so thick oil could have been saturating the air.

The entire castle rattled and shook. Screams echoed, fervent songs of pain and anguish. The darkness inside Paris responded, practically purring with approval the way Sex always purred for physical contact, enjoying every terrible note. Wanting out, wanting loose. Wanting to cause everyone around him to hurt, too.

Paris was on the path to giving in, to stepping out of the circle William had drawn and fighting with the shadows, hell, fighting with William, when Sienna trembled against him. He pressed against her more firmly. *Must protect,* he thought. That's why he was here. For her. To be with her. To ensure her safety.

She trembled again, this one worrisome in its intensity. He wasn't sure what was happening behind him or around him or even how long this would last, but she knew, and it terrified her. And yet still she had thought to protect him, he realized. Still she had wanted to hide

him. *Him,* not herself. His warrior core had been offended by that, true, but just then he could only thrill
over her concern. She cared about his well-being.

I want her, Sex said. Of course, the purring started up
again.

So do I. And he would have a taste of her. Finally,
here and now, the circumstances be damned. She was
too worried for sexual contact? Hardly. She needed a
distraction, and there was nothing better than desire.

Paris felt his way to her jaw, cupping her to hold her
steady while luxuriating in the silky warmth of her skin,
the delicacy of her bones. "Concentrate on my voice,
baby. Can you do that?"

A jerky nod.

He wished he could see her and discover whether or
not color was returning to those delicate cheeks. At her
ear, he whispered, "You're so soft. I've never felt anything softer. And your scent intoxicates me. I can't help
but think you'll be even sweeter between your legs."

Her breath hitched, her hands finding his chest and
flattening over his pectorals.

"When I drive my fingers deep inside you, you'll be so
wet for me, won't you, baby? I'll eat you up, drink down
every drop of your honey, and you'll scream for more."

Yesss, Sex said on a moan. *Pleassse.*

"Paris," Sienna breathed.

A needy plea for more? That's what his demon heard
in her tremulous tone. Paris found himself leaning down,
the rest of the world forgotten, his nose in her hair as he
sniffed the heavy waves. He scented the wildflowers and
the coconut, now mixed with something rare, a bloom
found only at night.

Oh, hell, yes. That was her arousal.

Sex liked it, too, tossing out his own special fragrance.

The two combined, the most wondrous bouquet enveloping Paris. Wondrous—and torturous. Instantly he was revved up, more than primed, more than ready, desperate to sink inside this woman and thrust his way to orgasm. All he had to do was rip open both their pants and kick her legs apart. He'd drill her deep and sure. She would be hot, dripping and so tight around him.

Sharp little nails burrowed past his shirt and into his skin, as if to hold him in place. He could feel the heat of her, pulsing, seeping into him, blending with his own and lancing straight to his cock. He ached unbearably. Before he even registered that he'd moved, he'd edged her legs apart with his foot and arched into her, fitting his erection against her feminine core.

Hello, sweet damnation. Either he'd just made the biggest mistake of his life, or the best. They fit together like matching puzzle pieces. He rubbed against her, slowly at first, just enough to tease and tantalize them both. The pleasure built, right alongside the pressure. Yeah, he definitely should have taken her earlier. His demon was ready to burst free of his skin.

Paris couldn't gauge Sienna's reaction through sound because of the surrounding screams, so he moved one of his hands to her throat, keeping his touch gentle. Nothing could stop him from *feeling* her moans, and the vibrations were so damn gorgeous.

"Paris." Her lips pressed against his ear. Definitely not a plea this time, but not a warning, either. "You can't want me."

He circled his hips, pressing, retreating, pressing. "What is this, then?"

"A treat for the only available woman in the room."

The words were like a slap across the face, and his volatile inner darkness responded poorly, rampaging through him and demanding he hurt the one who'd harmed him. He bit back the urge and snapped, "So a guy like me can only want what's available?"

"You didn't want me before, in the room. So maybe this is punishment." Anger threaded her tone.

Punishment? His hands clenched in reflex, his own anger becoming an echo of hers.

Sadly, she wasn't done. "Believe me, I understand the concept far better than I ever did. Maybe you didn't come here to save me, after all, but to wound me the same way I once wounded you."

He hadn't trusted her, couldn't, no matter how badly he'd wanted to, and even told himself he did, and now he saw that she couldn't, wouldn't, trust him, either. Not really. He'd suspected this would happen. That hadn't bothered him (much) before, but it bothered him now. He hated that there were so many barriers between them. Clothes, reservations, doubts and worries.

"I'm nothing like the women you're used to," she went on. "I know that. I know that I'm not pretty."

"You're right. You're beyond gorgeous."

A gasp. "A-and my lips are ridiculous."

"If *ridiculous* is the new word for a wet dream."

Her little fists hammered at his chest. "Stop! Just stop. You need sex and you're trying to make a sale. I did the same to you earlier, wanting to be with you one last time. I shouldn't have thrown myself at you like that."

His back straightened. She had offered herself to him, not because she had felt guilty, but because she had wanted him. She should not have admitted that. There would be no stopping him now. He would have her, one way or another.

He licked at her lips, saying, "Baby, I've never had to try. I breathe, and the women offer."

The abuse stopped, a mewling sound leaving her. "You're—you're trying to put me in my place, then. Trying to tease me with what I can never fully have."

Oh, you can have it, all right. "You know that's not true. Not because you trust me, but because of your demon." Wrath would have been all over any deception on Paris's part.

A pause the agonizing length of three heartbeats. "You're…right. How odd," she said, both awed and hopeful. Her nails once again found purchase in his chest. "I hated the fact that a demon was placed inside me, wanted to be free of him, ranted and railed and even planned to give him back, and yet I've begun to count on his ability to read other people's intentions."

Once possessed, always possessed. For the most part, anyway. So give Wrath back to Aeron? That would be a big fat hell, no. That would kill her. Again. "You can believe me when I say that I do want you, Sienna. You're all I've thought about for months. Resisting you in that room was one of the toughest things I've ever done."

A vibration in her throat signaled her moan. "You're really attracted to me, despite everything?" Wonder saturated her voice, dripping over him like warm honey.

He had a thing for warm honey.

"Yes." Backward, forward he arched, renewing the decadent contact. He wanted to push for more still, but didn't. Not yet. He wanted her focused only on the pleasure, all her fears about ulterior motives assuaged. "Let there be no doubt on that score."

Another vibration, this one reaching a deeper part of him. "Why me?" Her nails plucked free of his chest, her hands smoothing over him. "I mean, you could have anyone."

"Exactly. I could, and I chose you. For so many reasons. You're smart."

"Debatable."

"You're witty."

"No more than a thousand others."

"You're argumentative and can't accept a compliment."

"Hey!" She reached up and tugged at his hair.

Despite the grimness of their surroundings and circumstances, he found himself grinning. "You're beautiful."

Her fingers slid to his scalp, massaging. "Not just beyond gorgeous?" she asked dryly.

"You're exquisite, and I don't want to hear you put yourself down again. Do you understand?" He had killed others for doing so. Her, he would simply spank. "You may or may not be happy with the results."

"Why? Are you thinking paddling? Because I'm getting a few images in my head."

"Well, well. There's something else to like about you. You understand me."

A snort. One he relished, because he had caused the humor behind it. "You must be blinded by horny demon-colored glasses," she said.

And she thought there were thousands of others just as stubborn as she was. He'd just issued an order alongside a threat, yet she had ignored both and continued on her merry way.

"Has your demon ever let you be with the same woman twice?" she asked, the words layered with a husky edge of arousal, as well as a note of nervousness. "I'd heard you— Never mind."

She had gotten a lot of her info from the Hunters. He

stiffened, hating the reminder of her past, but that didn't stop him from admitting, "No one but you."

The warmth of her breath trekked over his neck as she angled her head, placing them cheek to cheek. "Why me?"

"Don't know. Sex doesn't know, either. I've asked."

"Well, he should have picked someone else. I have small breasts," she whispered, as though ashamed.

He cupped the pint-size morsels in question. They. Were. Perfect. His hands were big, her nipples beading against the centers of his palms, and damn if that wasn't the most exquisite sensation in the world. He fit his lips against her ear, nibbled on the lobe.

"I want them in my mouth," he rasped.

A groan of approval. Nails in his scalp now, digging deeper and deeper.

Paris kissed and licked his way to her lips. They were parted, warm, the sweetness of her breath sawing in and out, scented with the spice of coconut. He hovered there, still not taking what he wanted. What they *both* wanted. If he started this, he was going to have a hard time stopping. A *very* hard time. He'd been without a female for too long, and his demon was too needy, but…

He didn't want to take Sienna in a hallway, in front of others, he realized. Yeah, he'd done that shit before, and it had gotten old hella fast. He wanted this one all to himself, each of her cries for his ears alone, her every reaction to his touch his personal discovery. Her scent, his. Her skin, his. His, his, *his*.

Take what's yours! Take, take, take!

Well, as alone as he could get with a demon trapped inside him.

"Paris?" she said, her tone unreadable.

"Yes."

"A word of warning. I'm really bad at this."

Confusion rocked him, his brows furrowing toward his hairline. "At what?"

"Kissing."

Before he could contradict her, she fit their mouths together and sucked the breath right out of his lungs. She wasn't bad at kissing; she was hesitant, unsure and tentative, but he craved her too viciously to teach her better. He took over, unable to stop himself. His tongue thrust forcefully, demanding she concede to his mastery.

Concede she did not. After his teeth banged into hers the third time, she bit down on his bottom lip, hard, drawing blood.

He jerked back before she cut the thing in half. "Damn it, woman."

Sex performed some sort of kickboxing move against the side of his skull. Not in complaint or to hide from the violence, but in excitement, to get *closer* to the violence. *More, more! Kiss her more!*

"I might be bad at it, but I know when someone else is, too. Do it right," Sienna demanded.

Was she frickin' kidding? "No one's ever criticized my technique before."

"That's because they didn't want to hurt your feelings," she shot back. "You and I are past that stage, so I feel okay in admitting that I got a superior kiss from Carl Knickerbocker in the third grade."

Spirit again, and damn if that didn't rev him right back up, demolishing any lingering hint of anger. He wished he could see her face. Those hazel eyes would be sparkling, her skin flushed, her lips swollen. She would be passion incarnate. "Should you be giving pointers? You're *far* worse at this than I am."

"Someone has to teach you." She patted his cheek. "Guess we'll have to learn how to do this together."

More, more, more!

His lips twitched with his amusement. Funny, that. Amusement, when his body and his demon were on fire, desperate for this woman. *I'm on it.*

CHAPTER TWENTY

"Okay. Let's see what I can do to give little Carl a run for his money." Slowly Paris went back in, pressed his mouth gently against Sienna's, lifted, pressed again, teasing her with the contact, barely tasting. She softened against him, her nails scraping against his scalp, her hands tracing down, down, until winding around his neck to lock him against her.

He licked at the seam of her lips, sipping at her, giving her what she wanted, slow and easy, and when she opened for him he licked his way inside, deep, tasting more of her, taking more. Her tongue met his, connecting, dueling with long, languid strokes. They learned each other, learned every nuance of tongue and teeth, breath and flavor, and it was the sexiest damn thing he'd ever experienced.

During their first meeting, she had kissed him and used his distraction against him, shoving the needle in his neck. She could have done something similar now, but he wouldn't have cared. His body smoldered with passion, his blood already molten in a way it had never been. His heart was a war drum in his chest, pounding out its cry for more from this woman, this obsession. His limbs shook.

With the darkness so thick around them, his sight was still razed and his other senses picked up the slack. Sienna's floral bouquet was branded inside his nose, causing his head to swim all over again. His tattooed fingertips tingled, memorizing the satiny feel of her. His ears twitched, every sound she made a caress. And her taste…oh, hell, yeah…ambrosia in its most potent incarnation.

But then, that's what she was now, what Cronus had made her. A supplier. A walking ambrosia dispenser. Stick a straw in her vein and you could get high for eternity.

When consumed by humans, ambrosia killed. Had once nearly killed Maddox's woman. Sienna, though, was already dead and no longer human. By feeding her the nectar mixed with the bulbs necessary for the plant's growth, something that would kill even an immortal, she was, in essence, an ever-fertile breeding ground for the drug.

What ran in her veins was more addictive than what Paris used to pour into his alcohol. And if anyone immortal ever tasted her blood, they would be instantly addicted to her. They would need her, keep her, and fight to the death anyone who tried to take her.

Why in the name of all that was unholy would Cronus do that to her? Why would he make her such a target?

Something else for the two of them to hash out—with blades.

Don't think about that right now. You've got her. She's safe, and she wants you as much as you want her. He gripped her waist, lifted her off her feet, then pressed her more firmly into the wall. "Wrap your legs around me, baby."

She obeyed, and he rubbed his erection against her clitoris so hard she cried out. That was…that was… There were no words.

More.

All. Everything. There were a few words, after all. "Are you wet for me?" Usually he had a stream of lovely, meaningless praise to give. Sienna was lucky to get more than *mine, more* and *yes* out of him.

There was a beat of hesitation, then she whispered shyly, "I am."

Wanton abandon splashed with a hint of reserve…a sultry combination.

Their tongues rolled together, faster, faster still. Her kiss was like sex. Overwhelming, consuming, necessary. He couldn't get enough, didn't think he'd ever get enough. Everything he'd done to reach this point, absolutely worth it.

He'd been with so very many people, had done so very many things. Some he'd liked, some he hadn't. Ninety percent of the time he operated on autopilot, going through the motions to get what he needed while leaving his partners with a smile of satisfaction, even when he'd hated who he was with, loathed the smells, the grasping hands, the knowledge that he was inside someone he didn't know.

He wasn't on autopilot right now. Instinct drove him, a need to possess and to be possessed. A need to become one, as corny as that sounded. So he kissed her again, because he couldn't not kiss her. Because he had to know more of her taste, more of her. He slanted his head, angling for even deeper contact, moving his tongue faster, faster still, taking her mouth the way he wanted to take her body.

This time, she offered no complaint. All the while he rubbed against her. His nerve endings were so sensitized he thought they'd be raw by the time he finished.

"Yes," she moaned, and clearly, this time she liked

his fervor. "Paris…I'm going to… You have to…stop…
Don't stop…please stop. Paris!"

There would be no stopping. He pressed ever harder,
heard her cry out at the bliss, and hell, he was on fire.
Burning for her, desperate to sink so damn deep inside
her that she'd know she belonged to him.

More!

"Paris…stop…please."

There was that word again. "Stop." Her hands tugged
at his hair, forcing his head to lift.

"I want you," she rasped, "but not here. Somewhere
else. Somewhere private."

MORE.

He'd take her back to the bedroom, he thought, dizzy
with need. Yeah. That's what he'd do, because he had to
strip her, had to see her, had to get inside her now, now,
now.

He straightened, dragging her with him. One step,
though, just one step, and thousands of needle pricks shot
through his lower leg. Reason returned, and he jolted
back into the blood circle. He was panting, could feel the
warm flow of blood down his calf, would be surprised
if he had any muscle left. In the time it took to snap a
finger, the shadow-things had chomped on him as if he
was a steak and they were starving dogs.

That's what Sienna had endured?

Sex retreated into the back of his mind, the pain too
much for him.

Darkness…rising… Paris's hand was on his blade hilt,
squeezing, as he contemplated jumping into the midst
and slashing.

Sienna's fingers curled around his biceps, stilling him.
She, too, was panting. "Are you okay?"

"Hurt?" He patted her down, searching for injuries.

"Not me. You?"

"I'm fine." Her nipples were still beaded, her belly quivering. Need was still galloping through her, yet she'd had the strength to stop when he had not. Impressive. Irritating.

"Are you—"

Just as suddenly as the shadow creatures had arrived, they left. The castle ceased shaking, the screams died. Light swept back through the hallway. Paris had to blink against the burn in his eyes.

Sienna's cheeks were flushed a deep rose, her lips soft, swollen and parted, gleaming with his taste. He must have plowed his hands through her hair numerous times. The strands were tangled around her. She looked wanton and wicked, and so sexy his shaft throbbed against his fly.

He turned away before he fell on her, devoured her. In the center of the hallway, William crouched in his own blood circle, his head bowed. The female immortal was at her door, her eyes wide, unsure. The male William had protected was at his door, too.

The other male, the one William hadn't reached in time, was lying on the bedroom floor, a sea of crimson and…other things spilled around him. He writhed in agony, even as he fought to put himself back together.

"You know what those things were?" Paris demanded. When his world spun, he scowled and threw out an arm to catch himself on the wall. But it wasn't because of blood loss or pain.

Sex whimpered, spurting weakness straight into Paris's veins. Bastard had been primed and disappointed too many times in the past few days, and with the denial of Sienna the countdown to "meltdown" had begun. That meant, if he failed to have sex, and soon, he would rapidly fade until he was completely useless. Until he collapsed, the pheromones wafting from him, drawing people to him. Until someone simply climbed on top of him.

No way he'd let that happen. His reasons for resisting Sienna hadn't miraculously vanished, but they weren't going to stop him anymore. He'd take her however he could get her, because the alternative was taking someone else and he wasn't willing to do that.

"Yeah, I know what they are," William finally managed after catching his breath. Eyes of otherworldly blue lifted and pinned Paris in place. Tension crackled in the air between them. "A long time ago Cronus created them the same way Zeus created you, but I'd heard after Cronus's imprisonment that someone else had taken over their care. Cronus must have reclaimed them. And now I'm gonna have to have a chat with him about houseguests and manners." Utter menace poured from him.

Clearly he anticipated a chat for two, from which only one would walk away. Yeah. Paris intended the same.

"That ever happen to you?" he asked, whipping back to Sienna and jerking his thumb at the guy split open from neck to navel. Because of what had been done to Sienna's blood, the creatures would have gone crazy over her. Would have converged en masse, concentrated solely on her, not leaving until they'd drained every drop possible.

There was no reply.

"Sienna. What's—" Her eyes were glazed over, he realized, glassy and glowing a bright, vibrant red.

"Punish," she whispered.

Wrath had taken over her mind and body.

"Must punish them," she repeated in a voice she had never before used with him, all gravel, no passion. A second later, her wings burst from her back, clouds of midnight tipped with violet. They flapped up, down, stretching to their full width and scratching the wall, the floor.

"Sienna," he said. Calm, he had to remain calm. Otherwise Wrath would turn that need to punish on *him*. He snapped his fingers in front of her face. "I need you to listen to me, okay, baby?"

"Punish." Her wings glided faster, until she hovered in the air.

"Sienna."

Without another word, she darted straight at the only window, shattering the glass and disappearing into the night.

Paris made a swift dive for her but missed and ended up with half of his body ready to free-fall too many stories into that frothing lake of doom. Well, hell. He'd asked her to let the bastard take over, hadn't he? *Stupid.* No telling where Wrath would take her, or what the demon would make her do.

One way or another, he was going after her.

Never had to chase a woman this much. He pulled himself back in and studied the incline, trying to decide the best and fastest way down without drawing the notice of the gargoyles. And wouldn't you know it? There was only one way. He was gonna have to make the fifty-foot dive, after all, and pray his legs wouldn't shatter on impact.

Problem was, now that he was on the downward slide to gotta-have-sex-or-die, he *would* hurt himself and he wouldn't heal very quickly. Whatever. She was in danger; he would do what was necessary. He threw a leg over the pane.

"Stay here." He tossed the words over his shoulder. "See if you can help the immortals."

"Way ahead of you," came William's muttered reply.

When his other leg was in place, Paris counted down. Three. Two. So *stupid*. One—

And suddenly Zacharel was there, white wings spread and waving gracefully through the air. Snowflakes drifted around him, the perfect frame for his emotionless features. He arched a dark brow. "Would you like a ride?"

"Where were you when the shadows were here?" he demanded gruffly.

"I can answer, or I can help you."

So sick of his manipulations, but there's no denying I could use his help. And aren't I just the cutest damsel in distress ever? Aeron had carried Paris through the skies a time or two, so he knew there was nothing sexual about it. He only prayed Zacharel realized the erection he currently sported had nothing to do with their close proximity.

The angel wrapped his arms around Paris's waist. "You'll find good deeds are balm for the soul."

"That's just peachy." For a greater sense of being anchored, Paris wrapped his own arms around the angel's neck. Solid muscle, ice-cold skin. Even as primed and needy as Sex was, the demon stayed quiet. "But can we do this without conversation?"

"Can we? Yes. Will we? No. While you are my captive audience, I wish to discuss your unhealthy obsession with the dead girl and the fact that she will be better off without you."

O-kay. Paris brought his legs between them, pushed their bodies apart, and jumped.

CHAPTER TWENTY-ONE

BLOOD DRIPPED FROM SIENNA'S hands, caked her clothing and made her tennies squish disgustingly with every step she took. As with every other time Wrath had taken over her body and whisked her out of the castle, he had forced her to follow the shadows to their lair so that he could wage an attack and hurt the creatures far worse than they had hurt others. His crimson-bright gaze had shone through hers, cutting through their skin...or ooze...or whatever comprised their outer shell, burning them. He had laughed and laughed.

The shadows had been too sated from gorging to fight back, their helplessness an aphrodisiac to Wrath, making him crave more, more, *more,* and the moment he'd finished with the shadows, he had turned his sights on the other beings living in this hidden realm, rhapsodizing when they, too, screamed in pain.

When his hunger was finally satisfied, he tried to force her to walk back to the castle. For the first time, she had known what he was doing while he was doing it, her mind refusing to break its link with Paris, and she'd fought him—and fought hard. Ultimately, as replete as he'd been, he'd given up and retreated to the back of her mind. Now she was at the wheel and driving the (short) bus.

Sadly, her fighting wasn't yet done. There was an invisible cord connecting the castle and her neck, trying to pull her closer and closer. She wasn't sure how much longer she could resist. Her wings were shredded—not that she knew how to fly without Wrath's guidance—and though they would heal in a few hours, they were currently unable to hold her weight. Still, she dug her heels into the ground and managed to slow her momentum. Pain vibrated in her bones. She cringed as she turned... turned...and began to slip away in the opposite direction. Yes. *Yes!*

To go back, even to see Paris, to say goodbye, to kiss him one last time, to make love to him, was to imprison herself. And though she was tempted, oh, was she tempted, she had to do this. For him. For Skye. Before Cronus learned of her escape, thought to punish Paris and started pulling her strings all over again.

If she could reach Galen, interrogate and kill him before Cronus realized she was gone, she wouldn't have to seduce him, and the war between the Lords and the Hunters would at last end. Even if the keeper of Hope never told her where her sister was, he couldn't hurt the girl if he was dead. That would have to suffice.

Footsteps echoed, jerking her out of her mind. There were beings behind her, she realized, following her. She didn't have to glance back to know they were empty-eyed males with sagging, gray-tinted skin and jaws that split into rows of four, each loaded with razor-sharp fangs. They were killers without a conscience, the blood of their enemies their source of life.

A few weeks ago, Wrath had struck at their camp, leaving blood and death in his wake. Of course, that meant Sienna—the face the survivors had seen—had become Enemy One. They'd been gunning for her ever since, and would have attacked the castle if not for the Gargl.

The urge to run was nearly irresistible. From the glimpses her demon had given her of these creatures, she knew how they'd hunted in the past, knew how mercilessly they'd killed. Knew they enjoyed the chase more than they enjoyed the slaughter. So maybe if she kept a calm head, maybe if she stayed on her current path, they'd lose interest in her.

Yeah, maybe. Not.

"You took our ssslavesss, female. Now *you* become our ssslave."

That lisp came courtesy of his fangs, which sliced at the words as they emerged.

"The thingsss we'll do to you…" A calculated snicker. "The ssscreamsss you'll utter…"

Offering no reply, but remaining highly attuned to their every move, she forced herself farther and farther from the castle. Her surroundings became darker, the air thicker, scented with blood and other things. She bypassed piles of bones, crimson-colored ponds, caverns that sprang from the mouths of large, carved skulls. She had no weapons, and wasn't exactly sure where the realm's exit was—only knew it was here because Cronus had brought her through while she was semi-conscious, and besides, how else would Paris and his friend have entered?—or where in the heavens she would next find herself.

Should have questioned Paris. Hindsight sucked.

"Yesss, keep walking, female. You're headed ssstraight for our camp."

Truth or lie? Wrath was no help this time. Should she stop? Fight them? Her self-defense skills were laughable, considering she had trouble balancing her weight. No matter what she did or where she went, the men were going to attack her, and that was that. Waiting for them to strike merely delayed the inevitable.

A pain-filled grunt rent the air behind her, followed by another. Then another. The men must be fighting among themselves, she thought with a tide of relief, saving her the trouble.

A head—without a body—rolled past her. The empty-eyed stare flashed, disappeared, flashed, disappeared. She tripped over her own feet as another head rolled past. Her stomach churned, even as her relief tripled.

"Must you kill so needlessly?" a male voice asked. Emotionless, and yet there was something in the cadence, something that caressed her ears.

"Yeah. I must."

Paris! Sienna whirled around, her heart a thunderstorm inside her chest. Her gaze cut through the darkness. Where was— There! Her knees nearly buckled from the ensuing flood of happiness.

"Why?" The speaker was a dark-haired man dressed in a robe, keeping pace beside Paris. He had a sublime face, wicked in its heartless beauty. Majestic wings of white-gold stretched from his back. He looked like a fallen angel, but then, so did Galen. Still, if Paris trusted him, so would she. Snow wafted around him, but only him. The flakes seemed to absorb into his skin and crystallize.

"They were looking at her, threatening her," Paris said, but if he knew where Sienna waited, he gave no indication, "and my demon knew what they were thinking. They deserved a hell of a lot worse than they got."

"I caught you, saved you from painting the ground with your organs. You owed me a favor, and I asked for a single day without bloodshed."

"Yeah, but you didn't specify which day." With that, Paris dismissed the angel and at last focused on her.

Tall and strong, scowling, he strode toward her. He had bruises under his eyes and cuts that rode the length of his arms, but his gait, though slow, was steady. Bodies were piled up behind him. She'd thought only two of the creatures were following her, but oh, had she miscalculated. At least eleven had trailed her.

"Where the hell do you think you're going?" Paris demanded the moment he reached her.

Her gaze fell to his lips. Those lush, red lips that had kissed her and sipped at her and smashed against her own. Lips she craved all over her. "Somewhere else. I'm trying to escape, and doing an excellent job of it, thank you," she replied.

"Without saying goodbye?" He latched on to her bloodstained wrist, turned her arm left and right, searching for any damage. "Nice, Sienna. Real nice."

Was he actually mad about that? Guilt rose, followed by shame and even delight. She raised her chin, refusing to buckle under his stare. "If I had returned to the castle—and believe me, my body wants to return and even standing here is a chore—I'd be stuck there again. You said you wanted my curse broken. Well, I'm doing my best to break it."

He released her, sighed. "Fine. You did the right thing, but I hate the fact that if I hadn't come after you I never would have seen you again." He could have accused her of abandoning him, of leaving him there to suffer, or any number of other things. That he hadn't…

"I hate that, too," she admitted.

Clearing his throat as though uncomfortable with the direction of their conversation, he massaged his neck.

Those ocean-blues looked as if the sun shone behind them, glistening off the water. "Anyway, I don't want you out here by yourself. It's too dangerous."

"Well, I don't want me out here by myself, either." A wave of dizziness suddenly hit her, and she swayed.

He examined her from head to toe, some of the angel's frost setting up shop on his skin. "That's not just other people's blood you're wearing, is it? You're hurt."

Concern. For her. If she'd had any resistance left, she would have lost every bit of it in that moment. "I'll heal."

"Who hurt you?" Lethal menace in his tone.

"Wrath, when he burst through the window. The other times he took over, he made me walk to the parapet on the castle's roof. This time he was afraid you'd slow me down. So—" she shrugged "—he picked a faster route."

The long spikes of Paris's lashes fused together, barely masking the menace resting behind them. "Don't let him take over anymore."

Not the least bit intimidated by the warrior's growing anger, she rolled her eyes. "Earlier you wanted me to do just that."

"I changed my mind," he said, leaning down until they were nose-to-nose. "Don't push me on this, woman. I'm too keyed up."

They stayed like that for several seconds, breath mixing, emerging faster. She wanted him to kiss her again, to finish what they'd started.

"This area is not safe," the other man said, ruining the sensuality of the moment.

Paris jolted upright, his back going ramrod straight. "Sienna, meet Zacharel. He's a warrior angel for the One, True Deity. Zacharel, meet Sienna. She's mine."

A shiver rippled through her. Uh, had he just claimed her? Had he just warned the other male away from her, as if he were possessive of her? Pleasure warmed her up, chasing away the numbing cold the angel had brought with him.

Zacharel offered his hand to her, his fingers long and thick. "I will protect you," he said, the words somehow an invitation—and a vow.

"No touching," Paris snapped, pushing the angel away from her. "Ever."

Zacharel's neutral expression never wavered, nor did the intensity of his gaze.

She shifted uncomfortably, uncertain why he wanted to protect her. There was a note of truth in his tone, however, one she could not refute. Somehow she knew he would do everything in his power to keep her safe.

Or…maybe that was a trick. Maybe, like Galen, Zacharel built up hopes and smashed them down. Gulping, she looked to Paris for answers. "Is he…"

"Like Galen?" he asked, sensing the direction of her thoughts. "No. He's the real deal, as well as a self-righteous prig who will test every limit of your patience. He's also impotent. Now, where are you headed?" He cupped her jaw and forced her focus on him and him alone.

The heat of his touch…the rough texture of his palms…another shiver stole through her. "I'm not sure." Did she sound as breathless to him as she did to herself? "I was walking aimlessly, searching for the exit. You wouldn't happen to know where it is, would you?"

"Yeah. Two days' walk in the other direction."

"Oh." She'd have to pass the castle, then, and if she passed it, she would be drawn inside. No question. If she went inside, she wouldn't come out again.

"I'll take you," he said at the same time Zacharel said,

"I can fly you there in just a few hours. And I am not impotent. I have simply never experienced desire."

Whoa. Talk about an attention stealer. Questions immediately poured through her mind. Why not? Were angels asexual? How old was he? What kind of woman could break through that icy shell and jump-start his hormones?

Maybe when things settled down she would set the angel up with someone—not that she knew anyone—because no one should go without physical contact of some kind. It hurt.

When she'd first opened her eyes and discovered her new ghostly form, she had tried to touch someone, anyone. No one had sensed her, in any way, and her mind had threatened to snap from the lack of sensation.

"You're not flying her anywhere," Paris growled. He'd been watching her, she realized, gauging her reaction to Zacharel's offer. "I told you. No touching. Besides that, she stays with me, by my side. That's nonnegotiable."

She could have argued with him. *Should* have argued with him. They had no future together, and prolonging the inevitable would destroy her in the end. But the thought of two more days with him proved irresistible.

"I stay with him," she said with a nod.

A flare of satisfaction sparked in Paris's eyes as he, too, nodded his approval.

"After you have a woman, you quickly grow tired of her," Zacharel said. "Is that why you are so eager to be alone with this one?" He sounded genuinely curious rather than waspish, yet the words stung all the same. "If that is the case, then I will gladly allow you some time together."

She must have flinched, because Paris released her and spun for attack, two daggers in his hands.

"Do you *want* to die?"

Zacharel remained focused on her. "You have only to say my name, female, and I will come for you." He vanished.

CHAPTER TWENTY-TWO

PARIS LUNGED FOR ZACHAREL, encountered only air and let loose a dark stream of curses. The main one being, "Stupid cock block." He turned back to Sienna with narrowed eyes. "Say his name, and sign his death warrant." He didn't give her a chance to respond—not that she knew what to say—but returned to her side and swooped her into his arms. He started forward, his pace smooth, her weight seemingly insubstantial. "There's a cavern up ahead. We'll get you patched up before heading for the exit."

"How do you know there's a cavern?" She'd lived here for months, far longer than Paris had, yet *she* hadn't known about any caverns.

"I scouted out the area when I first arrived."

Such a warrior thing to do, and sexy as hell. She sighed and let her head drop onto his shoulder. The muscles bunched beneath her cheek. And now that they were heading toward the castle, the tug became less pronounced, allowing her to relax.

"You know," she said, "we've only been reunited a short time, but this is, like, the hundredth time you've had to carry me."

A snort. "Your math might be a little off, baby. Besides, I like carrying you."

Baby. She loved when he called her by the endearment, loved the way his voice dipped so huskily. Her chest constricted, and her belly quivered. He was the first to ever speak to her in such a way and, unlike the time he'd called her "sweetheart" so long ago, he clearly meant it to be something special just for her.

As she rubbed her cheek against him, his champagne-and-chocolate scent hit her, more intense than ever before, and derailed her thoughts. She pressed her nose against his hammering pulse, drinking in as much of the aroma as she could. Her nerve endings perked up, singing for his touch, his caress.

His gait slowed. A few steps later, he tripped.

Was he distracted by her, or injured? Concern overshadowed her arousal when she recalled the cuts on his arm. "Are you okay?"

"I'm fine," he replied gruffly. The reassurance was ruined a second later when he stumbled over a rock.

Definitely injured. "Put me down." She struggled against his hold. "I want to walk."

"Be still," he hissed, as though in pain. "Distract me. Tell me why you joined the Hunters. You told me before, that day I woke up in your cell, but some of the details are missing."

She struggled until the rest of her strength drained, and got nowhere. Even in a weakened state, he was stronger than she was.

Every new thing she learned about him made her want him more, and made him that much sexier.

Ultimately she relaxed back against him, conceding defeat only long enough to plan. Or not. Her thoughts derailed a second time as more and more of his scent permeated her skin. Desire for him began to overwhelm her.

"Sienna."

His question. Right. And, okay, fine. If he wanted to

carry her despite his weakness or whatever was wrong, she would let him carry her. Being close to him was a need. "I bought into their ideology. I was convinced the world would become free of hurt, disease, badness and evil if only you and your friends were destroyed."

"Killing us won't turn the world into a utopia. Humans make their own choices, bringing the bad and the evil on themselves. But let's say we *do* influence the world. Would that matter? People still have choices. They can resist, fight, and choose to act as they were meant."

"I know that." She licked her lips and imagined licking her way to his—then lower. "Now."

"Do you really?"

"If I repeat my answer, will you finally believe me?"

A moment passed in silence. A silence as thick and heavy as the air around them. "Yes."

She blinked in surprise, momentarily distracted from the subject at hand. "Why?"

"Because I *want* to believe you."

Not because he trusted her, she thought, and tried not to be disappointed. But then, asking for his trust would be like asking a human male to gift her with the moon and the stars. Impossible. And yet his faith, even given for that reason, was a promising start.

"Then, yes, I truly believe killing you would serve no purpose."

The edge of his jaw appeared chiseled from stone as he nodded. "Next question. Has Cronus ever told you why he enslaved you?"

A dangerous topic, but she said, "Yes."

He shifted his hand, his fingers brushing the underside of her breast. Just like that, the desire returned. "Well. Tell me."

Trying to seduce the information out of her? No need.

She'd lied to him once upon a time, and she'd already decided never to lie to him again. Trust was a precious thing, and she wouldn't turn her back on his, no matter the trouble she courted. "He wants me to return to the Hunters, watch their leader and steal his secrets."

Against her cheek, she felt his heart stop beating. Just stop. One second, two. Finally the organ kicked back into gear, but its strikes were too fast, too brutal.

"Will you?" he asked. They'd reached the entrance of the cavern, which just happened to be the mouth of one of the giant skulls. Paris had to hunch his shoulders to get inside without scraping his head on the teeth.

"Yes," she whispered, praying her inner torment over the fact remained hidden. "I will."

"For Cronus or for yourself?"

"For…all of us. For answers about my younger sister. She's missing, has been for years. For vengeance. I hate the Hunters. Hate what they do." *For you,* she added silently. "Though hopefully I won't have to do things Cronus's way." No reason to mention the mistress thing. Her plan to sneak in now, interrogate and kill could work.

Whether Paris believed her or not, he didn't say. He carted her to the center of the enclosure, where a natural spring rested, and set her on the ledge. He arranged her wings so that their tips wouldn't scrape the dirt floor.

A frigid breeze blasted through, filling up the entire space and making her shiver. Silent, Paris started a fire the old-fashioned way, sparking two rocks together and letting the flames catch on the twigs he'd gathered. Golden flames illuminated his face, bathing his features in a heady mix of light and shadow.

He was always beautiful, but just then he was mouth-wateringly exquisite. A mythical god of the heavens, no mere mortal worthy of him. Especially not her.

"I didn't come here to punish you," he said.

She remembered the accusation she'd launched at him while he'd had her pinned to the wall, her lips stinging from the brutal kiss he'd forced on her. A kiss she might have enjoyed under any other circumstances. But at that moment, as scared as she'd been of the shadows and of her feelings for him, she'd needed gentle.

Until gentle hadn't been enough for her riotous body.

"I'm glad," she said softly.

"You believe me? Just like that?" He snapped his fingers.

"Yes."

His gaze jerked to her, crackling with the same flickering heat as the fire. "Why?"

"Because I want to."

An angry shake of his head, dark hair whipping against his cheeks. "Or maybe because you're grateful to me."

She licked her lips, tasting him in the air, knowing they were now talking about something entirely different. "No."

"Or because you merely wish to keep me strong."

"No."

"Certainly not because you desire me," he said, his tone sharp as a whip. "Not because you hunger for me."

He wanted her to say it, wanted her to admit her desire for him while they were separated. That way, she couldn't claim passion spoke for her. More than that, he wanted her to say it without offering her the same admission. Not at first, and maybe not after. Either way, she'd be taking a risk. While a denial could save her pride, he might turn away from her, now and always. And while agreement could cause her major embarrassment, it could also bring her a pleasure unlike any she'd known before. So, no contest.

"Yes," she admitted. "Because I desire you, hunger for you."

Silence once again reigned, and she wasn't sure if he'd heard her or cared. Then his gaze shifted away from her, only to jerk back to her a second later, as if he lacked the strength to battle his own needs, the blue of his eyes mixed with glimmers of demon-red and black. Eerie and haunting, but not frightening. Not anymore.

"I wasn't sure what I would do with you when I found you," he said, his voice more gravel than anything. "Save you, yes. Definitely. Sleep with you, yes, that, too. I want you so badly I ache. All the time, I ache, but even though I want to keep you, part of me has always known that I would have to leave you afterward. I can't do permanent, even with you."

Even, he'd said, as if she were special. And the fact that he'd copped to his own feelings of desire caused her hunger for him to return in full force. Her entire body trembled, and had she been standing, she would have collapsed. "I know you'll have to leave me," she said. It wasn't something she could blame him for, because she couldn't stay with him, either."

He dragged in a breath, his fingers clenched on the rocks he still held. "I will not lie to you, and I will not cheat on you, and if we tried for something more, I would have to do both."

Like he'd done with that woman, Susan.

"Being with you may not affect my demon, may not strengthen me. I don't know, because I haven't had the same woman twice since my possession. If it doesn't work, I'll have to leave you sooner than expected and find…someone else."

There was no reason for him to know that the thought of him with another woman ate at her, leaving raw, oozing wounds. "I know."

"Because you saw…"

"Susan. Yes."

Sadness flickered in his eyes, then anger. He ran his tongue over his teeth, as though her response had somehow pricked his temper. "If that happens, I'll tell you. I'll tell you first, before I leave, and no matter what, I'll come back to you. I'll make sure you reach the exit. But after that, we have to… We say goodbye, once and for all."

The fire must have been doing its job, but the cavern seemed to warm in an instant, the cold vanquished. Perhaps her body had simply sucked that cold inside. She felt chilled to the bone. Paris wasn't going to protest her return to the Hunters. She wondered if he would object to her involvement with Galen, if it became necessary, but wasn't going to ask. As much as she wanted to know the answer, she *didn't* want to know the answer.

"Knowing all of that, do you still want to be with me?" he asked.

His tone implied he didn't give a shit about her answer. That he'd shrug and easily find someone else if she said no. But he was holding his breath, she realized, his cheeks flushing under the strain. He did want her, and he did care whether or not she wanted him back.

"I still want to be with you," she said. "Still want *you*."

He searched her face, clearly satisfied by what he saw, because he nodded. "Good. Now take off your clothes and get in the water."

CHAPTER TWENTY-THREE

PARIS WATCHED AS SIENNA dropped her shirt on the floor, where she'd already kicked her pants. Now she stood in her bra and panties. Plain, white. And yet, clinging to her perfect little body, they were the sexiest garments he'd ever seen.

His erection stretched past his navel, the base wider than his wrist. Yeah, he wanted her that badly.

More, Sex pleaded.

"The rest," he croaked. She was so beautiful...so strong. He'd come all this way, done all those terrible things, and yet she had freed herself from Cronus's hold. When Paris looked past his own masculine pride, he was glad about that. She had fought her demon and won, something he had never been able to do. Whatever happened outside this realm, she would be okay.

What happened inside of it, however...

Shouldn't do this, he thought, even as he repeated, "The rest. Now."

She unhooked the bra, dropped the garment on top of the others. Rosy nipples pearled from the lingering coolness in the air, topping off breasts he wanted in his mouth. Her thumbs slid under the waist of her panties and tugged. Down the exquisite length of her legs, until she was a whole lot of naked. His gaze was riveted on the dark triangle of curls shielding his favorite place in this realm or any other.

She shifted uncomfortably, her arms lifting and lowering as if she wanted to cover herself but kept talking herself out of doing so.

"You're perfect. So sweet and perfect." Slender, finely boned, with that deliciously freckled skin, each mark reminding him of a little drop of candy. He was going to lick her from top to bottom.

When they parted, there would be no part of her he hadn't tasted.

Frowning, she looked herself over. "How can you say that about me?"

"If you're about to insult yourself, I suggest you zip your mouth and get in the water."

His waspish tone had her blinking. "You're mad."

Hell, yeah, he was mad. "When I tell you how beautiful you are, and you express doubt, you're basically calling me a liar."

"No, I don't mean… It's just that…" She paused, reminding him of the babbling, uncertain woman he'd smacked into in Rome. The one who had fascinated him so completely, the one who'd prattled so charmingly. "Men just don't…"

Men. He cursed with enough heat to blister. "That's good, because otherwise I'd have to kill them." She was his and anyone else who looked at her, anyone else who thought to touch her— *Stop right there. Keep the possessiveness to a minimum. This is temporary. Has to be temporary.*

"Paris," she said, a hitch to her voice.

"Yes." He wanted to look away, couldn't look away.

"I think you're beautiful, too." With that, as if she hadn't just undone him, she turned toward the spring. He saw the elegant, and bruised, line of her back. Saw where those violet-and-jet wings grew in two perfect rows, saw the obsidian butterfly tattoo etched between them.

The curve of her spine made his mouth water. There were two indentions at the base, just above her ass. And speaking of her ass…had he ever seen anything more lovely? Enough to grab while he pounded deep inside her, toned, four freckles forming a starlike pattern on the right cheek.

He could worship there for hours, days.

More. Please, more. Need to touch.

A moan of bliss left her as she sank into the steaming water. She disappeared underneath the surface, saturating her hair, then came back up sputtering.

"Here." His arm shook as he withdrew a thin, wrapped bar of soap from his pocket. Embarrassment doused him when he noted he was trembling.

She accepted gratefully, her fingers brushing his palm. Beads of sweat broke out on his brow. "Thank you. You were smart to travel with one of these. I'll have to remember to do that."

Yeah. He wasn't going to explain his reason for doing so. He wasn't going there with her. Ever.

Telling her that he *always* carried a bar, that he never knew whose bed he'd end up in, or what kind of person he'd be with, or how dirty he'd feel afterward, or that he carried soap like other men carried condoms…not smart. A mood ruiner for sure.

And speaking of condoms, could he tell her the truth? He couldn't catch an STD, so he couldn't pass one on; pregnancy was rare between an immortal and a human, much less a dead human; and while he hated sleeping with strangers, hated being so intimate with them, his demon needed the skin-to-skin contact. So, no condom, even though his shaft had come into contact with thousands of people. She would be disgusted.

He shouldn't have pushed her for a sexual relationship when he had nothing more to offer her. He should have given her time to make a more informed decision, but he didn't have time. *They* didn't have time. In two days, he would lose her. And the thing was, Sex needed fulfillment now. So, yeah, if she would let him, he would take her.

He settled at the spring's ledge, need for her clawing at him. If they did this—they were so doing this—and Sex wasn't satisfied immediately afterward, Paris would... what? Do what he'd told her he would do and find someone else?

Don't think about that right now. He would lose control of his temper.

Already the darkness inside him swirled, craving a release of its own, making him feel as though he were possessed by two demons, each with separate needs. Sex, needing sex, and Violence, needing bloodshed. But Maddox carried the demon of Violence, so there went that theory.

Whatever. It doesn't matter. Only Sienna and this moment matter.

Sienna.

Soon she would leave this realm, the heavens, and hide from Cronus. No way would Paris allow her to hunt Galen. He would convince her to remain tucked away, and that was that. She would be safe, and Paris would return to his friends. To his war. To his old life.

A sick, pitiful existence, but, hell, after all the people he'd hurt throughout the centuries, he deserved it. Especially for what he'd done to Susan.

He'd truly admired and respected Susan. Had promised her fidelity even though he couldn't give it, and had slowly broken her heart. He wouldn't do that to another woman.

But... He yearned for more than random couplings. He yearned for monogamy.

He yearned for Sienna.

You can have her, Sex said.

Only to lose her.

No argument there.

Why have you allowed me to harden for her on multiple occasions, even though we've had her, yet you have never done the same with another? Over and over he'd asked this question, and always the answer was the same.

I don't know. It just happens.

A lot of things "just happened." While Paris hated the prospect of the upcoming separation from Sienna, she had easily agreed to their two-day limit. Had to be that way, yeah, but damn. Would a little fight about it have killed her?

Shit. He was being unreasonable, the darkness still driving his emotions. If he wanted this woman, he should have her. If he wanted to keep her, he should have her always. End of story.

Should, should, should. You couldn't live with shoulds, could you. Only woulds.

He shook his head, clearing his thoughts. He had a direct view of Sienna as she bathed. She lathered herself up, and damn if he wasn't transfixed as the bubbles cascaded down her breasts, caught on her nipples, then resumed their journey to her navel.

"Sienna, I have to tell you something." He ducked his head, too humiliated to face her. After this, she might walk, no chance of sex, but he had to do this or his conscience would never forgive him.

"You can tell me anything."

They'd soon find out. "After your death I had to...you know...and even on my way here, I..."

What are you doing? You know it's better if they never know what happens when we're done with them.

We. You mean *you*. *When* you *are done.*

"I know," she said, quieting both the demon and him.

No accusations, no making him unload the gory details. He liked that about her. A lot. She probably had no idea how rare that acceptance was, but he did. "The last time was a few days ago, I swear. I kept thinking I'd find you, and I wanted to be with you and only you when that happened."

"Paris, we weren't dating. We weren't committed. The last thing I said to you was that I hated you. And I'm sorry for that, I really am. So don't beat yourself up about your actions. You did nothing wrong." Water splashed as she closed the distance between them. She stood and warm, wet hands wound around his neck, twirling the ends of his hair.

He rested his forehead on the curve of her shoulder. Soft, soft skin, scented so sweetly his head did that fogging thing. Sex went crazy, too, perhaps even more desperate to touch and taste her than Paris was. "I wouldn't be so understanding with you. If you had slept with another man, even though we weren't dating, even though we weren't committed, I would...rage." He still wouldn't lie to her.

And what he would do afterward, when they split...

"At me?"

"No. Maybe. I don't know." His arms shot out and dragged her closer, needing her closer. Water soaked his shirt to his chest. Her nipples rasped at him, creating the most sizzling of frictions. "I want you all to myself."

She carried the sun under her skin, lighting him up every time he neared her. The jade and copper in her eyes were a lush, thriving valley he could lose himself in. Her mouth inspired every one of his most erotic fantasies.

Yes! This is what I've needed, what I've been craving.

What Paris had been craving.

"Since you," she told him softly, "there's been no one, and before you, years had passed."

Years. The concept baffled him as much as it pleased him.

"He was...the only man I've ever... I thought I would marry him," she said. "He was a Hunter, the one who recruited me." A pause rife with a thousand sharp edges, then, "I'm changing the subject, but only a little. I would like to express one more doubt about, um, myself, before we continue."

He stiffened, suspecting where she was headed and dreading it with every fiber of his being.

She hurried on. "I know we've been together before, and you know I'm just me. But this time it's different, because I know you better, know myself better, and I'm afraid that you'll... That I won't be... That I can't compare. To the others."

Yeah. Exactly where he'd thought she was headed. He dropped a kiss onto her collarbone, licked where his lips had been, then sucked hard enough to leave his mark. She gasped.

"I'm afraid *I* won't measure up, too," he admitted. "Here I am, the keeper of Sex. What if I can't please you? What if I can't live up to your expectations? And Sienna," he added before she had time to respond, "the others, they can't compare *to you*."

He'd been with thousands, yes, and he'd done his best to leave each one satisfied. He'd been using them, after all, so it was the least he could do. But making them come hadn't been for their benefit; it had been for his, something to ease the sting of his guilt. Had he actually cared about their pleasure? No.

"Oh, Paris." Those dainty, beautiful hands smoothed over his back. The motions were rhythmic, graceful, waking up parts of him he hadn't known existed. "How about this? Today you're just a man and I'm just a woman. There's no past, no future, only the present. We do what feels good. Nothing more. Nothing less."

Ah, hell. She kept that up and he would blow before he got inside her. She'd offered him the sexiest words he'd ever heard, ever hoped to hear, and it was another reason to like her. She did more than arouse him. She comforted him.

"Yeah. I'd like that," he said.

Me, too!

That's enough out of you. He settled his big hands on Sienna's tiny hips, lifted her out of the water and set her on the rocky edge beside him. The warmth of the water had flushed her skin, and now, droplets traveled all the places he wanted to go. He moved in front of her, crouching, rocking back on his heels before settling on his knees. Slowly he drew his hands along the tops of her thighs. He stopped at her knees, his thumbs dabbling underneath for several minutes before he applied pressure and opened her up as wide as he could get her. She was pink, wet and glistening.

He should tongue her nipples first, and he meant to. That had been the plan. Open her up, slide closer and pay proper homage to those sweet little buds. Except, now that he had a direct view of the prettiest feminine core he'd ever seen, there would be no starting up top and working his way down. He wanted *that*. Now. Wanted her dripping.

"I need you in my mouth. Down my throat. All over me. Tell me you need that, too."

"I—"

"Tell me."

"Yes. Please, Paris. Now."

CHAPTER TWENTY-FOUR

No teasing him, no tormenting him. His woman deserved a reward. Paris pressed a soft kiss where his thumbs had played, just behind her knees, then licked and nibbled his way up...up... A tremor moved through her, a perfect mimic of the vibrations Sex was throwing at him.

He leaned closer...closer still...breathed deeply, taking in the erotic scent of her desire. His blood fired, burning through him, scorching everything in its path and leaving only the desire. It was all he knew, all he wanted to know. Then he was there, right on her, licking his way up her center.

She cried out, the hoarse sound blending with his moan of rapture. Her arousal coated his tongue and he swallowed her, instantly addicted. His eyes closed as he savored. Wasn't just ambrosia he was tasting, either. Beneath the tropical syrupiness of the drug, there was a unique flavor all her own, something wine-rich and decadent. And for the first time in his life, he thought he could actually *taste* the aphrodisiac his demon released. Sweet as honey, rich with spice, it filled his mouth, coated his throat, seeped from his skin, blending with Sienna's succulence.

How many times had he dreamed of doing this to her, with her? Countless. He'd waited so long, and at times, he'd feared he would never know the reality. Nothing should have been able to live up to the languorous feasting he'd envisioned, but this not only lived up, it surpassed. She was everything he'd ever craved, and more.

Her fingers tangled in his hair, applying the most arousing sort of pressure. His woman wanted him back, attending to her need. There was no headier knowledge. He licked back up her core, but this time he didn't pull away. He swirled the tip of his tongue around her clitoris, teasing, taunting, driving her passion higher. Hell, driving his own higher.

He was starved for her, his cock throbbing against his fly.

"Not there," she instructed. "You're almost there. Please, just a little closer and you'll be there." The words gasped from her. Her hips undulated as she sought to place his tongue directly on that swollen clitoris.

And she thought she was bad at kissing and sex? Silly female.

He penetrated her core, sinking his tongue inside her, fast, faster, glorying as she panted his name, as her essence covered his face, as he swallowed her down, as her nails sank into his scalp, as her hips twirled and met his thrusts, as she arched into him, retreated, arched again.

"Paris! Yes, yes. There!"

When he felt her tensing, edging ever closer to release, he fit his lips over her clit and sucked, hard, at the same time driving two, then three, fingers deep, so deep. He scissored them, shifting depth and width in a constant stream of motion, and just when she reached the pinnacle of climax, he backed off a fraction, slowing his movements. Her moans tapered into incoherent mumblings, her hips following him, circling, trying to lure him back within those satiny walls.

"Paris! Finish me."

"I want to make you feel good."

"I do, promise."

"But you want more."

"Yes. Please!"

"Very well." A ruthless plunge of his fingers, scissoring over and over, his tongue flicking over that swelling bud, and she climaxed with violent force, her inner walls clenching on him. A scream tore from her, so loud and bracing it cracked her vocals. He loved it, reveled in the knowledge that he had brought her to this point.

His desperation grew critical, and he had to remove his fingers from her and clamp onto her thighs to hold himself steady, to stop himself from ripping at his zipper and slamming home.

He stayed like that until she calmed. Finally her shoulders sagged, and her head lolled forward. Those midnight wings trembled, glimmering like polished ebony. She was panting shallowly, her bottom lip cut from where she'd bitten down.

When her slumberous gaze met his, he brought his fingers to his mouth and licked at her arousal. He couldn't get enough of her, didn't think he would ever get enough.

Her pupils expanded, consuming those hazel irises and leaving only black. Black velvet, smooth and endless. He could lose himself and never care to be found.

"Take off your clothes," she whispered. "Please. Let me have you now."

He grabbed the collar of his shirt and tugged, ducking to free his head from the material's confinement. Her hands found his pecs a second later, her palms pressing into his nipples.

"Your heart is racing," she said, clearly awed by that fact.

In that moment, his heart beat *for* her. Only her. He'd

never craved a female this much. And that she knew what he was, what he'd done, and wanted him anyway... He moved in and fit his mouth around one of her rosy little nipples, sucking hard then easing the sting with a flick of his tongue. He turned his head and did the same to the other, leaving his mark on them both. Branding her, so that when she saw herself in a mirror she would know she belonged to someone else. To him, only him.

"Let me see the rest of you," she said.

He shook his head.

"Paris..."

Another shake. To remove his pants, he would have to stop touching her, and he didn't want to stop touching her. Couldn't conceive a good enough reason to *ever* stop.

"Please. I need to see you."

Trembling, he pressed his forehead between her breasts. He swallowed, found his voice. "You never have to beg. Not with me. Whatever you want, I will give you." Always before, he'd taken from his partners. With her, he wanted to give anything, everything. "But if I strip, I will lose control. Let me savor you, Sienna."

"Control is overrated. I want you, however I can get you."

Such beautiful words. "I wish we were at my home, and in my bed, and I had you splayed on my pillows. You deserve better than a dirty cave."

She cupped his cheeks and forced his eyes to meet hers. "After everything I've done to you, how can you say that?"

He didn't remind her that this moment had no past. He couldn't. The past flooded him, too. "Sienna, you ran to me when you were in trouble, when Cronus first enslaved you. Before *that,* you slept with me to strengthen me despite the fact that you were horrified by our potential audience, despite the fact that I was your greatest enemy. Before that, you were involved in a war and batting for your team, same as me. You did nothing I wouldn't have done, had the situation been reversed."

Tears filled her eyes, splashed down her cheeks.

"None of that. Not here, not now." He captured them with his tongue, kissing them away. Now the reminder came. "Just a man and a woman, remember?"

"I just…I always get emotional after mind-shattering orgasms," she said with a dry undertone, and he laughed. "Or I must, considering that was my first."

"Your other man didn't—"

Her smile was silky, wanton. "What other man?"

Good girl. He chuckled, surprising himself. Genuine humor between lovers wasn't something he'd ever experienced before her.

"I want you anywhere I can get you." Nibbling on her bottom lip, she reached down and pushed at his zipper. Her fingertips brushed the weeping tip of his cock, which stretched far past the waist of his pants. "Mmm, no underwear."

"I was…hopeful."

Now she was the one to chuckle.

He gripped her under the ass and urged her forward, even as he leaned back on his haunches. She slid from the rocky foundation, held up only by his hands. He positioned her core just over his erection. So hot, so wet, but he didn't push inside. Not yet.

"Kiss me," he commanded, even as Sex got his purr on. Guess the demon was so excited, he couldn't stay quiet a moment longer. At least he wasn't talking. "Like before. Own me with your mouth."

"My pleasure." A shiver rocked her as she meshed

their lips without any hesitation, thrusting her tongue into his mouth and feeding him all that she was. Owning him, just as he'd wanted.

"Can't hold back," he said. All thoughts of savoring her, this moment, fled. They had here and now, and not much else. He had to know the rest of her, had to join them. "Must be in you. Need to be in you."

"Yes. You'll own *me*."

He thrust deep and sure, filling her. They moaned in unison. Paris, Sienna, Sex. It was like coming home after a year in the desert, when you were so thirsty, so hungry, you felt as if you were drinking and eating for the first time. As if you were alive for the first time. His senses awoke, aware of her every need, attuned to her every nuance.

This was what he'd yearned for so desperately. Not just a communion with her body, but with her mind. Her soul, their every breath intertwined.

Yes. Yes, yes, yes.

She was tight, tighter than a fist, and he knew he stretched her. Knew he was too big for such a slender body, but that didn't stop him from moving her up and down, up and down from the root of his shaft to the very tip. She was so wet, the glide was smooth. Her nipples rasped at his chest, creating the most delicious friction. Friction that lanced spears of pleasure throughout his entire body.

He was utterly consumed by her. She was in his mouth, pressed against him, her weight sliding her down on him…down…all the way…her legs squeezing at his, her hands on his back, her nails scraping and clawing at him. Even the ends of her hair acted as a stimulant, dancing over his skin, tickling.

Paris kneaded his hands up her spine and stopped between her wings. Occasionally over the years, he'd had to massage his friend Aeron to work out the stiffness from battle. So he knew just how sensitive the slits in these wings could be. Keeping in mind that she had to be sore, he kneaded gently, rolling the muscles and tendons under his fingers.

A hoarse cry left her. "Paris! Oh, Paris!"

His name on her lips did it for him, totally, completely. He rarely ever told his partners his name, not wanting to hear them say it and increase his shame. But now, with Sienna, he was once again undone.

He pounded into her, harder, so damn hard their teeth banged together when she dove in for another kiss. Their tongues sparred with the same strength, the same intensity. His testicles were drawing up, the skin around them tightening. White-hot waves of pleasure and strength swam at the base of his spine, ready to burst through him, to devour him and brand her.

So badly he wanted to come, but he wouldn't, not until she'd exploded on him. Her pleasure came first, now and always.

He reached between their bodies and circled his thumb against her clitoris. And, oh, sweet heaven, that's all she'd needed. Another scream that cracked her vocals echoed around him, her inner walls milking him. He jetted inside her, pouring all of his desire, all of his need and passion straight into her core. Roaring, roaring, so caught up in the incredible sensations, uncaring about anything else.

And when, an eternity later, she collapsed against his chest, her legs lax against his, he continued to hold her, unwilling to let go. Just then, he wasn't sure he would ever be able to let go.

CHAPTER TWENTY-FIVE

HE'D BEEN ABUSED, his skin like pretty pink ribbons curling from a Christmas box.

Violated in the worst ways.

But Kane never gave the female minions what they wanted.

He was ashamed that he couldn't fight his way free, that his demon had somehow taken him over and held him down as surely as the chains shackling his wrists and ankles. He was a warrior, thousands of years old, with experience honed on the bloodiest of battlefields. This should be child's play to him. He should have escaped long ago.

More than any of that, however, he was humiliated by all kinds of other things he wasn't ready to acknowledge or face. The things they'd done to him...

Later. He would deal with it later. Maybe. Right now, all he could do was distance himself from what was happening to his body, as if it wasn't actually his body enduring the abuse. As if someone else had teeth in his thigh, hands where no others had been.

Drip, drip went his blood.

Kane had been tortured before. Many times, in fact. This was just more of the same, he told himself. Yeah. Right.

Disaster laughed, a cruel, happy sound echoing in his mind. If only that were the first time, but no. Disaster had laughed and laughed and laughed, a never-ending stream of amusement.

Hate utterly consumed Kane, kept him conscious. Every time he felt himself slipping into darkness, he thought about the demon High Lord inside him. Despite his instinct to remain distanced, he wanted to know every deed done to him. One day, he would return the favor in kind—a thousandfold. His demon would suffer this way. His demon would die this way.

Yes, one day.

His gaze pulled from the blood-spattered cavern wall above him and slipped down his body. He was a raw slab of scarlet. Dripping…dripping… Were those his ribs? Yes, he thought hazily. They were, one of them even pointing in the wrong direction.

One. Day.

Distantly he heard the pound of…horse hooves? Maybe. Whatever it was caused the minions on top of him, under him, even those around him who were awaiting their turn, to scatter in the winds, leaving him atop the boulder, naked, still bleeding…still dripping. Crimson, such a lovely yet horrifying color. Life and death, bound together.

He should be in tremendous pain, but there was nothing. Only a strange, welcome numbness.

A horse's whinny. Booted footsteps. He should care. Someone was here, looking at him, seeing him at his worst. He did care, but there was nothing he could do about it. No way to cover himself or hide what had been done to him. He wanted to kill this newcomer the same way he wanted to kill the minions and Disaster. Anything to wipe away all knowledge of this day. Forever.

A shadow fell over him, then someone was leaning down and peering into his eyes. Dark hair, eyes of the cruelest blue. "I know you. You are Kane, keeper of Disaster. Had a bad day, have you?"

Kane gathered enough strength to turn his head away. The action, small as it'd been, zapped every bit of that strength, leaving him cold, hollow. He had nothing left. Of course, the guy reached out and turned his head for him, forcing his attention to return.

"I'll take that as a yes."

Silence.

The guy grinned, and it was not nice. "Once, I could not have paid a Lord of the Underworld to visit me here. Now you guys keep popping up for free. By the way, your friend Amun called me Red while he was down here. Well, he thought it. Boy doesn't speak much, does he?" He gave a genuinely amused chuckle, and yet, there was bite to the sound. "Wish I'd picked up on that thought while he was in front of me, but then, I didn't have these, a gift from Amun before he left."

Red held up two hands—and they weren't attached to his body or any other. They were dark-skinned and held together by a strap of leather. A strap of leather he had wrapped around his neck, as if he were carrying boxing gloves. The insides of the hands had been scraped out, the flesh leathered.

They *were* gloves now. Human gloves.

Acid bubbled in Kane's stomach. Amun had come down here to rescue Legion and in the process had been infected by hundreds of demon minions, evil becoming a slick oil over his skin. The only solution had been to send him back down here to release them.

The gloves were the same mocha color as Amun's skin, possessed the same lines.

"What do you mean…gift?" Kane managed to work past his shredded throat. A throat scraped raw when the minions had stuffed things into his mouth. They hadn't cared that he'd tried to bite them, and hadn't tried to prevent him from doing so. They'd actually liked that. They had just— *You aren't thinking about this yet. You'll become as crazy as Amun was.*

"I won the mitts in a poker game," Red said, his tone casual. "You play? Wait. Don't answer that. Let me learn your secrets with my new, favorite toy." Grinning his not-nice grin, he stuffed his hands into the skin gloves and reached out.

Contact.

Those hands pressed against Kane's temples, cool and tough. Red closed his eyes, his entire body jerking as if hooked to a car with a lot of stallions under the hood. A moment passed, the only sound that of his heavy breathing.

Then another round of hoofbeats reverberated. Booted footsteps came next. A blond male with a similar toothy grin was leaning over Kane. "Whatta we got here? Another demon warrior?"

"Looks like." Red straightened, his blue gaze boring into Kane. "He's quite the mess."

"Will he heal?"

"Don't know." A shrug as if the answer wasn't important either way, then, "The man beside me is my brother. Amun called him Black. I call him Asshole. You may use whichever you prefer."

"Let me use the hands," Black said, rubbing his own with anticipation.

"Hell, no." A growl sprang from Red, an animalistic warning. "I just got them today, and this is my week to own them."

"I just want to borrow them for a minute."

"Please. You'll keep them, claim it's your turn already."

"Will not."

"Will, too."

I'm dreaming. I have to be dreaming. At the very least, hallucinating. Feral killers—and they *were* killers; they possessed the same hard edge as his friends—were not arguing like children.

"Fine. Just tell me what you learned," Black said, clearly sulking.

"He was with the Dark, and recently." Love and hate bathed Red's tone. "The Dark thinks this one will take White from us. The pair of them were captured, brought here and marked for death. A cave-in separated them. He doesn't know where the Dark is. The minions brought him here, tried to mate with him."

The Dark? Only person who thought Kane would take someone named White was William. And how did Red know—the hands, Kane realized. Those hands *had* belonged to Amun, then. Amun, the keeper of Secrets. Red had put those…gloves on, had touched Kane and dug deep into his mind, ferreting out information. A handy little weapon to have. He should be enraged, but he was still too numb.

Black popped his jaw. "White will have sensed your joy at finding a new demon, as did I. She will be here soon. We cannot allow her to meet this keeper." Emerald eyes bore into Kane. "You will not take her from us."

I don't want anything to do with her, dude.

"Shall we kill him and be done with it?" Red asked as if he were contemplating what to serve for dinner.

Black rubbed at the golden stubble on his jaw. "That would put him out of his misery. A good deed on our parts."

Kane wanted to help him with the answer. *Hell, yeah, you should kill me.* Because when this numbness wore off, when his body shrieked with the pain and his mind merged with his emotions, he was going to suffer. He was going to scream. He was going to rage.

Vengeance, he told himself. He could not have vengeance if he was dead.

"No, no killing," Black finally decided. "Not until I've had my turn inside his head."

"Agreed."

Then they would kill him a week from now, after Black had his turn. Seven days. Kane didn't know whether to laugh, thank them or just go ahead and start screaming and raging now.

The two freed him from the chains, but he didn't have the strength to move. He could only lie there, waiting, helpless to their whims.

"Green is going to rip into us for saving him," Red said. "You know how protective he is of White."

"True that." Black hefted Kane over his shoulder, unmindful of his exposed rib cage. "She's the only female he can tolerate."

The action disrupted some of the physical numbness, shooting sharp lances of pain through him. His mind began to fog, oxygen a faraway dream.

"But by then," Black continued, as Kane faded... faded... "I will have had my turn, so that is a moot point."

Kane didn't hear Red's reply. For him, it was finally, blessedly lights-out.

CHAPTER TWENTY-SIX

HIGH IN THE HEAVENS, Cronus stood at the foot of his bed, glaring down at his wife. She was still naked, still chained, but with two words, she had just changed the very foundation of their war.

"What did you say?" Surely he had misheard.

Her chin lifted haughtily, her eyes a shimmer of midnight hatred. "Beat me and let him go."

No, he had not misheard. His narrowed gaze shot to the male Hunter kneeling at his feet. Cronus had come here, as he'd come here every day for the past few weeks, and offered Rhea the choice. Watch a Hunter die or feel the hammer of his fists. Or in this case, watch two Hunters die—a male and the female who had refused to release him as Cronus dragged him from the cage. Always she preferred to watch a Hunter die. Always.

Except today.

What had changed? The Hunter in question? He was the only variable that was different. Did that mean she cared for the male? No, he assured himself after a heartbeat of bewilderment. Rhea cared only for herself. Did he mean something to her heavenly campaign? But what could a lone puny human do to aid a goddess? The answer was simple. Nothing.

That left only one option. She desired him.

Rage unfurled inside Cronus, iron fists that battered at his chest. His skin pulled tight against his bones, his marrow sharpening into dagger points and cutting at him. He gripped the human by the hair, jerking him to his feet and studying him anew. Late twenties, blond, handsome in a quiet, distinguished way only a mortal with a limited amount of time could manage. Lean, with only the barest hint of muscle.

Clearly, he wasn't a fighter. A scholar, perhaps. There could be no asking him, however. Like all the others, Cronus had already cut out his tongue. A must for these meetings. Allowing someone to speak to Rhea, to deliver a secret message Cronus could not decipher, would have been a huge tactical error.

Cronus never made tactical errors.

He looked at his wife. Her stubborn expression gave nothing away.

"Let him go," she said, chin going ever higher. "I've made my choice. I will be beaten in exchange for his life."

Let the male go? Alive and well, forgiven for his crimes against the greatest king Titania has ever known? The concept was inconceivable. Laughable. "And the female?" he snarled, tugging her hair to lift her head.

She whimpered, her obvious distress causing the male to grunt. How sweet, Cronus thought dryly. The humans cared for each other.

Eyes the color of a blood-soaked battlefield swept over the girl. "I don't care about her. Do whatever you wish with her, just let the male go."

Rhea's demon must be giving her fits. Either that, or Strife simply enjoyed the show. Well, it would be Cronus's pleasure to offer another blast of discord. "I do not approve of your choice, wife. Therefore, I think I will behead the man before I release him."

The queen sputtered for a moment, her chains rattling against the bedposts. "Are you completely lacking in honor, *husband?*"

"Of course. To win, one must do whatever is necessary. Besides that, I never promised to let your Hunters go while their hearts still beat, did I?"

"You bastard!"

"If you wish to save this one, you will tell me what's so special about him. That is our new bargain."

The male quaked with fear, his clammy sweat creating an acrid scent in the air. The female, still kneeling at Cronus's other side, reached for him, clasped his hand in a show of comfort and support. Her hair was cropped to her shoulders, and so black the tint had to have come from a bottle. Her eyes were brown, a deep chocolate, and filled with anguished tears. She was pretty in a delicate sort of way, and somehow familiar to him.

She wasn't the first female he'd brought to Rhea, nor would she be the last. There were several others waiting below in the dungeon. Now he wondered if he'd slain a sibling of hers, a sister perhaps, and that was why he thought he recognized her.

"Explaining my reasons was never part of our bargain," Rhea said in that haughty voice of hers, the one he loathed. The one guaranteed to make him see red. "Let. Him. Go."

Sure enough, Cronus's rage intensified. He returned his attention to the male. Shadows formed half circles under his eyes, his cheeks were hollowed out and there was blood dripping down his chin, all proof of his mortality.

Had Rhea once welcomed him into her bed? Was this man one of the many Cronus had felt his wife enjoying these past few months? Had this bastard climaxed inside her?

When her passions came upon her, she become wild and wanton, and unaware of—or unconcerned by—the damage she inflicted.

Each new deliberation tossed another smoldering log onto the fires of his rage, until the only thing inside his body was thick, black smoke with crimson flames trapped throughout. He couldn't see past them, could only choke on them. And only then did he realize that it was not the human who was quaking with such intensity; it was *him,* and the knowledge humiliated him.

The human had to pay.

"Look at me. Now."

Long golden-brown lashes lifted. Eyes filled with challenge and hatred stared up at him. Resentment, too. Did this human yearn for what he himself possessed? A connection to Rhea?

Well, that ended now. Before Cronus realized he had moved, he'd released the girl, palmed a blade— and slashed. He watched as the man's throat split in the center, blood welling and flowing. Watched as pain took the place of the resentment…watched as even that dulled…faded…and his body sagged.

The girl screamed, the shrill noise scraping at his ears, annoying him. Frowning down at her, intending to reprimand her, he uncurled his fingers from the man's hair and reached for her. *Thump.* The lifeless body hit the floor, and she released another scream, darting out of his way.

Not before he caught Rhea's gasp of horror.

His attention whipped to her, the girl suddenly forgotten. *His wife had just gasped.* Misery was to be her only companion in the countless eternity that awaited her, yes, but the fact that she'd dared to find that misery in the demise of some frail mortal failed to fill him with any kind of satisfaction.

Such a reaction meant he'd miscalculated, that she had, indeed, cared for the man. Even as his temper flared all the hotter, he struggled with understanding. Why care for a creature so limited by time and capability? A creature so fragile, so easily killed. As he had just demonstrated.

The black-haired wench scrambled to the body of the fallen male and gathered him close. She cried, her tears a flood of emotion. Obviously, she had cared for the man, too. But…why? What had he done to draw two women's loyalty?

Cronus's lip curled up in a snarl. The answer didn't matter, not really. The bastard was gone now, never to return. "Let him go," he commanded the girl.

She looked up at him, hatred shining in her eyes. She carefully laid the body upon the floor, pressed a kiss to his forehead and stood. Her steps clipped, measured, she approached Cronus, horrible sounds of grief rising from her.

Had he not taken her tongue, curses would have been hurled at him, he was sure. But she could not blame him for her lack. He had given her a choice. Return to the cage and die another day, or stay with the man, lose her tongue and die on this one. She'd chosen to stay.

"I am not a monster," he said. "The pair of you sanctioned the wrong side of the war, and you paid for it." One thing he'd learned while whiling away the centuries inside Tartarus: a king without a firm hand was a king without a throne.

What came next was expected. She threw herself against him, her fists pummeling at him, her fury and heartache infusing every blow. He didn't try to defend himself. There was no need. Did she truly think she was hurting him? That she *could* hurt him?

A resounding *no* to both, yet her relentless effort soon aggravated him. He had better things to do. "Stop, female."

Either she didn't hear him or she didn't care to obey. He set her away from him, a concession on his part, and one he did not often offer, but she just came back, a catapult of feminine ire. He could have frozen her in place with a wave of his hand, but he refused to venture down that path. Pride dictated she obey of her own accord or suffer the consequences.

"Do you wish to die, too?" he asked.

Somehow the question reached past her mania, and she stilled, a whisper of emotion-charged air separating their bodies. Panting breaths sawed in and out of her mouth, those heart-wrenching tears continuing to flow.

What came next was *not* expected.

With a cry springing from the depths of her soul, she threw herself into his blade. Her eyes widened with her pain; blood gurgled from her mouth. His blade. Oh, yes. He still clutched the hilt, the sharp, silver tip facing her— now inside her.

She did indeed want to die.

"Very well, female. Once again, I will support your choice." A tug of his arm, and she was freed from the intrusion. A flick of his wrist, and he killed her the same way he'd killed her man. Quick, easy. A mercy slaying, he told himself.

Her eyes rolled back in her head as her body slumped beside her man's.

A long moment passed in silence. Something burned in his chest. Regret, perhaps. Though why he would feel such a strong emotion for someone he did not know and did not care about was a mystery. Violence walked hand in hand with victory. In the heavens, you could not have one without the other.

"Well, well," Rhea said, and there was no longer a hint of remorse in her tone. No anger or betrayal, either. "My compliments on a job well done, darling."

He spun to face her. He was not met with tears, recrimination or even sorrow. He was met with glee. Lips he'd once kissed with reverence lifted in a smug grin. "How did that feel, murdering two innocents?"

He schooled his expression to blankness, unwilling to reveal his confusion. "Why so haughty, wife? It is your man bleeding all over my carpet, is it not?"

"No. It's not." She arched a brow at his flinching response. "Do you think I know not our prophecies? How it will be my Galen to take your head—unless you bind him to the female with wings of midnight."

He wiped his blade on the coverlet at Rhea's feet, a stark reminder of his prowess. One she would be forced to see for the rest of her stay here. "If *your* Galen takes my head, you die, as well."

Laughter layered with ice left her, causing a chill to crawl down his spine. "I know." And she didn't sound as if she cared. "I also know how your mind works. You expect Galen to want to use the winged girl and her new demon, but you doubt he will desire the girl herself. How, then, could you force a bonding? Let me think, let me think. Oh, yes, I know. By turning her into a walking fountain of ambrosia and addicting Galen to her blood. How am I doing so far?"

Not since Zeus ambushed him and drove him to his knees had Cronus experienced such fear. "Shut your mouth. You know nothing!"

Rhea continued on, her voice a silky caress. "You

could not infect a living girl with ambrosia; you could only infect a dead one. And who better to pick than someone the Lord of Sex desired? He will convince his friends to leave her alone, and she will convince him to leave Galen alone. Finally, peace will reign and your head will be safe. Yes? That's what you believe, isn't it?"

His heart slammed against his ribs. "Wrong," he croaked. "You are so wrong."

"How you disgrace us both with your lie. Did you think I would have no idea what was predicted all those centuries ago?"

Remaining silent, he once again schooled his features, unwilling to give her any more of a reaction.

"And did you truly think I would do nothing when I learned you'd given the demon of Wrath to a dead human girl, and she was growing wings of midnight?" Another grin, devious in its joy. "Well, what I did, husband, was learn everything I could about her. About her missing sister, Skye, and Skye's mate. The two people you just killed."

A moment passed as he digested her claim. When he did, he stumbled backward, shaking his head vehemently. "No. No."

"Why do you think I allowed you to capture me, hmm? Why do you think I allowed you to capture my people? How else do you think your spies learned where they were hiding? I have been waiting for just this day. The day you brought about your own ruin, the day you realized that because you carry the All-Key inside of you, I do, as well. Think your Sienna will aid you now?"

With that, Rhea vanished from the bed, the chains that had bound her thudding onto the vacant mattress.

CHAPTER TWENTY-SEVEN

LEGION PACED HER BEDROOM floor as if her feet were on fire. The Lords had already left the fortress, destination Rome, determined to find and kill Galen, thereby saving Ashlyn and the babies. That they hadn't come for her... she knew they'd never once considered trading her.

They were *that* honorable.

How did Legion repay them? By hiding herself away. And because of her actions, Ashlyn would suffer.

Sweet, sweet Ashlyn. What was Galen doing to her? If he hurt her the way the demons had hurt Legion... Stomach rebelling, she raced to her bathroom and hunched over the toilet. As many times as she'd thrown up the past day—week?—she was surprised when her lungs remained in her chest. Surprised, and disappointed.

She wanted to die. She would rather die than go through another pawing, having hands rip at her clothing, having things...done...to... "Argh!" She cut off the venomous thoughts before they could fully form. One unbidden image and she would collapse, hysterical, useless for days to come.

With a shuddering sigh, she rested her temple on the lid of the toilet. That beautiful blonde minor goddess had asked her a question. Who did she love most? The men who had saved her, or herself? Finally she copped to the answer. The men, definitely. They could have left her in hell, but they'd come for her, rescued her. She owed them.

But…if she gave herself to Galen, he would torture her. She'd poisoned him, after all. Had tried to kill him.

He would expect her to warm his bed. She knew that. Before she had poisoned him, she had slept with him. Her first time with a man, and she had liked it, had craved more, until…

She gulped, once again forcing her mind to blank.

If she went to Galen, she would willingly place herself in another version of hell. But then, that's what sacrificing yourself meant, didn't it? Enduring pain so that someone else wouldn't have to.

That's what the warriors had done for her, time and time again. Could she really do any less for them?

A shudder of revulsion worked through her, and she closed her eyes. She was decided, then. She would go to Galen. She would trade herself for Ashlyn.

There was no other way, no other choice.

And now that the decision was made, she had only to close her eyes and think of him, and she would appear before him. The Lords had forgotten that, like Lucien, she could move from one location to another with only a thought. Only difference was, she didn't have to follow a spiritual trail. Once she knew someone, she could appear before him anytime, anyplace.

Someone knocked on her door gently, as if afraid to startle her. She sniffed the air, recognized the sky-drenched scent of Danika, Reyes's woman. She must have come to talk to her. Probably meant to reassure her that she was protected and safe, that no one thought to use her as Bait.

"Go away," she shouted.

"No, I need to— Wait. You're speaking. You're speaking to me. It's been so long—"

"I said go away!"

"Legion, let me in. Please. I need to talk to you. Need to tell you—"

"Goodbye," she whispered, knowing she had to leave now or she would lose her nerve. Knowing she would never return. After the trade, after Ashlyn was safely returned, she would kill herself. She would rather die than be touched.

She pictured Galen—blond, beautiful and wicked. A moment later, the floor beneath her fell away.

CHAPTER TWENTY-EIGHT

SIENNA RIGHTED THE CLOTHING Cronus had given her when he'd first brought her to the castle. The shirt fit around her arms while tucking under her wings without having to wrap around the tops and drape over her shoulders. No fuss, no strain, but complete coverage. She was shaking.

What she'd just done with Paris…she'd never experienced anything like it. Not even with him. Nothing could have prepared her for the total body awakening. He'd pleasured her with soul-shattering thoroughness, had known exactly where to touch her, how to kiss her, what to say to ramp her desire up, up, oh, sweet heaven, up. She'd been completely into him, her mind focused on him, the rest of the world forgotten.

And yet, as beautiful as the loving had been, they were now, half an hour later, steeped in all kinds of awkward. For her, that had been way more emotional and meaningful than she'd been equipped to handle, and she had to wonder. Was it always like that for him, with everyone?

"So, uh, did being with me work?" she asked, then wished she could swallow her tongue, both dreading and excited about the answer. "For your demon?"

He nodded as he sat at the edge of the spring. "Yes. I'm strong now."

Despite the affirmation, her dread increased. He'd

closed off his expression, hiding his feelings behind a blank mask.

"Do you know how to use a weapon?" he asked abruptly. And clearly, that was the end of the demon conversation.

O-kay. So they weren't going to talk about what had happened. Which meant they wouldn't be talking about what came next in their relationship.

Two days does not a relationship make, idiot.

"What kind of weapon?" Dumb question. Whatever he said, the answer was the same.

"Any."

"Not really. When Wrath overtakes me, he kills using my body or whatever's available. I'm never aware when he does it—it's only after the fact that the memories flood me—so the skills aren't something I've retained."

"What about before your possession?"

"I was always a behind-the-scenes girl." Oh, damn. Why'd she have to go and mention the one thing sure to turn him into Mr. Distant? Or rather, Mr. Way More Distant.

But he surprised her. He showed her a small handgun thingy, then how to flip the safety. He released the clip, revealed the bullets and taught her how to put everything back together. "All you do is point and tap the trigger," he said. "Hollow points will do enough damage to whatever you're aiming at, no matter where you hit."

And what about when she missed, which was a very real possibility? Because just thinking about holding the gun made her hands shake. "So, you want me to buy one and carry it, like, all the time?" She'd never, in all her life or death, fired one.

"No." He leaned over and stuffed the metal in the waist of her pants. Cold, heavier than she would have guessed. "I want you to carry this one. The safety's on, so you won't hurt yourself."

"You're not afraid I'll shoot you in the back?" The joke fell flat, their relationship—or whatever—too new, and she blushed

Of course, he surprised her yet again. "No. I'm not." Utter confidence coated the words.

Relief swept through her. "I'm glad."

He cleared his throat. "Do I have your full attention?"

"Yes. Of course." And right then she knew, reality crashing into her hard enough to hurt. This was his way of saying goodbye. His way of preparing her to live without him. Her knees threatened to buckle, but she managed to remain upright. "Yes," she reiterated.

"Good. Now listen up, and listen well." His gaze drilled into hers. "I've done a lot of research about the living dead. If anyone threatens you, that means the person can see you. And if he can see you, he and his weapons will be solid to you. I won't remind you about the men out there, how they saw you and would have been able to touch you. If they can touch you, that means you can touch them. So you need to act first, and think about it later. That means you shoot the culprits without hesitation. Got it?"

"Y-yes."

"All right, then. Moving on." Next he withdrew a crystal blade. He stretched out his free hand and motioned her closer.

One step, two, until she was at his knee. Apparently, though, that wasn't good enough. He latched on to her hip and dragged her between the deep vee of his legs. Though he wasn't in a sexual mood, the touch excited her all over again.

He forced her to curl her fingers around the hilt, those

ocean-blues grave. "If someone gets in your grille, they deserve what they get. Go for vitals, where they're soft and you don't have to worry about cutting through bone. Like here." He moved her hand to his side, laying the blade flat a few inches above his hip. "And here." He moved her hand to the ropes of his stomach.

Touching him there reminded her of just how hungry she was, and not just for his body, causing her own stomach to growl. Her cheeks heated all over again. Was she cursed to always embarrass herself in front of this man?

His beautiful lips curled into the semblance of a smile. "Still haven't eaten, huh?"

Though a mere shadow of what it could be, that half smile lit up his entire face, dialing "beautiful" to "exquisite." She, too, lit up, her nerve endings pulsating. Gulping back her always increasing desire, she nodded. "I'm starving."

A moment passed. He cursed. "This goes against what few morals I have left." Frowning, he released her to dig around in his pockets. He withdrew a plastic baggie filled with dark purple powder.

"What does?" Holding her? Giving her weapons? Now that she was aware of her hunger, the pains started up, her blood heating to the point of boiling, her skin shrinking over her bones.

Don't think about it, and you'll be fine.

He set the baggie aside, stared at it for several minutes, and released a ragged breath.

Wanting to give him time to come to grips with whatever was bothering him, she studied the knife he'd given her. The crystal blade was jagged, rainbow shards trapped under the clear exterior. The handle was a dull copper, solid, and warm with his body heat.

"I've never seen anything like this," she said.

"And you never will again. There are only two in the world, and I've got the other one. That baby will kill anything, even a god of this world, and do whatever you command, as long as it's in your hand. Like, if you need to hide it, grip it and think *invisible.*"

Her eyes widened, and her jaw dropped. "I can't accept this. The two are obviously a matched set and—"

"Don't argue with me." His tone was hard, uncompromising. He withdrew a small flask from his other pocket, picked up the plastic baggie and dumped half of its contents inside.

She'd told him where she was going when they parted, and who she would be with. He had clearly forgotten, or he would be insisting she give the crystal back and pretend she'd never seen it.

"Paris, listen to me. I'm going after the leader of the Hunters. Do you understand what I'm telling you? You can't risk something like this falling into enemy—"

"Don't. Don't say another word right now. I've decided you're not going near that psycho, and that's that, so just take the knife and say thank you." He swirled the liquid in the flask before lifting the small round rim to her lips. "Now drink."

"*You've* decided? You can't—"

"Drink."

She had no choice but to obey; he'd already begun pouring the contents down her throat. And sweet heaven, she loved the taste. A diluted version of what Cronus gave her, but delicious all the same. She gulped back one mouthful, then another and another, the warmth sliding into her, dancing through her, easing her pain faster than a blink.

"Enough." He removed the flask before she could start licking at any stray droplets.

She moaned her disappointment, then closed her eyes for a moment and savored. Her skin plumped back up, and wow, she could have floated away on a cloud of bliss, forever lost.

"What is that stuff, anyway?" Cronus had never told her.

"Ambrosia."

Huh. A substance consumed by the immortals, she recalled reading, used for pleasure and the reaffirmation of power. As she now knew, myths often misled, straight-up lied or barely touched upon the truth. "Why do I—"

"Nope. No questions about this particular subject right now." He hooked the flask to one of her belt loops and tucked the baggie carefully in her pocket. "When you feel yourself going into withdra—I mean, when you feel yourself getting weak, take a few swigs. You'll perk right up."

"Clearly."

He met her gaze, the blue of his eyes frosting over in seconds, turning the ocean into a river of glass. "You said you could go a week with what Cronus brought you, right?"

So. She couldn't question him, but he could question her? She could have refused to answer, or demanded they trade answers. She didn't. "Yes." The change in him upset her, and she wouldn't add to his obvious stress.

"What you just drank should last a few days." He gripped her forearms and shook her. "I need you to listen to my next words. If you retain nothing else I say, retain this."

"Okay," she repeated, tensing as his anxiety bled into her.

"Never, under any circumstances, are you to allow

someone to taste your blood. Do you understand? They do, and you are to kill them before they can escape you."

"Who would want to taste my blood?" Humans? Impossible. They couldn't see her or even sense her. Vampires? Maybe. The nocturnal creatures existed, but they wanted *everyone's* blood. Why target a ghost of a woman?

A muscle ticked in Paris's jaw, a sign of his growing anger. "You'd be surprised. Now promise me. Promise me you'll kill anyone who does."

"I promise." Her hands fluttered to his shoulders, an offering of comfort. He was trying to tell her something without freaking her out. She knew it, sensed it. Trying to protect her, even though they were destined to part.

He released her to shove his hair off his brow. There were dark smudges on his fingers, she saw. Wanting to help him, even in so small a way, she took one of his hands and rubbed at the inklike spots. They remained. She frowned.

"They won't come off. They're tattoos," he explained, no inflection in his voice. He'd gone very still, had even stopped breathing at her first touch.

Why would he tattoo smudges on his fingertips? Her eyes met his, a tangle of confusion and an ever-present desire. She ignored the first and concentrated on the latter, lifting the tip of his finger to her mouth and sucking.

His pupils did their pulsing thing, stretching, snapping back into place, stretching again. The scent of dark chocolate and expensive champagne drifted from him, enveloping her, fogging her thoughts, electrifying her already sensitized nerves. She bit his pad lightly, and a hoarse groan left him.

"Do you have any children?" she asked, then had to

fight a wave of sadness. *I can't. Never again.* To distract herself, she sucked his finger deeper than before, swirling her tongue at the root and sliding the appendage out with a *pop*.

The sudden topic switch didn't faze him. "No. I always know when a woman is…I mean, Sex knows, and he wants her that much more, but impregnating a stranger is one of two things I've never let him force me to do."

Her head tilted to the side. "What's the other?"

"Lie with someone under the age of consent."

How vigilantly he must have to fight for such concessions. She knew firsthand how powerful a demon's compulsions could be. "Do you want them? Children, I mean. One day, with a woman you love?" *Stop this. It's too painful.*

He offered a casual shrug, or tried to. The lifting of his shoulder was stiff, jerky. "I want *you,* here and now," he said. "Let me have you. One more time before we head out."

One more time, a thought as arousing as it was depressing. Refusal, however, was not an option. She hadn't lied earlier. She would take him however she could get him. "Yes."

A slight whistling behind her, a cold splash through her, and then Paris's entire body jerked. His eyes widened, and his hands fell from her. He frowned, looked down. A blade hilt protruded from his chest.

Sienna screamed and whipped around, using her own body as a shield for his. Except, one blade had already gone through her, as if she were nothing more substantial than mist. For whoever had thrown the weapon, she wasn't. He could not see the dead, nor touch the dead, so neither could his blade.

The culprit was a large—really large—guy with pink hair and tattooed teardrops of blood under one of his eyes. He stood in the entrance of the cavern.

His punked-out features blazed with hatred. "How's that for not fighting fair?" he snarled.

Paris shoved her behind him, and she stumbled from the force he used, falling into the water and sputtering. Her heart raced out of control as the two men slashed each other with their eyes. A physical slashing would follow, no question. Both were familiar with the dance of death, an undeniable truth as they got into position.

"How'd you find me? You know what, never mind. I don't care. You tossed that dagger at my woman. For that I'm taking your throwing hand." With a tug and a grimace, Paris removed the blade from his chest. His eyes glowed bright red, casting a crimson spotlight on the man he clearly wanted splayed on the chopping block.

"Your woman?" A snort, a sneer. The newcomer reached up and slid two serrated blades from a crisscross at his back. "What woman? It's just you and me, demon."

"I don't give a flying flip that you can't see her." The words emerged on a growl, more animal than human. "She's mine, and you brought violence to her door. For that, you're losing your balls."

"Is that so? Well, I say you hurt me over my woman, so now I'll hurt you over yours." He grinned without humor, metal glistening and whistling as he twirled the hilts.

"Doubtful." Paris clasped the other crystal blade.

Another snort. "If you want to walk out of here alive, you'll tell me where my goddess is."

"You're the one who likes more pain and less talking, right?" Paris said. "Come on, then. Come get your pain."

Just like that, they were on each other. They fought faster than she could track. What she caught, like clicks of a camera: the pause as Paris pinned the punk, his boot coming down on a throat. The horrible suspension as a blade arched toward Paris's midsection. The heart-stopper of hope as Paris swung for a knee, connected. The terrifying beat of time as Paris hit the ground, his opponent snarling on top of him.

And what followed *that* was a ballet of hammering fists and kicks with enough vigor to snap bones. Knees going for sensitive places. Teeth ripping. Claws tearing. Metal clanging. They slammed into walls, rolled around on the floor, hacked at each other. Blood splattered in every direction. Never had she seen anything more brutal.

They wielded their blades beautifully, horrifically. *Annnd* yes, as promised, there went the newcomer's throwing hand. Blood sprayed anew. That didn't stop him from launching at Paris and going for Beat Each Other Senseless, round two.

So badly Sienna wanted to take out her new gun and fire, but the two were tangled together, and she was afraid she would shoot Paris. Having joked about nailing him in the back, she was now faced with the very real possibility and couldn't risk it. More than that, the bullet probably wouldn't hurt the punk, would probably soar right through him the way his blade had soared through her.

So…what could she do? Unsure, but knowing her current position helped no one, she slogged her way out of the water and stood. A cold blast of air hit her, making her shiver so vehemently her teeth rattled and ice crystals formed on her skin. A second later, the angel Zacharel towered in front of her.

"Stop them," she pleaded.

His green eyes were hard, unflinching and totally focused on her. "Come. We will leave them to their battle."

Her impromptu swim must have waterlogged her ears. She could not have heard him correctly. "Come with you, as in *leave* Paris behind?" Weren't the two men friends?

"Yes." He waved his fingers with definite impatience. "You grasped my meaning correctly. Paris would prefer you not be around such violence, I'm sure."

"Don't care. I'm staying." Warriors like him and Paris were unfamiliar with denial, and took every measure of resistance as a challenge, she was learning. Before this one could leap at her, she held her hands up, palms out, and backed away from him.

Cowardly, perhaps, but effective. He frowned at her.

"I'm staying, and that's final," she added.

Paris sensed the new threat and unleashed an unholy roar. He dove on Zacharel, knocking the robed warrior down. The angel didn't shove him off. Didn't touch him in any way, in fact, and yet Paris propelled across the cavern and slammed into the opposite wall.

The pink-haired punk was on him a second later, the fight speeding into a new level of ferocity. But through it all, Paris never dropped the blade that had done a meet and greet with his heart. He cozied the tip, and then the hilt, up to those extra-special soft spots in the guy's side and stomach, just as he'd showed her.

A pain-filled grunt, a black curse. Then the guy was slumping over and Paris was whipping back around, his crimson sights once again on Zacharel—who was now standing beside Sienna.

With a gasp, she skirted around the spring, creating as much distance between them as possible. "Back off, angel boy."

Black brows winged into his hairline. "Hardly, demon girl. I do this to save you, to save thousands of others."

Uh, what now?

"Walk to me, Sienna." Paris was panting, bleeding, shaking, and the crazy, animalistic glaze hadn't left him. "Now."

With every fiber of her being, she wanted to run rather than walk to him. And she would have, if the angel hadn't said, "I cannot let her do that, demon," and appeared at her side in the next blink, taking hold of her wrist and locking down.

CHAPTER TWENTY-NINE

OH, HELL, NO, PARIS THOUGHT. Two pansy wingers—one of them practicing, one of them fallen—were not gonna get the drop on him. He hadn't killed the fallen, not yet, he'd just hurt the guy a little. Or a lot. Whatever. Now he wanted the bastard to suffer for a long damn time.

His need to protect Sienna burned hot. The fact that the fallen had interrupted their sexual play, the fact that someone other than himself had seen her delicate features overcome with desire, were reasons to kill. Savagely.

Zacharel he actually kind of liked, but that didn't mean he'd tolerate interference in this matter. Only thing going for him right now was the fact that Sex was either asleep or hiding, and thankfully had no opinion.

"Let her go," he snarled. He was losing blood fast, his chest like a waterspout that had sprung a leak. Hurt like a son of a bitch, and he knew he'd go down sooner or later. He was determined to make it later, when Sienna was safe.

The angel gave a single shake of his head. "Your temper is too fierce."

So the hell what? "I've got myself under control."

"Do you really?"

No. "I said I did, didn't I? So let her go before I make you."

"By taking my hand? My balls, as you told the fallen?"

A pregnant pause, anger fighting to be freed from a man who clearly denied his emotions—but couldn't fully suppress them. One day he would erupt, no question. "What will you do to yourself when you accidentally hurt your female?"

One stomping step, two. "Back off. Now." The darkness inside him was so deeply rooted, he knew the stuff had moved in and set up shop and he'd never get rid of it, even when he and Sienna parted. Especially when they parted. Already he was going to sink into despair when he lost her, and if he allowed himself to relax with her, to like her that much more, he would only drag her down with him. That's why he'd fought his emotions so hard after having sex with her.

Now he was glad for that. If he had to murder the angel, he would, and the darkness would be shooting out happies over the deed rather than remorse.

"Your darkness," Zacharel said.

"You reading my mind?" The invasion would cost him.

"No," the angel replied, saving his life. "Your eyes. The darkness is there. Do you know what it is, warrior? Do you know what you play with? No? Well, allow me to explain. As a human body can grow a child, a demonic one can grow evil. That is what you have done. You have allowed your demon to birth another demon, for lack of a better word. This one is all yours, your baby, and like the other possessing you, he will never leave you."

Should have surprised him, didn't. Shouldn't have angered him further, did. Sienna had heard those damning words. "Unless you want a personal introduction, you better step away from my woman."

"Paris," she said, sadness dripping from her tone.

Sadness rather than anger, leaving him confused.

Whatever. If she tried to tell him that she wasn't his woman, that this second demon—or whatever it was—was a deal breaker, he'd lose it. When he had to let her go, fine, whatever, he'd reevaluate and dial back the possessiveness. But here? Now? There'd be no dialing back. He'd just pounded inside her, had just come inside her, branded her, and he still had her decadent taste in his mouth. She'd cried his name, had wanted more, and would have given him more.

"I still have your present," she reminded him. "Should I… Do you want me to…use it? I thought he was your friend, but…"

He blinked. She would stab the angel? For him? The thought probably shouldn't have cranked up his desire for her, but it did. And that she would do this after hearing Zacharel's condemnation of him was heartwarming.

"Not yet." Behind him, he heard the punk lumber to his feet. His hand tightened on his weapon.

"No," Zacharel said, stopping him. At last he released Sienna. "The red is receding from your eyes. That is good. You will not hurt the girl now. Therefore I will take the fallen elsewhere and return later. As for you, you will head for the doorway leading out of this realm." He vanished a moment later, the fallen going with him though Zacharel had never touched him.

As if his presence had been the only thing keeping Paris upright, he collapsed, toppling to his knees. Sienna rushed to his side and eased him the rest of the way down. Thick black spiderwebs wove through his line of vision. Any moment, and he'd sink into unconsciousness.

"I've got you," she said. "I'll take care of you. I won't let anything happen to you."

He didn't want to say what he now needed to say, didn't want to spoil what had happened before with what

had to happen now. He'd been here, in this very situation, a thousand times before. Injured and fading—with
only one way to heal.

"I have to... You have to... Sex, I need sex."

His demon was all over that, torpedoing out of hiding
to shoot blood into his cock. Happened so fast, Paris suspected the demon would battle whiplash for days. This
was uncharted territory, though. Until Sienna, he'd never
been with the same woman twice. Now that he had, he
knew it would keep him level, strong, but would being
with her more than once actually mend his body?

"Sex? But you're in no condition for that. You should
rest."

"No resting. I hate that it has to be this way, but I can't
change it." When he was injured like this, he needed
full-on, hard-core sex with as many different partners as
possible. But even if a hundred beauties had surrounded
him, he'd still only have wanted the one looming over
him, silent, her hands gentle as they explored his wounds.
A woman he shouldn't trust, especially while he was like
this, but one he couldn't, wouldn't, turn away from.

No matter what happened next.

"Please, Sienna. Ride me."

Only the slightest pause. "You don't have to beg me
for anything, Paris," she said, using his own words to
comfort him. "I told you I'd take care of you, and I will."

CHAPTER THIRTY

IF I EVER GET PARIS completely naked, Sienna thought wistfully as she unbuttoned and unzipped the black, flowing material of his pants, *I'll probably spontaneously combust.*

Not wanting to jar him, she stretched the fabric apart rather than tugging it down his legs, allowing the massive length of his shaft to spring free, just as he'd done earlier. No man should be so beautiful all over, a study of hard strength and dark sexuality no matter where you looked.

He threw an arm over his face, hiding his features from view. "I hate this."

She'd been reaching for him, but now reared back. "I'm sorry. I can find you someone else if you'd rather—"

"No," he rushed out. He must have heard the horror and distress in her voice. "I don't hate being with you, and I don't want anyone else."

Good, because she wasn't sure she could have followed through. Becoming his pimp would be a special kind of hell.

"What I hate is that we're chasing something meaningful and organic with something clinical and mechanical. Something forced."

Her first thought: he'd enjoyed the sex, too, and considered it meaningful. Joy careened through her, bright starbursts that warmed each of her cells. Her second thought: he was ashamed right now. The joy withered, cooled. They had so much working against them already, she couldn't allow him to add such an awful emotion to the mix.

"You're not forcing me to do this, Paris. Before we were interrupted, I was wet. I'm still wet." And she didn't mean from the water. "Why does this time have to be any less meaningful than the other when we were headed in this direction, anyway?"

He'd groaned at *wet*. Now his arm fell away, and he peered up at her with those amazing eyes of searing azure. "You're so lovely."

When he looked at her like that, all heavy-lidded and dreamy, she *felt* lovely. "Let me show you the rest of me." She pushed to her feet and disrobed, his gaze tracking her every movement.

Throughout the centuries, he had seen countless others naked. She knew that; she had seen them. He had been with tall women, short women, skinny, heavy, black, white and everything in between.

Sienna was nothing special, and yet, when he said, "Beyond gorgeous," with a fine sheen of sweat dotting his brow, she believed him this time. He was right. Her demon would sense a lie. The joy returned.

"I think the same about you," she admitted. Naked, emboldened by his praise, she straddled his hips and eased down. But she didn't impale herself on his thick length. Not yet. He needed the sex, and time was imperative, but he needed stroking more. Needed assurance that she was here, in this moment with him, all the way.

His arousal jutted out between her legs, her warmth all over it. She traced her fingers over the tip, and he sucked in a breath.

"Climb up here and straddle my face," he croaked. His

palms found her breasts and kneaded, rolling her beaded nipples through his fingers. "I want to taste you again."

The desire to do just that nearly slayed her. Blood rushed through her veins at an alarming rate and heated dangerously, chasing away any lingering chill. "I'll hurt you. My weight... Your chest is injured."

"How about this? I *need* to taste you again, and I don't care if my chest hurts."

She licked her lips. "How about this? *I'll* taste *you*."

He stilled, even seemed to stop breathing.

"Unless you don't want me to," she hurried to assure him.

"It's not that." The words sawed from him, hoarse and throaty, more grit than substance. "I haven't let anyone do that to me in more than a thousand years." He sucked in a breath. "No, that's not actually true. I let a slave perform the act on me on the journey here, and I hated every moment of it."

"Oh." Bafflement widened her eyes. All men loved receiving oral sex. Right? So why had he stopped the women from sucking on him? And he'd stopped them, she knew that he had. Every woman he'd welcomed to his bed had probably wanted to fit her lips over that cock and drink him down.

"But you," he went on, still on edge. "I will let you. If you want to."

She flattened her hands on his stomach, felt the cords of the muscles clench. "I don't want to make you uncomfortable or do something you don't like—"

"No. You misunderstand." His shook his head, all that astounding hair performing a ballet around his temples. Strands of black and brown and gold she longed to fist. "I didn't let the others do it because I was already using them and didn't want them doing me any more favors.

And the only reason I let the slave was because I needed answers, and that was the fastest way to get them."

Answers about me.

"And Sienna? The slave was…he was a male."

And that was not his preference. Sympathy washed through her. To have no control over your body and its reactions, to be forced to submit to a desire you yourself did not feel, had to be torture. "Just so you know, there's nothing wrong with that. And I won't be doing you a favor, Paris. You are a beautiful, charming, intelligent, sexy as hell man, and I'm dying to have you. Just as you are. With all the others you were simply practicing for this moment," she said, hoping to tease him into seeing the truth of her claim. "In doing this, I'll be pleasuring us both. I hope. I mean, I have about as much experience with blow jobs as I do with sex."

"If that's the case, I'm about to come my brains out. You'll be perfect."

"Quiet. Sienna's not done putting you in your place."

A smile bloomed. "Yes, ma'am. But, uh, what's my place?"

"The pedestal for the most admirable man I know. I don't care what you've done, or who you've done it with. You could have rampaged the entire world, could have raped viciously, constantly, but you don't. As for the sex of the slave, well, I hope you respect me in the morning, because I think you're even sexier now and I'm going to be very upset if I don't get my turn."

He licked his lips. "You want a turn?"

"More than anything."

Already his hips were writhing underneath her, as if he were imagining her mouth on him, working him over. "Please, Sienna. Please, do it."

"Yes. But only if you'll like it." She shimmied down

until her lips were poised over that beautiful erection. *This is mine,* she thought, dazed.

"I'll like it. I swear I'll like it."

"Let's find out for sure." Her tongue emerged, licking up and down his shaft, treating his length like a lollipop. Groan after groan left him, and she took that for approval. On her third upward glide, she fit her fingers around his base and her lips around the head. As she gloried in his flavor, her hand continued the erotic journey on his shaft.

Her wings arced down and around, the tips stroking his sides. For the first time, she understood the joy of having them. Surrounding him like this, she forgot about the rest of the world. Only they existed. Only the pleasure.

A curse roared from him as his hips jerked, thrusting him deeper. Immediately he apologized and backed off. "More. Please, more." He pounded his fists against the floor. "I have to have more."

She sucked harder, tasting him deeper, savoring, then swallowed him down as far as she could go. He was too big and stretched her jaw, but she didn't care. His entire body shook with the force of his enjoyment. She never stopped working him with her hands, either, one doing the stroking, the other tugging at his testicles.

But then she started wondering what those tasted like and released his cock with a *pop* to run her tongue over the tightness of his sac. He enjoyed that, too, especially when she drew one, and then the other, into her mouth.

Would she ever get enough of this man?

When he was shouting her name, she returned to the main event, taking him in, taking him down, his wild reaction spurring her on and on and on, her body lighting up, desperate for him, for all of him.

"I'm close, baby, I'm so close. If you don't want to taste me, you need to—"

In answer, she sucked him so hard her cheeks hollowed.

"Oh, yeah!" His hips jerked up, his muscles knotting on his bones, and a roar far louder than any that had come before ripped out of him. He jetted down her throat and she swallowed every drop, holding on until the very end, when he sank onto the ground, his panting breaths filling the entire enclosure.

"Ride me," he commanded in that voice full of gravel. "I need to be in you. Now."

"Yes. Now." She knew she had just repeated what he'd said, again, but that rich scent was seeping from him, surrounding her, blinding her to everything but him. And this. Oh, sweet heaven, *this*.

She lifted, surprised to find that she was shaking. A quick glance, and she saw that his wounds were no longer bleeding, and the skin had even sewed itself back together. And despite his recent climax, he was still rock-hard and ready for her.

Once again she straddled him, and this time she took him in, all the way, until she was sitting on him, her ass resting on the backs of his thighs. Now she was the one to cry out. Like before, he stretched her, but it was such a good, burning stretch and she was so damn wet, so damn eager.

He clamped his fingers on the rise of her hips and moved her, up and down, his strength a shock. Because when he moved her down, he slammed her, forcing himself as deep as he could go, lifting himself up to meet her halfway.

"Kiss me," he growled. "Lean down and kiss me."

Even as she rocked on him, she obeyed, her chest

smashing into his as she slanted her head and meshed their lips together. His tongue immediately shot inside her mouth, claiming her as his, owning her. His hands went to her back, sliding under those slits that housed her wings. It was as though he'd put his fingers and his mouth on her clitoris at the same time, using his nose and his chin and his beard stubble, anything and everything to stimulate her to the fullest.

Release slammed through her with the same force Paris used. Wild exhilaration pumped through her, the pleasure so intense her nerve endings were electrified. Pinpricks of white behind her lids, fire in her veins. A storm of satisfaction through every inch of her.

She didn't mean to, but she bit his lip until she tasted blood, and even that was a stimulant. Her nails dug into his scalp, holding him still for her abuse as she rode out the thunder and the lightning. But he didn't seem to mind, seemed to like it. One of his hands fell to her ass and pressed her down as he rose up, and then he was roaring, spurting inside her, sending her over the edge a second time.

When at last they calmed, they collapsed on the ground in a tangled heap of arms and legs, shaking together, gasping, desperate for air but not caring that they couldn't find it.

"Thank you," he panted.

"You liked?" she replied when she found her voice.

"Woman, you nearly killed me. I should be manning back up, putting us back on track, but I'm completely blissed out."

So was she. Each time together was better than the last. "I hope we do that a thousand times today."

"I hope that's an accurate guesstimate and not hyperbole."

"If anything, I *under*estimated. You're very good with my wings."

She felt the warm stroke of a chuckle against her skin. "I'm not too rough?"

"You're perfect." A kiss at the cord that bound his shoulder to his neck, a scrape of her teeth. "Ever been with a winged woman before?"

"Uh…I…" He hesitated, even as his skin prickled with heat beneath her mouth.

His shame had returned, and once again she experienced sympathy for all he'd endured. "I'll take that as a yes. Was she an angel, like your friend?" He needed to purge the memories and the feelings that accompanied them.

"Uh…"

"Another yes. A demon, too?"

Only the slightest pause. "Yeah." He ducked his head in the opposite direction, as bashful as a schoolboy.

Adorable. Just adorable. As strong as he was, as fierce as he was, he cared about her opinion. "Paris, it's okay. I know you have a past, and I wasn't pressing for details to embarrass you or to make you uncomfortable. I just wanted you to know there's nothing you could have done to disgust me."

Slowly he relaxed and turned toward her. Those dark shadows swirled in his irises, but as she watched, they thinned and misted away. Zacharel had said those shadows were another demon, an evil inside of Paris that he could never get rid of. She wasn't sure why he'd welcomed that evil, or "birthed" it, and she didn't care. To her, he was Paris, only Paris, and she would never again make the mistake of hating someone for a perceived malevolence.

"Thank you," he said again, tightening his hold on her.

"Listen, you. If I can't put myself down, you can't thank me for my stunning common sense."

One of his hands slid to her face, cupped her jaw. She'd meant to make him smile, but his expression had never been fiercer. "It's a deal."

Emotion clogged her throat, and she forced a cough. "How about I tell you something embarrassing about me, so that we're even?"

A rough, ragged, "Please."

"When I was little, I played beauty shop with my younger sister. I was the stylist and put her gorgeous honey-blond hair in a ponytail—then I hacked off the entire thing. She was the makeup artist, and painted my face with permanent markers. Our parents were horrified." A bombardment of nostalgia had her choking back a sudden sob.

Enna, Tommy from class says I have too many freckles, and that they make me ugly. Tears rolled down cheeks still baby-round.

Well, Tommy from class is stupid. You don't have half as many as me, and I'm the prettiest girl in the world. You said so.

A girlish giggle. *And I never lie!*

I miss you so much, Skye, she thought now. *I'll find you. I'll save you.*

Paris's thumb caressed the rise of her cheek. "I lost you there for a moment."

"I'm sorry."

"Don't be. I was just saying your story isn't embarrassing. It's cute. By the way, I think your wings are hot, and I'm curious to know why I never wanted to lick them when Aeron had them."

She placed her hand over his and forced herself to smile. Soon she would lose him, so she had to enjoy him while she had the chance. "Don't take this the wrong way, but I hope you get stabbed again. Like, real soon. I loved kissing you all better."

Finally, a surprised laugh barked from him. He pulled her down until her body covered his. "Baby, I'd willingly stab myself for that kind of kissing. But thankfully there's no need. I already have another owie and it needs your special doctoring skills."

CHAPTER THIRTY-ONE

BY THE TIME THEY WERE DRESSED and stepping out of their private cave into the big, bad realm where Zacharel the Chastity Belt waited, Paris had regained every bit of his strength and then some. His muscles were jacked with adrenaline, his bones fortified with steel. His steps were heavier from his increased weight, surer with his superior balance.

All because of Sienna.

"I used my energy escorting the fallen...someplace else. We'll have to walk to the doorway," Zacharel said to Sienna. His cheeks *were* a little gaunt, his bronzed skin now lacking any shine. "That is what you still prefer, yes? Before, you told me you would rather walk with Paris than fly with me, anyway, and though you will soon discover why that is unwise, it is the best I can offer at the moment."

"Yes, thank you," she replied, ever polite.

"If you're going to hang with us, make yourself useful." Paris took the lead, urged Sienna to follow him and forced the angel to take up the rear. "Guard her with your life."

A gust of wind danced around the angel, and only the angel, more chilling with every second that passed. "I plan to do so. No matter the threat against her."

An easy tone, but his expression implied Paris himself was a threat, and Zach would take him down if necessary.

Good to know.

During the trek to find Sienna, hardly any creatures had been out and about, and there'd been a small measure of light, a crimson glow from the moon. Now, there were a lot of those hungry, oozing shadows slithering in every direction, and the only light came from the occasional fiend—like the ones who'd followed Sienna, with every intention of harming her. They were staked to poles and burning alive.

Paris reached back and hooked her fingers around the waist of his pants. "Don't let go of me unless you have to fight." *I don't want her to have to fight.*

"I won't." Confident, unafraid.

That's my girl. Their little train crept through the wilderness, and, like now, some sort of campground. Tents stretched on either side of him. Sex kept his big mouth closed, and this time Paris knew beyond any doubt that the demon was sleeping off the pleasure rather than hiding.

A hiss. A snap of teeth.

Enemy.

Paris searched through the darkness, found the source just up ahead at the top of the closest tent, and leapt into action. He went low, sliding on his knees, running his blade along the trunks of the same vinelike creatures he'd encountered on the climb down that cliff. He was back on his feet a second later, watching as the remains slithered along the sides of the fabric.

No time to relax. Three more rained down. He kept his pimp hand moving, arcing, slicing, and from the grunting he heard behind him, he knew Sienna and Zacharel were doing the same.

A quick look to check on his woman—she had her gaze on his back, swiping at anything that made a play for him—proved she had no wounds, hadn't been hurt. One of the vines snapped in her direction, dripping fangs protruding from a pair of razored leaves. She was too busy protecting him to protect herself.

Paris swiped out his arm, and got a hunk of skin and muscle torn away. He sucked back a howl of pain. Okay, so now he knew what dribbled from those teeth. Acid.

"Fly her out of here," he commanded Zacharel, even as he spun, hands crisscrossing and chopping, pieces of vine flung away. He'd rather lose her that way than another, more permanent way.

"Told you. I expended the rest of my energy removing the fallen."

From the beginning, Paris had known he should off the punked-out bastard, but *noooo*. He'd sympathized with the guy's plight. Lesson learned, though. Show a softer side, and boom, you'd be punished later.

"I'm not leaving you," Sienna said while grabbing on to a stalk and hacking off the head with the crystal blade he'd given her. She was fast, but not fast enough, and soon they would be all over her. "Must have dropped the gun in the water. Sorry."

Darkness...rising... Paris dropped his daggers and went for his own crystal blade. A single mental command, and the metal elongated...becoming a torch crackling with flames. He pressed those flames against the leather walls, the material soon engulfed...and the sparks jumped to the next tent.

Shrieks blended with the blaze's crackle as he, Sienna and Zacharel raced away.

After a mile or so they slowed down and Zacharel said, "I thought you wished to remain inconspicuous."

"We needed to send a message." Thankfully, the shadow creatures got the message, too. Mess with Paris's ragtag group, and fry. They kept their distance. Only Sienna's presence prevented Paris from stomping over and doing some damage.

He wanted to hurt them, but he wanted her safe more. *You can always return for them.* True. When Sienna left him, he'd need a good fight to level him out.

Great. Now, at the thought of her leaving him, he was ticked all over again. He only began to calm a few hours later. Nothing and no one dared approach, and more than once his thoughts skipped back to what Zacharel had said.

Paris's darkness…his temper. Zacharel had implied that Paris would one day hurt Sienna. Yet, when they had been inside the cave and he'd been worked into a dark, consuming rage, he had remained totally aware of her. He hadn't let the action near her.

With the vines, same deal. He'd remained aware of her. Had sought to protect her, placing that need above the one to maim.

Good news, right? Except, what if *she* ever pricked his temper? What if all his darkness focused on her?

Oh, hell, no. That wasn't happening. Zacharel had made him paranoid, that was all. But doubts, once planted, could take on a life of their own, and Paris found himself sweating over the possibility.

Sienna affected him in a way no one else ever had. She accepted him as he was, good, bad and ugly. But if she ever betrayed him, if she ever lied to him, if she ever fought him or turned against him, he couldn't predict how he would react. Especially now that he knew the thrill of her complete surrender.

What are you doing, pondering the worst? He'd given

her a small measure of his trust. By succumbing to these fears, he would dishonor them both. He'd never minded dishonoring himself, but the thought of dishonoring *her* weighed heavily on his shoulders.

She'd taken him in her mouth, tasted all that he was, and loved his body with such shattering sweetness he would never be the same. She'd seen him at his worst. She knew his past, his future, and yet she still watched him with awe in her eyes, as if he meant something to her. He would not diminish that gift. And it *was* a gift.

A stumble over a rock propelled her into the side of his body and jerked him out of his head. He caught her with his free hand before she fell.

"Sorry, I didn't mean to space out," she muttered as she straightened. While the sex had strengthened him, it had clearly tired her.

He shouldn't have felt such pride about that, but he did. "You don't hear me complaining about having you in my arms."

Her lush, lovely grin flashed up at him. "True."

Zacharel might have rolled his eyes.

Paris gave him a mental bird before scanning the stretch of land ahead. There were miles of dark yet to travel, filled with lots of little landmines. Like the puddle he next had to jump over, then help Sienna do the same. His nose wrinkled. The water smelled like rotting corpses. Probably because…yep, he saw a pair of dull, dead eyes floating underneath.

A fly as big as his fist darted past, then another. One landed on his arm and immediately bit his biceps. He slapped the insect, meaning to fling it away from him, but he ended up smashing it, the damn thing splattering all over him.

The entire realm was a cocktail of creepy from some

of his favorite worst horror movies ever. Yeah. He dug the cheese. He also enjoyed romance novels, bench pressing buses and baking chocolate chip cookies.

He hadn't had time for that stuff in a while, and now... now he realized just how much he'd missed it. How cool would it be to throw in a DVD, kick back with Sienna beside him and watch the bloody good times roll. After that, they could curl up together and maybe read a few scenes from a romance novel.

None of that would happen, though. He and Sienna were parting as soon as they reached the exit. And what do you know. Now he wanted to kill something— simply hurting was no longer good enough—with his bare hands. Was actually praying some feral, foaming-at-the-mouth male would jump out and attack him.

This wasn't good. Meant his obsession with Sienna had reached the next level.

Paris maybe could have forced himself to let her go without much of a fuss before their time in that cavern. Now? Not likely. She was everything he'd ever wanted for himself and everything he hadn't known he needed, all rolled into one sexy little package. A warrior when she needed to be, a siren when *he* needed her to be, yet always soft and sweet and giving. And brave, so brave.

When that pink-haired punk had invaded their private space, she hadn't run. She'd stayed put. In case Paris needed her, and to keep Zacharel out of his face when things got dicey. He admired that about her. Hell, he was beginning to admire *everything* about her.

Suddenly Paris understood his man Amun in a way he never had before. Amun's woman was a former Hunter, too, and once upon a time she had helped murder their bestie Baden. Because of that, every single Lord of the Underworld had despised her and had wanted to see her guts spilled all over their fortress, Paris included, but Amun had stood his ground and defended what was his, and everyone eventually—reluctantly—climbed on board the welcome train.

Maybe, after he'd taken care of Cronus, he would do the same for Sienna—take her home and play house. Things would be difficult at first, sure. She hadn't killed anyone, but the Lords still didn't and wouldn't like her. They'd seen his cut and bruised body after her comrades had finished torturing him. They'd watched him suffer over her loss—and heard him curse himself for caring about her when she had never felt the same for him.

Until now. She'd changed her mind about him, and he'd changed his mind about her. He wasn't sure *what* had done the changing on his end, though he suspected it had more to do with simply wanting to believe in her, as he'd claimed. He wasn't even sure when the change had happened. All he knew was that she wasn't out to get him.

Accepting that once again drove home the point that his earlier fears, planted by Zacharel, were foolish.

Paris knew women, and he knew sex, and he thought he was pretty good at reading the former's emotion while engaged in the latter. More than that, he'd been with Sienna before. She might have wanted him back then, but that want had nothing on what she felt for him now. Total, all-encompassing and *real.*

He wasn't sure what had changed her mind, either, but he was glad that something had. He loved being with her. She eased him. In so many ways, she eased him. So what the hell was he supposed to do without her, while he hunted Cronus?

Who would he take to bed when the first wave of weakness hit him?

Oh…damn. The thought of being with someone else made him sick. Like, vomit blood sick. He wanted Sienna and only Sienna, and when they parted, and they would because he couldn't take her with him to hunt Cronus—too dangerous for her, considering the ambrosia in her system—he would have to take *someone*.

If he continued on this thought path, he would break down.

Maybe she sensed his turmoil. She twined her fingers with his, brought his hand to her mouth, and kissed the pulse hammering in his wrist. The world came back into focus with a whoosh.

"—did you do with that other guy, the fallen you called him?" she was saying to Zacharel. "Did he, uh, survive?"

"He lives, yes," the angel said, but offered no more.

"He'll come back for me." That kind of blame and hatred wouldn't fade. But by the time the fallen healed, Paris and Sienna would have already parted. She would be safe.

"Yes," Zacharel said. "He will."

A spike of fear added a layer of spice to the sweetness of Sienna's scent. Paris traced his thumb over her knuckles, reveling in the softness of her skin as much as in her worry for him. "He won't get the drop on me."

Suddenly a shadow at his left surged into motion, darting at Sienna with the speed of an arrow. The only color in the six-foot slash of darkness was the flash of bloodstained fangs inside its mouth.

Without missing a beat, Paris stepped in front of her, whipping out of Sienna's clasp to grasp the creature by the neck. He was surprised by the solid feel of flesh and heat. He commanded his crystal dagger to become whatever was needed to destroy a living shadow and stabbed, going deep into that mouth and feeling those fangs cut into his skin.

The dagger began to pulse with the light of the sun, bright enough to cause his eyes to tear. There was a howl of pain, a gurgle, before the writhing mass exploded into particles of mist and scattered on the breeze.

"Thank you," Sienna said on a wispy catch of breath. The roses had faded from her cheeks, making her freckles stark.

"We don't thank each other for this kind of thing, remember?" Protecting her would never be about the accolades.

Those exquisitely plump lips curled into a radiant smile he would see in his fantasies for the rest of eternity. Desire for her spun to new life.

She reached up, perhaps planning to trace a fingertip along the seam of his now aching mouth. Then Zacharel said, "May the Deity save me from such nonsense," and she dropped her arm to her side.

"I don't think your deity will have to worry about saving you," Paris snapped. "I'm pretty sure females will recognize the fact that you're not worth the effort from glance one."

The angel seemed pleased by that.

Polar opposites, Paris thought; that's what he and the angel were. Zacharel had never experienced a spark of arousal, so he had no idea what he was missing. Paris pitied the poor girl who finally gained his notice. She'd have to have balls of steel. Zach would fight her every step of the way to the bedroom, and probably even blame her for his introduction to passion.

Now that might be fun to watch.

If the circumstances had been any different, Paris might have unleashed Sex's special scent upon the angel.

More than likely even Zach would fall prey to the lush, candlelight-and-silk-sheets imagery that always consumed everyone else, and his horror at wanting Paris would amuse for centuries to come.

Sienna stiffened. As attuned to her every nuance as he was, Paris's attention whipped to her. The roses had returned to her cheeks, but they were too bright, as if she were suffering with a fever. Her eyes, now more emerald than gold, were glued ahead—on the castle that had just crested into view.

Her bond to the structure must be growing stronger, he thought.

Paris wrapped his arm around her and tugged her as close as he could get her, remaining careful of her wings. She didn't protest. In fact, she nuzzled her cheek against his neck, warm and soft and his.

He kissed her temple. "Don't worry. I won't let you go."

A sigh of relief and unmistakable gratitude. "Than— I mean, whatever."

"Good girl," he said with a grin.

Zacharel frowned at them. "Do you still mean to part?"

Paris lost his good humor, and shot the angel an I-hope-you-die-painfully glare. Now was so not the time to get into that.

"Yes," Sienna said in a tone as cold and biting as the wind buffeting against Zacharel. Then, contradicting the harsh affirmation, she rubbed a fist against her chest as though a hot poker burned there. "We're still going to part."

Indignation rose up, but Paris swallowed it back. That was the way it had to be. He knew it, had agreed to it. Shit, he'd even been the one to suggest it.

"This is good." The angel nodded his approval, the action allowing several snowflakes to catch in the satin of his hair.

"Why do you care?" Paris demanded. He still hadn't figured out the reason for Zacharel's continued presence.

A shrug of one strong shoulder. "I would not say I care. I simply know that the two of you cannot successfully sustain a relationship."

With that note of truth in his voice, it was clear the angel wholeheartedly believed what he'd said. "Our relationship isn't your business, so your opinions aren't welcome."

"Actually, the two of you were made my business."

Paris saw red. Demon-red. A volatile reaction when one was not needed, but he was helpless against it. Sheer will alone kept his hands at his sides rather than hammering into Zacharel's face. "By who?"

Wings of white and gold spread, the angel beside him one moment, then in front of him the next. Zacharel's feet floated above the ground, those wings flapping slowly, holding him steady. Paris had to grind to an abrupt stop to avoid slamming into him. Around them, snowflakes tumbled and swirled only to land and melt.

In case things got ugly, he shoved Sienna behind him. "What happened to being too weak to fly?"

"I have regained my strength."

"How?"

"The answer will not change what is about to happen."

He arched a brow, weapon at the ready. "Are you sure you want to go this route?"

"Some part of you hopes to keep her. Otherwise, you would not have reacted so violently to my observation." Before Paris could respond, he added, "Do you recall when I told you that if you continued on your current path, you would lose everything you'd come to love?"

He popped his jaw. Only the gentle caress of Sienna's hands on his back prevented him from hurling obscenities.

"I did not lie, demon. I never do. And now I think it's time I proved just how terrible an enemy I can be."

Paris blinked. Suddenly he hovered in the air, high above the castle's drawbridge, Zacharel cradling him against a hard chest honed on the battlefield. His heart pounded an unsteady beat.

"How the hell did you do that?" And where the hell was Sienna?

"With powers you cannot begin to imagine. But this is not what I wished to show you." One finger at a time, the angel loosened his grip. "I hope that you will soon learn I can help you…or destroy you."

"You better not do what I think you're going to do, you dirty piece of—"

His anchor vanished, and Paris free-fell toward the dilapidated slats of wood. He landed on the creaking boards with a hard slam and good loss of oxygen. Behind him, he heard the gargoyles screaming out their war cries, the flap of their wings, the scrape of their claws.

Zacharel had. He really had. "Son of a bitch!"

CHAPTER THIRTY-TWO

"Come. I will escort you to the exit."

Sienna gaped at Zacharel, who had just appeared in front of her. Paris and the angel had been standing in front of her, bucking up against each other, ready to throw down as testosterone charged the air, only to disappear without warning. The angel had returned the very next second. Without Paris.

"Where is he?" she demanded, though she wasn't too worried about the answer. Paris and Zacharel were friends despite their differences, and Wrath had yet to make a peep.

"I took him to the castle and dropped him on the bridge."

Reevaluation time. Paris and Zacharel were not friends on any level. Wrath, on the other hand, must think angels could do no wrong. "Why would you do that?" Sure, Paris would be carried inside and locked up. Sure, he would escape, and he would be fine. But none of that mattered to her just then. Fury rose, dark and hot and dangerous.

Calm down. Before she whipped out that crystal blade Paris had given her and went to town on angel flesh. She'd so had enough of males and their abuse of supernatural abilities.

Zacharel blinked as if the answer should be obvious

to one and all. "That, as you called it, is what one male does to another when they are arguing."

"No. No, it's not."

His lips edged down in the slightest of frowns. "That is what your Paris did to William of the Dark only this morn."

Well, she had no comeback for that, did she?

Zacharel shook out his wings, the white-and-gold feathers lifting slowly, elegantly. Snow glistened between the down. Her anger did nothing to lessen the impact of his beauty, the murky landscape somehow providing a suitable backdrop for him, dark where he was light.

No, not light, she mused. An aura of dawn radiated from him, causing him to glow.

"Well?" she prompted. "Will you take me to him?"

"Your eyes…" he said, his frown deepening.

"What about them?"

"I can see that Paris's darkness has taken root inside you already."

He spoke the words and somehow she knew they were true, the knowledge simply becoming a part of her. Paris's darkness, the one his demon had given birth to, was indeed inside her. A small twinge of worry was quickly followed by a shrug of unconcern. Wrath lived inside her. What was one more entity?

"You've ignored my first question long enough. Now I'm taking over. Listen up, and listen good. I want you to take me back to the castle."

The demand was unwise, unnecessary and counter-productive to her screw-Cronus plan, followed by her bagging and tagging of Galen, as well as her search for her sister, but that wasn't going to stop her. Paris would fight to reach her, that protective side of his demanding he witness her escape from the realm, she knew that now. If that happened, he would be harmed.

"You intended to part company in two days," he said, unwavering. "I merely sped things along."

She'd been looking forward to those two days with Paris, had wanted to make love to him again and again and brand him inside her mind, her body, until her every cell smelled like him.

"You keep reminding us that we can't be together." Suspicions tangoed with her thoughts as she crossed her arms over her chest. "Why is that?"

"Because you both need reminding." Simply stated, as if she should be ashamed for asking.

"Why?" she insisted.

"Why would you *want* to be with him?" Zacharel's dark head tilted to the side, his study of her intensifying. "Do you love him?"

Did she, when doing so would cause their break to hurt that much more? "I like him." A lot. Like, really, *really* a lot. And she respected him. Admired him. Craved him like a drug. He was witty and kind and protective and loyal, and even though he had every reason to despise her, he hadn't once treated her as if she were the enemy.

"We need you in the heavens, Sienna."

Did they, now? "Well, get in line. Lately, everyone needs me." And no one would explain the reason. She fisted her hands and propped them on her hips. "What is it you think I can do for you? Because right now, I'm having trouble taking care of myself."

"All I know is that you will herald our victory in the most gruesome war this world has ever seen."

Forget sputtering. She gaped. Her, responsible for winning a war. No pressure, though, right? She so couldn't deal with this right now.

Zacharel stiffened, glanced over one strong shoulder. "Cronus comes," he said. "He has the answers you seek, though I would not trust him were I you."

Stomach cramp. Not Cronus, not now, and not outside the castle. He would flip. Although, keeping him out of the castle would keep him away from Paris, so... "Get lost, angel boy."

At that, he quirked a brow. "I will allow you to leave with him. I don't think you will thank me afterward, however. Until we meet again, *demon girl.*"

He was gone a moment later, and what do you know, Cronus appeared a moment after that. No longer dressed as a Goth reject from hell, he now wore a gray silk suit tailor-made for his frame, all elegant lines and overflowing bank account.

Wrath stopped prowling and started slamming at her skull, very much wanting a go at him, but unable to figure out why. What he didn't do was fill her mind with images of the king's sins. Weird.

Cronus glanced left, right, and frowned. "Why are you outside the castle? For that matter, how did you *get* outside the castle?"

"Wrath took over," she said, lest he puzzle out that she had been aided by other immortals.

"Ah." Smiling, revealing his dazzling pearly whites, he extended a crimson rose in her direction. "For you."

"I, uh..." Not just stunned but completely flummoxed, she accepted the dewy bloom. "Thank you."

He inclined his head ever so slightly as he accepted her appreciation. "And that's not the only gift I come bearing. I have what you need." A clear vial filled with glittering violet liquid followed the same path as the rose. "My apologies for the tardiness in its delivery."

His apologies? Seriously? "Don't worry about it?" A question when it should have been a statement.

Cronus cleared his throat, clearly uncomfortable. "Drink."

Because she had no desire to confess that she'd already been fed, she took a small sip of what she now knew was ambrosia. What she didn't know was why she needed ambrosia, or why Paris had looked ill when he'd handed her that flask.

Cool coconut flowed down her throat, sprouted wings and flew through her entire body. And wow, it packed a powerful punch. Both strength and weakness blazed through her, cannibalizing off each other and leaving her in a fog.

"That's a good slave girl," he mumbled.

I love being patronized, I really do. "Why are you being so nice to me?" she asked, swaying as she returned the vial to him.

He waved his hand and the glass disappeared. "I must show you something," he said, and with another wave of his hand, her surroundings fell away. From warm to cold, dark to light.

From salvation to damnation.

CHAPTER THIRTY-THREE

SUDDENLY SIENNA WAS STANDING inside an unfamiliar chamber with white walls that stretched so high she could barely discern the domed ceiling above. Portraits hung everywhere. There was no furniture, just marble columns that boasted the occasional string of ivy, and stands that held sculptures and other crafted artifacts.

To stop herself from screaming from the mental calamity of the location switch, she bit her tongue until she tasted blood.

"This," Cronus said, splaying his arms and slowly pivoting, "is the Chamber of Futures." There was a reverent quality to his voice, one she'd never before heard from him. "Here, destiny takes shape and endless possibilities await, for this is where my All-Seeing Eye records her visions."

"All-Seeing Eye?" She was still so disoriented that it was nearly impossible to get the words out.

"A female who sees into heaven and hell, time and space, present, past and future." Every syllable held a new layer of urgency. "When one dies, another takes her place. Over the centuries, many have served me. There are no limits to how far back or how far forward these women can view. No limits to how high or low their scope."

To have such a power would be both a blessing and a curse, she thought.

"Everything you see here was created by my Eyes."

Sienna tucked the rose behind her ear, forgetting about his weird mood as she tripped her way to the nearest portrait. In it, an older, frailer version of Cronus stared back at her. He had gray hair, wrinkled skin, and wore a long white robe. This was the god she'd first met. Only this one was dirty, bruised and trapped in a cage.

"I have learned that everyone has several different futures, and the choices they make ultimately decide which road they will travel. Come," he added without a breath, taking her by the forearm and ushering her through the long, seemingly endless expanse of the room. "There is something you must see."

With every step she took, the portraits rearranged themselves, gliding over the wall, changing places with fluid grace. She didn't try to pull away from him. Dizziness held her in thrall, and she needed the anchor of his hand to keep her upright.

"These Eyes, they do not always understand what they see, for they cannot determine the context of the actions they record. They do not know if they see past or future, how to stop something or how to make it come to pass."

"And so you have to guess," she finished for him.

"Correct." He stopped, and so did the movement of the portraits.

In the frame now in front of her, warriors fought to the death in every direction. Not just any warriors, but familiar faces. There was Galen, his white wings outstretched, his long, bloody sword raised. Before him was Cronus, with a thin line of blood connecting one ear to another—his head about to slide from his neck.

Sienna's heartbeat quickened as she took in the rest. There was Paris, off to the side, watching what happened to Cronus with wide, shocked eyes. Blood caked him. His mouth was open, as if he were shouting something.

"This is one of the futures that await me," the king said. "Long ago, my first Eye warned me that a warrior with wings of white would someday slay me. I assumed it would be an angel, only to later realize there were other warriors, like the Lords of the Underworld, who were equally capable of doing so. And then my newest Eye painted this."

"Why didn't you kill all the Lords, then?" Sienna asked. She knew he'd already considered that route. A being like him wouldn't have been able to help himself. "Just to be safe."

He moved two steps forward. Again the pictures danced into new locations. "The reason is here." He stopped, as did the pictures. "Look."

Frowning, Sienna obeyed. In this one, a young Cronus sat on a throne of solid gold, the Lords of the Underworld lined up behind him, expressions reverent and stances determined. They were clearly protecting him, guarding him with their very lives. So badly she wanted to reach out and trace her fingertips over Paris's lips. How beautiful he was. How strong.

"This is my real future," Cronus said. "Or rather, the one possibility I must ensure comes to pass."

"How?"

"The answer lies in the two warriors missing from this army."

She gulped, studied every face. "Galen is missing. And...no one else."

"Do you see the keeper of Wrath?"

"Of course. Aeron is right—"

"I do not speak of Aeron. He is no longer the demon's keeper."

"Me?" she squeaked.

"Yes. You are the key to this future, Sienna."

Disbelief thrummed through her. "I don't understand." The angel had mentioned she would get her answers— and that she shouldn't trust what she heard. Seemed like an eternity had passed since he'd issued the warning. She wasn't sure what to believe, what to discard. "How am I the key?"

"Look closely at the bottom."

She leaned over, gaze homing in on the portrait's lower edge. Surrounded by a crowd of onlookers was a woman. Her profile was to Sienna, her skin freckled, her nose and cheeks and chin— Her eyes widened. Hers. Those features were hers. The woman's hair was brown and wavy, just like hers, and black wings stretched from her robe. She stood beside a kneeling man who had his arms wrapped around her calves, holding on as if she were precious to him.

Galen, Sienna realized. He wasn't missing from the painting after all.

"All those centuries ago, when my Eye spoke of my death, she also told me there was a way to save myself… or, to be precise, a woman who could help me do so. I looked for this woman around every corner. She never appeared, and I despaired."

What came next was going to hurt, Sienna thought, straightening. Didn't take a genius to figure that out.

"Eons passed, and I was imprisoned when the worthless Greeks conspired with my wife, whom they later betrayed. I knew I would escape, for that, too, had been foretold, though the Greeks were too foolish to believe. When I at last reclaimed my rightful place on the heavenly throne, I sought out the Lords, thinking to destroy them before they could destroy me."

He paused, sighed. "But newly returned to power as I was, I did not like the idea of killing the Lords and freeing their demons, thereby having more enemies knocking at my door. More than that, I *liked* the idea of controlling Zeus's warriors, of using the beings he created as my own personal errand boys as I searched for the one among them with the power to kill me.

"And oh, has that decision paid off. I have kept a close eye on their comings and goings and indeed, the Lords have proven surprisingly useful to me. That is why I know that the future you see before you in this painting, of me reigning in harmony with these warriors as my stalwart army, is already coming to pass.

"But still there is the matter of my predicted execution—and my predicted rescuer. Just when I had given up hope, you at last appeared, a woman who belonged to neither side of the war and yet also belonged to both sides. A woman who pledged her allegiance to Galen but whose interest had unmistakably been captured by Paris. A woman who had the power even in death to influence a warrior's every thought and action."

She could only shake her head.

"Oh, yes. He's thought of you, only you, and that's what brought you to my attention. I had never before noticed a human soul, but I had to know why he craved yours so very much. That's when I discovered you were the one the Eye had foreseen. You look like the woman in the painting, and you have the same past as the woman I was told would save me. Both of those revelations can mean only one thing. You are to be my salvation."

"I don't care about your salvation," she whispered.

"I know. But you care about Paris's, and if Galen dies, so does he." He waved his hand and another portrait appeared. In this one, Galen, Paris and a few other Lords lay in pieces on a blood-soaked floor. Her heart sank at the sight.

"And so we are back to your role as savior—mine, Paris's, in the end it makes no difference, as either path leads you to Galen. You should thank me," he went on. "I gave you Wrath. Made you strong enough to survive whatever the keeper of Hope chooses to do with you." His gaze pierced her, a swirling black that increased the intensity of her dizziness. "Galen adores power, and you are to be his mate."

"No." A gasp, a plea.

Merciless, he continued. "Because of your demon, you will know those who lie to him, who befriend him when they truly hate him, and you will stop them before they are able to harm him."

First sleep with him, and now protect him? "No! I hate him."

"I did not say you had to love him to carry out your task. Merely think of the alternative if you do not carry it out. Paris dies."

No. No, no, no. "What happened to learning Galen's secrets and betraying him?" Fury sparked to life. "What happened to finding my sister? And why would you want me to stop others from harming him if he's the man destined to kill you?"

Red flashed within the black of his eyes, scarlet pools of his own fury. "Let us say that I have my reasons, and my plans. So listen and listen well. There are but a few possible futures for me and thus, the world. The first is that I reign as king for eternity. The second, I am killed, which means my wife is killed. If we are both lost, *chaos* will become king and the Lords will die." He twirled his finger and the portraits began their dance anew.

A new frame stopped beside her and she looked it

over, her mouth going dry. Angels, so many angels, bloody tears raining down wings of white and gold. Men and women wearing togas fought each angelic warrior savagely.

And there on the ground at their feet were the Lords, bloody, broken…lifeless. She wanted to cry, to collapse.

"To answer your other question," Cronus continued, "I do wish to know Galen's secrets. I do wish for you to betray him. For this to occur, I need you to protect him, as well. As I said, I have my reasons and my plans, and by rights I should punish you for daring to question their logic."

All she could think about was Paris's death. Paris, dying. Paris, dead. Paris, gone forever.

Cronus added, "Before you think that my faithless wife had the right idea when she conspired to lock me away, before you think to put in place any plot that would result in finding a way for my wife alone to reign—" his voice went low, harsh "—know that if Rhea rules, your sister's killer will control the fate of your world."

Her head spun with even more disbelief, fury and dread. Cronus had just said…had just claimed… "But you told me she was alive," Sienna croaked.

"She was."

Was. Not "is." *Was.* "And now?" Another croak.

Wrath chose that moment to get his slam on, and this time, he snarled. *Something is wrong. I don't like this.*

His voice jolted her. He'd spoken to her before, of course, but usually he limited himself to words like *punish, kill, heaven* and *hell.*

Is he lying? As Zacharel had implied. *Please, tell me he's lying.*

I don't know. I don't know anything right now.

A whimper slipped from her.

"I have done my research. Skye became a Hunter," Cronus said. "Perhaps for the same reason you did—to right the wrong of her abduction. You could have met her, talked to her, and never have known it, for she was a child when you saw her last. Nor would she have known you. She eventually got out, but she was married to a Hunter. She was trying to get him out, as well. She… died with him."

"No." This was too much to take in. She couldn't process it all.

"And when Rhea learned that you, my winged savior, were searching for the girl, she had her…" His gaze skittered away. "Rhea had her killed."

Wrath released another snarl. *Something is wrong.*

"You're lying. You have to be lying." Sienna's knees shook and she barely managed to remain upright. That she could have been so close to Skye and not even realized it…that now she would never have another chance… "Prove it. Prove she's…that she's…gone." A lump of grief congealed in her throat. Her eyes burned, tears bubbling at the backs.

"Very well."

The air in front of her shimmered, crystallized, and then, as if she were looking through a magical peephole, she saw a bedroom, a black-haired girl sprawled on the floor, her throat slit, her body resting beside a man who'd clearly met a similar fate. A lake of crimson pooled around them, thick and black at the edges.

Sienna fought down her instinctive revulsion—how many gruesome images of those she cared for would she be forced to endure this day?—and pushed herself to think back. To the best of her recollection, she had not interacted with this girl during her time with the Hunters, but then, there were hundreds, if not thousands, of

Hunter compounds and cells, and she'd never had access to the database of members.

"That's not her," she said with a violent shake of her head. "My Skye had blond hair."

"So does this girl. You know the black is not her natural color. Her lashes prove this."

Sienna made herself look closer. Long brown lashes framed dulled brown eyes.

Enna, when you grow up and get married, will you still love me? Brown lashes fluttering innocently as Skye awaited her answer.

I'll always love you more than anything or anyone.

"No." Plump lips, soft and pink, and as big as Sienna's. A delicate bone structure, a stubborn chin. "No." Acid created a toxin of rage and sorrow in her stomach.

"Yes. When I...found her like this, I scoured her mind, her memories. This is your Skye."

"No!"

Her sister...lying on the floor. Ruined. Dead. Gone forever, like Paris would be. No longer a little girl, but a woman. Gone...forever... The words echoed in her mind, horrifying and shocking and sickening. Gone...

Is that truly her? she asked Wrath.

Yes. I can see her life, and you in it, but I cannot see her death. Why can't I see her death?

Sienna locked on the affirmation, nothing else registering. Skye was...was...dead. Dead. Her precious Skye was dead. "Bring her back." She pushed through the shimmering air and fisted Cronus's lapels, shaking him. "Bring her back the same way you brought me back."

"It is not always so simple, even for me." Guilt, so much guilt in his tone, all over his features, radiating from him.

Wrong, so wrong.

Enough with the babbling! "You're the self-proclaimed king of the gods." She shook Cronus all the harder. "Ruler of the Titans. Jailer of the Greeks. Leader of the Lords of the Underworld. What's one little soul compared to all that? Bring. Her. Back."

"There are laws of life and death even I must obey."

"Her soul—"

"Is no longer savable."

"I don't believe you."

"That doesn't change the circumstances."

"Bastard!" Her palm darted out of its own volition, slapping his cheek so sharply she would not have been surprised to find she'd peeled away his skin. "You lied to me. Said she was Galen's prisoner."

When he failed to retaliate, or block himself from further abuse, she struck again.

"You lied!"

"To ensure you obeyed me and kept Galen under control, I did what I felt I had to do," he at last admitted. "I knew you would not kill him if you thought only he knew where your sister was. And as I said, I have my reasons for wanting him protected for now. But no, Galen never imprisoned her. She never had a child with him."

Another slap, this one so hard she thought she fractured her own bones. Still he accepted the abuse without comment. "Her death could be another of your lies. Anything to jerk my chains, right?"

Wrong, so wrong, but she is dead. She is dead.

A blink and Sienna was standing in the very room Cronus had shown her. The woman's body, motionless at her feet. She could smell the coppery tang of blood and death. And here, in this chamber of fatality, there was no missing the resemblance to her mother.

To *their* mother.

Wrath released another snarl, another and another, something "wrong" continuing to prod at him. But he didn't know what the problem was, and Sienna didn't have the strength to reason things out with him. Grief slammed through her hard, knocking the breath out of her lungs. Breath she couldn't steal back, no matter how hard she tried. The fog thickened in her mind. Razors dipped in flames razed her chest, burning her up.

Her surroundings faded as she waded in and gathered the girl to her chest, clutching her close, letting her heart beat for both of them. The tears finally cascaded, falling, falling, a never-ending river of pain.

"I will return you to the castle," Cronus said, voice as gentle as if he were speaking to a babe, "and I will give you time to come to terms with what has happened. Your memories will no longer haunt you, and you will be able to leave the realm, should you wish it. In this, you have my word. But I will come back for you, Sienna, wherever you are, and I will expect you to aid my cause. And now…now that you've seen what my wife, Galen's ruler, is capable of, I think you'll want to, yes?"

CHAPTER THIRTY-FOUR

THE LORDS OF THE UNDERWORLD were here, on the island in Rome, and nearing the Temple of the Unspoken Ones at that very moment.

They would have a plan of attack, Galen thought. The most likely: all but one warrior would surround him, staying hidden in the shadows, and that one would approach him to speak to him. Unless, of course, they *all* thought to hide, shooting him full of arrows and bullets now and asking their questions later.

Wouldn't matter either way. The warriors must know they were walking into a trap. That Galen would not have set the meeting here if he could not use the Unspoken Ones to his benefit.

Once the Lords reached the threshold of the temple, the Unspoken Ones would have them, would whisk them here into their inner sanctum, as one, right in front of Galen, and lock them in place with invisible bindings, allowing him to do his thing.

However, Galen didn't want to go that route. It was too time-consuming, with too much risk. Not to his life, but to theirs. If he killed one of the Lords, none would ever complete the trade he'd demanded. All he wanted right now was Legion.

His hands fisted. If the warriors had failed to bring her, he would honor his word for once in his life. As he had told Lucien, he would take another loved one from the Lords, and another and another—until they broke down. He would not kill, but he would harm.

Every day Galen's need for Legion worsened. Hope had built up dreams of having her, of punishing her, of taming her…of *owning* her. Jealousy had tossed fuel on an already smoldering fire of resentment as he wondered where she was and what she was doing.

A rustle behind him had him tensing.

He whipped around. Standing between fat white pillars were all five of the Unspoken Ones. The furred one with a headful of hissing snakes in place of hair. The scarred one, with more muscles than three roided-up boxers fused together. The female, with the face of an ugly bird and horns lining the length of her spine. Lastly, the tallest two—one with shadows seeping from his skullet, and the other with blades that dripped poison spiking from the crown of his head.

Each creature was bound by chains they couldn't break. And yet, the tenuous bonds mattered only as long as Cronus lived. The moment he kicked it, these beings would be loosed upon an unsuspecting world. No one, not even Galen, would be able to stop the destruction they would undoubtedly mete out.

On an altar in front of them lay Ashlyn, pale and panting, sweating, like a virginal sacrifice of old. Only this virgin was heavily pregnant and about to give birth. The fright he'd given her had caused her to go into labor.

Oddly enough, Galen didn't like that she was in pain. She wasn't a bad sort, and hurting the fairer sex had never been a particular favorite of his. He'd do it, *had* done it—he'd do anything—but he never enjoyed it.

"Cut the babes from her belly," the horned, beaked she-devil commanded him. "I would have them for my own."

Babes? As in more than one?

"They must die," the scarred male snapped.

"No. We will use them as barter," one of the mountains of muscle said.

Ashlyn moaned in pain, in supplication, her glassy gaze pleading as she looked to Galen. "Please. Don't do this."

Begging the enemy. To do so, she must love those babies with her whole heart, even though she had yet to meet them. He thought he understood that. Nearly twenty-nine years ago, he'd inadvertently fathered a daughter; he had not learned of her existence until she was fully grown. Knowing she was of his blood had been all that was needed for him to…not love her, he didn't think he'd ever experienced that emotion, but to feel a sort of kinship with her despite the fact that she was as different from him as he was from the Lords.

His Gwendolyn. A Harpy. A female he could not bring himself to hurt. A female who would cut him down without a moment's hesitation. He liked that about her, felt pride in her ruthlessness.

Galen had done terrible things throughout his life. Betrayed his friends, killed for power, razed cities, purposely addicted his own people to drugs so that they would need him, follow him. He had destroyed their families when they dared to disobey him—or even so much as *thought* to betray him. He'd slept with females he shouldn't have, in ways he shouldn't have.

There was no line he hadn't crossed. No line he *wouldn't* cross. He had done all of that—and would do a thousand times worse—yet he had never cared about the consequences. Still didn't. Unlike the warriors he'd been created with, he hadn't come with a sense of honor, a bond of brotherhood or a need to help anyone but himself.

Baden, the first to be created, had gotten most of the goodness and the rest a mere trickle. Galen, the very last to be created, had gotten what remained—nothing but the cold and the dark.

Perhaps that was why he had gone after Baden first.

None of the Lords knew he had spoken with Baden before he'd sent his Bait to lure the man to his death. A private meeting Baden himself had arranged. None of them knew Galen had vowed to leave the immortal army alone, to stop the war, if Baden sacrificed himself.

Possessed by the demon of Distrust, Baden had not believed Galen's vow, but he'd made the bargain anyway, just in case. Galen knew it was because he'd blamed his demon for his instinct to mistrust, and hoped for the best—because of Galen's demon.

The Bait—Haidee, one of the keepers of Hate—had gone to the warrior, unaware that her victim knew where she would lead him. Baden had not wanted his friends to know he willingly rushed to his grave. He had not wanted them to witness the event, either, but of course they had followed him. There had been no stopping the war after that, even if Galen had wanted to. Which, of course, he hadn't.

"Gaaaaaleeeen." A low, pained moan echoed as Ashlyn writhed atop the stone. Her face was red, swelling, her breaths coming in shorter puffs.

"Don't look to me for aid, female." The next half hour was mission critical, and he could not allow her to distract him. "I told your man what he must do to save you."

"Please. Pleeeease."

A pang in his chest. If he told her the only way to ensure he would give the babies to their father was for her to crawl to him, she would find the strength to do so. She'd even kiss and lick his boots. She would do anything and everything he asked, no matter how vile.

Oh, yes, she loved her children. They were flesh of her flesh, blood of her blood, and they would love her in return.

Nothing and no one had ever belonged to him and only him—except Legion. Not that she would do anything necessary to save him, nor would he do anything necessary to save her. But. Yeah, there was always a but with him. He had been her first lover—and he wanted to be her last.

He wasn't sure what had happened to her during her forced stay in hell. Didn't know what she had welcomed, and what she hadn't. But she would no longer be his alone, that much he knew. Something else to punish her—to punish all of them—for.

"The babes," the female Unspoken said again. Was that…yearning he detected in her voice? Did she actually crave a chance at motherhood? "Give. Me."

The males turned on her, scowling, tossing obscenities, arguing over what should be done versus foolish desires. Whatever happened to the mother, Galen decided in that moment, he would not allow the Unspoken Ones to have or hurt those children.

Finally, a decent act on his part. One of goodness, without guile or selfishness. Never let it be said he was all bad all the time.

"G-Galen. I am h-here, as requested."

Every muscle in his body went taut, his blood instantly firing, blistering through him. A hallucination? He sniffed, taking in the earth, a hint of hellfire and the subtlest trace of sea salt. No hallucination.

Legion was here.

The wealth and variance of emotion he felt nearly overwhelmed him as he spun to search her out. And there she was, a few feet away. She stood at the edge of the temple grounds, trees stretched out behind her. She was lovely, though not exactly as he remembered. Tall, buxom, with a fall of pale hair and eyes of the smoothest brown. Her lips were chapped, as if she'd been chewing them, and she'd lost so much weight her T-shirt and sweatpants bagged on her.

The Lords hadn't taken proper care of her. For that, they would suffer more than he'd originally planned. She was to be punished, yes, but by his hand and only his hand. Anger became the front-runner inside him.

"Are you armed?" he asked, not expecting the truth.

"I—" Her hand fluttered to her throat, and her gaze skittered past him, widened. "Ashlyn." She raced forward, only to jolt backward when he stepped in her path, her desperation to avoid him palpable.

"You will stay where you are."

"L-let her g-go." The stutter told him more than her words. She was afraid of him. "You said y-you would."

"Legion, gooooo!" Ashlyn screamed, speaking through a contraction. "Tell Maddox—"

"Silence!" Galen snarled. He would accept no interference in this matter.

Legion grabbed her stomach, her skin taking on a greenish tint. Her chin trembled.

This fear of hers scraped at his nerves. Before, she had been brave and full of the fire she had been raised in.

"The warriors are almost upon us," one of the Unspoken said. "We will whisk them here the very moment we can. Now, give the females into our care, so that you may fight without distraction."

That had been their plan, and one he'd pretended

to agree with. Then and now, the thought of allowing anyone to touch his woman grated. And when he noticed Legion's reaction to the idea—a cold wash of horror in eyes glassy with unshed tears—he was decided.

"Back away," he told her. "Stand in the rubble at the edge of the trees. And if you so much as think about flashing away or running, I'll hurt the human."

The tears finally fell, but she did as commanded. He hated the increased distance between them, and blamed the Unspoken Ones.

"What are you doing?" one growled.

"Give them to us," another shrieked.

They had only one weakness that he knew of. They could not take what they wanted; it had to be given to them. Usually they used trickery to ascertain free will, as they had done to obtain the Cloak of Invisibility from Strider. When trickery failed, they resorted to scaring their victims into submission.

They would learn. Galen feared nothing.

"Don't move from that spot, no matter what happens," he told Legion, peering at her until she nodded to acknowledge she had heard him.

Then she gulped, raised her chin. "But only if...only if you give Ashlyn and the babies back to Maddox. Alive."

Of course, the Unspoken Ones reacted first.

"No!"

"Never!"

"She will leave you the moment you comply!"

"Do not be a fool!"

Legion glanced behind him. The greenish tint returned to her skin, and damn if she didn't look ready to scream.

"Eyes on me," he snapped, and she immediately submitted. Such lovely eyes. Rich and dark and boundless, even with their cascade of tears. "Do not look away from me."

A tremor in response.

He backed up until he stood beside Ashlyn, then twisted and bent, sliding his arms underneath her, picking her up. She was heavy, her muscles knotted from strain. Legion maintained the connection between them.

The Unspoken Ones demanded to know what he thought he was doing. He ignored them, carrying the girl to Legion's side.

"We gave you the Cloak, Hope. You owe us the females."

Had they meant to keep the humans as their due, then? He laughed with just a bit of humor. Probably. Something he would have done, as well, so he couldn't really blame them.

Wait. Yes, he decided. He could.

"Should you betray us now, we will hunt you. We will destroy you in the old way." The female let loose a cackling laugh. "Do you have any idea of the awfulness that entails?"

He ignored her, saying to Legion, "Vow to me here and now that you will not try to escape me, that you will go with me willingly and do everything I tell you, when I tell you to do it. A blood vow." One she would not be able to break, even if she wanted to.

For immortals, keeping blood vows became a compulsion.

Another tremor shook her. Those liquid eyes with their spiky lashes roved over him, causing his cock to fill and harden. He would have her. Tonight. "I w-will, but only if you vow to give Ashlyn and the babies back to Maddox, without hurting her. Or them. Today. And without fighting the Lords."

The girl had learned to bargain, to cover all the bases. A complication, but not anything that would stand in his way.

Galen placed the still panting, pregnant female on the ground as gently as he was able. She was in too much pain to notice or speak. As he straightened, he removed one of his daggers.

Legion shrank away.

That fear would have to be dealt with. He wanted his firecracker back. The one who had seduced him at the bar, screwed him in the bathroom. Bitten and poisoned him before he could finish.

Speaking of, she owed him an orgasm. And so many weeks had passed, she now owed him more than one. Interest was a bitch. But first, ensuring her cooperation. "In exchange for what I have asked you to promise, I vow to you here and now, this day, that I will give the female Ashlyn and her offspring back to her male Maddox, and I will hurt none of them. I will fight not with his friends, but give her and the babes over, unharmed by my hand or any other, and go on my way." He pressed the tip of the blade into his palm and cut so deeply he hit bone.

Blood welled. He smeared crimson on both sides of the blade, making sure to saturate the tip. Then he offered the weapon to Legion, hilt first. Part of him expected her to take it and slash at him, but no. She knew she was beaten, merely watched him, undecided about her next move. Cooperation was her only option. Unlike Lucien, she did not have the power to flash others alongside her, so she couldn't spirit Ashlyn to safety.

"Hurry." Any moment now, the Lords would arrive and it would be too late to walk away with what he wanted. He couldn't fight the Lords *and* watch Legion. And he couldn't run with her, avoiding battle, because she could flash away from him any time she wished. He needed her vow. "Before I change my mind." As if he would ever change his mind.

With a trembling hand, she accepted the blade. Nervously she licked her lips.

He waited, on edge.

Finally, he heard the words he craved. "In exchange for what you have already promised, I vow to you here and now, this day, to willingly accompany you to wherever you wish." Those glitter-ripe tears continued to rain down her cheeks. "I will do w-whatever you ask. And stay as l-long as you demand my presence."

She pressed the blade's tip into her palm and cut. Not as deeply as he had, but enough to ensure a successful exchange. Her blood welled, mingling with the droplets he'd left behind. He liked that, liked knowing some part of him was now inside her.

He reached out, clasped her hand against his, her wound against his. At the moment of contact, he felt a *pop* inside him, a tear on his soul, and though he'd never done anything like this before, he knew the vow had just made a place for itself inside him. Judging by her grimace, hers had just done the same.

At last, she belonged to him.

Legion flinched.

Had he said the words aloud? Or perhaps she, too, had snapped back to reality as the Unspoken Ones hissed and cursed and threatened behind him. Galen cupped her cheek with his uninjured hand, his thumb caressing the rise of satin-covered bone. She trembled, but didn't pull away.

He rattled off the coordinates to his home. "Leave now, make no other stops, talk to no one, and I will give the girl and her babies to her man as promised." And the Unspoken Ones could not stop her as they could the Lords. Well, all the Lords save the ever-annoying Lucien. "Hurry, I am almost too late."

She gulped, jerked from his clasp. He mourned the loss. Wanted to roar as she vanished before his eyes. *She goes to your home. You will be with her again.*

He had only to take care of two tasks. Ashlyn, and the Unspoken. They could lure anyone, him included, with their gazes, cast illusions and hypnotize. And they liked to do so; they also liked to play with their prey. Something they didn't need a willing spirit to do.

He knew, because he'd fed them some of his own men. The ones he'd disliked, the ones who hurt the innocent. Ironic, yes, considering all the things he himself had done, but also another of his very good deeds. He did them upon occasion, if for no other reason than to amuse himself.

Soon the Lords would be too close for him to divert. As promised, he couldn't, wouldn't, fight them, but the Unspoken Ones *could.* If he allowed that to happen, the Unspoken would forgive him for his unwillingness to share the females. Except, Ashlyn could be hurt during the battle, which meant Galen could not allow it. Soooo, he couldn't take care of the Lords or the Unspoken this day. Both would have to be dealt with later.

Keeping his gaze trained on the ground, he approached the pillars. Heard chains rattle. Stealthily he dug the Cloak from his back pocket and unfolded the material. The creatures tracked him, even as they hissed at him; he felt the heat of their gazes.

Acting quickly, he flared his wings and the Cloak at the same time. His feet lifted off the ground, and he spun…spun…letting invisibility overtake him as the razor-sharp edges of his wings sliced into the Unspoken closest to him while the Cloak extended like a tentacle and wrapped around the neck of the farthest, crushing his windpipe.

The first lost his insides, and hunched over with a howl of pain. The second couldn't breathe and collapsed, unconscious.

Galen was on the next two a split second later, a tsunami of movement, twisting, diving, cutting and doing a little more of that crushing. They couldn't see him, couldn't fight him, and oh, he had fun.

Less than a minute after his initial attack, all five were on the ground. The Cloak sagged in Galen's grip as he planted his feet on the ground, his body coming back into view.

"Shouldn't have taught me how to use the Cloak properly," he *tsk*ed.

He bent down and scooped Ashlyn into his arms. Sweat soaked her, her cheeks were puffed from the strain, and she clutched her stomach as she wheezed. Without the Cloak, he couldn't flash her, and with it, her man would not sense her. That left Galen with only one option. He stalked away from the temple without any explanation. Tree branches reached out, slapping at him. Twigs snapped under his boots.

"You. Will. Die," he heard one of the injured choke.

"That is *our* vow to you," another panted.

"Your screams will echo into eternity."

Ignoring them, again, he picked up his pace. After this, they might opt to aid the Lords. No matter, though. They were stuck here, so what could they really do to him, even with immortal help?

"Cry out for your man, Ashlyn."

That fall of honey hair remained plastered to her scalp as she shook her head wildly. A moment passed. She cringed and covered her ears with her hands, an action he understood. Wherever she stood, she could hear every conversation that had taken place there.

Using the arm wrapped under her shoulders, he angled his wrist to tug one of her hands away. "You heard my vow to Legion. I cannot hurt you or your man today. Call for him. Bring him to you."

Perhaps she meant to deny him a second time, but she opened her mouth and a scream of pain was unleashed. Birds flew from the tops of trees. Insects ceased mid-song. Animals of the four-legged variety raced for cover.

He could have set her down and left her there, but he didn't. Whatever the Lords had planned to do to him, they changed their minds when they heard that scream and came running. He heard the thunder of their footsteps and ground to a halt, waiting. A few seconds later, they ruptured the thick green foliage, becoming a half circle of menace around him.

They were closer than I realized, he thought. Interesting. They might have won this round, after all.

Maddox cared not for his own safety. "Give her to me." He sprinted the rest of the distance, and with a tenderness belying his savage expression, he took his woman into his arms. "Oh, my love. I am so sorry. So sorry."

Another pang ripped through Galen's chest.

She moaned. "Hurts."

"I know, darling, I know. Lucien," the warrior growled as his narrowed gaze landed on Galen. "Flash her out of here. Now. She's in labor."

"Maddox," she panted. "Don't want...to leave...you."

"Shh, love. Shh. We'll get you help. Let Lucien take you. Then he'll come back for me. He can't take the two of us at once, but I'll only be moments behind you."

"Promise?"

"Promise."

"If something happens and I can't get back to you—" Lucien began.

"What?" Ashlyn screeched. "Why wouldn't you be able to get back?"

Maddox gave the scarred warrior a hard look.

"Remember what Danika said to us." Lucien gently took the still protesting Ashlyn from Maddox's arms. "We won't be at the fortress."

Maddox maintained contact for as long as possible. When the keeper of Death and the pregnant female disappeared, he straightened to his full height and once again met Galen's stare.

Galen wasn't sure why he stayed, even then. Each warrior had weapons, and all of those weapons were trained on him. Guns, blades, a crossbow. His own daughter, Gwen, was the holder of the bow, an arrow notched and at the ready.

Ah, now he knew why he'd stayed. Deep down he'd known she would come, and he'd wanted her to see what he'd done. See one of his rare good deeds. And maybe... maybe even decide to like him.

"Why did you give her back?" Maddox demanded. Despite the fact that his woman had been returned healthy and whole, he reeked of rage.

"Why else? I now have what I wanted from you."

The warrior's brows lowered, surprise a slash of crimson in his eyes. "You have Legion?"

So. They hadn't brought her. She had come to him on her own. Another interesting tidbit—and enough to ripen every thread of possessiveness inside him. "She is mine, yes."

"How?"

He grinned slowly with glee. "How do you think?"

A flash of bone and scales under Maddox's face, his demon rising to the surface. "There's something you should know about Legion."

"And that is?" He knew what would happen next, knew exactly what the warriors planned to do. Knew it would hurt like a son of a bitch. He could have covered himself with the Cloak, could have flashed away. Instead, he stood there, his grin widening.

"You're not going back to her." Maddox raised a Glock, as Galen had known he would, and fired, nailing Galen in the chest.

On the heels of the bullet, blades sliced into his stomach, an arrow right into his heart. He met his daughter's gaze as he fell to his knees, reached back and at last grabbed the Cloak. "Now we're even," he told her, voice faint as he shielded himself from view.

CHAPTER THIRTY-FIVE

WILLIAM WATCHED AS PARIS was carted closer and closer to him by those horny, humping gargoyle fiends, amused as ever-loving hell. In fact, he nearly busted a gut laughing. Yeah, he knew taunting the new and improved Paris 2.0 was borderline idiotic, and that the warrior would come gunning for him in the next few minutes, but like William could really pretend to be sad about this, so, *bring it.*

"Dude," he said. "You've already got several money shots wetting your chest. Classic!"

Sex didn't say a word. Just gave William the finger and held steady, emotion seething in his eyes. Emotion in the form of badass shadows, yeah, but that failed to lessen William's amusement.

Paris was clearly planning to murder someone other than William before the day finished ticking out, because, also clearly, more was going on here than simple humiliation. And William suspected that someone would be…the suspiciously missing Sienna? Nah. She was already dead. Zacharel? Had that pisser come back for more? William really hoped so. Hoped Paris gave it to the winger but good.

William didn't have a good history with the skybound, and though they didn't seem to recognize his too lovely mask of a face, they'd jump him like a pack of rabid dogs if he revealed his *true* form.

Not that he ever would. Anyways. It was best not to go there, even mentally. Mind readers abounded in this realm.

Just as Paris disappeared around the corner, a grave and desperate Lucien materialized right in front of William, a screaming, panting Ashlyn clutched in his arms.

The words exiting her bleeding lips were things only back-alley whores and junkies in need of a fix would say. And maybe Lucifer, the self-proclaimed king of the underworld.

"Bad day?" Never had William heard the gentle beauty utter such filthy, vile things. And really, she'd never looked prettier to him. Rock on.

"Danika told us she needed to have the babies wherever you were shacking up," the keeper of Death said without preamble. Lines of tension branched from his eyes like little rivers of poison. "Following your spirit trail was not easy or fun, especially since my warriors have need of me. Show me to a bed now."

"Are you sure she said where *I* am?" William thumped his chest just to be sure.

"Bed. Now."

"Now!" Ashlyn yelled. "They're coming now. Please, please. Or I'm going to tell Maddox you tried to feel me up!"

"*So* cruel. He vowed to remove the best part of my anatomy if I so much as breathed in your direction." Despite his cavalier tone, William moved quickly as he led the pair up the stairs, down the hall and into the bedroom he'd cleaned for himself, intending to free the trapped female immortal and spend a few days getting to know her body in every twisted position he favored. So far, no luck.

Lucien laid Ashlyn down, careful, so careful. "I'll get Maddox now."

"Thank you. *Ohhhhhh, Gooooood.*" She squeezed Lucien's hand, and William heard the bones crack. When she came down from the pain an eternity later, she released the now-pale warrior. "Maddox. Now. Or I'm going to rip your face off and…and… *Ohhhhhh!*" The last was an evil screech better suited to a banshee from hell's darkest corridors.

"And tell Maddox he felt you up with it?" William said, always willing to help out.

"I'll be back in just a few. Take care of her." Lucien disappeared, his "or else" unsaid but no less evident.

"Well, hell," William breathed, scrubbing a hand down his face. Alone with the pregnant Bride of Chucky, as well as the Seed of Chucky. And he was supposed to do some good? Yeah. That was so not happening. Best he could do was stay right where he was and not vomit blood.

One by one, Lucien flashed the other warriors inside. Maddox first, then the others, then the women, then the two godly artifacts they had in their possession. Was the Budapest fortress under attack or something? Because damn.

Since no one touched the drawbridge, the gargoyles never came for them, so they were free to mill about— aka run like hell away from DEFCON Five.

And still, hours later, Ashlyn was in labor. The worst kind, at that. The babies wanted out, needed out, but they were stuck, and no one here was a stupid doctor, so no one knew what the hell to do to help her.

Maddox was barely holding himself together as he paced, shouting, punching walls. The others had stopped exploring and now congregated in the hall outside Ashlyn's room, pacing alongside him. Except for Danika, the brave soul who'd taken over as labor coach. She was inside the belly of the beast. Wait. She was peeking out the door.

"Get over here," the blonde screeched at William.

He was surprised he heard her. After Ashlyn's last round of curses, his ears were still leaking blood and brain matter. He'd taken up residence against the far wall, arms crossed over his chest, and was all about warding away intruders into his personal space. "Who, me?" Again he found himself thumping his chest.

"Yes. You. Standing around wasn't part of your job description when I told the guys Ashlyn would need you for this."

Smart-ass. "News flash, little Dani. I know nothing about human births." Still, he entered the room and approached the bed. Sweat soaked both women from head to toe, and both were pale, trembling. Scared, too, judging from the size of their pupils.

"But you do know about demon births, don't you?"

Sometimes he forgot that Danika was the current All-Seeing Eye, that she could peer into heaven and hell, past and present. And he'd also forgotten Maddox was half human, half demon, and one quarter asshole, capable of spawning demonic offspring with special needs.

"Okay, yeah. I'll take over." And he knew what to do now, which was a relief. For him. Ashlyn was about to experience the worst pain of her life. Pain she would beg to escape—even at the hilt of a sword.

"He isn't touching her," Maddox growled, stomping over to get in William's face. Bastard must have entered the room behind him.

William merely cocked a brow. "You want your woman to survive?"

"Of course." A hiss.

"Then get the hell out of the room! You, too, Dani, and tell your man to stand guard and keep everyone else out, too. And I do mean everyone. No matter what they hear." If they got a whiff of what he planned, they'd remove his hands with a rusty butter knife.

On the bed, Ashlyn was no longer writhing, no longer screaming. She was just a lump of flesh and covers. Getting weaker by the second…almost too late…

"Now!" William shouted. "I'm the only chance the three of them have of surviving."

The petite Danika put her arm around the hulking Maddox and somehow managed to drag him into the hall. William strode over and shut the door, closing himself inside with Ashlyn. Then he moved the dresser in front of it, knowing he'd need a few minutes' head start if anyone busted past Reyes.

Deep breath in, deep breath out. He was trembling as he unsheathed a dagger. "Sorry about this," he said, and got to work.

CHAPTER THIRTY-SIX

AFTER A SHORT STINT in the dungeon below the castle, Paris freed himself from the tunnel-visioned gargoyles' newest restraints and found his friends. As glad as he was to see them, he was also upset by what had gone down while he was away. Ashlyn kidnapped by Galen. Legion trading herself to save the pregnant female. Kane, still missing. No contact. A dead-end trail even Amun now had trouble picking up.

He plopped on a bench someone had dragged into the hallway outside Ashlyn's room. He was trying to keep himself distracted and calm. Zacharel had Sienna. Had probably shown her to the realm's exit. She was probably on her way...wherever, her bond to this place at last broken, her will her own.

This was for the best.

The best sucked.

I want her, Sex said with a pout.

Me, too.

"This castle is lacking something," Viola said as she eased next to him.

She was the first to speak to him in a conversational tone. His friends had been too preoccupied with Ashlyn to do more than bark orders for water, towels and a muzzle for...someone. William probably.

The goddess had given up her I'm-on-the-prowl dress and had changed into a glittery T-shirt and some kind of gray silk pants, the material so sheer he could see her underwear. Okay, so maybe she hadn't given up the gotta-get-me-some attitude altogether. She'd pulled her pale, silvery hair into a high ponytail, the length swinging with her every movement.

"Hello? Are you listening to me? Of course you're listening to me! I need permission to redecorate or I'm afraid I'll have to leave."

I want her! In just a few seconds, Sex was foaming at the mouth, bouncing around in Paris's head, desperate for the goddess rather than Sienna. Far more desperate than the demon had ever been, in fact. *I need her. I have to have her. Now, now, now.*

What was *that* about? They'd had Sienna earlier this very day. Sex should be shiny new until tomorrow.

Want, I want! Want, want, want!

Paris frowned. When Kaia strode past him a heartbeat later, her hips swaying with her every step, his cock following her like a heat-seeking missile, he really frowned.

Usually when he thought about taking a woman he'd already been with, his erection deflated like a balloon. Or, if he didn't remember being with a particular woman, he simply couldn't get hard while he was around her. Surely this didn't mean…surely he couldn't…

Want her, need her! Want all of them!

Yeah. He could. He could take Viola (who he hadn't already had) and Kaia (who he had), Paris realized, his cock twitching with need for both of them. Rather than exciting him, the knowledge filled him with dread.

How was this possible?

Your commitment to Sienna…I don't know…but I can have them all and I want them all.

But…but…Paris had dreamed of this, of finding a woman and being with her multiple times. Any woman.

All women. Sienna, as well as all the others. After his first encounter with Sienna, he'd thought she was his only hope for getting it. He hadn't understood, but then, he hadn't cared to understand. He'd accepted and he'd rolled. Yet now that he could have the same with some-one else—anyone else, apparently—he still…wanted only Sienna, he realized.

He'd never been with a woman like her. Someone who knew about him, but accepted him anyway. Someone who gave more than she took, even when he wanted her to take more than she gave. Someone with grit and fire who wasn't afraid to tell him off or apologize when she made a mistake. Someone who fought for what she be-lieved in, did what it took to win, *whatever* it took. A hated quality once. Admired now.

Suddenly Strider was in his face, navy eyes glittering as he pressed the back of Paris's head into the wall. "That baton in your pants better be for the goddess next to you and not for the redhead who just walked past you."

Liked him better when he was preoccupied. Rather than engage the guy further and risk a fight Strider would have to win to stay upright, Paris nodded. "Right. The goddess." Finally he understood Strider's annoying possessive streak. How the warrior would kill another man for even looking at what was his. Paris would kill male or female, god or goddess, good or evil, for making a play for Sienna.

There'd been enough truth in his tone to mollify the warrior. "Okay." As Strider straightened, he cracked the bones in his neck. "Okay, then. We're good."

Paris watched him walk away, and caught Gideon's amused gaze. The keeper of Lies must have sensed the layer of deception. No one smelled a steaming pile faster than Gideon. No matter how small that pile was.

Guilty, Paris looked away. This shouldn't be happening.

His demon cackled with glee, still wanting, still needing.

He felt dirty and disgusting and ashamed, was suddenly glad Sienna had chosen not to chase after him. If she saw him like this, he would lose it. He needed a shower. Needed to scrub his skin off, layer by layer, until the last drop of blood drained from him.

When the scent of chocolate and champagne began to waft from him, he cursed under his breath. *I'm not sleeping with Kaia or Viola or any other woman here.* He didn't give a shit what his body or his demon demanded from him. He wasn't allowing it. Wasn't putting up with it. *And you can't make me, can't lure them. Do you understand? You stop that right now, or I'll cut off my cock and laugh as we wither away.*

But...but...

No! No excuses, no pleading. He wasn't sleeping with anyone today, tomorrow or the next day. Or even the next. No way. *No one but Sienna,* he thought with a determination that shocked him. And he didn't care how weak it made him. His hands still tingled from touching all that soft, warm skin. He still had her sweet, tropical scent in his nose. He wasn't giving that up, wasn't welcoming someone else.

"Hello. I'm still here," Viola said, pouting like a child. "Don't you care that I might leave if you don't give me what I want?"

He so didn't have the patience to deal with her right now. "You can't leave the castle, okay? This is the safest place for all of you, safer than the Budapest fortress. Galen and his Hunters can't enter without serious injury, and if they try, we'll all be alerted."

Plus, he'd seen the crimson streaks over each of the

windows and doors, and knew William had smeared his blood there. That meant the shadow monsters couldn't come inside again.

"Who said anything about caring for our safety? We need portraits of me there, there and there." As she spoke, she pointed.

"I'll be sure and alert the decorator," he said darkly.

"And there."

Sex hadn't yet given up the quest to get inside her, and Paris's cock did that twitching thing. He gnashed his molars. The goddess was gorgeous, no question about that. Naturally feminine and sensual in a way most could never be, even with centuries of training. And once upon a time, Paris would have been all over her. Cancel out her personality, and she was just the type he used to go for. Lushly curved.

Now, having basked in a satisfaction so complete he would never be the same, settling for anything less held no appeal. Sienna's lean body did it for him. Made him hunger. Blinded him to others. Her scent, her taste, both had been specifically designed to ramp him so high up no one else could ever hope to reach him.

"You're beyond maddening," Viola said.

He was maddening? Right. "You can decorate all you want. Happy?" If he didn't change the subject, she'd keep that shit up all day and he'd end up introing her tongue to his blade. "So where's your dog?"

"My little princess is resting in my new room. Travel is so hard on his delicate constitution."

"Of course." Because all vampire Tasmanian devils possessed delicate constitutions. And what was up with calling a male "princess?" Paris scrubbed a hand down his face, tired, hungry and torn up inside. Screw this. As soon as he knew Ashlyn and the babies were okay, he was taking off, finding Sienna and making sure she was okay. *Then* he'd let her go once and for all so that, when he slept with someone else, he wouldn't be cheating, wouldn't destroy her sense of trust.

But maybe...maybe he'd be with her one more time first. Sex with her was a revelation, not just because she'd strengthened him, healed him and made him come harder than he ever had in his life, but also because sex with her wasn't about him. It was about *them*. Their needs. Their desires.

There was nothing dirty about it. Nothing tainted, one-sided or detached. They touched each other, kissed each other and pleasured each other because it felt good, because passion burned bright and inexorable.

"—listening to me?" Viola threw up her arms in exasperation.

He shook his head, almost told her the truth, and then stopped himself. He did, and her demon would give her fits. She'd probably follow him around like a lost little puppy. "Yeah, uh. I'm fascinated. Interesting stuff."

Maddox paced back and forth, back and forth in front of him. Reyes tried to stop him with a pat on the shoulder, but the warrior shrugged him off and kept going. Lucien tried next, but Maddox shrugged him aside, too. A mistake. In punishment, Anya tripped him as he passed her.

"Why do I always try to befriend the hopeless causes?" Viola said. "Could you be any more selfish, tuning me out when I have such riveting things to say? Then again, I guess I shouldn't be surprised. I mean, you're married because of me, and you haven't ever even thanked me."

"Mmm-hmm. Like I said, fascinating," Paris said absently. And then her words penetrated. "What's that now?" He twisted on the bench, pinning her in place with his narrowed stare. "Did you just say the word *married* in reference to me?"

"That's right. And I never repeat myself. Except for those times that I do, in fact, repeat myself. But that's usually only when I'm mentioning how silky my hair is, how sparkly my eyes are and how sexy my body is. Hey, do you think someone has a bag of peanuts? The spicy kind?"

I will not choke the life out of her. "Exactly who am I married to, and when did the supposed ceremony happen?"

"Oh, did I forget to tell you again? You're married to your ghostly girlfriend, the one you tattooed yourself for. That's how undead marriages are forged. Ashes to ashes, dust to dust, and all that. Well, that's how one-sided marriages are forged, anyway. She's not married to you, so she can tap whoever else she wants without violating any ancient laws and having to endure horrible punishment."

His jaw creaked open and closed as Viola continued to talk. And talk. "Shut up for a minute. How am I married to Sienna?"

Silence.

But then, Viola's glare said enough.

"Sorry," he muttered. "I'm just in shock. I can't be… What you're saying isn't… There's just no way…"

"You are, it is and there is. That's part of the reason you're able to interact with her now. You bonded yourself to her."

Bonded. His mind had short-circuited. He was bonded. He was married to Sienna. She was his. His woman. For real. His wife. Forever.

His.

Wife.

And apparently, despite the fact that his body could now breach any feminine core of his choosing, he couldn't do so without violating a law he'd never heard of, thereby sentencing himself to some kind of punishment. A punishment he wasn't sure who would mete out.

His demon's reaction to the other women now made sense. Sex had been on the right track. With Paris's commitment to Sienna, his infidelity would now feed the demon. Making love with Sienna would, too, though. He'd married her before finding her, and they'd since made love three times.

"You're sure?" he croaked when there was a lag in Viola's monologue. He wanted this, he realized. He wanted this to be true so badly he could taste his own anticipation. Could feel the hum in his blood, the song in his ears. He wanted to be bound to Sienna in the most irrevocable of ways.

Viola patted him on top of his head. "As if I'm ever wrong. But Paris, listen to me. We've *got* to get serious for a minute."

They weren't serious already? "So you weren't serious about the marriage thing?" He would kill her. Just press on her carotid and snuff her out.

"Of course I was serious." She cupped his cheeks, her expression sad. Then she sniffed, and licked her lips. "Hmm, you smell good." Closer…closer…she leaned in. Sniffed at his neck. "Really, *really* good."

Stupid demon.

"Now tell me the truth," she said, her voice lowering, going husky. "Do you think I'm the most beautiful woman you've ever met? And more important, do I look fat in this outfit?"

"I'm so going to give you to the fallen angel," he muttered, putting a little distance between them. Her hold on him tightened, her eyes already glazed with want. "That'll be his punishment for chasing me."

A slow, confused blink. "The fallen who?"

She didn't remember her own ardent suitor. Nice.

"What's wrong with me? Why do I feel this way?" she asked, just before a low moan left her. "I don't find you attractive, don't want to rock your world, and yet, I'm ready to climb on board."

A scream ripped through the entire enclosure, saving Paris from having to form a response. Everyone in the hall stilled, not even daring to breathe.

"Ashlyn." Maddox rushed toward the bedroom door, but Reyes tackled him.

The keeper of Violence fought for all he was worth, and several other warriors had to dive into the pile to shut him down. Paris was about to join the fray when he caught sight of familiar black wings at the entrance of the hallway.

His gaze shot up, and he met gorgeous hazels that were wider than usual. Sienna's face was flushed, her eyes red and puffed as if she'd been crying, and her mouth swollen. He was running at her a second later, leaping over the pile of his friends, tripping, getting up, and running some more.

SIENNA WASN'T MAD. What she felt was so beyond mad no single word could describe it. A mix of rage, guilt, sorrow and more rage, maybe. And then some more rage with a splash of heartbreak. And a lot more rage. Her sister was dead, and the queen of the Titans had killed her. Just slit her throat and left her on the floor as if she were garbage.

When Cronus had dropped Sienna here, all she'd wanted was to find Paris and throw herself in his arms.

Not to cry, she doubted she'd ever cry again, but to forget, if only for a little while. Instead, she discovered some strange beauty had beaten her to the finish line.

A beauty his friends probably liked. The group had apparently taken over *Sienna's* castle, and they were likely to tackle Sienna as they'd just tackled each other if she took a single step in Paris's direction.

The big, hulking giants were heavily armed, an army of menace, each soldier possessing a feral red gaze that spoke volumes. The main chorus being *I'll smile when I kill you,* but they never went for kill strikes. They were simply trying to subdue the one on the bottom of the pile.

What seemed an eternity ago, she had studied these men for nefarious purposes. Seeing them live and in person should have freaked her out. And maybe it would have, if Wrath hadn't just whipped up a party in her brain, tossing out image after image, all of them involving the handsy blonde.

With her smile, her laugh, her *everything,* she enticed men to fall in love with her. Their adulation was her nourishment. And then, when she had them at her feet, she left them, just moved on to the next one, and forgot all about them.

That's what she would do to Paris. And why wouldn't he fall for her? Sienna wondered. She was the most beautiful woman Sienna had ever seen. Hell, even *she* was tempted.

Paris appeared in front of her, gathering her in his arms, rubbing his cheek against hers. He smelled of desire she recognized, such heady desire. "I'm so happy to see you."

"You…you…"

"What's wrong, baby? What happened?"

Glaring up at him, she tugged from his hold. "I'm

gone a few hours—" and in that time had decided to be with Galen to save Paris's life, she thought but didn't add "—and already you've moved on." She gave a bitter laugh. Even knowing this would happen couldn't have prepared her for the flood of pain actually seeing it wrought. "You tried to warn me, didn't you, and I told you I understood." *Well, I don't!*

"Moved on? With Viola?" He grimaced. "Hell, no. We were just talking."

"Yeah, I know. Your body language said plenty." Before, she'd only seen his hard-on—and it had been pointed at the blonde. Now she felt it, hard and long and thick, and sweet heaven, she still wanted it. Still wanted him.

"Are you jealous?"

"Of course not!"

"You are. You're jealous." He laughed, awe and delight bubbling in the undertones. "Can I just tell you how much that turns me on?"

"Everything turns you on," she snarled, struggling to dampen her anger. He was just so damned pleased with himself. And her! "And I'm not jealous."

"You are, and I love it. Anyway, something's going on with my demon, that's all. I swear to you, I haven't been with the goddess and I won't be. Ever."

"She's a *goddess?*"

"Who holds no appeal for me."

He could be lying. He could be telling the truth. Actually, he was telling the truth, she decided in an instant, not needing Wrath's help. Paris wasn't the type to lie. Consequences weren't something he feared.

"It doesn't matter." Her shoulders sagged with defeat. "I shouldn't have come back."

"Doesn't matter? Are you giving up on me? On us?"

He gripped her forearms and shook her. "I know we said we'd part when you could leave the realm, but I want to revisit that decision. It's no longer an option for me. And I know you're going to have a difficult time believing this, but no matter how my body reacts to others, no matter what my demon wants, you are it for me. Do you understand?" Another shake, harder than before.

"Uh, Paris," Strider called. "Who you talking to, buddy?"

He twisted, and she peeked around him. The warriors had stopped fighting each other, and everyone but the scarred one and the blonde goddess were eyeing Paris as if he'd just flipped his ever-loving lid.

"They can't see me," she said.

He was saved from having to reply to her or his friends when the door in the center of the hall swung open and the dark-haired William stepped into the hall. He was pale, clearly shaken to his soul and bathed in blood.

She gasped. "What happened to him?"

William clapped to gain everyone's attention. "All right, listen up. I've got good news and bad news. Because I'm such a positive person, we'll start with the good. Ashlyn survived the birthing, and so did her personal horde."

The hallway echoed with breathy sighs of relief…none louder than Maddox's own.

"So what's the bad?" someone demanded.

After a dramatic pause, the warrior said, "I'm out of conditioner. I need someone to flash out of here and get me some. Hint, I'm looking at you, Lucien. And, yeah, you're welcome for my amazing contrib to your happy family. Little terrors clawed me up but good."

"William!" someone else snapped. "Stay on track, and

keep the unnecessary details to a minimum. We're dying here."

"That's gratitude for you. So anyway, come on, come in, and meet your nephew and niece, Murder and Mayhem. Or, if you want to call them by their nicknames, and I'm sure you will the moment they get their mitts on you, Pistol and Shank."

CHAPTER THIRTY-SEVEN

As HAPPY AS PARIS WAS with the births, as much as he wanted to meet the babies, he had to take care of his woman first. He tossed Sienna over his shoulder with the finesse of a bulldozer, shouted, "No one enter my bedroom, no matter what you hear," and stalked to the room he'd used before, passing through the hall of statues. Each of his friends cast him weird looks before he rounded the corner. Mainly because they were all laid out flat and hadn't recovered from Maddox kicking and shoving them out of his way, so they were dazed, but also because they assumed Paris had just spent a good five minutes talking to himself.

I want her still, Sex said with no small measure of surprise.

Don't worry. We'll get her.

Sienna had been stunned silent and remained still at first, but with his every step she worked herself into more of a lather. Soon she was slapping at his back, jerking at his hair and attempting to knee him in the face and balls. Up the stairs he went, down another hall, barely able to prevent his emasculation. He shouldered his way inside the chamber and slammed the door with a backward kick.

He'd been torpedoing his way into a black rage, but seeing Sienna had calmed him. Just like that. Zacharel could blow him, because clearly he would never hurt this woman.

She'd come back for him. That deserved a reward.

He set her on her feet, and she immediately launched herself into full-blown attack. To be honest, he was glad as hell. Anything was better than that moment of defeat. Her little fists pummeled at him, and he accepted the abuse. Until he realized she'd made an improper fist and was actually hurting herself. He wound an arm around her waist, spun her and slammed her into the hard line of his body to still her.

"Let me go!"

"In a minute." As she struggled, he pulled her thumb out from beneath her fingers and rearranged her fist. "Hit like this." Done, he released her.

She swung back around to beat at him some more, and this time the blows stung. "You aren't walking out of this room until I've killed you!"

That'd be a nice little trick, and maybe something to try later. "I'll let you do anything you want to me, but I'd like an explanation first. What's this about?"

"Argh!" She leapt away from him, paced like a caged lion. Energy radiated from her, practically lifting her hair off her head. "It's about the fact that all men suck! And in case you didn't realize, you're included in their numbers."

"I would hope so. Otherwise our romance would be missing something."

Her eyes glittered with jade fire, the gold lost. "Was that a crack about your penis? Because if so, you can do better." She stalked to the dresser and shoved with all her might, knocking the thing to the ground. Wood splintered. The granite surface shattered. The drawers spilled from their holders. Scowling, panting, she grabbed one and lobbed it at him.

He ducked, and the empty container smacked into the door. Both fractured. Another quickly followed, and he barely managed to dodge it.

"Why are your friends here? Aren't you afraid I'll spy on them and learn their secrets?"

"No." And he wasn't. Not anymore. He'd judged her harshly before, but he wasn't going to make that mistake again. "Just like you aren't afraid I'll sleep with anyone else while we're together."

Another drawer. "That's what you told Susan!"

"I know, and I've lived with the guilt ever since. I will *never* do that to you. Tell me you know that."

"Yes, I know that, but we weren't together a few minutes ago. Which means you went after the first tail to twitch in your direction the second we were separated. But I'm not your girlfriend, and I will never be your girlfriend, so I can't complain, can I?"

"No," he said quietly. "You won't ever be my girlfriend." *Because you're already my wife.* Those words. He'd never thought to use them in regard to himself. But now that he had, yeah, his possessive instincts flared, insisting on their due. Didn't help that Sienna was the sexiest female he'd ever seen. A live wire, sizzling, crackling, the essence of passion. Yeah, he was hard as a steel pipe.

Another drawer was flung his way. Only four more were left. He'd let her have them, and then he was going in.

"I'm so sick of this world, the lying and the tricking and the killing." One. "That woman is going to pay. Oh, she's going to pay so bad." Two. "I'm going to join in and do a little killing of my own. Not through Wrath, but with my own hands." Three. "That bastard Cronus thinks he can manipulate me, but he can't. I'm done with all of you!" Four. "And I'm not going to save you, so there! You can go to—"

Paris barreled forward, snagging her around the waist and tossing her on the bed. As she bounced on the mattress, her wings shot out to slow her momentum. He dove for her before she could catch herself and hover in the air, and for once he didn't try to be careful. He pinned her, trapping her legs beneath the muscled weight of his own and her arms over her head. She tried to buck him off, but all she succeeded in doing was rubbing his hard-on against her clit.

A cry of need parted those pretty lips.

More!

"You wet for me, baby?" He didn't ask for permission, but transferred the shackling of her wrists to one hand and shoved up her shirt and bra with the other, baring her breasts. Her nipples were red and swollen, begging for him.

"No," she said, and he knew she lied. "Not wet, not wet, soooo not wet." Yeah, she knew it, too.

He dipped down and sucked. She released another of those beautiful cries, her hips undulating against him. He kept sucking and she kept bucking against him, until he couldn't stand the pressure anymore and shoved his hand down her pants, past those panties and straight into the heat of her. She practically bowed off the mattress.

Yes, please, yes.

One finger, two, three. He thrust them home, as deep as he could get them.

"Paris... I... Oh, yes, yes!"

"There's my girl." She drenched his hand, just the way he liked, so hot and silky, fitting him so damn perfectly, even this way. "When you used your mouth on me, I wanted to have my face buried between your legs. I still do. And next time, I will. I'm going to have all this honey down my throat."

"Paris...I'm going to... I'm so close already." Her eyes were squeezed shut, those long lashes fused together. "Let go of my hands. I want to touch you, too. *Need* to touch you."

"You think those little taps you gave me weren't foreplay? And hell, baby, I was hard for you long before that."

"Yeah?"

"Oh, yeah. You still mad at me?"

"Yes, but don't stop."

"Got to. Gotta give you something more." He removed his fingers just before she climaxed, and she screeched in frustration. "Gotta give you something better."

Her inhalations rasped in, her exhalations stormed out, both quick and heavy. Need truly was riding her hard—but not as hard as he was going to. He was *drunk* with his passion for her, his head swimming with it, his veins burning with it.

He jerked her zipper down, but didn't bother with shoving her pants away. Couldn't. He was too busy undoing his own. He didn't shove those down, either, and once his cock was free, he poised himself at her entrance. She couldn't open her legs very wide, the material wouldn't let her, so when he pushed in, he had to bear down some of his weight. But when he was in, he was really *in,* her inner walls locked around him, tighter than any fist he'd ever made.

She screamed at the contact, and he loved the sound.

Every thrust was a slow grind against her, and yeah, his body rubbed her clit with every downward glide. No longer did her words make any sense. She was panting and incoherent and lost to an all-consuming fervor. Sex, too. Hell, Paris, too. His balls were drawing up tighter and tighter, yet still sliding against the tops of her thighs.

Her arms fought his hold—oh, baby, he hadn't let her go, had he?—but he kept a steady grip, her breasts thrust up, her nipples rubbing his chest, the friction sparking all different kinds of flames. Satisfaction, lust, clawing need, contentment. With his free hand, he cupped her chin.

"Look at me." He slowed his thrusts.

Took a moment, but ultimately she obeyed. Those hazel eyes were fever-bright, glazed, her pupils utterly blown.

"You're not done with me. Do you hear me? You are not done. You are mine."

"I'm…" Another scream, her inner walls milking him, her hips lifting…lifting…even lifting his weight, sinking him deeper than should have been possible.

Sex shouted at the amazing pleasure.

And like that, Paris erupted, the orgasm churning in his spine, shooting through his sac, up his erection and into her, pumping his seed straight into her body. A white-hot jet, again and again. He came so hard he saw stars.

When he was at last emptied out, he opened his eyes to find Sienna had collapsed on the mattress and he had collapsed on top of her, was probably smashing her. He rolled to his side, but they were still connected so he took her with him. Her head just kind of lolled into the hollow of his neck.

There was a long period of silence as they caught their breath and their heartbeats slowed, but all the while he knew one fact to be true: he'd never experienced sex like that with anyone else and he never would again. Hell, he didn't want to.

"I never had a temper before," she murmured groggily.

He ran a hand up and down the ridges of her spine. "Well, you've got one now, that's for sure."

She bit his collarbone, a playful nip. He expected Sex to respond, but the demon had gone to sleep. "We shouldn't have done that."

"I wanted to calm you down, and I did. Missionary accomplished."

Another nip. "I meant, we shouldn't have had angry sex."

He said, "Couldn't help myself. I liked your temper."

"I could tell. Is there a position you don't excel at, though? You're giving me a complex."

"If there is, will you help me practice until I do?"

"So many times you'll lose respect for yourself."

He laughed. He just couldn't help himself. He was... happy. She was teasing him, as if they were friends. They *were* friends. "I wasn't going to sleep with the goddess," he said. "I swear to you. Never will I sleep with that female."

She placed a kiss just above his heart. "Don't do that. Don't promise things like that. Because even as jealous as I was, and yes, I'm freely admitting to a stalkerlike rage, I would rather you slept with a thousand like her than weaken and die."

His chest got tight. Gently he pulled out of her sweet, sweet body, and they both moaned at the loss. He stripped her, stripped himself, then placed his gun on the nightstand beside the bed, and his blade under his pillow. Safety taken care of, he went right back to cuddling Sienna into his side. First, though, he gave her nipples a *Daddy's back* kiss.

"We're going to talk about that, and about what you were so upset about, because I know there's more to it than the goddess," he said. "In a few minutes. Right now, I want to say a few things, and then I want you to tell me something about you. I want to know you better." In all ways.

They weren't leaving this bed until he'd seen her brain naked, too, and that was that.

"O-kay."

"Susan Dille," he said. "I cared for her. I wanted something to work with her, but I was growing weak. Finally I caved and slept with someone else. I was miserable, she found out, and things only got worse from there. I don't want that with you."

"What makes me so different?" she whispered. "I mean, how can you be with me more than once?"

"I've wondered about that myself, and I think it's because my desire for you is more powerful than my demon."

"That's… Oh, Paris. That's the sweetest thing I've ever heard."

"Good. Now it's your turn for a confession. Start talking."

CHAPTER THIRTY-EIGHT

"I, WELL... HMM," Sienna said.

"Come on, baby." Paris combed his fingers through her hair. "Look past my terrible personality and hideous looks and throw me a bone. Teach me how to woo you properly."

She snorted. "I'd argue the hideous looks part."

"But not the terrible personality? Ouch. That hurts, baby."

Her next snort was half-bathed in laughter. "Well, this won't teach you anything but my stupidity. Once I tried to spray tan my freckles away and ended up looking like a diseased carrot."

"I adore your freckles, and my favorite fantasy involves licking every single one of them. More secrets, though. I want more." Was so hungry for them.

A heavy pause, and when she next spoke, she'd lost her air of playfulness. "The guy I was going to marry, well, I was going to have his baby, but halfway through—" a shudder rocked her "—well, I lost her. My baby girl. Afterward I just sort of broke down and my fiancée left. I was moved to a different division of the Hunters' enterprise."

"Oh, Sienna, oh, baby, I'm so sorry."

Tears filled her eyes, quickly masked. "I recovered."

No one ever recovered fully from that kind of loss.

"I never allow myself to think of her. That's probably unhealthy, but…"

"But it's how you survive. What did you name her?" He knew she'd given the little girl a name.

Another pause, then a hesitant, "Rebecca Skye."

He remembered when she asked him if he even wanted to have kids. Had she ever wanted to have another? Probably. The loss would have left a wound inside her, one that would never fully heal. He knew that kind of loss well. But pregnancy wasn't a possibility for the undead. Still, he wondered if adoption was. Perhaps she could take in one of the kids with unexplained abilities Anya had hidden around the world to save them from Hunters. Sienna would make an amazing mother, protective, loving, fierce.

"She's in heaven, I think. Not Cronus's heaven, or this heaven, or wherever we are, and not Zacharel's heaven, either. I've never told anyone this, but when I died, I knew there was someplace wonderful to spend eternity, as well as someplace terrible. Maybe Cronus is my personal hell, my something terrible, but Rebecca is in that other place, that far better place, where someone far better than Cronus or Zacharel's Deity rules. And now I want to talk about something else. Something light."

Light. He could give her light, even though he had a thousand questions about this "better place" and this "better" ruler, and her suffering and her dreams. "I enjoy watching romantic comedies, action adventures, horror, whatever. Anything but subtitles. That artsy crap is lame." He cupped the sweetest ass on the planet and found himself hard all over again.

"Tell me more." With a voice full of rasp, she said, "I want to know about you, too."

"I'll tell you anything you want to know." And he meant that.

"You and your friends…you're really close."

Those same friends would have told him she had a hankering for information so that she could use it against him. Paris knew better. "We were created together. We're family."

"Created?"

"Yeah. Zeus made us from the blood of his best warriors, steel, baser instincts, things like that."

"So you have no mother or father?"

"Nope."

"I'm sorry. Blood family isn't always hearts and flowers, but there's comfort there. I'm sorry you didn't have that."

"Just made me that much closer to my boys, but I did sometimes wonder what it would have been like. Then I'd think about what I did have, men who would die for me, and I would realize I've got everything I need."

"Having someone who is willing to die for you is rare. And several someones? Awesome."

"Yes. It is."

"I'm glad you have that. It's better than family."

How wistful she sounded. "You don't?"

"No. Never."

And didn't that just break his heart. *I might die for her,* he thought. *Might throw myself in front of a sword for her.* "Now I'm the one who's sorry. I mean, you died for me, but I haven't—" Oh, damn. Wrong words. He expected her to tense, waited for the mood to shatter.

She didn't, it didn't. "Yeah, I did, didn't I? You *are* lucky."

No animosity, just a kind amusement, a contemplative dreaming. There went his heart again, breaking into a few more pieces.

"When we met," he said, "you claimed to be writing a romance novel. You even had pages. I remember how they scattered at your feet when I slammed into you. Was that true? Were they yours? Since waking up in that cell, I figured they were a lie, but now that I know you better, I'm thinking differently."

"They were mine, yes. I love romance novels, and I did want to write one. Maybe I will one day. Not that there's a publisher for the dead."

"Well, you've already got a built-in audience of one. I want to read what you wrote, and what you will one day write. Promise?"

She licked her lips, her tongue caressing his skin, too, and oh, did he like that. "Have you, uh, ever fallen in love?" she asked, ignoring his demand.

Okay, all right. He'd let her lack of an answer about the novel slide. For now. "Once I thought I was, but it didn't work out. And there were a few times, after I was with a woman, that I would wish for more and hang around. A few times I even dated a woman without sleeping with her, hoping for some type of relationship, but all along I'd have to sleep with others, so I'd feel guilty and then I'd just stop seeing her so that the guilt would fade."

"I'm sorry."

"Don't be. Not your fault."

"Doesn't help that Hunters threaten everyone you love."

"Yeah."

"How do you deal, having a group of people hunting you, hating you?"

"It's not easy, I won't lie. Sometimes we push ourselves over the edge. Drugs, alcohol, sex, whatever our particular vice is, but we go on and we look out for each other." The warmth of her breath stroked over him, tantalizing him. "And lately we are Addams Family normal—you know, doing the hearts and flowers thing while navigating everything our enemies throw at us."

Her nails dug into his chest. "The Hunters…more than half of the organization is brainwashed. We're told over and over how evil you are, how you are responsible for everything bad that has ever happened to us, to everyone. How perfect our lives could be if you were gone. They show us pictures, horrible pictures of torture, disease and death, and they prey on our weaknesses. Like with my sister, telling me that little girls wouldn't be kidnapped if there were no demons in the world."

First she'd lost her sister, then her baby. He squeezed her tight. "I'm sorry for her loss." For all the crap she'd endured throughout her too-short life. Crap he'd only added to. "I should have told you that when you first mentioned her, but…"

"But we had only just reconnected and didn't trust each other."

He kissed her temple. "We've always known the Hunters were studying us. Is that how you knew I was in Rome that day? How you knew the romance novel would distract me, and what drug to use on me?"

"I knew through Dean Stefano, my boss, and he knew through Galen. Galen, I'm sure, knew through Rhea, Cronus's wife. Funny, but I never understood the chain of command until after my death."

Paris couldn't help himself and gave her temple another kiss. They were getting heavy again, and he didn't mind that, wanted to travel that road with her, all roads with her, but she didn't and he would honor her wishes.

"I'm going to switch gears for a minute, okay?"

Her relief was palpable as she said, "Please do." One at a time, she plucked her nails from his skin.

"I know you've never been married, but other than the douche who left you have you ever…wanted to be?" He tried to ask it casually, as if the answer was no biggie, but he couldn't keep the yearning from his tone.

Her reaction, when it came, was one of shock, and he wasn't sure whether that was surprise-party good or you-just-hit-my-car bad. She jerked upright, that dark flood of hair draping one bare shoulder. Her eyes were still more green than brown and they dominated her pixie face. The lips he'd kissed until they were puffed and red were parted.

"I…I…"

Balls to the wall. He would finish this. "I want you to marry me," he said. He wanted her tethered to him the same way he was tethered to her. Mentally, emotionally and physically.

"Paris…"

He threaded his fingers through her hair. "Don't say anything right now. Just think about it." Because, bottom line? No more talk of separating. They were staying together, and that was that. He wasn't letting her go, and he sure as hell wasn't cheating on her. No matter the cost to himself.

From now on, there was only one sheath for his sword. Would there be problems? Complications? Oh, yeah. Probably more than he was aware of, and he was aware of plenty. But he'd rather deal with those problems *with her* than be without her and have smooth sailing.

"I have to tell you something," she whispered, the defeat returning in an instant. "I lied. I won't kill her, and he can manipulate me. Otherwise, the rest of you are dead, too, and I can't allow that to happen."

"Won't kill who? Who can't manipulate you? Tell me, and I'll fix it." *I will slay her dragons.*

"You can't. Rhea, she…she… When my sister Skye was taken, we were swimming in the neighborhood pool. Mom told us never to go there alone, but I was fourteen and thought I could handle things, and Skye wanted to swim so badly. We were just supposed to walk to the park, but we went to the pool instead. It was so crowded that day, and I had to go to the bathroom, and when I came back out, she was being dragged away by a stranger. Everyone must have thought she was throwing a fit, because no one stopped them, and I couldn't get to them."

He opened his mouth to offer comfort, to tell her it wasn't her fault, that even though she'd gone against her mother's orders, she wasn't the one who had abducted the little girl, but she wasn't finished.

"Today I learned that all these years Skye has been alive. Until recently. She was murdered. Rhea murdered her. If I'd only found her earlier, but I didn't, and now I have to live with the knowledge that she…that I…" She was rambling, the words spewing out as if they'd been trapped for a long time and were now tangling on her tongue as they fought for freedom.

He ached for her. As he'd never ached for anything, he ached for her, and he didn't take the decision to slay her dragons lightly. He'd do what needed doing. "Go on, baby. Tell me the rest."

A shudder moved through her. She inhaled forcefully. "Cronus told me that Skye was Galen's prisoner, then he told me that he didn't actually know where she was, *then* he showed me her lifeless, bloody body."

Paris had known the bastard was low, but this…he had no words. His reckoning with Cronus needed to happen soon—with knives. No wonder Sienna had been so upset when she'd returned to the castle. "I'm so sorry, baby. If I could take away your pain, I would." Finally he told her what he'd wanted to tell her. "This isn't your fault. It was never your fault. You aren't responsible for the things other people do. Never have been, never will be. This is their shame, not yours. But I know it hurts, I do, and however you want to handle it, I will help you."

"He showed me because he expects me to spy on Galen and to…to be with him."

Spots of black flashed over his eyes. "When you say *be with Galen,* do you mean be with him sexually?"

A shameful nod, and maybe even a bit resolved, as if she deserved nothing better.

"That you'd even consider it tells me that you want to punish yourself," he said, comprehension a slap in the face. "For what you did to me, and what you think you allowed to happen to your sister."

Her chin jutted stubbornly. "Maybe."

"So, what else is it you did exactly, that some part of you thinks you need to be punished? Fought for a cause you believed in? Check. Slept with a man you were attracted to, despite everything else? Check. Saved him when you could have left him to a slow, torturous death? Check."

Her hand balled into a (proper) fist. "I told you that I hated you as I lay dying."

"Every couple says things they don't mean when they're fighting."

"Well, I meant it at the time! And before that, I drugged you."

"Yeah, and I planned to screw you and leave you like

I'd done to a thousand others." She flinched at his crudeness, but he kept going. "And guess what? At the time I was blithe about it. I loved women, and I protected them, but I still used them. In my mind, it was my right. I needed a wake-up call, and you gave it to me."

"No, you—"

"Don't make excuses for me. You've seen my past, and you know I've spoken true."

She snapped her teeth at him. "So you're saying you bear me no ill will? None at all?" A snort lacking any hint of amusement.

He fisted her hair a lot harder than he'd intended, but he didn't loosen his grip. "Baby, I'm saying I *adore* you."

Once again, she floundered for a response. The anger drained from her, and utter longing peered down at him. "Adore?" she squeaked.

"Your ears are working just fine."

The harshness of his reply had her sighing dreamily, something that puzzled and aroused him. "I was wrong earlier. *This* is the sweetest thing anyone has ever said to me."

And so I'll be stepping up my game now. If that made her happy, his A-Game was gonna make her blissful. "Nothing to say in return?"

"Well, yeah. Cronus says that my being with Galen is the only way to keep you and your friends safe."

Hell, no. When they'd lived in the heavens, Galen had been one of Paris's go-to guys. They'd hung together, fought together. Paris had admired the guy's emotional distance, his ability to do whatever was necessary to finish a job successfully. And okay, fine, they'd shared women, sometimes even at the same time.

He hadn't cared then. He cared now. Not just because

Galen was Enemy One, but because Sienna was his and his alone. She was staying with him.

"You're not going back to Galen." No way, not ever. Actually, Paris would die first. "And just a quick FYI. Apparently my friends plugged the keeper of Hope full of bullets earlier today. He's no good to anyone right now."

"But he'll recover, I know he will, and then...then..." The rest of the story flooded from her. The Chamber of Futures, the portraits, the three possible outcomes for the world. For Cronus. *For him.*

Too much to digest at once, but still, nothing changed his mind about Sienna staying put.

"We have time," he said. "We have time to figure this out, and we will. But you're not going to him. You're mine. Only mine. And I'm yours. I will never sleep with anyone else. Do you understand what I'm saying? Never. When I said you were it for me, I meant it. No one else, whether you're with me or not. And Sienna, you will be with me."

As he spoke, her mouth fell open, snapped closed. "Do *not* say things like that."

"Baby, I will do more than say it. I will blood oath it." He reached for the daggers under the pillow, but she threw herself over his body and batted the weapon to the floor. Then, clearly suspecting he'd just reach for another weapon, she swiped her arm over the nightstand and sent the gun flying.

Now, there was the shocker of a lifetime. He wasn't offended by her resistance, though. She wanted him safe, alive, thriving. Was even willing to sacrifice her happiness for his.

"Did you just challenge me?" he asked. They were flesh to flesh, male to female. Her wings spread, blocking out the rest of the room. She was all that he saw, all that he felt. Her breasts pressed into his chest, her nipples already beaded for him. Her core rubbed against his swollen length, and her legs splayed over his. "I think you just challenged me."

"No. I did not."

"You did. Quick fact—you mess with a man's weapons, and you might as well knee him in the balls. You'll get the same results. So I accept." Moving so quickly she couldn't possibly resist, he flipped her over, onto her back, spread her legs and shoved inside.

No preliminaries. Just straight-up, hard-core sex in the most basic fashion. She was wet, so very wet, so they had no problems.

"Paris!"

"Yeah, baby, that's it. Take me all the way in."

"Is this how you reward all challengers?" she asked between panting breaths.

"Only you."

Her moan of pleasure filled the room, blending with his hiss of inexorable bliss. By the time he finished with her, she would know the man she belonged with—because there would be no part of her that he left untouched.

CHAPTER THIRTY-NINE

GALEN APPEARED IN THE CENTER of the bedroom, and
Legion shrank deeper into her shadowed corner. She'd
been here for over an hour, having whisked herself to the
coordinates he'd given her. She had no idea what the rest
of the place looked like. Coward that she was, she hadn't
left the relative safety of the room. To her immense relief,
no one had entered, either.

Though she'd been tempted, she hadn't even explored
the rest of the chamber. Gorgeous pile after gorgeous pile
of shiny gold coins, glittering jewels and odd, ancient
weapons abounded. Weapons she couldn't use against
her captor, so what was the point of studying them?

While Galen had worn white at the temple, he'd since
donned a red robe. A *drip, drip, dripping* red robe. She
frowned. A copper tang coated the air. That's when she
realized. Not a red robe, but a blood-soaked one.

His knees gave out and he fell, barely catching himself
before a face-plant. His wings were tattered, and there
were blade hilts and arrows protruding from his chest.

All that blood…

—*hands grasping at her breasts, her thighs*—
—*teeth scraping over her skin*—
—*claws in her eyes, plucking them out*—
—*something hard between her legs*—
—*laughter, so much laughter*—
—*shackles on her wrists, her ankles*—

Bile burned holes in her stomach and escaped, quickly spreading through the rest of her. She covered her mouth with a trembling hand, fighting tears. The memories of her time in hell never left her, but sometimes they completely overtook her, dragging her into a different sort of hell. One of humiliation, degradation, helplessness and horror.

"Fox!" Galen's ragged shout rang out. "I need you."

Legion must have whimpered at the sound of that shout, because Galen's head whipped in her direction. His sky-blue eyes were rimmed with red, his cheeks streaked with dirt. Was he going to watch as "Fox" did things to her?

His expression softened. Only a little, but enough to stave off the encroaching hysteria. "You think I'm in bad condition, you should see the other guy."

Tendrils of hope reached out, tried to wrap around her. Hope for something better. Hope for a future with the man in front of her. Panic infused her, after all, and she fought them with all of her mental strength. Finally the tendrils thinned, vanished.

"Please don't hurt me," she croaked.

He frowned at her.

Rushed footsteps beyond, and the door swung open. A tall, slender woman with jet-black hair and angular features flowed inside. She was attractive, in a regal way, with eyes like the differing temperatures of flames, an odd mix of blue and gold.

But there was a gray cast to her skin, bruises under her eyes, and though she gripped a gun in both hands, she was trembling. A quick scan, and she found Legion. Lifted one of the guns.

Yes, Legion thought, strangely comforted all of a sudden. *Yes. An end. Finally.*

"No!" Despite his injuries, Galen dove in front of her.

The girl—Fox?—had her finger off the trigger in a heartbeat, the weapon lowered.

Disappointment settled on Legion's shoulders. Perhaps she should have ended herself long before now. Why hadn't she? Suddenly she didn't know, couldn't remember.

"You don't hurt her," Galen said, menace a strong undercurrent. "Ever."

Confusion joined the disappointment. He'd just… defended her.

Fox ran her tongue over her teeth. "She do this to you?"

"No. Now help me to the bed."

As Fox sheathed her weapons, her gaze remained locked on Legion, narrowed and hate-filled. Even as she approached Galen, wound her arm around the warrior and eased him to his feet, she kept Legion in her sights. He leaned his weight into her, and they inched their way to the bed. Slowly, carefully, he sat at the edge of the mattress.

Were they lovers? Legion wondered.

Visibly weakening, now wheezing, Galen said, "Get your tools and get this shit out of me."

With one last warning glare in Legion's direction, Fox flew out the door.

"Will she obey you?" Legion asked softly. "About me?"

Sky-blue eyes found her, the lids heavy, casting his face into the come-to-bed sexy realm, and she hated herself for noticing. "Yes. The only person you need to worry about is me."

So. He planned to save her torturing all for himself. And he would torture her. She had no doubt about that.

—something slicing between each of her ribs—

—rotted breath fanning her ear, trailing down her chest—

She wrapped her arms around her middle. *Distract yourself.* "Did the Lords do that to you?"

"Yes," he repeated. "As promised, I let them go without hurting them back."

"Th-thank you." Worry for them was another constant in her life.

A long moment passed in silence, allowing her thoughts to once again careen out of control. Soon she was imagining what would happen to her once Galen healed. "Why do you hate them so much?" she asked, just to fill the void.

"I don't hate them." He balanced his elbows on his knees and his weight on his elbows. "I'm simply looking out for myself."

"Why?"

"Who else will?" Then, "Enough about me. What happened to you in hell?"

The blood drained from her face, then the rest of her, leaving her cold and empty. "I can't...talk about it, please don't make me talk about it."

He stared at her, different emotions washing over his face. Fury, regret, hope, jealousy, fury again.

Fox rushed back in, the black bag she held slamming into her thigh with a loud *thump.* Legion curled her knees into her chest, doing her best to become a smaller target, but Fox was through intimidating, her focus on Galen.

She crouched in front of him, set down the bag, and dug inside. After cutting away his robe, she whistled as she looked him over. "This is going to hurt like a son of a bitch."

"Don't care. Do what's needed."

As she worked, Legion kept her attention on the back of her head. Maybe because Galen kept his on *her,* still staring at her, trying to see past her skin and into her soul.

Fox was demon-possessed, she realized. Having grown up among the dark lords of hell, Legion sensed the evil inside her, could feel the ooze of her...distrust. Yes. That's what she felt rubbing her nerve endings raw.

Distrust. A High Lord. The strongest of the strong, a leader of many minions. Legion was a minion of Strife, and the two demons had warred constantly, pitting their armies against each other. Distrust was no longer...right, though. The malice seeping from the girl's pores was warped, almost frantic. No wonder her skin was grayish and her face bruised. She must have to fight the demon every hour of every day to remain sane herself.

"So, you want to tell me what happened?" Fox asked. "What's going on?"

"No," Galen replied tartly. "I don't."

"Do it anyway. You take off for Rome to deal with the Unspoken Ones and get the Cloak, and I don't hear from you for weeks. I thought you were dead. Then suddenly you're back, and you practically are dead."

She'd removed everything that didn't belong, and was now cleaning the blood from his chest. As the crimson was wiped away, she began to piece together the tattoos on his chest, stitching his skin in place. A butterfly over his left pectoral, and one over his right.

Two butterflies?

Legion's gaze jolted up and clashed with his. He was still eyeing her through those narrowed lids, daring her to say something. She gulped, kept quiet.

"I got the Cloak, stole Maddox's woman and traded her for this one." He motioned to Legion with a tilt of his chin. "Hey! Can you at least pretend to be a woman and try for gentle?"

"Wuss. Why her?" Fox demanded, spreading some kind of paste over each of the wounds.

"Don't worry about her. She's mine, and she's not going to hurt me. Are you, Legion?"

If only. She shook her head.

"Say it. Say the words."

A tremor moved through her. "I'm not going to hurt you." She couldn't. Even if he chained her up and did... and did... *Bile, spreading faster and faster...*

"Because I'm commanding you to take care of me, and you have to obey me, don't you." Not a question.

"Yes," she whispered.

"Calm down, Gay Man," Fox told him. "Your heartbeat is jacked up, and it's causing you to bleed more heavily."

"You know I hate when you call me that."

He'd grumbled the admonishment, but he hadn't struck at her, and that shocked Legion to the bone. He must really like the woman, she thought. And was that... could that be...jealousy swimming through her?

No way. Legion wanted nothing to do with Galen. Nothing! *Hate him.* For what he'd done to Aeron, to Ashlyn.

A short while later, Fox had him bandaged up and lying flat on the mattress. She tucked the covers around him and stood there, brushing his hair from his face until he fell asleep with a last shuddering command. "Don't hurt her."

That's when Fox turned and leveled Legion with the evilest stare she'd ever seen—and she'd been chained to the devil himself a few times.

"Galen might think of you as his, little girl, but *he* is

mine. And I protect, and avenge, what's mine. You harm him in any way, and not even he will be able to stop me from harming you in kind."

CHAPTER FORTY

CRONUS SEETHED WHEN he discovered his Lords had found his hiding place, the Realm of Blood and Shadows, where he kept Sienna and the three demon-possessed warriors he'd locked there. They'd invaded his private castle. All except for Torin, the keeper of Disease, who was back at the fortress in Budapest, having refused to let Lucien flash him. Too much risk, he'd said, even if he was draped from head to toe with protective gear.

One touch of Torin's skin against his, and Lucien would be infected with the very disease running rampant in the other warrior's veins. Torin put his friends before himself, always, an attitude Cronus did not understand or respect. But the thought reminded Cronus there was a way to work this situation to his favor.

Torin would do anything to touch a female human without hurting her. Even accept a gift that wasn't a gift. A gift that was a curse. A gift that was a death sentence. A gift that would ruin Rhea's own plans. Not that he would know it. Cronus grinned.

Unlike Lucien, Cronus did not have to touch an individual to move him. Cronus simply spoke, and Torin appeared in front of him.

The warrior palmed two blades in his gloved hands and spun, searching for the culprit, even as he oriented himself to his new surroundings. He stilled when he noticed Cronus, though his gaze continued to rove, memorizing the details, the exits.

A field of ambrosia stretched for miles, scenting the air oh, so sweetly, the violet petals glistening under the gleam of a sun that offered the perfect amount of light and heat.

"Cronus," Torin said with a nod of his head. If he was upset or even thrilled about being pulled from his Budapest fortress for the first time in centuries, he didn't show it. No bowing, either, so of course, no scraping.

All of his current problems stemmed from his leniency with the Lords, Cronus mused. They issued commands and expected him to obey. Then, when he issued commands, they refused him, sometimes openly, sometimes by more stealthy means. His mistake was trying to connect with them, to become one of them. He should have proven his strength and demonstrated the consequences of defying him from the beginning. He wasn't their friend, would never be their friend. He was their king, their master.

And now he would prove it.

"You rang?"

Oh, yes. He would prove it. Cronus studied him, this warrior he was about to use. Torin had white hair that shagged around a wicked face humans craved for the rest of their lives if they were unlucky enough to catch a single glimpse of it. Emerald eyes, more sinful than anything. Lips that had never known a female's taste.

"Walk with me," he commanded, expecting absolute compliance.

And getting it. When the warrior reached his side, he pivoted and strode through the field, the lush leaves caressing his suit-clad legs. He ran scenarios through his mind, gauging the pros and cons of his decision.

"So...what's up?"

The impudent tone irritated him, but he made no comment. For now. "I have a new task for you."

A groan. "You and your tasks. Torture so-and-so. Kill so-and-so. Rally my boys and send them into the danger zone. So, fine. Let's hear this new one. I'm sure it will delight me as much as the others."

"Tone," he snapped.

"Yes. I have one."

Calm. "And you'll lose your tongue if you use it again."

Silence.

Excellent. "Today, Disease, I give you a gift. The greatest treasure in my possession. *Despite* your disappointing, offensive attitude."

Those green eyes rolled. "All right. I'll bite. What's this gift?"

"My...All-Key." He needed to give it away, but doing so irked considering the lengths he'd gone through to get it.

"Great, but I have no flippin' idea what that is."

Of course not. Save for four others, Cronus had murdered everyone who knew about it. The four? Anya, the minor goddess of Anarchy and its former possessor; her father, Tartarus, who had given it to her; Lucien, who knew every one of Anya's secrets; and Reyes, who had once dared to shackle Cronus and barter for his woman's freedom. And the quartet lived only because Cronus had a use for them. Had they ever spoken of the key, he would have stopped caring about their usefulness, and they knew it.

"This key unlocks any door, any prison, any curse. Anything. Nothing can bind you. And if anyone tries to take it from you, they will die." That did not mean Torin would be free of his demon. The two were bonded, two halves of a whole. One could not live successfully without the other.

"Sounds cool, but why me?"

Because Torin was solitary, spending more time alone than with his friends. Because he would never fall in love, nor betray his secrets to a female while they whiled away too much time in bed. Something that happened far too much for Cronus's liking. Something he himself had once been guilty of doing.

"Should you tell anyone about this gift," he continued, not deigning to reply aloud, "I will kill you as well as the one you told. Should you try and give it away, I will kill you and all those you love. And, when I ask you to return it to me, you will do so without hesitation. One moment of resistance, just one, and I will do more than kill your loved ones. I will hurt them in ways you cannot imagine."

Torin's purposeful stride never faltered. "Yeah, well, thanks for thinking of me, but I'd rather eat dirt."

Cronus sent a wave of power slamming into the man's temples, knocking him off his feet. He hit the ground, writhing from the pain of it, blood soon spurting from his ears.

Looming over him, Cronus said, "You were saying?" A wave of his hand, and the pain eased.

Torin lay there, panting, dripping with sweat. "I was saying dirt is delicious, thanks for the mouthful."

His lips pursed. Breaking the Lords would clearly take more than his usual strong-arm tactics. They smiled when he hurt them, laughed when he threatened. As much as that frustrated and angered him, it also fascinated him. Despite everything, they were honorable. When they gave their word, they stood by it. A foolish practice, really, but one he'd come to rely on where they were concerned.

Only when he threatened those they loved did they fall in line with him. But Torin could not simply cooperate because of fear. Not this time. Not with something as important as the All-Key.

"Do this, keep the key safe for me, and I will grant you a boon," Cronus said. "Anything you wish. Anything that is in my power to give, of course."

Suspicion danced in the warrior's eyes, and Cronus knew he was weighing his options. Refuse the king, and face punishment. Accept, and face potential trickery. Betrayal. But for the prospect of such a reward, he would not say no.

"I think we both know what you want," Cronus pressed. "A chance to touch a woman without sickening her and starting a plague."

Breath caught in Torin's throat, and Cronus knew that he had him. "Can you give me that chance?"

"In a way. What happened to the vial of water the angel Lysander gave you?" If there was but a single drop left, Torin could touch a woman, then feed her the droplet and save her, for the water healed any wound on any creature. Would he be able to touch her after that? No, but his condition would have been met.

"Gone. And the angels won't give us any more."

Unfortunate, but understandable. The angels had to endure terrible, terrible things to even approach the River of Life from whence the water came. Cronus himself had never dared go near it. "There is a woman...I will force her to meet with you. You can touch her all you desire, and she will never sicken."

"Yeah, uh, no thanks. I want to pick my own woman."

"That, I cannot give you, and that was not the bargain. You wanted a woman to touch. I can give you one."

A long while passed in silence while Torin considered the offer. "Is she dead?"

"No. She lives."

"Old? A child?"

"No. She is neither too old nor too young."

"How will I be able to—"

"Answers were not part of the bargain, either. Decide!"

Finally Torin nodded, as Cronus had known he would. "Very well. You have a deal."

He did not allow himself to smile. When the All-Key left him, its powers would leave Rhea. He could imprison her. Have her at his mercy—or lack thereof.

What he did not mention to Torin: the All-Key wiped the memory of the one who gave it away. Except Cronus's, and probably, because of their connection, Rhea's. Cronus had created the key, and so had ensured it would never adversely affect him. However, no one else, Torin included, was extended the same courtesy.

When Torin bent his knees, as if to push himself into a stand, Cronus shook his head and reached down. "Stay there. This might hurt a bit."

ON THE OTHER SIDE of the heavens, Lysander stepped from the cloud he shared with his Harpy mate, Bianka, his wings spread and gliding just enough to leave him hovering in place.

"I am failing you," Zacharel said, the words gritted. The snowstorm that followed him constantly increased in ferocity, the flakes catching in his eyelashes, between the feathers of his wings, weighing them down.

"You have not failed me, and you *will not* fail me. I

have complete faith in you. Now, what report do you have of the girl?"

He rallied and said, "While she thinks she will be able to walk away from Paris in a few days, the pair has grown closer. Worse, she now carries his darkness." He'd seen the shadows swirling in her eyes after he'd carted Paris away from her.

"The war grows ever closer," Lysander replied. "She will still be of great use to us."

"Are you sure? Cronus has tricked her, convinced her to aid him. I expected him to lie to her, but I also expected her demon to catch on. He hasn't. And now that Paris has learned of his marriage to her, he will fight for her to the death." He'd thought Paris would never learn of the connection, which was the only reason Zacharel had helped tattoo him. Had he refused, Paris would have done it anyway and begun resisting him ahead of schedule.

"Cronus is a greedy fool, but Paris has surprised me. He might have shared his darkness with her, but she has shared some of her light with him." Lysander thought for a moment. "If he wants her as I want my Bianka, he will not part from her easily."

Too true. Passion, desire, lust, whatever you wanted to call that wild craze to mate, still remained completely out of Zacharel's realm of understanding, yet he could not deny *something* took hold of the pair whenever they so much as looked at each other.

Like magnets, Paris and Sienna were drawn to each other. They fought for each other, and parting would destroy them on some fundamental level. That he'd once thought to convince Paris to willingly walk away from her had been foolish. Force would be needed.

"Whatever you wish me to do," he said, bowing his head, "I will do."

Lysander expelled a weary sigh. "We need her. No matter what, we need her. Do whatever you must to convince her to side with us. If that's not enough, simply take her."

IN THE DEPTHS OF HELL, Kane sank in and out of consciousness. As vulnerable as he was when he slept, he much preferred it to the crippling pain of having his guts tucked back inside his body and his flesh stapled back together. Then, when the staples failed, having that battered flesh cauterized with liquid fire. He felt like someone had parked a bus on his chest, done some donuts, then let the passengers stampede off.

And the laughter…oh, the laughter from his demon. Disaster loved this. Loved the pain, and the degradation, and the helplessness. Kane imagined this was exactly how Legion had felt when she'd been stuck down here.

He should have supported her better. Should have tried to help her. Not that Kane wanted help himself. Part of him still wanted to die.

The horsemen—Black and Red—were saviors as well as tyrants. When he'd screamed as they "doctored" him, they'd next taped a ball gag in his mouth. When he'd thrashed, they had chained him down. They weren't cruel about it, though; they were matter-of-fact, as if they were doing him a favor. A reason he wouldn't take them with him when he kicked it.

Red stood over him now, blowing cigar smoke in his direction. "You up for a little poker yet?"

Whenever the pair realized he was awake, they always asked the same question. That one. He shook his head, unsure why a game of cards was so important to them.

"Bummer." Genuine disappointment shone in his features. "Soon, though."

Kane nodded in agreement because he didn't know what else to do, and closed his eyes. Without any resistance on his part, he drifted back to his favorite place, a black void of nothingness.

CHAPTER FORTY-ONE

THE NEXT MORNING, AFTER spending the entire night making love to Sienna, Paris showered, threw on clothes someone had brought him from home, weaponed up and ensured Sienna's crystal dagger rested on the nightstand, ready for her use if it proved necessary. Though he hated leaving her, he exited the bedroom and entered a whole new world.

Apparently Danika, the current All-Seeing Eye, had foreseen that terrible things would take place at the fortress in Budapest, and she'd sensed staying close to William was the only way to survive. So here they all were, one happy family—though how his friends had so quickly installed a weight room, a wet bar and a media room in the castle, Paris might never know.

He concentrated on the changes as he stalked the halls, so he wouldn't think about his woman sleeping peacefully in his bed. Naked, sated, rosy from his mouth and his hands and his body. Wouldn't think about the breathy sounds she'd made, the way she'd cried his name and begged for more. Wouldn't think about the way she'd made *him* beg for more. The way they fit, so damn perfectly.

Maybe at first he'd been obsessed with her without really knowing her. But he was learning her. Underneath her prim and proper exterior, and even underneath that iron spine of stubbornness, she was soft and gentle. Delicate. She loved with her whole heart, and she fought to protect what she considered hers. Hell, she sacrificed her body, her time and her life for what she considered hers.

She was dedicated. That temper of hers was a huge turn-on. Every time she'd tossed a drawer at him, he'd gotten harder. How many females were brave enough to challenge him in a contest of strength? Not many. But she had, because when she looked at him, she saw past the face and the hair and the stained, corrupt past. She saw a man. Just a man.

He almost turned around and strode back to his room. He wanted her arousal on his face, and her nails going down his back. He wanted to be branded by her in every way. Then, anyone who looked at him would know. *He* belonged to *her*. And—

What the hell was that hanging on the wall? He skidded to a stop. Just like at the fortress in Buda, there were portraits lining the corridor walls. Only, every single portrait was of Viola.

Viola in a gown. Viola in leather. Viola lying down. Viola standing up. Viola looking over her shoulder. An endless stream of poses.

"Breathtaking, aren't I." A statement, not a question, coming from directly behind him. Viola moved to his side, a vision of loveliness in a pink tank and hip-huggers. "I fetched them from one of my homes."

"Uh, yeah. Sure. Breathtaking."

"Which one is your fave?" She tapped a fingertip against her chin, studying them. "I'm having a hard time picking between that one and—all the others."

"Uh...let me think about it."

While he pretended to look them over, Sex purred, wanting to be closer to her. A second later, Paris was sporting massive wood. Shit. He raked a hand through his hair, shamed. Even this was like a betrayal to Sienna.

Why are you doing this to me? he demanded of his demon. *I thought we talked about this.*

Cheating feels good. I want to feel good.

Well, cheating's not gonna happen. And I want you to think about this for a moment. Every time we're with Sienna, it's a two-for-one deal. Or hell, maybe more than that. She's a human, a ghost, an ambrosia supply, a former Hunter and a demon, all wrapped into one tasty package. And if we are untrue to her, we lose her. And you will never get a quintupping again.

Why, she's an orgy waiting to happen.

Exactly.

A layered pause. *Oh...well...hmm.*

"Well?" Viola insisted.

Right. What would pacify her? "I can't actually pick. They're all equally amazing."

"I know, right. I'll have one delivered to your room. You and your hand can spend countless hours studying the details. I had a few surprises painted throughout. You're welcome." She whistled as she skipped away.

He stood there a moment, thinking about the fallen angel who desired her. He really should help throw the two together. Because really, was there a worse punishment for the guy than ending up with *that* for eternity? Food for thought.

He beat feet to the next hallway, and wasn't surprised to find Anya taking down the pictures of Viola and replacing them with pictures of herself. The decorator wars were on, he supposed.

"Gwen, Kaia, seriously," the (minor) goddess snapped, having trouble hanging on to a frame and a hammer at the same time as she balanced on a ladder. "This is the most important mission of your lives and you're riding pine on the sidelines? Get in here, you lazy bitches!"

Not wanting to be recruited, Paris ducked his head and kept walking, hands shoved in his pockets. From the corner of his eye, he caught a glimpse of the Harpy sisters in one of the bedrooms, studying a life-size— and warped—drawing of Galen. Guy had horns, crooked teeth and three fingers on each hand. His clown feet were too big for his body, and rather then genitals, he had an X. A really small X.

Gwen was pretending to pull back a crossbow, aiming for his heart, and Kaia was shaking her head no and pointing to the man's groin.

Sex started in with his purring. Out of habit, maybe, because a few seconds later, those purrs faded. Best part? Paris never got hard.

A wary sigh echoed inside his head. *If we do this relationship thing, I'll need her often.*

The demon was willing to try. Paris couldn't help himself. He gave a fist pump toward the ceiling. *Believe me, I know. And we'll have her a lot more than just "often."*

What an amazing damn day this was turning out to be. A megawatt smile bloomed. Yeah, he had a whole lot of shit to do. Talk to Cronus, spank the guy's wife, kill Galen while he was at his weakest and find Kane, but first, he wanted to catch up with his friends and visit the newest additions to the family.

Down on the next floor, there was a table piled high with snacks. Without slowing, he snagged an apple and a box of Strider's Red Hots. A bite of apple followed by a few of the cinnamon candies, and you had a mouthful of delicious.

A lot of his boys were congregated in the hallway outside of Ashlyn's room, eating, talking, laughing and more relaxed than he'd seen them in a long time. This was what their lives should always be like, he mused.

William was in the corner, a dark-haired girl tucked into his side, the pair of them locked in earnest conversation. Gilly was a teenager on the cusp of womanhood who'd suffered unimaginable abuse as a child. Danika had taken her in, and the girl had been leery around everyone but William. For some reason she'd adored the bastard from day one.

Maybe because she didn't yet know that William had recently slaughtered her entire family. Paris wondered how she'd react when the truth came out. And it would; it always did.

Gilly had hated her mother, stepfather and brothers, but deep down she'd probably loved them, too, and it was hard to forget that kind of feeling. Most likely scenario: she would leave, and William would follow her, protect her. He wouldn't be able to help himself. The need to protect ingrained itself in a man's very soul, and once he felt it, it was hard to forget, too.

Now that William had shed blood for her, that need would be even stronger, as Paris well knew. Every time he'd taken a life, his desperation to reach Sienna had increased. But he had her now. They were together, and he wasn't letting her go.

When Paris reached the pair, he tapped the girl on the shoulder to gain her attention. She yelped in surprise, slapped him out of reflex and sank deeper into William's side. Not wanting her to assume he was angry or that he would retaliate, he kept his gaze on the warrior. "What's the word on the three immortals?"

He could have stopped by their rooms, they were just down the hall, but he'd rather find out through the gossip train that was William's mouth and save time.

Willy frowned at him. "For frick's sake. Apologize."

Frick? "She doesn't need to apologize to me." He gave her a reassuring grin. "I was recently informed that I have a very slappable face."

"I wasn't talking to her, I was talking to you. Apologize for startling her."

Oh. "Sorry, Gilly."

She offered him a soft smile in return. She was a pretty little thing, with dark hair and dark eyes, a sun-kissed complexion and the kind of curves no father ever wanted his daughter to have. "No worries. My bad. I lost track of my surroundings."

"Well, I can see why you'd want to tune things out rather than pay attention to Willy's ugly mug."

She chuckled and Paris faced William, saying, "So, the immortals?"

William shrugged. "No change. I've tried everything I can think of, and believe me, it was very impressive sh—uh, crap, but a no-go all the same. They're locked tight in those bedrooms."

"Any word on Kane?"

"Uh, yeah, about that." With his free hand, William massaged the back of his neck. "He's alive and he's in hell, but he's out of enemy hands. You guys want him back, though, you'll have to go down there and get him."

Something was off in the guy's tone. "How do you know this?" Not even Amun had been able to get to the truth.

"Just do. Group's leaving tomorrow, and by the way, you weren't invited. My guess is they think you're a crazy psycho who makes out with himself, but that's just a guess."

Whatever. "Who's going?"

"Amun, Haidee, Cameo, Strider and Kaia."

Mostly girls. Were their taskforces changing or what? "You're not going down there with 'em?"

"As if. I mean, sure, the captors kind of made it a condition to Kane's release, but…nah. I don't think I will. Got stuff to do, you know. Me and my Aussie have an intimate evening planned."

Intimate with his conditioner. Figured. "Who are *the captors?* And why are they insisting you go?" He didn't bother touching on William's refusal, because honestly? That didn't mean shit. If his appearance was a condition for obtaining Kane's freedom, he'd make an appearance. End of story.

William looked down at Gilly, his expression all gentleness and reverence, and gave her a little push. "Be a darling and find me some gummy bears."

Her eyelids, usually at half-mast and always halfway to the bedroom when she gazed at the warrior, narrowed. "So patronizing." Still, she stomped away, just as he'd wanted, affording them a bit of privacy.

"Be sure to watch your mouth while you're searching for my sweets," William called after her. That's when Paris caught sight of his T-shirt. It read, Save a Virgin, Do Me Instead. "Talking back isn't attractive."

"You're right. I should respect my elders." She didn't turn back, but she did extend a hand and flip him off.

Paris chuckled. "What are you teaching that girl?"

Suddenly serious, William gritted, "How to survive. Now, returning to our convo. Kane's captors happen to be some serious badasses I used to know down there."

Badasses tripped a memory. "You're talking about the Horsemen of the Apocalypse, right? Because yeah, Amun might have mentioned you're their baby daddy."

"That damned Amun." Electric eyes gleamed with the promise of retribution. "What a sissy gossip!"

Back to cussing were they, all the darns and fricks out of the equation?

"Oh, and speaking of gossip," William continued, his expression now anticipatory. "Have you seen Blood and Gore yet?"

"Who?"

"Pistol and Shank. I rename them every hour or so. Keeps things fresh."

Yeah, but what were their real names? "That's why I'm here. I want to meet them."

"Well, why didn't you say so?" William threw an arm around his shoulders and ushered him through the sea of familiar bodies. "Out of the way, mutants. My boy P is going in next."

"But it's my turn," Cameo said, and damn if that wasn't a whine in her voice, mixing with all the world's misery. She stepped in front of them to block their path to the door, her arms crossed over her chest. "Did you know that seven thousand babies die every year of—"

"*That's* why you're getting skipped." William offered her a sugar-sweet smile. "Besides, I delivered those hellions and almost had to take an eternal dirt nap because of it. I pick the order, and I say Paris is next."

Cameo frowned. She was one of the most beautiful women Paris had ever seen. More beautiful, even, than Viola, with long black hair and liquid silver eyes. Lips as plump and dewy as a rose.

"Did you know that about one percent of all births are stillborn?" she asked. The whine was gone, leaving only the misery.

She was also a major downer.

Stab me in the heart already, Paris thought. Because she played hostess to the demon of Misery, the sound of her voice was always enough to tear a guy up. Throw in her death statistics, which she'd been offering unsolicited more and more, and watch a party deflate like a balloon.

"Someone get this girl a lollipop and shove it deep in her mouth, stat," William shouted, urging Paris past her to the door. He didn't knock, but barreled inside. "All right, ladies. Our turn."

Reyes was sitting beside the bed, dark and menacing, with Strider the blond giant at his left. Both warriors were cooing at the thickly blanketed bundle of joy Reyes held.

Ashlyn was propped up on the bed, pale, shaky and clearly weak. Maddox sat beside her, holding the other bundle.

"Out," William added. "Paris wants to see Smith and Wesson."

"Don't call them that," Maddox said. Paris had never heard the keeper of Violence use such a gentle tone. It was more startling than being punched in the face.

"What do you want me to call them? Shits and Giggles? Fists and Kneecap? Nah, I don't like that one. Hammer and Nails? Dude, these kids are hard-core gangster. They need kick-A names, not that blah, blah sh—crap you gave them."

Slowly Reyes stood, waited for William to close the distance and gently placed the bundle in his arms. The dark warrior patted Paris on the shoulder as he left, and Strider did the same. Only, he stopped and said, "Meet me in the gym when you're done," before leaving.

Battling a wave of foreboding, Paris nodded. Then the two were gone, the door closed behind them, and he pushed the upcoming chat from his mind. He made his way to William, who seemed perfectly at ease holding such a fragile being. Only in secret had Paris ever allowed himself to contemplate having a family, because no way had he wanted to father a kid with a one-night stand. Now, with Sienna, who had been denied the chance to be a mother...

He wanted to give her this.

At William's side, he peered down at the first demon-human hybrid infant to join their crew—and what he saw nearly shocked the piss out of him.

"Gorgeous little fiend, isn't she?" William said, beaming down. He tickled her belly. "Oh, yes, she is. Yes, she really is."

Gurgling happily, the baby waved her little fists. Her eyes were open and clear, a vibrant, crackling orange-gold, and so freaking intelligent, despite the fact that she peered up at William with total, absolute adoration. And yeah, she was gorgeous. Already had a cap of honey-colored hair, the corkscrew curls spiking up from her head. But the real shocker? She had a mouthful of teeth. Really, really sharp teeth. And those cute little fists? Topped off by curling claws.

"Will she ever be able to pass as human?" he asked quietly, not wanting the probably sensitive mother to hear.

"Maybe, maybe not," Ashlyn answered anyway. "Time will tell. Either way, they are both beautiful beyond imagining."

Figured that she'd heard him. She herself might be human, but she could hear any conversation anywhere, no matter how many years had passed. That was her curse. And weren't the twins in for a real treat, never able to hide anything from mom.

"What's her name?" he asked.

"Ever," William said with no small amount of disgust. Ever did a fist pump in the air. With pride? Or anger?

"The name is perfect, just like her," Ashlyn said. Her

eyelids were fluttering closed, as if she were having trouble staying awake.

"Go on to sleep, sweetheart," Maddox told her. "I'll take care of everything."

"Thank you," she said as she sighed, head already lolling to the side.

"Want to hold her?" William asked Paris.

"Ashlyn? No, thanks." Maddox would brain him, same as Paris would brain any warrior who tried to hold Sienna. Not that any besides William and maybe Lucien could even see her at the moment.

William rolled his eyes. "You know what I meant. The *baby*. Ever."

"Oh, uh, yeah. I totally knew what you meant."

"Do you have to be so loud?" Maddox snapped in that quiet, gentle voice so at odds with the roughness of his features.

Paris held up his hands, palms out, whispering, "No way on the holding of the kidlet." He was too big, and too hard to do anything but bruise the little girl. Besides, Ever growled in his direction, her lips peeling back from her fangs, and it was very clear she was happy where she was.

He moved around to the other side of the bed, where Maddox held the boy. Of course, the warrior beamed with pride as he smoothed the blanket from the kid's face. Like Ever, the baby looked months old. He had a cap of black hair and his eyes were the same shade of violet as his daddy's and diamond-hard. Two little horns peeked from his skull, and there were patches of scales on his hands. Those scales were black and as smooth as glass.

With focused intensity, the boy studied Paris. And Paris had no doubt the kid had sized him up in a single heartbeat, learning his weaknesses, his flaws, and his bad habits, and was preparing for attack.

"What's his name?"

"Urban," William answered before Maddox could, and again he was all about the disgust.

Ever and Urban. Cute, in a Hollyweird sort of way. "What made you pick those particular names?"

"We didn't," Maddox said. "They did."

His eyes widened. "They can speak?"

"No, but they are very good at communicating."

And that would be…how? "So, I hear the birth was troublesome. How'd William save the day?"

Maddox stiffened, even as William shook his head and placed Ever in the bassinet beside the bed. When he straightened, William rocked his hand over his neck in a slicing motion. A kill-that-line-of-convo-*now* gesture.

"That goshdarn mothertrucking a-hole cut my woman up, ripped the babies out and sewed her back together." Maddox's nostrils flared, so heavily did he breathe. "Without anesthesia."

William popped his jaw. "There wasn't time. They were clawing their way out, and waiting any longer would have killed your Ashlyn for sure. And better a dagger slice, which is smooth, than the savage tearing that comes with claws. And by the way, you're welcome. They're all alive."

Well, all right, then. Like a coward, Paris abandoned ship, leaving William to endure Maddox's wrath on his own. He made his way to the gym on the bottom floor. Strider was there, as promised, running the treadmill like a man possessed. Which he was.

Blond hair was plastered to his scalp, and rivers of sweat ran down his deeply tanned skin.

The white-haired Torin was at the far side of the room,

bench-pressing enough weight to have fractured the marble floor. Shock rooted him in place for a moment. Torin never approached the masses, too afraid of someone accidentally touching him.

How'd he get here, anyway? Last Paris had heard, Disease had turned down Lucien's offer for air travel. And when the hell had Torin gotten so ripped? He usually holed up in his room, covered from neck to foot in black. Now, without a shirt, Paris saw the guy had the chiseled body of someone who could kick his ass.

Both men stopped what they were doing when they realized he'd entered. Paris whipped off his shirt, his gun holster and his blades, stored them on a bench and moved to the treadmill beside Strider.

"What'd you want to talk to me about?" He hit a few buttons, and then the thing was lifting and moving, giving him a grueling incline and a sprinting pace that felt unbelievably good. He hadn't exercised like this in a long time.

"What's this I hear about you having an invisible Hunter on the premises?" Strider asked, catching a towel Torin had thrown at him. He wiped his face, his gaze remaining on Paris. "The Hunter possessed by Wrath, I might add."

Shoulda known. "She's not a Hunter, not anymore, and she's not up for discussion."

"Like hell she isn't. My woman is here."

"Yeah, and your woman can take care of herself."

Pride flickered in Strider's navy eyes. "True enough. Fact remains, though, that an unseen enemy is the most dangerous. Your girl can do all kinds of damage to everyone here."

He cranked the speed up another thousand notches,

until his boots were hammering into the base and rattling the entire machine. "She's not out to hurt us."

"Yeah, so, I've got some wiring to do," Torin said from behind them. "You boys have at each other." Footsteps, and then it was just the two of them.

"You're telling me the girl who drugged you, who watched your torture, is no longer a threat to you or anyone?" Strider asked skeptically. "Please."

"We worked it out." Sweat beaded on his skin, too, dripping, dripping. His muscles burned just right, soaking up the strain, loving it.

"In the sheets, no doubt, but all that means is that you're thinking with something other than your brain. You gotta know that."

Don't challenge him, don't challenge him, don't you dare challenge him. You had to be careful around Strider. His demon took exception to any hint of confrontation, and then Strider had to battle it out, doing everything in his power to knock you senseless, or he'd suffer for days as punishment.

"Everyone accepted Haidee," Paris reminded him, "and she was a Hunter."

"Now she's the living embodiment of Love. It's kinda hard *not* to like and trust her. Your girl, we can't see or hear her. Can't judge her actions and her words for ourselves. Can't see how she is with you. And do you really need another *you're thinking with your man junk* speech?"

Darkness...rising... "I'm asking you to step off," Paris said, "before things get nasty and we have to work this out the hard way." If he had to go the challenge route to stop his friend from verbally slamming his woman, he would.

Silence. Then, a grisly, "I feel—"

"A burning sensation when you pee?" *Now you're just being mean.*

"Real mature," Strider said, but he calmed down a notch. "Me and you, we got history. More than the others know, more than the two of us ever want to acknowledge. But we both know it's one of the reasons we went our separate ways when the two groups split for while, me with Sabin and you with Lucien."

Heat seared Paris's cheeks, and it had nothing to do with physical strain. "We said we'd never talk or think about it." And he'd always kept up his end of that agreement.

"Apparently, times change. You were weak, dying. There were no humans around, and you refused to let any of us help you."

"Shut up." His happy day was going down the drain fast. "Just shut up."

"So, my demon took up the challenge, and I took care of you. Now I'm asking you to take care of your friends in turn. Get rid of the girl," Strider went on, ignoring the demand. "We lack one artifact, just one, and once we get it back we can start searching for Pandora's box. We can finally save ourselves. Not only can she spy on us, steal from us and hurt our more vulnerable members, she could ruin our future. Just think about it. For me."

Strider threw his towel in the hamper and stomped from the room.

CHAPTER FORTY-TWO

FOR SIENNA, THE NEXT few days passed in a blissful haze punctuated by moments of mourning. Except for two things, all was right in her world. But she wasn't going to think about those two things. She would erupt into one of her rare and shocking rages, and rip the entire castle apart.

Instead, she would think about the fact that Paris *adored* her. She would think about all the times she and Paris had made love, and how each time he had been more frantic to get inside her than the last. He'd taken her in ways that scandalized, delighted and thrilled, and in the quiet afterglow, they had talked.

No subject had been off-limits. They discussed the Hunters—where certain facilities were, the names of some of the higher officers, the location of the cavern where Galen supposedly met with Rhea and the pair performed rituals for "the greater good." Then they'd talked about themselves, about where they would travel and what they'd do if there hadn't been a war to fight.

Paris picked the mountains, with the cold and the snow and a soft rug in front of a fireplace. She picked the beach, wanting to watch him rise from the water, glittering droplets sliding along the ropes of his stomach and catching in her new favorite place on his body—because the waves would have stolen his swimsuit.

Of course, earlier this morning he'd strode out of the

shower, dripping wet, no towel in sight, with a wicked smile on his face, and she'd laughed at his antics (after she caught her breath). She was desperately trying to guard her heart against him despite his demand that they stay together, because she knew she still had to leave him for Galen, that she had to stop Rhea from taking the Titan throne, that she couldn't kill her greatest enemy because doing so would kill Cronus, and as he'd said, if he died, chaos would reign and *Paris* would die.

The only way to save him was to control Galen, and thereby Rhea. Not the best revenge, but it was all she could allow herself.

She wished Skye could have met Paris, wished the girl could have seen the good in him, that man and demon were not truly one and the same, that the demon was dark and dangerous, destructive, but the man was fun and caring, worthy of respect. Just like Sienna was not the sum total of Wrath's deeds, but a woman who fought for what was right.

Once upon a time, Sienna had considered giving the demon back to Aeron. But if she did, she would die—for real and forever—and she would be unable to avenge her sister, even in the smallest way. Plus, she needed him. He still hadn't figured out what was "wrong" with Skye's death.

Don't cry, Enna. Boys are stupid, Mama said so, and if that fathead Todd doesn't want to go to the dance with you, he's the stupidest ever!

I miss you so much, Skye. Sienna turned the corner—and barreled into a speeding golf cart. After crash-landing on her butt, she saw the cart was blue with orange flames painted on the sides, and the minor goddess of the Afterlife/keeper of Narcissism was at the wheel.

"Sorry, I'm sorry." Most times Sienna didn't bother watching where she was going, because only Paris, Viola and Lucien could see and touch her. Everyone and everything else she ghosted through and no one ever even knew. But because the cart belonged to Viola, Sienna could feel the metal that had just flattened her lungs.

"I'm late," Viola said, waving a piece of paper in the air. "You, too? Do you need a ride?"

As always, Wrath shot Sienna's mind full of images. Viola, breaking hearts. Viola, double-crossing others to save herself. Viola, unconcerned by the pain she left in her wake.

Punish...

A whisper rather than an urge. For some reason, Wrath had been on his best behavior lately, never trying to overtake her, his hunger under control though she'd done nothing to feed him.

"Sienna. Female...ghost person. Do you need a ride? Time is a serious issue right now."

"I would love a ride." She needed a few minutes alone with the woman, so this was actually perfect. "I've been looking for you." No longer did she bear any ill will toward the woman. After all, Sienna had watched Paris interact with her, and the guy could barely mask his impatience to escape.

But having done all of that watching, Sienna now knew how to deal with the goddess. She also knew Viola was one of the few people who wouldn't curse her outright, who would hear her out.

"Well, hop on and stop standing there all lost in your thoughts. I don't want to miss the good part."

Sienna didn't ask what "the good part" was, because the woman would have explained in minute detail about how everything pertained to her. She simply unfolded from the floor and slid into the plush leather seat, careful of her wings.

"Well?" the goddess prompted, stomping on the pedal. They jolted into motion, cutting corners, honking at nothing, flashing their lights. "What did you want to talk to me about?"

To begin: flattery. "As intelligent and powerful as you are, you're the only one capable of helping me."

"Well, of course I am. Here's a well-known fact. I'm more than made of awesome. I am the original awesome." From behind the wheel, Viola flicked her pale hair over her shoulder. She wore a gown of shimmery gold, the material cinched just under her breasts and flaring at her hips. Red-carpet worthy, for sure. "Soooo?"

"I'm trying to figure out how best to ask for what I need."

"Try opening your mouth and forming words. That's what I do, and I can assure you my methods are always stellar."

Sienna ran her tongue over her teeth, not allowing herself to issue a snappy retort. She didn't think Viola meant to be so haughty, but hello, a girl could only take so much. "Well, I'm running out of time."

And there was the main reason for her recent string of temper tantrums. Her time here was ticking, ticking away. Soon she would have to leave. Not just because she had heard some of Paris's friends plotting her downfall, and not just because those same friends hated her guts and would never trust or forgive her, but because she really was going to Galen, keeping him away from Cronus, so that Cronus could keep Rhea away from his throne, no matter how sickening the tasks she had to perform.

"Do you want me to buy you more time?" Viola asked,

as if such a thing were possible. They reached the stairs. Without pause, she took them. Bounce, bounce, bounce. "You'd have to pay me back. I mean, with two-hundred-percent interest, but—"

"No, I...well, when I leave, Paris will weaken." Her head slammed into the roof of the vehicle. *Oh, please, please don't let my next death be in a tragic golf cart accident.* "I don't know if you know this, but he has to have sex every day or his body shuts down. His demon is...needy, you know."

"Yada, yada, boring." Landing smoothly, the cart erupted into full speed. (Twenty-five miles per hour.)

She bit her tongue to hold in her retort. "When I leave I want you to make sure Paris sleeps with the women Lucien brings him, and that he *keeps* sleeping with them."

And there was the second reason for her temper tantrums. Due to pressure from Sienna's staunchest haters, Lucien kept disappearing and reappearing with a new woman in the hope that one would entice Paris away from her.

While Paris could easily ignore his friends, the persistent and determined Viola would find a way to get her way. Otherwise, she would be a failure, and the goddess would never allow herself to be a failure.

"What I'm hearing is, I'm the only thing standing between your man and his certain death," Viola said. "So what's in it for me if I save him?"

For a moment, Sienna couldn't reply; there was a giant lump in her throat. This was killing her. She wanted Paris all to herself, now and always, and oh, she really did love the man, didn't she? Body, heart and soul, she loved him. She'd been falling slow and steady, but now she was flat on her face, nothing but a puddle of love.

He was everything to her. Her light when things became too dark. When she cried, he comforted her. When she laughed, he laughed with her. He treated her as if she were a special treasure. He protected her, cared about every ache and pain she might experience.

She would tear the world apart to keep him safe. She would willingly suffer without him, as long as she knew he was out there, alive.

"What would you like from me?" Sienna wasn't going to quibble. What the goddess wanted, she would give. It was as simple as that.

"You're Wrath, right? Well, when I call on you to slay one of my enemies, you have to slay him. No questions, no hesitation."

"As long as the enemy in question isn't someone Paris or his friends know and like. Or want alive."

The goddess thought for a moment, nodded. "We have ourselves a deal."

"Good. Now, I have one other request for you." She outlined what she wanted.

Viola shot her a sly smile. "Wicked, and quite shocking coming from you. I had no idea you were into that. You look so mousy. But it's always the quiet ones, isn't it?"

"Will you do it?"

"You'll owe me two slayings, same conditions."

"Done." It was done.

"Now, hold on tight because I'm cranking this baby up. I'm just certain they won't start without me, but these Lords sometimes defy logic, so you never know."

"Oh, good." A woman with curly dark hair, a face as innocent as a cherub's and wings of the purest white appeared just in front of them. "I found you."

Viola slammed on the breaks, and the cart skidded to

a stop mere inches from crushing the newcomer under the tires. "What's with all the ladies jumping in front of me and keeping me from where I want to go? Jealous much?"

"I seek Sienna."

"Me?" Sienna's heart suddenly felt as if it had been injected with adrenaline. That had been a close call, sure, but that wasn't why she was palpitating. "Heaven," she whispered, the reverent yearning in her voice flowing straight from her demon.

"Yes, you. I'm Olivia," the angel said with a sweet smile. A white robe draped her from shoulders to ankles, making her look as if she'd just stepped from a dream.

Viola jumped out of the cart and hurried past Olivia. "Have fun girls, I'm needed elsewhere." Pale hair streaming behind her, she disappeared into the ballroom about a yard ahead.

"I recognize you," Sienna said, even though the two of them had never met. She stood on shaky legs, closed the distance—*heaven, my heaven*—and reached out, pinching a strand of those curls between her fingers. Soft, silky. "Wrath loves you, I think."

Olivia's smile went full-on sunshine as she scratched Sienna behind her ear. "How's my darling boy doing?"

Wrath purred like a kitten.

"He's, uh, good."

"I'm glad. He really is a sweetheart, isn't he?"

Wrath?

The demon rolled to his back, kicked up his legs and shook as great tides of rapture swept over him.

"Let's you and me chat later, all right?" Olivia said, arm dropping to her side. While Wrath pouted like a toddler, the angel added, "Aeron sent me to find you. He wanted to speak to you himself, but he can't see you and conversing with the woman who has his Wrath through a third party would be a little too painful. Maybe one day. But I digress. He's ready to leave this castle and hunt for Legion, but won't because Paris is about to have an aneurism. At least, that's what Aeron said, and he thinks you're the only one who can calm his boy down."

Paris. Worry instantly flooded her, her demon's preoccupation with the angel overshadowed. "Where is he?"

"Just follow the trail Viola blazed." Stepping to the side, Olivia motioned toward the ballroom.

Sienna darted into motion, flying through the open doorway and once again stopping dead in her tracks. A group of the warriors and their mates stood under a banner that said only INTERVENTION in big block letters. They each held a piece of paper. Viola had taken her place in the center, shifting eagerly, ready to say her piece.

Sienna's gaze locked on the warrior named Aeron, the man who'd once hosted Wrath. He had closely cropped dark hair, beautiful violet eyes, and his body, which had once been covered in the tattooed images of the victims of his blood rages, was now slowly being covered with tattoos of his angel.

Seeing him, Wrath went crazy inside Sienna's head, wanting to reach out, to touch the warrior. *Friend. My friend.*

I know, but now's not the time to catch up with him. Honestly? She wasn't sure any time would be right. The guy scared her. He looked like he ate kittens for breakfast and thumb tacks for lunch. His dinner wasn't something she dared contemplate. Organs might be involved.

Wrath pouted. The demon had wanted back inside of Aeron as much as Sienna had wanted to get rid of him. But she had changed her mind, and she hoped Wrath had, too. He wasn't begging to escape her. For all she knew, he was as addicted to Paris as she was.

Friend. Talk to friend.

Soon, she promised. Wrath whimpered, and she had to force herself to look away. Paris stood in front of the group, his back to Sienna. His sun-bronzed skin was bare from the waist up, and his muscles were knotted. At his sides, his hands were fisted.

Anya was reading her letter out loud. "—you're okay, I guess. I mean, if Lucien says you're good people, you're good people. I think you've got a really hot body with a lot of delicious brawn and sinew, and even though I wouldn't do you without having an emergency medical exam afterward, a lot of women with low self-esteem would totally hit that."

"Anya," Lucien said with a truckload of exasperation.

She glanced up at him, all innocence. "What? You said start the letter with praise before going into the root of the problem. Now zip it so I can finish. You already got to read yours." She cleared her throat, glanced back down at the paper. "Making out with an invisible woman is a disease. And really creepy. If I see you with your hands squeezing air one more time, I'm going to sand-paper my corneas."

"Enough," Paris said with quiet menace.

"My turn," Viola said.

Ignoring both of them, the lithe goddess of Anarchy continued. "Add in the fact that Inviso-babe is a Hunter, and you've got a recipe for *oh, shit.* Which isn't good for your health. Or ours. Mainly ours. That is why we humbly request that you enter some sort of treatment program before that woman enters you in a death program with guns, knives and a rack. And by *rack* I don't mean boobs."

Wow, that hurt. It shouldn't. Sienna had brought this on herself, deserved it one hundred percent, and had done nothing to earn their trust. *Still.* Ouch. Her lover's friends had hosted an intervention to get Sienna out of his life.

One of Paris's hands slid back, around his waist, his fingers curling around the hilt of a knife.

He was going to blow a fuse, she thought, and she didn't want him at war with his friends because of her. Not now, not ever. So, yeah, she was leaving. Sooner rather than later.

Her chest constricted, heralding the sharp lances of pain from a breaking heart. Didn't matter, though. She would take one more day with him. Just one. Then, bye-bye forever. "Paris," she said, doing her best to mask her hurt.

He spun, those electric-blues she loved so much crackling with fury, the malicious shadows dancing through their depths.

Gently she said, "Come up to the roof with me," and waved him over. "I need to practice my flying." Truth, and the reason she wasn't leaving the fortress right this second, was instead allowing herself this extra day with him. She had to be prepared for anything. And, yeah, she wanted to say goodbye properly—in bed. "No need to worry about the vines there. The gargoyles eat the walls clean, and William's blood is on the outer rail, I checked, so the shadows won't bother us, either."

"My friends are… They need…" He was dragging oxygen through his nose so intensely his nostrils were flaring.

"No, they don't. You are not going to be mad at them over this." A command she had no power to enforce, but one she would see through.

"Yes, I am."

Behind him, Viola relayed the conversation only she and Lucien could hear, clearly thrilled to be the center of attention. Sienna tuned her out. Only Paris mattered right now.

More forcefully, she said, "Paris, I'm not offended by this." She was destroyed. "Now come here. I need a cheerleader, and I'm thinking you'll look great in a skirt, holding poms."

He didn't crack a smile. That unholy, malevolent rage still held him in a tight grip. So, really, there was only one other thing do to.

"Catch me," she said, sprinting to him. He would never forgive himself if he fought his loved ones.

"No, don't come near me while I'm like...*this*. Humph."

She'd launched herself at him. Those strong arms did indeed catch her, winding around her and clamping on like shackles. Tremors vibrated from him and into her.

Acting fast, she nipped at his ear. "If you hurt them, you'll get blood on my castle walls—well, more blood, and I'll be very upset." Only once before had she ever tried to use feminine wiles, and that had been the first time they met. Now she lifted her head just enough for him to see her face, and batted her lashes. "Please come to the roof with me. Please."

He peered at her for a long while, silent, before finally relaxing. He pressed a kiss straight into her mouth, daring the quickest of tastes, the tease, before striding out with her still clutched in his arms.

"My eyes," Anya whined. "Oh, my eyes."

"I think we just made a huge mistake," Lucien said gravely.

Paris never looked back and neither did Sienna.

CHAPTER FORTY-THREE

THE MOMENT PARIS STEPPED onto the roof, he sensed the evil waiting to attack. Thanks to William's blood, the shadows couldn't get inside the castle or pass the rail, just as Sienna had said, but what waited for him wasn't exactly a shadow.

Wanting no part of the coming action, Sex retreated faster than ever.

Palming his crystal blades—nope, make that *blade,* he had just the one now—Paris maneuvered Sienna to her feet and behind him. The sky was a strip of black velvet with no pinprick of stars, the moon a crimson hook in the corner, just as before. Moisture clung to the air, hot in spots, cold in others.

Either Sienna sensed the menace, too, or she knew not to distract him. She remained quiet. His gaze arrowed over, lit on a darker patch of onyx, and shit, another dark patch, then another, gliding together, coalescing, elongating…until a man stood before him, shrouded by the black, the mist like a veil in front of him.

Sienna gasped. In fascination or horror, he wasn't sure.

Guy was handsome, if you liked serial killers, with cold black eyes, more muscles than even Paris sported, and shoulders wide enough to take down the entire first line of defense in a game of touch football.

Paris crouched, a coiled snake ready to dart and bite.

Dude had made a mistake, approaching now. Since Paris had walked into that intervention and realized his friends were still gunning for him to ditch Sienna, fury had been a seething tide inside him.

He understood their reasons. He did. And he couldn't blame them. But doing what they'd done out in the open, just to hurt her, was taking things too far.

He commanded his crystal to become a weapon capable of killing such a creature, and the thing instantly morphed into—a klieg? Someone play whaa whaa whaa for Debbie Downer, because seriously. Kinda felt like he was going to a shootout with, well, a freaking klieg.

Shadow Man laughed, the sound all creepiness and no joy. "I know what you wonder. I can bypass the blood, yes. And I will if I must. My phantoms feed from the immortals, and that is payment rendered for their stay. Yet now you house the Lord of the Dark, their enemy, and keep my boys from their due. That is unacceptable."

"Your phantoms aren't feeding on my friends." He recalled the warrior lying in a pool of his own blood, what was left of his insides spilled on the floor. The prisoner's pain had been unbearable to witness, so Paris could just imagine what the guy had felt.

"Other arrangements must be made, or I will force you out of my realm. You will not like my methods, I assure you."

There was a time for physical confrontation, and a time for bargaining. "What else would they like to eat?"

"Immortals." Clipped, angry. "Only immortals."

"Then we've got a problem." He inched backward, edging Sienna to the door.

Shadow Man lurched forward, that dark mist stretching and gliding like wings. Paris swung the flashlight, his thumb flipping the on switch. White light cut through the darkness, but just before reaching his opponent, the man rolled through the air and out of the way.

When he stilled, they faced off. Paris twirled the thin flashlight in his palm. "That all you got? Huh?" A taunt meant to buy Sienna enough time to blast inside. He hoped she understood that, but he couldn't hear footsteps, couldn't hear the door slam.

"If I showed you what I've got, it would be the last thing you *ever* saw."

"Prove it."

Like that, they were on each other, a choreographed dance straight from *Star Wars*. Funny that they both knew the moves. Paris used the klieg like a light saber, twirling the golden stream as he contorted his body left and right to dodge the sashay of those misty wings.

Finally, contact. When the light sliced through one of Shadow Man's legs, there was a sizzle, a rise of steam, and the big guy released a firing-squad shout, his anger like little bullets that pelted against Paris's mind, causing him to stumble.

That stumble cost him.

One of those dark wings whipped out and hit his arm with so much force the flashlight flew from his grip. Not mist, after all. Then that big body engulfed him, closing around him. Screams, thousands upon thousands of screams, echoed around him. So loud his eardrums burst and warm blood poured down his lobes.

Releasing a scream of his own, he covered his ears and fell to his knees. Ants were crawling all over him, surely eating at his flesh, ripping it away, consuming him bite by tasty bite.

Another firing-squad shout sounded, and the darkness instantly lifted from him. Took him a moment to orient himself, and what he saw made him want to vomit. Shadow Man was a few feet away, and Sienna was holding him off with the flashlight. Their mouths were moving, but Paris couldn't hear what they were saying.

Until...*boom,* his eardrums healed and the volume came back on in an explosion of noise.

"—how many would you be willing to settle for... consuming?" Sienna was saying, trying not to reveal her disgust.

"Five. A day."

"They never got five before! One," she snapped. "A week."

"Three. A day."

"Three. A week."

A moment of silence before Shadow Man nodded. "Agreed. First payment must be given *today.*"

"Yes, but only if all of us—the Lords, their loved ones, the babies, the immortals, me—are safe, no matter where we go in this realm or what we do."

Another moment of silence, another nod. "And so the deal is made. But best you hurry, female. I might change my mind before the first payment is delivered." With that, the black mist thinned, broke apart and disappeared altogether.

Sienna rushed to Paris's side and sank to her knees, patting him down, checking for injuries.

"Are you okay?"

He hung his head. He hadn't saved her, hadn't helped her. She'd had to save him. She'd had to help him. He'd let her down in so many ways. What kind of warrior *was* he?

"I'm sorry, baby."

"What? Why?" She handed him the flashlight.

A quick mental command, and the crystal blade returned. He stashed the thing at his waist. "I let you down.

You could have been hurt." And Zacharel had warned him about that, hadn't he? That Paris's temper would get the better of him and he would hurt his woman. He'd thought that meant he would strike at her, which he knew would never happen. But, no. The angel had known better. His temper would cause him to lose focus, to allow *others* to hurt her.

Yeah. Well. That was so not happening again. He'd keep himself level no matter what the hell he had to do.

"Paris, you've never let me down," she said with feeling.

Yeah, he had, but that stopped now. His thigh muscles burned like a son of a bitch as he stood. He helped her do the same. Inside the castle, he tucked her into a corner, checked the only window in the small alcove to make sure William's blood was still smeared over the top—it was—then cupped her cheeks.

"Stay here for me, okay? I've got to tell Lucien to find us three acceptable, uh, meals."

"They don't have to be immortal," she said. "He finally admitted that immortals taste better, but anyone will do."

Then Paris knew exactly who to use. Last he'd looked, there were Hunters stashed in their Budapest dungeon.

"Who are—"

"Don't you worry about that." If she knew the men, well, he wasn't sure how she'd react. "In fact, why don't you go to our room instead of staying here? I'll join you in a bit. Okay?" He kissed her before she could reply, and left her there.

Didn't take him long to locate Lucien. The warrior was still in the ballroom, and when he caught sight of Paris he apologized all over himself, his mismatched eyes filled with regret.

"We'll talk about the intervention later. Right now I need you to do something."

He explained what he needed, and the warrior was Johnny-on-the-spot, disappearing and returning a few minutes later with a Hunter clutched in each hand. Humans were easier to transport than immortals.

The men, both in their late thirties by the looks of them, were grimy, weak and had no fight left. Paris claimed them, and Lucien went back for a third.

Maybe this should have settled heavily on his shoulders, but these men had been captured while trying to slaughter his friends and their lovers. They would have cut the throats of the females without a moment's hesitation.

They deserved what they got.

When Lucien returned, they muscled their loads up the stairs and back into that small alcove. Sienna hadn't moved an inch, and Paris cursed under his breath. But she didn't say anything when she spotted his burdens, even though her mouth opened as if she had plenty to unleash. She just watched with wide eyes as he and Lucien stepped onto the roof.

"Stay," he commanded, shutting the door in her face. He didn't want her to see what happened next.

He and Lucien approached the edge and looked down. A whole lot of airtime before reaching the rocky, blood-soaked ground. Whatever. He still wasn't gonna feel bad. But he did wonder, again, if Sienna knew these guys. If she'd understand why he'd picked them. If she'd understand that he would use the information she'd given him to find more Hunters, to bring them here and use them in the same way, for as long as necessary.

Drop them, a disembodied voice he now recognized said on a sudden wind.

Only then did the Hunters begin to struggle. Paris and Lucien shared a moment of oh, shit before shoving them over. Shadows immediately darted from the sky, surrounding the men, catching them, and then devouring them. Screams, more pain-filled than the ones he'd heard while inside Shadow Man, rent the night. Then, silence.

And so the deal is sealed, another wind proclaimed. *You are safe. For now.*

He wasn't sure he could trust the Shadow Man, but Sienna would have caught a lie, so there you go. "Thanks," he said to Lucien.

"Of course." A pause, a sigh. "Listen. I *am* sorry about what happened, and I will talk to the others. I've never liked what we were doing to you, how we were pushing you, and I'll make sure your woman is respected. She's who you want, she's who you'll get."

His throat tightened up. "Thanks," he repeated.

Lucien drilled a hand on his shoulder, a love pat with more strength than he probably realized, before taking off. As he exited, Sienna entered.

"Hey," she said, expression blank.

"Hey," he replied. Trepidation, foreboding, yeah, he felt them.

"So the toll's been paid?"

He nodded mutely.

"Good. I saw their sins. Those men were awful, had done terrible things. Wrath wanted a go at them."

That was it? That was her response? She wasn't going to question him, castigate him? Was just going to accept? "I love you," he said. He couldn't hold the words back. There was no hiding the truth any longer, not even from himself.

Her jaw dropped. Those beautiful hazels were once

again all about the emerald, the chocolate completely overshadowed. He was more into this woman than he'd ever been into another. So into her that he would die for her. Willingly, happily.

She just fit him. Made him happy. Relaxed him, excited him, challenged him.

"I—I…" Twin pink circles appeared on her cheeks. Arousal, maybe. At least, he hoped.

"No, don't say anything." He motioned her over, said huskily, "Just come here."

She stumbled over to him, and he drew her close for a hug. Breathing deeply, he drank in her tropical scent, letting it brand him, remake him. There wasn't anyone or anything that could keep him from this woman. She was his. Now and always.

He placed the sweetest of kisses against the wildly hammering pulse at the base of her neck. "Let's practice your flying, okay?"

"O-okay."

She loved him back; she had to love him back. If she didn't, he would seduce her, romance her and woo her until she did. *Most important battle of my life.*

He set her away from him, and they spent the next few hours working on extending her wings properly and quickly enough, as well as getting her feet off the ground. Having never flown himself, he repeated the things Aeron had told him, the things he'd learned simply from watching the warrior, and he was happy to note Sienna made progress. But shit, he knew there was a lot he didn't know.

Eventually Sex came out of hiding, enjoying the contact, pushing Paris to take things to the next level.

Not yet. This is too important.
You told me "often."

And you've been getting often, you stupid shit.

"She'll never learn to sustain flight like that." Familiar male voice. Behind him.

Paris didn't bother turning around. "What do you suggest?" He was willing to take suggestions in this, and only this.

Zacharel sidled up to him, his fingers stroking his stubble-free chin. "I can only teach her the way I was taught. She must stand at the edge of the roof and spread her wings as far as she can get them."

"What if I fall?" she gasped. "I won't be able to catch myself in the air."

"You will not fall," the angel said, and the layer of truth in his voice was as convincing as ever.

Sienna met Paris's eyes, and he nodded. Flying was important. Flying could one day save her soul. Because yes, as the shadows had proven, even souls could be ravaged.

Gulping, she brushed past him. The moment her fingers trailed over his, he grabbed on to them, linked their hands and decided to walk with her. Her trembling increased with every step.

"Afraid of heights, baby?" he asked, when they reached the flat edge.

"I shouldn't be, but that's a long way down."

"S'all good. We won't let anything happen to you. Promise."

"Step back," Zacharel commanded, and though reluctant to sever contact, Paris obeyed. "Now stretch your wings," the angel said to Sienna.

Those black gossamer wings extended to their full length, lovely in a way he'd never before noticed. A deep, rich purple veined the black, swirled in the center and stretched to the tips.

"Excellent. Now, try not to let this next part frighten you." Without any further warning, Zacharel pushed her off the ledge.

She gave a horrified gasp as she tumbled from the roof, heading down…down…

"Noooo!" Paris's stomach bottomed out as he launched forward, meaning to dive off after her.

The angel stopped him with a right uppercut to the jaw, sending him propelling backward. Sex whimpered at the pain exploding through his head, but refused to retreat, refused to hide.

"You said she wouldn't fall!" Paris shouted as he stood, intending to try again. He was going after her, and that was that.

"She didn't fall. I pushed her."

"If she's hurt—"

Zacharel vanished, reappearing a second later with Sienna at his side. There was a green tint to her skin, and when she realized solid ground held her up, she hunched over, gagging, trembling uncontrollably.

"You…bastard…" she got out.

"This is the only way to learn." No emotion layered Zacharel's voice. Just a whole lot of *what'd-I-do-wrong*. "This is how we are taught. Besides, you are a soul. Had you made contact with the ground, I doubt you would have burst open like a melon."

"You doubt!"

"Find your brave core, demon girl. Step back up and we will try again."

Paris delivered an uppercut of his own. The angel's head whipped to the side, blood leaking from the gash in his bottom lip, but he merely straightened and blinked in confusion.

"You do anything like that again, and I will end you." Paris didn't wait for a reply, but gathered Sienna in his arms and carried her to their room.

CHAPTER FORTY-FOUR

"WHY DON'T you take a shower and relax, baby?" Paris said as he set Sienna down on their bed. "I'll be back in a few."

She had no idea what he was planning or where he was going, but she nodded. She could use a little alone time. Her heartbeat was currently engaged in a world-record race.

He kissed her forehead and was off, shutting her inside. Shower, yes, that's what she needed. After all, she had just plunged toward certain death, unable to force her wings to work, and the only reason she had survived was that the angel who'd tried to off her had caught her seconds before the splat.

Punish, Wrath said.

The first time he'd ever wanted to hurt an angel. Either he'd taken the shove personally or his hunger had returned.

On her stumble into the bathroom, she noticed that Viola had come through for her. A ring rested on the nightstand, its only stone a huge amethyst in the center. Good. Yeah. Good. Not heartbreaking.

The warm water relaxed her somewhat, but she had no desire to linger. Just shampooed, soaped up, rinsed off and towel-dried. About five minutes had elapsed. What a day. And yet, despite the near-death experience, she had a feeling that, when she looked back, this would be her favorite day of all time. Paris had said he loved her.

Not saying it back had nearly destroyed her, especially as he'd worked her over, his hands sliding along her wings, caressing yet firm, as he taught her what he knew about flying. But she was leaving him tomorrow, never to return, never to see him again, and well, yeah. Not going there.

When she emerged from the bathroom, she saw him sitting on the edge of the bed, facing her, his elbows resting on his knees. He wore an expression she'd never seen on him before, one of such glowing tenderness her knees almost buckled.

"Come here," he said.

Dropping the towel, naked and glistening, she obeyed without hesitation, stopping between his spread legs. His big hands settled on her hips, his thumbs lightly rasping over the flare of her waist. She shivered.

"Where did you go?" She tunneled her fingers through his hair, adoring the soft strands as they lifted and fell.

"Just out in the hall. I was going to lose it, and I didn't want you to see. Punched a few holes in the wall. Now I just want to hold you for a minute. Okay?"

Always. "Yes."

He tugged her closer, his arms tightening around her, and then he laid his head just over her breast, his warm breath trekking over her skin, his ear pressed into her heartbeat. They stayed like that for a long while, until she was shaking with the need to touch him, to be with him fully.

He must have sensed her desire because he urged her forward, taking more of her weight, more, until he lay flat and she was on top of him. Then he turned both their bodies sideways, rolled her and settled her in front of him, so that he cradled her. His chest to her spine, his erection pressing between her cheeks.

"Let me love you," he whispered. "I want to fill you and move in you and come in you. I want to be so deep in you, baby. So damn deep." His hand moved between her breasts, angled, and kneaded the upper, rubbing against her nipple, creating the most delicious friction.

"Yes," she repeated. Her brain was fogging, her every thought belonging to him, to what he was doing.

His other hand moved between her legs and found the center of her desire. "All this honey. All mine." One finger burrowed into the gap her legs created and penetrated her, then another.

She rocked with his inward strokes, arching into him. "I love the way you work me."

He nibbled on her ear. Slid a third finger home. Moan after moan cut through her throat, booming through the room.

"Get me all wet, baby. I want you all over me, coating me, drenching me."

She continued to rock…rock against him, losing herself, happy to lose herself, never wanting to be found, desperate to remain here, with him, always, lost, so lost.

"So perfect. More."

She squeezed her eyelids shut, her ears picking up sounds she'd previously missed. The hard rasp of his breath, coming faster and faster. The shift of his hips against the sheets, the slow grind of flesh against flesh. "Paris."

"I'm going to do you so good." His voice was guttural, almost totally animal. "I'm going to be in you, and I'm going to have you down my throat, your taste in my mouth. You're going to welcome me inside, aren't you."

"Oh, yes. Please, yes."

He removed his fingers, and she cried out, her desperation for him cranking out of control. How he'd get everything he wanted, she didn't know, but at least she wasn't empty for long. He clutched her upper knee and parted her legs, and without a pause in the glide of his hips, he slid as deep as he'd promised. She cried out again, this time in relief, stretched and filled and nearly insane with her need for more.

He moved in her, even as he traced her lips with his wet fingers—wet with *her*—and slid two digits inside her mouth. "Suck them."

She did, oh, she did, tasting herself, the erotic act new for her, but so damn arousing. She rolled those fingers around, sucked on them as commanded, bit down on them. Then his fingers were gone and he was angling her face, and his mouth was pressing against hers, his tongue darting inside, taking the taste of her into himself. All the while he moved in her, so, so deep, then almost all the way out, then so, *sooooo* deep.

This was more than sex, some distant instinct told her; this was a bonding, a mating. He was all over her, in her, and she was all over him, in him. This man…oh, this man. She couldn't get enough, would never get enough.

"Where am I?" he suddenly demanded. His thrusts were becoming jerkier, slamming inside harder, harsher.

"Here." A moan of passion. "With me."

"Where am I?"

"All over me. In me."

"Yeah. That's right. All over you. In you. I'm yours, and you are mine." He dove back in for another soul-stealing kiss, shattering her, claiming her. "You like this."

Not a question, but she answered anyway. "Love. This." As many times as they'd been together, he'd never been this intense, this focused on ownership. And hell, she wanted to own him, too. She reached up and back and fisted his hair, holding on tight, not caring when the strands pulled.

He hissed in a breath.

Her hips arched back, with force this time, slamming into him. Both of them groaned at the bliss. She edged ever closer to release, and he was right there with her.

"Take me, baby. Take all of me. Yeah. That's it. You know the way."

Pressure, building and building, consuming. Just a little more… "Paris!" One more hard slam and she was shooting into the stars, pleasure flooding her in a rush, a storm. Her inner walls clutched at him, grabbing on to him, letting him know he was where he belonged, that this was right, that they were right.

He rolled her all the way to her stomach, pressing her face into the pillows, and hammered harder, faster. A roar ripped out of him, as rough as his thrusts, and he filled her up, coming and coming and coming some more. She was right there with him, launching into a second orgasm, one that snuck up on her, but took her ever higher.

When she came back to earth, she blinked open her eyes. Had she passed out? She must have, because Paris was on his side, and she was on her side, and they were facing each other, but she didn't recall moving. His breathing was a little off, so she didn't think very much time had passed. He'd drawn the sheet over their bodies and was peering over at her, as if memorizing her features.

"I want to leave with you," he said. "Go somewhere Cronus can't find you. Where no one can hurt you."

Her heart lurched. No one—meaning his friends. "I

told you. I don't want you to be mad at anyone on my behalf."

"They disrespected you."

"And I deserved it."

"No!" He threw a punch, his fist going through the headboard, wood shards raining. "*I* told *you* not to talk like that. And the next time you do, I'm putting you over my knee. They aren't perfect, not a single one of them. We've all done things. Things that would shame hardened criminals."

"Well, they're reformed."

"So are you. I'm not saying I want to leave them forever. I love them. Need them. I just want to give them time to accept you. And just so you know, if I ever treated their women the way they've treated you, they would retaliate."

She had to change the subject. *Had. To.* He was melting her resolve. Being what she needed, saying such wonderful things. And he meant them. His tone was all about the serious.

"Hiding from Cronus," she said. "I don't think that's possible."

Gradually he relaxed. "There are medallions. Whoever wears them is hidden from him and all his followers. He gave them to us once, then took them away. I can steal one."

And enrage the beast, placing himself in eternal danger? "No. I have to do this, Paris. I have to go to Galen, and Cronus is going to take me. I just have to," she finished lamely. *For you, for me.*

"That's it?" Anger returned to those electric eyes. "You're not even going to think about it? When the very idea of my enemy breathing the same air as you drives me to commit murder?"

Her own anger sparked. "When it comes to putting you in danger? When it comes to making sure you survive? There isn't anything to think about."

He softened, but only slightly. "Same with me. I don't want you in danger. Ever. And you think about this. I will waste away without you. Yeah, I know I'm the king of manipulation, playing on your emotions, but I will do *anything* to keep you. I will kill. I will lie. I will betray and cheat and steal. I will topple mountains."

"Paris, I—"

He wasn't done. "All my life I have fought and I have fucked, and I thought I was happy until you pissed me off and woke me up and I realized I'd simply existed and accepted. And you might have gotten my attention through my demon, but you kept it because of *you.* I could have anyone right now, and no, that isn't ego or a front, it's just me telling you that now that Sex knows I'm committed, he's making me hard for every damn female in the place, or he was, and he can again, but I don't want them and I won't take them."

Careful, girl. This man, *this man she loved,* could talk her into anything. There could be no spending the rest of the night with him. She had to leave. And she had to leave now.

The knowledge shattered her.

"Sienna, baby. I know I'm coming on strong. I know I'm pushing for a lot. Just…give me some time, okay? We'll figure this out. There's a solution, there has to be. Trust me."

So many pieces of her, scattered and broken, never to be fitted back together. "I do," she croaked. "I trust you." The truth, but it wouldn't stop her.

"Good." He must have assumed she'd agreed to give him time.

She didn't correct the mistake.

"Now, I want you to listen to me. Do you remember when I told you not to let anyone smell your blood, to always clean yourself up if you are injured?" He waited for her nod before he went on. "That's because Cronus has made you into an ambrosia spout. Your blood is a drug for immortals and highly addictive."

"That's not—" Yeah, no reason to finish that sentence. Anything was possible. She was living—er, undead—proof of that. Bitterness rose, joining the anger and the hopelessness. "How did he do it? *Why* would he?" Even as she spoke, she knew the answer to the latter.

Why—so that she could more easily "seduce" and control Galen. That's how she would keep his interest. How dare he do this! she seethed. How dare he turn her into a…a…walking narcotic!

Punish…PUNISH.

Yes. She would punish. Would that stop her from doing what needed doing? No. Not when Paris's life was at stake. But, oh, she and Cronus would have a reckoning one day.

Wrath grunted his approval.

Gruff, Paris said, "I'm sorry about what happened, baby. I wish I could go back, stop him."

Melting… "Is there a way to fix me?"

"Not to my knowledge."

She leaned into Paris, pressing her lips into his. He wanted to continue the conversation, she could tell, but he was into the kiss and accepted her tongue, taking it as his right—and it was. While he was distracted, she reached for the ring Viola had left her. Slid the metal onto her middle finger.

Tears burned the backs of her eyes. *Do it.*

"Sienna," Paris said. He cupped her jaw as he liked

to do, as gentle as if she were a precious treasure he couldn't bear to bruise. "Talk to me. Tell me what you're thinking. Please."

Do it. Do it! First, one more kiss, just one more. She dove back in, filling her mouth with his special taste. All that heat and chocolate. What lay ahead of her was an eternity of misery, but then, that was her punishment, wasn't it. For what she'd done to him before. Part of her even thought Wrath approved, for the demon was now purring in the back of her mind, as he'd done for Olivia, feeding off Sienna's sorrow.

Do. It. Still she hesitated. Was she going to talk herself out of this? No, oh, no. She was talking herself into it, she realized when her next thought hit. Paris had to fall out of love with her. He just had to. He had to forget the vow he'd made her, and live. Live happily.

And so she did it. She did the one thing guaranteed to make him hate her.

She positioned her ringed finger at his throat, just as she'd done once before, that day they'd first met. His pulse was erratic, a drunken drumbeat.

DO IT. A tragic "I'm sorry" left her as she struck. She shouldn't have said that. Should have been cold, heartless.

His eyes flared wide. "What the—" Comprehension bled into his irises, even as they glazed. The liquid had broken the blood/brain barrier instantly. Rather than shout at her, curse at her, he slurred out, "Don't leave me. Don't…leave… Stay…mine…please…"

Though he fought the effects, he couldn't stop them, and his eyelids drifted shut. His arms plopped to his sides. He was very still, his chest rising and falling evenly. Took everything she had to climb out of the bed. To dress in clothing Cronus had provided for her, choosing a long-sleeved T-shirt that fit around her wings, black leather pants and combat boots. She quaked the entire time, tears pouring down her cheeks.

She claimed two daggers, and neither of them were crystal. Those she left on the nightstand, resting next to each other. They were his. He would need them. She strapped the weapons on her wrists, hilts down. A shake of her arms, and those blades would slide right into her palms.

For a moment, she closed her eyes. *Had to be done, had to be done,* she chanted. Didn't make her ache any less, or feel any better. Or any less guilty. Why couldn't Paris have looked at her with anger there at the end? Why'd he have to be so understanding?

She refused to delude herself. He would come after her.

She had to stop him.

Though she almost broke down and sobbed when she exited the bedroom, she somehow managed to pick herself up and scour the castle. She found Lucien down the hall, in the room he'd claimed for his own. He sat in a velvet-lined chair, a glass of something amber in one hand, the other wrapped around Anya, who perched in his lap.

He sensed the intrusion immediately, his gaze arrowing straight for Sienna. He set his glass on the floor.

"What's wrong?" Anya demanded. "You tensed."

When he registered Sienna's identity, he relaxed, his scarred face easing off the *someone's-gonna-die* throttle. "Anya, sweetheart, will do you something for me?" he asked, tenderly running his fingers through her fall of pale hair.

"Anything, Flowers." She licked up his neck, humming ecstatically. "You know that."

He fisted a thick lock and lifted her head, forcing the pleasuring to end. "Will you go to the kitchen and make me some hot chocolate? With whipped cream *and* marshmallows?"

"Wait. What?" Her red lips pulled into a frown. "I thought you wanted me to do something totally, absolutely freaky to your body, and I was one-hundred-percent racer ready for that. Hot chocolate—"

"Anya. Please. I have a craving."

Her eyes narrowed. "Are you pregnant?"

"Anya."

"What? It's a legit question right now, considering what you're willing to give up, but fine. My man has a craving." Off Anya went, grumbling, leaving Lucien alone with Sienna and not realizing it.

"I drugged Paris," she admitted. And wow, what a way to kick things off poorly.

Scowling, Lucien jumped to his feet. "Did you hurt him?"

"No, no. Of course not." She leaned against the door, no longer able to hold herself up. "Cronus wants me to go…to Galen…to spy for him, to control him." Why was this so difficult? She'd drugged the man she loved; this should be as easy as breathing. "It's the only way to save Paris, and you guys, from certain death. The longer I stay here, the more likely the chance Galen will get to Cronus, and Rhea will take the throne." And the harder it would be to leave Paris.

His blue eye swirled, hypnotizing her, while his brown one seemed to lock her in place. "I could accuse you of lying, of saying this so that we won't suspect you of rejoining your flock and sharing our secrets."

Her tongue thickened with the need to curse, but she plowed ahead anyway. "Yeah. You could. And that's fine, more of the same, but Paris, he trusts me and he wants me to stay. He wouldn't let me go."

In the ensuing silence, she noticed something. Wrath was quiet now; he'd truly fed from her pain and her actions, and wasn't concerned by Lucien in any way. And also, maybe she'd gotten it right before and Aeron had already won this battle. Maybe the Lords were exempt from the demon's brand of justice. Whatever. Didn't matter. She wasn't going to be around them anymore, was she? Wrath could feed off her sorrow for eternity.

"Paris will want to come after me," she said. "You know he will."

A dark brow knitted into Lucien's hairline. "So he can retaliate for being drugged?"

"No. To save me from Galen."

His lips pursed as he considered her words. "What do you want me to do?"

"Stop him." The words were shards of glass in her throat. "I have to stay with Galen, have to somehow find a way to control him."

"Here's a tip. Kill him," Lucien suggested.

If only. "Cronus says I can't, that if Galen dies you guys die, too. This is the way. The only way." As she spoke, she straightened her shoulders. Her determination grew, turned her into a rock.

Sienna wasn't weak, and she wasn't a coward. Not any longer. She was doing this, even at the expense of her own happiness. "Don't let him come for me. Keep him here, and keep him strong. So. Yeah. That's all I came to say."

A long, torturous pause as he considered his reply. "You know what you're asking, right?"

"Yes." To mask the newest flood of tears, she looked down at her booted feet. "You're a good friend to him, and I'm glad." *Getting choked up again.* "I'm glad he has you. Take care of him, Lucien. If ever there's information I obtain that can help you, I will somehow send it on. Trust it or not, but it will be there if you want it."

"Sienna—"

"Just...take care of him, like I said." No need to open the door. She simply stepped through it and pounded her way to the roof.

There was only one thing left to do.

CHAPTER FORTY-FIVE

SIENNA'S WINGS LIFTED properly and were no longer dragging against the floor. Her shoulders ached, but the shooting pains were nothing she couldn't handle. She was determined. Still rock-solid. Unbendable.

She would do this. Wouldn't waver.

She pushed her way onto the roof, the cloying darkness of the realm once more enveloping her. No sign of that shadow guy...thing, but of course, his blood toll had been paid and he'd vowed to leave everyone alone. Whether or not he'd keep his word, she couldn't be sure. Wrath had sensed the menace in him, yet the images the demon had shot through her head had been grainy and, well, shadowed, confusing them both.

Nothing had been clear, so she had no idea what the shadow guy was capable of doing. She trusted him because she had no other choice.

In the center of the parapet, she stopped and spread her arms. There was no hesitating to take a breath. No reflecting on what could have, should have, been. "Cronus! Cronus! I summon you!"

A flash of white at her left. Heart thumping, she spun. The angel Zacharel had taken shape, lovely in his heavenly glory, glowing with an aura that pulsed with energy, yet seeing him caused a tremor of fear to crawl down her spine. His expression was devoid of emotion, those white-and-gold wings spread regally, his robe pristine.

Wrath reacted as if he'd just spotted Olivia. *Heaven!*

"My people need you, Sienna," Zacharel said. "I told you this."

She raised her chin. "And I told you to get in line."

"Why do that when I can simply take what I want?"

"If you could settle for my unwillingness, you would have taken me already."

He inclined his head at her logic. "Then come with me of your own accord. You are the key to our victory."

So sick of those words. "Why am I the key? *How* am I the key?"

"I do not know."

So sick of nonanswers. "Well, then, you don't get the key. Besides, I didn't think angels and demons ever worked together."

The slightest softening around his emerald eyes. "High Lord demons, like the one inside you, were angels once. I know—knew—your Wrath. Once upon a time, his justice was not perverted or warped, but fair and right."

"That doesn't change my mind." Where the hell was Cronus? "Paris comes first, and this is my way to save him." And if Paris himself hadn't changed her mind about her current path, Zacharel had no chance.

His brow furrowed as he tossed her words through his mind. "Why do you love him?" He sounded genuinely baffled. "Why do you sacrifice yourself and your happiness for him?"

"He is strong."

A snort. "Others are strong."

She remembered doing the same thing to Paris, contradicting everything he said. Had *she* been this annoying? "He's smart, and giving, and caring, and kind, and—"

"He is a killer."

Though her eyes narrowed, she continued as if he hadn't spoken. "He is protective of me, and he makes me feel special. He takes care of me. And he sacrifices for me, too."

"You wish a sacrifice to be made? Done. Name your price and I will see to it immediately."

Hope ignited. "Can you save Paris from the fate Cronus showed me? In two of the potential futures, he dies. Can you save him and his friends?"

"No," Zacharel replied honestly, and that shouldn't have surprised her but it did. "The roadways have already been paved, the vehicles placed upon them and in motion. There are no breaks."

As vivid as the metaphor was, the reality was inescapable. Hope burned to ash and floated away. "Very well, then. Cronus!" she shouted. "Cronus!"

Zacharel skimmed a fingertip along his brow. "The Titan king has lied to you, you know. Lied about so many things."

Breath caught, froze in her lungs. "About Paris?"

"No."

Then nothing else mattered. "Cronus!"

He heaved a ragged sigh of frustration. "Help us, Sienna. A war brews in the heavens. Good versus evil. You want to be on the side of good."

Been there, ruined lives because of that, she thought. "Cronus!"

"We will never lie to you," he said, floating closer, "and you will have a chance to avenge the wrongs committed against you and those you love."

Wrath really liked that idea, and slammed against her temples to gain her undivided attention.

Don't need to sell that any harder. The thought of

working on the side of the angels—for real this time—
was hard-core awesome, and yeah, part of her wanted to
be all over it. But. Yeah, always a but. "I'm sorry, I really
am, but I drugged a good man to do this, and you can't
guarantee his safety, so I can't help you."

Zacharel studied her for a long while, silent. Then,
"Very well. I will allow you to leave with the Titan.
When you need me, and you will, simply speak my name
and I will come for you."

And take her straight into the heavens. "Find a way
to save Paris and his friends, and I'm yours. See, I've
learned something in this new, immortal world. Everything has a price, a toll. The Lords are mine. Their lives
for mine, or no deal."

"Very well," he repeated just before he disappeared.

A split second later, Cronus materialized in front of
her, and oh, was he pissed. His scowl broke up the clean
lines of his face, turning regal features sinister. At least
he'd given up the goth mesh and tailored suits in favor
of his white robe.

"You summoned me, and then you blocked me?" Eyes
a shimmering mix of ebony and scarlet, he snarled, "How
did you block me?"

Just as before, Wrath went silent, unable to see into
Cronus's past. Frustrated them both. Much as she raged
about the sick things the demon had made her do, she'd
come to rely on his keen insight into the people around
her.

"I didn't block you," she replied honestly, the words
laced with venom. *I hate this man,* she realized. For
everything he'd done to her, and everything he was doing
to Paris. "I summoned you to tell you I'm ready. I want
to go to Galen. But first…"

Steps unhurried, she approached him. Her arms were

lowered at her sides, and she gave a little shake. The blades slid into her hands, as planned, and the moment she reached Cronus, she whipped into a frenzy of motion, shoving him back, into the castle wall, the tip of her weapon poised at his jugular.

He could have thrown her off, but the threat happened so quickly, he could only widen his eyes in astonishment.

"You fed me ambrosia, *made* me ambrosia."

Finally he shoved, propelling her backward. Only by frantically flapping her wings did she prevent herself from flying over the rail.

"And the problem?" He brushed a piece of lint from his shoulder. "I did what was required to make this work. You were right, you aren't pretty enough to capture Galen's attention, and we need his attention."

No apologies, the bastard.

One day...

He went on silkily, "Now, allow me to capture yours."

She blinked and her surroundings changed, from dark to light, bleak to ostentatious. Befuddled, she sheathed her weapons.

Above, a teardrop chandelier hung from the center of intricately carved woodwork. At her sides, thick red-velvet curtains spilled over the windows, with chairs and lounges made of the same material scattered throughout. A rosewood desk, candelabra, tables with swirling bars of gold at their bases. Below, a plush wool carpet with the loveliest blooms woven in jewel tones. The scent of jasmine and honeysuckle saturated the air.

"What is this place?" she asked.

"This," he replied, "is your new home."

She wouldn't cry. She *wouldn't*. "Galen lives here?"

"In Rhea's realm of the heavens? Yes. Usually his men occupy every room, but many of them are currently missing." Steps light, Cronus closed the distance between them. He gripped her forearms, forcing her to peer up at him. "In exactly sixty seconds, you are going to enter that room." His gaze shifted to a closed doorway behind her.

Why the wait? Then again, who cared? "All right."

"Galen will not accept you as you are, not any longer. You stink of Paris, his enemy."

And she was supposed to convince the horrible man otherwise? Fabulous.

"There's only one way to avoid that," Cronus added.

Sickness in her stomach, ice in her veins. "And what's that?"

"This."

She never saw him move. One moment Cronus was holding her, the next he was stabbing her in the stomach. Sharp pains tore through her, and she glanced down through widening eyes. His hand was wrapped around a blade hilt he had slammed into her belly.

Wrath roared at the injustice, and in that moment, the demon had no need to see into Cronus's past to experience a desire to strike. *Punish!*

"Why would you... Why...?" Blood trickled from her mouth. *One day, I really will kill him.*

PUNISH. PUNISH. PUNISH.

"I told you. Galen would not have wanted you otherwise." Cronus stepped back, taking the weapon with him. Again he offered no apologies for his actions.

Hate him. Blood wet her shirt, poured down her skin. Her knees shook, collapsed.

PUNISHPUNISHPUNISH.

Eyes narrowing, she inched toward him, once again palming her blades.

He grinned. "Unwise to waste your remaining energy

on me. I suggest you crawl to the doorway I showed you and find Galen. Otherwise, I'll return to Paris and kill him myself."

With that, he abandoned her, leaving her alone and slowly bleeding to death.

Spiderwebs wove around her vision. Zacharel had been right, she thought dazedly. Cronus had lied and betrayed her time and time again, and like a fool she'd let him. Had come to regret her decisions. But she couldn't cry out for the angel.

Her desire merged with Wrath's. Somehow, some way, she would finish Cronus, Rhea *and* Galen, and save Paris, and tell the rest of the world to screw itself.

CHAPTER FORTY-SIX

PARIS JOLTED UPRIGHT. Fog enveloped his mind, and a great sense of doom had taken up residence in his chest. He patted the spot beside him. Cold, empty.

"Sienna," he called, thinking she might be in the bathroom. He needed to hold her, to know she was okay. A sense of foreboding was overtaking him.

Silence.

"Sienna." He shouted her name this time, and with the reverberation of his voice, the fog thinned and memories flooded him.

Sienna had left him. Left him to go to Galen. He threw his legs over the side of the bed, ignoring a wave of dizziness.

Need her, Sex said.

I know. I'll find her.

"Don't get up," a familiar voice intoned. Lucien had just flashed inside the room.

Paris tensed, did his best to focus. His friend had pulled a chair beside the bed, stretched out his long legs and locked his fingers over his stomach. Though the position was relaxed, his dark hair shagged and tangled around strained features and grave eyes.

"Have to." Paris performed a quick scan of the room, checking off things he'd need. Clothes. Boots. Weapons. His gaze landed on the nightstand where both of his crystal blades rested. He gritted his teeth. She was out there, unprotected.

Fear momentarily overwhelmed him, and he dropped his head in his hands.

Need her!

I know, damn it! You think I don't know?

"She came to me, you know," Lucien said. "Asked me to keep you here."

He lifted his head and met his friend's multihued stare, his fury rising on a swift tide. "Did you hurt her?"

Lucien blanched, the scars on the side of his face seeming to rise up. "No."

Okay, then. Okay. "What did you say to her?"

"We'll get to that. Apparently she also went to Viola and asked the goddess to make sure your demon was properly fed."

He popped his jaw. Sienna wanted him to have sex with another woman. The knowledge might have undone a lesser man, and yeah, it angered and upset him, but he understood her motive. His well-being above hers. It was the same for him, which was exactly why he was going after her. Then he would find a way to bind her to him permanently, through fair means or foul.

She's ours. Sex might have been reluctant at first, but he was totally on board now.

No argument from me.

Once Paris had thought he would be able to let her go. He'd thought he could never ask anyone to spend 24/7 with him. Had thought the complications would be too great to overcome. Well, he'd thought wrong. When it came to Sienna, there was nothing he wouldn't do, nothing he wouldn't endure—or demand she endure.

Paris stood, swayed.

Lucien followed him up.

He rolled his shoulders, gearing for battle. "You gonna try to keep me from her?" *Nothing and no one keeps me from her.*

"Hell, no." The warrior whipped out his Glock and checked the clip. "I'm going with you to get your girl."

SIENNA CRAWLED toward the doorway. She left a trail of blood behind her, but finally reached her destination. She expected to ghost through. Instead, she met resistance. A solid wall. *Damn it!* Lifting up to curl her fingers around the knob was a production. Already she was light-headed and weak, but with every second that passed she grew more so.

Two things drove her. Hatred for Cronus, Rhea and Galen, and love for Paris. She could do this. She would do this. She'd come so far, wouldn't stop now. Fat white stars winked through the spiderwebs. Breathing proved difficult, the air seeming to thicken each time she inhaled.

Knob, twisted. Door, butted with her shoulder. Hinges squeaked. Yes! Success.

One hand in front of the other, knees dragging in behind her. Past the threshold. One hand in front of the other, knees still dragging. Stars, stars, so many stars, outshining the webs completely.

Rustling a few feet away. A female's whimper.

A male's curse.

Galen? "Help…me…" Sienna managed.

Feet hit the floor. Footsteps echoed. The slide of feathers over wood planks. Then a handsome blond male was crouching in front of her. Hello, Galen, the man from the portrait. He was bare-chested and covered in blood-stained bandages. He had a blade poised overhead, as if he meant to strike at her, but then he hesitated, his nostrils flaring, his eyes instantly glazing over.

"Who are you?" he croaked.

Her heartbeat sped up, which in turn caused her to bleed out faster. Her thoughts were like mist, impossible to grasp. "I'm...Wrath. Hunter." And why wasn't her demon flashing images of Galen's crimes through her head? Was he as weak as she was? His strength reliant on hers, as hers was sometimes reliant on his?

Across the way, she saw a pale-haired female peek from the shadows of a corner. Her features were tight with strain, her skin colorless. Was this Legion, the girl the Lords were searching for? The girl who had traded herself to save Ashlyn?

The girl Galen had risked his life to obtain?

Hell, Wrath said with a whimper.

"Why are you here?" Galen demanded. "How did you get here?"

Sienna wished she'd come up with a story beforehand, wished Cronus had given her one. Now she had nothing. No words to soothe him and convince Galen of her trustworthiness. At least until she could defend herself.

"Help," was all she said.

Legion crawled forward. "Wr-Wrath? I can't see you, but I feel you."

My hell.

"Stay back, Legion," Galen barked, and the girl instantly scampered back to her post. He never removed his attention from Sienna.

What had he done to Legion to create so much fear in her? What did he *plan* to do to her? No matter what, Sienna couldn't let him hurt the girl. Had to find a way to get her to safety.

As if he read her mind, he said savagely, "She's mine. You touch her, and you die—after I play with you a bit."

Sienna glared at him. So many threats had been tossed her way lately, his was just white noise.

He licked his lips, bent down and sniffed. "You smell so good." His words were beginning to slur. "*So* good."

She remained motionless, part of her wanting him to taste her blood, the rest of her repulsed by the idea. But this was it, the way she would control him, and as much as she despised Cronus for it, she was suddenly a little grateful. When Galen was under the ambrosia's spell, Paris would be safe.

And then she would rewrite the predicted future, creating a fourth road. As she'd promised herself, she would kill both the king and queen of the Titans. There would be no locking them up, no mercy.

Another sniff, a shudder of pleasure and then Galen jolted back, stumbling to his ass. "Fox," he shouted, crab-walking the rest of the way from her. "Fox!"

Damn him. Sienna drew on what modest strength she had left and edged toward him. Had to get him to taste. Had to... She reached out a bloody hand.

"Fox!" His eyes widened with horror when he hit the wall, unable to move as she inched...inched...

Footsteps behind her, a hard hand fisting in her hair, jerking her backward. So she was visible to more than just the master of the house, she thought dimly as her strength ebbed. Evidently Cronus had worked his magic on Galen's henchmen, as well.

"Kill her," Galen croaked. "*Kill* her."

KANE KNEW HE WAS DREAMING. Why else would he see Amun and Haidee facing off with the two horsemen, daggers clanging together, grunts and groans filling the air? Why else would Haidee's skin be changing to straight-up blue ice, her hair into icicles? Why else would William be buffing his nails as he leaned against a wall?

Why else would a beautiful female with long silver-blond hair cascading over one shoulder and eyes of the purest lavender be looking down at him, frowning, tugging at the shackles on his wrists and ankles?

Hell. Maybe he *wasn't* dreaming. Maybe she was an angel. "Dead?" he rasped. After all, he'd willed himself to die, and maybe, finally, blessedly, his soul had left his body. Maybe he was free of his demon. Maybe he was being sent to that secret realm in the heavens where the deceased Baden and Pandora lived. A realm where the demon-possessed were to spend the entirety of their afterlife.

Baden, once his best friend. Once the keeper of Distrust. Aeron had spent a little time in that secret realm, had spoken to Baden, and even to Pandora, who hated them all with a passion that hadn't dimmed through the centuries.

Aeron had escaped with his Olivia. Kane, however, did not want to escape.

"Dead?" he asked again. Even as he spoke, his brain flashed a neon sign into his awareness. *Mine.*

The female, surely the loveliest creature he'd ever beheld, said only one word. "No." But he felt the force of her voice in every single one of his cells. Pure, enchanting, intoxicating.

Mine. A roar now.

Angels couldn't lie, so he knew she had told the truth. Even though there was no actual layer of truth in her voice. So, if he wasn't dead, he was alive. The thought didn't please him. He hated that such a beauty was seeing him like this. At his worst, violated, injured, weak.

"Kill me, then," he commanded.

Mine. Louder than before. He didn't understand the possessive instinct, and didn't want to understand it. He might veer from his current path.

Silence, such heavy silence. The calm before the storm. Because, in the next heartbeat, Disaster protested. Loudly. Screaming and screaming and screaming inside of Kane's head.

No, he wasn't dead.

Kane reached up to cover his ears, and succeeded. His arms had been freed from the chains, he realized distantly. That's what the woman had done. Unchained him.

"No," she repeated. "I won't be killing you."

Mine.

Shut up. He returned to his dream theory. This was a dream, only a dream, which meant she had to do whatever he wanted her to do. Right? "Kill. Me."

Her hands slid underneath his shoulders and pushed him up, up. He felt her heat, the smoothness of her palms. Smelled the fragrance of patchouli, deep, rich and musky, erotic and earthy. Deep in his nose, clinging to his sinuses, spreading into his stomach, his bloodstream.

MINE.

A growl was rising up his throat, threatening to spill out of his mouth. His arms went limp and fell uselessly to his sides, and yet he still had to fight the urge to reach up and grab on to her. He wanted his mouth on her, wanted his body in hers.

He wanted…and so he would have.

MINE, SHE IS MINE.

The blonde—who was suddenly no longer a blonde, but a lovely black woman—no, a sultry Latina—got all up in his face, dark eyes piercing him. "I am not here to end your life, but to save it," she said. "I will take you to the human world—and in return, *you* will kill *me*. I'll have your vow first."

Disaster stopped screaming and started laughing again.

CRONUS WALKED THE CHAMBER of Futures alone, his emotions balanced on the razor's edge of destruction. He'd searched everywhere, yet he hadn't found Rhea. The Hunters he'd captured and locked away were now missing. Rhea had somehow freed them, he knew. And Sienna had not yet done her job with Galen.

If he had to raze the entire world to save himself, he would.

One way or another, he would obtain what he wanted. Dominion over the human world. Control of his wife. And life. *Eternal* life. He was an immortal, a king, the most powerful of his people—even if a few out there left him trembling.

He stopped in front of a vase one of his Eyes had sculpted and painted so long ago. In it, Rhea's hated daughter Scarlet, the keeper of Nightmares, was in the process of removing his head. So, yes, there were two predictions about his death. Two supposed murderers. Two different places, in two different times.

Why?

He had never been able to figure out this particular mystery. Only one person could kill him, true? Unless Galen and Scarlet worked together? But the pair despised each other, fought for opposite sides. Proof: Scarlet had recently invaded Galen's dreams and convinced the man of his own impending downfall. Those dreams had driven the keeper of Hope to attack her man, Gideon, which had enraged her further.

Cronus blinked as an idea took root. Could the answer be that simple? Had Scarlet somehow invaded his Eye's dreams? Had she shown her a false reality? He and Scarlet had been enemies since her birth, and hurting each other had become something of a game.

Perhaps, he thought. Yes, perhaps. Which meant he was most likely on the right path. Galen was the biggest threat, and so Galen had to be corralled.

Sienna now knew exactly how ruthless Cronus could be to ensure his goals were met, and she would come through for him. If she failed, he would make good on his threat. Paris would die. And he would make her watch.

CHAPTER FORTY-SEVEN

A STAY OF EXECUTION, Sienna thought, but only because Galen's bodyguard, Fox, had done what he had not and tasted her blood. As the woman had dragged Sienna out of the bedroom and into a cellar room boasting only a long table with a drain underneath it, she'd gotten blood on her hands. Sienna had made certain of that. She'd promised Paris she would kill whoever tasted her blood, and she would do her best to see that through.

And as the woman lifted her onto the table, she'd caught the sweet coconut scent of ambrosia. She'd licked, closed her eyes and moaned in bliss. Then, of course, had come the feasting. Fox had fallen on her, lapping at her, biting her. And when she'd finished, she hadn't rendered the death-blow but had carted Sienna to her bedroom and tied her up in a corner.

That had been...how many days ago? Sienna had lost track. Time passed too slowly for her—and yet too quickly—measured only by the number of visits Fox paid her. Her initial injury had healed, but Fox kept making new incisions, taking more blood, keeping her weak.

What was Paris doing right now? Resenting her? Hating her? Had Lucien managed to keep him inside the castle? Yeah. Probably. The Lords had made their feelings about her clear, and they would jump on this chance to deepen his negative emotions.

Don't go there. It's bad for your mental health. Besides, she needed to plan. First up? Getting Legion out of here. Second, returning and force-feeding Galen her blood. 'Cause no way he'd trust her after she absconded with his woman, and she really needed his trust. She couldn't kill him if she couldn't get close to him.

Legion's frightened face flashed through her mind. Not Galen's woman. Galen's *perceived* woman.

Wrath stretched inside her head. Like her, he was growing weaker. He needed to feed himself, was desperate to punish someone, and Galen was the perfect candidate.

She wiggled on the floor, rubbing her bound wrists against the wall behind her. Unfortunately, her wings kept getting in the way. And there was a gag in her mouth, so she couldn't call for help. Not that she would have. Zacharel would sweep her straight into the heavens and expect her to march to his Do What I Say band. So not happening.

The bedroom door swung open, and Fox stomped inside. She wore combat boots, black leather pants and a bustier. Her hair was pulled back in a ponytail, and she was licking her lips. She'd come to toke up.

She fell to her knees in front of Sienna, removed her gag, said "Miss me?" and palmed a blade.

Come on, fight her. Do something. "You're pathetic, you know that? Galen had the strength to resist me, but not you. Are you embarrassed?"

Fox was too enraptured by the pulse in her neck to reply, and never even bothered to check her restraints, something she'd done every time before. The addiction was getting worse, then. Good.

"I bet you're not. You're too stupid to—"

With a growl, Fox lunged, lowering her head. Sienna jerked her knees up, knocking the female in the temple and sending her flying to the side. Sienna lumbered to a stand, which was difficult to do with her arms shackled behind her and her ankles held together. Not to mention the Tilt-a-Whirl inside her head.

Scowling, Fox jumped to her feet. "You're going to pay for that."

What she would do next, she didn't know, but then, it didn't matter. Suddenly Legion was there, behind Fox, unnoticed—and swinging a frying pan. The cast iron slammed into Fox's skull, a loud *clang* echoing. Fox's eyes went wide, rolled back, and her knees collapsed.

Legion dropped the pan as if the handle was on fire and stood there, panting, staring down in horror.

"Grab her knife and cut me loose," Sienna commanded, taking over. "Hurry, we don't have a lot of time."

Shaking, crying now, Legion remained exactly as she was. "I—I know you're here, but I can't—I can't see you, can't hear you."

No. No, no, no. If Legion couldn't see her, Legion couldn't touch her. Sienna tried everything she could think of to make herself known. All the while Wrath slammed against her temples, desperate to escape. Finally, not knowing what else to do, she allowed him to take over.

For the first time after ceding control to the demon, Sienna was aware of her surroundings, of her body and her mind. She wasn't sure if it happened because she was stronger or Wrath was weaker, but she felt her skin change, from smooth to scaled. Felt her teeth sharpen and her nails elongate.

A second later, Legion gasped. "Wrath."

"Hell." Sienna's voice was lower, gruffer than ever before.

The girl worked up the courage to bend down and pick up the knife, then close the distance between them. Delicate hands cut the rope away, freeing Sienna's arms.

Through the demon she commandeered the knife. Bending down proved to be a huge mistake, though. The dizziness cranked out of control, and she ended up sprawled on her stomach. She drew up her knees and sawed at the rope, cringing as every inch of her throbbed.

"I knew she hadn't killed you," Legion's soft voice proclaimed. "I could feel my Wrath. I would have come sooner, but Galen commanded me to stay in his room for however long he had to stay inside it. Turned out to be three days. He left this morning, nullifying the order, and I followed Fox to the kitchen and then to her room."

Sienna's mind caught on only one fact. Three days. Paris would have had to sleep with at least one woman to maintain his strength. More likely two. *Don't think about that, either.* A breakdown would stop her from doing what needed doing.

Completely free now, she anchored the blade at the waist of her pants, pushed to a stand, and held out a hand to Legion. The girl hadn't moved, was frozen in place, her expression one of great misery.

"Where is Galen now?" Sienna asked, still using that gruff voice.

"I don't know. He hasn't returned."

Good. That was good. "We're leaving." She waved her claw-tipped fingers. "Me and you, right now."

Blond hair fluttered around slender shoulders as she shook her head. "I can't."

"Can. Come on."

"No, I can't. I took a vow." The misery increased. "I have to stay with him."

We'll see about that. Vow or not, Sienna was taking

this girl to safety. *Now.* Arguing would waste time. Fighting would be ineffective. As weak as Sienna's body was, Legion would escape her in seconds. *Sneaky route, here we come.*

"All right. We go without you," she lied. "Need another weapon first." Though she almost fell a thousand times, she managed to pick up the pan, straighten—and brain the girl the same way she'd brained Fox. *Clang.*

Legion crumpled, landing on top of Fox. Yeah. That was gonna leave a mark.

Getting the girl, who was no lightweight, positioned properly on her shoulder was a nearly impossible task. At the last moment, Sienna found the strength to pull through and level out. But the burst cost her. Wrath lost his hold on her, her image returning to normal and her body now moving under her own steam. She stumbled her way into the hall.

A long hallway. Papered walls, freshly polished furniture. Only the best. A spiral staircase loomed ahead. Miles away, as far as she was concerned.

Then, at the far end of the hall, Galen took a corner as if he were wearing skates, all speed and furious grace. He was armed like a tanker, and menace rippled off him. Had she spotted him on the street, she would have run like hell and prayed for a quick death. Now, she could only watch as he barreled toward her, intent on taking Legion back.

No, he would never trust her now. Her only hope was to engage him, and force her blood down his throat. Then he'd want her alive. *Right? Please be right.*

She was about to set Legion down when she caught sight of Zacharel on one side of her and the shadow guy from Cronus's realm on the other. Dang it, how many people were after her? These two were closing in. Galen noticed them, too, and shouted a black curse. They would reach her before he did.

And then it happened. *Contact.* The black mist enveloped her first. She and Legion were swept up into a world of dizzying screams. Beneath those, she thought she heard Zacharel's roar of frustration and anger. A mistake on her part, surely. The angel was emotionless.

Wrath retreated to the back of her mind, and just as Sienna opened her mouth to release a scream of her own, the noise quieted. Wrath caught those grainy images again, and had no idea how to react. She tried to fight her way free, but the black mist held tight around her, blocking the view of her surroundings.

"Female." Shadow Guy's voice was raspy and coaxing. "I have a bargain to propose to you."

Legion slipped from her grip. Sienna reached for her, but couldn't quite get to her, the girl remaining inside the mist, floating, spinning. Eyes closed, she slept on.

"Do you have a name?" she asked.

"Yes."

When he offered no more, she snapped, "Well, what is it?"

"Some call me Hades."

The king of the dead? High Lord of the Underworld? Greek god? The one Hunters feared above all others? *That* Hades? *I am not intimidated.* "I'm listening," she said, because she had no idea what else to say.

"Your man needs you."

Her stomach bottomed out. "What do you mean?"

"He refuses all women and grows weaker by the moment. I will take you to him. *After* we reach an agreeable end to our negotiations."

Paris, weak and growing weaker. The news that he'd remained faithful to her shouldn't have relieved and delighted her, but it did. It so did. "How do I know you're telling the truth? What would you want in return?" More bodies to feed his shadows?

"Unlike that fool Cronus, I have no need to lie. And part of me hopes you turn me down so that I *can* force you. Your screams will join my others, and the symphony will thrill me for centuries to come. I'm feeling magnanimous, however, and we will try your way first."

This can only end badly.

He continued, "I heard what the angel said to you. I heard what Cronus said to you. You are a key to victory, and I want you to play for my team."

Argh! Once, no one had wanted her. Now everyone did. "Nope. Sorry. I've already picked my side."

"I thought you would say such a thing. But I heard you bargain with the goddess. She asked for a boon, and you agreed. I will accept the same arrangement."

"You want me to slay one of your enemy?" Shocking. He should have no problem doing that on his own.

"No. I simply wish for a boon, to be named later. Anything I desire, as long as it does not hurt your man or his friends. Do you agree?"

"I can't go back to Paris. You'll have to do something else to save him."

"I cannot, but you can. All you must do is allow me to take you to him. So simple, so easy."

Hardly. "Leaving him nearly killed me."

"Staying away from him *will* kill him." His voice became a caress. "Let me take you to him. You may be with him, strengthen and save him, and then you can convince him to give you up, for no one else has been able. No one else *will be* able."

I'm so weak. Can't leave him in danger. "The girl goes with me, and that's nonnegotiable."

"Of course. For a second boon."

Sweet heaven, how many would she owe when this was over? "Very well, but only if the same conditions apply."

"They do. And so the new bargain is struck." Though she could make out no faces in the dark, the shadows thinned in one area, light seeping through to reveal a hint of a grin. "I take you to your man, who is searching for you, and the girl to Aeron, the one searching for her."

Sienna blinked, and next found herself inside a tent located somewhere outside the Realm of Blood and Shadow. Too much light seeped in from the tent's cracks. But then she spotted the fur rug and her location ceased to matter. Paris was sprawled on top of it. He was still. *Too* still. Fear nearly drilled her to her knees. Until she inhaled. Warm air, scented with champagne and chocolate, fogging her up in the most succulent of ways. His demon's special scent. Her mouth watered, and her blood quickened. Her own injuries were forgotten as warmth pooled between her legs.

"Paris," she whispered. His skin was fever-bright, flushed and beaded with sweat. He was gloriously naked, and thickly aroused. His eyes were calm behind his lids, his chest barely rising with his breaths. "Oh, Paris." *I can't let him get like this again. Have to do something.*

"Sienna?"

She rushed over to him and kissed him, knowing even so small a gesture would help revive him. The more their tongues dueled, the more aggressive he became. When his lids flipped open, eyes of brilliant red pinned her. With a growl, he grabbed her by the waist and tossed her to her back. Her heart sped into a superbeat as her wings flared to avoid being crushed.

He ripped at her clothes, shredding them. The very

moment she was naked, he had her legs spread and was inside her, thrusting hard and deep.

As he worked her, he threw back his head and roared. She arched up and took him even deeper. Brutally, wondrously.

She'd missed this, missed him. Needed this, needed him. Her nails went to his ass and guided him into a faster rhythm. The passion swept her up, overwhelmed her, consumed her, broke her heart and fit the pieces back together. Her love for him knew no bounds, had no limits.

Just as climax loomed, he stopped. Just stopped, and peered down at her, panting breaths bursting over her. The flush had drained from his cheeks, and realization now flooded his eyes, followed by concern and horror.

"Oh, baby. Did I hurt you?" His thumbs dusted over her lips with exquisite care.

"Talk later. Make love now." So close. Any second now, she would hurtle into satisfaction.

His cock jerked inside her, as if the command had sparked all kinds of naughty desires. "How are you here?"

"Later!" She squeezed at his massive length.

"Yesss." His hips pistoned once, pistoned again, and then he was slamming in and out, and they were both moaning. Then his lips were on hers, and their tongues were intertwining, and she was swallowing his taste, and it was better than ever, and she couldn't get enough, never wanted this to end, and…and…and… Oh!

Little pleasure bombs exploded through every inch of her. His name left her mouth over and over again, the chorus joined by his shouting of *her* name as he came. He jetted white-hot, giving her every drop of his passion.

She relished the moment, savoring him, thrilled by all that he was.

When he fell on top of her, she cradled his weight, exactly where she wanted to be. Where she wanted to stay, forever. She'd left him once. She didn't think she could leave him again.

"I love you," she whispered. "I love you so much."

"You better," he murmured against her ear.

That's my man. Such a Paris thing to say, and she grinned.

He disengaged and rolled to his side, but kept her close, his arm wrapped around her. "And now that I'm not dying," he announced, expression growing somber, "we talk."

CHAPTER FORTY-EIGHT

PARIS KEPT HIS BODY LAX, not wanting to make Sienna uncomfortable, or aware of the fact that he basically had her in a choke hold. A gentle choke hold, one that did nothing to impair her ability to breathe, but a choke hold all the same.

She wasn't going anywhere, and that was that.

Thankfully, Sex was out for the count and unable to comment.

"All right," she said. "Let's talk. I'll start. Do you hate me now?"

"Hate you? Baby, that might be the stupidest thing you've ever said. No offense."

"None taken. I'm too relieved. After what I did to you…"

"All you did was remind me that I need to up my game where you're concerned." And honestly? Her actions had given him hope that she felt as deeply for him as he felt for her.

"You're not mad at me for going to Galen?"

When he would have done the same thing? "Only at myself. I should have sated you so sublimely, you were never again able to walk."

"A little more practice on your end," she teased, "and that'll be a possibility."

"Witch."

When she reached up to brush her hair off her face, he

saw that she was cut up and bruised. He swallowed back a bark of fury. Having been restrained a time or twelve throughout his life, he recognized the markings for what they were. Rope burns. "Did Galen do this to you?"

Dread shuttered her features. "No, and I don't want to talk about it."

Very well. He wanted to reassure her about a few things first, anyway. But he *would* find out who had harmed her afterward, and as soon as he did, he was going on a rampage for revenge.

"That means you're ready for talk, part two," he said, all hint of his amusement gone.

"I—I don't know about that."

"Too bad. You need to know that I didn't sleep with anyone while we were apart." No matter how weak he'd gotten, no matter how many females his friends had shoved at him. Finally, all but Lucien had continued on their quest to find Sienna.

Mental note: tell Death to call off the search party.

Speaking of, he was pretty sure Lucien had popped in while they were having sex, thinking to protect him from whatever had come to kill him, then had popped back out when he realized what was going on.

"I know." The tips of her fingers traced languid circles around his nipples. "I trust you. But Paris, you were so near death." She kissed his chest, just above his heart. "I don't like that you allowed yourself to get in that condition."

"Don't care. And just so you know, Sex missed you, too. You wear a lot of hats, and he wants to do them all."

She chuckled, a warm, rich sound that acted as manna for his ears. "Right now I've got my stern taskmaster hat on, so you two better listen. I have to leave. I just have to, but I need to know you're taking care of yourself and—"

"No."

"Don't be that way."

"Try to leave. Just try it. See what happens."

"Paris—"

"You stay or I let myself fade. End of story. Promise me."

Such heavy silence. "I have a plan I have to see through."

"Plans change. Deal."

She banged her fist against his chest. "You are so frustrating."

"Tell me what I want to hear, Sienna."

A sigh slipped from her, seeming to drain the fight out of her. "Fine. I'm staying with you, but we're going to have to brainstorm a solution to our Cronus and Rhea problem, our Galen problem, and our you're-gonna-die-prophecy problem. Because, did I tell you? Cronus told me that if Galen dies, you and your friends die. If Cronus dies, you and your friends die."

"I'm not saying I doubt what you've heard, but I do doubt the source. But even if what he said is true, there will be a way around this prophecy. There always is. I'm not worried in the least." In fact, he was overjoyed. And were those *tears* in his eyes? Yeah. Yeah, they were. If that made him a wuss, that made him a wuss. He didn't care. She was here, she was staying. She was his.

He glided his arm from around her neck to her lower back, splaying his fingers over her curves. "Thank you," he said, but the words weren't enough. They didn't convey enough. "And now that we're officially together, I want to tell you some things about me. I want everything out in the open, nothing hidden. I want to share all that I am."

She must have sensed the direction he headed. "You don't have to. What happened in the past is the past."

"Full disclosure. I want you to know what you're getting with me. That way, if Wrath ever shows you something, or my friends ever say anything, we'll already have dealt with it."

"Whatever you say won't change the way I feel about you."

"I'm glad, but I'm doing it anyway."

Her sigh caressed his skin oh, so deliciously. "All right."

She loved him. She'd copped to the feeling. This would be okay. "I'm an ambrosia addict. But I haven't touched the stuff since before reaching you," he rushed to add. "And if something ever happens and I'm exposed to your blood, you don't have to worry. I will *not* hurt you."

Her silky hair tickled his chest as she nodded. "I know you won't hurt me, but Paris, I drugged you. I didn't know about your addiction, or I would have found another way to knock you out. I am so, *so* sorry, and I will never forgive myself."

He hated the implication that she would have left him still, but he drank up her concern for him. "Forgive yourself right now. That's an order. But I will, of course, be spanking you before *I* forgive you."

The most adorable noise escaped her, a snort and a laugh combined. "I accept the spanking. Deserve it."

His lips twitched with the sweetest kind of humor. "You can't accept your own punishment, baby. You'll have to fight me."

She purred, actually purred, and the vibrations had him rock-hard again.

Tell her the rest, so you can move on to the good stuff.

He lost his half grin. "Okay, here's part three. I know you told me you've seen my past, but I'm not sure if Wrath showed you everything. I told you about that one slave, but he wasn't the only one. I've…been with men."

Not even a pause. "Oh, yeah? Well, in college I kissed a girl. She was my roommate, it was raining outside, dark with the occasional flashes of lightning, romantic yet scary. You know how it goes."

That she wasn't going to make a big deal about it, that she again just accepted each facet of him…no wonder he loved this woman. "Did you like it?"

"I kinda did," Sienna said in a scandalized whisper.

Mmm, but he liked her scandalized. Wondered what he could do to ramp that up, what would make her nervous but too excited to say no. Finding out, well, he'd never looked forward to a bedding more.

"Later, after your spanking, we're gonna do a little role playing. I'm going to be your sweet, innocent roommate, Parette, and you're going to demonstrate that kiss on me." *And then I'm going to talk you into doing things you've only ever dreamed about.*

"Incorrigible beast."

"But you love me anyway."

"I love you *always*."

Before he could respond, there was an explosion of white light at the front of the tent. In a flurry of movement and frothing rage, Paris grabbed both the crystal blades, pressing one into Sienna's hand. He was standing a moment later, unconcerned by his nakedness.

Cronus had arrived, and if his fearsome scowl was any indication, he was ticked. First instinct: attack. Paris tamped it down. Barely. Second: recon. Answers, he needed answers.

The king's narrowed gaze slid past Paris and onto

Sienna, who had just finished righting her clothing. "You ruined everything," he growled.

Paris moved in front of her, blocking the king's view. Cronus merely pointed to the side of the tent, and Paris was propelled there on a powerful gust of wind, his arms spread, his legs spread, invisible ropes tying him in place. Though he fought, he couldn't free himself.

Helpless. Just like that. Panic was like bitter pills in his mouth, and he swallowed so many he might just overdose.

Darkness...so much darkness...I will hurt him. I will kill him. He struggled so viciously his muscles began to tear from his bones. That didn't slow him.

A scowling Sienna popped to her feet. *Use the crystal,* he projected with the last vestiges of his control. She didn't; she stood her ground, her chin held high.

"I'm not going back to Galen," she announced.

"Even if he were addicted to you, Galen will not trust or follow you now. He hates you. You took his prisoner, damaged his soldier, and he is not the type to forgive or forget. To him, every offense is to be returned a thousandfold."

Those gossamer black wings extended. "There's another way. We'll find it. Just give us time."

"Time? *Time.*" Menace pulsed from Cronus. "You once asked me why I wanted you willing. The answer was simple. Eventually you would have turned on me. Now you have and that's no longer a concern. So, no, I'm afraid you're out of time. Now I will destroy everything you hold dear."

Paris snarled as Cronus vanished and reappeared in front of Sienna in a single blink. He snagged her by the hair. At last Paris managed to free himself, both shoulders popping out of joint. He was running for them. Nearly upon them.

Just before he reached her, Sienna shouted, "Zacharel! I summon you."

Cronus reached out and stabbed Paris just before Paris reached them. Sienna gasped. The pair vanished, her gaze locked on Paris as he fell to his knees, a searing pain consuming him.

CHAPTER FORTY-NINE

"WE ARE *NOT* DOING THIS again," Sienna shouted, worried for Paris, desperate to return to him. "I'm sick of everyone flinging me where they want me to be." Black, all around her. In her nose, in her lungs, pouring through her bloodstream. No color, no life, just an endless void. "That ends *now*."

"You failed to take the easiest route, and now you'll have to live with Plan B," Cronus said, his voice slithering from the nothingness.

I won't ask. His plans mean nothing to me.

"Zacharel!" she called again. Work with the angels? Why not? She would learn to fly properly, and finally, once and for all, control her own destiny.

A flicker of light. A return of the dark. Another flicker, lasting just a bit longer. She caught a glimpse of big, puffy clouds, glued to an endless expanse of night sky. A star here, a star there, twinkling from their perches like eyes trained on her, watching her every move. She must be in another realm. One without a single living creature in residence.

She turned a full circle, and found Cronus standing a few yards away. His arms were crossed over his chest, his legs braced apart. She was suddenly very grateful she'd maintained her grip on the crystal blade Paris had given her.

"Another reason I wanted your willingness," Cronus

said. "If you had turned on me, you would have become Rhea's soldier and therefore been under her protection."

Now he wanted to talk? Well, he could take his confessions and shove them. "I'm warning you. Return me to Paris. *Now*."

He arched a mocking brow at her. "Or what?"

"Or I will fight you." *Planned to, anyway. You just sped things along.*

A booming laugh, sharp and bitter, even anticipatory. "You could try."

"Return me to Paris," she repeated. "This is your last chance."

He continued on as if she hadn't spoken. "Rhea did not kill your sister. I did."

Her heart skipped a beat as denial rushed through her. "No." A lie, surely. One meant to punish her. Because, if he were telling the truth, she would have helped the very man who'd destroyed her precious Skye, leaving her bloody and broken, her last memory of a knife slicking through her skin. She would have bled for the man who had destroyed an innocent. She would very nearly have sacrificed her own life and happiness for *her sister's killer...*

No!

And yet, Wrath's earlier insistence that something had been wrong suddenly made sense. The moisture evaporated from her mouth. A knot grew in her throat, and she had trouble drawing in the necessary oxygen. Dizziness took center stage in her head.

"I held her in my hands, and I slit her throat. I watched the life drain out of her. I killed her husband first. Made her watch. I can prove it." He reached up and jerked a chain from around his neck. A butterfly carved from a black diamond dangled from the center.

In the next moment, the shield that had prevented Wrath from seeing his sins crumpled to nothing. She clutched her temples, squeezed her eyes closed as the scene unfolded inside her head. Cronus, holding Skye and a human male at his sides. Making them kneel. Stabbing the male. Skye, fighting, shoving herself into his blade. Skye, bleeding. Cronus, finishing her off. Skye, dying.

Nausea rolled through Sienna's stomach, a churning acid threatening to boil up and out. A fury drenched in seething flames and sharpened by jagged bits of glass.

"I have lived for millennia," Cronus said. "Think you I have not learned a few tricks along the way?"

We will punish him. A whisper. *WE WILL PUNISH HIM.* A scream.

I will, she replied. A vow. *Oh, I will.* For Skye. For Paris. For herself.

"You ruined my plan, and now I will ruin yours," he seethed. "I will bargain with Galen. For his eternal allegiance, I will hand you over, his to punish as he sees fit. If you run from him, I will bring you back to him. And if you think to flee to your demon lover, I will make Paris suffer before I kill him. And have no doubt, I will kill him. He thinks to take revenge on me for everything I've done to you."

The king had made that kind of threat one too many times.

Hatred joined the sickness, as did a dollop of darkness. Violence waltzed between those shadows, the urge to maim and destroy so strong she felt as if she were drowning in them. She didn't fight them; she embraced them.

He *would* be punished. Here. Today.

Hold, Wrath said. *Not yet...not quite yet...*

She didn't know what Wrath planned; she only knew she trusted him to lead her in vengeance.

Cronus added blithely, "Did you know four artifacts are needed to find Pandora's box? Galen has one, and the Lords have three. That will change. I will take the All-Seeing Eye, the Cage of Compulsion and the Paring Rod, and I will bestow them on Galen. All four artifacts will be his. He will be so grateful for my gifts, he will vow never to harm me. He will find the box, and your precious Lords will die."

Hold...

"You trust Galen that much, do you? You actually think he'll keep his word? That he won't try and take *your* demon, too?" She flashed a patronizing smile. "I bet he's as trustworthy as you are. So, after you do all of that for him and he goes in for the kill shot, what will you do, hmm? Are you going to fight him? Or finally accept your death sentence as your due?"

Cronus stalked to her, but stopped midway, his ears twitching. A smug, eerie laugh bubbled from him. "Speak of the devil. Or in this case, the man who masquerades as angel. Galen approaches, woman. And never has a warrior been angrier. He wants what you stole from him, and he will extract his pound of flesh from your body."

Hold...

"Bring it," she said. Because, yeah, she was going to punish Galen, too. Punish him for every crime he'd ever committed against Paris. For everything he'd done to Legion. Everything he'd ever *thought* to do. At long last.

The king's nostrils flared. He clearly wasn't fond of her lack of fear.

Well, too bad.

Hold...

"No worries, baby. We've already brought it," Paris said from behind Cronus.

The darkness fell away, as if a curtain had been jerked to the floor. Bright light exploded, the sun shining so vividly. Her eyes stung, but she kept them open. Paris was pale and bloody but steady on his feet. He stood with the rest of the Lords behind Cronus, who spun to face them. They were armed for war. Unlike in the painting, they weren't here to protect him.

Even better, an army of warriors whose white wings proclaimed them angels stood behind them, and *they* were armed for war. Zacharel claimed the helm. Every time she'd encountered him, his lack of emotion had amazed and even disturbed her. Now, she was grateful for it. He was determination itself, as cold and cruel as the snow falling from him, clearly willing to do *anything* to meet his goals.

"You broke the rules, Cronus," the warrior angel said flatly, "and now you will pay."

What rules?

"Mind if we join the party?" another voice—a female voice—said from behind Sienna. "I've been waiting for this moment for far too long."

Sienna whipped around to see a beautiful brunette who could only be Rhea. The regal Titan queen stood beside Galen, who was glaring at Sienna as if he would come for her first. An army of Hunters flanked them, and she recognized a few faces.

I've picked my side. Beware, she projected through her narrowed eyes.

"What is this?" Cronus demanded.

"The first battle of the new war," Zacharel replied gravely.

"Well, then. It begins. I'll need my own army, won't

I?" He waved his hand and a great throng of his people appeared, Titan gods and goddesses enveloping him, hiding him in a sea of stunning, flawless faces and immaculate, jewel-studded gowns and togas. They were obviously confused by the sudden change of scenery and none were armed.

When they spotted the unrest surrounding them, they wised up fast. Weapons of every kind appeared out of thin air.

"To the death!" Cronus shouted.

As if his voice was the starting bell, the armies rushed each other.

Now! Wrath shouted at her.

Sienna opened her mind to her demon, allowing him to take over, and threw herself into the thick of the action.

CHAPTER FIFTY

PRIORITY ONE: SIENNA.

For once, Sex didn't hide deep in a corner of Paris's mind. The demon, on a high from their woman's body, pumped strength straight into his veins as he rushed toward her, the wound from his stabbing having already healed. The darkness inside him frothed and writhed, guiding him but not consuming him. The three of them were one.

When he saw a man, a Hunter, coming up behind Sienna with a Glock raised and aimed, he roared, quickened his pace. Met the guy with an arcing blade to the throat before a single shot was fired, even as he spun his woman behind him.

Zacharel had warned him that up here, in this realm between realms just above the heart of the heavens, *everyone* could see her. And if they could see her, they could touch her. If they could touch her they could hurt her. And like him, she could be killed, her body too injured for Wrath to repair it, especially considering the damage done to her during their separation—which she still hadn't told him about.

Paris's first casualty of the battle crumpled. One down. Only about a thousand more to go. "Can you fly to safety?" he asked, nailing another Hunter. There went number two.

She offered no reply. Fearing the worst, he swung his

sword to take down any threat in front of her. Only, she had worked her way back in front of him. He spotted the back of her head, her wings tucked safely out of the way, and realized she was engaged in her own battle. Either she had allowed Wrath to overtake her or she had learned some new skills in the hour they'd been parted. He was betting on the former. Good.

Clasping only the crystal dagger, she danced through the crowd with lethal menace, her focus on Cronus and the men and women surrounding him. Hunters fell all around her. She spun, she ducked, she darted left and right. Her wings flared suddenly, and she lifted high, higher, cutting someone down below her.

A true angel of death. Paris had never seen anything so beautiful. He trailed behind her, and anyone who turned their sights on her, he killed savagely. No hesitation. No regrets.

A throwing star sliced his forearm. There was a sharp sting, a warm trickle of blood. Neither slowed him, and he didn't bother checking for the culprit. There were so many people, so many bodies, so many wings and weapons.

The gods and goddesses wore bejeweled robes and hummed with electrical energy that lifted his hair. Some could shoot fire from their fingertips, some could shoot ice. Besides Cronus and Rhea, he'd never really had a beef with the Titans, but the angels, who were, miracle of miracles, on his side, *did* have a beef, so…*the enemy of my friend is my enemy.* Anytime Paris spotted a Titan, he slew first and decided to ask questions later.

Why Titans versus angels, though? A turf thing, maybe? Like, the heavens belonged to the wingers and they weren't going to tolerate encroachers anymore? Made sense, but even if the reason had been something as lame as "We don't like the Titans, whaa, whaa, boo-hoo, they're mean," he'd be in this at full throttle.

A group of Hunters surged toward Sienna, claiming his complete focus and rage. They seemed to recognize her as one of their own. Or rather, a traitor to their kind. Their abhorrence was evident, as was their spotlighting of her, as though Rhea and Galen had placed her at the top of the must-kill list.

Moving faster than human eyes could track, Paris twisted and turned, arms always crossing, swinging, cutting. Grunts and groans sounded. Screams, too. Ahead, a Hunter aimed a .40. Even as he continued forward, Paris threw his crystal blade as if it were a deadly boomerang. And actually, it was. It changed shape midflight and sliced through the Hunter's wrist before the shot could go off, taking both the hand and the gun, before hurtling back to Paris's waiting grip.

Except, he'd missed the other Hunter with the other gun, currently aimed at Lucien. Paris went to throw the blade, but the shot boomed out, nailing Lucien in the side. Blood spurted. The warrior shouted, but didn't go down. Kept fighting.

The other Lords closed ranks around him, protecting him. Good men. The best. They'd fought together a long time, in the heavens and on earth. They knew to stay close, to fight with their backs to each other and to draw tighter when an injury was sustained.

But Lucien gathered his strength and flashed himself directly behind the Hunter who'd harmed him. The man was dead before his body hit the ground.

"Look out," Paris shouted as another Hunter came at his friend. His boots hammered at the ground as he raced to intervene.

Lucien ducked. The human's dagger swiped nothing but air. And then Paris was on the guy, slamming into him, propelling him down, down. He punched once, heard bone crack, twice, *felt* bone crack, then finished him off with a swipe of his blade.

"Thanks," Lucien said, helping him up.

"No prob." He scanned the area, even as he threw himself into another fight. *Shit.* He'd lost sight of Sienna. Humans and immortals were still standing, weapons locked in battle. The injured had slinked off to the sidelines to protect themselves from further harm. Of course, warriors, being warriors, hunted them and took care of business.

Meanwhile, body parts were flying and blood was pooling. And was that a wing at his feet, white threaded with gold? Yeah. Damn. Poor angel.

Find Sienna. A command from his demon, his darkness and himself.

He barreled in the direction he'd last seen her, leaving a trail of death in his wake. This was why he'd been created, after all. To fight. To kill. He rolled with the violence, bending, straightening, darting as needed. Throwing punches, slicing through skin and into organs. He experienced several more stinging pains and trickles of blood, but still he kept going.

From the corner of his eye, he thought he saw Maddox fall. Then Reyes. And was that Sabin? They would be fine, he told himself. Like Lucien, they were strong. He would not believe otherwise.

A few feet ahead, Gideon was sliced through the stomach and bleeding like a sieve, fighting off two giants. Strider was...nowhere. Gone. But there were Kaia and Gwen, Haidee and Scarlet, hacking through enemy lines with grins on their faces.

My boys are fine or the girls wouldn't be so happy,

Paris assured himself. He quickened his steps and took one of the giants from behind, the decapitation allowing Gideon to center his efforts. There were just so many Hunters, so many immortals. If they could hurt his friends, then Sienna would be—

There! He caught a glimpse of those black wings. Blood dripped from their tips, and he wasn't sure if it was hers or someone else's. Urgency rode him, guiding him faster and faster. A war cry echoed as a male plowed toward her from the right. Paris noticed and launched himself at the man, catching him around the waist. They skidded across the floor. A swift twist of the guy's neck, and that little battle was over.

Paris hopped to his feet and headed for his woman. She took down a big bruiser of a man with a swing of her dagger. Crimson stained her arms to the elbows. Her shirt was torn, her side bleeding.

The darkness inside him thickened.

Zacharel appeared in front of Sienna, cutting a clearer path for her and challenging the Titans who clashed with other angels in front of Cronus. Big shocker, Cronus was fighting, too. Rhea's men had come from the other side, and were currently hacking at him as if he was a piñata and they wanted the candy inside him. And yet, they hadn't managed to inflict a single injury on him. He was too strong, too fast. Too damn powerful.

Then those Hunters were down, and it was Cronus against Rhea, no one standing between them, the rest of the battle raging behind them. Both held two short swords, and both raced toward each other. *Contact.* Metal clanged against metal, even sparking.

"Bitch!"

"Bastard!"

"If your man kills me, you'll die, too," Cronus spat.

"Worth it," the queen gritted.

All around, the humans and angels—and hell, even the Lords, because yeah, Paris felt it too—experienced an increase of fury. As if their emotions fed off the king's and queen's. Teeth were bared. Claws unleashed.

Paris had a strange thought that the entire world was probably shaking from this. Earthquakes, tornados, tsunamis, volcanic eruptions, storms of any and all kind. What would he find when he returned there?

Head in the game.

Kill, he thought. He threw himself back into the fray. Dagger, swinging. Bodies, falling. Sienna, close by. Finally he reached her. Of course, that's when Galen appeared. He was soaked in crimson, shaking with rage. And he swung a long broadsword at Sienna's neck.

She hadn't noticed, too busy finishing off another Hunter.

"No!" Paris leapt between the two combatants. Because he was taller than Sienna, the tip of Galen's sword cut through his chest rather than his neck. Skin, muscle, bone, all three split. Warm blood poured as his knees buckled.

A high-pitched scream of unholy rage and denial nearly busted his eardrums. Sienna had noticed. He thought maybe his heart had taken some of the impact, too, because the organ skipped one beat, then another.

His vision fogged. Bodies became blurs of movement. Black—Sienna and her ire. White—Galen and his brute force. The two engaged, a whirlwind of motion and menace.

Come on, come on. Paris wasn't going down like this.

He pushed to his feet, but was immediately tossed back down. Someone had barreled into him, was punching at his face. Got his lip but good, the tissue slicing on his teeth. Though Paris couldn't see who it was, he suspected the culprit was human, and kicked out. The weight left him, and he got back on his feet.

The male came at him again. "I've always wanted the honor of killing one of your kind."

Paris still held his dagger and swiped. Contact, gurgling. Another body joined the ever-growing pile.

Sienna…Sienna… There! Still fighting Galen. Her motions were slowing, and there were seemingly thousands of new streaks of red interspersed with the black of her broken wings. She was hurting, weakening. Eyes narrowing, homing in on his target, Paris kicked forward. More Hunters rushed him, but he kept his eye on the prize and hacked at whoever got in his way. Then it happened.

Galen pinned her to the floor, ready to render the final blow.

"Where is Legion?" the keeper of Hope shouted, going to his knees, putting his weight on her shoulders.

"Never…tell…" Her voice held no trace of Wrath. Which meant the demon wasn't guiding her right now. *She* was in control. She would feel every injury.

Hurry! Get to her! Paris stumbled, righted himself, kept moving. Closer…but not close enough…so damn far away.

Another human, tossed aside.

"Where is she?" Galen.

"Where you'll never find her." Sienna.

Just beyond them, Cronus drilled Rhea's sword with so much force, the queen lost her grip. The king pounced, fisting her hair and forcing her to her knees. And there was nothing she could do about it, weaponless as she now was.

With his free hand, Cronus withdrew a thin link of

chain from the pocket of his robe and bound her wrists behind her. Struggling the entire time, she spat curses at him. He hooked the chain around her ankles. A hog tie. A good one. The queen wouldn't be going anywhere until he let her.

A sharp lance of pain seared between his shoulder blades. Someone had just stabbed him in the back, Paris realized distantly. Once again his knees gave out. This time, he couldn't get to his feet. Commanding his crystal blade to elongate, he shoved the length backward, nailed the one who'd taken him down, then he began crawling. He *would* reach Sienna. He would, even though every inch he gained left a thick trail of blood behind. In fact, he'd lost so much he wasn't sure how he was still conscious.

Galen swung around, removing his weight from Sienna, but she stayed where she was. Prone, motionless.

What had the bastard done to her? "No. *No.*" On his hands and knees, Paris worked his way to her. "Hold on, baby. I'm coming."

Cronus and Galen circled each other. Both were cut and bleeding profusely. Both were limping.

"Well, well. Our showdown at last," the king said. He coughed and spit out a tooth. He was without a weapon, having dropped them to confine his wife.

He couldn't flash away, too injured to do so.

Galen raised his sword. "Well, well, indeed. You didn't bring what you promised me, and now you are defenseless."

"Am I? I think not. If you want your woman," the king continued, "you'll walk away now. I will bring her to you, and you may keep her. But you are never to defy me again. So walk away. *Now.*"

Sienna twitched. Twitched again. Relief consumed

Paris. Almost there, almost... Slowly she rose, shook her head and took stock of the scene playing out in front of her, clearly still consumed by Wrath's influence after all. Cronus had his back to her. Galen was in front of Cronus, but paid her no heed.

The crystal dagger she held glinted in the light. And it elongated as his had just done, thickened, the end becoming a hook. Becoming a scythe. Becoming the only weapon capable of killing the man who ruled from the Titan throne. Paris realized what was about to happen and froze.

Oh, damn. Anyone looking from behind Galen, which was the view from Danika's painting of this moment, would see only Cronus. They wouldn't see the slight female behind him. The female who would change the world with her next action.

"I will never bow to you," Galen snarled. "And I will get my woman on my own."

"You'll get her after I kill her, then."

Galen roared, his weapon shaking in his grip.

"Actually," Sienna said, even as Galen swung, "*you'll* be the one dying." She, too, swung.

Her weapon was longer, stronger, and far more powerful, and she beat Galen to the punch.

Cronus never knew what hit him.

His head detached, flew, and his body collapsed. Rhea screamed, but for a split second, she looked nearly triumphant. "Worth...it," she whispered, and then she, too, went silent, suddenly motionless.

My woman. Pride joined Paris's relief. *My woman did this. Won this.*

As the throngs began to shout in revelation, a dark, screeching form rose from the king's body, its crimson eyes glowing, its fangs long and sharp, and a tail swishing behind it. A similar form rose from Rhea, only hers had a stooped back with horns and claws so long they could have been sabers.

Their demons were escaping.

Crazed, Greed and Strife shot high into the air, disappearing into the night. Two of Pandora's demons would once more be unleashed upon the world.

"Someone should go after them," Paris tried to say, but then Sienna screamed, hitting her knees, and he no longer cared about anything else. Her arms spread wide, her back arched, contorting her. Her head fell back, and she released another scream, then another and another.

At last Paris reached her. At last she quieted, her voice box razed. She remained in that position, shaking, shaking so badly. He wanted to gather her into his arms, to offer comfort, but he put himself in front of her. He was her shield. Now, always.

Galen stood there, panting, and maybe he would have attacked, but the battle had ended as suddenly as it had begun. The few remaining Hunters realized they were outnumbered and took off in a dead sprint, though where they thought they could escape to up here, he had no clue. Bloody gods and bedraggled goddesses sank to their knees. Some bowed their heads; others simply looked stunned.

The angels came up to flank Sienna, daring the keeper of Hope to make a move.

"All hail the new queen," a goddess suddenly said.

The rest of the Titans repeated the phrase, their voices rising in fervor, as one by one, they kneeled in front of Paris. He wasn't sure what was happening; surely they would not refer to him as the new queen. He had his moments, sure, but maybe it was a Titan thing, like how Viola called her male pet "princess."

"They speak to the girl behind you," Zacharel said, moving to stand beside him.

Sienna? Sienna was *queen?* Of the Titans? Still crouched, he swung around to check on her. The dizziness increased, and he realized his line of sight was completely blown.

The angel added roughly, "Choices decide our fate. And though I was not made aware until now, she was to be the king's greatest asset—or his only downfall, depending on the choice she made."

"But *he* would...have known. His Eyes...would have...told him." Every word scraped his throat, burning. Every word weakened him further.

"I am sure they did," Zacharel said. "In their own way. Perhaps he did not look closely enough, or perhaps they did not show him everything. And now Sienna has taken the godly throne. *This* is why we wanted her on our side, why *everyone* wanted her on their side. The powers Cronus stole from so many others over the centuries have now become hers."

Do I know how to pick 'em or what? This was one more hat for her to wear, he thought with a faint laugh that caused blood to bubble up his throat, spilling out of his mouth.

A fog drifted through his mind, but it couldn't hide the revelation that he was dying. Already he'd lost too much blood, and with every second that passed, breathing became more difficult. But Sienna would be safe, always safe, and that was all that mattered. He couldn't ask for more than that. Except for a future with her. He would have liked that.

The rest of his strength draining, he allowed himself to fall backward, his head landing in her lap.

"Paris?"

Darkness that had nothing to do with his anger closed in. "I...love...you," he croaked out.

"Paris!"

"Save...friends...don't let...die." The darkness consumed him, and he knew nothing more.

Except...

"Paris!"

Her voice jerked him back. A flash of white. Darkness. A flash of white, lasting several seconds longer. Another flash, lasting...lasting...his body and demon seeming to stretch apart, disconnect...until he heard Sienna's voice and everything snapped back together.

"—not leaving me! I won't let you. Remember when we talked about having someone to die for? Well, you're mine. You're my someone. If you pass, I'll follow. Somehow, I'll follow." Oh, was she pissed. That temper of hers was coming out to play. "Do you hear me?"

The ground rumbled beneath him.

He smiled, because in that moment he realized something wondrous. Everything was going to be okay. Sienna was stubborn to her core. She had defeated Cronus, outwitted Galen. This was nothing.

They would be together, one way or another. She would make sure of it.

CHAPTER FIFTY-ONE

SIENNA HATED TO LEAVE PARIS in bed, and didn't want him to wake up without her by his side. His body was in the process of healing from the massive wounds he'd sustained during battle, and when he opened his eyes, he would want answers. Answers she would happily give, just as soon as she learned them.

So, after brushing her knuckles over his beautiful face—though he turned toward her, he gave no other reaction—she hurriedly left the chamber they shared in the Realm of Blood and Shadows. Then she stopped. Wait, wait, wait. She could flash now, couldn't she?

In fact, that's how she'd gotten Paris and all of his friends back here. She'd entertained a simple thought: *I wish we were home,* and boom, she'd blinked and every single one of them had materialized at the castle. Shock had drilled her to her knees, and her mind had gone into a tailspin. For hours after that, her mind had reeled with the possibilities—Hawaii, Russia, Ireland, Key West, plus everywhere else she'd ever wanted to visit—and she'd ended up flashing all over the world by accident.

That had been, what? Two days ago. Two days that seemed like an eternity, but she'd finally gotten control of that particular ability. She didn't think she would ever get used to some of the others.

Power swirled inside her, so much power her skin felt too tight for her body and her pores felt stretched, as if at any moment she could shatter into a thousand pieces. Apparently, taking Cronus's head meant she was entitled to nearly all of his powers, and definitely all that he'd owned. Like, say, his home in the heavens and even his harem—from which she'd promptly freed everyone.

One of the females inside—Arca—had asked her if Paris had sent her. In exchange for Arca's aid, he'd vowed to free her after saving Sienna. She'd said yes, and now that debt was paid.

On top of everything else, Cronus's allies were hers—as were his enemies. But she wasn't worried.

She could also *feel* the darkness inside her now, the darkness Zacharel had told her about, the darkness Paris had given her—a darkness Wrath loved to devour. He'd never fed from her, but had begun to feed from Paris, taking that part of him and lessening its hold on him. Zacharel would have to approve.

With a sigh, she flashed into Lucien's room, ready to begin her daily checkup on all of Paris's friends. He and Anya were in bed, sleeping peacefully. His injuries were less severe than Paris's, and he had finally crawled out of bed this morning, only to stalk into the entertainment room, toss Anya over his shoulder, and vanish them both.

Maddox and Ashlyn were also in bed, but they were cooing to their babies, who kicked and gurgled in their adoring parents' arms. Maddox was bandaged pretty heavily, was pale and bruised, but he was smiling. The little boy, Urban, met Sienna's gaze and winked.

Winked? Surely not.

Strider and Kaia were—having sex. Oh, oh, ick! *My eyes.* Sienna moved to the next room.

Sabin and Gwen—*someone save me.* They were also going at it. What was with the people in this castle? Had Paris's demon somehow rubbed off on all of them?

Gideon and Scarlet were snuggled together, talking. And a stranger conversation Sienna had never heard.

"I hate you."

"I hate you more."

"I hate you most."

Moving on.

Amun and Haidee were in the kitchen, baking cookies. Haidee had flour streaked on her cheeks, prints on her breasts and butt, all courtesy of Amun and his wandering hands.

Reyes and Danika were in their bedroom. Like Paris, Reyes was sleeping off his injuries. Danika was painting.

Sienna knew Danika was the current All-Seeing Eye, and purposely didn't look at the colorful scene being created. She didn't want to end up like Cronus, obsessed with what was to happen and doing everything in her power to prevent it, all while forgetting to truly live in the present.

All she'd been willing to listen to was Danika's claim that the Lords' fortress in Budapest would soon be too dangerous to occupy, though she didn't know why, and that the whole crew needed to stay here for the time being. Sienna had, of course, given her blessing.

Cameo was in the entertainment room, polishing her daggers while the TV played an episode of *1000 Ways to Die*. Yes, the warriors had found a way to rig the immortal realm to receive a satellite signal.

Aeron and Olivia— Not again! Seriously. The castle was more like a zoo with monkeys. Wrath gave his customary heaven/hell coos, and there was still a hint of yearning in his tone, but no more of the whimpers.

Happy to be with me? Sienna asked the demon. *At least a little?*

You aren't so *terrible.*

She laughed. Wrath talked to her more and more now, real conversations rather than a spew of single-minded words. He'd helped her on that battlefield, guiding her actions but not overtaking her completely, just as he'd done with Fox, allowing her to work with him and do what was needed. She suspected he felt that this way, he helped protect his Aeron and Olivia.

Legion was in the room they'd chosen for her, as well, but one of her wrists had been chained to the wall. A long link allowed her to move freely about, but the cuff itself kept her from flashing to Galen to keep her vow to him.

I'll have to fix that, Sienna thought.

Hope will fight to the death to win her back, Wrath said.

Yeah. Probably. But that was a worry for later in the day.

Viola and her princess dog thing were in there with Legion, and Viola was regaling the chained girl with stories about herself. A captive audience. Seemed about right. Poor Legion, though. The princess was licking her feet.

Torin was in his room, sitting in front of a bank of computers. There was a faraway expression on his face, and she wondered what he was thinking about.

In a snap, she knew. Could actually hear what he was thinking.

—supposed to do with the All-Key now? Cronus won't be asking for it back, he's dead, and crap, what's up with Paris's woman being queen of the Titans? Are you kidding me with that? She's a former human and dead besides. Not to mention a former Hunter. And we already know how whacked it is to be ruled by those with demons

inside them. Do we bow to her now? Damn, this is weird and I have no clue—

Enough! she thought, and the volume on his mind was completely shut off. Much as she didn't want to know the future, she didn't want to know more than her fair share about the present, either. Invading people's thoughts was so uncool. Mrs. Manners would not approve.

Sienna hadn't spoken much to the Lords in the past two days, too busy tending Paris and adjusting to her new position, but now she knew most of them were still uneasy about her. Fine, whatever. That would take time. Time she was willing to give them. Anything to be with Paris.

Next, she appeared in front of the three rooms occupied by Cronus's immortal prisoners. Cameron, Winter and Irish. Unlike all the times before, she saw no flashes of their crimes inside her mind. During the battle in the heavens, Wrath had fed to the point of sickness and currently had no appetite.

Cameron spotted her first, and alerted the others. She wasn't surprised that they could see her now. Everyone else could, too. They strode to those air-shielded doorways.

Cameron sniffed, caught her scent and growled. "Ambrosia. Again. I know you. You're that bastard's invisible spy."

"Well, good news," she replied. "That bastard is dead, and clearly I'm no longer invisible."

All three blinked at her. Irish gave no reaction, but the other two laughed without humor.

"Yeah, right."

"Whatever."

"I'm going to set you free," she said, and that shut them up fast. They stared over at her, suddenly serious.

She hadn't done this earlier because she hadn't been sure it was the safest course of action. How would they react to her as queen? Try to kill her? But then she'd decided, so what if they did? *My powers are greater than theirs.* "If you harm the Lords of the Underworld, your brothers by circumstance," she stressed, "you will regret it. They are mine, and I protect what's mine. Do you understand?"

Stiff, disbelieving nods.

"Ask around," she said. "You'll discover that I can hurt you in ways that will haunt you for eternity."

She stepped forward, touched Winter's door. The shield fell away, and Winter gasped. A second later, the girl was gone. She repeated the process with the men, and they, too, left in a snap.

So easy, when only a few days ago, such a thing had been impossible. Go figure.

Sadly, she still was not done with her chores.

William was not in his room, but a human girl—Gilly, she recalled—was sleeping soundly in his bed, her dark hair spilled out over his pillow. The scent of sex was *not* in the air, but fear was, with an overlay of comfort. Gilly had come here, afraid for William, who had also been injured during the battle. He had soothed her until she'd fallen asleep beside him, then he'd left.

Now he was perched on the rooftop of the castle, popping gummy bears into his mouth and talking to another man in hushed tones. Hades. Instantly both males sensed she was there, as proven when they glanced in her direction.

"Hello, girl I helped time and time again," William said, his sly humor evidently intact despite his battle wounds.

"Hello, girl who owes me many favors," Hades added.

Black mist enveloped him, veins of fire running through what appeared to be wings.

Maybe her new powers had improved her vision, because suddenly she could see things she hadn't noticed before. He had long jet-black hair, eyes of pure black, no pupils evident, and a face even more handsome than Paris's. Well, a face that other women might consider more handsome than Paris's. She didn't.

His muscles were huge, and there appeared to be tiny stars tattooed all over his chest.

I like him, Wrath said.

That kinda scares me, just so you know.

"If two equals many in your world, yeah," she replied dryly. "Have you decided what you want me to do yet?" What left her uneasy was the fact that he could ask for the world and she would have to give it to him, as long as it didn't harm Paris or his friends.

Hades shook his shadowed head, his grin serial-killer wicked. "Soon," he promised.

"Great," she said, and left them to their secret conversation. A blink, and she was up in the heavens, standing inside Zacharel's cloud.

It amazed her that the angels lived in the clouds, and those clouds were actually like homes. Furniture, hallways, gardens. Whatever the owner desired. Zacharel's had the requisite bed, but it had a man with pink hair and blood-inked tears chained to it. A blindfold was wrapped around his eyes, a gag stuffed in his mouth, and a sheet draped over his waist. The rest of him was naked.

Don't look. Not my business. On that nightstand was an hourglass-shaped jar with some kind of gooey substance in it. She did not want to think about what he did with the stuff.

"Zacharel," she called, gaze already returning to the

pink-haired man. Her eyes narrowed. This was Paris's assailant from the cavern…and, she saw with her new and improved vision, he was no man at all, but a fallen angel. Since when were his kind held hostage in the very place they'd chosen to escape from? She watched as he struggled for freedom.

Zacharel walked through the far doorway, and he was naked and wet, and oh, sweet Lord, he was gorgeous. Just…wow. A muscle mass to rival Paris's, and he must be smuggling tube socks in his stomach, because damn. He had muscled roll after muscled roll. Small brown nipples, and some serious man business, and no body hair.

Only flaw that he possessed was a black spot as big as her fist on his chest, just above his heart. The spot bled out in a few places, as if ink had been smudged. Wait. Nope. Not the only flaw. Whip marks seemed to wrap around his ribs, red and raw. And could she really call the snow still falling from his wings a sign of perfection?

He stopped when he spotted her. A second later, a white robe draped him. Also, his bed—and its prisoner—had vanished. "I had a do-not-disturb barrier outside." His emotionless tone had returned. "How did you get in?"

"Um, sorry about that," she said. "I just, uh, kind of willed myself here."

No chastisement. Just a tight "What do you want?"

"I wanted to thank you." He was the reason Paris and company lived. "You gave me water from the River of Life. I didn't know what you had to do to obtain that water at the time, but I do now, and I'm aware you had to make some sort of sacrifice."

Tidbits of information came to her at the oddest times now, and only this morning, she'd realized angels had to give up something they loved to even approach the water. And to leave with a vial? They had to bleed. A lot. Maybe that's why he'd been whipped.

After the battle, as Paris's energy had drained right along with his blood, Zacharel had traded her a vial of the stuff for a simple promise to help the angels in the coming war. Apparently, the battle against Cronus was not the one he needed help winning.

"I will do everything I can for you," she finished. There were limits to what she could do, of course. She couldn't bring her sister back, though she'd tried. She couldn't find Kane. She couldn't heal others. Cronus had never been the all-powerful entity he'd made himself out to be.

"You have much to learn about yourself," the angel said. "You will spend the next few weeks with us, and we will teach you what you need to know."

"As soon as Paris is up and around. He'll be coming with me," she said. And she prayed she was right, that he would want to.

"He shared his darkness with you, and you want him still?"

"Of course. I am a light for him, a way out, and somehow his darkness is my light."

"That is—"

"Enough about this, I know. I want him with me, and that's that." She disappeared, having one more stop to make before she could return to Paris.

Galen's home.

He and Fox were seated at their kitchen table, piles of guns and ammo spilled out around them. They were polishing metal, checking clips, fitting bullets.

Wrath growled, but didn't say anything.

Galen looked upset. Fox looked strung-out. Her nostrils flared, and she sniffed, hard, and then her head was whipping around. Her gaze landed on Sienna and she jumped to her feet, about to lurch in Sienna's direction, obviously craving another taste of her.

With a flick of her wrist, Sienna willed the female to the very table where Sienna herself had been snacked on, chaining her there.

Galen jolted to his feet, his chair skidding behind him. "You!"

"Me."

"I want my women back. Legion *and* Fox."

"And I want you to release Legion from her vow to you."

"Never."

"I thought you'd say that." She glided over and eased into Fox's seat. He made no aggressive moves toward her, but then, he knew what she could do now.

Maybe she should have killed him for all the wrongs he'd committed. But most of his Hunters were dead, decimated in the battle, so perhaps he'd suffered enough. Also, she didn't want his demon loose, like Greed, who had belonged to Cronus, and Strife, who belonged to Rhea, the two now out there somewhere, no doubt plaguing the world.

"As you know, the Unspoken Ones were bound to Cronus. Now that he's dead, they are free. I tried to keep them chained, but by the time I realized who and what they are, that I, too, could bind them, they were long gone." Her gaze was piercing. "They want your blood, Galen. They want it bad. They'll be coming after you hard-core." And really, she was surprised they hadn't gotten to him already. "Do you really want to put Legion in that kind of situation? That kind of danger?"

A long moment passed. His answer would reveal his true feelings for the girl.

His shoulders sagged. He sank back into his seat. "No. I do not."

He cared for her, Sienna realized. Truly cared for the girl.

"I…release her," he gritted out. "Release Legion from her vow to remain with me, obey me."

Double wow, but she didn't comment. She didn't know what to say. So she moved them on to their next order of business. "You have something I want."

He didn't pretend to misunderstand. "The Cloak of Invisibility."

"Yes."

"It's mine. *Mine*."

How she wished she could make him give her the artifact, but free will was a greater power than what bubbled inside her. Whatever Cronus had told her, that's why he'd worked so hard to convince her to do what he wanted. Immortal or not, king or not, you messed with free will, and you would be punished. Severely. She was pretty sure that's why she had ultimately defeated him. Because he'd taken hers, he'd lost his own in turn.

"What will it take to convince you to give me the Cloak?" she asked. She'd learned a thing or two about bargaining.

His eyes narrowed on her. "Protection. You must protect me from the Unspoken Ones."

And wouldn't the Lords just *love* that? "For a year," she said.

"Eternity."

"Two years."

"Eternity."

"One year," she said, her own eyes narrowing.

He popped his jaw. "Very well. Two years of protection. Maybe in that time, I'll kill you and take those kingly powers for myself. Protect myself."

By that time, she would have found Pandora's box, but she didn't tell him that. "Make a play for me, Galen, and you'll find yourself in a special prison for immortals for the next two years."

He paled.

Yeah. He caught her drift. He'd be rotting next to the Greeks he'd once betrayed. "Give me the Cloak."

His motions jerky, he pulled a small square of gray material from his pant pocket and tossed it at her. "There. Yours."

There was no time to bask in her victory.

"Sienna!"

She heard Paris's bellow across the vast distance between them. Her cheeks flushed with pleasure as she stuffed the tiny, folded Cloak in her bodice. He was awake! "Gotta go," she said, and willed herself back inside her bedroom.

CHAPTER FIFTY-TWO

PARIS WAS JUST ABOUT TO GO on a rampage when his woman appeared beside the bed. He caught his breath and fell back against the pillows. Her dark hair tumbled over one shoulder. She wore a gown threaded with gold and emerald, jewels sparkling in the material. Her hair was brushed to a luxurious mahogany shine. Those black wings arced over her shoulders.

She had never looked more beautiful.

He sighed with happiness as she threw herself on top of him. "I'm so glad you're awake!"

Her slight weight settled on him, her hair creating a curtain that made them the only two people in the world. He rejoiced. They belonged together.

"Is it true you're now the boss of us?"

She snorted. "You have such a way with words. But yeah, I am kind of the boss of you. Titans kept appearing out of nowhere to pay their respects, and I finally had to make a royal decree for space."

Queen Sienna. He liked it. "I guess that makes me King Paris."

A tinkling laugh escaped her. "I've always known you were destined for greatness."

"I'll get to boss my boys around, of course."

"Of course."

He grinned, so damn happy he could burst. "I knew you'd bring me back, baby. So, am I an undead soul?"

She lifted her head, a soft smile lighting her delicate features. "No, you're very much alive, and you still have your demon."

Yeah, he could feel the bastard waking up, stretching, demanding Sienna, only Sienna. Sex wasn't after random grind anymore. The demon had embraced Sienna and all the different facets of her personality, and didn't want to lose her. She was their lottery ticket.

Maintaining his grip on her with one hand, he patted himself down with the other. No injuries. He was completely healed. "What happened up there?"

She kissed his cheek, his neck. "After you passed out and I flipped my ever-loving lid, Zacharel calmed me down and told me about my new status and abilities. He also gave me a vial of water from the River of Life. For a price. I gave you and all the Lords a sip and you guys have been healing ever since."

"What price?" he asked.

"Well, all along the angels have wanted me in the heavens, helping them with their war. I told him that I was willing to help, but I wouldn't be living there. I will stay with you. If you'll have me. Except, we do have to stay up there for a few weeks so I can learn how to use my new powers. There's where I was just now. And I'm rambling, aren't I?"

"I love when you ramble. But did you really just say the words *if you'll have me?*" He couldn't help himself. He kissed her hard and fast, staking his claim. "I will have you today and every other. And I will help you help the angels. And yes, I will go with you, wherever you need to go."

A relieved breath left her. "I'm glad. Oh, and just in case it comes up, the darkness inside of you is now inside of me, too."

"What?" He sputtered, paled. "I'm sorry, so sorry. I didn't—"

"Don't worry about it...*husband*."

Everything stilled inside him. His heart, his lungs, the synapses in his brain. "You know I married you?"

"Of course." A sly smile lifted her lips. "I know a whole lot of stuff now. Like, world-changing stuff."

"World-changing, smorld-changing. You're okay with being bound to me forever? Because I get the impression it's not a two-sided marriage until you say so."

"I'm saying so, and I'm better than okay with it."

He *so* loved this woman. "Good, because I feel the same. *Wife*."

Her smile quivered as if she were fighting tears. She told him about Arca, and rather than displaying his customary guilt and shame because of his past actions, he kissed her tenderly. She loved him, too, and she had forgiven him. She saw the best in him.

"Thank you," he said. "With all of my heart, thank you."

"Welcome. Now, back to the darkness," she said, probably trying for a business tone but failing. His woman was a softie, a Twinkie with a cream filling, and he loved that, too. "Wrath feeds on it, and that helps keep him calm. And you know what that means, right? We're perfect for each other in *every* way."

"I so agree with that. We're a family, you and me, and I love you more than I can ever say."

"That's good, because that's how much I love you."

He planted a quick kiss on her mouth. Anything more, and he'd be all over her before he had all the information he needed. "So where are we right now?"

A wicked glint in her eyes as she said, "Back in the Realm of Blood and Shadows. All the Lords but Kane are here. Amun and Haidee found him, fought for him, but then they lost him again somehow. But don't worry, I'm on the case now. I'll find him once and for all. And I'm, uh, kind of a big deal."

He grinned.

"Now, on to the next topic. I want to show you something," she said. Rolling to her side but remaining within his embrace, she swirled her hand in the air above them. Shimmers of light, a thickening of the particles, and then colors bloomed around a mist.

He saw Baden. Red hair, muscled body.

Joy and grief bloomed inside him.

He saw Pandora. Black hair, leanly honed body.

Guilt and shame.

He saw Cronus. Brown hair, muscled body.

Smugness.

He saw Rhea. Black hair, slender body.

Vindication.

Their mouths were moving, but he couldn't hear them. They stood between thick, white pillars in a temple.

"I'm dead," Sienna said, "but I live. So I can do what even Cronus could not when he had the throne. I can travel there. I can talk to them. And I think I can even get your Baden back."

Tears suddenly burned his eyes. A puss once again, but whatever. This was a dream come true, all of it. "I would love that. *Thank you.*"

Her eyes misted, and she cleared her throat. "Okay, so do you want the good news or the bad news next?"

There was more? His chest constricted. "Bad. Give me the bad, no matter what it is."

"With Cronus dead, his enemies are now mine. I'm not exactly sure who they are, so I'm not exactly sure who to trust. Also, the Unspoken Ones are free, and I have to protect Galen from them."

He breathed out a gust of relief. He wasn't sure what he'd expected, but that wasn't it. "We'll deal with the enemies as they come. As for Galen, we'll discuss it."

She planted another kiss on his neck. "Great, because that's the perfect transition into the good news."

He would never grow tired of her caress and angled his head so that she'd kiss him again. "What?"

"Well, this is a two-parter. First, the Hunters have been all but obliterated. Second, Galen gave me the Cloak of Invisibility."

"Wait, wait, wait. Back up. *What?*"

"You are currently enemy-free."

"I don't…" Have any words, he realized. He experienced shock, then excitement, then disbelief, then shock again. He'd been fighting the Hunters for so long. *Thousands* of years. To suddenly find out he would never have to battle another? Almost too much to take in.

When he found his voice, he managed to croak, "Why would Galen give you his only artifact?"

"Well, when Cronus and Rhea died, the Unspoken Ones were freed, as I told you. They are now after him. He gave me the Cloak and in return, I offered him my protection. He hated doing it, and I whittled him down to only two years."

"You should have saved yourself the hassle. One, everyone here wants him dead no matter what, and two, with the Hunters out of the picture, we're good without the Cloak. We won't need to use it to sneak into enemy territory."

"You're welcome," she said, chin going in the air.

"Sorry, sorry. I'm grateful, I swear. That came out wrong. I just hate the fact that you were around him, and now you have to protect him." Which meant *Paris* had to protect him, too.

She softened. "You still need the Cloak. You can't be sure no one else will rise up against you, and it's better for you to have every weapon at your disposal, rather than someone else's."

"Such a smart girl."

Our girl.

Definitely.

"Besides, we can now search for the box," she said, beaming.

All four artifacts, he mused, awed by this woman of his. She was right. They needed the artifacts, not only to keep them out of enemy hands but to find Pandora's box and destroy it before anyone could use it against them. The goal they had been working toward so single-mindedly and for so long was nearer than ever to being met. "Let's not go searching for the box just yet," he said, tugging at her clothing.

"Such a smart boy." She met his waiting mouth with her own, licking and kissing and sucking on him. "We'll search later. Much later."

Yes! I'm on board!

IN A CORNER OF SIENNA'S MIND, a man's thoughts bubbled up. *What's up with this crap? Here comes another apology I have to make.*

Strider's voice, she realized. He was walking toward their bedroom, even then.

I tried to talk Paris into booting his girl, just like I tried to talk Amun into booting his, and both of them suffered for it. Not to mention how their women must have felt. So that's it for me. I'm done. No more getting involved with my boys and their women. But then, the

*only single ones left are Kane and Torin, but Torin is a
recluse so he doesn't count. And if ever Cameo brings
home a guy, well, all bets are off. Guy will have to prove
himself worthy, no matter what. And damn, I'm almost
there. Kaia better thank me properly for this, since she's
the one who insisted I do it. I hate apologizing, and Paris
is the vengeful type. He'll make me get on my knees and
beg, I know it. This is gonna be embarrassing. And painful!*

Knock. Knock.

"Go away," Paris shouted, hands clenching on Sienna's
ass.

"I need to talk to you, man," Strider replied, voice
muffled through the doorway. "Also to Her Highness,
who I assume is in there with you. I don't really have to
call her Your Highness, do I?"

"Yes, you do. But talk later."

"Now. So, uh, yeah. I'm sorry. See ya." *Yep, hurt just
as bad as I thought it would,* Strider thought.

His footsteps faded away.

"What was that about?" Paris asked.

Sienna's own thoughts filled her head. *I will not laugh.*
"Me. He was saying sorry for the way he messed with
you about me. Apologizing to both of us, actually."

"I love you, baby," Paris said.

Her lips stretched into another grin. "I love you, too."

When they were both naked, he sank inside her.
He was home, finally home. And he was at peace. His
woman was with him, and she wasn't leaving him. They
were going to be together.

Whatever else came, whatever else happened, they
would be together, just as he'd wanted since the beginning.

EPILOGUE

ONCE AGAIN ZACHAREL found himself high in the heavens, Lysander beside him, the pair of them peering down at a very content Paris and Sienna.

"I gained her cooperation," he said, "but not the way you wished. Paris will be joining her here."

"This is not the travesty I had feared it would be," Lysander replied. "When dealing with people and their emotions, allowances must always be made. I sometimes forget."

Emotions. A waste of energy in Zacharel's estimation. You lived, you warred and one day you died. Anything else was unnecessary.

Lysander continued, "I am surprised they complement each other so well, even more surprised they actually aid each other both emotionally and physically. I never would have guessed."

Nor he. Paris should have dragged Sienna down. She should not have had the determination and strength to pull him up. "What happens now?"

"Now, I will begin Sienna's training, and take responsibility for Paris. And you, in turn, will heed the Deity's newest order."

"Very well." The Deity's newest order—or rather, sentence—had come only this morning. Zacharel had been summoned to the Deity's temple, where a second punishment for his prior sins had been heaped upon his head, as if the eternal snowfall wasn't enough. "You must admit you have the easier task."

"True. I do not envy you, my friend."

Zacharel was to lead his own army of warriors. Warriors just like himself, only far worse. Men who had defied the rules one too many times. Men who would—supposedly—teach him the value of following heavenly laws.

They were like no other angels he'd ever dealt with. Some took lovers. Some cussed and drank. Some were tattooed and pierced, and as dark in spirit as many humans.

If he trained them well, the Deity had proclaimed, the snow would cease to fall from his wings, and he would be allowed to remain in the heavens himself. If he failed, if they failed, they would all fall together, forever banned from the only home they'd ever known.

Whatever it took, Zacharel *must* remain in the heavens. His greatest treasure was here, and he would rather die than be parted from it. He did not consider his attachment emotional, but rather, essential to his survival.

You might not survive even if you remain up here, he thought, rubbing the dark spot growing on his chest.

"If ever you need me," Lysander said, pulling him from his musings, "you have only to call."

"Thank you. I feel the same. If ever you need me…" *I might not be around to help.* At that moment, the Deity's parting words echoed in his mind. *Your life will soon*

*change in ways you cannot even imagine. I hope you
are prepared.*

Was he? He and his men would find out together, he
supposed.

* * * * *

*The adventure is only beginning
for Zacharel and his army of heavenly bad boys.
Don't miss WICKED NIGHTS,
the first book in Gena Showalter's scorching new
ANGELS OF THE DARK series,
coming soon from HQN Books!*

Lords of the Underworld
Glossary of Characters and Terms

Aeron—Former keeper of Wrath

All-Seeing Eye—Godly artifact with the power to see into heaven and hell

Amun—Keeper of Secrets

Anya—(Minor) goddess of Anarchy; beloved of Lucien

Arca—Messenger goddess

Ashlyn Darrow—Human female with supernatural ability; wife of Maddox

Baden—Former keeper of Distrust (deceased)

Bait—Human females, Hunters' accomplices

Bianka Skyhawk—Harpy; sister of Gwen and consort of Lysander

Black—A Horseman of the Apocalypse

Cage of Compulsion—Godly artifact with the power to enslave anyone trapped inside

Cameo—Keeper of Misery

Cameron—Keeper of Obsession

Cloak of Invisibility—Godly artifact with the power to shield its wearer from prying eyes

Cronus—King of the Titans, keeper of Greed

Danika Ford—Human female; girlfriend of Reyes

Dean Stefano—Hunter; Right-hand man of Galen

dimOuniak—Pandora's box

Ever—Daughter of Maddox and Ashlyn

Fox—Current keeper of Distrust; servant of Galen

Galen—Keeper of Hope and Jealousy

Gideon—Keeper of Lies

Gilly—Human female

Greeks—Former rulers of Olympus, now imprisoned in Tartarus

Green—A Horseman of the Apocalypse

Gwen Skyhawk—Harpy, daughter of Galen and wife of Sabin

Hades—Father of Lucifer and William

Haidee—former Hunter; beloved of Amun

Hunters—Mortal enemies of the Lords of the Underworld

Kaia Skyhawk—Harpy; sister of Gwen and Bianka; wife of Strider

Kane—Keeper of Disaster

Legion—Demon minion in a human body, friend of the Lords of the Underworld

Lords of the Underworld—Exiled warriors to the Greek gods who now house demons inside them

Lucien—Keeper of Death; leader of the Budapest warriors

Lucifer—Prince of darkness; ruler of hell

Lysander—Elite warrior angel and consort of Bianka Skyhawk

Maddox—Keeper of Violence

Olivia—An angel; beloved of Aeron

One, True Deity—Ruler of the angels

Pandora—Immortal warrior, once guardian of *dimOuniak* (deceased)

Paring Rod—Godly artifact with ability to render soul from body

Paris—Keeper of Promiscuity, also known as the Lord of Sex

Princess Fluffikans—vampire Tasmanian devil; pet of Viola

Púkinn—aka Irish; keeper of Indifference

Realm of Blood and Shadows—A sinister, hidden section of Titania

Red—A Horseman of the Apocalypse

Reyes—Keeper of Pain

Rhea—Queen of the Titans; estranged wife of Cronus; keeper of Strife

Sabin—Keeper of Doubt; leader of the Greek warriors

Scarlet—Keeper of Nightmares, wife of Gideon

Screeching—Immortal equivalent of tweeting

Sienna Blackstone—Deceased female Hunter; current keeper of Wrath

Skye—Sister of Sienna

Strider—Keeper of Defeat

Tartarus—Greek god of Confinement; also the immortal prison on Mount Olympus

Titania—The city of the gods; formerly known as Olympus

Titans—Current rulers of the heavens

Torin—Keeper of Disease

Unspoken Ones—Reviled gods; prisoners of Cronus

Urban—Son of Maddox and Ashlyn; twin of Ever

Viola—Minor goddess of the Afterlife; keeper of Narcissism

Warrior Angels—Heavenly demon assassins

West Godlywood—Titania's premier hotel

White—A Horse(wo)man of the Apocalypse

William the Ever Randy—Immortal warrior

Winter—Keeper of Selfishness

Zacharel—A warrior angel

Zeus—King of the Greeks